PENGUIN BOOKS

DARK EAGLE

John Ensor Harr is a writer, historian, and consultant in the management and communication fields. He is the author of two books on the Rockefeller family. Harr is married, has five children, and lives in Forked River, New Jersey. *Dark Eagle* is his first novel.

D0063995

John Ensor Harr

DARK EAGLE

*A Novel of Benedict Arnold
and the American
Revolution*

PENGUIN BOOKS

PENGUIN BOOKS
Published by the Penguin Group
Penguin Putnam Inc., 375 Hudson Street,
New York, New York 10014, U.S.A.
Penguin Books Ltd, 27 Wrights Lane,
London W8 5TZ, England
Penguin Books Australia Ltd, Ringwood,
Victoria, Australia
Penguin Books Canada Ltd, 10 Alcorn Avenue,
Toronto, Ontario, Canada M4V 3B2
Penguin Books (N.Z.) Ltd, 182–190 Wairau Road,
Auckland 10, New Zealand

Penguin Books Ltd, Registered Offices:
Harmondsworth, Middlesex, England

First published in the United States of America by Viking Penguin,
a member of Penguin Putnam Inc., in 1999
Published in Penguin Books 2001

1   3   5   7   9   10   8   6   4   2

Copyright © John Ensor Harr, 1999
All rights reserved

Map illustrations by James R. Harr

THE LIBRARY OF CONGRESS HAS CATALOGED
THE HARDCOVER EDITION AS FOLLOWS:
Harr, John Ensor, date.
Dark eagle : a novel of Benedict Arnold
and the American Revolution / John Ensor Harr.
p.   cm.
ISBN 0-670-88704-8 (hc.)
ISBN 0 14 10.0178 x (pbk.)
1. Arnold, Benedict, 1741–1801 Fiction.   2. United States—
History—Revolution, 1775–1783 Fiction.   I. Title.
PS3558.A62492D37   1999
813'.54—dc21   99-20824

Printed in the United States of America
Set in Bulmer
Designed by Francesca Belanger

Except in the United States of America, this book is sold subject to the
condition that it shall not, by way of trade or otherwise, be lent, re-sold, hired out,
or otherwise circulated without the publisher's prior consent in any form of binding
or cover other than that in which it is published and without a similar condition
including this condition being imposed on the subsequent purchaser.

This book is affectionately dedicated to my late father—
Raleigh W. Harr—whose life nearly spanned the century.
He was born in 1900 and died in 1997.
He served his country in the navy in two world wars.
And gave me my love of history.

ACKNOWLEDGMENTS

I have had the good fortune to find myself involved with a succession of women in writing and publishing this book, despite the conventional wisdom that the audience for novels of history and war is provided by men. Always there was constant encouragement from my wife, Nancy, and such friends as Maggie Kennedy. Then there was my old friend from the literacy wars, Benita Somerfield, who introduced me to Jean Naggar and her all-female literary agency (save for Russell). Jean then connected me with the wonderful Kathryn Court, publisher and editor in chief of Penguin, and the marvelous assistant editor Laurie Walsh.

Of course, there were plenty of men who offered encouragement and insights along the way—others at Viking Penguin, friends such as Joe McLaughlin, Peter Johnson, Datus Smith, John Peterson, Anderson Clark, Sol Karpman, and my sons Jonathan, Jeffrey, and James. Special mention is due to James for his excellent maps.

To all of both sexes I give my profound thanks.

CONTENTS

Contents

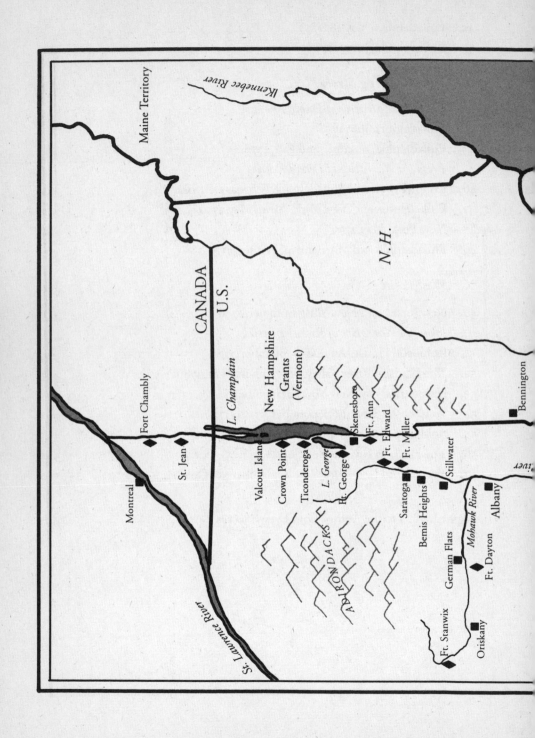

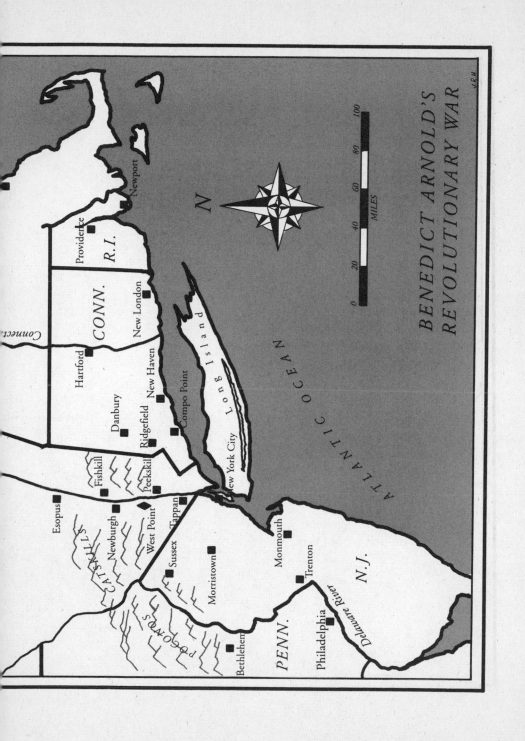

BENEDICT ARNOLD'S
REVOLUTIONARY WAR

CAST OF CHARACTERS

Eyewitnesses

Richard Varick: Aide to General Schuyler and Benedict Arnold
David Solebury Franks: Aide to General Arnold
Thomas Stanley: Aide and nephew by marriage to General Burgoyne

Principal Characters

Benedict Arnold: Leading combat general of the Continental Army
Peggy Shippen: Youngest daughter of Judge Shippen; Arnold's second wife
John André: Intelligence officer of the British Army

Supporting Characters

CONTINENTAL ARMY

George Washington: Commander-in-Chief
Alexander Hamilton: Aide to Washington
Philip Schuyler: Commander of the Northern Department
Horatio Gates: Successor to General Schuyler
James Wilkinson: Aide to Gates
Nathanael Greene: Washington's most reliable general
Henry Knox: Commander of artillery
Charles Lee: Second in command to Washington
Marquis de Lafayette: Major-General; Washington's protégé
Benjamin Lincoln: Major-General (promoted over Arnold's head)
Arthur St. Clair: Major-General (promoted over Arnold's head)
Daniel Morgan: Commander of the Virginia Riflemen
Nicholas Herkimer: Commander of the Tryon County militia
Matthew Clarkson and Henry B. Livingston: Aides to Arnold
Dr. William Shippen: High-ranking medical officer; Judge Shippen's cousin

BRITISH ARMY

Sir William Howe: Commander of the British forces in North America
Sir Henry Clinton: Successor to Howe; André's mentor
John Burgoyne: Commander of the British Army of the North
Will Phillips: Artillery officer; second in command to Burgoyne

Baron von Riedesel: Commander of the Hessian forces in Burgoyne's army
Barry St. Leger: Commander of the western wing of Burgoyne's army
Sir Guy Carleton: Governor-General of Canada
La Corne St. Luc: Burgoyne's Indian adviser
Philip Skene: Loyalist officer; founder of Skenesboro
Beverly Robinson: Loyalist officer; owner of Robinson House
Oliver DeLancey: Loyalist officer; André's friend

Other Characters

Judge Edward Shippen, Jr.: Leading citizen of Philadelphia; Peggy's father
Margaret Shippen: Judge Shippen's wife; Peggy's mother
Elizabeth, Sarah, and Mary: Peggy's sisters
Edward Shippen III: Peggy's brother
Hannah Arnold: Benedict Arnold's sister
Punch: Arnold's manservant
Becky Franks: Peggy's best friend; David Solebury Franks's cousin
King George III: British monarch
Lord George Germain: British Secretary of War
Charles James Fox: Member of Parliament; Burgoyne's friend
The Earl of Derby: Thomas Stanley's brother; Burgoyne's nephew by marriage
Joseph Reed: President of Pennsylvania; Arnold's implacable enemy
Hon Yost Schuyler: Frontiersman
Squire Joshua Smith: Arnold's gullible friend

AUTHOR'S NOTE ON SOURCES

When in the course of human events one is presented with a true story rich in drama and tension, with strong components of conflict, ambition, love, and betrayal, there is no point in straying from the truth in the telling of it. Every English speaker knows of Benedict Arnold, if only because his name has come into the language as a synonym for "treason." His career is reminiscent of a Greek tragedy. Unfortunately, it has also become somewhat clouded by myth and legend. Few of us know very much about the man—his exploits as the best combat general of the Continental Army, his passionate love affair with Peggy Shippen, the reasons why he took his fateful step, and what actually happened.

Although Arnold's story offers great insight to an understanding of the American Revolution, it is only in the outward aspects that it is a period piece. It touches upon many issues that are alive with us today.

Arnold's career has been well told in several biographies. I felt that it was time to tell it in the form of a novel, so that one could impute thoughts and dialogue and broaden the audience for this remarkable story. Doing so also requires some use of dramatic license here and there, but in ways that do not affect the essential story. The reader may be assured that in all important respects this account of Arnold's career is painstakingly true.

I owe my appreciation to the historians and biographers who have written so well of Benedict Arnold, in particular Carl Van Doren, James Flexner, Willard Sterne Randall, Claire Brandt, and Ray Thompson. And ever useful were the guardians of source material at the Library of Congress, the New York Public Library, the British Museum, the Historical Society of Pennsylvania, the New-York Historical Society, and the William L. Clements Library at the University of Michigan. I am also deeply appreciative of help given to me by the Whitehall Historical Society (formerly Skenesboro), the naval historians at the Smithsonian Institution, and the National Park Service people at the Saratoga National Battlefield, Fort Stanwix, Fort Ticonderoga, Morristown, and Philadelphia.

DARK EAGLE

PROLOGUE

Letters to the Author from Eyewitnesses

NOTE: Richard Varick, David Solebury Franks, and Sir Thomas Stanley, KB, were such invaluable eyewitnesses that their initial responses to the author have been printed in full and brief excerpts from their accounts appear at appropriate places in the following narrative. Their full accounts have provided much of the basis for the telling of this story of Benedict Arnold's career.

From Richard Varick

Prospect House, Jersey City
August 1st, 1826

My dear Sir,

I have reflected much upon our recent conversation and am moved to write this letter to you in an effort to reach a proper understanding. First, I pray you will forgive what I fear was intemperate behavior on my part, at least to some degree, on the occasion of our meeting.

I attribute this, in the first instance, to what I can describe only as a form of shock at the abrupt reminder of a man who, I will freely admit, I once greatly admired, but came to detest more than any other man save one, for nigh on half a century.

You do understand that Benedict Arnold nearly ruined my life. His perfidy reduced me to a state of torment for years, my reputation shattered by the poison of suspicion. I survived only because of my own fortitude and the intervention of George Washington himself.

I can look back on my career now and flatter myself that I not only outlived the curse of Benedict Arnold, but have made a tolerably respectable life—as the chief amanuensis to General Washington; as attorney general of New York State and codifier of state law; as the second mayor of New York City, a position in which I served eleven consecutive terms; as a close associate and friend of

Alexander Hamilton's, the greatest of all Americans (except perhaps for Washington himself); as one of the four founders and former president of the Society of the Cincinnati; as a founder and former president of the American Bible Society; as one of the original land developers of this fair city. During those many years, indeed since my own formal acquittal of any complicity in Arnold's treason, I have endeavored to banish all thought of the villain from my mind. I have rarely spoken his name, certainly not to the idle curiosity-seekers who have attempted many times to draw me out on this subject.

And now, Sir, you come to me in the 74th year of my life and ask that I not only think and speak of Benedict Arnold again, but that I plumb my memory to the depths and recall details of my regrettable association with him and my observations of his actions of nearly half a century ago. You will recall that I first thought you were playing some improbable prank, coming to me just after the eerie coincidence of the deaths of both Thomas Jefferson and John Adams on the same day—and that day being July 4th of this year, exactly fifty years after the great document forever associated with their names was adopted.

I do not include you in my reference to "idle curiosity-seekers." I now understand that your enterprise is meant to be a serious one. Nevertheless, I have misgivings about your design. We know Arnold's fate. He is befouled and begrimed in the Seventh Circle of Dante's Inferno, unless, by some cunning stroke, he has made an ally of Satan himself. His very name has come into our language as a synonym for "traitor." You can blacken that name no more than Arnold himself has done. Therefore, I ask: what is the purpose of constructing a narrative of his career? To make excuses, or even to attempt the impossible—to exonerate him?

There is another matter that concerns me. If I am not mistaken, I sensed in our conversation that you believe that Mrs. Arnold was his conspirator in treason. Perhaps you think that by sharing his guilt you can lessen it. But there is no evidence of her involvement. Quite the contrary. I knew Peggy Shippen Arnold, and a more fair and lovely wife and mother never existed. Both Washington and Hamilton attested to her innocence. No one can doubt the word of two such men.

I do not wish to prejudge you. By now, you may have divined that I have decided to cooperate with you, for the present at least, despite my reservations—or more accurately, because of them. I flatter myself that my testimony will help ensure that you avoid an errant path. Moreover, since our meeting, I find that I cannot dismiss Benedict Arnold from my mind, and surely this is an augur of sorts after so many years of repressing every thought of him. It is as if a floodgate were suddenly opened. Every memory of those times comes rushing back to me as clear and fresh as if the events had occurred but days ago. This has led me reluctantly to the conclusion that it is right that I should bear witness now, the more so because, I fear, the time is not far off when I will never be able to do so.

You asked if I could identify any other living persons who were witnesses of the time. Clearly, you should have started your quest a quarter century ago. If this were 1801 instead of 1826, you could have spoken with Hamilton, for he knew Arnold and was a witness to much of what happened. For that matter, you might have journeyed to England to interview the traitor himself on his deathbed, and Mrs. Arnold as well. The only other person I know of who could be of truly substantial value to you is David Franks, whom I believe still survives. He served as a member of Arnold's military family after the Battle of Saratoga. Thus David was an eyewitness to the period when Arnold was military governor of Philadelphia, an important time for this was when Arnold met and married Peggy Shippen and soon began his treasonous liaison with John André. I last heard that David resides in Philadelphia, and it may help you to locate him to know that he uses his entire name (he did in former times, at least)—David Solebury Franks—to distinguish himself from his uncle, the wealthy Philadelphia merchant who was condemned as a Tory.

To save you any confusion as to the respective roles that David and I played, please let me clarify. I was never officially an aide-de-camp to Arnold until the very end, in the late summer of 1780, when General Philip Schuyler recommended me as personal secretary and I joined Arnold just as he assumed command of West Point. It was the worst mistake of my life. Unbeknownst to me or to David, Arnold was already embarked upon his treasonous course. It is nonetheless true that, like David, I was a witness to the climactic events of that brief period. But I can also speak of two earlier times, of the events leading to the Battle of Valcour Bay in 1776 and, a year later, to the Battle of Saratoga. During those momentous conflicts, I was muster-master of the Northern Department and an aide to General Schuyler, who seconded me to special duty with Arnold on both occasions.

I also briefly reported to General Horatio Gates after he displaced Schuyler as commander of the Northern Department on the eve of Saratoga. I mention this because I believe one of the most important services I can render is to acquaint you fully with the intense rivalry between Schuyler and Gates. Unless one understands this, one cannot understand Benedict Arnold, for that rivalry colored everything that happened in the Northern Department, especially when, having vanquished Schuyler, Gates turned his venomous ambition and spite upon Arnold, his unsuspecting and erstwhile friend. It was in the north that Arnold won his fame, where almost all of his military heroics took place. It was in the north that the true turning point of the Revolutionary War occurred—the Battle of Saratoga. And what happened there profoundly affected Arnold's later infamous career.

Allow me to clarify an earlier allusion in this letter, when I wrote that I detested Benedict Arnold more than any other man <u>save one</u>. That man, of course, is the murderer of Alexander Hamilton. There was a time when I could not have imagined that any human being would ever be the match of Arnold in villainy, but Aaron Burr has succeeded. He has, as you know, managed to survive the *murder of Hamilton and his own treasonous escapade, and now practices law in the City of New York. I cannot prevent you from seeking Burr's opinions, if you wish to expose yourself to his poisonous mind, but if you do so, Sir, I do not wish to hear of it.*

I shall say no more for the present. I know that you wish me to go back in time and begin those recollections of more immediate use to you. I will begin examining my old letters and diaries, which have lain these many years in a trunk in my attic, and then will commence writing my narrative. Once you have returned the enclosed legal agreement to me, properly signed, witnessed, and notarized, I will send you sections of my narrative as completed.

With that, I am, Sir,

*Yr most Obedient Servant
Richard Varick*

From David Solebury Franks

*Philadelphia
October 15th, 1826*

My dear Sir,

I shall be delighted to cooperate with you in your endeavor to construct a narrative of the life and times of Benedict Arnold. There were moments many years ago when I thought of attempting such a thing myself, but alas, my talents do not lie in that direction. It is most certainly a story that should be fully told.

I am grateful to Dirk Varick for bringing us together. When you and I met in Philadelphia a month ago, I was as surprised as Dirk at hearing that infamous name of Benedict Arnold brought up for discussion in any serious context. But I understand and approve of your intentions.

I was in New York a fortnight ago on some business with my former colleagues at the Bank of North America, where for a time I served as chief cashier. Prompted by your design, I took the opportunity on my return to call on Dirk, whom I had not seen nor heard from for many years. It was a sentimental visit, a pleasure to see Dirk in passable health and to see his most imposing residence in Jersey City.

You readily discern that Dirk and I react in a quite different manner to your plans. There is good reason for this, aside from the fact that he and I are men of very different temperaments. Dirk had his heart set on a career in public life, not only as a lawyer but also as a man of some political ambition. The onus of suspicion that fell on both of us when Arnold's treason was revealed thus proved to be much more difficult for Dirk than for me. At this time, Dirk was a more intense object of suspicion than I, perhaps because he was senior to me and served as Arnold's personal secretary. Dirk and I each testified for the other at our joint court-martial, at which we were both acquitted of complicity. Nevertheless, his reputation was in ruins, whereas I quite freely went on my own merry way.

Dirk was not rescued until General Washington took pity and brought him up to Newburgh in 1782 to be in charge of the massive task of organizing and codifying all of the General's letters and papers for the entire war. That act of confidence by Washington miraculously cleared Dirk's reputation and enabled him subsequently to proceed on his political career. As you doubtless know, he held high offices in New York State and became Mayor of New York City, and probably would have gone on to even higher office had it not been for the death of his good friend Hamilton and the anti-Federalist sentiment that swept the country. But Dirk survived that as well. His legal practice has flourished and he has done well in all of his private endeavors.

Meanwhile, I flirted for a time with a career in our diplomatic service and found it seriously wanting in every way save for the dubious pleasures of traveling abroad. I then returned to where my talents lay, in banking and commerce—making money, not to put too fine a point on it! And I am happy to say that I also have done quite well.

There is something else about the differing reactions of Dirk and myself to the Arnold affair. I was as appalled at Arnold's fateful action as Dirk was—and everyone else on the North American continent, for that matter. But Dirk was outraged that anyone could think that he—a man of such rectitude!—was involved. I, on the other hand, understood their suspicions completely. After all, Dirk and I were closer to Arnold at the time than anyone other than his wife. We saw and commented to each other about some strange things going on, but never in our dreams did we imagine the true explanation for them. But what galled and embarrassed both of us is that we should have known! And it was quite natural for everyone else to think that we did know.

To understand this difference between us, you must fix first of all on the fact that Dirk is a Dutchman. I say this not in a pejorative way at all, but somewhat affectionately, as I could only wish others would do when they learn that I am a Jew. Dirk is a Dutchman, which is to say that he is frugal, stiff, proper, proud—and unforgiving when he or someone he cares about is slighted. But he is the most scrupulously honest man I have ever known. You voiced concern to me that he may not cooperate fully with you. From my recent visit with him, I can tell you to rest easy on that score. Whatever his initial reservations, he is much taken with the task now, and you can expect a full and honest account from him, despite his abhorrence of Arnold.

It is so like Dirk to believe in the innocence of Arnold's wife, the former Peggy Shippen of Philadelphia, all the more because Alexander Hamilton told him it was so. But I knew her much longer and much better than Dirk did. During the Philadelphia period, the odd circumstances made me much more than a military aide to Arnold. I became a sort of factotum to the Arnold family and something of a confidant to Mrs. Arnold.

Peggy Shippen Arnold! One of the most beautiful (and troubled) women I have known in my seventy years on this earth. Engaging, talented, charming— yes! She had an almost magical appeal about her. It is truly no exaggeration to say that all the young men who came into her presence fell in love with her in some manner or degree—Hamilton, Lafayette, John André, all the handsome British officers during the occupation of Philadelphia, myself certainly, even solemn old Dirk! But innocent? No! I had confirmation when General Washington selected me to escort her to her parents' home in Philadelphia after Arnold's treason was uncovered. The first night, we stayed in Paramus, New Jersey, at the home of her close friend, Mrs. Theodosia Prevost, the lover of Colonel Aaron Burr. But I am ahead of myself—I shall wait until this point in my narrative to convey what happened on that occasion, or perhaps you may wish to speak to Burr himself. Of course, I do not discuss such things with Dirk—the mere mention of Burr's name turns him choleric with rage.

I am afraid you will find that neither Dirk nor I can help you much with the character of John André, although we saw him several times after his capture. We both have a high opinion of him because he forthrightly told his captors that neither of us had anything to do with the treasonous plan. They didn't necessarily believe him, but at least he was honest about it. It is also clear that he did not inform on Peggy, though I'm not sure anyone ever asked him about her. Of course, all the Americans liked André, Alexander Hamilton most of all—André was courageous and honest, and he seemed charming, intelligent, and gifted as well.

You are aware, I believe, that I can be of assistance to you only from a point after the Battle of Saratoga to the end. I became Arnold's aide only after he was so terribly wounded and all his young patrician aides left him to go on to other things. Thus I was not a witness to Arnold's military heroics, though I certainly have no reason to doubt them. He was an uncommon man, at times a wicked and difficult man quite apart from the treason. He had his redeeming qualities, too. I am candid enough to admit that I was a party to some of Arnold's schemes in Philadelphia that got him into such trouble, though, as far as I am concerned, he did nothing worse than what others in command habitually did in those days—until his fateful decision to commit treason.

At any rate, I am your witness to the decline and fall of Benedict Arnold, if a man who had taken Peggy Shippen as his bride could be said to have fallen. I shall set to work preparing my narrative and sections of it shall be forthcoming in due course.

Until then, I am, Sir,

Yr most obedient Servant
David Solebury Franks

From Sir Thomas Stanley, KB

Knowsley, Lancashire
England
22 November 1826

My dear Sir,

I thank you for your letter of clarification received but a few days ago. I admit I was puzzled at being asked to assist in the compilation of a narrative of the career of Benedict Arnold, considering that during the rebellion in North America I had met that famous character personally on only one occasion and otherwise had merely seen him at considerable distance, when we were opposed in arms.

Your determination that the story should include a faithful and informed account of the British side during the war is certainly laudable, given that this was the anvil against which the brilliant reputation of General Arnold as a soldier was forged. I am pleased to cooperate for the reason, I frankly state, that it serves my own purposes. For many years I have availed myself of every opportunity to bear witness to the truth of the role played by my late uncle by marriage, General John Burgoyne, KB.

As you are doubtless aware, he was very badly dealt with by the ministry of the time, in particular by the Secretary of War, Lord George Germain, to say nothing of several of his fellow officers. When he returned to England after the Battle of Saratoga, he was the victim of vile and unjust criticism, certainly not to the extreme that General Arnold brought upon himself, but a terrible ordeal nonetheless, which he was able to surmount (and thenceforth to lead a productive life) only because of his great strength of character.

Thus, I welcome another opportunity to state the true facts. As General Burgoyne's principal aide-de-camp in both the 1776 and 1777 invasions of the Colonies from Canada, the one culminating in the Battle of Valcour Bay and the other the Battle of Saratoga, I have intimate knowledge of much that transpired on our side. The relevance to General Arnold is certainly there, not only for the reason I cite above, but also for the extent to which his exploits preoccupied British leadership and, for my uncle, became something bordering on an obsession. I think this is not well known to very many people.

Another point of relevance is that I came to know John André quite well, and Peggy Shippen, too, when I served in our army during the occupation of Philadelphia, having stayed in America whilst my uncle and his ill-starred army returned to England on parole.

In any event, I will begin examining my partial diary of the time and my notes, and will send you segments of my narrative as they are finished. I am, Sir,

> *Yr most obedient servant*
> *Sir Thomas Stanley, KB*

PART I

Independency

~~~~~~~~~~~~~~~~~~~~~~~~~~~~~~~~~~~~

Chapter 1

St. Jean-sur-Richelieu
Canada
June 18, 1776

The horses pawed the ground nervously, frightened by the acrid stench of the black smoke spiraling upward from the remote frontier hamlet. Everything that could burn had been put to the torch—the wooden portions of the fort, the houses, the sawmill, the shipyard and docks.

Utterly drained of energy, Captain James Wilkinson slouched next to his horse, clutching her reins and murmuring soothing words. She was a beautiful chestnut mare. Of the many horses he had known since his boyhood days on his father's farm in western Maryland, Wilkinson loved this one the most. She had become his best friend, his constant loyal companion. Through all the horrors of the long retreat, the spirited mare had done everything he had asked of her. All she wanted in return, seemingly even more than feed and water, was his attention and approval.

Numbed as he was, Wilkinson soon realized that he was hanging on the reins for support. He eased up, feeling the return of involuntary trembling in his legs. Exhausted nearly to the point of collapse, he could not remember the last time he had slept in a bed or bathed or changed his clothing. Even the smoky air could not mask the rank odor that emanated from his own body.

He glanced up at his commander. Brigadier-General Benedict Arnold sat astride a handsome bay, its black mane flashing as it reared its head. Wilkinson took small solace in seeing that Arnold's restless energy had waned as well, his face weathered and lined, his uniform mud-stained and torn. Wilkinson knew that Arnold had slept even less than he had the past week, burdened as he was by a twice-wounded leg that still had not completely healed. Wilkinson was waiting for the signal to help Arnold to the ground, knowing that his chief would stay in the saddle until the last possible moment, so painful and difficult was the act of mounting or dismounting.

Arnold was staring at the burning town and fort several hundred yards to the north. Wilkinson looked in that direction, half expecting the vanguard of the British Army to appear suddenly through the smoke and haze to threaten the escape of the last American troops from Canadian soil. For the past day and a half, Wilkinson had ridden at Arnold's side up and down the line of dispirited American soldiers that at times stretched for more than five miles. Only the southernmost dock had been spared from the torch so that the retreating men could board their barges and scows and longboats and head up the Richelieu River to the safety of Lake Champlain and American territory. Without boats, the British could pursue them no further, so dense was the wilderness on either side of the river from St. Jean south to Lake Champlain. And Arnold had made sure there would be no boats, having ordered everything wrecked or burned that could be of any conceivable value to the enemy.

Tears had come to Wilkinson's eyes more than once at the pitiful spectacle of the American soldiers as they staggered toward safety. Nearly six thousand men had already embarked at this dock—the lame, the wounded, the diseased, with the able-bodied among them manning the oars against the gentle current. Arnold and Wilkinson had been present at dawn when Major-General John Sullivan clambered aboard his longboat, his scowling face matching the bitterness of his final remarks to Arnold. Wilkinson remembered the day only two months ago when Sullivan had arrived as the new commander of the American army in Canada, determined to complete the invasion successfully—only to see the odds turn decisively against him early in May with the landing at Quebec of a large British relief force from England.

One of Wilkinson's duties was to make true copies of Arnold's correspondence, and from this he knew that his chief had been the leader among the officers in urging Sullivan to retreat before it was too late. It was an uncharacteristic stance for Arnold, who already had built a reputation as an aggressive commander. Wilkinson had seen a more practical side to his chief when Arnold had argued that there no longer was any choice, that the army must be saved. Sullivan had resisted, wanting to make a last stand at Montreal. When Wilkinson brought that message to Arnold, the captain was witness to his chief's explosive temper. Arnold raged about in his tent, denouncing Sullivan as an incompetent fool. He soon calmed enough to dispatch Wilkinson with another letter to Sullivan, again making the sober, lucid case for retreat. Sullivan finally agreed, accepting Arnold's offer to use the troops under his command as the rear guard.

The evacuation of the army had been agonizingly slow, and Wilkinson thought it a miracle that the British had not come down before it was complete.

The laggard pace of the American exodus was caused in part by Arnold's insistence on loading the boats as much as possible with materials salvaged from St. Jean—tools, parts of unfinished boats, stocks of seasoned lumber. Then more time was required for the wrecking and torching of the town and the fort—that had to wait until almost all of Sullivan's army had passed through to the embarkation dock.

Wilkinson's sense of impending danger had grown with each passing hour. Now, the madness of loading still more lumber was delaying the departure of the last boat, the one that the final contingent of eighteen Americans depended on for their escape. Even Arnold seemed aggravated by the delay as he turned his gaze from the town to the men on the dock who were loading the heavy boards, placing them in the center of the boat so that the oars and poles could be manned around the perimeter.

"Let's move it along, Sergeant," Arnold rasped. "Move it along, if you please."

Sergeant Elijah Cale wiped his hands on his dirty, torn shirt, his face blackened by soot and a week's growth of beard. He glanced at his hand-picked crew of fifteen men, the last of the rear guard, some of them lugging timbers to the boat, others onboard to receive them. Only a third of the large pile had been loaded.

"General, we can take but a few more," Cale said. "We could swamp the boat."

Arnold reined around to face Cale. "Damn," he muttered, almost under his breath. "I *want* that wood."

From the set jaw and the look in his eyes, Wilkinson knew that Cale's opinion of the idea of loading more wood was no higher than his own. Wilkinson could not fathom Arnold's obsession with transporting the wood. Wasn't there plenty to be had everywhere in the forests that abounded in the region? In a moment of sarcasm, the thought crossed his mind that Arnold might order some of the men to stay behind so that more wood could be loaded in their place.

Arnold barked his instructions in a decisive voice. "Keep on. Load as much as you can. Then set fire to the rest. Arrange the boards so the dock will burn, too, as we leave." Cale gave a sardonic glance as he touched a finger to his forehead in acknowledgment.

Wilkinson groaned inwardly. This could take another half hour. Almost as much as his own fate, Wilkinson was concerned about the future of his beloved horse. If *he* were in charge he would have given no thought at all to the damned lumber; he would have found *some* way to get the horses onboard, even though Arnold had said it was impossible, given the size of the boat and its sloping sides and the number of soldiers remaining. Wilkinson could see no way around it—the horses would have to be abandoned.

He remembered the day when he found the two horses, a stroke of luck that had earned him a triple reward—he became Arnold's aide-de-camp, obtained the rank of captain at the age of eighteen, and rated a horse of his own in order to serve as a courier for the man who had volunteered to cover the retreat. The horses were the two best the unfortunate *seigneur* owned on his estate near Boucherville. That's why he had kept them well hidden from the armies that criss-crossed the region. Arnold needed a mount, having taken a nearly disastrous spill when his horse had slipped on moss-covered rocks near where the Richelieu emptied into the Saint Lawrence River. The animal had to be destroyed, and at first it seemed that Arnold's military career might be over as well, his leg momentarily caught between the horse's flank and a large flat rock. The wound he had received in the failed assault on Quebec had barely healed, and now the same leg was bruised and bloodied anew. Once again, Arnold was lucky—no bones had been broken, and he was soon able to walk, though dependent on crutches and unable to mount a horse for more than a week.

Wilkinson had located the horses by bribing a disgruntled *habitant*. Arnold had commandeered them, writing out a chit that he told the distraught owner could be redeemed later for payment. Clutching the paper in his hands, the owner wept as Arnold and Wilkinson rode away. It was surprising to Wilkinson that the owner had seemed most devastated by the loss of the mare, murmuring over and over, *"Mon gentille châtaigne, si jolie."*

That had given Wilkinson the idea for a name for his new horse. He called her "Joliete," even though he knew the word had a slightly pejorative meaning in French, as in describing a maiden who knew she was pretty and acted it out in an affected way. But he like the sound and decided that it was apt in any case—Joliete certainly knew that *she* was pretty, and she was a flirt, too, showing off and prancing about until assuaged with attention and favors. Wilkinson long ago had learned that every horse has a distinct personality, and he thoroughly enjoyed Joliete's sprightly manner.

Wilkinson knew he would have to say good-bye to his beautiful mare. He and Arnold would take their saddles with them, but the horses would have to be abandoned. Undoubtedly, they would be picked up by the oncoming British. Wilkinson hoped that the lucky British officer who inherited Joliete would treat her half as well as he had.

He noticed that Cale had loaded only a few more timbers before setting his men to work to arrange a pyre of the remaining ones. Now they were packing in small pieces of wood and some shavings. Next they would ignite the fire the same way they had the buildings of St. Jean—by sprinkling lamp oil about and applying a torch.

Arnold wheeled his horse and spoke to Wilkinson in a toneless voice: "Let's take one more look." He flicked his wrist in the direction of the town. "I want to see how close they are."

Wilkinson found his voice. "The enemy, sir?"

Arnold gave his aide a quizzical look, as if to ask, *Who else would I be talking about?*

"But . . . but, sir," Wilkinson stuttered, "the men are lighting the fire. We'll be ready to go in just a few moments."

"Not until that blaze is well along," Arnold said. "We have time. I want to make sure."

Make sure? Of what? Wilkinson suddenly felt as nervous as the horses. "It could be dangerous, sir."

Arnold ignored Wilkinson's comment. He glanced back at the dock. "Sergeant Cale! We're taking one more look. Have everything ready to cast off as soon as we return." He dug in his heels once and began to canter toward the town.

Exasperated, Wilkinson hastily mounted and caught up. He now realized what Arnold was trying to do. He recalled that in the final letter to Sullivan, Arnold had vowed to be the last American soldier to leave Canada. Obviously, he could fulfill that vow right now at the dock. But Wilkinson discerned that it wouldn't count for Arnold unless he made sure that the British *also* knew he would be the last American to leave. What swelling vanity!

Wilkinson remembered his pride when he had become Arnold's staff aide only six weeks ago. He had heard often of Arnold's exploits from men who had served under him—the capture of Fort Ticonderoga; the capture of the British naval sloop right here at St. Jean to give the Americans control of Lake Champlain; the epic march when Arnold had brought his small army across the Maine wilderness to Quebec in near-winter conditions. There he had joined the other wing of the invasion force, led in from the west by General Richard Montgomery. Wilkinson had heard many versions of what happened next—the daring assault on Quebec in a raging blizzard on the last day of the year, how the attack had been betrayed and had failed, with Montgomery slain and Arnold down with a musket ball through the calf of his left leg. But Arnold had fought on, laying siege to Quebec. He had kept the royal governor of Canada, Sir Guy Carleton, penned up in the walled city for four months—until the situation changed abruptly with the arrival of the British relief army under General John Burgoyne.

The stories were so vivid that Wilkinson almost felt he had witnessed the exploits himself. But he *had* seen with his own eyes how brilliantly Arnold had managed the retreat. With an uncanny sense, Arnold seemed to know just when and where to skirmish with the advancing British, to draw them away from the main army with a feint, to delay them and keep them off balance with lightning moves, while Sullivan's army made its ponderous way to safety.

Arnold's courage and tactical sense never seemed to falter in action, but at other times Wilkinson found his changing moods unsettling—impulsive generosity one moment, harsh demands the next. More than once he had seen

Arnold reach into his pouch to give a coin to a soldier who had done well. In contrast, there was the time when Arnold, an apothecary in his former life, had ordered every man of the rear guard to be inoculated against smallpox, which required dipping a pin into the serum of a victim's festering sore and then pricking one's own skin beneath a fingernail. Many of the men had balked, fearing they would catch the full-blown disease, and Arnold became enraged, threatening twenty lashes for each man who refused the inoculation. Wilkinson had tried to avoid the dangerous procedure himself, but finally submitted. He lived to see Arnold vindicated. Sullivan's predecessor in command, Major-General John Thomas, had adamantly refused Arnold's pleas to order inoculation of the entire army. Two weeks later, Thomas was dead—of smallpox. Meanwhile, only a few men of the rear guard had died from the inoculations and the rest remained remarkably healthy, as the disease continued to ravage the main army.

Arnold slowed his gait as the two riders reached the edge of the town. Wilkinson yanked out the rag that served him as a hankerchief and clasped it over his nose and mouth against the thickening smoke. He tried not to think of the possibility that he and Arnold could suddenly find themselves in the midst of the British advance party. To calm his jittery nerves, he began to focus on just how he might find a way to leave Arnold's service, assuming he were able to survive this last foolhardy act. He had been glad of the opportunity to ride with Arnold, to fight at his side, to learn from him. For weeks, the frenetic activity had given Wilkinson a kind of delirious joy, a sense of importance he had never known before, fueling his own ambition to become a great soldier. But life with Arnold had become just a bit too adventurous.

Wilkinson glanced at the stoic Arnold, who was a relatively new brigadier, having been promoted only last January, very nearly on his thirty-fifth birthday, as a reward for the epic wilderness march. Achieving that rank before the age of thirty was the goal Wilkinson had set for himself. It occurred to him that one way to escape Arnold, see less of the dangerous front-line duty, and be promoted all at the same time would be to secure a staff position with a general of the next higher rank. Wilkinson had learned that playing the staff aide game was a quick route to promotion. If he could find himself a major-general to serve, he would become a major at least, perhaps a lieutenant-colonel. Who? Certainly not the sour and dyspeptic John Sullivan. Who could it be?

Arnold reined his horse to a halt. He glanced around at the docks and shipyard on one bank of the river and the moat and the stockade surrounding the fort on the other. Embers glowed and in some places flames still licked at charred timbers. The fort had consisted of two linked compounds, all of it destroyed except a stone building in each compound and portions of the stockade where sod had been piled up as a defensive measure.

Arnold wore a satisfied smile. "It'll be a long time before Burgoyne builds any boats here," he said. He pointed to one especially long dock, now a black-ened, sagging hulk. "That's where the *Royal Savage* was tied up," he said, re-ferring to the naval sloop he had stolen from under the noses of the British. He pointed to the forest beyond the first compound. "We left our boats hidden upstream and sneaked through the forest right there."

"Yes, sir," Wilkinson mumbled, wanting to say that this was not the time to retell war stories. Only the day before, Wilkinson had been among a group of young officers listening to Arnold recount in detail his coup of a year earlier, how, with only thirty-five men in two small boats, he had surprised the St. Jean garrison at dawn, capturing all fifteen British soldiers and the *Royal Savage*. He emphasized that the action made him the first American officer to set foot on Canadian soil. His group had sailed away only hours before the Seventh Regi-ment of Foot, the Royal Fusiliers, had arrived from Montreal, too late to protect the fort. And then, only six months later, the entire Seventh Foot—more than six hundred officers and men—had been captured at St. Jean by General Montgomery when he brought his western wing of the American invasion army north to Canada. Arnold had a point in telling the story, an almost mysti-cal notion that his escapade of a year ago and Montgomery's coup fore-shadowed the present situation. Just as happened then, Americans were narrowly escaping capture by the British. But, Arnold said, once again it would be the Americans in the end who would do the capturing—if the British under John Burgoyne pressed too far.

When the group broke up, Wilkinson had not been surprised to find that the other young officers shared his own view: given the great disparity between the opposing armies, the Americans might just succeed in escaping, but they certainly wouldn't be doing any capturing.

Mercifully, Arnold did not take the time to express his vision again, but in-stead resumed the slow ride along the cinder path northward through the town. They had come through the worst of the smoke, but now the air had a particularly noxious odor, arising from several barrels of pitch-tar still burning where a storehouse once had stood. Soon the horses began to ascend a small rise on the far side of town.

Wilkinson's heart jolted—he thought he heard the faint sound of drum-beats in the distance. Instinctively, he allowed Joliete to fall behind a few paces, ready to jerk the reins about and gallop back. He imagined breasting the hill to see British redcoats staring at them at point-blank range.

Once atop the rise, Wilkinson knew that the sound of drums was not a flight of his imagination. The enemy was indeed visible, but the line of grenadiers was about a quarter mile away, well out of musket range, and it stopped at the sight of the two riders on the hill. Wilkinson saw three men on horseback come up to the front of the British line. They stared at the two Americans in the distance. Then one of them beckoned, and the grenadiers be-gan to move forward on the double, brandishing their muskets.

Arnold did not move. Wilkinson said: "Those horsemen, they could catch us before we could push off in the boat."

Arnold shook his head. "Those troops are infantry, not cavalry. Those officers won't get out in front of their infantry." He laughed. "I wish they would. I like those odds—three against two. Better than anything we've seen in a long time."

He raised up in his stirrups, his weight on his stronger leg, and stared intently. "I wonder who we've got here," he murmured. He pulled a spyglass from a case attached to his saddle and trained it on the British horsemen. After a few moments, he let out a triumphant cry. He turned to Wilkinson, white teeth flashing in a big smile. "By God! It's Burgoyne himself! I'm sure of it."

Involuntarily, Wilkinson said, "That's not possible."

"Oh, yes it is! You won't see Carleton here, but Burgoyne's the field commander. And he's not afraid of us. He wants to be in on the kill. Here, take a look." Arnold handed the glass to Wilkinson.

"The one in the middle, you mean?" Wilkinson asked, staring through the eyepiece. "Yes, you can see he's a high-ranking officer! He's looking at us now through his glass. How do you know it's General Burgoyne, sir? Have you ever met him—or seen him?"

Arnold was amused by the thought. "Gentleman Johnny and I don't travel in the same circles. Until now, at least." He raised his body as high as he could in the stirrups and held his right arm upward in a Roman salute. After a few moments, he waved his arm back and forth. Then, very deliberately, he made a conventional salute.

Wilkinson glanced at this bit of theatrics and then returned his eye to the spyglass. He watched as the high-ranking officer said something to the man on his right and handed over his telescope. Then he stood in his stirrups and returned the salute. With that, the three horsemen began to move forward at a walk.

"He returned your salute!" Wilkinson shouted, handing the spyglass back to Arnold. Then he saw the front line of grenadiers kneeling and taking aim from about two hundred yards away. "Oh my God, General, they're upon us!"

"Hardly," Arnold said. "But it's time." He turned his horse around and began moving south at a trot. Wilkinson galloped off, but pulled up to wait for Arnold, his moon-face contorted in a look of desperation. "Hurry, sir!"

"They can't run as fast as a horse can trot," Arnold said. "And they're already tired."

The first volley crackled and Wilkinson imagined he could hear bullets whizzing past him. Several hundred yards further on, he looked back over his shoulder at the crest of the hill and saw the grenadiers coming. No horsemen. Arnold was right about that. As the two men rode silently back through the smoke to the southernmost dock, Arnold drew out his prized Scottish pistol and began loading it.

The pile of lumber blazed, giving off intense heat, and the landward side of the dock was beginning to burn as well. Most of the men were in their places on the boat. Having heard the shots, Cale and the rest were standing by on the edge of the dock, muskets at the ready. Wilkinson dismounted and assisted Arnold to the ground. Arnold set his pistol down and began unbuckling the girth of his saddle, indicating to Wilkinson to do the same. Arnold pulled his saddle and blanket down and called to the men on the dock. "Get these saddles onboard."

He leaned down painfully to retrieve his pistol. Clutching his horse's bridle by the cheek strap, he shouted to the men in general: "We leave nothing for the damned lobsterbacks!" Then he fired a shot into the horse's brain. The big bay staggered and fell, its sleeky muscled legs twitching on the ground.

Arnold turned expectantly to Wilkinson, who was gaping in horror.

"You know we can't take them with us," Arnold said, matter-of-factly, reloading his pistol.

Wilkinson stared at him numbly. He wanted to shout that *he* had found the horses, they were *his*—but that would've been absurd. He understood Arnold's policy when it came to destroying fortifications and a shipyard that could be of real value to the enemy. But why slaughter these beautiful animals? Would it make *any* difference to the cause if they lived? Wilkinson looked at the expressionless faces of the men on the dock and in the boat, but found no solace there.

Arnold came up and said quietly, "I love them as much as you do. But we have no choice." He handed the pistol to Wilkinson.

Joliete had bolted away a few paces when Arnold had fired his shot. Wilkinson moved up to her. He whispered, "Run, Joliete, run!" smacking her on the rump. The horse took another few paces.

Arnold came up, cold fury in his eyes. He took the gun and pointed it at Wilkinson. "I could shoot *you,* for insubordination," he said. "You know that, don't you?"

The British grenadiers emerged through the smoke at the edge of the town, followed by the three horsemen. Several of the soldiers took aim and fired their muskets. This caused Joliete to take tentative steps back toward Wilkinson, her head bobbing up and down.

"Let's go!" Arnold roared. "Get on that boat," he snapped to Wilkinson.

Wilkinson turned, choking back a sob, and stumbled to the dock, his shoulders hunched, following the others as they scrambled on board. Joliete tried to follow him, but Arnold grabbed her bridle and shot her behind the eye just as she tried to buck away. The mare fell, but tried to get up again. Arnold angrily jerked his thumb at Cale, who came up and fired his musket into the mare's head.

Arnold waved Cale on board, shoved the pistol in his belt, and limped to the dock. He took the stern line and climbed over the side of the boat carefully. Along the gunwales, men pushed away from the dock and the boat drifted into the current, oars dipping into the water. Arnold had been the first American to invade Canadian soil—and the last to leave. He knelt at the stern, staring back at the smoking ruin of St. Jean and the oncoming enemy soldiers.

From the narrative of Richard Varick

I first laid eyes on Benedict Arnold when he arrived at General Schuyler's manor house in Albany on June 24th, having ridden the hundred miles from the fort at Crown Point to report on the condition of the army. He was surprised to find that General Horatio Gates, late the chief administrative officer for Washington's army at Cambridge, was also a house guest of Schuyler's.

I was somewhat in awe of Arnold for his reputation, but I quickly came to detest Gates. It seems he had been in Philadelphia attempting to gain influence with the Congress for advancement. He had selected General Schuyler as being vulnerable, for the reason of the dislike the New Englanders held for him. This was because Schuyler, as the leading man of Upper New York, had been active in the effort to annex the territory directly to the east, known as the "Hampshire Grants" or "Vermont," a version of the French name for the Green Mountains. The New Englanders furiously opposed this.

Shrewdly, Gates got the backing of John Adams and other New Englanders for a resolution naming him commander of the American army in Canada. He had come north in arrogant fashion to oust Schuyler and replace him. Schuyler pointed out that there no longer was an American army in Canada—it had fallen back to American territory, to Schuyler's jurisdiction as commander of the Northern Department. Therefore, the best Schuyler could do was to put Gates in command of the remnants of that army, succeeding John Sullivan—but Gates would still be subordinate to Schuyler.

Gates ranted and fretted, but in the end had to submit, contingent upon receiving clarification from Congress. I wondered what Arnold thought of all this, as he stood by patiently, prepared to deliver his report. What he had to say cooled the ardor and temper of Schuyler and Gates immediately. The military situation was grim indeed.

Arnold left the next day to prepare a Council of War for when Schuyler and Gates reached Crown Point. It was nearly a week before our ponderous column moved out, Schuyler and Gates unhappily sequestered in a carriage together while the rest of us rode horseback, a train of wagons bringing up the rear with our baggage and some supplies for the fort.

Chapter 2

Albany to Crown Point
June 25-July 8, 1776

Benedict Arnold's main objective on his trip back to Crown Point was to inspect the ship-building facility at the wilderness hamlet of Skenesboro, a place that would be vital in the strategy he thought should prevail in the coming conflict. He had not seen Skenesboro since having captured it more than a year before, easily routing the small band of Loyalist defenders under Major Philip Skene, founder of the town and owner of all the surrounding land, reportedly more than thirty thousand acres. While Arnold was on campaign in Canada, General Schuyler had taken over Skenesboro in order to transfer his ship-building activity from the Hudson River to a location with deep-water access to Lake Champlain. Skene was in no position to object. He was now serving with the British Army in Canada, confident that he would be reclaiming his lands after a British victory.

Arnold had also decided to make the return trip in a more civilized fashion, instead of riding the entire distance in a single day, as he had on the way down. He accepted the invitation to spend the night at Schuyler's summer home on a point of land at Saratoga, on the banks of the Hudson nearly halfway to Crown Point. As he rode northward toward Saratoga along the left bank, Arnold passed through miles of Schuyler's land, past his farms, forests, grist mills, lumber yards, and docks. What unimaginable wealth! Arnold thought about the feud he had seen erupting between Schuyler and Gates. He knew instinctively to avoid any sign of partiality. He wanted to remain on good terms with both men, realizing that each would be depending on him in the coming struggle with the British. In a way, Arnold admired Gates's spunk in challenging so powerful a figure as Schuyler—but he disliked the means. Arnold hated slavering to politicians. In his mind, the only correct way to win advancement was by sheer competence—by excelling above all others. In his case, that meant brilliance on the battlefield, to earn rewards from grateful countrymen.

After a restful night in unaccustomed luxury at Schuyler's country house, with its charming gardens and sweeping views of the river, Arnold crossed to the east bank of the Hudson at the ford just north of Batten Kill. This way, his journey would take him past the line of forts dating back to the French and Indian War, first Fort Miller, then, twelve miles further, Fort Edward, near where the Hudson made its big turn to the west, and finally Fort Anne, deep in the wilderness, the last settled place before the final twelve miles to Skenesboro. He found the forts woefully dilapidated, with more settlers in view than soldiers. Well out of harm's way for the present, the forts had only small militia garrisons.

The wilderness between Fort Edward and Fort Anne was marked on the maps as "The Drown'd Lands." The route through it merited being called a road instead of a trail only because some effort had been made to assist the traveler in traversing many of the marshy places and creeks that abounded in the thick forest. Most of the hundred or so bridges that Arnold crossed consisted only of a few logs felled over creeks or small marshes, but Skene also had built boardwalks across some of the larger wetlands.

Skenesboro was located on the west bank of Wood Creek, near where the creek emptied into South River, the southernmost reach of Lake Champlain. South River provided a narrow, sinuous water route stretching more than thirty-five miles to the main body of the lake at Fort Ticonderoga. Arnold dismounted at the outskirts and surveyed the town. He was impressed by what he saw. Schuyler indeed had added several wooden structures and ship-building platforms to the two stone buildings, sawmill, and docks that Skene had put in. There was a curious lassitude about the place. Arnold could see two boats in an early stage of construction, but no one working on them. He spotted a large party of men resting in the shade of a building. This was no ten-minute work break on a still, hot day in late June. These men seemed nearly comatose, except for a few playing a game with dice.

"Who are you men?" Arnold growled, as he walked his horse up to the group.

It was a considerable time before one man roused himself to say: "Albany County militia. Who the hell are you?"

"Oh, you're solders, are you," Arnold said, waiting until some nods acknowledged the fact. "I wouldn't have guessed it. What do you do when you see a brigadier-general of the Continental Army?"

After much exchanging of glances, the men began to get to their feet. "That's better," Arnold said. "Now. It's two o'clock in the afternoon. Why are you loafing instead of working? There's a war going on. We need those boats."

There was mumbling, but no intelligible response. "All right, listen to me. I'm going to count to ten. Any man who's not hard at work by the time I finish gets fifty lashes. You understand me? Laid on his bare back, by God. One . . . two . . ." The men began to move toward the ship-building platforms. Arnold grabbed one soldier's arm. "Where's Colonel Wynkoop?"

"He's in the—there he is now," the man responded, pointing to the largest of the two stone buildings. Arnold saw a corpulent figure, blinking in the sunlight, passing a hand over his eyes. With very careful steps, he began coming down the long flight of stairs. Arnold went over to him. "Colonel Wynkoop?"

"*Commodore* Wynkoop, if you please. And who za devil are you? Vat are you up to?" The man mopped his brow and began scratching his belly. His face was flushed and a strong smell of alcohol emanated from him.

"I'm General Arnold. I thought you'd like to see those men get some work done."

"You haf no right to order my men around. Ve report to General Schuyler."

"So do I. I'll have to tell him what I've seen here."

Wynkoop's huge body wavered back and forth, giving Arnold concern that it might come crashing down on him. Steadying himself, Wynkoop said: "Ja. Vell—vy don't you come in? Out of ze sun. Ve'll talk. Ja?"

In the next several hours with Jacobus Wynkoop, Colonel of the Albany County militia, self-styled "commodore" of the American fleet, and longtime Dutch friend of General Schuyler's, Arnold found no reason to change his initial opinion that the man was a pompous fool. But he was pleased when Wynkoop told him that a barge was to be rowed up South River at dawn to fetch more supplies from Ticonderoga. Arnold and his horse could be taken aboard.

General Schuyler's caravan spent the night of July 6th at star-shaped Fort Ticonderoga. The condition of the troops there was disturbing, even more so when the newcomers were told that these were the comparatively healthy of the lot. Most of the sick and wounded were twelve miles north at the charnel house that Crown Point had become. It was midafternoon the next day by the time the caravan came in sight of Fort Amherst, the name given by the British to the rebuilt fort at Crown Point after the retreating French had blown it up in 1759.

General Arnold stood with Dr. Lewis Beebe at the gates of the fort to welcome their superior officers, the bitter Sullivan having disdained to do so. Arnold watched as the caravan threaded its way through the tattered tents and brushwood hovels in which the sick and wounded had found pitiful shelter. On one side of the grassy peninsula leading to the fort a graveyard stretched, a new one of freshly turned mounds of earth.

Arnold saluted Schuyler and Gates as they alighted from the carriage, and then shook each man's hand. Major Varick came up and dismounted. Arnold could tell from the blanched faces that the three men were stunned by the foul odors of disease and death that dominated the air. They would soon become used to it. Equally depressing was the shambles the fort had become, several of its large redoubts collapsed, log walls rotting in many places, and a number of buildings blackened and partially caved in from a fire the previous year.

After greetings were exchanged, Arnold said: "Most of the standing buildings serve as a hospital—for the worst off. Would you like to inspect that first? Or go to your quarters? We have good, safe rooms for you."

Schuyler found his voice. "I'd like to rest for a while." The others nodded dumbly.

"Very good," Arnold said. "We'll have dinner in an hour. In the officer's mess, which is still intact." He turned to Schuyler. "By the way, sir, the mess is the room we'll use for the Council of War tomorrow. It's the only decent large room we have. Is noon a good time to begin? That'll give us at least three hours before dinner."

"Very good," Schuyler managed to say.

After a restless night, Benedict Arnold arose before dawn. He strolled past the docks on West Bay where two of the American warships were moored; the third, he knew, was on duty at the northern end of Lake Champlain. A fresh breeze came from that direction as Arnold rounded the northern point of the peninsula, carrying the fetid smell of the encampment away from him as he walked along the narrow strip between the outer wall of the fort and the lapping waters of the lake.

Arnold climbed onto a small wooden deck connected by a catwalk to the fort. The structure protected one of the pipes through which fresh water could be drawn. Tired and somewhat dispirited from the constant scene of misery that Crown Point had become, Arnold sat on a bench and gazed at the expanse of the lake to the north, imagining a British armada coming down. He knew that even if nothing were done to augment the American naval strength on the lake, it would be at least a month before the British could mount an effective challenge to it, so thoroughly had the shipyard at St. Jean been destroyed. Plenty of time for Arnold to go home to New Haven to see his three young sons. When he had sought permission during his visit to Albany, General Schuyler had asked him to wait until after the defensive strategy was agreed upon and work begun. That seemed reasonable enough, but Arnold feared that if the preparations were to be anything close to what he knew they must be, he would be so busy he would never get away.

He had last been home almost a year ago. His wife, Margaret Mansfield Arnold, had died in June, at the very time Arnold was engaged in his escapade to St. Jean to capture the garrison and the British naval sloop. Peggy was long in the ground by the time word reached Arnold. He hurried to New Haven to find there was no apparent cause for her death, just that she had succumbed to a sudden chill. Stunned by the inexplicable loss, he was uncharacteristically immobilized for weeks. It was an agonizing time, especially in trying to explain their mother's absence to the children—the youngest son, Henry, the one who looked most like Peggy, was barely two years old when she died. Finally, Arnold took the only solace he could, an abrupt return to duty. He left the children and his affairs in the care of his sister Hannah and journeyed to Cambridge for a meeting with General Washington. The result was the offer to take command of the eastern wing of the invasion of Canada, which Arnold eagerly accepted. Now, after nearly a year of frequent and often perilous action, he ached to go home once again, to get some rest and see his sons and revisit Peggy's grave.

He heard someone coming down the catwalk from the fort, and turned to see General Schuyler approaching with careful steps. Arnold began to rise, but Schuyler waved him down. "Please, don't disturb yourself. I'll join you if I may," he said, sitting down next to Arnold and breathing the fresh air deeply. "I think you've found the only place of serenity in the entire fort. A most pleasant and sparkling morning."

The two men sat silently for a while, enjoying the scene as the sun broke through a low bank of clouds cresting the ridgeline of the Green Mountains across the narrowness of the lake to the east, brightening the pink and blue sky. From the window of his bed chamber, Schuyler had observed Arnold walking along the docks and resolved to join him for a private conversation. He needed Arnold to act in some way as a counterweight to Gates in the Council of War. He wasn't sure exactly how, and it would be unseemly in any case to speak directly to a junior officer of such matters, as if they were conspirators. Schuyler began thinking of how to raise the subject without actually raising it.

He had experienced a momentary stab of panic when Arnold had asked for home leave, fearing that his best commander would never return, that he would be tired of this one-sided war and decide to resign his commission to be with his children, to resume his successful career as a merchant or use his seafaring talents to enter the profitable business of privateering. But Schuyler quickly realized that Arnold had a zest for war and would hardly withdraw when his reputation had soared so in such a short time. He clearly would be in line for promotion to major-general within a year or less.

In truth, Schuyler needed Arnold badly and was somewhat in awe of him. He knew that the American position in the north, endangered as it now might be, was owed to Arnold, to his exploits in the spring of '75—the capture of Skenesboro, Ticonderoga, and Crown Point, and the raid on St. Jean that had won control of the lake. Those successes made it possible to launch an invasion of Canada. Schuyler had been embarrassed at having to command the invasion from his manor house in Albany, confined by a series of chest ailments and repeated attacks of gout. And so he had sent Richard Montgomery and his army north on the lake and river to take St. Jean and Montreal and march on Quebec, there to meet his death. And he had acquiesced in Washington's plan to send Arnold across the trackless wilderness of Maine on the eve of winter to mount a surprise attack on Quebec from the other direction. Like almost everyone else, Schuyler had thought that an impossible assignment. But Arnold had done it, had made the epic march, attacked Quebec, been wounded, maintained a siege for months, and then covered the retreat masterfully when the odds turned decisively against the Americans. Schuyler needed this kind of ability now, given that his corps of commanders in the north was perilously weak and rent by dissension in the persons of Gates and Sullivan.

For his part, Arnold was in awe of Schuyler, but for different reasons, not as a military commander, though he credited Schuyler with leadership attributes and basically sound ideas. He admired Schuyler's wealth and position, a station in life to which Arnold aspired. He felt that such would have been his birthright, had it not been squandered by his father and grandfather. He was eager to earn it back now, earn it by sheer achievement in a glorious war for liberty. And it did not escape him that the support of so prominent and powerful a man as Philip Schuyler could be useful to his ambitions.

At length, Schuyler broke the silence. "A lovely lake," he said. "The fish can be tasty. But not like the seashore."

"How so?" Arnold asked.

"No oysters. No clams, no lobsters."

"Indeed." Arnold smiled.

Almost casually, Schuyler said: "I've been thinking about our Council of War." Arnold looked up expectantly. "I have some new dispatches," Schuyler went on, "and I want to begin by giving everyone the latest information. These matters may have an important bearing on our decisions. So we'll have an open discussion of them." Schuyler turned to Arnold. "Then, General, I shall call on you to speak."

"Yes, sir." Arnold nodded. Nothing unusual there. It was the custom, after the presiding officer opened the meeting, for the general officers to speak according to their rank, junior officers first, the most senior man last. Under that custom, Arnold would be the first to speak. The juniors were expected to be limited and circumspect in their remarks, setting the stage for the presumed wisdom of the elder generals.

Schuyler resumed in a monotone. "I want more than the usual preliminary comments from you. I shall ask for your full analysis of our present situation and your recommendations as to what actions we should take." Seeing Arnold's puzzled expression, Schuyler added: "No one is more experienced in the northern campaign than you, on the ground, as it were."

Arnold spoke in a neutral tone: "You flatter me, sir. But—forgive me. Won't General Sullivan take offense?"

Schuyler shrugged. "He may, but, alas, he no longer matters. We shall certainly listen to any opinions General Sullivan may offer in the discussion. But in his present mood, I don't think he can view our problems very calmly or dispassionately. Understandably, he's most upset at being superseded so abruptly. I wish he would stay because we're so short of general officers. He'll leave tomorrow to go to General Washington's headquarters in New York Island to present his complaints and plead his case. And then probably on to Philadelphia to the Congress to do the same."

No loss there, Arnold thought to himself, his mind already racing to how he would fashion his presentation.

Schuyler's homely features contorted into something resembling a grin. "I daresay you have given our situation considerable thought. I could not imagine it otherwise. Am I correct that you have recommendations very much in mind?"

"Yes, sir, I do."

"Good. It is not my intention to discuss your views now. That would not be proper without the others present. I shall of course reserve judgment, but I flatter myself that your tendency of thought will not be dissimilar from my own."

"I suspect so, sir." With the army still numbed by the harrowing final weeks of the Canadian campaign, there had been no serious effort among the officers to discuss strategy for the next phase of the struggle. Yet, from his talks with Schuyler before the Canadian campaign began as well as recent encounters, and his observations of what Schuyler was already trying to do, at the shipyard in Skenesboro as well as elsewhere, Arnold reckoned that their thinking probably *was* very much along the same line.

"The truly important thing—" Schuyler halted, and then resumed in a fervent voice. "It's absolutely *vital* that we achieve a unified position. We *cannot* afford divided counsel against such odds." Schuyler slumped, apparently in deep thought. "I speak to you frankly," he finally said. "In his anger, Sullivan could be nasty. That's no matter. He'll be gone. But General Gates . . ." his voice trailed off. "I haven't had an opportunity to discuss the subject with him."

Arnold smiled inwardly. Schuyler and Gates had spent a good deal of time together in recent days. What Schuyler really meant was that he had no *wish* to discuss the matter with Gates.

Schuyler spoke again: "Our corps of commanders is very thin. Sullivan will be gone. Baron de Woedtke—I'm sure I tell you no tales—is hopeless, poor wretch." The last was a reference to a foreign officer commissioned a brigadier by Congress to fight in Canada. Now he was whiling away time at Crown Point, seemingly intent on drinking himself to death. "Gates, alas, is not happy at all with the situation. We have a few good colonels. David Waterbury is the best and he is likely to be made brigadier at any time. Beyond that we have no senior men other than militia officers." Schuyler gave Arnold a meaningful look. "It's vital that we have a unified approach. I'm afraid it won't be easy. You understand?"

Arnold nodded slowly. It was clear that Schuyler did not want to invite opposition from Gates and a possible stalemate. It would be better for Schuyler if both he and Gates were to react to someone else's views rather than present their own. Let Gates spend his ammunition shooting at Arnold's presentation and out of the debris Schuyler might be able to fashion some compromise that could be agreed upon. Arnold was not at all unhappy with the arrangement. At the least, he would have a full opportunity to make his case.

Schuyler slapped Arnold on the knee. "Well, once we have achieved our plan of action and assignments are made, you shall have your home leave. No man deserves it more."

Chapter 3

Fort Amherst
Crown Point, New York
July 8, 1776

Having spent several hours scribbling his notes, Benedict Arnold was the first of the officers to enter the room for the noon Council of War. Because he would be making a major presentation, he chose the chair at the foot of the conference table, where he would have good eye contact with everyone.

A few moments later John Sullivan shuffled in, giving Arnold a baleful glare as he took his seat. *Yes, of course, blame the messenger,* Arnold thought. When he had returned from Albany, Arnold had seen no reason not to forewarn Sullivan that he was being replaced by Gates. It had seemed the decent thing to do—give the man a chance to absorb the shock and prepare himself instead of keeping it a secret. But Arnold had experienced relentless anger from Sullivan ever since. Aware that Sullivan could be troublesome in the conference, Arnold decided to make another try at breaching the gap.

"I'm sorry that you'll be leaving us tomorrow, General," he said.

"*I'm* not," Sullivan grated. "I can't wait to get this damned pesthole behind me."

Arnold was surprised to see that the next entrant was young James Wilkinson. Arnold was now without an aide, having dismissed Wilkinson as soon as the retreat from Canada had been completed. It had to be that way—Arnold could not tolerate an insubordinate act by anyone, much less the man closest to him in the field. He had not done it bitterly. He had not put Wilkinson on report, and his last words to him had been: "I don't know whether to condemn you for disobeying orders—or admire your spunk." He now leaned over with raised eyebrows, as if to ask: *What the hell are you doing here?*

Wilkinson had not sat at the table, but on one of the chairs against the wall that were reserved for aides. He leaned forward, hand cupping his mouth so that Sullivan would not hear him. "I'm attached to General Gates, sir— temporarily at least," he whispered.

Arnold smiled sardonically. Gates had only been in Crown Point a day, but

Arnold had already noticed Wilkinson sucking up to him. He had to hand it to Wilkinson. He was brassy and he was a survivor. Arnold whispered back: "Let's hope he doesn't ask me for a recommendation."

Wilkinson gulped, and then said: "I've come early. To notify General Schuyler that Gates will be delayed."

Wonderful, Arnold thought. *Schuyler will love that.*

Schuyler soon entered, followed by a host of officers—Baron de Woedtke, Dr. Lewis Beebe, Richard Varick, four colonels, and several aides. Schuyler sat at the head of the table, Sullivan at his left. The empty chair to his right, the seat of honor, was waiting for Gates. After everyone settled down, Schuyler glanced around. "Where is General Gates?"

Wilkinson delivered his message in a tremulous voice, earning himself a steely glare from Schuyler. The silence hung heavy as Schuyler drummed his fingers on the table. Quite apart from being top commander, a patrician of his stature did not like to be kept waiting by anyone. At length, Varick rose: "I'll see if I can find General Gates, sir."

"No, no." Schuyler waved Varick down. "He knows when we're starting. We'll give him a few more minutes. And then we'll begin without him."

Arnold glanced up at the ceiling, its timbers charred from the fire of a year ago. He peered through one of the two windows of the room, seeing troops moving aimlessly about in the compound. He knew it would never work to start the meeting without Gates. Even though Gates was second to Schuyler, circumstances made him the heavyweight of the meeting, the new man with a congressional appointment, the on-site commander of Crown Point and Ticonderoga. Arnold's gaze fastened on Varick, the normally stolid muster-master and aide to Schuyler, who now was squirming at the insult to his chief more than Schuyler himself was.

Gates finally made his entrance, striding importantly into the room. Puffing from the exertion, he took his seat, nodded at Schuyler, and then beamed a smile around the table, as if satisfied at making a point.

"So glad you could join us, General," Schuyler said drily. He paused a good while before announcing his agenda. He told the group he would begin by bringing news from the latest dispatches to everyone and summarizing the military situation before asking General Arnold to present his analysis and rec-ommendations. This last raised a few eyebrows, but Schuyler immediately launched into an attempt at the impossible—to bring a measure of cheer to the meeting. He leaned back in his armchair with a pleased expression: "It is amazing how swiftly news can travel, when it is truly important—only a matter of days from Philadelphia by the fastest couriers and less from New York!" Schuyler now leaned forward intently, treating the others to a proud smile. "Last evening I received dispatches from both places. Today is July eighth. I have the honor to report to you that only six days ago, on July second, the

Continental Congress voted to declare complete independency from Great Britain!"

There were murmurs around the table, the exchanging of glances, a few men mumbling "Hear, hear!"

As if to deflate the import of Schuyler's news, Gates said: "I've been expecting this for six months and more."

Varick impulsively blurted: "This will stiffen our resolve!"

"It might stiffen the resolve of the British even more," Sullivan said wryly.

Arnold could see the disappointment clouding Schuyler's face. Apparently, he had expected that his news would release whoops of joy and the raising of toasts to a glorious future. Aside from Varick and himself, the general reaction treated it more as an act of defiance against impending doom. Arnold's own view was more pragmatic. Brave declarations were nice, but what truly counted was *earning* independence on the battlefield.

Schuyler tried once more: "This noble declaration means that the *former* Colonies are now emphatically known as *States!* Thirteen free and independent States. And collectively, for the purpose of conducting the war, we are the United States of America!"

Still nothing more than nods and murmurs. "I have no other details, no text, but I shall keep you informed when more comes in," Schuyler mumbled. "As for the other dispatch, from New York, I am afraid the news is rather ominous. On the last days of June a great many sails of British warships and transports were sighted, bound for New York Bay. Over the first few days of July the vessels began arriving by the score. It is clear that General Howe has moved his army down from Nova Scotia to attack New York, as anticipated. And many more vessels arrived directly from England, apparently a large reinforcement armada under his brother, Admiral Sir Richard Howe. As you know, General Washington was aware of the danger to New York and has been moving down from Cambridge and Boston into defensive positions on Manhattan and Nassau Islands for weeks."

Gates commented: "This doubtless means that Washington will send us precious little help. We'll be on our own up here."

When Schuyler made no response, Gates sniffed and looked around the table. He spoke in a slightly admonishing tone: "May I suggest that we all keep this news from New York to ourselves. We have entirely too many faint hearts here as it is. You all know how energetic the rumor-mongering can be among the rank and file."

Schuyler seemed about to challenge this idea, but again he let the remark pass. "Before I call upon General Arnold," he said, "allow me briefly to summarize our situation." He then relentlessly intoned what everyone already knew, detailing the gap between the pathetic, scourged American army and the large force that Carleton and Burgoyne had assembled at St. Jean. A stream of reports from spies and deserters revealed that the enemy had as many as ten thousand British, German, and Loyalist troops and more than five hundred Indian scouts and warriors. Most interesting were the additions to this army—hundreds of seamen from the Royal Navy and a host of shipwrights, riggers, blacksmiths, and carpenters.

Exactly. Burgoyne intends to build himself a naval force that will sweep us from the lake, Arnold thought.

The ensuing silence was broken by Gates: "And, as I understand it from Dr. Beebe and Major Varick, we are now reduced to fewer than six thousand men, which is bad enough, but—nearly half of them are unfit for duty. Am I correct, gentlemen?" Beebe and Varick both nodded dejectedly.

"Well, now, what is the answer?" Gates asked the group in general. He then addressed Schuyler in an oily and somewhat patronizing tone: "My dear General Schuyler, since as we all know you are the great man of the entire upper Hudson region, Albany and Tryon Counties, and all the rest, pray tell why we have not seen the militia and volunteers from these places. Why have they not flocked to our aid, just as the stalwart men of New England came to the aid of their embattled brethren in Massachusetts but a little more than a year ago? By the time I arrived there, to take charge of organizing our new army, we had more than twenty thousand men!"

Arnold did not feel that he knew Gates very well, having spent only limited time with him the year before in Cambridge. Gates could be a jovial companion in the evening, if one were in the mood for many laughs, great quantities of drink, and a steady barrage of bawdy jokes and sarcastic criticisms of people not present. But Arnold well remembered the pompous, needling style of the man at other times—as when he had belittled Washington's decision to send Arnold north through the wilderness to Quebec. It was precisely the scorn of such men that had steeled Arnold's determination to succeed. Arnold did not envy Schuyler. Up to now, Schuyler had avoided acrimony by simply ignoring Gates's comments. But the question had been put directly to him, and everyone was waiting to hear his answer.

"This is a sparse area, General," Schuyler said. "A fraction of New England's population. And no one has come from New England to help us—save for you, of course. The few troops we have from that region are all Continentals, no volunteers. Now that you are with us, perhaps that will change. We know of your reputation there," he concluded with veiled sarcasm.

"Ah, but it is not *their* homes and hearths that are threatened," Gates responded in kind. "My question concerns *this* region."

"It's too early to expect a general turnout," Schuyler said stiffly. "We certainly shall have the Albany County militia, though they have been much preoccupied recently in putting down Loyalist uprisings. As for the Tryon County militia, I doubt that we will see them until the autumn at best."

Gates pretended to be shocked. "For heaven's sake, why?"

"Loyalist sentiment is strong in the Mohawk Valley and the Indian population quite large," Schuyler pointed out. "The Tryon County leaders believe that the enemy may very well decide to go up the Saint Lawrence to Lake Ontario for a long flanking movement—to land and march to the Mohawk River to recruit more Loyalists and stir up the Indians to ravage the entire valley all the way to Albany."

"A prodigious long way to go," Sullivan grunted.

"Yes, but another water route with no mountain barrier, and only the Tryon County militia and the small garrison at Fort Stanwix to stand in their way. I'm happy to report, however, I recently met with the chiefs of the Iroquois Confederacy and secured their promise to stay neutral. Some, the Oneidas and Tuscaroras, even favor our side."

Gates rolled his eyes. "I don't know why anyone would take the word of those savages," he said, as if Schuyler were foolish for even trying.

"I believe they will honor their pledge," Schuyler said testily. "My only fear is what might happen should Thayandanega reappear." No one needed a translation for this reference to the fierce Mohawk chief, known to the English-speakers as Joseph Brant, who had been taken to London by the British to be flattered and seduced at the court of George III.

Schuyler went on: "If the enemy does not go to the Mohawk Valley and if the Indians stay quiet, I will expect the Tryon County militia to join us. In fact, if we can hold out until the harvests are in, I believe many other settlers will come to us. My efforts to that end shall not be wanting."

Gates barely concealed a snicker. "Hold out until the harvests are in? Why should the enemy wait the entire campaigning season before attacking us?" When Schuyler did not respond, Gates sniffed: "All this talk of the Mohawk Valley! I should think a much more likely possibility would be that Carleton and Burgoyne might pass us by the other way, striking east to descend the Connecticut River Valley and ravage New England."

What nonsense, Arnold thought. *The enemy is going nowhere but here.* He began to fear that either Schuyler or Gates would explode if their icy exchanges went on much longer, endangering his chance to rationally lay out the strategy he knew must be followed. Then he became aware that Schuyler apparently had had enough, too. He was calling for Arnold to speak. "Please proceed, General Arnold," he said.

"Thank you, sir." Arnold leaned forward, shuffling the papers in front of him, taking a moment to gather his thoughts. "Let me begin by saying, with all respect, that I do not believe the enemy will deviate from the a straightforward attack down the lake. To attempt the Mohawk Valley, as General Sullivan points out, would be a very long way for a large army to go—at least three times farther than the direct route."

Schuyler seemed about to argue the point, but subsided.

Arnold continued: "And for the British to strike for New England, they first would have a long and mountainous march and then the countryside would very likely rise up against them, as happened at Boston a year ago."

Gates scowled. "Your point is a telling one, General. The New Englanders would rise up—as I fear the Yorkers will not."

That was too much for the proud New Yorker. "I will tolerate no more such insults, General!" Schuyler burst out, his face reddening.

Before Gates could lash back, Arnold hurried on: "Gentlemen, if the enemy moves in either direction, east or west, we certainly will know about it in enough time to react. In the meantime, we must prepare for what all of the evidence suggests that the enemy will do. Namely, build a fleet at St. Jean to overwhelm us on the lake and strike for their main obstacle in the north—Ticonderoga."

"What evidence?" snarled Sullivan.

"The most obvious is the unique character of the enemy's force, as General Schuyler has described it. All those laborers and skilled craftsmen. The large contingent from the Royal Navy. And the materials for making boats that Burgoyne has brought all the way from England. There's more. The news that General Schuyler brings us from New York completes the picture. It suggests that the British really are intent on the 'grand strategy' that we've all heard about."

Arnold proceeded to recount the elements of the British strategy that the Americans had learned about in scattered reports from London and Canada—the idea of severing New England from the rest of the Colonies by securing the water route from Lake Champlain down the Hudson River to New York Bay. The plan called for two invading armies—one coming down from Canada, the other driving up the Hudson from New York City. When the two armies met at Albany, the radical head of the rebellion—New England—would be amputated and, the British believed, the war all but won.

For his clinching argument, Arnold reminded his listeners that those two armies would now be in place if Howe succeeded in taking New York City—*and* that the rumored author of the "grand strategy" was none other than General John Burgoyne. He concluded: "All of this dictates what our defense in the north must be. We must do everything in our power to delay the British advance from Canada, especially on the lake. I believe there is every chance we can keep the enemy from attacking Ticonderoga until well into September, perhaps even October. At that point—"

Arnold was interrupted by Sullivan, who came to life with a derisive scoff. "Delay them through the *entire* summer? General Gates has already raised that question. How on earth can we *delay* them?"

Arnold's response was even in tone. "By maintaining control of Lake

Champlain. As long as possible. And the only way to do that is to match the British in building warships. For each they build at St. Jean, we must build one at Skenesboro."

At this, Sullivan exploded in laughter, glancing at each man around the table in turn, as if inviting them to join him. "Build *warships*! In this wilderness! Well, yes, you have all the forests for wood—but nothing else. The supplies, the craftsmen, the seagoing men, they're all two hundred miles away in the coastal towns. This is the most preposterous idea I've ever heard!"

Baron de Woedtke, Dr. Beebe, and several of the colonels joined tentatively in the laughter, and Wilkinson rolled his eyes and gave a small smile. Schuyler and Varick remained impassive, while Gates, who Arnold thought might join in the scorn, seemed to be reserving judgment, his eyes narrowed in thought.

Arnold continued in his calm voice: "Certainly it will be difficult. But it can be done. There are three points to consider. First, we have an advantage. We have the only warships on the lake now. Only three in number, it is true, and poorly designed for the task. The British must start at the beginning. And they've already lost a month of the campaigning season. We laid waste everything we could in the retreat from Canada, and I gave special attention to the shipyard at St. Jean. We ruined it as much as human hands could do. It will take the British weeks to get that yard in working order. And they've only just started. They've lost two weeks because of the heavy rains. The roads and trails to St. Jean have been quite impassable—and remember, they must portage everything around the rapids and falls at Fort Chambly. They must build their boats at St. Jean to have access to the lake.

"Second, it is true that most of the men and supplies we will need are hundreds of miles away. But whence came the British craftsmen and seamen? From England. Thousands of miles away. Surely we can do as well. It will take all of the influence that General Schuyler and General Gates can bring to bear. I believe that with a concerted effort, our friends on the coast will rally to our need. We cannot afford to waste any time, but we are not behind in this race. Not yet."

As Arnold spoke, Sullivan's sneer was replaced by a sullen expression, his brow gathered in a frown. Beebe and de Woedtke were now warily attentive. Taking his cue from Gates, Wilkinson listened intently, suddenly aware that this discussion could turn out differently than he had first expected.

"My third point," Arnold continued, "is that we have more resources in this region than it may seem at first glance. We transported a great deal of the seasoned wood from St. Jean and burned the rest. Skenesboro is the perfect place, a decent shipyard that is already being expanded, because of General Schuyler's foresight. It's well protected from any possibility of a British raid, and it has deep water and direct access to the lake. Moreover, General Schuyler has been turning out boats at his Hudson River shipyards for nearly two years and more recently at Skenesboro."

"Those are merely small boats for transporting men and supplies," Gates interjected, "made by house carpenters. They'll be quite useless in battle."

"We needed transports then and we need warships now," Arnold said, "so we must convert. There are two gundelos already under construction on the ways at Skenesboro." Arnold used the army term for the gondolas—heavy, flat-bottomed boats with oars, capable of carrying three cannon.

"As much as a year ago, General Arnold and I discussed the possibility that one day we would have to convert from transports to warships," Schuyler said quietly.

Arnold selected one of the papers from his notes and spread it out on the table. "I have taken the liberty of compiling a list of what I think our goals should be in building warships. First of all, it would be a magnificent stroke if we could build a large fully rigged ship of two hundred tons or more, a square-rigger, perhaps a frigate, capable of carrying many more cannon."

Schuyler shook his head dejectedly. "I fear that is truly beyond us, General. It would divert us, perhaps fatally, from building a larger number of smaller ships, the kind that are truly possible."

Disappointment clouded Arnold's face. "I suggest this only because I fear the British will do everything they can to get a powerful ship on Lake Champlain. By building it from the ground up at St. Jean or breaking an existing ship apart to transport it around the falls to be reassembled."

Schuyler spread his hands. "If so, that would add to the delay you spoke of so eloquently. We do have the *Royal Savage*."

To Arnold's mind, comparing the *Royal Savage* to a frigate was like comparing a pistol to a cannon. She was a notoriously difficult boat to sail, hard to even get away from a dock unless the wind were just right.

"Leave aside the question of a large ship," Schuyler urged, "and let us hear the rest of your list."

Arnold was tempted to argue the point further but decided to choose another time. "I would want to see us build at least ten of the gundelos," he continued, "similar to the two already under construction. These would be the workhorses of our fleet. For maneuverability and greater power, I would want eight row galleys, half again as long as the gundelos, slender, with keels, much more commodious and carrying more cannon, swift under two lateen sails when the wind is right, but also propelled by long oars or sweeps when the wind is contrary, as many as thirty-six of the sweeps."

Quieted for a time, Sullivan found new reason to scoff. "What is this talk of gundelos and galleys? Are we to make our men into galley slaves? Are we back in the days of the Greeks and Romans?"

Arnold had vowed to himself to use only reason and logic in his presentation, avoiding loud persuasion or angry reactions. Though he found Sullivan's jibes profoundly irritating, the only important people in the room to him were Schuyler and Gates, and he knew Schuyler was already favorably disposed. So he managed to keep his equanimity once again: "You may well ask, General Sullivan, why it is that the Pennsylvania navy consists mainly of row galleys designed by Benjamin Franklin. It is because they can maneuver in a restricted area such as the Delaware River and the estuary, no matter what the wind does. There are portions of Lake Champlain that are narrow, not even as wide as the Delaware River. The row galley is an ideal vessel for such places. I discussed this with Dr. Franklin when I met with him in Montreal last February. He made sketches for me, and I have worked on a design for the past two months, whenever I had a moment to do so. I can tell you that our men will be glad to pull their oars when it means victory or saving their lives."

Gates pursed his lips: "Pray tell me just how this ship-building effort you recommend will delay the enemy's advance."

"The British will not want an even match on the lake. They will want their fleet to be superior to ours before they come out. If we can keep up to them in building ships—or at least come close to that and make sure they know about it—the entire summer will pass. Then when they do come out, they will face a naval battle. Only if they win that battle will they be able to attack our second line of defense, Fort Ticonderoga. If we have delayed them long enough, they might not even attack, especially if they see that they cannot take the fort by storm, but must lay siege to it. They will begin to fear the onset of winter. They will realize that the freezing of the lake will mean the cutting of their supply lines to Canada. They will imagine what it would be like trying to march on Albany in the winter snows."

"This is a fantasy," Sullivan growled, but Gates waved him off. He said: "You seem very confident, General Arnold. How do you justify that?"

Arnold thought for a long moment. "I don't wish to underestimate the enemy—nor the task we face in carrying out such a massive effort. The British *will* bring their fleet out at some point. We *will* have to fight them on the lake. But I believe they will be very cautious—and therefore much time will pass. We know that Sir Guy Carleton is in command, much to the displeasure of General Burgoyne. And Carleton—well, you know much better than I, General Gates, from your own personal experience. Am I correct that he is a much more cautious commander than Burgoyne?"

Gates nodded slowly. "Yes, this is so. John Burgoyne is a gambler. He's disposed to attack. And Carleton is conservative. And the wiser for it, I believe."

"And so Carleton is likely to hold Burgoyne in check," Arnold said. "I believe we can build a fleet strong enough to defeat the enemy on the lake—*if* we can get the help we need, the experienced sailors, and if the fleet is well led.

Even if we lose a naval battle, we will have delayed the enemy. And the *certain* advantage of delaying an enemy assault on Ticonderoga until well into the autumn season is that we will have more time to prepare the defenses. More time for our troops to regain their fighting trim. And the harvest will be in and we can expect more militia and volunteers to come to us. More of a chance that we can force the enemy to lay siege, as winter comes."

No one commented. Arnold fell silent. He had made the case as best he could. Gates, who was staring at the ceiling in deep thought, finally asked a question: "General, you refer to a naval fleet as our first line of defense—and Fort Ticonderoga as the second. What about Crown Point?"

"I would abandon this place," Arnold said. "We could still use West Bay and the docks for a time, but the fort itself is a shambles, I don't have to tell you. The effort it would take to restore it would much better be used on Ticonderoga, a far superior and more defensible place. Even if that were not so, I don't think it wise to divide our forces and defend two forts when we'll be hard pressed to defend just one."

Gates and Schuyler exchanged an uneasy glance. The logic was irrefutable, but such a decision would not be well received in the south.

The silence returned. Arnold braced for attacks on his plan. Then Gates spoke: "Only God knows if it will work. Naval warfare is foreign to us. But our circumstances are unique. We must try it." He turned to Schuyler. "I am satisfied, I think General Arnold has outlined exactly what we must do. And I compliment him for it."

Taken by surprise, Schuyler could only nod and say: "I agree."

Gates smiled sweetly at Sullivan. "Unless, of course, General Sullivan has a better idea?"

"Thank you, General," Sullivan said sarcastically, "but I will not bore you with my own fantastical notions. Since I will not be here to see them executed."

Ignoring Sullivan, Schuyler rapped on the table excitedly. "Well, now, we are agreed on what we must do. My first decision is that you, General Arnold, are the perfect man to take charge of the ship-building effort at Skenesboro."

"But you have a commander there."

"Ah—yes, but he will be reassigned. Now, I know I speak for General Gates as well as myself when I say that we shall do everything in our power to solicit the help we need from the main army and the coastal towns."

"If I am to be responsible for construction at Skenesboro," Arnold said, "I very much will need a first-rate person to follow up on the requests that you and General Gates will make, to act as an agent scouring the coastal towns constantly."

"Yes, well—" Schuyler's eye lighted upon Richard Varick. "I shall appoint Major Varick to that important role. Under your supervision."

Varick looked as if someone had just stabbed him with a bayonet. "But, sir . . ." He began a protest, and then subsided.

Shocked, are you? Arnold thought. *You'll do just fine, my boy.*

Rubbing his hands in glee, Schuyler rattled off more decisions and called for a planning session the next morning, delaying his departure for Albany for a day.

Chapter 4

Carlisle, Pennsylvania
June–July, 1776

"We could always try to escape," Despard said gloomily.

"Out of the question!" John André snapped.

Despard frowned and spoke dryly: "Yes, I know, we're officers and gentlemen, and we've given our word and all that." He leaned forward. "But when your life is threatened continually, when you're made to live in miserable conditions, when everyone in the world seems to have forgotten you—surely there comes a time when you have a right to save yourself in any way you can."

It was a new thought for André, and he pondered it. A nice moral choice. He truly believed he would die before he would allow his honor to be stained. "We *have* given our word, Jack. And in return our captors give us some degree of freedom to move about, to live in a comfortable room instead of being stuffed into a cell or a prison ship. If any of us break that trust, all future British prisoners would be treated terribly." Seeing Despard still shaking his head, André decided that the only effective response to him would be on practical grounds: "It wouldn't work anyway, Jack. We'd never get through the wilderness. We'd have to steal horses to try it and the penalty for that is a hangman's rope."

Despard sniffed and gazed morosely out the dormer window to the scene below of the muddy, rutted main street of the frontier settlement of Carlisle. It was Sunday and a few churchgoers were straggling home. He and André did not attend services. There was no Anglican church in Carlisle, which seemed inhabited entirely by Scotch-Irish Presbyterians, all of them partial to the rebel cause and all apparently refugees of one sort or another from the British Isles, or the descendants of refugees, and therefore hostile to all things English.

André and Despard had been among the prisoners taken at St. Jean the previous December when the Seventh Regiment of Foot had surrendered the fort to General Montgomery. Their first place of imprisonment had been

Lancaster, but after three months someone of authority in Philadelphia decided that the five hundred prisoners, an entire regiment, constituted a potential menace to the Lancaster populace, which had been thinned of able-bodied males by recruitment to the militia and the Continental Army. The solution was to deprive the regiment of its leadership by dispersing its officers to other towns, sending ten of them forty miles west to Carlisle. These men were not received well in the rude frontier hamlet, and they soon looked back upon Lancaster, which formerly had seemed unspeakably dull and provincial, as an idyllic place compared to Carlisle.

There had been some hostility in Lancaster, too, but also some friendly and intelligent people. The elderly chairman of the committee of safety there, Edward Shippen, Sr., had treated the prisoners in a kind and even-handed way. He was a man they could entrust with their letters to home and their requests for drafts on their funds in London. André and Despard had purchased fowling pieces, handsome light guns for bird shooting, from an old German gunsmith. They found they could freely roam the countryside on bird-hunting excursions, within their six-mile limit. André was placed in the home of Mr. and Mrs. Thomas Cope, a congenial Quaker family. He had become fond of eleven-year-old John Cope, who showed some talent for drawing. André tutored young John in both drawing and the flute. When the time came, John's father could not bring himself to accede to André's request to take the boy with him to Carlisle to continue his education, and so the parting had been a sad one indeed.

Carlisle families would not accept British officers in their homes, fearing they would thereby seem less patriotic than their neighbors. The officers had been somewhat dubious in any case about residing in what they regarded as squalid hovels, but now they were dismayed because they would have to pay much more for their lodgings, splitting up among the three taverns that were the only substantial buildings in the town, apart from the church and the jail. André twice had been able to secure funds from his holdings in London through the medium of Mr. David Franks, a Philadelphia merchant who served as the official agent for imprisoned British officers, relaying the money through Mr. Shippen in Lancaster. This had enabled André to secure the best accommodation, a large room on the third floor of Mrs. Ramsay's tavern, taking Despard as his roommate. And André soon found himself the creditor for some of the other officers, who either did not have funds to draw on at home or didn't wish to take the risk of losing their money in transit.

Unless the ten captive officers went out as a group, they rarely could stroll about the town without being insulted, or rudely shoved aside, or even spat upon, and more than once a stiff reaction had brought about a one-sided fist fight. Those were the only times the local committee of safety intervened at all, and then only to rescue the victim before he was killed. And so, the miserable captives could do nothing but stoically endure frequent abuse.

What should have been a joyous day for André and Despard turned out to be one of crushing disappointment. This occurred at the end of May when Lieutenant Edward Burd and four mounted men of his Lancaster militia arrived with the news that the British officers were to be released and exchanged for American prisoners. Burd would escort them as far as Lancaster where several militiamen would be detailed to take them on to Philadelphia. Not surprisingly, the ten British officers went wild with joy, dancing about in the street. Locals crowded around, glaring sullenly, torn between their desire to be rid of these unwelcome guests and chagrin at seeing them suddenly so happy. Burd held up the scroll he had received from Elias Boudinot, commissioner of prisoners in Philadelphia, and began reading the names in alphabetical order. But the first name he read was "Ferris."

André and Despard listened with growing consternation, and when Burd finished they stood there transfixed, stunned. Burd had read only eight names. They were not included! They began remonstrating and Burd kept shaking his head, trying to explain that the exchange quota allowed for only eight officers and that the names had been drawn by lot. It was too bad, but André and Despard were simply the unlucky ones. That caused Despard to lose his poise entirely, alternately pleading and screaming that there must be a mistake. The locals began pressing in, growling and muttering at the behavior of the two distraught officers. A melee threatened, held back only by the militiamen who maneuvered their horses around André and Despard. At Burd's behest, the other eight British officers slunk away to their lodgings to pack their gear. Burd was adamant that he could take only those listed, but promised André and Despard that he would send a query to Boudinot along with the prisoners and their escort.

The two men sat glumly in rocking chairs on the porch of Mrs. Ramsay's establishment, watching their ecstatic colleagues appear one by one to dump their baggage into the wagon brought by Burd's group. Another altercation threatened when the three tavern owners came running out, shouting that they were owed money by some of the departing prisoners. A good deal of wrangling ensued when Burd made it known that officers who had not paid up would have to stay behind. In the end, André loaned sufficient funds to three of his erstwhile colleagues.

"You're a bloody fool!" Despard whispered in his ear. "If you'd held back we'd have gone in their place!"

"That would be a rotten thing to do," André said.

Despard groaned. "Well, why didn't you at least use some of the money to bribe that stiff-necked rebel to take us with them—to Lancaster at least?"

"Jack, you're a poor judge of character," André responded. "Burd would've been mightily offended, and we'd be worse off than we are now. He'll be back in a week or so to fetch us when the matter gets straightened out in Philadelphia."

"And you trust far too much," Despard rejoined.

The two men verged on tears as they watched the wagon roll away, the officers sprawled on their baggage, demeanors sad for the moment out of deference to André and Despard. A couple of them kept shouting their thanks to André, saying they would repay him as soon as they caught up with each other. Before the procession was out of earshot, however, all that could be heard was laughter and whoops of joy, causing André and Despard to sink deeper into depression.

They had even more reason to despair in the weeks that followed. No one appeared from Lancaster to liberate them, and the locals taunted them more than ever, possibly because they were an easier and more concentrated target as the only two left. The rowdiest types in town also seemed to have a special dislike for André as the personification of the English gentleman, with his handsome face and figure, courtly manners, impeccable uniforms, and artistic talents and interests. Despard wore a uniform, too, but otherwise in appearance he resembled the frontiersmen more than he did André. An Irishman five years André's senior, Despard had been a soldier since the age of fifteen; he had a lean, saturnine face with a blue cast to the jowls, and his speech tended to be clipped and brief, with a trace of a brogue remaining.

The next serious incident occurred late in June, when André and Despard availed themselves of their main out-of-doors pleasure, taking their fowling pieces and a beautiful hunting dog that André had purchased to the countryside on a pleasant day to shoot birds, but really more just to walk the fields and forests out of sight of Carlisle and its citizens. On the way back to town they saw a crowd of perhaps fifteen men running toward them in an agitated state. The mob seized the two British officers and began roughing them up, tearing their uniforms and emptying their pockets. As they were dragged into town, André and Despard learned that the reason for the anger of the mob was a new rumor brought back to Lancaster by a recently released American prisoner. He charged that André had turned American prisoners over to the Indians at St. Jean, who had roasted the poor fellows alive. Any suggestion of Indian atrocities sent tremors through this frontier town, although, in truth, the Indians were as much sinned against as sinners. Years earlier, during Chief Pontiac's war, hoodlums had massacred more than thirty Indian women and children who had been jammed into the Carlisle jail, ostensibly for their protection.

A hangman's noose ominously appeared, and Despard flailed his long arms about, managing to quiet some of the men enough to hear André's denials. "Does he *look* like someone who would be dealing with savages?" Despard shouted. Then Mrs. Ramsay appeared, stout of figure and ferocious of mien, shaming the ruffians to silence with her stentorian voice. André and Despard slipped behind her skirts into the relative safety of the tavern and their upstairs room, where they stood trembling, drawing out their swords in readiness. When no pursuit came thundering up the stairs, they slumped on their beds, and Despard said: "Thank God you're a paying customer or the old bitch would've let us be hanged."

One result of the debacle was that the two men soon learned that they were not entirely without sympathizers in Carlisle. That night a boy surreptitiously returned their undamaged fowling pieces to them. André gave him a guinea, but later he and Despard smashed the guns so that no ruffian of Carlisle would ever inherit them. Then it became clear that an unnamed citizen of Carlisle had carried word of the incident to Lancaster when Edward Burd and his men showed up two days later, sent by Mr. Shippen.

André and Despard were overjoyed and rushed out to greet the militia lieutenant. He waved a greeting, then held up his hands in protest. "Wait, wait!" he shouted. "Before you say anything, I want to tell you that I'm not here to take you out."

"What?" André and Despard exclaimed in unison. Burd dismounted and waved off his troops. "Tie up your horses and relax somewhere till I call you." He turned to the two devastated British officers. "I'm here to restore order. After what happened the other day."

"Great," Despard moaned. "How about saving us from *dis*order by getting us out of here?"

"Look, I'm sorry. I tried, I really did. We haven't heard from Commissioner Boudinot. And Mr. Shippen—well, he's a stickler for the rules."

Despard glared, but André said, "It's all right, we know it's not your fault. How can we help you?"

"We've investigated that rumor about you," Burd said, glancing at André. "It's totally false. What I want is your side of the story, and then I want the committee of safety to round up those responsible."

"You'll hang them all, right?" Despard said sarcastically.

"No," Burd replied, with a half smile. "But I'm going to scare the hell out of them. Now, I may need you to help identify them."

André shook his head. "I think we should stay out of it."

Burd thought for a moment. "I think you're right. Let's see how it goes first. When I'm done I'll find you and tell you what happened."

Only an hour later, Burd found André and Despard in the public room of Mrs. Ramsay's tavern and sat down at their table, accepting André's invitation to join them for a repast of soup, ham, bread, and ale. Reaching into his inner pocket, Burd tossed a packet on the table. With a smile, he said, "I didn't know you were a spy, Lieutenant André."

Despard blanched and André looked puzzled. Burd continued: "The miscreants presented these letters as evidence. Said they were written in a mysterious code."

"These are just my letters to my mother and sister in England," André said. Then he laughed. "Ah, I see! Written in French!"

"Yes. I told them it was a very mysterious code indeed. I rounded up a dozen of the culprits and I tell you, I wasn't surprised when four turned out to be members of the council of safety. They hung their heads and mumbled some apologies and promised never to do it again. I told them that was good because the next time there would be a long sentence to hard labor." Burd took a long pull on his ale, then said: "I thought of bringing several of them over to apologize in person, but I decided to check with you first."

"I don't think so," André said. "It would just be embarrassing for them and for us. Let it lay and hope they keep their word."

"I hope they do, too," Burd said, "because there's something else you should know. My company is leaving Lancaster again, I'm sorry to say. I'm not sure who'll be left to come over and punish these fools, if there is any further trouble."

Despard groaned at that: "What do you mean, *if*? We're likely to be murdered here before much longer."

"I'm sure not," Burd said. "It's unpleasant, I know, but these are isolated, ignorant people—just relieving their own tensions. They know if they do you real harm, Mr. Shippen will make sure they pay."

"Yes, but that would be too late, wouldn't it?"

Burd shrugged. "I told my men not to say anything about our leaving the area, but they're probably boasting about it, even as we speak."

Despard was curious about Burd's militia company, the Lancaster Rifles. Burd told him he had already served with the Continental Army, during the siege of Boston the previous year.

"Where are you going now?" André asked.

"To General Washington's army again. The call is out. Looks like there'll be some heavy fighting this summer."

The two prisoners were hungry for news, Despard voicing their bitterness over the fact that there wasn't a soul in Carlisle they could trust, that they heard nothing but rumors.

Burd told them the reason his unit had been called up—the fact that General Howe apparently intended a major assault at New York Island, his army having sailed south from Nova Scotia and passing by Boston. General Washington was on the move to defend New York.

"We were taken at St. Jean," André said. "What's the news from Canada?"

"You probably have St. Jean back by now," Burd said. "Our people are retreating out of Canada altogether. That exchange you unfortunately missed came about because of American prisoners paroled in the north by the governor general of Canada."

"I wish he'd released just two more," Despard said.

"I was under the impression there were some peace negotiations going on," André said, as he resealed his letters with wax borrowed from Mrs. Ramsay.

"There have been," Burd said, "but it's over now. There's every sign the Continental Congress is going to vote for independency."

"That'll do it," Despard said. "We'll be fighting to the finish."

"Yes, I'm afraid so. Your people are going to invade from the north, too. Down the lakes to try to take Ticonderoga and Albany. There's going to be a lot of fighting this summer."

The three men were silent for a while, putative enemies who were half-smiling at each other. Then André asked: "How do you really feel about it? Independency, I mean."

"It not an easy question to answer," Burd said. "It makes this truly a civil war, and that's very bad. Everyone has to make a choice, for or against. And that means Americans will be fighting Americans—as well as fighting you. Even families will be divided. Look at old Ben Franklin, one of the strongest pro-independency men. And yet his son, the royal governor of New Jersey, he's a Loyalist. My grandfather, my father, and I all hoped it wouldn't go this far. It's inevitable now, and we've made our choice. Other family members will go the other way. My uncle in Philadelphia, for example, the Judge. He stands to lose everything. He's kept his opinions to himself, but I'm sure he's Loyalist at heart."

"I wish it hadn't gone so far, too." André said. "But we're soldiers. We don't deal with policy. We just have to do our duty."

The three men chatted for a while longer, on a first-name basis by now. Finally Burd had to leave for the long ride back to Lancaster. He told André and Despard that his company would go through Philadelphia on the way to New York. "I'll get to say good-bye to Betsy—my fiancée," he said. "I'll also see Mr. Boudinot and try to press him as hard as I can. And I'll make sure Mr. David Franks knows about your situation here. I'll see that your letters get sent off, too, John."

"Thanks for everything, Neddy," André said. "I hope you come through it all safely."

"And you two as well."

After Burd and his men rode out of sight, Despard said: "A nice fellow, our Neddy Burd is—for a rebel. But let him go. He's no use to us here, for God's sake. What we need is some law and order right here in this damned place."

As if Neddy Burd's lecture had been taken to heart, there was less overt hostility in the days that followed. A few rather pretty girls gleamed like rough gems among the drab women of Carlisle, and several times André had noticed one of them looking at him with eyes that suggested an emotion quite the opposite of hostility. André was not interested, certainly not in provincial women, and he was well aware that any flirtation would enrage the males of the town.

On the other hand, he knew from frequent complaints that Despard was sex starved, not having had a woman since a furtive, groping encounter with a camp follower in St. Jean. When he ogled the pretty girls of Carlisle, they averted their eyes in distaste, and André would jab him in the ribs with his elbow.

As far as André was concerned, Despard chose the worst possible time to succumb to his lust. In the late afternoon of Friday, July 5th, word reached the outpost of Carlisle that the Continental Congress in Philadelphia had voted on July 2nd to declare that the thirteen Colonies were free and independent of the mother country. This brought forth a spontaneous celebration as citizens streamed from their homes to mill about in the streets, shouting and dancing. A liberty pole and banners made their appearance and reckless frontiersmen fired their muskets and pistols to the sky. Spirits were imbibed liberally, and impromptu parades snaked up and down the main street, many of the cele- brants shaking their fists and shouting epithets up to the third-story dormers from which André and Despard occasionally peeked, wisely having decided to forgo their daily exercise of strolling about town. They remained indoors as the frenzy continued all night, all day Saturday, and again well into the night. After André dozed off Saturday night, Despard tiptoed down the stairs to keep a rendezvous he had managed to arrange with a local whore in the basement of Mrs. Ramsay's tavern.

André was awake when Despard returned to the room to boast about his assignation. Exploding in anger, André shouted: "You stupid arse! That'll get us killed quicker than anything else."

"No, John," Despard said. "She's a whore. Nobody cares. We were cele- brating their declaration of independency, each in our own way. Her for money, me by fucking them."

The next morning André was at his desk writing letters when Despard finally awoke and began dressing. André was still fuming about Despard's assignation of the night before. "Here I was, worried to death, wondering where the hell you were," he told the puffy-eyed Despard. "They're all crazy over the news from Philadelphia. I hate to think what would've happened if they'd caught you with one of their women. And you used money I loaned you!"

"Don't be such a damned prude. I keep telling you, she's just a whore. No one cares. Not too expensive, either. How about it? I can arrange a rendezvous with her—just for you."

Despard chuckled at André's look of disgust and contempt. For some time he had suspected that André's effete manner and his obsession with young John Cope of Lancaster might indicate a different orientation altogether. He had kept his thoughts to himself. He didn't want to seem to be suggesting any- thing, and besides, as long as André was paying the rent he didn't want to of- fend him too much. He contented himself with a somewhat snide question as he watched André turn back to his writing: "Another letter to little John Cope?"

When André made no reply, Despard stretched out on his bed. "I don't understand why you waste time writing so many letters."

"I write a lot of them and you don't write any," André said.

"That's because I don't have anybody to write to," Despard said softly. He went on, in a louder voice: "The damned rebels just throw your letters away. You've written a hundred since we've been prisoners and you've never gotten more than five back."

"Ah, but those five were precious," André said. "They may throw some of them away. But writing them is better than doing nothing. We've got a lot of time to waste." He was working on a letter to his eldest sister, the only one of his family he felt he could burden with the truth about the miseries of life in Carlisle. He had just written that the men of Carlisle were "crapulous, greasy, worsted-stocking knaves." A nice and accurate bit of invective, he thought.

"How about some music?" Despard asked, fingering his flute, his sole artistic interest, but enough to cause André to choose him as his roommate. "We could try that Rosetti duet again."

André leaned back and sighed, looking at the windows, which were all open in an effort to capture some breeze on this warm Sunday in July. "I don't think so. They could hear us, and you know what that means." The men of Carlisle were contemptuous when they heard the mellifluous strains of dual flutes coming from the third floor of Ramsay's tavern. On one occasion a barrage of eggs and cabbages and clods of earth hurled upward had caused the redoubtable Mrs. Ramsay to make another appearance at her doorway. André and Despard had noticed that the ruffians were careful not to break any of her windows by throwing rocks.

André resumed his writing and soon heard heavy breathing, suggesting that Despard had lapsed back into sleep. Probably due to his exertions in the cellar last night, André thought. He finished the letter and sat still for a while, his mind wandering to memories of home. He thought of the dreamy months he had spent at Buxton and Lichfield as an admirer in the literary circle of the renowned poetess Anna Seward. Six years his senior, Anna had attempted to educate André in the ways of love as well as poetry, to a strangely unsatisfying result. She had then promoted a love affair between André and her seventeen-year-old ward, the languorous Honora Sneyd, a blond and blue-eyed beauty, but also one made somewhat pale and inert by consumption.

At the age of twenty-six, André had such regular and well-placed features that some might have regarded him as pretty more than handsome, with lively brown eyes, a fair complexion, and a ready and generous smile. He had the polished manners and appearance of fortunate birth, but he was not of an aristocratic background. His father, a successful merchant, had left his native Switzerland to establish a countinghouse at the hub of world trade, Warnford

Court, London. He married a visiting Parisian lady of good family, who bore him five children. John, the eldest, enjoyed the bounty of his father's trade in the Levant and the West Indies—an education at the University of Geneva, where he added German and Italian to his fluent English and French, and began to refine his native talents in the various arts. He learned drawing and painting under a Swiss master, he became an excellent dancer and musician, and he began to write poetry and plays.

When his father died in 1769, André joined his uncle in managing the family business and quickly found that he loathed it. The bills and papers and implements of gain stifled his artistic nature, and so he began his apprenticeship with Anna Seward and his attempted affairs with the poetess and her ward. When these paled, he decided that he had to get away entirely. He hated business, had no interest in the church, and lacked the conviction to attempt a career as a painter or poet. But he saw romance and adventure in the military life, and so he had purchased his commission in the Seventh Foot in 1772, entrusting the business entirely to his uncle. André obtained permission to study military science and mathematics at the University of Goettingen, on the condition that he also tour the Continent to use his linguistic abilities in secretly reporting observations of the state and techniques of the various armies. It was his first brush with military intelligence, which in time would become a passion for him. In this way, he managed to linger on the Continent until his regiment sailed in 1774 to take up duty in Quebec. He joined the regiment there, by first sailing to Philadelphia and then traveling northward overland through the Colonies. He started a military journal, illustrating it profusely, and then began making drawings and paintings of the Indians and the flora and fauna he encountered in the New World, as the regiment moved deeper into the wilderness to Montreal and then to garrison the fort at St. Jean.

André opened the large leather pouch on the table before him, in which he kept his journal and illustrations, as well as some personal items. He shuffled through the drawings and paintings, holding up a favorite one of a dancing Indian, a wondrous figure, nearly naked, his bronze skin daubed in vermillion and blue and green and black. André took another one, a portrait of an Indian sachem, and chuckled as he recalled how the braves standing behind him as he painted it had grunted in wonderment as the head seemed to take on a life of its own.

After Despard awoke again and the roommates had taken some breakfast, André returned to his desk. He soon found Despard peering over his shoulder. "Ah, your military journal, John," Despard said. "Not much to draw of interest to the army in these parts, eh?"

André looked down at the street. "Things seem to have died out since last night. It's Sunday, after all. No reason not to take our walk. I'm going crazy cooped up in here."

"Think we could risk it?"

"Yes. Let's go. We'll stay close."

The two men exited via the private back entrance to avoid any drunks who might still be celebrating in the public room. They walked several blocks with no incident, breathing the fresh air deeply. By the time they turned back, however, they saw that a number of men had emerged onto the main street, including the worst of the rowdies. And some of them plainly were still drunk.

"Oh, God," Despard moaned. "Here we go again. Have they no respect for the Sabbath?" The two men increased their pace; Mrs. Ramsay's door in sight, André was acutely aware of how flamboyantly the uniforms they were required to wear stood out, the scarlet coats with blue facing, the white breeches and polished leather boots, all in stark contrast to the homespun garb of the locals.

It all happened suddenly, the taunts, the jeering, a line formed to bar their way. When Despard tried to break through, he and André were seized, their arms pinioned. The leader was a man they had not seen before, a bearded, scar-faced fellow. He pulled out an enormous hunting knife, its blade stained with rust and dried blood, and held it up to André's face. "Take a good sniff of my blade, laddie, and lick it or I'll cut your throat," he growled.

André, his jaw set, glared at the man. "Go ahead, you pimping coward."

Just then a strange weapon flashed through the air, beating upon the ruffians and thrust into the face of the knife-wielder, who André and Despard soon learned was named Jared Potter.

The weapon was a broom, and it was formidable in the beefy arms of Mrs. Ramsay. She kept screaming Potter's name as he fled down the street, she waddling in pursuit. The other men doubled over in laughter, and André and Despard quickly took the opportunity to slip through the door and flee up to their room.

Later they learned that Potter, now a trapper, had formerly been an apprentice to Mrs. Ramsay's husband and had disappeared into the wilderness months ago, owing her money and having committed other foul deeds.

"She wasn't saving us," Despard said. "She just wanted to get him." Nevertheless, the two men gave Mrs. Ramsay a gift of a box of spermaceti candles with a thank-you note. The next morning she frostily returned the gift.

"She doesn't care about *us,*" André said. "She just doesn't want any blood spilled at her front door."

"And she wants to keep getting her rent," Despard said. "But I don't care. She's better protection than Neddy Burd and his militia."

"That could be a problem. I'm getting low on money. And that last draft I sent is well overdue."

Despard was somber, thinking of Mrs. Ramsay suddenly becoming an enemy rather than a protector. "The world has forgotten us, John. We're going to rot away here."

"Maybe the war will be over soon, considering what Neddy Burd was talking about, those two invasions we've got going."

"Otherwise—start thinking the unthinkable. Think about escaping."

"No," André said stubbornly.

Chapter 5

Philadelphia
July 8, 1776

For some time Judge Edward Shippen, Jr., had felt himself being physically swept away by a revolution—no, by *two* revolutions, which were occurring almost simultaneously. It was not that he was a participant. Far from it. He was a man on the fringes, an uncomfortable and melancholy witness to events that changed his world dramatically, a man utterly powerless to influence those events, and so left to think only about how he and his family could survive.

For the past week he had been drawn to the main scene of action, as a moth to a candle's flame. He would take his daily constitutionals from his attractive house at No. 98 South Fourth Street to the vicinity of the State House Yard, only two blocks away. The Yard occupied a full block bordered by a seven-foot brick wall. Fronting to the north on Chestnut Street was the imposing State House, where the sessions of the Continental Congress were held.

The Yard itself could be a pleasant place to stroll, or at least it used to be before all of the revolutionary fervor began. It had been declared "a public green and walk forever" when acquired by the Pennsylvania Assembly in 1732, but precious little had been done to make it "green." The grass was patchy from overuse and no plantings had been put in, despite occasional pressure from some citizens, the Judge included, to landscape the place. Only a few ancient walnut trees provided shade on a hot day. The Judge would walk by the southern gate on Walnut Street and enter only if the place was not too crowded with orators or demonstrations or militia musters. Otherwise he would stroll around the block to pass by the front entrances to the building to see who was coming and going, never tarrying but moving along as if he had some mission of his own. The Judge was just past fifty years of age, but he seemed older as he walked along with his bandy-legged gait, hands clasped behind his back. His handsome face was increasingly lined and often wore an unconscious frown, brought about by worry and irritability over recent events.

While strolling by a week ago, on Monday afternoon, July 1st, he had been forced to flee from a sudden and violent thunderstorm to the safety of the Coach and Horses Inn across Chestnut Street from the State House. Later he learned that at that very time the delegates of the thirteen colonies were taking a preliminary vote on the subject of independence. Nine in favor, four opposed.

The vote was carried over to the next day. Of the four negative delegations, South Carolina succumbed to pressure, reluctantly changing its vote "for the sake of unanimity." New York, with no instructions from its legislature, abstained. Judge Shippen was walking past the State House again that morning and saw Caesar Rodney of Delaware arrive, ailing and mud-stained after an all-night ride from Dover, to break the tie in his delegation. Ominously, two of the most prominent men of the five-man Pennsylvania delegation, John Dickinson and Robert Morris, deliberately absented themselves, knowing they could no longer prevent a step that they regarded as premature at best. And so Pennsylvania had also voted for independence. Twelve Colonies for independence, one abstention—and New York would not be long in making it unanimous. The irrevocable step that had been brewing for over a year had finally been taken.

All that evening and late into the night, Judge Shippen heard the noise of celebrations erupting spontaneously in the streets. From the rear of his extensive property, he could see the flicker of a bonfire that had been ignited not a block away and hear the cacophony of bells ringing throughout the city. He listened intently and concluded that the massive State House bell was not among them. Good thing—its resonance surely would cause the building's rotting steeple to collapse. Two days later, on July 4th, the delegates wrangled all day to amend Thomas Jefferson's prose and approve the final version of the Declaration of Independence, causing even more rowdy celebrations.

On the afternoon of Saturday the 6th, Judge Shippen had tea at the home of his cousin, Dr. William Shippen, who lived only a few doors away at the corner of Fourth Street and Locust. William was a pro-independency man, though not nearly as vociferous as his elderly father, also a doctor. And his brother by marriage was Richard Henry Lee of the Virginia delegation to Congress, the strongest southern ally of John and Sam Adams in pushing for independency. From Lee, William had procured one of the copies of the Declaration that had been hurriedly printed, and the two cousins pored over the text.

"Much stronger than I thought it would be," William mused. "I'm satisfied."

The Judge shook his head. "It's quite radical. Is it really necessary to excoriate the King for every wrong known to mankind?"

"He deserves it. The King and his ministry have been totally uncompromising. You saw the text of that terrible speech he made to Parliament. They think we're wayward children and need to be spanked. People are tired of that, Edward."

"Well, I'm with John Dickinson. This is premature and dangerous. The King is sending peace commissioners. We could still resolve our differences through negotiation."

William laughed. "I don't think so! Not now."

"But the British reaction is likely to be quite violent."

"What do you think is already happening? For heaven's sake, we're at war. The British have attacked Charleston. They're going to invade from Canada. We all know about that huge fleet of warships and troop ships that Admiral Howe has brought to New York. And they've even fired on our city." The last was a reference to the foray by the British warship *Roebuck* in May when it had sailed up the Delaware River to fight an inconclusive engagement with the row galleys of the Pennsylvania "navy" that Benjamin Franklin had designed. It was the first time that the City of Brotherly Love had ever received hostile fire.

Edward held up the document. "This will bring them here with a vengeance. They'll want to hang every member of Congress."

William frowned. "You've got to give this some thought, Edward. I know it's especially difficult for you. But you were so clear and strong in your opposition to the worst of the laws, the Stamp Act, the Townshend Acts. Why not come along with the tide now? Accept independency and show some support for it. Otherwise, life could get very unpleasant."

Judge Shippen sighed. "I can't do that. Loyal opposition is one thing, and I'm prepared for that. Armed rebellion is quite something else. I've been a man of the law all my life. I know very well that bad laws can be passed. You have to work to repeal them within the governing system, not overthrow the system with violent rebellion. That's the way to anarchy, to the jungle. You know what Hobbes wrote. Without law, the life of man is 'solitary, poor, nasty, brutish, and short.' "

"The old system is dead. We must go on to something new, or we'll never get the militia properly organized and armed. You know what'll happen on Monday. The proprietary government, the Charter of 1701, the Assembly, everything will be abolished."

"I know," Edward said gloomily. It was a reference to the second revolution that was underway, one that preoccupied Philadelphians even more than the Declaration of Independence—and would destroy everything that generations of the Shippen family held dear. The proprietor himself, William Penn, had written the Charter of 1701, and a Shippen ancestor, also named Edward, had served as the first governor under Penn.

It had always been a source of pride for the Judge to reflect how strong the family connection to the Penns had remained through four generations. After returning from his education in law at the Middle Temple in London, he had gradually assumed all of his father's hereditary offices when Edward Sr. abruptly retired and moved to Lancaster to profit in the fur trade he loved so much. His son had become judge of the Vice-Admiralty Court, town clerk, protonotary of the Supreme Court, member and clerk of the Common Council, and finally was awarded a seat on the Provincial Council, the highest governing body in Pennsylvania. Its role was to advise the governor, who was always appointed by the proprietor, and membership was virtually limited to families long associated with the Penns—the Shippens, the Willings, the Allens, the Tilghmans, all related and interrelated by marriage.

Judge Shippen had been forced to stand by helplessly as the strength of the proprietary government had eroded gradually over the past decade, as the Assembly became radicalized and assumed more power, as the Quaker leadership weakened, as Scotch-Irish and German immigration increased, and as the growing movement for independence had ultimately split the Assembly and finally rendered it totally ineffective. Now the radicals had succeeded in mounting an election of delegates to a constitutional convention to design an entirely new governmental system in Pennsylvania to replace the Charter of 1701. An indication of how radical a system this convention would produce could be seen in the fact that *only* those who disavowed allegiance to George III and swore to support a government "on the authority of the people only" would be allowed to vote.

The prospect was dismal for Judge Shippen. All of his income-producing offices would disappear, in fact had already diminished nearly to the vanishing point. He might be able to continue his law practice, but clients would drift away when they were not even sure what laws were extant.

"What will you do?" William asked quietly.

"I'll stay neutral as best I can and stay out of trouble—try to keep my family safe and just survive," Edward said with a wan smile. "War is an abomination. I really fear the British will be so outraged by that Declaration that they'll come directly here to punish the city."

"No, they're going to New York," William said. "I'm sure they'll come here sooner or later. The greater danger for you, I should think, is—well, everything about you suggests authority and position, Edward. Unless you show some overt support for independency, the radicals will condemn you as a Tory. I don't know that you can successfully maintain a neutral posture. You'll end up being disliked by both sides. Now, this new government will be dominated by the radicals. For suspected Tories, that could mean a very uncomfortable and nerve-wracking time. Perhaps confiscation, fines, even imprisonment."

"I'm well aware. That's why I'm thinking of leaving the city."

"Really!"

"Yes. My father suggested that we remove to Lancaster. I don't like that idea. I have my eye on a farm in New Jersey. In Amwell, not far from the Delaware River and Bucks County. A lovely place, with good water and sweet meadows."

"Well, that should be safe enough if the British come here. Forgive me, I do have trouble seeing you and your family on a farm."

"I don't know why. I could open a country store."

William hid his smile. "Have you discussed this with the family?"

"Only with Margaret. She rather fancies the idea. The children, though—all my daughters are confirmed city girls. And my son—he'd like to run away and join the British Army. They'll just have to adjust themselves. And what will you do, Cousin?"

"Well, unlike yours, my profession is rather in demand. I'm negotiating for a position with the medical department of the Continental Army. Whether I take it depends on the rank and responsibilities."

Edward shuddered inwardly as an image flashed through his mind of his impeccably dressed, somewhat dandified cousin in a field hospital wearing a bloody apron and holding a saw in his hand. "Dear William," he said, "if it comes, I wish you good fortune and Godspeed."

"And for you the same, my dear cousin."

The next morning the Judge persuaded his family to attend services at Christ Church, the principal Anglican church in Philadelphia, although it was twice as far from the Shippen home as St. Paul's, the nearby "parish of convenience." Edward Sr. had left the Quaker circle of friends, the faith of his ancestors, to become a Presbyterian, which perhaps was fitting in his Lancaster environment. But his son had gravitated to the Church of England. It seemed so right for a man of his station to belong to the established church—established in England, that is, if not in the Colonies. Attending Christ Church on this day afforded the Judge an opportunity to converse briefly with several of his friends, including the former attorney general Benjamin Chew and the most recent mayor, Samuel Powel. There was nothing new to learn except that, to the Judge's surprise, Powel now seemed to favor independency.

The elderly black houseman, Reuben, was waiting with the carriage after services to spare the family the walk home in the oppressive heat. The Judge assisted his daughters and wife into the carriage and then announced that he would prefer to walk. Attending Christ Church also gave him the opportunity to once again pass by the State House, with only a slight detour. His heart was gladdened when his youngest daughter, Margaret, called "Peggy" to differentiate her from her mother, leaped down and said she would like to walk with him. She was his secret favorite, cool, grey-eyed Peggy, only just turned sixteen, and yet the only other member of his family who seemed to have a head for figures and business, and a lively curiosity about what was going on in the world to go with it.

For her part, Peggy adored her father, and they often had long talks about serious matters. On this day, however, Peggy prattled on about inanities until they reached the State House Yard. The buildings were quiet on the Sabbath, and they nodded to acquaintances as they walked along, a pleasing picture of a proud and kindly father and his lovely young daughter. There was some activity in the Yard, preparations for the occasion at noon tomorrow when

Colonel John Nixon, head of the Fourth City Battalion of Militia, would read the text of the Declaration of Independence to all citizens who cared to hear. The twenty-foot-high circular wooden platform, erected in 1769 by the Philosophical Society to observe the transit of Venus, was being decorated. A liberty pole had been erected.

"Rather clever of them to schedule the public reading on the very day of the election," the Judge commented sarcastically.

"Father, I don't understand why we voted for independency," Peggy said earnestly. "And I don't understand this election at all. What does it mean for us?"

The idea of trying to explain any of it to anyone was wearisome. "Why worry your pretty little head about it?" the Judge said, and then instantly regretted it. It was just the sort of condescension that Peggy hated. She frowned, but before she could say anything the Judge hastily indicated an unoccupied bench beneath one of the walnut trees. "Let's sit here for a moment and rest, my dear." He had begun to perspire in any case; it would be nice to be quite still for a while to let the slight breeze cool him. He quickly explained to Peggy about the intense pressure brought on the middle colonies and South Carolina by the New Englanders and the other southern colonies. John Dickinson and Robert Morris, both honorable men who opposed independency, had absented themselves because of this pressure and because they knew they no longer represented sentiment within the Assembly—thus by default allowing Pennsylvania to vote for independence, two delegates to one. Peggy thought this still seemed cowardly on their part, and she was aghast at her father's description of tomorrow's election.

Mouth puckered, she asked: "You cannot even vote unless you sign that beastly oath?"

"Yes."

"You won't do it, will you father?"

"No, of course not."

"Will they win?"

"Who? The radicals? Of course they will. They'll be the only ones voting."

Peggy contemplated this for a moment, brow furrowed. "Then—those who do *not* vote will, in effect, be voting *against* independency."

The Judge smiled. It was clever of Peggy to see this. "Yes, you're right. What they've done, unwittingly, is to create a referendum. If you count the eligible voters who *don't* vote—"

"How many would that be?"

"We'll have to wait and see." The Judge was doing some mental arithmetic. "They've broadened the electorate. The number of citizens in all of Pennsylvania must now be close to three hundred thousand." The Judge was up on such things, having himself signed the naturalization papers of more than twenty thousand German immigrants throughout his career, collecting three fourths of the two-dollar fee each of them paid. "Every man over twenty-one who is a taxpayer is eligible to sign the oath and cast a vote. I would guess—about sixty or seventy thousand."

"And I shall guess that no more than ten thousand will vote!" Peggy laughed merrily.

"Quite a few more than that, I should think. But it will make no difference. The convention will happen and we'll have a new government, very different from the old, I'm afraid." The Judge suddenly decided that Peggy would make a good test case before broaching to the entire family his plan to leave the city. He told her about the farm he had contracted to buy in New Jersey. "It will be a very nice contrast from the city, I believe."

"Oh, yes," Peggy said. "It should be much more pleasant out in the country, away from this beastly heat."

"I don't mean just for the summer. We'll live there until the war is over." To Peggy's stunned expression, he quickly explained his concerns over growing anarchy in the city and a bloody battle that would destroy it.

But Peggy was wailing. "To *live* there! On a *farm?* Forever? But all of our friends—oh no, Papa, no!" Tears were forming in her eyes.

The Judge fared little better at dinner. He surveyed his children as Reuben's wife, Lucille, served the table. Of the girls, only the second eldest, auburn-haired Sarah, insisted on her actual name, though she was sometimes called "Sally." The eldest, Elizabeth, was "Betsy"; sweet, shy Mary was "Molly"; and blond, petite Margaret was "Peggy." Each was prettier than the last. When Peggy was born in 1760, the Judge had written to his father that "another of the worst sex has arrived." But he added: "She is entirely welcome."

The only surviving boy (two had died in infancy) was Edward III, who insisted on being known as Edward, disliking "Neddy" and all other variations. He was a handsome, flush-cheeked boy, but somewhat scatterbrained and impulsive. He and Peggy were the most ardently pro-British in the family. When the Shippens had entertained George Washington at dinner in 1774 during the First Continental Congress, Peggy's outspoken comments had embarrassed her parents, but Washington, a gentleman, had only smiled and nodded at the impetuous sentiments expressed by the charming girl. Sarah and Molly also were Loyalist in their views but seemed much more interested in the young men who swarmed around them than in the events of the time. The Judge was sure that these attitudes were not politically motivated but were social in nature—all of his children's friends were of the traditional ruling class of Philadelphia. By the same token, one could understand why Betsy was pro-independence, given her engagement to Neddy Burd, who would soon go off to George Washington's army with his Lancaster rifle company. Out of sympathy for Betsy, Mrs. Shippen tended to favor her side. The resulting schism in the family circle often required the Judge to act as mediator, as he had so frequently in his profession.

The usual dinner-table prattle of gossip and teasing was so intense that the Judge actually had to rap his fork against his glass to gain attention. He had decided not to delay in telling the family of his plans: even though Peggy had promised not to say anything, she was so distraught that the Judge doubted she could conceal the news. As he described his plan to move the family to New Jersey, the reaction was adverse and noisy, and the Judge and his wife looked at each other with raised eyebrows, waiting for it to die down. Then the Judge began to extol the pastoral virtues of the 340-acre farm he was buying, and added that Cousin John Allen had a farm only nine miles away.

"Only nine miles away!" Sarah wailed. She could not imagine going nine *blocks* to see any of her many friends in Philadelphia. Only Betsy among the children seemed contented with the news. Because of her engagement, her social life was much more restricted, anyway. The Judge began to see another good reason for his plan. Times were growing loose, and he considered some of the female friends of Molly and Peggy to be somewhat forward. And there were entirely too many swains mooning about. A more isolated rural life would be safer and healthier in another way. He said nothing of this, instead dwelling on the need for a safe haven from the carnage that surely would be visited on Philadelphia one day by an attacking British Army.

This brought forth an outburst from Edward III. "We have nothing to fear from the British! They'll be coming to liberate us! I'd like to join them myself. I'd like to shoot a few rebels."

Betsy gasped. "And would one of them be your own cousin?" She broke into tears, grasped her napkin, and fled from the dining room, Mrs. Shippen hastily following her.

The Judge stood up. "You and I are going to have a little talk, young man. Right at this moment, if you please!" He grabbed his son's arm and led him into the library.

The next day the Judge vowed to stay away from the State House Yard, having no desire to hear the words of the Declaration again. But curiosity got the best of him. He was to meet the sales agent for the New Jersey farm, who was available every Monday afternoon from two to four at the Indian Queen Hotel and Tavern at Fourth and High Streets, just two blocks beyond the Yard. So the Judge left early, at one, to pass by the Yard on his way, confident that at least he would miss the reading that was scheduled to begin at noon. The place was packed and the Judge slipped in the southern gate, intending to stay on the fringe of the crowd. The ceremony must have started late because Colonel Nixon was still bellowing the text from the other end, though the Judge could pick up only an occasional word at that distance. Nixon had elected to speak from the rear balcony of the State House, rather than use the wooden platform.

Among the dignitaries in the crowd at the far end of the yard, the Judge could identify delegates to Congress: tall, sandy-haired Thomas Jefferson; the bulky Dr. Franklin; Caesar Rodney; John Witherspoon of New Jersey; and many others. The leaders of the independency faction in Pennsylvania were conspicuous—Joseph Reed, Charles Thomson, Timothy Matlack in his uniform, though his Fifth City Battalion had not yet been formed. The crowd was composed mainly of members of the bewildering series of committees that had been formed and reformed over the past two years in the process of undermining legitimate authority—the Committee of Observation, the Committee of Correspondence, the First One Hundred, the Second One Hundred, the Committee of Privates, the Committee of Mechanics and Artisans, the Council of Safety (newly formed to replace the old Committee of Safety, which had been deemed too weak in its performance).

The only person the Judge knew in the immediate vicinity was Nicholas Biddle, who sidled over and whispered in his ear: "What are you doing here? There are hardly any of the respectable citizens present."

The Judge smiled. "Well, then, what are *you* doing here?"

Biddle smiled back. "Just curious to see what we're in for."

The crowd interrupted Nixon with frequent cheers, but finally his oration wound down. The Judge recalled a dream he'd had the night before, a vision of a waxen candle, unlit, but nevertheless melting under some intense heat. That was how he felt now, melting away, everything he held dear melting into nothingness. A band was playing and people were milling about, smiling and congratulating one another. The Judge spied the sales agent he was to meet, standing at the far end of the Yard, and he began to work his way toward him.

He nearly collided with Timothy Matlack, to his mind one of the most obnoxious of the independency leaders. The Judge had once ruled against Matlack in court, and the man had held a grudge ever since. Matlack stopped, and a big grin slowly spread on his bearded face.

"Well, well, if it isn't the eminent Judge himself," Matlack said. "Fancy seeing you here. Good day to you, sir. A *very* good day it is!"

"Good day, Mr. Matlack."

"*Colonel* Matlack, if you please."

"Indeed."

"I'm sure you're here to sign the oath so that you can vote," Matlack said, with a trace of sarcasm.

"No, I have other business."

"You're not going to sign the oath?"

"No, I am not."

Matlack's face now took on a cold expression. "I thought as much. I tell you that you will have cause to regret that one day. I promise you."

PART II

Valcour Bay

From the narrative of Richard Varick

Arnold and I did not become friendly for some time. He was brusque and demanding, and sent me off on my mission with nary a good word. I left Ticonderoga on July 15th to scour every coastal village and city from Boston to Baltimore, begging, buying, and borrowing supplies of every description for Arnold's ship-building effort at Skenesboro, constantly pursued by urgent messages from him, demanding the moon. I did not return to Ticonderoga until mid-September, then only because the huge battle for New York between General Washington's Continental Army and Sir William Howe's British invasion force not only dried up all supplies but also made it next to impossible to ship anything to the north from points south of New York City.

I also had the nagging doubt that the bits and pieces I was sending north could ever truly become warships. I saw nothing but rolls of cordage, barrels of pitch and tar, piles of oakum, great bundles of linen canvas, tons of iron, balls of heavy sewing twine, tools of every kind, blocks of lignum vitae for special fittings, powder, shot, swivel guns, and even cannon. But when I reached Ticonderoga a sight greeted my eyes more wondrous and enchanting than any Christmas morning. I saw the miracle of a magnificent, fully completed row galley, the <u>Washington</u>, riding proudly at anchor, as well as three finished gundelos and a fourth at the rigging dock.

Arnold greeted me warmly and praised my performance, which of course made me think better of him. That and his amazing accomplishments. He said I had seen nothing yet—wait until I saw the yards at Skenesboro. "Come with me to attend the launching of a new gundelo, the <u>Philadephia</u>," he said. I eagerly accepted. We left Ticonderoga after midnight to benefit from the cooler night air, traveling by longboat down South River.

As I look back on it now, I can honestly say it was one of the most incredible journeys of my life.

Chapter 6

Skenesboro, New York
September 16, 1776

Light shimmered across the lake from the glow of lanterns and torches at Fort Ticonderoga until the longboat turned southeastward and the bulk of Mount Independence eclipsed the view. Now there was only starlight, the moon having vanished below the horizon, as the ten oarsmen gently dipped their sweeps to the count of the coxswain and pulled at an easy pace against the tepid current. Arnold, the veteran campaigner, promptly went to sleep, reclining against his knapsack in the very prow of the boat. He had counseled Varick to take advantage of the cool night air, but Varick was too excited to sleep.

He had been invigorated by what he had seen and heard since his return to Ticonderoga. The black despair of June had been replaced by a new sense of hope. Everyone at the fort recognized that the plan Arnold had proposed at the June meeting, and was carrying out so energetically, was working—so far at least. The British had lost two full months of the campaigning season and still showed no signs of coming out. With the harvest season begun, recruits were beginning to show up at Ticonderoga, including several companies of the Tryon County militia under General Nicholas Herkimer, arriving only days ago. Morale in general had improved remarkably.

General Gates had taken care to protect that morale by denying entry to the fort of several boatloads of American soldiers, who had been captured in Canada and had been paroled by Sir Guy Carleton on condition that they not take up arms against the King for a year. Their infectious joy at being freed and going home would have been highly damaging, Gates decided.

The choice of Arnold to lead the fleet in battle, as well as supervising its construction, had been unanimous. Both Schuyler and Gates sent messages to the south expressing their pleasure that Arnold was in charge, Gates commenting that he was "convinced that General Arnold will thereby add to that brilliant reputation he has so deservedly acquired." Before these dispatches could have reached their destination, General Washington made it unanimous in a message suggesting Arnold for the command, saying that "none will doubt of his exertions."

But Arnold nearly missed his opportunity. Varick had heard about the vicious dispute that erupted that summer, having to do with captured baggage and supplies that Arnold had sent from Montreal to St. Jean for safekeeping in the care of two officers of the invasion army, Colonel John Brown and Colonel Moses Hazen. When he arrived at St. Jean he found the goods plundered. Arnold brought charges against Brown and Hazen, but while he was busy later building ships at Skenesboro, his enemies managed to load the court-martial with their cronies and charged that it was really Arnold who had stolen the goods. He had no chance of locating his witnesses, who had fled during the confusion of the retreat from Canada. The court found against Arnold, whose response was to challenge every single member to a duel, one by one.

General Gates moved in with alacrity, abolishing the court and sending the whole affair off to the judgment of Congress, where he knew nothing would happen for months. In his transmittal letter, Gates referred to Arnold's "warmth of temper," but said that "the United States must not be deprived of that excellent officer's services at this important moment."

This incident fitted in with rumors Varick had heard of other disputes involving Arnold. It seemed that the very aggressiveness and decisiveness that served him so well in battle had also created more than a few enemies for him. *Fortunately,* Varick thought, as he finally dozed off, *I'm on his good side—now at least.*

Both Arnold and Varick woke with a start as the longboat crested a sandy spit. "Halfway island, Gen'l," the coxswain said, as he jumped into the knee-deep water and waded ashore. "Time for breakfast." The oarsmen all alighted as well, heading for the bushes to relieve themselves. Arnold and Varick painfully clambered over the gunwale, stretching their cramped limbs, as several of the men set to work lighting a fire to boil coffee and fry bacon.

The first pale light of dawn broke over the lush greenery of the Vermont territory to the east of the stream and the rugged terrain of New York State to the west, as Arnold and Varick settled themselves on a log to eat their breakfast and sip their coffee. Arnold was anxious to hear more about what Varick had seen of the British forces and the fight at New York City. The night before, Varick had described the awesome sight of the forest of masts in New York Bay created by the hundreds of British vessels at anchor, and the fact that the British had immediately taken Staten Island as their base, not only meeting no resistance but able in two days to recruit an entire regment of Loyalists. Then they invaded Long Island and completely outflanked the American defenders.

"The day before I left," Varick told Arnold, "General Washington decided to give up the City of New York and retreat up the island to better defensive positions in the broken country to the north. Good thing, too. That same day, the British landed in force, crossing the East River to Kip's Bay. They would've surely sealed off our troops if Washington hadn't moved north."

"So they're fighting for Manhattan Island now," Arnold said.

Varick nodded. "I don't like to be pessimistic, sir, but there was no mistaking the look of desperation I could see on the faces of our men, both officers and troops. They were badly mauled on Long Island. It's a miracle that most of the army was able to cross the river and get safely to Manhattan. General Sullivan was captured," Varick added with a small smile. Sullivan had been quickly added by Washington to his army.

Arnold shook his head. "No! He should've stayed here. I'm tempted, but I won't comment anymore. What do our people say, about the size of the enemy force?"

"Well that's it, sir. The British have over thirty thousand troops. We're outnumbered, two to one."

"They have a lot of the Germans, don't they?"

"About nine thousand, I was told."

Arnold spat. "Imagine that! Hiring other people to do your fighting for you."

"They say those Germans are the best fighters in the world."

Arnold snorted. "They'll have a surprise or two coming, believe me." After a pause, Arnold asked: "What about the countryside?" To Varick's puzzled expression, he said: "The people. Aren't any of them rising up, coming to Washington's army?"

Varick shook his head. "No, sir. It's nothing like Boston last year. I don't know why. Maybe they fear the British are invincible. The Loyalist sentiment is very strong. New Jersey is a no-man's-land. Complete anarchy. Armed bands of ruffians fighting and raiding, calling themselves Loyalists or patriots. I was able to visit my poor abused parents several times as I went back and forth. They live in daily fear."

The two men were silent for a while, and then Varick said: "Sir, I forgot to tell you who came ashore with the British at Gravesend Bay. You'll never guess."

"Who?"

"None other than Joseph Brant. Back from London." Varick added sarcastically: "And now an eyewitness to the power of the King's arms."

"That means he'll be here stirring up trouble for us."

"Yes, sir. I alerted General Schuyler of course, and he sent word all down the Hudson Valley to be on the lookout for Brant and apprehend him if he tries to come north."

Arnold barked a laugh. "They won't touch him. He's an Indian, for God's sake. He'll pass through like a ghost."

"I suppose," Varick said. "I wonder who's worse. The Indians or the Germans."

"The Indians," Arnold said emphatically. "No comparison."

The two men rose as the crew began to return to the boat, several lingering to douse the fire with sand. Soon they were making slow progress on the water again as Arnold and Varick both dozed off.

They woke when the sun breasted the forest on the Vermont side, beating down mercilessly. Arnold loosened his tunic and surveyed the square, open, stolid face of Richard Varick, his shock of blond hair falling on his brow. *A rare, reliable man,* he thought. "Dirk, you've done well," he said.

Varick looked up, coloring slightly.

"You've praised what I've accomplished," Arnold said. "I want to tell you, it would've been impossible without you." Varick's face was scarlet as Arnold continued. "You sent more materials than I thought possible. And you solved the terrible problem of the workmen, when you signed Casdrop and Loftus on. Even though we had to pay them too much."

Thomas Casdrop of Philadelphia had built Franklin's row galleys. He recruited thirty carpenters, riggers, and shipwrights and led them to Skenesboro for the unheard-of wage of five dollars per day. Varick's other coup that summer had been the hiring of John Loftus of Boston, who brought twenty-five Irish workers from the Massachusetts coast. Varick had feared that agreeing to the five-dollar wage would result in a court-martial for him, but, despite Gates's anger, the sum had been approved.

"Thank you, sir," Varick mumbled. "I'm glad Casdrop and Loftus have done well."

"A lot of bloody fist fights at first," Arnold said. "Casdrop's Presbyterians against the Papists from Boston. But they've calmed down. Especially after I allowed Loftus to set up his own line of supply from Boston." Arnold smiled at Varick's baffled look. "Rum, cider, and ale," he explained. "Good stuff, too— and cheap for the workers. Loftus runs a pub every night in the basement of the big stone house."

The shock was apparent on Varick's face. "Yes, it stretches the rules," Arnold said. "But it's good for morale and keeps 'em out of trouble. This place can be a hell hole—swamps on two sides, mosquitoes as big as birds, mountains that cut off the breeze. They miss their wives after a hard day's work. So the pub is good for them. Waterbury keeps it under control," Arnold said, referring to his on-site commander, David Waterbury, who had just been promoted to brigadier. "Besides, you know an Irishman can't do a damn thing the next day unless he has a potful the night before."

"But, sir, it's against—"

"They're civilians," Arnold snapped. "Army rules don't apply the same way. Here to do a job on contract and that's it. As they frequently remind me. Now, I said you did well, but there's one place where you failed miserably."

Varick immediately knew what Arnold was talking about—the lack of men with seagoing experience. He had dealt with that complaint before. Shaking his head, he said: "You have to believe me, sir. It's impossible to find sailors who'll come up here. They laugh at the idea of five dollars a day, compared to what they think they can make going to sea in a privateer."

Arnold sighed. "Sometimes I think that's where I should be," he said morosely. "So what's the result? We draft men from the army to form crews. I end up with the scum of every regiment, and I'm expected to train them and make sailors out of them. It's our greatest weakness."

"I know, sir. I'm sorry."

Arnold had calmed down. "I know it's not your fault. I've spread the men from Marblehead among the ships," he said, referring to Massachusetts men who were experienced in fishing and the coastal trade. "I've got a few commanders with some experience, Waterbury, Wrigglesworth, Rue, one or two others." Arnold glanced at Varick and smiled. "How about you? You'd make a fine sailor. Want to join up?"

"Oh, no, sir," Varick said emphatically. "I have no seafaring experience at all."

"That qualifies you for this navy! You've learned a lot about boats this summer. In two weeks I'll have you as good as any of my captains. Think of the glory—you'll go down in the history books."

"I can't swim. And I don't think General Schuyler would let me go."

"No, I don't suppose so."

"Sir," Varick spoke hesitantly, "if I might inquire . . ."

"Go ahead."

"Well, General Gates's message to Congress said you were entirely skilled in maritime affairs. I was wondering how you ever acquired that skill, I mean, given all the other things you've done."

"I grew up with it. We lived on the shore. In Norwich. And my family had several trading vessels."

Varick nodded as Arnold leaned back again and looked vacantly at the sky. "Of course, my father went broke and lost the ships—and everything else. So I apprenticed myself out to an apothecary. After I finished my term, Dr. Lathrop gave me a stake and I opened up my own shop in New Haven. From the beginning, I wanted to go beyond drugs and potions, to general merchandise and trading. Books from London, wines and perfume from France, silks from India, as well as spices, mustard, sugar, tea, coffee." Arnold made a shape with his hands. "The sign over my shop said, *'B. Arnold, Druggist, Bookseller, Etcetera, from London.'* I bought my stock on two trips to London. Then I wanted my own ships to get into the Atlantic trade, Canada to the Caribbean. And I wanted to sail them myself. I didn't trust anyone else. My father-in-law, Samuel Mansfield, the former High Sheriff of New Haven, was my partner. The old man ran the shop while I went to sea."

"Still, it's a big step, isn't it, from merchant seafaring to warfare at sea."

Arnold laughed. "Business is a kind of warfare. Especially if you're determined to succeed. I've had many battles over credit and payments; I've been sued many times and I sued right back. I fought battles at sea, too, against the sea itself and twice against raiding parties."

"And now, it's deadly warfare at sea. What will it be like, General?"

"My boy, it will be pure holy hell. You can't imagine. But I can't wait. We're going to show them something."

Varick marveled inwardly that Arnold actually *lusted* for the forthcoming sea battle. He silently thanked the Lord that his feet would remain firmly planted on the ground.

It was late morning by the time Skenesboro came into view, and Varick drank in the sight, so different from his last visit. There were more buildings and busy activity everywhere, at the sawmill, the forge, the various sheds for specialized work, the platforms on which gundelos sat in various stages, one of them clearly the finished and resplendent *Philadelphia,* due to be launched on the morrow, and beyond, the ways where row galleys were taking shape, one nearly finished, another well started, and a third showing only the keel and some ribs. A large group of men hovered about one of the gundelos—it looked as if they were just completing the stepping of the mast, a function Arnold had decided would be performed at this site, with the final rigging and armoring done at the Ticonderoga and Crown Point docks.

As the longboat coasted toward the dock, a stout, red-kerchiefed man at the gundelo site waved and bawled out: "Top o' the mornin' to ye, sor!"

"That's Loftus," Arnold said, waving back.

"I remember him well," Varick said. He could see Casdrop further down, with his crew scattered among the row galleys. Then he saw General Waterbury coming down the steps of the main stone house, buckling his belt, ready to greet his chief, as a sergeant shouted orders and the militia guard formed up.

After a heavy midday meal and wine with the officers at the post, Arnold announced that his inspection would take place late in the afternoon when it would be cooler. He retired for a nap, as did Varick, but his curiosity stirred him and he soon got up to look around on his own.

In the first shed Varick entered, woodcarvers were at work on trestle tables. An old German with a wispy beard cheerfully showed him the templates he used to produce the various sizes of sheaves out of lignum vitae and how they fitted into block shells carved from white oak. Across the room Varick watched men turn the graceful sweeps, each handle carved at one end, the flat, thin blade tapering at the other. At another table, a worker was making trunnels—tree nails—octagonal pegs of white oak eight inches long. Although the shipbuilders made extensive use of iron bolts and nails, they favored trunnels for some heavy-duty purposes. Pounded into holes slightly smaller than their width, they made stout, rigid joints.

In the next shed, men were laying out a sail on a pattern marked on the floor, unrolling long strips from the three-foot-wide bolts of linen canvas. One crew stitched the lengths together with waxed twine, side by side. Another group worked on bolt ropes at the margins, turning over the cloth to make hems, and still others pierced eyelet holes along the head of the sail to sew in rope grommets.

One large shed was filled with the skeletons of ships yet to be assembled—beams, planks, and timbers of every size, men shaping them with adzes, axes, and saws. Stacked along one wall was precision work—seventy-eight braces to form the configuration of a single gundelo hull, Varick was told, the upright part of the L-shaped braces curved to different radii, each brace carved from a single piece of white oak.

Next, Varick entered the forge and immediately was perspiring from every pore. Begrimed, glistening men pounded away at red-hot iron, making everything from the smallest nails and bolts to the ponderous anchors, six feet long.

Outside he was momentarily shocked by the bright sunlight and the seeming cold after the intense heat of the forge. A shout and a familiar voice drew him over to one of the gundelo platforms. John Loftus jumped to the ground, wiped his palms on his leather apron, and said: "Mr. Varick, good to see you, sor!"

"John Loftus, good to see you. I hear you're one of the foremen of this yard."

"Aye, that I am. I think your General made me so to keep me out of trouble."

The two men stood in the shade of the hull and chatted for a while. Loftus chided Varick for not telling him very much about Benedict Arnold beforehand. "He's a difficult man, to be sure," John said. "Very demanding, he is. And the blazin' energy! He'd like to build a navy as big as England's right at this joyful little spot. Once we made him realize we're not part of his army, but free men here on a contract, we've got along fine."

Varick asked how the work was going. "We've used all the seasoned wood," Loftus said. He slapped the hull behind him: "This green wood is hard to work and it warps—we use so much pitch and tar and oakum you'd think these tubs would sink to the bottom as soon as they hit water."

"You don't sound too high on these ships."

"No, don't mistake me. They're sturdy enough. Just big bateaux, really—fifty-seven feet long, fifteen abeam. Fully loaded and manned, they draw about four feet, ride three feet out of the water. But *big*—as much as thirty tons, I'd say. They'll take a lot of punishment. It's just that I get this strange feeling now and then. Here we are turning out boats faster than I ever thought possible. The general's organized the work very well. But what are we building them for? To fight a war and probably to be blown apart and sunk. Each one that gets launched, I wonder what's going to happen to her. And worse, to the poor bastards who'll be sailing her."

Before Varick could make any reply, Loftus glanced past him and said: "Well, we've got company, sor. They'll want us to join them." Varick looked around and saw Arnold, Waterbury, Casdrop, and Benjamin Rue climbing on board the *Philadelphia*. Rue was to be her captain; he had arrived that morning with ten of his crew, coming overland from Lake George. The inspection was about to begin.

Arnold tried but found little to gripe about, and, from the expression on his face, Loftus knew it. When Arnold finally sat down on the afterdeck, his feet dangling into the well of the ship, the others joining him, Loftus sent one of his men off to fetch a trayful of tankards of ale. Varick lingered for a while, slapping his hand against the heft of the mast, savoring the sweet, clean smell of newly sanded wood and the immaculate details of construction. His eye roved again over the ingenious rig that Arnold and Loftus had designed at the bow to convert land cannon to marine use. The twelve-pounder would be secured in stout wooden tracks running back thirteen feet, with block and tackle attached to the gun carriage on either side and a thick breeching rope to contain the massive recoil of the gun.

Varick admired the smooth curve of the ship leading to the bow, the gunwales lined with shot garlands, curved wood beams with spaces hollowed out the size of melons where the twelve-pound balls would rest until needed. All the tools and gadgets the gunners would need were in their places—the spongers, rammers, ladles, wormers, handspikes, crowbars, tompions, water buckets, shot gauges, linstock, and gunner's picks. On the portside of the cockpit, the cookstove was already in place, with its brick lining and bed of rocks and cast iron cookware properly hung. Looking aft, he could see that everything was equally shipshape, the smaller recoil tracks for the two nine-pound cannon that would be positioned amidships to aim off of each side, the bentwood frames for the awnings, the storage racks, and the hooks where the fascines would be suspended, long rolls of wood slats or saplings to fend off fire from small arms.

Will swelling pride, Varick turned to join the others. Nothing like this had ever happened before. It would be the first time that an American fleet would do battle at sea. *Arnold was right about the glory,* Varick thought. Whatever happened, American schoolboys would read about this for the rest of eternity.

The ale arrived and Arnold hoisted his tankard in a toast. "To the *Philadelphia*! And to victory!" Amid murmurings of "Hear, hear!" all took a deep swig, followed by much smacking of lips and wiping of foam. The ale was delicious in the pleasurable afterglow of success and accomplishment, in the warm air and slanting bronze sunlight of that September afternoon.

"That's damned good ale, John," Arnold said.

"Boston's best, sor, brought all the way up here at no small expense."

"Well, you can afford it," Waterbury observed drily. He had a ruddy face and sported a walrus mustache, a rarity among the English speakers, who favored the clean-shaven look, in contrast to the Canadians and Germans, who loved facial hair. The fact that Schuyler and Gates had assigned the new brigadier to Arnold as his number two indicated the importance they placed on the naval defense.

"John, how about a small supply of this ale for our journey back to old Ty," Arnold said. "And some cold cider, if you have it."

"I do, and it will be my pleasure, sor."

Arnold glanced at Waterbury. "And some provisions? Some of that good ham and corn and yams we had today. And some bread and butter."

"Of course."

"We might as well travel in comfort while we can." Arnold turned to Rue. "Can one of your boys man the cookstove?"

"They'll fight for the chance, rather than pulling on an oar."

"We may need it for warmth, too. The season is turning, gentlemen. You can smell it and feel it, even if you can't see it in the leaves yet. I think our hot spell is over. It'll be damned cold tonight, and tomorrow we'll wish we had the sun back." Arnold was holding court; he had the rapt attention of the others. "The days are shorter and the nights are cool. How long can Carleton and Burgoyne drag their feet? You'd think that if we have to fight a sea battle they'd make sure we do it in the summer so that you can fall in the damned lake and not freeze to death."

There was some involuntary shuddering at this, as Arnold turned to a boat-by-boat review of the growing fleet. He cast his eye along the row of construction platforms. "Naming the gundelos after the cities and states hasn't done us much good, has it Dirk?" He was referring to whether the honor had helped stimulate the flow of supplies to Skenesboro.

Varick allowed himself a small smile. "It was a definite help in a few cases, General."

"What's the next one on our list?"

"Baltimore," Waterbury said.

"The damned Marylanders haven't done a thing for us, have they?"

"Nothing, sir," Varick said.

"To hell with them, then. Goddamned Papists." Arnold half smiled. "Sorry, John," he said to Loftus. Then he grinned. "We'll call the next one the *Spitfire*."

Varick wondered what the future schoolboys of Baltimore would think of that.

Arnold began talking in a serious vein. "I know you're all wondering just when we'll be fighting this sea battle we've been preparing for. I can't tell you that. I do know it will be soon. The British are close to running out of time. I've heard some say that perhaps they won't come out at all. That's nonsense. The time will come—within the next two weeks, most likely. They've delayed to build a large vessel, but I can't worry about that. She'll be ponderous and we'll be highly maneuverable. I don't know how close we are in firepower. We always knew we'd have to outmaneuver and outthink them to be successful.

This probably will be my last visit here. We've got to stay on the alert constantly. We need to bring the fleet together and work on our plan for meeting the enemy. The most important thing is for no one to think that the nearness of battle means we can begin to slack off here at the shipyard. What we need to do—what we *must* do—is redouble all our efforts. Work longer days. I've got thirteen warships now. I'd like many more than that, but I'll settle for the ones under construction here now—especially the galleys. Everything has been working well so far and we've had good luck. The best thing that can happen is that I'll be able to meet the British not only with the *Philadelphia* in the fleet, but with these three galleys and two gundelos here." Arnold jerked his thumb toward the line of construction sites.

Then he looked every man in the eye in turn. "I'm counting on every one of you. I want your best."

From the narrative of Sir Thomas Stanley, KB

The summer of '76 was one long exercise in galling frustration for my uncle, General John Burgoyne, and his loyal subordinate, Major-General Will Phillips, our chief of artillery. They were eager to begin the invasion during the good campaigning weather of the summer, to defeat Arnold's makeshift navy, take Crown Point and Ticonderoga, and drive down the Hudson River to take Albany and entrench ourselves before winter set in.

We were aware of the enemy's doings most of the time, through our network of spies, deserters, Loyalist informers, and Indian scouts. Burgoyne and Phillips had two angry meetings with Sir Guy Carleton, early in August and a month later, in early September, because they were convinced that we had naval superiority over Arnold. But Sir Guy was extremely cautious, fearing that if Arnold somehow should prevail at sea, our troops, advancing unprotected in their bateaux, would be vulnerable to slaughter.

Carleton placed his confidence in Captain Thomas Pringle of the Royal Navy. The first major delay was caused by Pringle's insistence on building a massive "radeau," a huge gun-raft, the <u>Thunderer</u>. His entire outlook immediately became clear to us. If, by any wild chance, Pringle were to lose a naval battle to the rag-tag Americans and their homemade fleet on this remote lake in the wilderness, he would be the laughingstock of London, his career destroyed. Therefore, clear superiority was not enough for Pringle—it had to be <u>crushing</u> superiority. This was confirmed when he next insisted on leading his fleet with a three-masted, eighteen-gun frigate. It took a month to bring the eighty-foot <u>Inflexible</u> up from Quebec, break her apart, and transport the pieces around the rapids to be reassembled.

Incredibly, it was not until early October that Carleton declared we were ready to advance. My uncle did not enjoy travel by sea at any time, but especially now as he was not feeling well, so we did not board one of the warships, but instead rode with the main scouting party of British troops and Indians down the western shore of Lake Champlain.

We had military superiority—but Arnold had a surprise for us. I will never forget what we saw on the morning of October 11th.

Chapter 7

Valcour Bay
Lake Champlain
October 11, 1776

The horse picked its way delicately over the rocks, a soft fir branch slapping at Burgoyne's cheek. A few feet further and he was in the brilliant sunlight and the panorama opened up before him, an image that would remain fixed in his mind the rest of his life.

Ahead of him were the three scouts on the promontory, their faces split by huge grins. Major-General Will Phillips had already dismounted and was looking down in awe. He turned and shouted jubilantly: "It's true, by God!"

The scouts had come in that morning, shouting that the Americans were trapped, not five miles from the forward camp. Burgoyne had awakened with a fever and a racking cough. With a small escort, he had already started on his way to the nearest medical help back at the base camp when Phillips caught up to tell him the news. That banished all thought of seeing the surgeon from Burgoyne's mind. He insisted on turning around and heading for the alleged trap, despite the protestations of Phillips.

Now he was glad he had come. Below was the American fleet, neatly anchored in an arc across a small bay at the mouth of a narrow channel, formed by an island less than a mile offshore. It was the entire American fleet—Burgoyne were sure of that because of information gleaned from prior intelligence reports. He could even begin to identify most of the ships. Two schooners, one sloop, one cutter, five large row galleys, and nine gunboats. He knew that they were manned by some six hundred men, most of them strangers to boats and water, and that their commander was Brigadier-General Benedict Arnold.

Beyond the island, Burgoyne could see the sparkling waters of Lake Champlain and then the deep blue-green shape of Grand Isle in the distance. To the left, where Phillips was now pointing, he could make out the sails of the British fleet under Sir Guy Carleton and Captain Thomas Pringle of the Royal Navy, coming down under a brisk northerly, half again as many vessels as the

Americans had, with much greater weight of cannon, and manned by nearly a thousand experienced seamen.

Burgoyne considered Arnold the most audacious and aggressive commander on the American side. Now he began to doubt that assessment, shaking his head with a puzzled expression. Lieutenant Stanley had dismounted, and he peered up at his uncle with concern. Burgoyne did not look well at all; his complexion was ashen and he seemed to sway slightly in his saddle. He began to speak in a soft voice, as if to himself, but Stanley was right next to him and could hear every word: "What the devil is he trying to do? This makes no sense. He's sailed his fleet two thirds of the way up the lake from Fort Ticonderoga and tucked it into this channel. We'll either blockade him and starve him out or if he chooses to come out and fight, we'll blow him to bits."

Suddenly drained of all energy, Burgoyne sagged in his saddle. He seemed convulsed by chills, trembling violently. And then he slumped and fell from his horse. Fortunately, Lieutenant Stanley was in a perfect position and alert enough to break the fall. The men gathered around Burgoyne's prone figure, one of them bringing several blankets over to warm him. Stanley cradled his uncle in his arms and Phillips was on his knees staring intently at his face.

"He's awake," said Phillips. "Here, bring more of those blankets."

Burgoyne struggled to a sitting position. "Just dizzy for a moment. I'm all right."

"Like hell you are," Phillips growled. "You should've gone to base camp."

"Did I fall?"

"Yes, but Lieutenant Stanley caught you. He saved you a broken head."

"I'm all right now."

Phillips leaned close and spoke in a low intense voice: "Jack, listen to me for once. Listen to common sense. You've *got* to get help. We're taking you back."

"No."

Phillips fumed for a moment. "At least let us take you down to the shore where the troops are. It's windy here. We'll send for the surgeon to come here if you won't go to him. It'll take twice as long, but if—"

"And if I fall asleep down there you'll have me packed up and on my way. No thank you. I'm staying right here. This is a good place. I want to see what happens. Here, help me against that rock." Several of the men half carried Burgoyne back a few feet to prop him against a large smooth boulder, tucking blankets under and around him.

"What is this place?" Burgoyne asked. Phillips fished his map out of his breast pocket and managed to consult it, despite its violent fluttering in the wind. "That's Valcour Island out there. Yes, there's Cumberland Head, where you can see our boys coming down," Phillips said, pointing to the north. Then he glared at Burgoyne, shaking his head, as he struggled to refold the map.

Burgoyne managed a grin. "Go on, Will, tell Cudlip to deploy his men."

Standing now, Phillips wore an exasperated expression. "Mark you, Jack, I tried. It's on your head now. I'll be back as soon as I can."

Stanley spoke up: "Perhaps we can get a small fire going, out of the wind over there behind those rocks. We can make him some tea."

"Do that," Phillips said, "and if he passes out again bundle him up for the trip to base camp." He mounted his horse, paying no heed to Burgoyne's protests, and headed down the slope to where the scouting party stood by, two companies of the 24th Foot and a band of Ottawa scouts under the command of Major Peter Cudlip.

For perhaps half an hour, Burgoyne lay back exhausted. As soon as the fire was kindled, Stanley came over to squat nervously next to him. At Burgoyne's call, Stanley fetched his telescope from the leather pouch attached to his saddle. Burgoyne focused and scanned the American fleet. He began a running commentary, identifying the *Congress* at the center of the line. "There, I see Arnold," he said. He passed the glass to Stanley, who also caught a good glimpse of Arnold, a powerfully built figure in a blue and buff uniform moving animatedly about the deck of his flagship. It was the second time that Burgoyne and Stanley had laid eyes on Benedict Arnold—both times through a spyglass at a distance of perhaps a half mile. On the first occasion, when Arnold made his long-distance salute at St. Jean the previous June, Burgoyne had been certain Arnold would be captured.

Burgoyne raised his knees to provide a more stable support for the glass as Stanley returned it, but it was no use. His eye teared and the gusting wind and his own weakness shook the glass so that the image seemed to dance.

He began to shiver, laying the telescope down. A few minutes earlier he had been perspiring, so that now the damp blankets brought a knife's edge of chill to him. He pulled the blankets tight, trying to trap his body warmth and end the violent shuddering. The men hovered about, not sure what to do. Phillips was right. He was very ill. He prayed it was not the pox. Could it be swamp fever? Very nearly as bad. Burgoyne began perspiring again and started to mumble. He fought off delirium, wrenching his mind back to the fact that the long delay in attacking the Americans would finally end this day. The American attempt to block the British advance on Lake Champlain would be crushed, and it would happen months later than it should have.

The northerly wind had the feel of winter about it. Except for the long, low line of dark clouds on the northern horizon, it was the kind of bright autumn day in which everything seems unusually vivid, the yellow and orange and russet streaks in the foliage of the island and the mainland, the scudding whitecaps in the deep blue of the lake beyond. Benedict Arnold paced on the afterdeck of his flagship, the sleek seventy-four-foot row galley *Congress*. The nervous edge of anticipation among his men was palpable, the way it always was when there was no turning back, when battle was imminent and certain.

It had been a long wait. Nearly four months of boat-building, recruiting, training, maneuvering, spying, planning, all now drawing to the inevitable climax. Two row galleys and one gundelo remained unfinished, unable to join the fleet in time for the battle. There was nothing more Arnold could do to prepare. Now they would have to fight.

He cast his eyes to the right and to the left, along the long concave arc of his fleet, eighteen warships in all, positioned facing south across the mouth of Valcour Bay, a distance of less than a mile from the sandy spit at the south end of Valcour Island westward to the rocks and cliffs of the New York mainland. He knew that the British fleet and the vanguard of the British Army were moving down, blocked from view by the bulk of the two-mile-long island, but very visible to Arnold's lookouts and couriers, who streamed like ants up and down the slope of the island bringing word to be shouted down the line of American ships.

He knew the risk he was taking by coming this far north and concentrating his fleet in Valcour Bay—but it was a calculated risk, the only way he could see to gain an initial advantage in the coming battle. The move was contrary to Gates's orders to stay on the defensive, repeated in every planning session, and emphasized in the last one. But were they *orders*? Arnold chose to regard Gates's nervous conservatism as *advice*. What did Gates know about strategy and fighting at sea? His last advice had been to "avoid any wanton display or unnecessary risk." If Arnold were not certain he could win a naval battle, he should return to Ticonderoga, Gates said. But why build boats and put cannon on them if you're not going to maneuver? Just put the cannon on the battlements of the fort, if the boats are going to end up there, anyway. Arnold was not going to cower under the protection of Ticonderoga's guns. He saw his mission as the opposite—to protect Ticonderoga as much and as long as possible by meeting the British far from the fort.

Arnold's number two on board the *Congress,* Lieutenant Joshua Brooks, came up to him. "Excuse me, sir. I believe we have company. On the shore over there." He pointed to the New York mainland.

Taking the telescope from Brooks, Arnold scanned along the water line. He could see slight signs of movement, occasionally a red tunic flashing amid the foliage. He spotted an Indian, then a second one. He put the glass down and said: "Good work, Lieutenant. That'll be one of their scouting parties."

"Can they alert the British fleet?" Brooks asked.

"Not unless they have cannon. Musket fire'll be drowned in this wind. Looks like they're trying to conceal themselves."

"Why?"

Arnold laughed. "They don't want to scare us out of our trap! They won't start firing until the action begins. Have the fascines lowered. Both sides. It won't be long before they ford some men over to the island up channel—to surround us! Pass the word up and down the line."

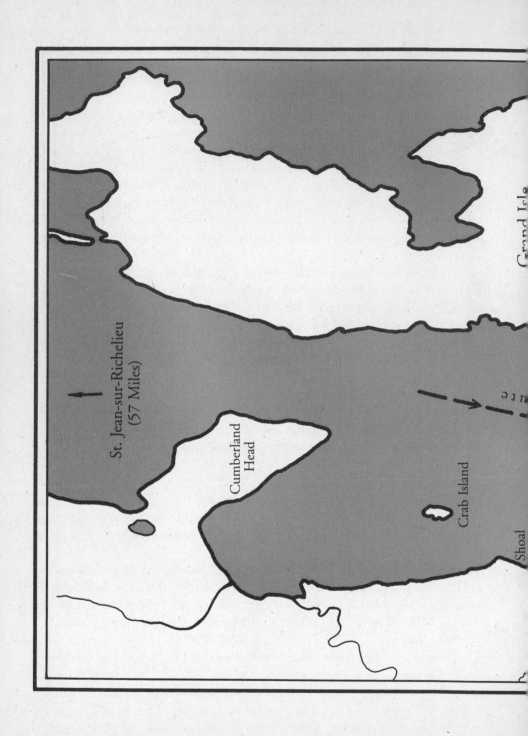

St. Jean-sur-Richelieu
(57 Miles)

Grand Isle

Cumberland
Head

Crab Island

Shoal

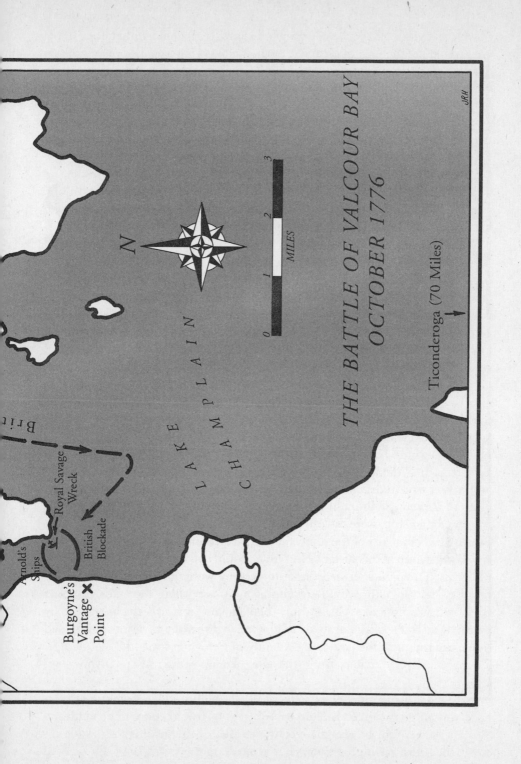

N

MILES

0   1   2   3

THE BATTLE OF VALCOUR BAY
OCTOBER 1776

Ticonderoga (70 Miles)

L A K E   C H A M P L A I N

Royal Savage Wreck

British Blockade

Arnold's Ships

Burgoyne's Vantage Point ✕

Brit

JRH

He was glad to have the company on shore. It guaranteed that none of his men would get the idea of escaping the battle by swimming ashore and disappearing into the wilderness. He pulled out his pocket watch. Past eleven o'clock. At dawn he had made sure that the crews had a hearty breakfast. Now he passed the signal for the midday rations to be handed out. If the men were going to be looking at cannonballs soon, they might as well have full stomachs. Arnold was not a particularly religious man, having long thought that the only reason for fervent prebattle prayers was to cancel out the other side's prayers. He knew that the enemy's guns were superior to his, by just how much he wasn't certain. He took satisfaction only in the knowledge that he had done everything humanly possible to prepare these vessels and these men. Despite himself, Arnold began whispering a silent prayer.

The rocky ledge where Burgoyne was perched was several hundred feet above the water and about a half mile south of the tip of the island and the American line. Arnold's fleet looked like so many toy boats in the reflecting pool at Hyde Park. The American line of anchorage across the mouth of Valcour Bay seemed designed to protect the bay, but there was nothing to protect, for the bay was the beginning of a channel that ran back more than two miles to shoal water at the northern end. A perfect trap, a bottleneck, and Arnold had put himself into it.

To the northeast, beyond the profile of Valcour Island, Burgoyne could see that most of the British armada was now through the narrow passage between Cumberland Head and Grand Isle. With this brisk wind, the battle—or the blockade—would be joined within the hour. He could see the ship-rigged *Inflexible* leading the armada, with the flagship *Maria,* the schooner *Carleton,* and a fleet of oared gunboats following her in formation. The cumbersome gun-raft *Thunderer* brought up the rear, and clustered around her, as if she were a mother ship, were the canoes of the Indian scouts and scores of bateaux bearing the vanguard of the army, more than a thousand strong. So clear was the day that even at this distance Burgoyne could make out the crimson of their uniforms. The plan specified that if the enemy were not encountered on the first day the vanguard would encamp at the place where the Little Bouquet River enters into Lake Champlain, then moving forward the next day by bateaux, the bulk of the army to follow in stages as the invasion progressed down the length of the lake to the vicinity of Crown Point and Ticonderoga. There would be action, Burgoyne now knew, sooner than anyone had expected.

He felt a rising glow of excitement. It was still possible to make a difference, despite all the time Carleton had wasted. If Arnold chose to do battle, he and his men would be slaughtered by nightfall. If there were a blockade instead, the bateaux with the troops could move right on past, the main body of the army to follow—there was no threat to them on the lake with Arnold bottled up. Intelligence reports held that the Americans had no more than six thousand effectives to garrison Ticonderoga and defend the region below it to Albany—and nothing but scattered militia south of Albany all the way down to the Hudson Highlands and beyond that to Washington's army, which from all accounts was taking a severe beating from General Howe. And then there was the fact that Gates was in command at Ticonderoga, which only increased Burgoyne's anticipation. He did not hold his former subordinate in high esteem; it would be a pleasure to teach him a lesson. It could be a bloody battle at Ticonderoga if Gates showed courage, but the fort could not hold out under assault by superior artillery and seasoned troops who outnumbered the defenders two to one. Then it would be on to Albany. With any luck it could be taken before the first serious snowstorm—if only Carleton would move decisively. Then, Burgoyne thought, we could consolidate our position and lines and be primed to strike southward in the spring for the juncture with Howe—and final victory.

Burgoyne nodded off for a moment, and then suddenly awoke, an elusive thought ticking at his brain. He surveyed the scene below once again. "Something is not right here," he said, looking sharply up at Stanley. Then he began trembling with chills again, and he gratefully accepted when Stanley proffered a tin cup of tea wrapped in a cloth. Burgoyne sipped the hot liquid carefully. A horse scrabbled up the rocky slope. Phillips dismounted and sat down on a bed of blankets.

"Everything's ready," Phillips said, reaching for a cup of tea. "We've got the men spread out along the shore and couriers on the way to bring up the rest of the men from base camp—and the surgeon. Cudlip has a party ready to ford the channel at the other end and take up positions on the island. There's no way out," he chortled.

Burgoyne nodded absently, clutching his tea as if it were his sole connection to life.

"They know we're here," Phillips continued. "Couldn't help that. They don't know how many we are, though. I told Cudlip to keep the men quiet and keep out of sight as much as possible. No shooting. I don't want to scare them out of the trap."

Phillips appraised the limp figure of Burgoyne next to him. "You look awful, Jack. Anything I can do for you?"

Burgoyne shivered again. "How about two naked wenches to keep me warm?"

"Will Indian wenches do? Only kind we have around here."

"Well—no thank you."

Phillips chuckled at the thought of Burgoyne huddled under a blanket with Indian girls liberally greased with bearfat, as was their custom—John Burgoyne, the finest dresser in the West End; high-stakes gambler; playwright; uncle by marriage of Tom Stanley's older brother, the Earl of Derby; man about town, at age fifty-three still much admired by the ladies (although a loyal husband); member of Parliament; so dapper and engaging in London society that he was known everywhere as a gentleman of the first rank. His troops affectionately referred to him as "Gentleman Johnny," but in polite society only a few intimate friends called him that to his face. Now only his fine prominent nose and fevered eyes could be seen under the cowl of his blanket.

"I never should've come after you," Phillips sighed. "I should've let you get on to base camp and get some help."

"And I'd have never forgiven you. After all we've been through? Not to see the end of it?"

"Doesn't help you if you're dead, Jack. For God's sake, you're sick, man! It could be the pox."

"It's not the pox."

"Well, whatever it is, it's damned serious." Burgoyne made no reply. Phillips went on. "Listen to me. You can't ride in your condition. I've got some lads making a carrying basket for you. You should leave the minute it's ready."

"Why? You've got the surgeon coming here."

"It'll be hours. You could met him halfway if you left now. Besides, what can he really do? You've got to get to hospital, in Montreal. As soon as possible. Maybe nothing will happen here. Just a blockade that may take days. Arnold's going to surrender. It's hopeless."

"I'm not so sure," Burgoyne said. "From what I know of Mr. Arnold, he's not the surrendering type."

Phillips scowled. "They damn well better give up—or the poor bastards'll be bloody pulp by suppertime."

Burgoyne looked down at the line of American boats. He noted that some of them had a network of anchors strung out so that they could be moved back and forth by hauling on the lines instead of relying only on the wind. He saw that the island blocked Arnold's view of the advancing British fleet, but knew he would be well aware of it with the American lookouts on the island shouting messages down the line of boats. And the British, as their vessels began to come abreast of the island heading due south, could not see the Americans.

Burgoyne suddenly glanced at Stanley and nodded. "Now I see it," he said.

"What?" Phillips asked.

Burgoyne looked at the homely, craggy face of Phillips. "They're not trapped, you know."

"What?"

"The Americans. They're not trapped."

Phillips was irritated. "Well of course they are. Just look at what your eyes can see."

"I am. You're trapped when you're driven into a trap or lured into one. They weren't. They *chose* to come up here. This is Arnold's plan."

"What plan?"

"Desperate perhaps. But clever. You've got to admire it."

"What the hell are you talking about?"

"You've got to assume that they regularly get information from spies and scouts, just as we do. So Arnold knows he's outgunned. So what is he going to do? He has to make a stand somewhere. His purpose is to defeat our navy and stop our invasion, and failing that to hurt us and slow us down as much as possible, to hinder our attack on Ticonderoga. So he comes all the way up here to the northern part of the lake, ready to engage us as far from the fort as possible. He gets an idea and tucks his fleet in behind this island, hoping to surprise us. He knows the prevailing wind this time of year is northerly. That makes any idea of meeting us head-on in the lake very unattractive because we'd have the advantage of the wind coming down from the north. It's what our seafaring friends call 'the weather gauge.' He wants to reverse that, to get the weather gauge himself. And his luck holds out because we've got a strong northerly today. That means when our fleet sails past, he'll attack with favorable winds at his back while we have to come *into* the wind."

Phillips was astonished. "He's going to attack us?"

"That's right."

"No!"

"Yes."

"But we outgun him, two to one!"

"That's why he's got to try something daring."

"I don't believe it!"

"Look at our fleet out there. Do you think they know that Arnold is anywhere near? They're sailing by without a care in the world, no enemy in sight. They've got a surprise coming."

"We've got to warn them!"

"How?"

"We'll open fire."

"It would work if you had some of your cannon, Will. They won't hear musket fire, not in the teeth of this wind."

"Damn! What good is an artilleryman without any artillery? We can try— we've got to do something. I'll tell Cudlip to open fire, build some bonfires."

"No time for that," Burgoyne said. Shaking his head in exasperation, Phillips mounted and disappeared down the trail again.

Exhausted, Burgoyne leaned back. He was impressed. Despite the odds against him, Arnold had been able to find a possible advantage. No telling how long it would last or how much good it would do him. The odds still made it look like a suicide mission. With a half smile, Burgoyne spoke to Stanley: "I might have to revise my opinion of old Horatio Gates. Amazing that he would countenance this kind of plan." After a while, he added: "On the other hand, he doesn't have to be on any of the boats. Maybe it's all Arnold's idea. That would be more like it."

He watched through slitted eyes as *Inflexible,* leading the way, began to edge past the island, sails full-bellied and stiff in the wind. It would begin very soon.

Chapter 8

Valcour Bay
October 11, 1776

Down the shore, Burgoyne saw small puffs of smoke and heard faint reports of musket fire as Cudlip's troops took aim on Arnold's fleet. More of the British ships were sailing proudly past the point of the island, running before the wind, oblivious to the nearness of the enemy. The Americans began tensing their cable lines. Three boats broke out sail and prepared to move ahead, among them the largest American warship, the sloop *Royal Savage.* Incredibly, well more than half of the British fleet sailed past before their enemy was seen. Then slowly, one after another, the ships began the attempt to come about into the wind, wallowing and floundering. The ship-rigged *Inflexible* was far out of useful range, dead in the water, sails flapping, now trying to put down anchors to avoid slipping further downwind. But some of the oared gunboats soon managed to come into range, and *Royal Savage* forged out to meet them. The first fire of the battle came from her, great billows of white smoke, and then, a measurable instant later, the roar of the cannon blasts and a faint echo from the rise of the island and the mainland.

Phillips had returned, squatting beside Burgoyne. He pulled out his gold watch. "It's just past noon," he said.

The *Royal Savage* blasted away, but she was exposed and soon nearly surrounded by a wolfpack of gunboats. She damaged some of them, and was supported by fire from the nearest American gundelos, but there were too many attacking ships. Her panicky crew tacked to return to the line, but mishandled it and ran her aground on the sandy spit of Valcour Island. Burgoyne let out a whoop of joy. He could imagine Arnold's frustration. He and his landlubbers were up against Captain Thomas Pringle and the trained officers and sailors of the Royal Navy. Yet the small group on the promontory watched with mounting awe as Arnold, despite the early loss of his largest warship, held his own against the British superiority in ships, training, and cannon. He worked his initial advantage to the utmost, maneuvering skillfully in the tricky wind and water currents caused by the channel and the island, sometimes with the aid of the spring cables he'd had his men lay down, keeping his crescent line intact throughout most of the battle and thus able to concentrate crossfire on any British ship that ventured forward to attack. Because of the crescent line and the narrowness of the bay, not more than two or three of the smaller ships at a time could attack any closer than two hundred yards. Clouds of smoke from scores of cannon booming almost at once covered the scene, parting intermittently in the gusty wind as if a veil were lifted, allowing Phillips to scan with the spyglass and provide a running account. He reported anxiously on the foray of the *Carleton,* the twelve-gun British schooner, as she moved toward the American line, attacking alone. American fire raked her, bringing down spars, rending her sails, pounding her hull until she began to list. She wallowed helplessly, but the American cannon just didn't seem big enough to sink her.

Then, with great excitement, Phillips described the heroics of a sailor who climbed out on the bowspirit of the *Carleton,* right in the midst of American fire, to run up a replacement jib in an effort to bring the bow of the schooner around. This failing, he was able to toss lines to men in two longboats, who had rowed up from the British flagship *Maria* and were screened by the *Carleton*'s hull from American fire. They gradually hauled the damaged schooner around until her remaining sails could catch the wind and move her out of danger.

"He's just a boy!" Phillips shouted, referring to the heroic sailor. "A midshipman, by Jove! Thank God he survived. What a career he shall have!"

The British warships formed a line at a range of two to three hundred yards and slugged it out with the Americans, each side scoring an occasional hit. The *Inflexible* was still unable to make enough headway to join the battle, and the ketch-rigged *Thunderer,* with its massive twenty-four-pounders and a crew of two hundred men, finally appeared past the point of the island, moving slowly to the west to try to come within range. These two vessels together had nearly as many guns as the entire American fleet. Twice British gunboats exploded when American shots hit their powder magazines. The British seamen were trained and superior fighters at sea when it came to boarding enemy vessels, but the only way they could attempt this in the narrow bay was not by grappling two ships together, but by rowing men up in the longboats. The Americans countered this tactic with grapeshot and chain fired from the swivel guns mounted on the gunwales of their ships. After several longboats were shattered, their men bloodied and drowning, the effort was abandoned. But even without the two largest ships, the cannon of the other British ships were generally larger than those the Americans had, and this began to tell gradually. The gundelo *Philadelphia* was slowly sinking. The galley *Washington* was listing, her deck awash. Phillips studied the *Congress* through the glass, reporting that her decks were slimy with blood, that he could see Arnold everywhere at once, aiming cannon, sending signals, exhorting his men, clearing away wreckage.

It was a strange sight, as if it were a picture unfolding. Except the cannon blasts, the sounds and smells were faint from the half-mile distance, despite the leeward position—no odor of saltpeter or fresh blood, no screams of the wounded. It was a pretty scene of boats maneuvering in a background of brilliant colors, of fluffy white clouds of smoke. Burgoyne shook his head. Of all the forms of fighting, he took battle at sea to be the worst, the sense of being an isolated target, of being trapped. As if the fear of a limb being torn away by enemy fire were not enough, there was the fear of falling spars and masts from above and the fear of drowning below.

It was a changing picture that he watched. By late afternoon the wind, though still northerly, had abated considerably. The line of dark clouds on the horizon had dissolved into a grey overcast advancing from the north, now obscuring the sliver of moon and the first stars of twilight. The lake was calmer now, slate grey, the whitecaps gone. Still the two sides blazed away at each other. All afternoon the cannonade had ebbed and flowed, at times a deafening, echoing roar.

At one point a vicious hand-to-hand fight broke out between the crew of the grounded *Royal Savage* and a band of Cudlip's men who had occupied the island. Soon outnumbered, most of the Americans escaped by longboat or by swimming to the closest American warship.

As the wind died down still more, *Inflexible* and *Thunderer* were able to move toward the line of battle. As if watching these ponderous vessels inch their way forward, the other boats slackened their fire until there was an eerie quiet. Then, at five hundred yards, *Inflexible*'s big guns opened fire, a deeper booming sound than anything heard before. She was now in range, but safe from enemy fire herself, and *Thunderer* was coming into range as well. The equation of battle changed instantly, and the Americans began pulling back, deeper into the confines of the bay. It was nearly six o'clock now and rapidly growing dark. *Inflexible* ceased fire, the awesome example plain. No point wasting ammunition in the dark. In the morning light there would be plenty of time to take the American boats apart, piece by piece.

Inflexible and *Thunderer* anchored in positions that divided the mouth of the bay into three segments. Longboats began paying out cable from either side of the stern of *Inflexible* so that she could be hauled broadside in either direction for tomorrow's cannonade. Other British warships took up positions filling the gaps. The mouth of the bay was sealed. The Americans were blockaded, trapped after all. The battle was over. Tomorrow they would surrender or die.

For a time the men huddled on the cliff were silent as darkness closed in.

"I don't know whether to celebrate or not," Phillips said at length. "They put up a hell of a fight. And I don't think the Royal Navy quite lived up to its reputation. But it's over now."

"That it is," Burgoyne whispered, looking utterly spent.

"Jack, are you ready for hospital now?" Phillips asked, a touch of sarcasm in his voice.

Burgoyne nodded. Repeatedly during the afternoon Phillips had remonstrated with him, but Burgoyne refused to leave. It was time now. When food had been offered to him, he'd nearly gagged. He ached in every bone, and beneath the blankets he was a sodden mess, as if, for long hours of all-out exertion, he had fought in the battle himself. Barring the wounded, he was sure he felt worse than any of the exhausted men on the boats below. "It's unfair, but sometimes obstinate people are fortunate," Phillips said.

"What does that mean?"

"I learned a while ago that the vanguard of your army put ashore north of here for the night. Another big contingent on Grand Isle. A little delay, courtesy of Mr. Arnold. For you, Jack, it means that help is just a few miles away instead of twenty. We'll get you to a surgeon quite soon. My guess is he'll have you off to a hospital in Montreal tomorrow."

Burgoyne sighed. Not a pleasing prospect. "Is Arnold still alive?"

"Oh yes! If I'd seen him take a cannonball, you would've have heard about it!"

"I've revised my opinion of Mr. Arnold. Haven't you?"

"Aye, that I have."

"Do me a favor, Will. See that he's well taken care of. That's one rebel I should like very much to meet."

He'd called them the scum of every regiment. Of all the officers, only he was experienced as master of a vessel at sea. And yet his men had fought well. Surprisingly well. Arnold smiled. One advantage for a commander in fighting at sea was that there was no place for the men to run or hide. On land, many's the time he'd seen militia pull foot, but not at sea. The British fleet was even stronger than he expected, and yet he had fought them to a standstill for the better part of six hours. But what of tomorrow?

He lay stretched out in his tiny cabin aboard the *Congress,* a few moments alone, of deserved respite to try to gather his thoughts before the conference of his captains. Although he was in superb physical condition, his muscles ached from the rigors of the day. One side of his swarthy face glowed an unnatural red, and his black hair and eyebrows were singed from repeated exposure to the flash of powder. Now swathed in oil-soaked linen, his hands were blackened and burned from a half day of wrestling with hot, smoking cannon. As much as anything else, he had come in to rest his left leg, the one that had taken a musket ball in the assault on Quebec and then had been damaged again months later when his horse had slipped. Before dressing his hands, he had stripped the leg bare and gently massaged the blue-red scar of the bullet wound. He remembered the surgeon's words: "The ball entered above the tendon Achilles, in the muscle between the tendon and the bone." A quarter of an inch either way and Arnold would have been crippled for life or lost the limb. The legacy of the two wounds was that the leg was prone to tire easily and ache after exertion. But his former leg wounds were nothing compared to the horrors he had seen on the lake this day. Nearly a third of the men on the *Congress* alone had been thrown overboard dead—those that were gut shot, or with splinters in their heads, or limbs crushed or blown off. And more would be consigned to the water before night was done. Even now, the moaning of the wounded on deck was pitiful.

The toll had been heavy on the officers whose duty it was to expose themselves bravely to enemy fire to set an example for the men. The *Philadelphia* had sunk and the gundelo *New York* was unsalvageable. The galley *Trumbull* was in good shape, and the *Washington* had been saved though she had taken heavy punishment. The *Congress* had been hulled seven times, and only desperate work at the pumps and by the carpenters had saved her.

The *Royal Savage* was gone. Arnold had been bitterly angry at her crew for running her aground, but even more so for abandoning their ship without destroying her. He thought then that the British would have her intact. Instead they set fire to her after dark, apparently fearing that the Americans might succeed in landing a party to refloat her and return her to action. The fire had grown until it reached the powder magazine, and the *Royal Savage* had blown apart, a blazing beacon against a pitch-black sky. All of Arnold's papers were aboard her. Most important were the account books that documented the expenses that he had borne personally for nearly a year for the expedition to Canada. There would be trouble over that, getting Congress to reimburse him without proper documentation. Nothing compared to the trouble Congress would get from him if it failed to do so! But that was a problem for another time—not worth considering until he found some way of surviving the massed guns of the British fleet.

He tried to concentrate on that unpalatable subject. There would have to be a decision soon. His senior officers, Waterbury and Wrigglesworth, had survived the battle. New captains had been named for the boats that lost them in battle. Now they were all coming to the *Congress* for a conference. He knew that someone had already arrived. He'd heard the clunk and scraping sounds of a skiff coming alongside.

The problem was that there were no good choices. The situation seemed to boil down to surrender or be annihilated. There was the chance that he could hold out for a few days by pulling back further into the bay. The British would not bring their big guns in too far for fear of a sudden maneuver that might endanger them. And why should they? Arnold's men had rations for only a few days. The British Army would move right on past in its fleet of bateaux and canoes—Arnold could do nothing to stop them, bottled up as he was. He had considered trying to slip at least some boats out via the northern channel, but that was hopeless. He had scouted that area the day before. One could find a path through the rocky shoals at that end, but certainly not at night, and during the day enemy warships and troops would be all about. The idea of trying to escape by land was also out of the question, with a growing number of redcoats and Indians occupying the shoreline and the island, the Indians with their war whoops a constant reminder. Besides, Arnold reflected, his mission was to prevent or delay the progress of the British army, not to flee or surrender.

Arnold tried to imagine what conceivable combination of conditions could favor him tomorrow if he chose to fight. He was always ready to believe that anything was possible, but it was hard to see what it could be in this situation. The only way to fight without simply being slaughtered was to keep *Inflexible* and *Thunderer* out of the battle. He had done that successfully today, but now they commanded the entrance to the bay like twin fortresses.

Arnold had no doubt that his officers and men would vote for surrender if given the chance. He knew full well the earnest arguments that would be made in conference. They were blockaded by a superior force with their ammunition running low—down to twenty or thirty rounds in some of the boats. Carleton had the reputation of being a decent and generous man. If they surrendered, he would undoubtedly free them on parole, on their pledge not to bear arms for a year, as he had the prisoners taken at Quebec and during the American retreat. Surely that was better than a painful death! A hard argument to overcome. Then there was the fact that the men knew all the bad news from New York. General Washington was in full retreat, giving up all of New York Island and pulling back to New Jersey and Westchester County. The huge British force under General Howe was threatening to smash Washington's army totally, and might well have done so by now.

To Arnold that was reason to redouble one's efforts, but he knew that the officers would conclude simply that the cause was lost. Why fight on without hope?

He did not go to war to surrender. To Benedict Arnold the war was a heaven-sent opportunity to prove his mettle, to win back the status and prestige and wealth of his family that his father has squandered. It was the chance to pay the British back for their insolent treatment of the colonists, to fight for freedom, that most glorious of causes. It was the chance to break out of the mundane life of commerce, of husband and father, to lead men in battle and gain fame and honor. One did not accomplish such things by surrendering.

A British cannonball had conveniently torn a window in the side of

Arnold's cabin, much larger than the tiny ventilation ports. The flickering glow from the burning *Royal Savage* cast the shadow of Arnold's face on the opposite wall. He swung over to look out. The fire was beginning to die down. He saw a longboat approaching, a lantern at the bow. It looked like Waterbury coming over from the *Washington,* several others with him. The wind had fallen off to the merest breeze. A fine mist filled the air.

Arnold continued to study the scene, and an idea began to form in his mind. At length he began to rise. It was time to meet with his officers. He knew now what they were going to do. It was a slim chance perhaps, but the only one worth taking that he could see.

Chapter 9

Military Hospital, Montreal
October 30, 1776

"Oh yes, he's quite improved now. Although I must say, when he arrived I would not have wagered two shillings he would survive." Dr. James Babbidge spoke in a waspish tone, giving Phillips the impression that he was being held accountable for Burgoyne's illness.

"What was it?"

"Eh?"

"His illness. What is it?"

"Swamp fever, it appears." Babbidge did not sound as if he were totally convinced himself. "Fortunately, with the army away, we were able to give the general our full attention."

"Yes, most fortunate indeed," Phillips murmured, toying with the obvious rejoinder that Burgoyne would receive full attention no matter what the circumstances. Sitting in this tiny confining office with Babbidge, the head surgeon, was giving him a headache. "What about the future. How soon will he—"

"He'll be very weak for quite some time—although I should think he could leave our care within the fortnight. I suspect he will have an occasional recurrence, probably with milder effects. If he takes good care of himself he should, on the whole, be fine."

"Thank God for that," Phillips said. "Has he been kept informed of the progress of the campaign?"

"My dear fellow, he was delirious, quite incoherent, for more than two weeks. He passed a crisis only a matter of a few days ago. I forbade any correspondence or visitors, military or otherwise, until yesterday."

"Was no one of his military family with him through all of this?"

"Of course. There were several at first. Lieutenant Stanley was here every day. But he's taken ill himself, poor fellow."

Exactly the sort of thing that happens in hospital, Phillips said to himself. "How is Lieutenant Stanley?"

"He's recovering rather well. I allowed him to see the general this morning, for the first time since he took sick."

The desire to leave the stuffy room suddenly was overpowering. Phillips said: "I'd like to see the general now, if I may."

"No reason not to, sir. You mustn't stay long, though. Come, I'll take you myself."

Burgoyne was in a corner room on the second floor, clearly a room always held for the highest-ranking patient in this building of stark walls and bare, polished floors. The room had a small rug on the floor and a fire in the grate. Burgoyne was dozing, and Babbidge left, agreeing after whispered discussion that Phillips could simply wait by the bedside until the patient awoke. On a table on the far side of the bed were a dispatch box, several pouches, and a stack of papers. Some letters were scattered on the bed. Phillips was shocked by Burgoyne's appearance. His face had a greyish pallor, and he had lost considerable weight. Phillips sat in the chair by the bedside. As he watched, the eyelids flickered and opened. Recognition grew in Burgoyne's eyes, followed by a wan smile.

"My God, can it be?" he croaked in a small voice. "The ugliest major-general in the British Army? What a joyful sight! I must still be delirious. It's good to see you, Will."

Phillips gently clasped the fingers of a raised hand. "Well, I'm glad to see it's the same old Jack Burgoyne. You had us frightened there for a while, m'lad."

With an effort, Burgoyne pushed himself to a half-sitting position. Phillips helped him adjust the pillows. "I must say, compared to a few days ago, I'm feeling tip-top." He shot a quizzical look at Phillips. "What is today? Practically November, is it? I had you placed in Albany by now. What are you doing here?"

Phillips waved his hand at the papers and letters. "I see you've been keeping up."

"Not really. Young Stanley was finally allowed to see me this morning, but he knows less than I do. I read some yesterday and this morning, first time in weeks. There's nothing much recent. I didn't get much mail from home, I'm afraid." His face took on a haunted look. "I'm terribly worried. Charlotte's taken a turn for the worse. That's why she hasn't written in over two months."

"Jack, I'm so sorry. What is it? How did you—"

Burgoyne picked up one of the letters. "It's from our nephew. You know him, James Smith-Stanley, the young Earl of Derby. Tom Stanley's older brother. He tries to be tactful. But the meaning seems clear enough. I judge it to be quite serious."

Phillips was silent, feeling awkward. He was never much good at comforting others. What does one say?

Burgoyne had fastened his gaze on Phillips again. "You didn't answer. Why aren't you in Albany? What's going on?"

"We're not going to Albany."

"*What!* Why not? What happened?"

"I'm sorry I'm the one who has to bring you the news. You're not going to believe what I have to tell you. Are you sure you're strong enough? This may shock you."

Burgoyne glared balefully at Phillips. "Of course I'm strong enough. Now suppose you quit this nonsense and tell me—" Burgoyne stopped as he saw the resigned look in Phillips's eyes.

"You took Ticonderoga, of course."

"No."

"The devil you say! Why not, in the name of—wait a minute. Don't tell me—"

"No, no, we didn't lose. We could hardly do so. We didn't fight."

Burgoyne absorbed that in silence for a moment. "Well, for a while I thought I was having a nightmare. I guess we should be thankful. It certainly would be the pit of humiliation to suffer a defeat at the hands of Horatio Gates, our former comrade-in-arms. Especially when you outnumber him, what? Three to one?"

"Mmm, I doubt it. Perhaps two to one."

"Then why not attack? Ticonderoga and Gates are yours for the taking after you swept Arnold and his fleet from the lake."

"You know what happened to them, do you?"

"Yes. I just read a copy of Carleton's report to the War Office. A rather terse report, I must say. He wrote Lord Germain that the enemy fleet was destroyed. Dated October sixteenth, I believe."

"I read that, too. Carleton showed it to me. True enough, but far from the whole story."

"Well, for heaven's sake, tell me what happened. The morning after I left—did they surrender?"

"The morning after you left, they were gone."

Burgoyne was incredulous. "What do you mean, *gone!*"

"Just what I said. Vanished. Disappeared. Nothing but four or five hulks they left behind, half sunk. When I looked down at the bay that morning—well, I don't think I've ever been so surprised in my life. Hold it now, Jack. I don't want you to get agitated. Just lean back and let me tell you the whole story. I never saw them again, but I learned what happened, from Pringle on our side and General Waterbury on theirs. He was Arnold's number two. We captured him—and about a hundred men."

"What about Arnold? Did you capture him, too? Is he dead?"

"You're getting ahead of me. Go back to that night in Valcour Bay. Waterbury told us that when Arnold called his captains together to tell them what he planned to do, they all thought he'd lost his senses. But he convinced them they had no better choice. It turned misty that night, and then a very nice fog that would do London proud. They slipped past the blockade, single-file, as nice as you please, right up close to the shore where you were perched that day. Clearly, Carleton and Pringle left too much of a gap toward that shore. The rebels were very clever about it. Lines all greased. Oars muffled with burlap. Each boat had a hooded lantern in the stern so the next fellow in line could follow. I think Waterbury said there were twelve boats in all. They gave their wounded something to chew on, they all kept very quiet, and they got away. Quite audacious. Nobody on our side heard a thing. Nobody saw a thing."

For a long time Burgoyne shook his head slowly from side to side, the trace of a smile forming on his lips. "I don't believe it."

"I said you wouldn't. But it's true, by Jove."

"I can imagine the expression on Carleton's face. So what happened then?"

"They were about twelve miles down the lake at first light, putting in at Schuyler Island to try to repair some of the damage to their ships, when Carleton and Pringle realized they were gone and set out after them, mad as hell. Really more embarrassed, I should think. It turned out to be a day of light, tricky winds, and each fleet could only make about six miles the rest of the entire day. The next morning, the thirteenth, the chase resumed with us still about three or four miles behind. Then Arnold's luck ran out. You know, he'd been quite lucky with the weather. He had the northerly on the day of the battle and then fog that night to aid his escape. But on the thirteenth, he was still moving slowly in light airs on his part of the lake when we caught a northerly gust and came booming down to catch them. About half of Arnold's boats came about to engage us so that the other half could get away. Mainly, it was two of their large galleys, Arnold's flagship *Congress* and *Washington*, Waterbury's boat, which was already half-sunk. Plus four or five of the gondolas that were too water-logged to make much headway. The other boats continued on toward Crown Point. We surrounded Arnold's pitifully small remaining group and began blazing away. In less than an hour Waterbury struck his colors, just as he was about to go under. And then all our boats concentrated on Arnold. And he kept holding out. *Inflexible, Maria,* a half dozen more of our boats, all kept pounding away. I tell you, *Congress* was nothing but a floating pile of wreckage—so Pringle says—and still Arnold kept fighting back."

"I told you he wouldn't surrender easily."

"He didn't surrender at all. He got away again. He outmaneuvered us. The wind shifted around to the east, and Arnold suddenly got his oars going and pulled right into the wind through a hole in our line. Two of his gondolas were able to follow. We couldn't sail into the wind, and they made it across the lake to the opposite shore. The lake's quite narrow there, a spot called Buttonmould Bay near Split Rock. They beached their boats and set fire to them, colors still flying. They all got ashore with their muskets. Arnold stayed until he was sure their boats were destroyed, and then they left. They had a skirmish with one of our Indian parties, but they made it down the shore and crossed over to Ticonderoga. Their other boats and crews were already there."

Burgoyne stared ahead blankly. "This Arnold is getting to be quite a problem. A remarkable fellow, really."

"Indeed. You know how stuffy Pringle is. He said he's never seen anyone fight like that."

"Well, I shan't meet Arnold this time. A pity. I was looking forward to that." Burgoyne glanced at Phillips. "Carleton was right. He didn't tell Germain the embarrassing details, but the enemy fleet was defeated. What prevented you from going on to take Ticonderoga?"

"First of all, it took a bloody week to bring the army down. Even when you're unopposed and have all the bateaux you need, transporting eight thousand men and all their provisions and equipment in that wilderness is quite something. Crown Point was abandoned, the rebels wrecked it. We moved down and set up camp near Ticonderoga and surrounded the place. And Carleton diddle-daddled away a few more days, trying to decide what to do."

"Decide what to do! It's perfectly obvious—"

Phillips held up both hands. "Easy, Jack. Obvious to you and to me. Even to Carleton. The truth is, he just didn't want to do it. You could tell the way he was talking. He went on and on to me about how tragic the war is, spilling the blood of Englishmen and all that."

"Yes, I know he feels that way. So does Howe. And his brother even more so."

"You were no stranger to those views yourself."

"Yes, but that was in Parliament, before the fighting really started. I was opposed to some of the policies that led to the war. But when the shooting starts, it changes everything. We have no choice. We have to win on the battlefield."

"Well, I wish Carleton understood that. An old Indian sachem began telling him the snows were coming. The Indians had lost interest. They wanted to go home. Of course, it *was* cold as the devil. But we could've done it. The enemy tried to make Ticonderoga look imposing, with flags all over. I wasn't impressed. I could see a way to position artillery that might have been devastating. But Carleton talked himself into quitting. He said it's too late in the season. He didn't want to leave long supply lines through the winter. He said we'd accomplished our primary objective, pushing the Americans out of Canada and taking control of the lake. Best thing, he said, was to go back to Canada, and then see what it looks like next spring. I think he imagined himself somewhere between Ticonderoga and Albany, in the wilderness, in the dead of winter, buried by snow."

"It's his commitment to Canada, too," Burgoyne mused. "That's the reason we couldn't get him to move all summer. Staying there at St. Jean and building boats was a way of postponing the campaign. We could've moved much earlier. But once we'd pushed the rebels out of Canada, the urgency went out of it for Carleton."

Phillips nodded. "Another thing was Arnold. Carleton was impressed by him. He said to me, 'If they're going to fight like that all the way, then what's the use?' Can you imagine that? After I heard that I stopped trying to persuade him. Hopeless!"

Burgoyne grimaced. "Funnily enough, Arnold lost the battle. We destroyed his fleet. But he won the campaign because he delayed us so long we gave up."

"Perhaps it makes no difference after all," Phillips said. "The way Howe seems to be treating Washington, the war may be over now for all we know."

"What's the latest news?"

"Well, Howe keeps winning victory after victory. Washington's fleeing for his life. Howe may have trapped him somewhere in the Jerseys by now. Or he could be crossing the Delaware River to take Philadelphia and hang all the members of Congress. It could be all over."

"Perhaps, but I don't belive it," Burgoyne said. "Howe can take Philadelphia, but that doesn't necessarily mean winning the war. Washington could still hide in the countryside somewhere and Howe won't be able to corner him. I don't think this rebellion will die quite so easily. No, our plan is the right one."

The two men were silent for a while. Then Phillips spoke: "I didn't wait for the boat ride back from Ticonderoga. They'll be coming through here in the next few days. Eight thousand men! Some of the regiments will be going back to England, Carleton said. Some of the Germans, too."

"I'm going home with them."

Phillips was taken aback. "You can't do that!"

"Why not?"

"No one knows when the river will freeze. They'll be in a hurry. The ships can't wait."

"I'm in a hurry, too, I'll be on the first ship."

"The doctor says you'll be in hospital another fortnight."

"He is quite mistaken, I assure you."

"How can you think of crossing the ocean in your condition—in the winter? You may very well kill yourself. Remember what you told me about the last time, when you sailed home from Boston last winter."

"I know. I hated every minute. There was one particularly bad storm. I thought we were done for. But I have no choice now. I've got to go."

"Charlotte?"

"Yes. I'd never forgive myself . . ." Burgoyne heaved a deep sigh. He was sitting more erectly now, arms clasped around his knees, seemingly lost in thought. At length, he said: "I have a terrible memory of what happened when I arrived home from that awful voyage a year ago. I'll never forget what greeted me when my ship dropped anchor in Portsmouth harbor. It was January fourth. Young Lord Stanley was there to greet me—he wasn't yet the Earl of Derby. He had nothing but bad news to tell me. His father, my oldest friend in the world—Lord Strange—had died a month earlier while I was tossing about on the ocean. We were schoolmates. He was Charlotte's older brother. It was through him, of course, that I met her. And he braved the old Earl's wrath when Charlotte and I eloped. We spent five years on the Continent, in many ways the happiest time. Lord Strange finally worked out a reconciliation of sorts with the old man, and so we returned to London and I resumed my military career—and the old Earl ended up being rather proud of this particular soldier!"

Indeed, Phillips thought. Everyone knew that Burgoyne owed his seat in Parliament to the backing of the powerful Stanley family. But his military laurels he had entirely earned on his own. Perhaps all he was referring to was financial help, enabling him to repurchase his commission. Phillips had never heard Burgoyne speak so much of personal matters, and he was intrigued. Now he feared that Burgoyne, who was beginning to ramble, would discourse at length on something he enjoyed talking about—his brilliant career in the Seven Years War, which had made him the youngest brigadier-general in the British Army and brought him a commission to raise a new regiment, the Sixteenth Hussars, soon known as "Burgoyne's Light Horse." And that in turn had led to something more than an acquaintance with the then Prince of Wales, now King George III.

Phillips became aware of a throat clearing and turned to see Babbidge at the doorway, making signals with his eyes. Clearly, it was time to leave and allow the patient to rest.

"Jack, the surgeon is here. I'm afraid I must leave you to your rest."

"No, stay a moment longer."

"I'll be back tomorrow."

Burgoyne watched narrowly until Babbidge disappeared from the doorway. "When you come back tomorrow," he hissed, "I want you prepared to get me out of this miserable place and on to Quebec. Young Stanley, too."

"Well, I'll be back, you can count on it."

Phillips rose, ready to depart, but slowly sat down again as Burgoyne resumed his narrative in a monotone, his eyes staring blankly ahead. "When Lord Stanley met me at Portsmouth, it was not only the death of Lord Strange he had to tell me about. I scarcely had time to grieve. He said that both Charlotte and her father were gravely ill in London. He and I sped off to London. I spent the next day at Charlotte's bedside. And then the next morning Lord Stanley and I called at his grandfather's townhouse. The old earl was on his deathbed, surrounded by physicians who were worse than useless. It was very touching. In Lord Stanley's presence, the earl clasped my hand and spoke most warmly and forgave me again for marrying his daughter without his permission. He died the next day, January seventh. He was eighty-seven."

"And so the grandson became the Twelfth Earl of Derby?"

"Yes."

"I take it you and he are on good terms."

"Yes. He's thirty years younger than I. With his father and grandfather both gone, he is, in a small way at least, something of a son to me. A capital fellow, really."

To be sure, Phillips thought, and I understand why, of all the young officers in the British Army, the one chosen as one of General Burgoyne's aides-de-camp is Thomas Stanley, the younger brother of the new Earl of Derby. "And what of Lady Charlotte then—she recovered, I take it?"

"She *improved*. I don't think you could say she ever really recovered. She's been so thin and pale. The problem was, as you know, I was scarcely home a month before it became clear that I would be asked to take charge of the new expedition to relieve Carleton at Quebec."

"Yes, that's when you called on me."

"Exactly. I wanted you badly, for my number two. I didn't know what I was getting you into. I submitted my plan, Lord Germain liked it, and it was clear that I was to be in command. But his orders to Carleton never arrived until it was too late. It would've been very different if I had been in command. Instead, here we are, another frustrating year in North America with damned little accomplished."

"It wasn't your fault."

"If I'd known how it would turn out, I never would have accepted. Before I left last spring, Charlotte begged me not to go. She said I'd been over here once before and that was enough for anyone. I told her it was my duty. Then she said—well, the one thing she feared most was that I would be killed on campaign. Next, that she would die alone—while I was away. So you see how it is. I really have no choice. I've got to get back."

"I understand. But I'm afraid of it. If you're not well—"

"Promise me you'll come back tomorrow and help me. Please alert Lieutenant Stanley. And travel with us to Quebec. I'm afraid you'll have to stay in Canada. Carleton will be glad to see me go, but he'll want you to stay." Burgoyne smiled. "Someone has to do the work."

"I'll be back—to see what the doctor says."

"I will brook no argument—from you or the doctor. Besides, you know me. Spend a winter in this deadly province? Not on your life. When I get back I'll have a go with Lord Germain about next spring. If Howe hasn't won the war, we should do this invasion again, and this time do it right. And that means I will clearly and absolutely be in command of the invasion. Otherwise, old friend, you won't see me here."

Part III

The Winter of 1776

Chapter 10

Eastern Pennsylvania
December 11, 1776

Despard groaned when the stage creaked to a halt only two hours after he and André had boarded it at daybreak. He rubbed condensation from the window to peer out and see a man with a trunk standing in front of a small wayside inn. Another passenger, apparently. Despard looked across at André, who showed no sign of irritation. For a while it had seemed as if they would have the coach to themselves the rest of the way to Philadelphia, which would have suited Despard just fine. Easier that way. No need to explain anything to anyone. It was the strangest trip he had ever taken, and he was anxious to have it done.

The stop provided an opportunity to use the "necessary" at the inn, the driver hoarsely announced, the last chance before reaching the Middle Ferry crossing to Philadelphia, but Despard decided it was too damned cold. André showed no disposition to move. If he can last so can I, Despard told himself. With luck, the trip would take only another two or three hours.

Deliverance had finally come for André and Despard when Edward Shippen sent an escort to bring them to Lancaster, where he handed them safe-conduct passports to Philadelphia signed by Elias Boudinot. Shippen told them that no escort could be spared for the rest of the trip—they would have to travel alone by public coach to Philadelphia. After having paid off Mrs. Ramsay, André was down to his last few coins, so Shippen provided the two British officers with enough in Continental dollars to pay their fares.

The door to the coach opened, admitting a wave of frigid air. The new passenger, a gentleman swathed in several coats and mufflers against the biting cold, was still chattering with the driver about loading his trunk. Exasperated, Despard pulled the door shut. Finally, the stowage completed, the door opened again and the new passenger began his climb into the coach, wedging himself and his garments through the doorway. After stepping on André's toes and much heaving and puffing, he struggled into the seat next to Despard.

He removed his fogged spectacles to wipe them, revealing rheumy blue eyes and a dazed expression. "Bless me, I was near to frozen! Thank you, gentlemen, thank you," he said, although André and Despard had done nothing but wait for him to climb on board.

The stage lurched forward, and André leaned over to rub the mist from the window and gaze at the bleak landscape as they pulled out of the courtyard. Nothing of note. There was, of course, no possibility of his attempting to draw as long as the coach was in motion. He sighed. At least this was the final leg of the journey. What would await them in Philadelphia? He turned back and was surprised to see the new passenger staring at him, round-eyed with astonishment. André looked down. His act of leaning over had parted his cloak, revealing the scarlet tunic of his uniform.

The new passenger changed his expression as soon as André's eyes met his. He smiled weakly and glanced sideways as Despard, pretending not to notice what was now obvious to him—not only the red tunic but also the black leather of elegant knee-high boots, the white gloves, the relative youth of his fellow travelers, their military bearing, the very *look* of them. He could restrain himself no further. He spoke in a tremulous voice, Adam's apple bobbing: "Pardon me, gentlemen, would I be correct in assuming that you are British officers on the way to exchange?"

Despard and André exchanged glances. Finally Despard spoke sarcastically: "No, sir, we are the advance guard of Lord Cornwallis's army, on our way to invade Philadelphia."

André's glance was a rebuke to his companion. "We are indeed on our way to exchange, sir, and I can assure you, you have nothing to fear from us. Allow me to introduce myself. I am Lieutenant John André of His Majesty's Seventh Regiment of Foot, the Royal Fusiliers, of late an American prisoner of war in Carlisle. And my companion is Lieutenant John Despard, of the same."

The traveler now smiled easily as he worked his way out of one of his greatcoats. "And my name is Joseph Stansbury, citizen of Philadelphia, tradesman in pottery, ceramics, glassware, and fine crockery of every description, at your service, gentlemen." André could see that the passenger was not as old as he had thought—probably not past forty. "I was not afraid," Stansbury continued, "merely surprised. I thought the exchange had ended."

André and Despard were instantly alert. "We were sure there were more," Despard said. "How many were there?"

"A great many. It was strange. It was becoming commonplace to see British soldiers in Philadelphia. It seemed there were more of them than American soldiers. The British could have taken the city! But it all ended, a week ago or more. I've been away from the city for four days. And for a few days before I left I'd seen no British soldiers at all."

"Forgive us," André said, "but we know so little. We've been prisoners for an entire year. First at Lancaster where we were treated decently. Then we were sent to Carlisle, a primitive place. Have you been there?"

"Good heavens, no! Carlisle, indeed! I shan't wonder that you feel deprived."

A torrent of questions about the exchanges burst forth from André and Despard—how many men, could Stansbury identify any officers or regiments, where were they going, why and how had it happened? Stansbury waved his hands. "Gentlemen, please, I am not privy to any special information. I only know what was common knowledge in Philadelphia—as of four days ago, that is."

"But we have no knowledge at all," Despard cried. "Nobody tells us anything. Just wild rumors."

"A great many Americans were taken prisoner in the recent battles in the north," Stansbury explained. "Long Island, Manhattan, Fort Washington, White Plains. So many prisoners that a large exchange was agreed upon. We knew about it in Philadelphia because many of the released Americans were Pennsylvania men. They've been coming to Philadelphia on their way home and the British having been passing through the city on the way to their lines."

"Wait a minute," Despard said bitterly. "Those men who were captured in those battles. That was just a matter of weeks ago. Look at what happened to us! It isn't fair."

"Just be thankful that someone finally remembered us," André said. "Thank God for that. We could've been left to rot in Carlisle forever."

"You were given no escort?" Stansbury asked.

André explained the circumstances of their release and added: "The council of safety said we wouldn't really need an escort."

"But—your uniforms!"

"They said we had to remain in uniform, much safer that way."

"All the British I saw had escorts. They traveled in groups for the most part. And I should think that now it's especially important. The situation has changed. You know about Lord Cornwallis, apparently."

"We've heard rumors," André said. "At Lancaster, at Pottsville. We were marooned there for more than a day by the storm. This is our fifth day on this trip! We heard that General Washington has retreated all through the Jerseys, that he's falling back across the Delaware to take up positions defending Philadelphia. That it's Cornwallis pursuing him and Howe not far behind. Is this true?"

Stansbury made no reply. He suddenly seemed uncomfortable, glancing out the mist-streaked window.

Despard clutched his arm. "Is it true? Dammit, man, we've got to know!"

Stansbury spoke in a flat, neutral tone. "How do I know you are who you say you are?"

André was taken aback. "Really! Who else could we be? I certainly don't— wait a moment." He rummaged in his inside pocket and pulled out a document stamped with an official seal. "Here."

Stansbury examined the document. It was André's safe-conduct passport to Philadelphia signed by Boudinot and countersigned by Edward Shippen. Stansbury handed it back. "Please forgive me. It was foolish of me. It's just that—one can't be too careful these days."

After hearing this, André peered shrewdly at Stansbury. He said: "Mr. Stansbury, would I be correct in assuming that you are favorable to our party?"

Despite himself, Stansbury's eyes darted about furtively. "I was born in England. I was educated there. I make my living selling fine goods made in England. Now my inventory is running low. What I have left is precious. Now I have to sell some of the crude imitations made here." He heaved a deep sigh. "The war is an abomination. Yes, sir, you are correct! I am loyal to my King!"

"Then tell us, man," Despard said. "Is it true? Has Washington retreated across the Delaware? Where is Cornwallis?"

Stansbury spread his hands. "I'm sorry. I only know what is common knowledge about the war. I have no special information. For weeks we thought the British Army would arrive any day. We heard they'd won every battle— except for General Arnold in the far north. There was nothing to stop them all through New Jersey. General Washington was on the run. For weeks, the weather was beautiful, like September. Perfect campaigning weather. But nothing happened. Until about a week ago. Then some of Washington's troops began crossing the Delaware, mostly the sick and wounded, I believe. Then more started coming. I decided to leave the city. I thought the British would be hot on their heels. A major battle in Philadelphia. Or the rebels fleeing and setting fire to the city. I was frightened. I admit it. So I went to stay with my sister at her farm near Paoli. Miserable, at least for the likes of me, and still not far enough away. We got news every day from travelers, fellow refugees from the city, you might say. The last I spoke with, only this morning, said there's still no sign of the British Army."

It was typical of Carlisle that André and Despard had heard very little there about Washington's losses and his retreat. Another spontaneous celebration erupted when news reached town that General Arnold had stopped the British in the north, but the story seemed so unlikely that André and Despard had dismissed it as a wild rumor. "You mentioned General Arnold," André said. "What really happened up there?"

"Quite extraordinary. There was a naval battle, of all things. On Lake Champlain. Benedict Arnold built a fleet right out of the raw wood of the forest and stopped the British on the lake. They went back to Canada for the winter."

The two British officers glanced at each other, shaking their heads. "That really seems hard to believe," André said.

"I know. But apparently it's quite true."

Despard spoke: "Well, one invasion didn't work, but the other seems to be doing rather well. What's it like in Philadelphia? What sort of defenses do they have?"

"Everyone was beginning to panic. There was mass confusion. People of every political persuasion seemed to agree that it was all over, that the rebellion was hopeless. Still, there could be a terrible battle in the city. You could hear the bellmen moving about, ringing their bells and calling for citizens to help build redoubts for the defense of the city. People were placing wagers on the day and the hour that Congress would flee to another place. No telling what people might do. I was in jail once already—suspected of disloyalty, though I had done nothing wrong. Friends were able to get me out after a few days, but I want no more of that! So I decided it was time for me to leave."

Despard glanced at André. "I don't like this, John. The worst imaginable time for two British officers to go moving about this city without an escort. It's full of their troops. And they're not going to be in a very good mood. It could be dangerous."

"We have passports. All we have to do is get to Mr. David Franks." André turned to Stansbury. "Do you know Mr. Franks? He's the American agent for British prisoners. He'll see that we're taken care of."

"Of course I know him. He's a good customer. One of the wealthiest merchants in Philadelphia. He has a lovely mansion, Woodford, out in the Northern Liberties. I'm afraid he's gone. He was hounded by the radicals as a Tory sympathizer, like so many others."

"Gone. Where?"

"I'm not sure. Probably to New York."

"Well, that explains why no money has been forthcoming," André mused. "We'll have to report to the City Hall, to the Council of Safety, just as Mr. Shippen told us to do. They'll arrange the details of just how we reach British lines. It's their responsibility. It might not be easy, with things so much in flux. There could be a delay—but in the meantime, we could learn some useful information."

Despard scowled. "You just be damned careful about that. Or I'm going on alone."

André paid no attention. He turned to Stansbury. "Why are you going back to Philadelphia, then?"

"I don't get along well with my sister," Stansbury said in a small voice. "Truthfully, I couldn't stand it. I changed my mind, despite the danger. Everything I have is in my shop. All my precious china and crystal and crockery. So easily destroyed! So fragile!" He looked out the window morosely. "I just decided that if it's going to be destroyed, then I shall be destroyed along with it."

André smiled. "When our army takes Philadelphia, your shop will not be damaged. I guarantee it."

"But, if there's a battle, you may not be able to help it. And to tell you the truth, I'm more worried about looting by the citizens—or fire. A deserted shop would be a more likely target. That's why I'm going back. Don't you think it's right that I should be there?"

"I'm sure of it."

The three men fell silent. The stage rocked along. It was warmer now inside the coach. André felt drowsy. He leaned over to stare out the window, looking for sites of possible military interest that he could commit to memory for later sketching. He felt a surge of excitement at the opportunity before him. He had been to Philadelphia twice before, the first time in September 1774 when his regiment was assigned to North America. He debarked at Philadelphia and stayed only two days before traveling overland to the far north. After the regiment surrendered the fort at St. Jean, André, as quartermaster, was assigned by his captors to gather up the regiment's baggage and bring it south to the place of captivity at Lancaster. This provided André another opportunity for a leisurely trip, this time down Lake Champlain and the Hudson River and overland to Philadelphia, where his second visit was very different from the first. On this trip he had been afforded gracious hospitality by such luminaries as General Philip Schuyler in his mansion in Albany, and in Philadelphia he had been the guest of David Franks, the wealthy merchant. He had pushed his good fortune by delaying the last leg of his trip, to the place of captivity, for weeks. He met and flirted with Franks's niece, the lovely, statuesque Rebecca, and through her met other beautiful young ladies of the "little society of Third and Fourth Streets," as André called them, including Peggy Chew, daughter of the attorney general, and fifteen-year-old Peggy Shippen. The last, André had realized, would be one of Edward Shippen's granddaughters and the sister of Neddy Burd's fiancée. He dimly remembered meeting the other three sisters and their father, Judge Edward Shippen, Jr.

This third visit to Philadelphia would be different in still another and more important way. He patted his large leather pouch on the seat beside him. André had become a keen observer of everything in enemy territory that might conceivably be of interest to the British Army. He was using his skills as a poet, artist, and draftsman, and his training in the military sciences, to carefully record conversations and people he met, to draw maps, to sketch pictures of towns, road intersections, rivers and streams, bridges, ferries, buildings, anything that might be of interest. He had lately retrieved a map of Philadelphia from his collection. He had drawn it while spending nearly three weeks in the city the previous year. Now would be his chance to refine and improve the map and pinpoint the locations of targets of military interest.

It was this that made Despard uncomfortable. He argued that if any rebels ever searched them and found André's journal and drawings, they could accuse them both of spying. And there was only one penalty for spying—death by hanging. André brushed this aside. They were in uniform and passing through enemy territory quite legitimately, he pointed out, and no one had asked them to wear blindfolds. It was their duty to observe everything they could.

André's zeal in doing so was part of his transformation from a charming, easy-going young man into something of a warrior as a result of the grim experience as a prisoner of war, especially in Carlisle. Now an exciting opportunity presented itself, one that could make timely use of André's new intensity. The British had not yet attacked Philadelphia. Whatever André could record or sketch of the defenses of the city—redoubts on the perimeter, the river forts, artillery, the number and disposition of troops—could be of great value to Lord Cornwallis if André were able to reach British headquarters before the attack commenced. It was a remarkable opportunity that the Americans had simply handed to him.

André gradually became aware that Stansbury was humming a tune in a low voice and singing snatches of lyrics. It was a pretty little tune, and André asked what it was. Blushing, Stansbury confessed that it was his own composition and that his diversion from commerce was amateur song writing and poetry.

"My word!" André exclaimed. "The same is true for me! Not so much songs as the writing of plays and poetry." With great delight, the two men began querying each other, and soon they were reciting snatches of their poems.

Despard, who had no interest in poetry, rolled his eyes in disgust. Seeking a way to divert the two poets, he commented on the increasing traffic and asked if they were nearing Philadelphia.

"Indeed we are," Stansbury said. "And you'll notice that most carriages are going in the opposite direction. Many people *leaving* the city, but very few going *to* it."

André could see that what before had been an occasional wagon loaded with household goods had become a stream of refugees by the time the coach reached the banks of the Schuylkill River. Here they went through a checkpoint. The American officer chatted with the driver and gave only a cursory glance inside the stage.

The three passengers alighted to stretch their legs while waiting for the ferry barge to disgorge its load of passengers and wagons from the other side. André and Despard stood near the coach, their cloaks wrapped tightly against the chill, but also not wishing to advertise their uniforms. Although they had perfectly good credentials, they did not seek any unnecessary and prolonged conversation about their status. One never knew when a guard might turn out to be overly officious. The two men gradually became aware of an interesting scene about fifty yards upriver from the Middle Ferry dock. A mixed work gang of soldiers and civilians was busy unloading logs from several wagons. The logs were of uniform length, about twelve feet, and the workers were lashing half a dozen together at a time and then nailing and lashing strips of planking at right angles to the logs, as if to make a small raft. When each "raft" was completed, it was pushed into the water and guided into place to be lashed as an extension to the section before it. There was similar activity on the opposite bank. The two work parties were inching toward each other.

"What are they doing?" Despard asked.

"Building a bridge," André murmured, his eyes glittering with excitement.

"Some bridge," Despard sneered. "Look at how it practically sinks when they walk on those boards. You'd never get a wagon across that."

"It could be for only one purpose," André said. "Retreat! Washington is building that bridge so he can get his army out of Philadelphia by the back door when we attack! It's almost as if they've given up already. I've got to get this to Cornwallis."

The driver shouted, and the passengers clambered aboard the stage, which then pulled onto the ferry barge. As soon as they crossed the river, signs of the outskirts of a growing city were evident. More houses were visible as they traveled eastward on a heavily rutted road.

Something about the nearness to home prompted Joseph Stansbury to begin defending Philadelphia verbally, as if André and Despard had attacked it. "It's a very nice city, really," he said. "You would find it provincial, of course. I believe it's the second-largest city in the Empire, English-speaking city, that is—the largest after London." His smile beamed. "Thirty-five thousand people. Did you know that?"

His traveling companions nodded and grunted, both preoccupied with looking out the windows. Stansbury rambled on. "The people are very nice, really. We don't have ruffians the way you do in Boston and New York. It's the influence of the Quakers, you see. They founded the city and they've always controlled everything. Until the war. Now their power is gone. I used to be snide about them, laugh at their funny speech and funny clothes. They were not among my customers at all, you see. They *are* tolerant people, and peace loving. That's why Philadelphia is known as 'the City of Brotherly Love.' Most of the Quakers simply will not accept war. Turn the other cheek, you see. That's why they lost power. We had an election a while back and power is now in the hands of the so-called patriots. Terrible people! They don't have a majority. Far from it! Only six thousand people voted! I think most people are loyal to the Crown, whether they speak up or not. They don't want this war. But things are different now with the radicals in power. Very intolerant they are. I tell you, I miss the Quakers. Now the Presbyterians are running things. Watch out for the Presbyterians, boys."

"We know all about them, from Carlisle," Despard said. "What is your religion?"

Stansbury was surprised that anyone would ask. "Why, Church of England, of course."

"I see. Those are the Loyalists."

"Well—many of them, certainly. But there are many loyal folk who do not belong to my church. It's not always easy to tell where people stand. Most try to keep their own counsel. My church—the Anglican Church—always had the higher classes. Most of my really good customers. Now, with the war—"

"Can you point out the City Hall to us?" André interrupted. They had passed through a parklike square and were now traveling along a broad, tree-lined street. There were many more houses to be seen. The wagon traffic had thinned out considerably.

Stansbury squinted out the window. "Yes, of course. We're on High Street now. City Hall is at the very end of it, near the river." He turned back to Despard. "One can't be too careful, you see. Not with these new people. I never thought I'd miss the Quakers, those solemn souls, but I do! Now I'm afraid that if someone accuses me again of being a Loyalist I could be tarred and feathered—or worse. There are Loyalists still in jail—the new Walnut Street prison. Many of our most prominent men have left the city. Good customers they were. Some have gone to Canada or to England and some have gone to New York to urge General Howe to come here to take the city and restore sanity."

"Well, it seems he's intent on doing just that," Despard said.

"Yes, thank God for it. I hope he's in time. I hope it can be done without bloodshed and destruction."

Despard gave him an amused and sardonic glance and then spoke to André: "If David Franks is no longer here, what are we going to do? Don't we need to tell the driver to stop at the City Hall for us?"

"No, let's go to the inn. We have to eat and get lodgings, anyway."

"And what do we use for money?" Despard asked sarcastically.

"Gentlemen, if I can be of assistance," Stansbury said.

"Thank you, sir, but we shall be fine. It's the council of safety's responsibility to feed and house us until we are exchanged," André said. He ignored Despard's glare.

Stansbury suddenly leaned forward and pointed. "That house on the corner there. That's Joseph Galloway's house. My chinaware is in there. Lovely blue and white Nanking pieces. Galloway's a great leader, trying to find a new way of union with Great Britain so we can stop the fighting. The house next door, that's the residence of Governor Richard Penn, descendant of the Proprietor himself, but he's gone, of course. One of the great houses of the town. Built by the Masters family. I put all the crystal service in. You can imagine how elegant it is!" As the coach passed the house, Stansbury pointed. "Look over there. Just a block over on Chestnut Street. See! The largest building with the bell tower and the weather vane. Red brick. That's the State House—where the Congress sits. I'm sure they're gone by now."

André and Despard craned their necks to look out as Stansbury continued his travelogue. "And there—that row of stores and the courtyard and house beyond—that's all owned by Benjamin Franklin. A great man, a genius, but a strange one. He's very pro-independence."

André was surprised that for a city virtually under siege Philadelphia seemed almost deserted. Perhaps it was the cold weather. Some wagons passed by. Small knots of people stood on some of the street corners. Few soldiers were to be seen. The coach was now passing through what obviously was a market area, long rows of stalls in the center of the broad thoroughfare.

"Here's the City Hall," Stansbury said, "this last building in the middle of the street at the end of the market."

As the coach sharply veered to the left onto Second Street, André and Despard caught a quick glimpse of a square, nondescript building. Stansbury was now peering in the other direction and pointing excitedly. "My shop is back that way. Down Blackhorse Alley, second shop on the left as you go in. I couldn't see it. Oh, I hope everything is all right." Leaning over quickly to the other side of the coach, Stansbury said: "And here is my church. Christ Church. Beautiful!" André caught a quick glimpse of an imposing building with a steeple rising out of his line of sight even as he bent down to increase his angle of vision.

After several more blocks, the coach turned to clatter into the courtyard of the St. George & Dragon Inn, its final destination.

An hour later, having bid farewell to Stansbury, André and Despard were in the public room of the inn, finishing off a platter of cold ham and bread and a tankard of ale each, all they could afford with their meager funds.

"I still think we should've let Joseph Stansbury loan us a few pounds or their Continental dollars or whatever," Despard muttered.

"We'll never see him again."

"So? He's a Loyalist. Let it be a contribution. Besides, we may end up sleeping in his shop tonight."

André had formed a liking for the talkative little merchant during their short time together. "No, it would be dangerous for him. Why compromise him? Besides—"

"I know. It's the responsibility of the council of safety. You're so damned sure of that. Why didn't we go straightaway to City Hall then, so we could get some new passports, some more money so we could eat decently and get our lodgings?"

"I want to look around first. I won't be able to do that so easily if they decide to give us an escort." From his leather pouch, André had taken his crude map of Philadelphia. He drew his index finger across a line on the map. "This is the 'neck' of Philadelphia, the narrowest part between the two rivers, the Schuylkill and the Delaware. That's how we came—from the ferry to that square and then across High Street."

Despard shook his head. "It's like a game to you."

"What?"

"This spy business."

"It's important."

"I understand that. But you have to take it seriously, be prepared for it. Spying while you're walking around in uniform is a kind of madness."

André smiled. "We'll be careful."

"Otherwise—think about having a thick rope around your neck."

"No, not when you're in uniform. It's only when you're *not* in—"

"I don't trust any of that." Despard was a born worrier. His thin face with its perpetually arched left eyebrow often looked more haunted than supercilious. He clutched his cloak more tightly around him and rolled his eyes to see who might be watching them, but the chilly public room was almost empty at this hour. They had not been able to reserve lodgings for the night because the proprietor wanted payment in advance. Only with difficulty had they convinced him to take custody of their baggage. Despard examined his pocket watch. "It's nigh on to two o'clock, John. Perhaps this office in City Hall might be closed. Perhaps they'll be too busy to do anything about us. Then we'll *have* to go to Stansbury. Unless you want to stand around on a street corner all night."

"All right. Let's go."

When they emerged from the inn the two young British officers were surprised to find that the sky had turned as dark as night. "Could be a hell of a storm coming," Despard said. "Come on." He began striding south toward High Street.

"Wait a minute." André grabbed his arm and pointed to the left, down Coombs' Alley. "The Delaware River is very close. Let's walk down that way and take a look."

"John, for God's sake!"

"Why not?"

"That's where their troops will be. They're all crossing to this side, if you believe Stansbury."

"Exactly. That's the point. Let's go see."

"You're crazy! If they catch us snooping around—"

"Don't worry so much. Nobody's paid any attention to us. This may be the only chance I get. I need it for my journal."

"Damn your journal," Despard said, but he reluctantly followed André who was already walking toward Front Street, where a grassy expanse opened up to a wide view of Water Street and the riverfront. Despard was amazed to see the size of the Delaware compared to the skimpy Schuylkill to the west of the city where they had crossed earlier. In contrast to the scarcity of people to be seen on the city streets, there were scores of men in various uniforms moving about. Some were busy positioning artillery pieces facing the New Jersey shore. Others were moving crates of material from boats to warehouses, loading up a train of wagons. Many of the men were busy hauling boats up on the bank or making them fast to wharves that studded the riverfront. The most striking feature of the scene was the multitude of small boats of every kind—sculls, skiffs, flatboats, longboats, barges, small sloops—so many that there seemed to be no room for more, but out on the river more boats were coming.

André and Despard turned to walk slowly down Front Street, but with their eyes riveted on the riverbank to the left in fascination at the scene of activity. "It's worth it already," André said. "It's clear what Washington is doing. He must have his army spread out for miles in either direction to scour every inch of the New Jersey shore and bring all boats to this side."

"To be expected."

"It needn't stop us. There are several places upstream where the river can be forded. Our engineers can always build boats or we can bring them overland from New York."

Despard shivered. "I understand this river freezes over nearly every winter. Feels like it might happen soon. When it does our side can just walk across."

André nodded. "Before that happens it would be useful for us to get the navy up to these docks—to supply our troops and the city. Last time I was here I heard that the Americans have fortified the river down below the city toward the bay and the ocean. There are mudflats and more islands not far south of here. They've got at least two forts. By now they probably have booms and chains and chevaux-de-frise across the channels. I'd love to borrow a horse and take a ride down that way. Be excellent for my journal!"

When the expected protest did not come from Despard, André turned to look at his companion. He found him staring in fright at something over André's shoulder. Following his gaze, André saw a group of American officers emerging from a tavern on the diagonally opposite corner. They were laughing boisterously, but one of them had stopped to look intently at André and Despard.

"I think it's time to go to City Hall," André said. "It's very near, just two blocks over, if I have my bearings. Come along." They turned and began striding briskly toward their destination.

Chapter 11

Philadelphia
December 11–13, 1776

Judge Edward Shippen, Jr., sat in his favorite wing chair in the one room that was recognized as his special territory, the library, the smaller of the two ground-floor rooms that flanked the entranceway and fronted the street. With the chair positioned properly just beyond the window curtain, it was a vantage point from which he could observe much of the street without being seen himself.

At this moment he was in an agitated state and was willing himself to be calm. An hour had passed since he had managed to dispatch the first contingent of his family on the journey to the "Cottage," the modest house he had purchased in the Northern Liberties, near the fashionable suburb of summer homes at the Falls of the Schuylkill. It was barely within the six-mile travel limit imposed on the Judge under the conditions of the parole he had signed as a former officeholder of the proprietary government. Those who had not signed, mostly Quakers whose faith forbade them to sign oaths, had been exiled to a life of severe hardship in Virginia.

With so many people fleeing the city, it was impossible to hire a drayman or rent a wagon. Fortunately, the Judge owned two work wagons as well as a two-wheeled carriage and a handsome four-wheeled phaeton of the kind known as a "chariot" in Philadelphia. He had never quite been able to move up to the next and highest step—a commodious coach requiring liveried servants instead of a single driver. Not more than a dozen Philadelphia families owned such coaches. The Judge was now happy that he had been unable to join this elite company. Such ostentatiousness was a certain way to attract attention, and the Judge's daily life for some time had centered on the constant need to avoid attention.

His two elders daughters, Betsy and Sarah, had gone in the carriage and the larger of the work wagons under the protection of Edward III and Reuben, along with a goodly load of provisions, clothing, and furnishings. It would be a cold ride and the darkening sky concerned the Judge, but the girls were well bundled up and the trip should not take too long. As for the "protection" afforded by his scatterbrained son and an old black man, he was not so sure.

Reuben and his wife, Lucille, were the only two slaves the Shippens owned. Other household labor needs were supplied by a stream of indentured servants, usually German immigrants. The Judge was lucky that he still had two such servants bound to him, a German couple named Ernst and Ilsa. Indentured servants came and went, but Reuben and Lucille were always there, one of the symbols of stability for the Shippens. The Judge was uncomfortable with the idea of slavery, and once had offered his slave couple their freedom, but it had only confused them. As far as the Judge was concerned, their status as slaves was a technicality. His reasoning was that it made no difference to Reuben and Lucille whether they were legally free or slave. They would remain with the family until they died, dependent on the Shippens for the necessities of life just as the Shippens depended on them for some of the comforts of life.

The current source of agitation was the seeming inability of Mrs. Shippen and the two youngest daughters, Molly and Peggy, to get themselves organized for *their* trip to the house of refuge in the countryside. The Judge and his wife would take them in the phaeton, followed by the smaller work wagon bearing their baggage, to be driven by Ernst, who would also bring Ilsa and Lucille. It had nearly drained the Judge of emotional energy to get the first group moving; he had just come from the upper floors of the house where his efforts to speed up the second group had completely enervated him. There were times when the overwhelmingly feminine nature of his household was a delight; under the exigencies of war, those times were becoming rare.

The wailing and complaining of the last several days, ever since the Judge had announced his intention to remove the family once again to a safe haven, had been made bearable only when he had perceived a certain amount of grim humor in the situation. The fluttering of the females in his household, once their routine was threatened, reminded him of a hen house. And it was true that the family's first flight to safety had been something of a fiasco. The Shippens had moved to the New Jersey farm the previous July in the expectation that the British would attack Philadelphia in revenge for the Declaration of Independence. But the British failed to oblige, and then, as the months passed, the Judge became aware that the farm, instead of remaining a sanctuary, was very likely in the path of the Americans retreating from New York as well as their British pursuers. Life in New Jersey had grown dangerous in any case. The legislature gradually filled with radicals and had begun passing laws that could deny liberties and rights to anyone not avowedly a "patriot." Judge Shippen had been specifically threatened by an officious local magistrate.

Only his wife, Margaret, had discovered a love of nature in the remote countryside, tromping off for long walks. Her husband had quickly abandoned his notion of starting a country store, and the daughters, all sophisticated city belles, were desolate with boredom. Peggy had written to a cousin about how "extremely painful" country life was. There were shouts of joy when the Judge decided it was prudent to vacate New Jersey and return to the attractive three-story family home in Philadelphia.

Now, less than two months after returning home, the family again was threatened by imminent battle and again its patriarch chose to flee rather than subject his loved ones to the whims of war. By carefully monitoring his behavior, the Judge had become that rarity—a genuine neutral in thought and deed. He often woke in the predawn darkness thinking of the perils of the time, and then was unable to go back to sleep. In the middle of a friendly conversation or an excellent meal, his mind would go contrarily to his fears and turn his stomach sour, despite all his efforts to prevent it. He would become angry at his children over some trifle, and then indulge them too much to make up for it. He had rarely acted that way before, but the fears were so vivid to him. He could picture his family caught in the city during or after a major battle, with all the rapine and looting and death and fire that would ensue. It was always his wife and four daughters who suffered in these visions while he stood by helplessly.

There was also the nameless, underlying fear of a decline into the kind of anarchy that already prevailed in New Jersey under the advancing British, a breakdown of civilized society with food in short supply, money becoming worthless paper, neighbor turning against neighbor, men simply taking what they wanted by force. Refugees fleeing across the river from New Jersey brought horror stories with them, vivid stories of plunder and murder and rape. Except where the British Army existed in force, New Jersey was a no-man's-land, with marauding bands of patriots and loyalists viciously attacking each other. The behavior of the British and Hessian troops was also a constant menace, despite repeated orders from General Howe's headquarters forbidding plunder and mistreatment of civilians. New Jersey's civil government had simply dissolved, officeholders fleeing for their lives, with the election of William Livingston as governor only days ago seemingly nothing more than a last act of defiance. One of Howe's attempts to restore order was issuance of a bombastic proclamation, calling on New Jerseyans to sign an oath to King George III and thereby receive protection. Hundreds flocked to sign, but the "protection paper" they received all too often was ignored by lower-ranking British and Hessian officers and their troops as they raided and destroyed beautiful homes and treated civilians with contempt or worse.

The Judge knew that his fear stemmed in part from the fact that he had lost all of his offices, and consequently by far the greater share of his income, and that somehow made him feel worthless to his family, with the sense that he had failed, even though he could not help it. After all, the offices he had held no longer existed, abolished by the radicals along with every vestige of the old proprietary system. He was not able to build something with his hands, or protect his family physically, or even cultivate a plot of land. What good was he?

The war already had a devastating personal impact on the Shippen family when they heard in November that Neddy Burd had been killed in action in one of the battles on New York Island. The pall of gloom and despair in the household had miraculously lifted two weeks later when word came that Neddy was alive and well. He had been captured and was now held on a British prison ship in New York harbor. The sense of loss was replaced by a nagging fear that he would be mistreated. Would he survive? Would he ever be freed to return home to his beloved Betsy?

In addition to being nearly paralyzed with fear at times, the Judge had to bear the added burden of pretending that everything would be all right, in order not to increase the alarm that his wife and daughters already felt. They were so fragile, so vulnerable, so unprepared for the harshness all about them, so much made for a better world. All he could do was fight for survival as best he could, for their sakes. And the only way he knew to do that, the only way he *could* do it, was to avoid involvement with either side, to stay neutral. As his cousin William had warned him, he found that this was a path of constant fear and worry because the neutral in due course would be disliked by both sides, not trusted by both sides, regarded as a physical and moral coward by both sides. Already he had caught himself lapsing into obsequious behavior in the presence of extremists of both the Loyalist and rebel sides, and he hated himself for it. Yet it might well be that his best chance for survival would be to play the role of the doddering fool.

At present the menace was a physical one—the likelihood that the British Army would forge across the Delaware River at any moment and a cataclysmic battle for Philadelphia would commence. Perhaps it would be salvation—a quick end to the war. The Judge's neutrality went so deep that he didn't care who won the war, just so that someone would, soon.

The strongest rumor current in Philadelphia was that the council of safety was determined to put the city to the torch rather than allow it to fall into British hands. Would George Washington, that seemingly kind and decent Virginia planter, would he allow that to happen? The answer was probably yes, the Judge decided, if Washington saw any possible gain to it. After all, it wasn't *his* city, and the Judge had detected a certain hard streak in the Virginian who had seemed to fill his parlor with his large and ungainly presence during his only visit to the Shippen home, in 1774.

One of the Judge's perennial nightmares was the vision of his house being burned down. He loved his house with an inordinate passion—to him it was irreplaceable, and the thought of someone deliberately destroying it, or its being seized by one army or the other for a billet, was an abomination. The house dated from 1745, built with money given by his father as a wedding gift; the family had grown up there. It was a handsome four-bay house, wider than the three-bay homes of some of the Judge's affluent friends, including Samuel Powel. It sat on a large lot, the center of the block, allowing for a garden to one side and an orchard and extensive back buildings to the rear. It was built of red and black bricks from kilns right in Philadelphia, built right up to the sidewalk in the Georgian fashion, with marble steps and landing, and Doric columns and a classic pediment framing the massive front door. The Judge could not afford the more ornate Ionic columns—that would have required the services of a turner and carver in addition to the carpenter.

On the ground floor, in addition to the parlor and the library, the house had a dining room and the large center hall with its stairway to the upper floors and passageway leading to the back buildings—the two kitchens, the privy, servants' quarters, laundry, storeroom, smokehouse, woodshed, stables. On the upper two floors were eight more rooms—bed chambers and sitting rooms. The Shippens also had decided against expensive interior finishing and carving, yet the fireplace mantels and the broad polished mahogany stairway with its matching wainscoting were handsome. The extravagances were in the Wilton carpeting, the elegant chandelier in the large parlor, some fine furniture pieces imported from England, and the Charles Willson Peale portraits of the Judge and his wife (the budget had not allowed for further commissions to paint the children).

In his sanctuary, the Judge had one of the finest libraries in Philadelphia, more than one thousand volumes purchased with part of the wedding settlement he had received from his future father-in-law, Tench Francis. The heavy plate and other valuables had been packed in barrels and sent to presumed safety at his father's home in Lancaster. Should he save his books? It seemed hopeless. What good were the voices of Plutarch and Livy and Ovid, of Shakespeare and Milton and Voltaire, what good were they in a world gone mad?

The clock in the hallway began chiming the hour of five, and the Judge roused himself from his chair. He had hoped to leave at least two hours earlier; now the journey would have to be made in the darkness. As he rose, he suddenly saw some men converging at his doorway. One of them was pushing a cart containing two trunks. Fear clutched the Judge's heart as he heard knocking at the front door. In the absence of Reuben, he would have to answer it himself; Ernst would be at the rear of the house, loading the wagon. As soon as the Judge came into the hallway he caught sight of Margaret and the two girls, followed by Lucille, coming down the stairway, all dressed for outdoors. At last they were ready to go. They stopped in wonderment at the sound of the knocker.

The Judge opened the door. He saw two young men who came to attention, doffed their tricorn hats, and bowed slightly. The third man, obviously a porter, had put the trunks to the pavement and was hauling them up the steps. It had begun to snow, and the freezing wind whistled through the doorway. The Judge shivered, not entirely from the cold.

One of the young men, a very handsome fellow carrying a large leather pouch, looked vaguely familiar. He smiled and asked: "May we come in, sir?"

Involuntarily, the Judge stepped back and the two men entered. The porter pushed the trunks into the hallway and then left, pulling the door shut and leaving the two men standing at attention.

They and the Judge stared awkwardly at each other for a moment. The group of women halfway down the stairs stared at the men standing below. They stared back. Finally the handsome young man said, "We have a message for you, sir." He handed a paper to the Judge, who grasped it and looked about, bewildered and apprehensive. Who *were* these men?

As if reading his thoughts, the handsome young man threw back his cloak, revealing in full his uniform, and said: "I believe we met once before, sir. Almost a year ago. I am Lieutenant John André, of His Majesty's Seventh Regiment of Foot, and my companion is—"

"Lieutenant John Despard, of the same," Despard interrupted. "At your service, sir." With difficulty he had torn his eyes away from the young ladies on the stairway. Once again his loins ached—nearly six grim months had passed since his frolic with the frontier whore in Carlisle.

The Judge was very nearly experiencing vertigo. British officers! What had happened? Had the British already taken Philadelphia? Why were they in his home?

"You *are* Judge Shippen, am I correct, sir?" André asked.

"I am, indeed," the Judge said in a faltering voice, the first words he had spoken.

"I'm sorry if we startled you, sir," André said gently. "Perhaps if you read the note."

The Judge did so. He looked up. "To be quartered here? By order of the council of safety? I don't understand. It's impossible. We're leaving. The entire family is leaving. Who *are* you? Why did they send you here?"

André patiently explained the status of Despard and himself as former prisoners of war in transit, in need of lodgings for at least one night, perhaps several, until the council of safety decided on the best way to get them across the Delaware and into British lines, in order to complete their exchange.

"But why here?" the Judge repeated.

"We reported to the City Hall," André said. "We were seeking Mr. David Franks, but they confirmed that he had left the city. A man named Timothy Matlack then asked if we knew anyone else in Philadelphia." André paused a moment, suddenly feeling guilty. "I'm afraid I mentioned your name, sir—as well as that of Mr. Benjamin Chew."

"You mentioned my name?"

"Yes—well, we did meet, briefly, a year ago. You may not recall it, sir." André smiled and nodded at the ladies on the stairway. "And I met Mrs. Shippen and your daughters."

Despard said: "Mr. Matlack said he was sure you would be delighted to take care of several of your friends. He told us to tell you that exactly. I'm afraid I don't quite understand it myself."

André spoke. "I took it to mean that you were loyal to the Crown and that—"

"That's not true!" the Judge said. He could picture the bearded, mocking face of Matlack, one of the most radical of the patriots, who took delight in tormenting Loyalists. "Matlack persists in thinking so, but it's not true! This is his idea of a jest."

"Please, father," Peggy spoke up in a high, firm voice. "We're not *dis*loyal, either!" She remembered Lieutenant André very well from the previous winter, when he had managed to linger in Philadelphia for the better part of a month before reluctantly leaving for Lancaster. Peggy then had thought he was the most charming and handsome man she had ever seen, and she had felt pangs of jealousy over the attention he paid to Rebecca Franks. She had seen André a number of times, but recalled that he had been in the Shippen home only once, briefly, when he arrived with Rebecca and several other friends to pick up Molly and Peggy to go sleigh riding.

With her parents seemingly immobilized, Peggy began to take charge. She came down the stairs, removing her long velvet coat and matching hat. She took the cloaks and hats of the two officers, conscious of their eyes upon her, and ushered them into the parlor. The others followed tentatively.

The Judge had regained his composure and apologized to the embarrassed André for not having remembered his previous visit. Peggy continued to move about arranging things. She whispered in her father's ear that they could not leave for the refuge now, they had no choice. He should not worry about the rest of the family. They would think the second group had not come because of the late hour and the threat of snow. Tomorrow word would be sent to them. Then Peggy set Lucille to lighting candles and lamps and locating Ernst to begin rekindling the fires. After hurried consultation with her mother, Peggy sent Lucille to the kitchen to see what could be prepared for supper and told Ernst what goods to remove from the recently loaded wagon.

Candlelight dispelled the gloom and a fresh fire brought a measure of warmth and cheer to the parlor. The Judge had reverted to his customary thoughtfulness as a host. He apologized again for his confusion. By way of amends, he suggested that the two guests join him for a glass of light sherry in the library, but Mrs. Shippen intervened with the thought that the two young men should be assigned rooms first so that they could relax and refresh themselves. Peggy suggested her brother's rooms on the third floor. As the only male child, he had a bedroom and adjoining sitting room. Because he and Sarah were gone, the only occupant of the third floor was Peggy. Mrs. Shippen agreed and added whispered instructions to Peggy to relocate to Betsy's second-floor bedroom.

André had been watching Peggy's performance with an amused and observant eye. He remembered her as a pert and attractive child, but she had grown up considerably in a year's time. She was lovely, with a tiny waist and a swelling bosom. She had a level gaze, a small full mouth, and skin with the incredible freshness of youth, all framed by thick, lustrous blond hair. A vision of Honora Sneyd came to his mind, but this girl was even more beautiful, and she had a quickness and intelligence that the languorous Honora had lacked. He saw that Despard had been gazing at the other girl, Molly, who was silent and demure, like Honora in manner, but completely unlike her in appearance. Molly had dark hair, pale skin, and emerald green eyes. André could not decide whether Molly or Peggy was the prettiest, but Peggy clearly was ahead in self-assurance. He decided he would like to sketch them both.

On their way to the third floor, Despard whispered excitedly in André's ear: "Why didn't you tell me this was a house of beauties? Old Timothy Matlack didn't know how nice he was being! God, I could be a prisoner here! Which one do you want—the brunette or the blonde?"

"You keep your eyes and hands to yourself!" André hissed. "All we need—"

"All right, you take the blonde. She has an eye for you, I see it. I get the brunette. I don't know if I can control myself. I could make love to her on the parlor floor with her mother and father watching!"

"This is a family of quality. Just behave yourself."

From below, Peggy watched them mount the stairs. She felt a deep thrill of pleasure. What a marvelous turn of events! She knew that Timothy Matlack had meant it as a slur to her father, a crude attempt to frighten him, and she was sorry for that. But what a favor he had done for Peggy! One moment she faced a cold, dark ride to a remote place that was certain to be grim and lonely. Now the house was alive again! She remembered the blond-haired André as everything she had dreamed about in a British officer—and no Rebecca to distract him! She had thought she would never see him again, but now she caught him looking at her several times, and it made her feel as if she would swoon.

After an awkward start, supper proved to one of the liveliest meals in the Shippen household for a long time. It took hours, but Lucille outdid herself in producing a meat pie and potatoes and bread for a hot meal. The Judge uncorked a bottle from his dwindling supply of claret. The falling snow could be seen through the windows, giving the dining room a cozy atmosphere. Peggy sat there glistening, dreaming of being snowbound with Lieutenant André while her parents inexplicably were detained by the snow in some other, unspecified location.

A good deal of warmth entered the conversation immediately as André and Despard spoke of Edward Shippen, Sr., of Lancaster, and Lieutenant Neddy Burd, and told how helpful both had been and how much they liked and admired them. The two guests had been told of Neddy's fate and had been sensitive enough not to dwell on the miseries of their own imprisonment in

Carlisle. André vowed that as soon as he reached British lines he would do everything he could to get news of Neddy and to see that he was well taken care of—and, if the opportunity presented itself, to visit him in his imprisonment.

Partly to dispel the gloom over Neddy, André was every bit his best charming and witty self at the table, just as Peggy remembered him. Despard joined in occasionally, but could scarcely take his eyes from Molly. André spoke about London, about fashions and hairstyles, about art and music and the theater. He apologized several times for the fact that his information, for the most part, was eighteen months old. But it seemed fresher than anything the Shippens had heard in that span of time, and it was embroidered and enlivened by the stories André told.

Judge Shippen found that he was enjoying himself for the first time in months. It felt good to laugh again, but his insistent nagging conscience would not let him escape entirely. Every so often he felt a stab of concern for the other members of the family. Had they arrived safely at the refuge house? Would they be frightened because the rest of the family had not joined them? And then there was Timothy Matlack. Judging by the good time everyone seemed to be having, Matlack's little jest clearly had not worked. It was an ominous sign, nevertheless, of what the ruling clique in Philadelphia really thought of Judge Shippen. Despite all his best, honest efforts to remain neutral, they saw him as a Tory. This first overt act had been harmless enough perhaps, but what would come next?

Later that night, André found the sitting room on the third floor to be ideal for catching up on his drawing and entries in his military journal. It had blessed privacy, a table where he could spread out his materials, and a serviceable oil lamp and good supply of candles. Once again Timothy Matlack unwittingly had been kind. If they had stayed at the St. George & Dragon Inn as originally planned they probably would have ended up sharing a room with three or four others. Drawing and writing would have been impossible.

The realities of polite behavior had come home to Despard. He realized that he would have no chance of finding himself alone with Molly. This converted his lust to a kind of wistful mooning as he paced about the room. Every so often he would go out to the landing and look down the stairwell on the slight possibility that she might emerge from her room for some reason. In between he helped André recall some details of sights they had seen, and then, bored, cold, and weary, he collapsed into bed in the next room, leaving André hard at work. André filled page after page until he could keep his eyes open no longer.

The next morning, André and Despard left early to report to City Hall as instructed, just in time to miss an argument. Judge Shippen, noting the bright sunshine and the fact that the snow barely covered the ground, decided there was no reason not to proceed with the interrupted plan to take his wife, daughters, and servants to the house of refuge. He had to go in any case to tell the rest of the family what had happened—Ernst did not know the way. His idea then was to return alone to stay as host to the two young officers as long as that was necessary, comforted in the knowledge that his family was safe and keeping Lucille at home to do the work. He thought this was an excellent variation of the plan, and so he was genuinely surprised when Peggy and Molly were shocked by the idea. At first they spoke reasonably about wanting to stay at home to assist in tending hospitality to the two unexpected guests. Gradually their resistance to leaving escalated from pleading to anger to shrieking wails of discontent. Peggy even showed signs of moving into one of her terrifying fits. She moved the heels of her hands down her temples as if her head were exploding. She moaned about "hot irons" on her head.

"I'd like to take the rod to them," muttered the Judge later to his wife. She knew very well that he had not attempted corporal punishment since Edward III was six years old. "Am I simply to give in constantly?" he grumbled, after discovering that his wife agreed with the girls that she and they should stay until the guests departed. "Doesn't anybody understand what I'm trying to do?" the Judge asked no one in particular as he stalked out of the house alone. It had been a pattern for years that in the face of united female opposition the Judge almost always surrendered.

Supper was a less lively affair that night. André's mind was on all he and Despard had seen and learned during a long day. Judge Shippen was tired and upset over the fact that he had encountered still another argument once he and Ernst reached the refuge house. His son and two daughters wanted to return home with him when they learned about the unexpected guests. This time the Judge remained adamant.

The news that was shared at the table was not cheerful. General Israel Putnam had been named military commander of the city. Martial law had been declared. A curfew had been set for eight o'clock in the evening. It was strongly rumored that Congress would flee to Baltimore within the next day or two, and would vote dictatorial powers to General Washington.

The two British officers had learned an astonishing amount of information just by waiting endlessly at City Hall for appointments that rarely materialized. "People hardly paid any attention to us," André explained. "They kept running in and out and shouting things to each other. We just listened. Finally they sent us over to the State House, where the military headquarters is located. Still, it took us a long time to get anyone's attention."

The Judge wanted to know if Timothy Matlack seemed curious about how his clever idea had worked. "We never saw him," Despard said.

André described the total confusion at the State House. "I don't see how then can accomplish anything," he said. "We saw General Putnam arrive to

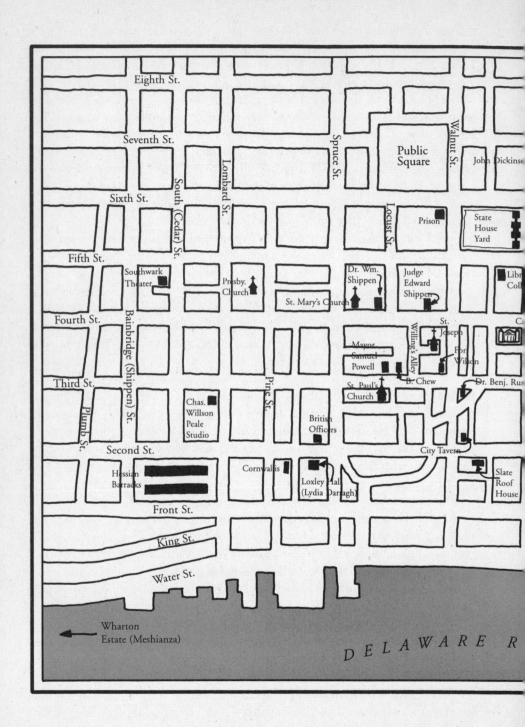

Eighth St.

Market (High) St.

Arch (Mulberry) St.

Seventh St.

Race (Sassafras) St.

Public Square

Vine St.

Callowhill St.

Sixth St.

Gen. Howe 1777
B. Arnold 1778-79
(190 High St.)

Du Simitiére
Gallery

Fifth St.

Fourth St.

Indian
Queen

Friends
Meeting
House

Third St.

Elfreth's Alley

Christ
Church

City
Hall

Second St.

St. George
& Dragon
Inn

London Coffee
House

Front St.

N

Water St.

0   1/8   1/4

MILES

R

PHILADELPHIA
1776-1780

JRH

take over, but nothing seemed to change. Of course it's none of my business, but I think giving supreme powers to Washington—or whomever—is the soundest idea I heard all day."

"Which probably means they won't do it," Despard said. He described how he and André had taken a walk at midday for a change of scenery and had come across the Walnut Street prison just a block from the State House and only two blocks from the Shippen home. "A handsome building," he said. "Looks as if it isn't quite finished."

"It isn't," the Judge said. "The master carpenter, Robert Smith, is dying, poor fellow. Of the cancer."

"Doesn't prevent them from using it," Despard said. "We watched them herding some prisoners out into the yard. They began tying them together with rope. They were going to march them off to Baltimore. Some chap said they were all Loyalists."

That was enough for the Judge. He adjourned supper and invited André and Despard to join him for a glass of Madeira in the library. After pouring the wine into small crystal glasses, the Judge sat in his favorite wing chair, moving it around slightly to face his guests, who sat opposite on the sofa.

"I was sorry to be abrupt at table," the Judge's voice was somber, "but I thought the conversation might be going too far—for the ladies, I mean."

Suddenly feeling guilty, André and Despard began mumbling apologies.

The Judge continued: "I'm most interested in what you learned about your own army. Will there be an attack on the city? And when?"

André and Despard exchanged glances. André spoke: "It seems that Lord Cornwallis is quite near the Delaware crossings with a large army, probably exceeding ten thousand men. His advance patrols appear to be occupying the river towns now, with the Americans having pulled over completely to this side. General James Grant is not far behind with another ten to fifteen thousand men. General Howe is directing the entire campaign."

"As for when the attack will occur," Despard chimed in, "who knows? It depends on so many things. The weather, how Cornwallis and Grant will cross, where they'll attempt it. One can only speculate."

"There seems to be no question that they will attack?"

André shrugged. "Not a single person at the City Hall or the State House doubts it, and we saw and heard a lot of people today. Everything about the situation is favorable. Lord Cornwallis has such a strong advantage, and he's an aggressive commander. This rebellion could be over very quickly."

The Judge nodded. "It would be a blessing to end the war quickly—but not at the expense of this city. I've heard the council of safety intends to burn the city before letting Cornwallis have it. Did you hear any more of that?"

André shook his head. "Nothing. I don't think that rumor is well founded. It would make no sense."

"Would Cornwallis burn the city *after* taking it? There was a terrible fire in New York after your army occupied the city."

"It was not set by us," André protested. "I wasn't there, of course, but I do know that General Howe would never countenance such a thing. No army does that anymore. Take a city and sack it. Not in modern times. We need quarters for our own troops. And we have to live with each other once this is over. No, if that fire was set by anyone, it was rebels—or someone with a grudge. Or it was accidental."

The Judge rose and refilled the glasses. He began describing his dilemma—whether to take the rest of his family to the country house of refuge or to bring the entire family home. He alluded to the fact that he could not leave until André and Despard were gone.

"We realize that, however unwittingly, we disrupted your plans, sir," André said, "and for that we truly apologize." The Judge began to protest, but André rushed on. "Rest assured, we will leave tomorrow. We finally were able to speak to one man who told us exactly what to do—to go under the custody of the couriers who leave hourly for General Washington's headquarters. From there, he told us it would be a simple matter to arrange our exchange, probably at a place called Bordentown. We will do this tomorrow—we will insist upon it."

The Judge was elated, then immediately felt guilty. "I don't wish to be inhospitable."

"Not at all, sir. You and your family have been most gracious. And I think you are right to take them to a safer place. One never knows what will happen if there is fighting here, a stray cannonball if nothing else, so it's much the wiser course. And you should do it soon—the attack may come at any time. For our part, we are most anxious to reach our side before the attack commences."

The three men sat in silence for a moment. Then André smiled and continued: "If we get back in time and there is an attack, I want you to know that I shall personally make certain that this house remains safe and secure." As in the case of Joseph Stansbury's shop, André knew there was little chance he could assure any such thing, but the older man's anxiety was so evident—surely it was harmless to assuage it for a time.

That night, from three floors away, André heard the ghostly chimes of the hall clock, tolling the hour of midnight. The oil was long since used up, so André worked by candlelight, straining his eyes, anxious to complete his entries. Hoping he would be reporting to General Cornwallis by tomorrow afternoon, he was writing down the details of the light horse troop he had seen forming up in the State House yard that afternoon. He heard a floorboard creak and glanced up to see an apparition in the doorway.

It was a figure in white, a wraith dimly seen. André was startled. It came closer, soundlessly, and it became Peggy, a shy smile on her lips. "You're awake. I'm so glad!" she said.

André jumped up. All he needed now was to be caught in this compromising position by the Shippens. No sign of anyone coming up the stairs. He could hear Despard snoring softly in the next room.

"My dear Miss Shippen! What are you—"

"Peggy! Please call me Peggy."

"Yes. Peggy. You shouldn't be here. It's past midnight. Your parents would be furious. "

Peggy kneeled on the sofa that bordered André's drawing table, her eyes luminous in the candle glow. "I know it's wrong," she said, "but my father told me you would be leaving early in the morning. I was afraid I wouldn't see you to say good-bye. I couldn't sleep thinking about it. Please forgive me."

André smiled inwardly. He could forgive her, but would her parents forgive her—or him—if they discovered her alone in a room with him past midnight and clad only in a long nightgown and filmy robe? It was possible that Peggy could be taken advantage of—to his surprise, he found the prospect was tempting. But she was safe with him. No one else would believe that, however. He laughed to himself, thinking what Despard would do in this situation.

Peggy curled up on the sofa, pulling her robe more tightly about her against the chill. She knew her behavior was shocking. She was shocked herself! But it was her last chance. "I wanted so much to talk with you. The last time you were here, there was always someone else around. And now—we've had no real chance to talk."

"I know. These are difficult times. When I come back it will be different."

"Will you come back? Truly?"

"Yes, I think so."

"How will it be different?"

"It will be peaceful. I won't be in this peculiar status. I can call on you—at tea or something. Then we can talk."

"Do you promise?"

"Yes, I do promise. *If* I come back. Now, really, you must go."

Peggy looked at the materials scattered across the table. "What are you doing?"

"I keep a diary. And I make sketches of what I see."

Peggy picked up the drawing closest to her hand and appraised it. The scene was familiar to her. She had heard Despard describe it at the supper table—a group of men building a log bridge, with a detail showing how the logs were lashed and the planks applied. "It's very well done." She looked up with a knowing glance.

"You're much too inquisitive for your own good, young lady."

Peggy laughed merrily. "I'm on your side, you know that." She picked up another drawing as André began to come around the desk to her. The drawing was a rough sketch of her father. It was an extraordinary likeness. The handsome head and the kindliness were there—and the weakness. Peggy was stunned at how good it was. "I remember you made a sketch of Peggy Chew last time you were here," she said.

"Yes. I don't know how I missed you." André took her hand and drew her to her feet. "Really, Peggy, you *must* go."

"The sketch of Father is so good. You're marvelous," she whispered. "Did you make a drawing of me, too?"

"Not yet."

"Not yet?"

"When I come back, I promise I shall draw you—if you go promptly to your room now."

Peggy's skin felt alive all over her body, and her lip trembled. He could so easily take her in his arms now. She wanted him to—and then she didn't. What she was doing was wrong. She should save herself for her husband. Her mother had drilled that into her from earliest memory. Lieutenant André would think she was a harlot. She must show that she was not. She broke away suddenly as if from his embrace.

"I'll remember your promise," she said. And then she was gone in a flash down the stairs.

André shook his head and smiled wryly. It was a relief to have her gone—and yet he recognized that he missed the presence of the sprightly girl.

Back in her room, Peggy drew back the shutter and gazed out the window. There was moonlight, and the snow cover was light blue in contrast to the pitch-black shadows, an eerie sight. She threw off her robe and let the cold air penetrate her gown. She felt thrilled to the depths of her being. It was almost as if they had made love. She was only sixteen, but she was a woman, eager for the adventures that lay ahead. Her life would be special, she knew it. Nothing about the war frightened her. Only good things could happen to her. She knew it.

From the narrative of Richard Varick

When Arnold returned to Fort Ticonderoga after fighting the naval battles on Lake Champlain, his reception was mixed at best. Gates's anger dominated the reactions, anger that Arnold had disobeyed his orders and hence had sacrificed his fleet. Others among us realized that the fleet was doomed in any case, given the superiority of the enemy, and that Arnold had performed heroically against the odds.

When Sir Guy Carleton's massive army came down to threaten us and then suddenly decamped to return to Canada for the winter, Arnold came to be re-garded by nearly everyone, even Gates, I think, as a hero. The battles at Valcour Bay and Split Rock had delayed the British advance only a matter of a few days. But the totality of what Arnold had done—including planning and conducting a ship-building race with the British in the wilderness, which cost the enemy the entire summer—merited credit to him for being the man who stopped the enemy invasion from the north.

It was at this time that the Indians began to show their respect for Arnold's military prowess by giving him special names. The Iroquois tribes knew him by the lugubrious title of "Heap Fighting Chief." The northern Indians, the Abneki, Ottawa, and Huron tribes, called him "Dark Eagle," which I thought wonder-fully captured both the heroic and dark sides of Arnold's nature.

Our fighting strength in the north dissipated quickly after the enemy de-parted. All the militia disappeared and an urgent call came from Washington to send him our Continental regiments. Gates and Arnold volunteered to lead seven depleted regiments southward, for the reason that both wanted to get to Philadel-phia to visit Congress—Gates for his political reasons and Arnold to settle his fi-nancial claims.

Chapter 12

**New Jersey and Eastern Pennsylvania
Mid-December, 1776**

Benedict Arnold gazed out the window at the blinding blue-and-white vision, intense blue sky above, a snow-covered landscape below. It was clean and beautiful, the snow thick and undulating in great drifts, not a speck of the earth to be seen, only a few stark trees and houses and barns rising out of the white blanket.

The relief column from Ticonderoga had been marooned by the blizzard for two days in the hamlet of Sussex, in far northwestern New Jersey. General Gates had met in the courthouse with the mayor of the town to negotiate as many billets as possible for the eleven hundred troops, but most of the men had to hunker down in sheds or barns or burrow into the snow to pitch tents. Gates, Arnold, Wilkinson, and two dozen ailing soldiers occupied a vacant farmhouse; Arnold using his experience as a former apothecary to treat the men with potions, salves, and purges.

"We've got to make up our minds about this," came the hoarse voice of Gates from across the parlor.

Arnold turned and took a seat at the small table opposite Wilkinson. "The snow stopped long ago, and it's warming up. We may be able to move out tomorrow."

"But to where?" Gates's voice was anguished. "This is a fool's errand. I want to know where I'm going. We have no idea where Washington is, if he hasn't surrendered or been captured already." Gates was lying on a sofa, blankets wrapped around his fevered body, a compress of salve latola that Arnold had prepared stuffed around his throat.

"We have no reason to believe that," Arnold said. "We've got to keep going until we know." He was concerned about Gates's health. Gates had been only mildly uncomfortable during the first part of the journey, marching from Ticonderoga to Albany, but when the expedition boarded boats to travel downriver to Esopus, he began to feel worse. Once the column began to move overland again, southwesterly through the Hudson Highlands in the shadow of the Kittatinny and Shawangunk Mountains, giving the British a wide berth by slicing through the far northwestern corner of New Jersey, Gates had been quite sickly.

The march had been especially rough during the long stretch through high country from Esopus to Sussex. Coming to Washington's aid "as quickly as possible" meant at best a slow, shuffling gait and plenty of rest stops. The roads had been treacherous, the mountain passes brutal to climb and descend, the weather raw, and the men exhausted. Pushing them harder would only have increased the number who deserted or dropped out along the way, too sick to go on. The march was a Sunday stroll on the village green compared to Arnold's wilderness trek across Maine to Quebec a year earlier, but that had been at the beginning of a campaign, not the end.

Part of the time on the grueling march, Arnold had basked in the newfound pleasure of being widely recognized as the man who had stood up to the British. He found that he had emerged from the wilderness a popular hero. Along the way, people would turn out in the villages to see the "fighting general," the one they knew would always be in the front lines with his men, who would face the enemy with indomitable courage. Someone had done a good job of spreading the word about what had happened in Canada and on the waters of Lake Champlain. It was probably men who had served with him, men who had been disabled or paroled or mustered out or gone home on leave—or had deserted. Whatever the source, everyone seemed to know what he had done, and that was astonishing to Arnold.

It was not a matter of his feeling that he did not deserve the praise. He damned well deserved it, but Arnold had expected few other people to understand that. Not counting his earlier exploits and the many skirmishes on the retreat from Canada, Arnold had fought the British in three engagements—the attack on Quebec and the naval battles at Valcour Bay and Split Rock. Technically, he had lost all three, and one did not expect to become a hero by losing battles and covering a retreat. But the epic scale of it all had come through in the making of a new legend. Arnold had dispelled the widespread fear of British invincibility at a time when that fear could have become overwhelming, given the beatings that Washington's army was taking. Under Arnold, Americans had attacked units of the finest professional army and navy in the world and given them a hell of a battle, and most had survived to come back and tell about it. The stark fact was that the threat from the north was removed, for a year at least, and Arnold was given credit for that everywhere.

The first few times the column had been delayed when people poured out to cheer Arnold, Gates had been expansive about it. To Arnold's secret amusement, Gates soon became annoyed at being ignored in favor of his subordinate. The final straw had come at Esopus when the New York State legislature had dedicated the day to Arnold and given him a special citation. Gates's illness began to worsen at that point.

Now, Gates had dozed off, snorting occasionally, then he woke with a start and stared at Arnold with dead, blood-streaked eyes. "We've got to decide," he muttered.

Arnold responded: "My suggestion is we cross the Delaware as soon as we can and get down to Dr. Shippen's medical camp in Bethlehem. Our sick and wounded can get better help there and we'll rest for a day or two. They'll surely know where Washington's camp is." At Esopus they had been told that a hospital camp was being set up well out of harm's way in the Pennsylvania town of Bethlehem by Dr. William Shippen, second-ranking medical officer of the Continental Army. Its purpose was to treat the sick and wounded of Washington's retreating army, with the idea of getting them back into action as soon as possible. "You could use some attention from Dr. Shippen yourself," Arnold told Gates.

"No thank you," Gates rumbled. "I prefer your gentler ministrations." Gates hated doctors. *All they want to do is bleed you,* he thought. He hated to have blood taken.

"I'd like to go," Wilkinson said. "I'm *sure* I can get through."

Arnold sighed. Gates's idea had been to send his aide off alone to find out exactly where Washington's army was and come back to report. *Talk about a fool's errand,* Arnold thought. Naturally, Wilkinson, being young and impetuous, saw this as a glorious mission that would get him away from the drudgery of the march. "I reckon there are five or six armies in New Jersey right now," Arnold said, "to say nothing of the loose cannons, who'll shoot anybody on sight." He was referring to the bands of ruffians that abounded in New Jersey. "You want this young man to find his way through all of that? He'll never make it."

Gates had hauled himself to a sitting position. "How do you figure so many armies?"

"Well, we've got one army here—if you could call it that. There's Washington's army, if he hasn't already crossed to Philadelphia. There's at least three

British armies, one under Cornwallis, another under Grant, and Howe's reserve corps at Newark. And Charles Lee is probably in New Jersey somewhere by now, coming to Washington's aid just like us. That makes six."

General Lee, second-in-command of the Continental Army, had six thousand troops and had been left behind in Westchester County when Washington began his long retreat to the south.

"I doubt it," Gates said. "It would be dangerous for Charles to try to move between the British armies. He should have come down long ago when he had a better chance."

"You say it's dangerous for him, yet you want this boy to do it?"

Wilkinson, who now enjoyed the rank of major as Gates's aide, was miffed at being called a boy and by having Arnold belittle his mission. "It'll be much easier traveling alone," he said stubbornly. "I can make it."

"Yes, that's what we'll do," Gates said, suddenly in a decisive mode. "Major, you can leave whenever you're ready. Early tomorrow, I should think. And remember, I want facts, what you see with your own eyes, not rumors. In the meantime, we'll do what General Arnold proposed—cross the river and get to Bethlehem. That will probably take us four or five days. You can meet us there, or if we haven't arrived yet when you return, continue north toward the gap along the Pennsylvania side of the river until you run into us."

Anxious to prove that Arnold was wrong, Major James Wilkinson rode an incredible distance in two days, nearly eighty miles in direct measure, but his was a torturous zigzag course all the way down to the Delaware River opposite Yardley in Bucks County. As he had been confident was the case, Wilkinson found that an expert rider on a strong horse could, with relative ease, evade any individuals or groups that looked dangerous. He had learned from stragglers that Washington's army had completed its withdrawal across the Delaware to Bucks County, preparing to meet the expected British effort to take Philadelphia. Mindful of Gates's stricture that he see with his own eyes, Wilkinson had come all the way to the river to make sure. Screened by a copse of bushes, he slumped in his saddle and stared at the black swirling waters and icy banks. Chunks of ice floated by in the current. Wilkinson had been told that the river was at least fifteen feet deep, a half mile wide. There could be no question of trying to cross it—there wouldn't be an operating ferry or any kind of boat within fifty miles in either direction. He couldn't see Washington with his own eyes, but he had learned *something* at least. He turned his horse around to begin the long journey back to join Gates and the relief column.

Then another thought occurred to him. He had also learned on his way down that General Charles Lee and his army were in central New Jersey to the west of the two British armies, with the Watchung Mountains and the Great Swamp as a screen against the enemy, who, in any case, seemed to be concentrating totally on eliminating Washington. Wilkinson could report his findings to Lee and ask the second-in-command of the army if he had any advice for Gates.

This would mean traveling due north, covering two sides of a triangle to the rendezvous with Gates. It could be well worth it. Among other things, it wouldn't hurt to get to know Lee. Wilkinson knew that if he ever became Lee's aide-de-camp, he would be promoted again, perhaps all the way to colonel! With that resolve, Wilkinson began riding northward, keeping a wary eye out and watching for a house where he could stop and frighten a farmer into giving him supper.

The next night, Wilkinson gave a mortal scare to an American officer at a tavern in the village of Pluckemin. He was sleeping when Wilkinson arrived, and he was certain the British had found him. It turned out he was on General Lee's staff and was due to leave in the morning on furlough. He told Wilkinson that the army was encamped at Vealtown under General John Sullivan, who had been named Lee's second-in-command, having been freed in an exchange after his capture at the Battle of Long Island. Lee was spending several days away from the army, with a small guard at Mrs. White's Tavern in Basking Ridge, the officer said. He hinted that the reason was an assignation.

Wilkinson promptly left on a fourteen-mile ride to Basking Ridge, arriving past three in the morning. He had an audience with Lee almost immediately and then had slept for a while before joining Lee for breakfast. Although it was nearly ten o'clock, General Lee still wore his nightshirt as he scribbled away at a table in the main ground-floor room. James Wilkinson sat across the table, scanning the maps on which Lee had drawn possible routes of attack against the British. From what Wilkinson had seen and heard on his riding expedition, the idea of attacking the British seemed dubious in the extreme. But who was he to question the second-ranking commander of the entire army, especially if he might be in his service some day?

Lee looked like an elderly clerk in a countinghouse, his long, lean frame curled over the table as he scowled at his exertions. He wrote the date, December 13th, 1776, and held a stick of wax to a candle to seal the letter. "There you are, my boy," he said in a high-pitched, creaky voice. It was a letter to Gates for Wilkinson to deliver. Later, Wilkinson would recall that at that moment he had wondered whether Friday the 13th would be a lucky or unlucky day.

As he put the sealed letter in his courier pouch, Wilkinson happened to glance out the window. He nearly froze in fear at what he saw. Red-coated British dragoons were riding into the courtyard, brandishing their sabers.

"General, the British are here!" Wilkinson shouted.

"What, what?" Lee sputtered.

They heard gunfire, apparently from several of Lee's small guard of six men, who had been lolling about outside. Lee shouted, "My God, what shall I do!" He leaped up and nearly knocked Mrs. White over, she having appeared with a frantic expression on her face.

"Follow me, General, I know where you can hide!"

The door burst open and a blast of gunfire came through the opening. Wilkinson could hear the screams of men who apparently had encountered the deadly sabers. The others present—two French officers; a civilian visitor; and Lee's aide-de-camp, Colonel William Bradford—had already bolted. Snatching his pistols from the table, Wilkinson fled up the stairway where Lee had disappeared. At the top landing he saw Mrs. White trying to squeeze the general into a compartment between a chimney and the breastwork of the fireplace, with little apparent success.

Wilkinson headed down another corridor to the room where he had napped earlier. He closed the door and pushed a table up against it, standing now with his back to the wall, pistols cocked, ready to kill the first man that entered. Or perhaps surrender. He wasn't sure.

More shots were fired through the first-floor windows. Wilkinson heard a booming voice from the courtyard, shouting for General Lee to surrender or the house would be burned and everyone put to the sword. After a few moments, Wilkinson heard footsteps padding down the stairs. He glanced out the window and saw that the owner of the powerful voice was a young officer of robust build who was waving his saber about impatiently. One of the French officers had been captured and the other was not to be seen. Then Wilkinson saw Bradford tiptoe out, but instead of his uniform coat he had found an apron to pose as a servant. Practically bowing and scraping, he told the fearsome officer that General Lee was coming down to surrender, and then casually minced away to disappear around a corner of the building. Soon Lee emerged at the doorway, still in the nightgown, but also carrying his hat and coat. "I trust you will use me like a gentleman," he said.

"Cornet Banastre Tarleton, His Majesty's Sixteenth Light Dragoons, at your service, sir," the young officer said sarcastically. "Come, we have an appointment with General Howe!" Two of his men pushed Lee atop a horse and the whole party, now numbering a dozen red-coated dragoons, immediately galloped off in triumphant high spirits.

Within two minutes after the dragoons disappeared, Wilkinson rushed down, grabbed his pouch, and ran into the courtyard. Dodging around several corpses and a screaming guard with blood spurting from the stump of his severed arm, Wilkinson reached the stable. Bradford was cowering there, still in his apron. The two men mounted and rode off toward Vealtown to alert Sullivan.

It was not until the following morning that Wilkinson finally found Gates, Arnold, and the column, preparing to move out from their bivouac in the tiny town of Mount Bethel, only a mile from where they had spent the entire previous day crossing the Delaware via the Portland ferry. He was shocked to see how bad Gates looked, his face an ashen pallor as he struggled to climb into the closed carriage that Arnold had commandeered to transport him.

Gates seemed to revive at the sight of his aide. The trio went back into the small house where Arnold and Gates had spent the night. Gates eagerly listened as Wilkinson began his report, almost incoherently at first, until Arnold calmed him down and made him take a mug of coffee. Wilkinson hastily described the hazards of his ride and what he had learned about Washington, but reserved his main attention for the dramatic tale of Lee's capture by the British and the miracle of his own escape. Gates was shaken by the news, while Arnold wondered how much of the tale had been embroidered, particularly the image of Wilkinson barricading himself in his room, ready to shoot anyone who entered. Arnold did not have a high opinion of his former aide's valor.

Gates was devastated. He was an old comrade and friend of Lee's from their service together in the Seven Years War. Arnold wasn't so sure the news was all bad. The populace would undoubtedly see Lee's capture as another terrible blow to the patriot cause, but Arnold knew that many of his fellow officers disliked Lee, an eccentric and cantankerous man who made little effort to hide his belief that he, a military professional with a long record of active service, should have been named to command the Continental Army instead of the man he regarded as a bumbling country squire from Virginia.

Gates scarcely heard the rest of what Wilkinson had to say, his description of the terrible mood of defeatism that he had encountered everywhere and the news that General Sullivan, now in command of Lee's army, had set a line of march due west to cross the river at Easton and reach the medical sanctuary at Bethlehem.

Gates was slumped on the couch and began muttering. "I can't go on. This news is the last straw. I can't go."

Arnold softly said: "I was hoping to get you to Bethlehem to get some help."

"No, no doctors. I just need rest. I need to sleep for three days, at least. I'll keep Wilkinson and a small guard and just stay right here until I feel better. Go on, Ben, take the troops to Bethlehem. I'll rejoin you when I can. Otherwise, you lead them on to General Washington."

Dr. Shippen had secured an excellent facility in Bethlehem, as well as setting up auxiliary locations in Easton and Allentown. The base in Bethlehem was the Single Brethren's House of the Moravian Order, a well-built, three-story building, eighty by fifty feet. The brethren were paid for the use of the entire building, and carpenters among them also found jobs—building coffins for the daily death toll among the troops.

The people of the region were not pleased at all with the continual arrival of wounded and diseased soldiers to their community. This area of Pennsylvania had been settled mainly by members of German, Dutch, and Swedish religious sects, who, like the Quakers of Philadelphia and Bucks County, were pacifists and therefore neutral concerning the war that, heretofore, had been waged safely to the east of them. Their neutral stance edged toward hostility because they blamed the patriots more for the war than they did the British and Loyalists, in the belief that they had stirred up all of the trouble in the first place—and were now losing. But what money could not buy, the humane and charitable religious tenets of the local people provided—more in the way of food, clothing, blankets, and bandages than Dr. Shippen had expected. Despite their misgivings, the local people would help any human being in need.

Shippen established a quarantine ward on the top floor, beds on the other floors to which the litter cases could be immediately assigned, an operating room, and a screening system for the walking wounded and diseased. The arrival of General Arnold and eleven hundred exhausted men all but overwhelmed the facilities that Dr. Shippen knew were more organized and commodious than anyone could have expected. Every soldier was screened by his staff under his constant guidance, and scores of local women and older children turned out with blankets and food and water to succor the ailing men who stretched in a long line outside in the cold air.

Shippen was interested to meet Arnold, the man he had heard so much about, but they had little time to talk—there was too much to do. Arnold was at Shippen's side for the better part of two days as his men were examined, and more than once he was useful for his own knowledge from his experience as an apothecary. Shippen noted with approval Arnold's constant attention and concern for his men and his ability to bolster their spirits by a slap on the shoulder or a joking remark or compliment.

On the morning of the 19th, as the first of Sullivan's four thousand troops began stumbling into Bethlehem, Arnold formed up his column to move out, fortified with Shippen's detailed instructions on how to reach Washington's last-known encampment, near Newtown, more than fifty miles to the southeast.

A cold drizzle was falling as Arnold headed the column out, his horse moving at a walk. He had an oilskin wrapped around his shoulders to give his greatcoat some protection from the rain. He wore a floppy campaign hat, a muffler tied around it and under his chin to secure the hat and protect his ears. Water dripped from his itchy growth of beard. Sometimes Arnold walked alongside the horse, not so much for a democratic show for the men or to spare the horse, but for a change of pace, to avoid a case of crushed balls or piles. These long rides were deadly.

The rest and attention the men received in Bethlehem had done them a lot of good, but now they had to endure the miserable, chilling rain. And Arnold could feel that it was getting colder. Snow was likely before they reached Washington's camp. Arnold hated the defeatist talk that now was to be heard on all sides, and he hated the tiresome, cold, boring march. After Carleton and Burgoyne had withdrawn to Canada, Arnold's only thought had been to get home to New Haven to see his boys and his sister, Hannah. But when the urgent call for help came from Washington, Gates had volunteered to lead the troops that he and Schuyler decided could be spared from the Northern Department. Gates had no desire to linger through the winter in Schuyler's territory in any case; he wanted to get south to see his family and renew the pressure on his friends in Congress to oust Schuyler. Because he was not feeling well, he prevailed on Arnold to go along as second-in-command on the march. It was clear that Schuyler wanted Arnold to take the assignment, too. Then Arnold realized the advantages for himself—the chance to see the chief and find out what he had in mind for Arnold's future, and, even more important, to get to Congress himself to deal with the assaults on his character from Hazen and Brown and their ilk, and to get reimbursed for all the personal funds he had laid out for the cause for nearly eighteen months. Seeing his family would have to wait.

Arnold was saved from some of the weariness of the march by an old trick of campaigning he had mastered, the ability to pass a good portion of a tedious day by sinking into a sort of trancelike state on his horse. He was not quite sleeping. Anything untoward in the line of march would alert him instantly. But he was nevertheless removed from the here and now of the dirt and chill and grime and transported to a world of the mind, a place where he experienced alternating waves of emotion—from euphoria to anger to sadness.

He often thought of home, of his dead wife, of his three young sons. Throughout the past eighteen months, he had kept his mind off of Peggy's death with a steely determination—until now. He wished that at least he could have been home when it happened, to comfort his sons. How bewildered they must have been. Thank God for his sister, Hannah, who kept the household together for him.

He missed Peggy, or rather he missed the Peggy who once had been, in the early years when their marriage had been warm and loving. Yet she had grown away from him, in a mysterious way, cold and remote. On trading voyages and later on campaign he had written to her regularly, but almost never received a letter in return. Even her death had been strange. All Hannah could say was that she succumbed to a sudden chill and was gone. Arnold knew differently. Margaret Mansfield Arnold had been dying for a long time, not physically, but in withdrawing from life, from him. Now her death was the physical confirmation of a state that already was, a state that left Arnold alone and with an aching need for love.

Christmas was only six days away. It would be nice to be home then, to see the boys and bring them some presents, to visit Peggy's grave, to give the loyal Hannah some support—but it was impossible. He would have to deliver the troops to Washington and perhaps still fight a battle before year's end.

Arnold quickly slipped out of his trancelike state when he became aware of a horseman cantering toward him. At first he thought it was the ubiquitous Wilkinson, finally come to tell him where Gates was and exactly where Washington's headquarters might now be. But it was another young officer who reined up and saluted. "General Gates's compliments, sir. He is presently at the White Horse Tavern at Coryell's Ferry. He has lodgings for you there, sir. The general invites you to join him for supper at your convenience."

Chapter 13

Neshaminy, Pennsylvania
December 21, 1776

"Thank God we had Arnold up there."

Arnold was startled by the words. He was certain they had slipped out of the commander-in-chief's mouth inadvertently, given the trace of embarrassment that Washington now showed, as if he suddenly noticed that Arnold was present. The words were all the sweeter for that. It was a true indication of what the chief thought of him.

Washington's unexpected comment had come in the middle of a gloomy conference about the prospects of the cause. A dozen men were gathered around a table in the dining room of the large farmhouse that the chief had taken over for his headquarters. Aside from the newcomers to camp—Gates and Arnold—the group was about evenly divided between Washington's inner circle and visitors from Philadelphia. The inner circle included the stiff-legged former ironmonger from Rhode Island, Nathanael Greene; Henry Knox, the bulky former bookseller from Boston who now commanded the artillery units of the Continental Army; and the chief's two senior aides, Tench Tilghman and Robert Hanson Harrison, both of Maryland. Joseph Reed, adjutant general, was not present, being on duty at the Delaware River defenses. The Philadelphia visitors included the city's military commander, Israel Putnam of Connecticut; Dr. Benjamin Rush, Pennsylvania delegate to Congress; Thomas Mifflin, who had distinguished himself in the losing struggle for Long Island; and John Cadwalader, fresh from having raised nearly one thousand new troops for Washington, known as the "Philadelphia Associators."

The gloom hung heavy as the men discussed the paucity of officers, a subject that was nearly an obsession for the chief. There was the embarrassing capture of Charles Lee by the British, though Arnold detected that the laments voiced around the table were not very deep in their sincerity, except possibly on the part of Washington and Gates. Then there was the pending resignation of Reed, a man on whom Washington relied heavily. He would leave the army late in January in order to take up his political career, an act virtually equivalent to desertion in Arnold's eyes. Reed belonged to the faction of radical patriots in Pennsylvania and would become deputy chairman of the new Supreme Executive Council, a scheme that placed a committee instead of a governor in charge of the state.

It was common knowledge that Washington innocently had opened a letter from Lee to Reed, which revealed plainly that both men were scathingly critical of their chief. Yet Washington refused to speak ill of either man. *A measure of his character, no doubt,* Arnold thought. *If it had been me, I would've strung 'em both up by the heels.* Particularly in view of the way that Lee for weeks had ignored or evaded Washington's pleas to bring his army down from Westchester County to join him in confronting the British. For that matter, Arnold wondered, why had Washington split his army in the first place?

A good many lower-ranking officers had been lost as well—lost to resignation, disease, wounds, death, and capture. The resulting shortage was one reason for the somber mood. *Good officers were needed,* Arnold thought. One should be careful to specify that. And what was left? He looked around the table. There was Greene, who had managed to allow twenty-eight hundred American troops to be taken prisoner at the disaster of Fort Washington on the northern cliffs of Manhattan Island, across the Hudson from Fort Lee. There was Knox, who had made his reputation by taking the Fort Ticonderoga cannon that Arnold had liberated almost a year earlier and moving them overland to Boston in the winter, a prodigious feat. Putnam was an old fool best retired, and the same ought to be true of the sickly John Sullivan, though he was much younger. Rush was a garrulous know-it-all, and Cadwalader and Mifflin seemed to Arnold to be nothing more than society busybodies, despite Cadwalader's recent success in raising troops. The only true professionals in the room were he and Gates—and possibly Washington.

The problems confronting the chief extended far beyond the shortage of good officers. Congress had fled to Baltimore. The presence of a large British Army across the Delaware River had put Philadelphia in the grip of panic. New York City and environs and most of New Jersey were gone. The cause of the revolution was in such desperate straits that merchants had taken to rejecting paper money—Continental dollars—for their goods. Everywhere the moods discernible in the populace were indicative of the dire state of the rebellion—joy among those who opposed it and gloom among the patriots. Fence sitters were leaning toward the British in large numbers. The army had dwindled to a dangerous level. Gates and Arnold had brought fewer than a thousand scarecrows into camp instead of the 1,500 trim fighting men that Washington's imagination had anticipated. Washington knew that Sullivan, who had yet to reach the camp, had only 2,300 troops instead of the expected force of twice that size. Adding these to the diminished number already in camp gave Washington a final return of 7,659 men, less than half of the British force across the river. Moreover, at least a third of Washington's troops were unfit for duty, and three out of five were due to go home, their enlistment terms over on December 31st. Pleas to the men to reenlist were falling on deaf ears. Congress had authorized new regiments, but they existed only on paper. Frantic calls to the states to provide militia went largely unheeded, except for Cadwalader's success.

In the midst of all this gloom, Washington offered one note of cheer, a rather important one. It seemed the immediate pressure had eased—it was now certain that Howe had decided to go into winter quarters, and it was clear that Lord Cornwallis was moving regiments back to the New York City area, leaving occupying garrisons at key locations.

At that juncture, Greene had interposed a reminder that was also a source of relief—the fact that the retreat from the north had ended for the season, with the withdrawal of Carleton and Burgoyne.

That was when Washington said it: "Yes. Thank God we had Arnold up there."

The words had slipped out, no doubt of it. Hours earlier, at dinner, there had been formal recognition by the chief of Gates and Arnold, who had not arrived in camp until late midday, delayed by the weather. He had spoken briefly of the importance of what they had done, but when he offered a toast he paid homage to Schuyler, Gates, and Arnold in equal measure. Gates seemed miffed by the mere mention of Schuyler's name, and Arnold had been disappointed not to be singled out for a special mention. Schuyler and Gates had contributed, to be sure. But he had done the real work, the hard, dangerous, bloody work. He had built the navy and he had fought the battle.

Now it was clear that Washington *did* understand that. Everything was righted in an instant. Arnold felt his cynicism and bitterness drain away, the dislike that he had been building up for Washington. These men around the table he had been disparaging in his thoughts now were turned to him, nodding and smiling. Cadwalader lifted his glass in salute. He heard Greene and Knox murmuring, "Hear, hear!" Even Gates gave him a thumbs up sign. He felt a rush of affection for Gates. If it hadn't been for him, Arnold wouldn't have been there at all.

That had happened two nights before at the White Horse Tavern. Even though Arnold arrived later than the other officers, he had taken the time to scrape the hair from his face, painfully, and to luxuriate in a hot water bath. The column was now only about a day's march from joining the main camp, and it was time to think about getting spruced up in any case. Arnold had his trunk brought up from the baggage train and selected a fresh uniform. He cleaned his black hair and retied it in a neat pigtail at the base of his skull in the naval fashion that he favored while on campaign. Feeling like a human being again, he descended to the public room where Gates sat at a large table with the usual crowd of aides and other officers.

There was a buzz of greeting for Arnold, but Gates rose, carrying his tankard of ale and a courier's pouch with him. He beckoned Arnold to a corner table. He wanted a private conversation, and that was interesting. Gates signaled the proprietor behind the cage who pulled a tankard of ale for Arnold. A young boy in a dirty apron brought it over, and followed later with slices from the haunch of venison at the main table, a bowl of potatoes and parsnips, and slabs of bread. He kept the ale coming, too, at the rate of two tankards for Gates to every one for Arnold.

Having heard the distinctive roar of Gates's laughter while coming downstairs, Arnold knew that he must have recovered considerably from both his illness and the shock at the loss of Lee. When he was in good spirits, no one loved a joke more than Horatio Gates, the bawdier the better. Arnold could see that Gates was all set to play the role he savored so much, that of the fount of all news and gossip, normally a monopoly for him because, exercising the prerogative of command, he sat astride the main line of communication. Since arriving, Arnold learned that Gates had been holed up at the White Horse Tavern for several days, having sent Wilkinson out again to determine Washington's exact location—the hamlet of Neshaminy, close to Newtown. And of course, to make sure that all communications came directly to Gates from headquarters. Gates's face was ruddier than usual, his nose framed by a lacework of tiny exploded capillaries. His eyes were bloodshot and were glistening from drink and his exertions at the other table.

"I don't think I've ever seen you look so sweet," Gates said.

Arnold laughed. "Sweet as a babe, after a lovely bath. Sorry to be late. I had to come a few miles farther." It was a reference to the fact that he'd had to lead the column alone. "I'm certainly happy to see you looking so much better. How did you recover so fast?"

"Simple. Plenty of rest—and no doctors." Gates's demeanor now turned serious. He began talking about the capture of Charles Lee. "Wilkinson had more to tell me about Lee. At breakfast that morning with him, Lee was denouncing the chief. For some reason Lee was still harping on the loss of Fort Washington. He said he'd advised evacuating it but Washington and Greene insisted on holding it—and we lost a whole damned army." Gates put on his thick reading glasses and rummaged in the pouch at his side. "Look at this," he said, extracting one of the letters. "Lee wrote it the very morning he was captured, gave it to Wilkinson before Tarleton's dragoons arrived."

Arnold saw that it was a letter to Gates. He read:

Basking Ridge, Dec. 13th, 1776

My dear Gates,

The ingenious maneouvre of Fort Washington has unhinged the goodly fabric we had been building. <u>Entre nous,</u> a certain great man is most damnably deficient. He has thrown me into a situation where I have my choice of difficulties; if I stay in this province, I risk myself and army; if I do not stay, the province is lost forever . . .

Arnold looked up, shaking his head. "I think General Lee stayed one day too long in that province," he murmured. Arnold was uncomfortable with denunciations of Washington. He was reserving judgement, hardly knowing the man. He had met with him several times in Cambridge before leaving for Newburyport to organize his expedition bound for Canada. That was well over a year ago.

He glanced back at the letter. The final paragraph read:

In short, unless something, which I do not expect, turns up we are lost; our counsels have been weak to the last degree. As to what relates to yourself, if you think you can be in time to aid the General, I would have you by all means go; you will at least save your army. It is said that the Whigs are determined to set fire to Philadelphia. If they strike this decisive stroke, the day will be our own. But unless it is done, all chances of liberty in any part of the globe is forever vanished. Adieu my dear friend! God bless you!

Arnold dropped the letter on the table, puzzled. "Set fire to Philadelphia! How would that save the day for us?"

Gates waved a hand, dismissing Arnold's questions. "Never mind that. What's important is *not* in the letter. Wilkinson said that at breakfast Lee carefully traced two routes on a map—one from Vealtown to New Brunswick, the other to Princeton. He wanted to mount a surprise attack against the British, would you believe it! Trying to decide which was the best target. And Wilkinson said he was leaning toward Princeton. What madness! With his pitifully reduced army! If he attacked Princeton, he'd be going against Cornwallis's fifteen thousand troops. If he'd gone against New Brunswick, he might've had some initial success, with surprise. But he would've aroused the British, revealed himself. He would've been crushed like a walnut between Cornwallis and Howe."

"But he would've drawn Cornwallis away from the chief," Arnold mused.

Gates shook his head. "I've known General Lee for a long time. He is not one to voluntarily undertake a suicidal mission."

"So it was just more talk," Arnold said.

"Yes—unless he was deluding himself that he could pull off some brilliant maneuver and show everyone that he should be in command instead of Washington."

The two men were silent for a while. Arnold was beginning to think that Gates's friendship with Lee was only skin-deep, or that, for Gates, ambition was considerably more important than friendship. Gates had been naked in his drive to oust Schuyler and take over in the north. Perhaps he now was feeling that he hadn't set his sights high enough. With Lee out of the way, who would be the logical successor to Washington whose reputation was sinking fast? Gates of course would think that he would be that man, he who, like Lee, thought Washington was "damnably deficient" and made no bones about saying so, unless he was in the august man's presence.

Gates was not through with the subject of Charles Lee. He asked pointedly: "What do you think possessed Charles to go off to that tavern in an area flush with enemy units and miles away from the protection of his army?"

Arnold smiled, thinking that Gates had just done the very same thing, though, true, it was not an area "flush with enemy units."

"Made no sense," Gates whispered darkly. "Unless—he *wanted* to go over to the enemy. Perhaps it was an elaborate ruse. Perhaps he was so disgusted he wanted to give it up."

Despite himself, Arnold laughed. "I shouldn't think so. If someone wants to go over to the enemy, they could find a better way than that. And get something for it, I'm sure."

"Yes, I suppose you're right, " Gates mumbled. "Damned shame. The way things are going, a few more weeks and Congress might very well have dismissed Washington and put Charles in command. I tell you Washington is leading us all on the road to doom."

Arnold managed to keep his expression neutral and say nothing. One moment Gates was accusing Lee of being a traitor, and in the next he was putting him in command of the entire Continental Army!

Noting Arnold's lack of response, Gates asked: "You don't think so? Consider this." He extracted another letter from the pouch. "Here's a letter from Washington to me, I got it just this morning. You won't believe this. He's as crazy as Charles is. He seems to be planning a maneuver of some kind."

"What do you mean?"

"Well, he's not altogether clear, but let me read: *'If we can draw our forces together,'* he writes, *'I trust under the smiles of Providence, we may yet effect an important stroke, or at least prevent General Howe from executing his plans.'* And later he refers to *'giving the enemy a stroke in a few days.'* " Gates put the letter down and drew back. "See what I mean? Madness! I don't see how we can reorganize this army north of the Susquehanna. *Give* Philadelphia to the British, for God's sake! Let the Whigs burn it!"

Arnold thought for a moment. "This is very different from what Lee was talking about. We know that Cornwallis is taking troops back to New York, leaving garrisons in place. Those garrisons could be exposed. And we know that the chief is going to lose most of his troops by year's end. Think of the men we're bringing down. We've come all this way and yet these troops are of no value to the chief—*unless* he uses them before December thirty-first." He felt a surge of excitement. "We don't know what he has in mind. It could be a brilliant stroke, if he keeps the advantage of complete surprise."

All the while Gates was watching Arnold, shaking his head in derision. "I forgot who I was talking to," he said. "You'd approve of anything as long as it was an attack."

Arnold flushed. "That's not true! If it wasn't for me Sullivan would've lost his whole army trying to hold Montreal. I argued for retreat. We had a hell of a time getting them out as it was."

Gates belched loudly. "All right, let's not get into a squabble." He studied the hawklike visage of the man before him, with his prominent nose and swarthy complexion. They had clashed violently after the battles on Lake Champlain. Gates's orders to Arnold had been specific. Stay at the southern end of the lake and stay on the defensive. Instead, the crazy, bloodthirsty bastard had sailed two thirds of the way up the lake and attacked! Later, Gates had backed off, realizing it could be argued that what Arnold had done was to make the most of what he had. He had stood up to the British. He had fought like a man demented, everyone said that. It was a bit much for Gates to listen incessantly to Arnold receiving plaudits for his heroism on the lake when he knew for a fact that what the man had done was to disobey orders. But there was no way to make an issue of it after Arnold was acclaimed a hero by everybody. And no point to it, really. Arnold was a man who would have his uses. At the right time and the right place, when you wanted to hit the enemy hard, he was your man. In the meantime, no sense getting into a pissing contest with him. He was just a bit crazy.

Gates drew another paper from the pouch and tossed it over to Arnold. "You think the chief can do no wrong? Read about your new orders."

Arnold read the paper. It contained orders for him to leave immediately to be second-in-command of an army that General Joseph Spencer was trying to pull together in the New England states. A large British flotilla and army under Sir Henry Clinton, Howe's second-in-command, had left New York harbor, landed at Newport, and occupied the Narragansett Bay area and much of Rhode Island. It appeared their intent was to ravage New England. The orders were signed by Washington.

Arnold leaned back, bitterly disappointed. "We're just a day from camp," he said bleakly. "He brings me all the way down here just to send me halfway back?" It seemed clear that "immediately" meant that at first light Arnold should head north. "I was counting on seeing the chief. I was counting on getting to Congress. Damnation!" He picked up the paper and reread it, trying to calculate time and distance. He would have to retrace his steps northward and loop well around the British, probably not able to cross the Hudson until King's Ferry. A thought occurred to him. "Do you suppose I could spend Christmas at home?"

Gates shrugged. "New Haven is a long way. Even if you made it in time, you'd just be passing by the front door. If Clinton's going to attack you've got to organize up there."

"Who else is he sending? Just me? As if I'm an army?"

"Your reputation precedes you." Gates smiled. "After all the chief's belly-aching about getting the troops down here, you can be damned sure he's not sending any troops."

"God, to be under old 'Granny' Spencer," Arnold moaned. Like Putnam and David Wooster, Spencer was another old veteran of the French and Indian War. Then Arnold nearly bit his tongue, realizing too late that Gates also was called 'Granny' by the troops for his habit of peering owlishly through his glasses.

"I think you should just decline this assignment," Gates said, his face impassive. Part of Gates's discomfort over Arnold's newfound fame was the thought that Arnold might be growing so much in stature that he could be another rival to contend with.

"I can't do that," Arnold said. "He *is* the commander-in-chief."

"Yes," Gates murmured. "But he's not God." He drummed his fingers on the table and seemed lost in thought. "Spencer *is* the wrong man. Perhaps I should be up there instead."

Arnold had given up trying to figure out what Gates was really thinking. He had worked hard to displace Schuyler. His frequent criticism of Washington could be understood to say loudly that he should replace the chief, especially with Lee gone. And now he wanted the command in Rhode Island!

"You'd be happy to be my number two there, wouldn't you?" Gates asked Arnold, a small smile on his face.

"Yes, of course," Arnold said guardedly.

Gates took the copy of Arnold's orders, folded it carefully, and put it back in the pouch. "I'll give this to you tomorrow night."

Arnold looked up. "What do you mean?"

"I'll give these orders to you when we reach camp."

"How can you do that? They'll know when it arrived here."

"I realize that. I'll tell the chief I made the decision to hold this, that we need to discuss it further."

"Thank God we had Arnold up there." The words still reverberated in Arnold's mind. It was past ten o'clock and the meeting was over. Washington had excused his fellow officers but asked Arnold to come with him to his quarters on the second floor. Arnold sat there now, holding a glass of port the chief had poured for him. The light was low, only two candles and the flickering embers of a dying fire. This was Washington's sitting room. In the shadowy gloom Arnold could see leather pouches piled on the floor and maps spread in profusion across a large table. He was well aware that it was a signal honor to see the chief without staff aides present. Washington sat in an armchair in a relaxed posture, his coat unbuttoned, kneading his eyes. Now he yawned and picked up his glass of port, dipping it toward his guest.

"I was a little disturbed that General Gates brought you on to headquarters on his own authority, despite my orders," he said. "It does give me the chance to tell you personally that I am very much aware of all that you have done. You've shown an enterprise that is sadly lacking in some other quarters. I know what your detractors are saying, too. The bold and vigorous man always attracts jealous critics of this sort." Washington might have been speaking of himself and his many critics. "Your actions speak much, much louder than their words."

Arnold swelled with pride, but he was careful not to show it. He said merely, "Thank you, Excellency." He had been well briefed by Tilghman on the chief's penchant for formality.

Washington looked up with large luminous eyes. He resumed in a monotone: "I also know that you've given up your prosperous trading business to wear your uniform. That your trading schooner was burned. And I know that while you were on campaign—you lost your wife. I know of no man who has given more for the cause of liberty."

"Thank you, Excellency," Arnold murmured again. There was a silence. He decided to take the plunge. "You mentioned my detractors. That business was referred to Congress by General Gates. I am most anxious to clear my name, to petition Congress on that matter and on my finances. For well over a year I haven't been reimbursed—"

"Ah, but this is not the time." The chief waved a hand. "I don't think you'd find Congress a very coherent body just now. If you could find Congress at all," he added, with a small smile. Seeing the disappointment on Arnold's face, he said: "I do understand the importance of this to you. And I shall give you leave to go to Congress at the first opportunity. There is no possibility now."

Arnold nodded, already resigned to the fact.

As an afterthought, Washington added: "I did allow General Gates to go. He'll leave on furlough tomorrow. He'll probably go home for Christmas, to his estate near Shepherdstown. His real interest is in finding Congress. I expect he'll be in Baltimore before long. Though I might've had uses for him here." Washington sighed. "He was rather insistent."

Arnold was taken aback at this news. He felt a bit of rancor toward Gates, having heard nothing from him of these plans.

"Will he take Wilkinson with him? What is he now—a colonel?" Arnold asked.

Washington laughed. "Oh, yes, that very ambitious young man! Gates wanted to take him along. But it's not official business. So Major Wilkinson made the right choice, though he was tempted. He's staying here."

After a moment, Arnold spoke: "Excellency, if I may make so bold—well, General Gates told me in the strictest confidence that you were contemplating some maneuver against the enemy."

Washington's eyes grew cold. "I wonder who else he's been talking to."

"No one, sir, I'm certain. I noticed, for example, that you made no mention of it in the meeting this evening."

"No. Much too large a group. There were some talkative people present. Everything would depend on surprise. I haven't decided yet."

"I'm very much in favor of it, sir."

Washington smiled. "Somehow I knew that you would feel that way. Others are not so sure."

"If there is to be any maneuver, I would very much like to be part of it."

"I knew I could count on you for that, too. Don't think I haven't thought of it. But I want you to take this assignment to New England. Your presence will mean more there than any other officer I could think of. Obviously, I can't send any troops."

"Did General Gates . . . ?"

"Yes, he intimated that perhaps he should be in command in New England. He seems to want to be everywhere," Washington said, with just a trace of sarcasm, "everywhere except where I want him to be. Now that I'm losing Joseph Reed, I'd like Gates to be adjutant general again. He's resisting. In the mood he's in, I thought it just as well to let him go."

For the moment Arnold said nothing, not sure how to comment on such matters. Finally, he asked: "So General Spencer will be in command in Rhode Island?"

"It has to be that way. But you're the man I'm relying on. You understand?"

"Yes, Excellency."

"You have young children, don't you?"

"Yes, sir. Three sons."

"How old are they?"

"The oldest, Benedict, is eight. Richard is six and Henry is four."

Washington raised his eyebrows. "That young? Really. All right, I want you to leave tomorrow. So that you can be home for Christmas. New Haven, isn't it? That's on your way to Rhode Island. You might just make it. Spend a week at home."

"But I thought—"

"No man deserves it more. Tilghman tells me you haven't been home since you were in Cambridge, before you left on the expedition to Canada. That seems a long, long time ago. You've done a lot since then."

"Yes, Excellency, but—what about Clinton and his army? Shouldn't I—"

"I should have told you. The situation in Rhode Island looks less urgent than we thought at first."

"Less urgent?"

"Clinton has taken most of Rhode Island—but, of course, that isn't saying much. It appears that this is not intended as an invasion force, as we first feared. More likely the British just want another ice-free harbor—and another town to help house their troops for the winter, now that Howe and much of his army are retiring to New York. They're overloaded there, ever since the fire." Washington noted Arnold's puzzled expression. "Of course. You weren't there. You'd have to see that incredible sight to believe it. By the time they were finished they had over four hundred ships—transports and warships. Anchored all over New York harbor." He shook his head gravely. "What I could do with one tenth that number." He sighed. "So, it appears that they want Newport for more room and having more ships at another station to help in their blockading of the coast."

"Should I be thinking about attacking Clinton?"

"I doubt it. Unless you perform a miracle in raising an army. Clinton has four to five thousand men, according to our information. Probably not enough for him to mount a serious invasion of New England, but ample for holding Newport with his navy at his back. Of course, we could be mistaken. If he ventures out more than he already has, that's another matter. Go to Boston. See how much of an army you can raise from New England. If all is quiet—well, you'll be in winter quarters, too."

Washington rose and lifted his glass in a toast. It was a clear signal that the meeting was over. "General Arnold, you have a great future with the Continental Army. And for your country. I know your qualities now. They will be put to extremely valuable use."

Arnold left feeling exuberant and light-headed. He was cynical enough so that he usually could see through puffery or sham. This was different. He had found himself fighting not to use too reverential a tone in talking with the chief. Something about the man inspired reverence—his bulk, his gravity, his insistence on formality and the prerogatives of rank, the knowledge of the burdens he labored under. It was not comfortable to be with him, but it was a rare experience. And Arnold now knew one thing with certainty. He knew that he was very high in the chief's esteem. And that was useful—considering that assignments were to be made for the next season, promotions were coming up, and he had affairs with Congress to settle.

Chapter 14

New Haven, Connecticut
December 25, 1776

The man and his horse were as one, so long had they been together, married in weariness, misery, and cold. Arnold felt a thrill of elation as his horse padded down Water Street and he came in sight of home. He had vowed to himself that he would be there for Christmas, and he had made it.

After delays in several towns when officials and citizens turned out to see and greet the "fighting general" as he passed through, Arnold changed his route several times and tried to travel incognito. His escort of six Rhode Islanders, all due to be mustered out on December 31st, also slowed his progress. They knew it would be impossible for them to make it home for Christmas, no matter how hard they tried. As a result, they lacked the motivation to exert themselves beyond the minimal safe response to the exhortations of their commander. So Arnold had forged ahead alone, carrying with him the final pay for the six men. At this point, he guessed that they were as much as two days behind him, bringing along the wagon with his baggage.

Arnold had arrived at Norwalk, thirty miles from New Haven, after dark. The weather was raw and windy, yet not nearly as cold as it might have been on Christmas Eve, so he decided to continue on his journey without stopping for the night, despite the fact that he had been in the saddle since daybreak. First he had errands to perform. For a fee, a farmer gave him supper and strangled a plump goose for him, which he slung over the rump of his horse. He finally located the toymaker's shop and pounded relentlessly on the door until he got a response. It was one time Arnold made himself known. The toymaker's anger evaporated as soon as he learned who was at his door. Arnold filled a sack with toy soldiers and cannon and tied it to the pommel of his saddle. He then found himself in an argument with the toymaker, who was refusing payment. It soon dawned on Arnold what the man wanted instead. He wrote a note of appreciation to the toymaker and signed his now-famous name with a flourish. The man's friends would truly believe that the "fighting general" had stopped at his shop. Not a bad deal, Arnold thought, as he set out on the last leg of his journey.

More than six hours later, he turned onto his two-acre property in New Haven, heading for the stables set back a good distance behind the white clapboard house. A half-moon shone brightly between drifting clouds. Arnold now tried to resolve the dilemma that had been nagging at him. Should he pound on the door and rouse Hannah and the boys? Or should he sneak in quietly and try to get a bit of sleep himself before they woke? Either way he would probably scare the hell out of them, he supposed. There was no sign of any kind of light within the house. Arnold's nearly total exhaustion decided the question. Lacking the energy to pull out his watch and try to read it in the dim light, he reckoned that it was not much past four o'clock. At least two more hours until dawn. He would sneak in if the key to the back door was still where he had hidden it more than a year ago. First the horse needed to be stabled and given feed and water.

He climbed wearily from his mount and began tugging on the stable door. It slid open, wood rasping on wood. Arnold led the horse into the pitch darkness. He could tell that his two carriage horses were in good shape by the snorts and whinnies of fear that came from their stalls. He was groping for the rack along one wall, where a lantern and flint should be, when he sensed another presence. He heard a scuffling sound, and a bolt of fear shot through him as he whirled about. A solid blow hit him on the chin and sent him sprawling, nearly unconscious, lights exploding in his brain. He retained enough presence of mind to roll along the ground, scrabbling out of the way as his attacker tried to pounce on him. He struggled to his feet and then a lunging shape plowed into him, knocking him through the doorway to the ground outside. Arnold managed to lift both feet and to kick out with all his might, catching his attacker full on the chest and stomach as he lunged again. In the moonlight, Arnold now could see that the assailant was a black man, barefooted, clad in a nightshirt and pants. Arnold's blow had sent him crashing back into the stable wall, sliding to the ground with the wind knocked out of him. Triumphantly, Arnold jumped up, looking for his pistol to kill the intruder, but it was in his saddle holster and the horse had bolted across the yard. He spotted a length of wood on the ground and grabbed it.

"You goddamned nigger!" Arnold shouted, standing over the man, club upraised. "You runaway bastard. Hide in my stable, will you? Attack me, will you? I'll beat you to death, you son of a bitch." He began flailing away with the club. The man warded off the blows as best he could, screaming and pleading all the while. As his words began to filter through, Arnold gradually slowed his pace and then stopped. "What the hell did you say?"

"Please, suh, I protecks them. The lady, she hire me." The black man looked up plaintively, his face glistening with blood and tears.

"*Who* hired you?" Arnold asked, gasping for breath.

"The lady in that house. Please, suh, I protecks them, the lady and those boys. I sleeps in the stable."

"Don't give me that." Arnold fetched the man another blow. "You're a runaway slave. And you picked the wrong place to hide."

"No, suh!" The man was indignant. "I be no slave. I be *free*! The lady, she hire me."

"If she hired you, what's her name?" The black man looked confused. "I thought so," Arnold shouted, and resumed swinging his club.

The black man screamed and tried to roll out of the way. He got to his knees and assumed a praying posture. "Her name be Miss Hannah! She be Miss Hannah!"

Arnold stopped the blows and sank to the ground himself, exhausted. "Why in the hell did you attack me? I'm General Arnold. This is my house, for chrissakes!"

The black man looked even more frightened. "I din't know. Please, suh, I just tryin' to protecks them. The lady, she frightened, she say you see anybody comin' 'round at night you jump on 'em! I just—"

"All right, all right," Arnold groaned. "Shut up and listen to me. I open the door and bring a horse *into* the stable. That means I belong here. If I take a horse *out* of the stable in the middle of the night, then I don't belong. Then I'm a thief. You understand that?"

"Yes, suh."

"So I brought a horse *into* the stable. Why did you jump me?" All Arnold got was a blank stare and an expression of confusion. "You're a goddamned runaway slave," he said.

"No, *suh!*" the man said sullenly.

"Where you from?"

"Tortola."

Arnold knew the island. Sailing up from Antigua once, he had taken refuge there from a storm. "You were a slave there," he said.

"Yes, suh. Long Look Plantation. But Mistuh Nottingham—he be a Quaker—he free all his slaves five years ago. I show my paper to Miss Hannah."

"What's your name?"

"Abednego."

"Abednego what?"

"Abednego Pickering."

"What do people call you?"

"Punch."

"That makes a lot of sense. Why?"

"I dunno. Ever since I were a child."

"Well you throw a mean punch—Punch." Arnold touched his tender jaw gingerly. "At least when no one is looking. If you broke my jaw—I'll still kill you."

Arnold tried to flex his mandibles and a jolt of pain shot through him. His anger rose again as he stared at the wretch before him. It was preposterous. He had been in the saddle all day and night. Bone weary, he had made it home for the pleasure of spending Christmas with his children. He had tried to put his own horse in his own stable. And this miserable scum had attacked him. General Benedict Arnold, the hero of the hour, had been attacked and struck by a Negro stable boy. If a soldier in the army had done that he would have been court-martialed and hung. The outrage of it brought Arnold to his feet and he began swinging the club again, raining blows down upon the hapless Punch.

"You miserable bastard! How dare you hit me? Get out of my sight."

Punch, trying to ward off the blows, protested. "But—that lady, Miss Hannah, she hire me."

"I just fired you. Get out!" Arnold watched as Punch scuffled away, his bare feet scraping the ground, his tattered nightshirt flapping in the wind. "You're lucky I didn't kill you!" Arnold shouted after him.

Let him find someone else's stable to crawl into, Arnold thought. Serve him right to freeze to death. He stood there, fuming, his free hand twitching. He realized there was no doubt the man's story was true. It would be like Hannah to hire an indigent Negro stable boy and expect him to defend the property. He touched his jaw again. It ached, but nothing seemed to be broken. As Punch's figure retreated, shoulders drooping, almost out of earshot, Arnold relented. *What the hell,* he thought, *it's Christmas.* "Hey, you! Punch! Come back here." Punch reluctantly turned. "See that horse over there? Let's see what kind of stable boy you are. Bring him here."

Punch brought the horse to Arnold who very deliberately took his all-metal Scottish pistol from the saddle holster. He tucked it into his belt as Punch watched nervously. Then Arnold swung the goose over his shoulder and unfastened his saddlebags and the sack of toys from the pommel. "Listen to me, Punch. You can stay. Go back to sleep in the stable. First I want you to take care of this horse. Brush him down. Get him some hay and water. Be careful with my saddle. Understood?"

"Yes, suh!"

Arnold turned to go to the house and said over his shoulder: "And Punch—if anyone tries to sneak in, you be sure to protect us." Punch nodded glumly.

The key was still behind the loose brick in the foundation of the house. Arnold took the time to relieve himself, then went up on the back porch. He opened the door as quietly as he could and entered the kitchen. There had been no sign of life from the house, no light and no sound. Arnold thought the commotion in the yard would have waked the dead, but the stable was pretty far back and downwind of the house. He put his burdens down on the kitchen table and walked through to the front hall, pausing only to light a candle.

He tiptoed up to the second floor landing, carefully avoiding the steps he knew would creak. Hannah's bedroom was the first one on the left. He thought it was going to be all right, that he could make it to his room and the blessed bed, but then the door suddenly jerked open and a terrified Hannah appeared, a pistol wobbling violently in her trembling hands. She was a comical figure in her flannel nightgown and nightcap, wisps of grey hair sticking out, her eyes round with fear. Arnold was in no mood to laugh. The pistol might go off. After all he'd been through, this would be a terrible way to go. He snatched the pistol from her. "Hannah! It's me, Ben!"

It seemed as if it took her a full minute to comprehend, but it was only a few seconds. Sobbing with relief, she embraced him. There was much clucking and cooing, and then she drew back to study him, noting his disheveled appearance and the bruise and scrape on his chin. "Ben, what happened?"

"I got my Christmas present from you early." To her puzzled look he said: "Punch and I met out at the stable. I'll tell you about it later." Arnold had become aware of a small boy rubbing drowsy eyes and then staring up, awestruck at the frightening sight of the martial figure towering over him. It was Benedict Jr., eldest of his sons. Arnold handed the pistol and candle to his sister, knelt down, and said tenderly: "How much you've grown. Don't be frightened, young Ben. It's your father, come home at last." He picked the boy up. "Let's go find your brothers."

All thought of sleep was banished. Two hours later Arnold sat at the kitchen table, his fatigue made all the more numbing by the warmth of the fire Hannah had kindled in the stove. He watched the sky lighten through the window as his sister busied herself making gruel, biscuits, and coffee. She began frying eggs. Time and the toys had overcome the awe and the shyness of the three boys toward a father they had not seen in well more than a year—shouts of excitement could be heard as they played war in the parlor. Hannah had prattled on endlessly, giving her brother all the detailed news from home, and Arnold responded to what seemed like a thousand questions. She set a platter of eggs and ham and biscuits before him, and he began to eat, slowly at first, and then ravenously.

He kept munching biscuits with honey and sipping coffee until, finally sated, he became barely conscious again, basking in the warm glow of being home in his own kitchen, the weariness and anxiety and pain of war shed for a time, blissful sleep beckoning. Hannah finally took pity on him and led him upstairs to his own bed.

Benedict Arnold's homecoming was positive for him in body, mind, and spirit. He fattened himself on Hannah's good cooking. He spent long hours with his sons, telling them stories and reenacting battles on the parlor floor. He slept and rested more than he had at any other time in his adult life, and he could feel the energy and verve and clarity of mind returning.

He soon discovered that he was a hero in his own hometown as well as everywhere else. Traffic increased considerably on Water Street when residents of New Haven learned that he was home. They came by on foot or in carriages, slowing their pace in hope of catching a glimpse of their famed fellow townsman. Occasionally Arnold would emerge from the house, grinning and waving to the cheers of the onlookers. Even the next-door neighbor, Arnold's mother-in-law, Mrs. Mansfield, who had grown somewhat acerbic in the wake of the loss of both her husband and daughter, greeted him with smiles and congratulations.

Several times he spotted men who had served under him in Canada. Never before had they received such warm greetings from their former commander. There was a jubilant reunion when John Lamb and Eleazer Oswald rode into the courtyard a few days after Christmas. Lamb was a veteran artillery officer who had lost an eye and part of his jaw when he had taken a cannon blast nearly full in the face in the same assault on Quebec Lower Town in which Arnold had been wounded. Oswald was an adventurer, a younger crony whom Arnold had known for several years. Arnold had been unable to give him a commission, but Oswald had gone on the march to Quebec anyway, as a volunteer.

Arnold came to terms with Hannah about Punch. The only other household help she had was a dim-witted Irish maid. Arnold decided that the well-mannered and well-muscled young man from Tortola could be useful, especially after he displayed proper contrition over his egregious error in attacking the master of the household. Arnold noted with satisfaction also that Punch, despite his youth and strength, had considerably more lumps and contusions than he did from their strange encounter. Arnold almost balked when he learned that Hannah was paying Punch a silver dollar a week in addition to room and board. Grumbling that there was something to be said for slavery, Arnold finally acquiesced.

The first time that Arnold went to the cemetery to visit Peggy's grave, he went alone, very early in the morning when there would be no one there to see him. He knelt down, the cold dampness of the earth seeping through the knees of his breeches, and pondered the strangeness of it all, her withdrawal from life years before her death. He had tried to talk about the children to her but got little more than blank stares in return. She had withdrawn from them, too, and perhaps that was a blessing now that she was gone.

Arnold wondered whether his rise to fame would have made any difference to her. Only twenty months ago he was an obscure captain of militia, struggling to marshall his company on the green in New Haven. Today he was a brigadier-general in the Continental Army, the most famous one by far. He was certain to become a major-general in the promotion list that was due to be issued by Congress within the next month or two. Another year of leadership on the battlefield and he would be promoted to the next rank, perhaps second only to Washington himself in the entire army, certainly the leading combat general. Everything was going according to plan, even faster than he had hoped. The war was the perfect outlet for his bursting ambition, and he was progressing in what he had set out to do—to become the most famous leader, the indispensable one, the savior of his land, to be showered with esteem and riches by grateful countrymen.

Would all of this have made a difference to Peggy? Would it have made her as warm and loving as she once had been? Or had he lost her love much earlier, lost it through his driving ambition? He wasn't sure of the answer. He was only sure that it now no longer really mattered. Margaret Mansfield Arnold was gone. When he tried to see her in his mind, the image was indistinct. All that was left was an aching void in him, and that would be filled some day. Arnold rarely spent time thinking about what might have been. He was much more concerned with what would be, what he would achieve, how he would bend those around him to his will, how he would shape the destiny of his country and the world. And Peggy was no longer part of that, never really had been.

Affirmation of his new status and a sweet measure of vindication came to Arnold on the fifth day of his home leave when the entire town of New Haven assembled on the green to honor him in a celebration arranged by the council of safety. Arnold, Hannah, Mrs. Mansfield, and the three boys arrived in the Arnold family carriage with Punch at the reins, elegantly decked out in livery that Hannah had managed to piece together. The six Rhode Islanders, who had finally arrived and were bivouacked on the Arnold property, had cleaned their uniforms with Hannah's aid and now marched smartly alongside as Punch threaded the carriage through the cheering throng.

The enthusiasm of the crowd clearly was heightened by the news of General Washington's startling victory at Trenton early on the morning after Christmas. His gallant army had crossed the Delaware River amid ice floes to march on the unsuspecting Hessian garrison and capture nearly one thousand enemy troops while losing but a handful of his own. It was a miraculous reversal of all the gloom and despair of the preceding months when the cause seemed lost forever. For Arnold, it was perfect vindication of what he had thought Washington should do, but it pained him that he was not part of the action when it could so easily have been the case. He consoled himself with the thought that he might be able to devise something as dramatic for General Clinton in Rhode Island.

Now he was the focus of New Haven's celebration and it was the pinnacle of triumph for him. He watched the beaming faces of his three sons and Hannah's glow of pride as speaker after speaker extolled his heroism and his virtues. In the crowd, Arnold saw the faces of men who had refused to do business with him when he was a merchant apothecary, men who had found his aggressiveness and ambition to be offensive. Now they were cheering him. He saw the constable who had arrested him as a young man when, in a typical act of bravado, he had danced along the roofpeak of a burning house. The constable was cheering him. He saw the town fathers who had tried to prevent him from taking supplies from the New Haven magazine when he was set to march his militia company off to Massachusets after Lexington and Concord. They had voted to stay neutral in any conflict, but Arnold had brushed them aside and taken the magazine. Now those town fathers were cheering him, too. Only Major-General David Wooster was missing to complete the vindication for Arnold. Wooster, elderly veteran of the French and Indian War and one of the ineffectual successors to Arnold as commander in Canada, had been scornful of Arnold as an amateur and an upstart back in the early days. He had sided with the town fathers in the dispute over the magazine. If Wooster were here, with his thin legs and gravelly voice, he, too, would have paid homage to Benedict Arnold.

On the second day of the new year, Benedict Arnold stood in his yard saying good-bye to his family and a few friends. Hannah pleaded with him to stay longer, at least until his thirty-sixth birthday on January 14th, but he told her it was his duty to go. The six Rhode Islanders were ready to march out. Technically no longer in the army, they had agreed to stay to escort General Arnold to General Spencer's headquarters near Providence.

Arnold pulled Lamb and Oswald aside and spoke earnestly to them. "John, I've been thinking about your idea of forming a new artillery company. One thing I've noticed since I've been home. New Haven looks just about defenseless to me. Just the old-timers militia on duty here. We'll call it 'The Artillery Company of New Haven.' I think we need it."

"Good!" Lamb said. "I'm glad you like it, because I need some help if I'm going to try it." Lamb adjusted the black eye patch that covered his left eye, on the side of his face that was a huge red scar, part of his jaw gone. It was a shame, Arnold thought. A good man, one of the best. He wanted to get back in the fighting and had applied for a commission in the Continental Army now that his year's parole had passed, the condition of his release by the British after Quebec. Because of the severe injury, it was not certain the army would take him.

Oswald wasn't as enthusiastic: "What for? The British aren't coming here."

"Don't be so sure," Arnold said. "Why do you think I'm going to Rhode Island? They've got a lot of troops at Newport."

"Let's see," Lamb said, "all we need is somebody's authority to do this, and some officers, men, cannon—"

"Authority, hell!" Arnold laughed. "It'll be your company, but we'll do it on *my* authority. I'm the king of New Haven! Haven't you noticed? I can do anything I want. As for officers, that's easy. John, you would be in command as colonel and Ozzie would be your second, with the rank of captain. As for men, I think we can find plenty of lads around here eager to play war if they don't have to leave home."

"When I wrote to headquarters asking to come back to duty," Lamb said,

"I suggested this idea of a new company to General Washington. He approved it in principle, but wrote they couldn't provide any help until Congress came up with some money. I'd have to get it started locally."

"That doesn't surprise me. It'll take months. But they'll reimburse us in the end if the chief has approved it."

"I don't have that kind of money," Lamb said. "Think of all the expense—field pieces, uniforms, ammunition, pay for the men, headquarters."

"We'll do it on the cheap. No uniforms, no headquarters. And maybe we can get our hands on some cannon, either cheap or we'll just take them. I'll put up whatever money we need."

"You will?"

"Yes, but try to hold it down. You two think this over. Scour the countryside, locate every field piece you can, and find out how we can get them. It won't be easy—but you'll find some, even if they're old ones. If we have to buy, then find out how much. I won't be so far away this time. I should be able to get back for a visit pretty soon and we'll see if it's worth going ahead. Agreed?"

The other two nodded enthusiastically, and Arnold clapped them on the shoulders. Then he went over to pick up each of his three sons in turn, to kiss each boy and whisper something in his ear. He kissed Hannah and turned to where Punch had his horse ready. "Punch, I want you to protect everything while I'm gone, you hear?"

"Yes, suh!" Punch said with a big smile.

Arnold mounted his horse, took up a position ahead of his escort and the team and wagon, and led the way out, responding to the shouts and arm wavings that came from his family and friends, from the knot of onlookers, and from Mrs. Mansfield on her front porch. He gave a cheerful salute and a final good-bye gesture.

PART IV

The Grand Strategy

From the narrative of Sir Thomas Stanley, KB

A terrible shock awaited my uncle when we were met in Southampton on December 19th by my brother, the Earl. The Lady Charlotte had died weeks earlier, only a few days after our ship had sailed from Quebec on the voyage home. General Burgoyne insisted on going directly to her grave, standing there for an hour in a driving rain, totally dejected, alternately cursing himself and begging her forgiveness. That had brought on the fever again, but within a week he was able to leave his bed and make the obligatory call on Lord Germain at the War Office. He had then gone on to Bath, the fashionable spa and resort in the west of England, to recuperate.

There Burgoyne soon regained his strength and, tired of doing nothing but winning at cards and taking the waters, he summoned me to Bath to join him in working on refining his ideas for prosecution of the war. The paper he had delivered to the War Office a year earlier had been a rambling opus of more than one hundred pages entitled <u>Reflections Upon the War in America</u>. Only a few pages of it had been devoted to what came to be known as our "grand strategy"—a pincer movement with two armies converging, one south from Canada, the other north from New York City, to secure the water line from Lake Champlain to New York harbor, and thus amputate New England from the rest of the Colonies.

Many people believed that the war was all but won, given Sir William Howe's victories, but my uncle disagreed strongly. He found distraction from grief over the death of his wife in working furiously on his new document, entitled <u>Thoughts for Conducting the War from the Side of Canada</u>. He concentrated on the strategy this time, refining it and adding new elements, such as a third army coming in from the west.

Finally, he was ready to seek Lord Germain's endorsement and go to work preparing for a new invasion of the rebellious Colonies, one that would be much better planned and staged than before. It was a brilliant piece of work, outlining a campaign that stimulated dreams of glory in my head.

Chapter 15

London
January 27, 1777

Time passed slowly in the oppressive quiet of the chilly, cavernous anteroom. General John Burgoyne stood at a tall window and watched light snowflakes drift by. From this vantage point in Whitehall, he could see the Queen's House in the distance beyond the Horse Guards parade ground and St. James's Park, and closer, to the right, St. James's Palace and Marlborough House. In the gathering dusk, only a few people could be seen walking in the park, hurried and bundled up against the cold, their breath visible in the wintry air. When Burgoyne had risen to go to the window, his aide, Captain Stanley, had also left his chair, and stood nearby, hands fidgeting.

Burgoyne paced back and forth and then stood rigidly still except for hands clasping and unclasping behind his back. Now he was at the window again, sighing heavily. He was a striking figure in the finely tailored dress uniform of a lieutenant-general of the British Army, the black mourning band on his sleeve a somber contrast to the scarlet tunic and the gold braid that adorned it. Burgoyne was widely known as an amiable and gracious companion. But he did not care to be kept waiting, least of all by a man he disliked.

The door to Lord Germain's suite of offices clicked, sounding impossibly loud, and Burgoyne wheeled about. Germain's deputy secretary, Christopher D'Oyly, appeared. He nodded and smiled and minced away, apparently bent on some errand.

"D'Oyly!" Burgoyne snapped.

The secretary stopped with an expectant air. "Sir?"

Burgoyne extracted his gold pocket watch and studied it. He looked up. "We've been waiting the better part of an hour."

"I'm so sorry, General," D'Oyly gushed, patting his long grey wig, "but the minister is so terribly busy. It won't be but a moment longer, I assure you."

"There are no other callers here at all."

"The minister is anxious to see you. He wants to get away himself, to the country. But it's the paper he must deal with, you see."

"Speaking of which," Burgoyne said drily, "are you certain he's seen my paper?"

"Of course, sir. I gave it him myself." D'Oyly waved a few fingers and left, picking his way carefully across the polished parquet floor.

Burgoyne pocketed his watch and glanced at Stanley. "Ten minutes to four. At four o'clock, we're leaving. To hell with him." He sat down in a large brocaded chair next to the window. It had taken him nearly a week to arrange this appointment with Germain. In combination with being kept waiting so long, it seemed ominous, as if Germain were willing to see him only as a formality, in the most begrudging way. There had been no indication of that when Burgoyne made his earlier courtesy call. Germain had been solicitous over Lady Charlotte's death and the state of Burgoyne's health, and had offered condolences more than once. He had not seemed disposed to discuss the progress of the war at any length, insisting only that Burgoyne should rest until he was fully recovered.

D'Oyly returned, nodding and smiling, and reentered Germain's sanctum. Burgoyne, one hand at his forehead and apparently deep in thought, didn't even look up. Stanley involuntarily shuddered when he began to hear distant chimes—St. Margaret's Church or St. James's?—tolling the hour of four. Again Burgoyne seemed to take no notice, and, despite the chill, Stanley began to perspire as he grappled with the question of whether it was his duty to point out the hour to his commander. He kept silent.

The door clicked again and D'Oyly, half bowing, beckoned. "This way, gentlemen, if you please."

The two men followed D'Oyly through several small offices to reach the large opulent room where Germain sat at his huge desk scribbling away with a quill pen. At sixty, Germain was just six years Burgoyne's senior, but he looked twenty years older. Still long-limbed and impressive in stature, he was giving way to fat with puffy eyelids and loose jowls. "Sit, sit," he rumbled. "Sorry for the delay. I had to finish my comments for His Majesty." Glancing up, he raised his eyebrows and explained: "The latest from Howe in America." He called to his departing secretary: "One moment, D'Oyly." Germain placed a number of documents in a mahogany dispatch case and handed it over. "You know what to do," Germain said. "And I'll be leaving for the country shortly—" a weak smile in the direction of his visitors "—just as soon as we are through here."

As D'Oyly left the room, Germain suddenly turned jovial. "My, my, Jack, you certainly look much better than last I saw you. I was right, wasn't I? A little rest did you a world of good. You need more. I didn't expect to see you for another month."

"Minister, you know my aide, Captain Stanley, I believe."

"Yes, of course. How are you, my boy? I trust your brother is well?"

"Yes, my lord."

Burgoyne spoke: "Are you at liberty, Minister, to say something of the news from Sir William?" He used the correct address, knowing that Howe recently had been made a Knight of the Bath, a reward for his success in North America.

"Oh, yes, nothing we can do about it, I'm afraid, else I would have gone to see the King myself. Howe went into winter quarters in December. He's dispersed all the rebels from the Jerseys, they've fled across the river to God knows where. Now he feels he's stretched his lines as far as he prudently can in this winter season."

"So he did not take Philadelphia."

"No, it appears not."

"And Washington and his troops are still intact."

"Well, hardly so. Howe hasn't *captured* Washington, if that's what you mean. I wish he had, but he hasn't. He reports that Washington is down to a few thousand effectives. And most of those are due to go home, would you believe it! Their enlistment terms are up, apparently. What a pitiful way to carry on a war."

Burgoyne felt a tremor of excitement. Howe had *not* achieved total victory! He was vindicated in his stubborn belief that a strategy for the 1777 campaigning season would be needed. He remained silent, certainly not wishing to show any pleasure that the war would continue at least another year. Burgoyne considered how to choose his next words, and the silence stretched. Germain leaned back in his ornate chair, taking care not to disturb the thick curls of his wig, and made a temple of his fingers. "Pray, gentlemen, what can I do for you?"

By a lengthy pause and his tone of voice, Burgoyne managed to convey the fact that he was nettled by the reception. "My paper, Minister," he said. "We're here to discuss my paper."

Germain sighed. He picked up the document, which had been lying on his desk together with the previous year's effort. "Yes, yes. I've read it, of course. I hardly know what to say. I did warn you not to tax yourself about this."

Burgoyne scowled, but said nothing. Germain continued to toy with the document. Then he said: "It's basically the same plan as last year, though I see you've added an ingenious element or two. But, surely you can see that time has simply passed this by." Germain looked up and then began a low chuckle. "Last year we had *reflections*. This year, it's *thoughts*. Perhaps next year, it'll be *ideas*!" He emphasized the word with a hint of sarcasm, and gave Burgoyne a toothy smile.

Burgoyne stared back. He suddenly felt that it was all hopeless. "Perhaps we have nothing to discuss," he said curtly.

"Come, come, Burgoyne," Germain said in an irritatingly soothing voice. "I realize this is important to you. But I—"

"It's important not just to me, Minister, but to you, to the ministry. I say to you that it is the only—"

Germain cut him off. "Yes, I know, the only way to win the war in one fell swoop. What I'm trying to say is that we hardly have need for any such elaborate designs now. As soon as weather permits, General Howe will track down Mr. Washington and his rabble and administer the coup de grâce."

"I'm not sure of that at all."

"Why on earth not? I just told you. Washington is down to a few thousand effectives. Howe says their Continental Congress fled Philadelphia in panic, like a band of thieves. Half of Washington's farmers are going home, will have done by now. He can't *force* them to stay and fight. They'd revolt! Hah, hah, the rebels fighting the rebels!" Germain enjoyed this thought hugely. "Now, what do we have against them, poised to finish this business next spring, just as I've promised Lord North and His Majesty? We have an army of thirty thousand men! The largest fleet ever to cross the ocean! They haven't a hope!"

"Minister, it could happen as you say. I pray that it will. But you said yourself that Washington has not been caught. His army may be diminished now, but he'll be in winter quarters somewhere, too. He has months to raise new troops. They seem to flock to him when their situation is most dire. He had twenty thousand men surrounding Boston when I was there. In one of my dispatches, I referred to them as 'rabble'—and I've regretted it ever since. Everyone has begun using that term, and it's misleading, makes us too complacent. Of course, they *are* rabble in a way, but they also can fight. I've seen them, close up. At Bunker Hill. In Canada on their retreat when they were outnumbered and ravaged by disease. They won't quit. Consider this, Minister. In that action on Lake Champlain, Benedict Arnold and his men *knew* Howe had taken New York and that Washington was in retreat. And still they fought like devils. They won't quit. We can only defeat them by a plan that—"

"You want another army of twelve thousand men?" Germain interrupted, his face growing red. "And yet another army to come in from the west? You want Howe to move north from New York? Why not a dozen more armies? My God, man, you *know* what it costs to raise and train and equip and transport one *regiment,* let alone a bloody army! The King would have apoplexy. Those wolves in Commons would start howling all over again."

"Far better to bear the cost in one season and end it rather than continuing to delude ourselves," Burgoyne said stiffly.

"Well, that's exactly what I thought I'd done *last* season. My dear sir, I'm afraid *you're* the deluded one! We'll end it, never you fear. And without need of this plan."

"You must at least take this up with the Cabinet."

"I must do nothing of the sort. I decide what goes to the Cabinet and what does not. And in this case, I've decided. As for you, sir, you've done your duty as you see it, and I thank you."

It was a clear dismissal, but Burgoyne sat silent for a long moment. With considerable effort, he restrained his temper. He sensed more than saw Captain Stanley sitting next to him in mute astonishment at the peremptory treatment being given to his commander. Burgoyne was puzzled. He and Germain had collaborated well the year before, aside from the lamentable delay in sending orders to Canada that would have put Burgoyne in military command, as promised. Why was Germain so stiff and insolent now? Was it only an un-shakeable conviction that the war was won? or was it something more? At length, Burgoyne spoke in a low monotone. "Minister, let us assume that Howe destroys Washington's army next spring, as you anticipate. That will leave New England untouched, still in a state of insurrection. That's where all the trouble began. That's the radical tinderbox of this rebellion. My plan would cut them off, leave them no hope." When Germain made no response, Burgoyne continued. "This is a serious matter, Minister. Of the utmost importance. Perhaps you'd like to think about it for a week or so. Read the paper again."

"You don't seem to understand, Burgoyne." Germain's tone was exasperated. "You and Carleton had your chance last summer. I gave you an army to do essentially what you're now proposing. And you failed."

"Failed!" Burgoyne shouted. "You know as well as I—what do you mean *failed*!"

"Well, you didn't succeed, did you? While Howe was knocking the pins out from under Mr. Washington, you and Carleton were sitting on your thumbs all summer. Now you're not needed."

"What are you saying! I didn't come here to defend myself from preposterous charges! If you want a court of inquiry, sir, I'll be glad—"

"Nobody's talking about a damned court of inquiry. *I'm* the court of inquiry!"

"It ill befits a man of your record to—"

"Careful, sir," Germain snarled. "You asked to see me, I granted you an interview, and if you can't accept—"

Burgoyne rose, trembling with anger. "Good day to you, sir!"

"Good day," Germain snapped.

For weeks, vivid images had cascaded through Captain Stanley's head as he and his uncle worked on the exciting new plan for the coming year—images of deep forests, war-painted Indians, men locked in combat, General Washington humbly offering his sword to General Burgoyne, who naturally was attended by his faithful aide-de-camp. Stanley luxuriated in the vision of riding with his uncle at the head of the victorious army as it paraded before cheering throngs in London, along the Strand where their carriage was traveling now, only the parade would be headed in the opposite direction, toward Whitehall and Parliament and Westminster Abbey. But incredibly, in the space of a few moments, all of the images were gone, all were ashes.

Burgoyne was still seething with anger, hardly able to speak after having told the driver to go straightaway to Brooks's Club. Finally he calmed himself enough to ask what Stanley thought of the interview.

His aide hesitated, then ventured: "I'd say we were rather roundly snubbed, sir."

"I'd say you have a talent for understatement," Burgoyne snapped. He looked up. "I'm sorry, Tom. I know you were counting on this, too."

"I—that's not important, Uncle John. I just feel so bad for you."

Burgoyne smiled grimly and slapped Stanley's knee. "What galls the most is that I should have known," he said, frowning now. "All the signs were there. The way the bastard kept us waiting! He put me in the position of a supplicant. Germain, of all people!"

Stanley knew exactly what his uncle meant, just as every officer in the British Army knew the story. It had happened twenty years earlier, during the Seven Years War, when Burgoyne had made his reputation and Germain had lost his. At thirty-four, Burgoyne was an aging captain then, but he distinguished himself in several spectacular raids on the French coast, leading to the commission to raise a new cavalry regiment, the Sixteenth Hussars. His methods were so novel that the then Prince of Wales, now George III, had come to the training camp to watch in awe. Later Burgoyne led the regiment brilliantly in the Peninsular Campaign, including among his exploits the capture of an entire walled city and eight thousand enemy troops, thereby becoming the youngest brigadier-general in the British Army.

In the meantime, Major-General George Sackville had failed to respond for a full thirty minutes to a direct order from his superior officer to lead his cavalry in a charge against the disorganized French infantry at the crucial point in the Battle of Minden. By the time Sackville moved, the precious opportunity was gone. As a result, he was court-martialed, cashiered from the army, his name stricken from the Privy Council. Yet, in the ensuing years, Sackville had inherited his father's lands and title, and thenceforth known as Lord George Germain, managed to ingratiate himself with the King to reach his new position of power. The irony of what had just happened, Stanley understood very well, was that the hero had been forced to seek the coward's approval—and had to endure the humiliation of a rude rejection.

Chapter 16

London
January–February, 1777

Once at Brooks's Club, Burgoyne and Stanley seated themselves at a scarred wooden table and ordered ale. When the foaming tankards arrived, Stanley asked: "What will you do now, Uncle John?"

Burgoyne glanced around morosely. "I'll probably spend a long evening playing whist or twenty-and-one. I'll probably drink too much. I'll probably find myself a wench." As an afterthought, he added: "Don't think I'd sully your aunt's name. I'm just talking soldier to soldier."

The two men fell into a mournful silence that soon was broken by a rasping roar of a voice. "Well, well, if it isn't Gentleman Johnny and his favorite subaltern!" The voice belonged to a disreputable-looking man with hair askew, soiled collar, waistcoat partly unbuttoned to free a bulging middle, blue jowls that bespoke an inadequate shave, and a faint unpleasant aroma about him. It was Charles James Fox, member of the House of Commons and an outspoken opponent of the war. He slid into a chair and asked, "Mind if I join you?" He snapped his fingers, got the attention of a waiter, and made a circular and dipping motion with his forefinger to communicate successfully that he wanted the same and that another round should be fetched at once.

"Please, Charles, do join us," Burgoyne said drily.

"Don't mind if I do. My, my, you lads are certainly looking glum."

Captain Stanley viewed the interloper with distaste, though he was careful not to show it. He knew that Burgoyne and Fox had been fond of each other ever since the days when Burgoyne was a member of the small band in Parliament that had opposed the heavy-handed British policies toward the American colonies. But he and Fox were opposites in other ways, and Stanley could not understand the attraction. Burgoyne was fastidious, patronizing the best tailors in London, powdering his hair, and changing his linen daily. It was doubtful that Fox changed his linen once a week and, as for his hair, he simply ignored it. Stanley decided that Fox got away with calling Burgoyne "Gentleman Johnny" in public and to his face only because he so obviously was not a gentleman.

"It has not been an auspicious day, Charles," Burgoyne observed. "Perhaps it will improve if you'll play twenty-and-one with me."

"No, thank you." Fox wagged a finger in Stanley's face. "For years my losses have played a considerable part in keeping your uncle in his grand style. Take my advice—never gamble with him." He turned to Burgoyne. "It didn't go too well with Germain, I take it."

"How the devil did you—"

"Jack, you know that I'm aware of everything that goes on in London. Everything important, that is." Fox turned to young Stanley again. "It's really very simple, my boy. All you have to do is know a few facts, and then if you circulate in the right places, observe keenly, talk to the right people, you'll soon know a great deal more. For example, it wasn't at all difficult to learn that the general was meeting with his secretary of war today. To find out what happened, all I needed was one look at your faces." He turned to Burgoyne with a bland smile. "Now, tell me what really happened."

"Then all you have to do," Burgoyne told Stanley, "is ask a lot of nosey questions."

"Come now, Jack, you can trust me. I take it Germain was unpleasant to you."

Burgoyne drew back. "That blackguard pimping dog!" he grated.

"Oh, my goodness." Fox glanced around in mock horror. "Speak a little louder, Jack, perhaps we can get an affair of honor going here."

Despite himself, Burgoyne chuckled at the thought of the impossible idea of fighting a duel with Germain. "It could never happen. Germain has no honor. That's how he saves his skin."

"Let me see." Fox rolled his eyes toward the ceiling. "I have it! Germain turned down your plan to win the war."

Burgoyne drew back with an air of amused exasperation, shaking his head. Fox pressed on. "Aha, I'm right! What is your plan, Jack?" Burgoyne's expression did not change, and Fox said: "Really, I may be against the war, but I'm not disloyal. I promise not to write a chatty letter to Dr. Franklin over there in Paris. I understand that esteemed gentleman, whom I had the honor to meet several years ago, arrived there just before Christmas, to represent the American cause." Still not getting any response, Fox turned to Stanley again. "Your uncle and I do have one point of difference. Once, a long time ago, we were staunch comrades in fighting the stupid policies that led to this war. He was the best spokesman in Commons on that subject. Except for me, of course. And Burke. But once the fighting started, the old war horse couldn't resist. He had to go dashing off."

"I have difficulty convincing Mr. Fox that once rebellion is a reality," Burgoyne said to Stanley, "it becomes a matter of national honor."

"Honor!" Fox exclaimed. "Germain has none and you have too much. 'Tis a quality that should be more evenly spread about."

"Leave honor aside. The only humane thing to do now is to win the war as soon as possible."

"Perhaps. But *don't* tell me about your plan, please. I've changed my mind. I don't want to know about it. But you *can* tell me why Germain turned you down."

"Well, of course, he thinks we've all but won the war."

Fox stroked his bluish stubble. "I thought so. I can understand that. It seemed every few weeks we'd get word of another victory of Howe's in the New York campaign. Long Island, Brooklyn, New York Island, White Plains, Fort Washington, now all of the Jerseys. You weren't in London for much of that, Jack, you don't know what it was like. Our armies seemed invincible. People kept pouring out on the streets, celebrating."

"Yes, I'm sure. But no one talks about how hard the rebels fight, do they? They don't talk about the Battle of Haarlem Heights, Valcour Bay, the fact that we didn't take Ticonderoga, or that Howe has stopped at the Delaware."

"Has he really? I didn't know that. Well, you can see that all the rest outweighs what you're saying. The rebels do fight hard, but nevertheless, they keep getting beaten. Everyone thinks we've won."

"Do you think so?"

"I'm not sure. I'm talking about the populace."

"The King and his ministers should know better."

"Perhaps. You know how they believe what they want to believe."

Captain Stanley spoke up in a hesitant manner. "Lord Germain did mention another reason . . . I mean, for rejecting the plan."

"Yes, go on," Burgoyne said.

"He made that obnoxious charge that you've already had your chance and failed."

"Yes." Burgoyne shook his head in disgust.

"I wondered why you didn't speak of what really happened, that it was Sir Guy's decision, not yours."

"Germain already knows that. Besides, I respect Carleton. He's no field commander, but he's a decent man. I wouldn't give Germain the satisfaction of hearing me criticize Carleton." Burgoyne glanced sharply at his aide. "There's bad blood there. It goes all the way back to Minden. Carleton was a member of the court-martial."

"As a matter of fact," Fox said, "the liveliest rumor in London right now is that Carleton is out to undermine Germain and take his place. And that you, Jack, are really here as Carleton's agent."

"That's absurd!" Burgoyne snorted. "Anyone who believes that doesn't know Carleton. *Or* me." He thought for a moment. "That *could* explain the cold reception we got from Germain."

"Exactly. And it suggests that there's only one thing you can do now," Fox said.

"What's that?"

"Go over Germain's head."

"You're joking. The prime minister doesn't understand military planning at all."

"No, no, forget my old friend Lord North. That *would* be hopeless." Fox spoke sarcastically of the man who had once sacked him from a minor post in the treasury. "I mean go where the real power is. To the royal personage himself."

Fox and Stanley watched as Burgoyne contemplated this new and intriguing thought. "You used to have a relationship there," Fox prompted, "before you started associating with the likes of me."

"Well, it's come back a bit," Burgoyne mused, "since I went to war. Before I left last spring, he offered to make me a Knight of the Bath. I've never told anyone that, except Charlotte."

"What happened?"

"I declined."

"In heaven's name, why?" Fox asked. "Why not wear the red ribbon? Sir John Burgoyne, KB, that's not bad."

"I felt I hadn't really earned it."

"There's that sense of honor again! Let him give you another chance to be worthy."

"It would be rather bad form to go over Germain's head."

"Jack, you're not playing quoits here. This is real life. It would be a delicious thing to do. Just what Germain deserves."

"I should pay a courtesy visit in any case. But I just can't walk in and hand the King my plan and start pleading my case."

"Well, no, you could be a bit more subtle than that. Pay your courtesy call and find an excuse to see him again. Several times. That shouldn't be too much of a challenge for a master planner like you."

The moment that Burgoyne was in the presence of the round-faced monarch, the idea came to him. George III had put on some weight since Burgoyne had last seen him. After courtesies were exchanged, Burgoyne managed to bring up the subject of exercise.

"Oh, you sound like our physicians, Burgoyne," the King moaned. "Always harping!"

"But, Your Majesty, your health is of the first concern to us all."

George III gazed sharply at Burgoyne. "I daresay you could profit from exercise yourself, what, what?"

Burgoyne felt resentful, but then he realized he had the opening he needed. Moreover, he said to himself, the King was right. In nearly three months of inactivity since he had fallen ill in North America, he had not only gained back his normal weight, but also was beginning to go to flab, with signs of a double chin. "You are absolutely correct, Your Majesty," he said. "May I suggest, the best way to gain physical exertion in these winter months is by riding horse."

The King's eyes opened wide. "Zounds, Burgoyne, a capital idea!"

"It's best to have regular schedule, weather permitting. Perhaps if someone were to accompany you."

"Yes, of course." The monarch thought for a moment. "Why not you, Burgoyne? Could you do it?"

"I'd be honored and flattered, sire."

Thus it was that several mornings a week, through to the end of February, curious citizens of London might have noticed their sovereign sallying forth on horseback in the company of one of the most illustrious officers of the British Army, cantering along the bridle paths of Green Park and occasionally Hyde

Park, with members of the Royal Horse Guards always at a respectful distance keeping a careful watch on their master. Burgoyne, an expert rider since his early youth, took care the first week to keep the rides short for fear that discomfort to the royal bottom would cause a quick retreat into indolence. Even so, there was some groaning at first, but the King, an accomplished rider himself, though out of practice, began to enjoy the outings. The crisp air brought a healthy flush to his cheeks, and he actually began to appear thinner. The growing familiarity between the two men brought Burgoyne more invitations to royal social functions than he had ever experienced before, but it was on the morning rides that private conversations occurred.

The two men would canter briskly, then walk their horses for a while as the King caught his breath. Then they would talk, and, as Burgoyne expected, the conversation was mostly about the war in North America. Early on, Burgoyne found an opening to bring up the subject of his plan. The King accepted a copy and promised to read it, but made no mention of it in the weeks that followed. Meanwhile, Burgoyne delicately picked away at the optimistic view that the King had inherited from Germain. He described the tenacity of many of the Americans, how they could lose a battle badly and yet survive to fight again. As a prime example, he said it was hard to believe the Americans were beaten when they would fight against a superior force as ferociously as Benedict Arnold had at Valcour Bay after he and his men knew that Washington was in full retreat.

"But he's just one man," the King said. "Their most enterprising and dangerous fellow, Germain tells me. I was very displeased that he was not captured."

That was too close for comfort, Burgoyne having been the one who had reported to Lord Germain that he'd nearly captured Arnold at St. Jean. Thereafter, Burgoyne stayed away from the subject of the previous northern campaign. He conceded to the King that the tide seemed to favor British arms, but that one should be prepared—it would be a mistake to count the rebels out. Occupying their cities merely left them roaming the countryside. Washington was still at large and had at least three months to build another army.

Burgoyne though he might have shaken the King's overconfidence a bit when the monarch began to dwell on another subject—his concern over the apparent lack of fighting spirit on the part of some of his commanders. He gloried in Sir William Howe's successes, but he was well aware that Howe had not pursued Washington as aggressively as he might have done. He spoke of Howe's older brother, Admiral Richard Lord Howe, who had argued incessantly with Germain about peace conditions before he would agree to take command of the British Navy in American waters. And Carleton, of course, was that oxymoron, a notorious moderate. The King even mentioned how hurt he had been when Burgoyne had opposed the ministry's policies toward the Colonies several years earlier in Parliament.

As much as Burgoyne basically agreed with the King's point, he realized that this was dangerous ground. He did not wish to become known as a critic of his fellow commanders, despite his private reservations about most of them, and yet he wanted his own point of view to be clear and distinctive. He spoke judiciously and somewhat pompously: "At heart, this is a *civil* war, Majesty, the worst kind of all. War should always be a last resort. The military commander who does not understand that, who does not first seek peace under honorable conditions, is worthless, in my view. Once peace is impossible, however, war must be pursued with vigor. Even then, your commanders are to be praised for their moderation, sire. It's one thing to defeat these rebels in battle, but quite another to live with them afterwards. We must win their loyalty back, and in that respect moderation becomes not only a virtue, but a necessity. So long as it is coupled with resolute determination to end the conflict successfully and as speedily as possible. That's my guiding principle." The King merely nodded absently, but Burgoyne was satisfied that at least he had been able to state his philosophy concisely.

On another occasion, the King raised the question of using the Indian tribes against the colonials. He referred to criticism of this practice in Parliament and even in the ministry. "They say it's a French sort of device," the King sniffed, "using these savages against white men. What say you, Burgoyne?"

"It's akin to our using soldiers from the German states, Majesty. Unfortunate, but necessary. We need the Indians as scouts and fighters. They're favorable toward our side. The Colonials would use them if they could, you can be certain of that. The trick is to make sure that wanton acts of savagery do not occur. I can promise you, sire, whenever any Indians are under my command, they behave in a civilized manner."

"Good," the King responded. "I really don't care what they do so long as it succeeds."

After weeks of exercise, Burgoyne began to despair that he would ever really shake the King's stubborn optimism. Then the news of Washington's victory at Trenton arrived in London. The next morning Burgoyne hurried to the palace but was told that the King was in conference. For more than a week Burgoyne could not see the monarch. Then more details of the fiasco at Trenton arrived, as well as the news that the Americans had moved on a week later to fight with spirit at Princeton and outmaneuver Cornwallis. The next day Burgoyne dutifully called at the palace again, and this time found the King prepared for the morning exercise. Instead of leading out at a fast pace the King walked his horse and began the conversation at once.

"You've heard the news, Burgoyne. These are minor affairs to be sure, but most distressing. Howe says he was overextended. Now, he's lost most of the Jerseys. He's pulled back all the way to Brunswick and Amboy. Most ominous, this means that what you said is true, that Washington's army is still intact, and that these rebels mean to persist."

"I wish it were otherwise, sire, but I'm afraid that your analysis is correct."

"I wanted so much to end the conflict this season!" the King blurted out. "It pains me that my subjects in America consider me a tyrant. I'm not! I'm a patriot king! I'm stern, to be sure, but that's for the good of my subjects. You understand that, don't you Burgoyne?"

"Of course, sire. I should point out that not all your colonial subjects, by any means, are rebellious. Only a minority. I truly believe most remain loyal to their sovereign."

The King put his foot in the stirrup. Burgoyne waved a page away, helped the monarch to his saddle, and gracefully mounted his own horse. After moving out at a slow pace, the King whispered hoarsely, "What truly concerns me, if the war extends beyond the coming season, is the French." He glanced meaningfully at Burgoyne. "They've been waiting all these years to get back at us. Mark my words, they'll stab us in the back if we let this go on much longer."

"Exactly the reason we must make certain it ends this coming season, sire."

They moved along at a faster pace and in silence for a while, Burgoyne's hopes rising as he noticed the King apparently in deep thought, his mouth working. The monarch reined to a sudden stop. "I've read your plan, Burgoyne. I like it. You're certain it will work?"

"I am supremely confident, Your Majesty. It is the right plan. It will succeed."

The King grimaced. "Another army of ten thousand men?"

Burgoyne had specified twelve thousand in the plan, but he let it pass. "Half of them are in Canada already!" Burgoyne's eyes lit up. "I see it as an army of nations, Your Majesty! Carleton can recruit at least one good regiment of Canadians. And the Indians, we can get the Ottawas and the Hurons, and the Iroquois tribes, too. Joseph Brant is there now. We have fine Loyalist troops in the north now, Sir John Johnson's rangers and Colonel Butler's regiment, and more will flock to our banner once they see what we're about. I'd like several regiments of the Brunswickers and Hessians. And at the heart, of course, our good British regulars!"

The King caught Burgoyne's enthusiasm. "By God, I like it. And I should enjoy seeing my entertaining of Joseph Brant pay dividends."

"The only thing, sire—with all due respect, Sir Guy Carleton should not command the invasion. His duty is to Canada. He should secure the base and—"

"I've already had a word with Lord Germain," the King said. "I can tell you, he is not at all happy with me. He says that if we have to do this, then Sir Henry Clinton should lead the Canadian invasion. That you can replace him in New York as Howe's deputy. Sir Henry arrived here just a few days ago, you know."

"Yes, I know." Burgoyne ground his teeth, feeling a deep inner sense of rage at Germain. Such an idea was nothing but pure spite. Clinton had already failed at Charleston, and he knew nothing of the northern territory.

The King clasped Burgoyne's shoulder. "I squelched that idea. Of course it shall be you in command. We're going to do it! I shall miss you on our morning rides. You've got work to do!"

That evening, Burgoyne sought out Fox at Brooks's Club, led him to a table, and ordered a bottle of the finest port. He leaned on his arms and beamed at Fox.

"It worked, I take it," Fox said.

"It certainly did!"

"You'll be in command?"

"Yes, indeed!"

"Well, it was just a matter of time, whether saddle sores or your plan would win. I must say I've enjoyed the thought of Germain looking out his office window and watching you frolicking with the King."

The port came and Burgoyne lifted his glass in salute. "I owe it to you, Charles, to your inspiration."

Fox drank ruefully. "Please don't say that."

"Why not? It's true."

"Because I don't want to be responsible. For one thing, I hate to see you go back there. For another, I'm not certain any plan—I'm sure your plan is the best and please don't tell me what it is—but no plan is going to work."

"What are you saying!"

"I'm telling you, I'm convinced we can't beat them on their own ground. Those affairs at Trenton and Princeton helped you make your case with the King, I'm sure. But they also indicate what we both know. We should give it up and patch things as best we can."

"What nonsense! I've been a military man all my life. I've been over there twice. You hardly ever set foot outside of London, and you don't know a musket from a broom. And *you're* telling *me* we can't beat them?"

Fox spread his hands out on the table and examined his fingernails as if he had just discovered they were dirty. "I agree, you're much more experienced in these matters than I. But I know just one thing, and you know it, too, deep in your heart. They're right and we're wrong. And that means they'll never quit. They'll win in the end."

"That's preposterous! I don't accept that at all!" Burgoyne frowned. "I grant you, there's some right on their side as well as ours. Now they want to break the authority of Parliament totally. Complete independence! We can't allow that! The only thing to do is end it on the battlefield, quickly. I tell you, I'll be home victorious by next Christmas Day."

Fox shook his head.

"Care to make a small wager?"

"You know I've sworn off gambling with you." Fox smiled. "On the other hand, when one has a sure thing—how much?"

"Fifty guineas."

"That's not so small."

"Well, it makes it worthwhile."

"All right, a pony it is!"

"Let's find a stakes-holder."

"We don't need that."

"Well, if I should lose, you might not get paid."

"If you lose, you'll be back eventually. Unless you've stopped a musket ball. In which case, I don't want to collect any money."

Burgoyne felt a surge of affection for the rumpled, ridiculous figure sitting before him. "Come on! They've got a new betting-book. Let's inscribe it."

They went to the betting-book and wrote the terms down:

Lieutenant-General John Burgoyne wagers Charles James Fox fifty guineas he will be home victorious by Christmas Day, 1777.

Chapter 17

Boston
March, 1777

It was dark when Benedict Arnold rapped sharply on the door of Paul Revere's shop at the head of Clark's Wharf, not far from North Square. Shivering, Arnold pulled his greatcoat tightly about him. Gusting winds from the north roared through the streets of Boston. Impatient, Arnold rapped again and tried to peer through the frosted window panes. Finally the door opened a crack. It was one of the apprentices. "Sorry, sir, we're closed now."

Arnold shoved a foot in the aperture. "The master is expecting me at this hour," he said.

"Be you General Arnold, sir?"

"Of course I am."

The door opened wide and Arnold was ushered into the shop. The apprentice quickly closed the door behind him and slid the bolt. "This way, sir. The master's at his work bench." He led the way down a corridor to a curtained doorway and stepped aside for Arnold to pass.

Revere was striking a blow with a marking die on a silver cup as Arnold entered. The workbench was strewn with silver objects in various stages of creation or repair. Behind Revere was another bench littered with tools. In one corner was a small furnace with a smelting pot, vented to the outside. There were large windows on one wall and a skylight overhead. To the right, through a double doorway, Arnold could see a larger workroom with several benches.

A broad smile spread across Revere's pleasant face as he put down the die and hammer. "Ah, General Arnold." He took off his leather apron and slid from his stool. "Very good to see you, sir!"

During his trips to Boston, Arnold had enjoyed coming to know Revere, a man of Huguenot ancestry with a stocky frame, dark complexion, and brilliant white teeth. Revere was the kind of man that Arnold approved of—he was a staunch patriot, and he at least had made an attempt at a military career as a lieutenant-colonel in a Boston militia regiment, though his greatest contribution was in the many skills he had mastered, including, most recently, the making and repairing of cannon.

"I'm most anxious to see what you have for me," Arnold said.

"I think you will be pleased. Come." Revere led the way to an adjoining sitting room and office. In one corner Arnold saw the uniform fitted to a clothing dummy. He went to it immediately and stared in wonderment. It was the finest piece of work he had ever seen. He touched the cloth. The buff facing was smooth and creamy, the tunic of a rich blue and soft to the touch. The epaulettes were of a thickly woven gold thread.

Meanwhile Revere busied himself lighting an oil lamp on his desk and pouring two glasses of Madeira. He came over to Arnold and gave him a glass. "To your good health, sir."

Arnold lifted his glass. "Thank you, sir. To your good health—and your superb workmanship." The two men drank.

"Not my workmanship, I'm afraid," Revere said, indicating the uniform with a wave of his hand. "I merely arranged it. I did secure the materials and the services of the best tailor in Boston."

"Indeed," Arnold said. He had been told that if he wanted anything of the finest quality, Paul Revere was the man to see. If he couldn't make it, he would arrange it—for a commission. He had brought Arnold, the tailor, and the material together to a perfect result.

"Not something to wear in the wilderness," Revere said.

Arnold smiled. "No, but for honors and promotions, and to join the finest company, it will serve well."

"Yes, a uniform for glory days. Come, there's more." Revere went to his desk and Arnold followed. Revere held up a pair of silk hose. "Such a uniform deserves refinements of the highest quality. It is my privilege to include a dozen pair of these fine hose at no extra charge to you, sir."

A warning bell clanged in Arnold's brain, a throwback to his many years of experience as a merchant and trader himself. "I'm most grateful to you," he murmured. He wondered how much the estimable silversmith would escalate his bill and what kind of clever arguments he would use to justify it. The haggling would be of a polite nature, but Revere would meet his match in Benedict Arnold.

"But wait, there's more." Revere lifted a strip of red velvet cloth from his desk as if he were a magician performing a trick, and Arnold was dazzled. On the desk lay a sword and an elegant sword-knot woven of the same thick gold thread. Arnold withdrew the sword from its scabbard and hefted it. It was perfect, of exactly the size and weight that he had described to the silversmith. It resembled a saber, but smaller and lighter, of the type commonly known as a hunting sword.

"It's of Swedish make," Revere said. "Note the fine finish and the quality of the blade."

Arnold returned the sword to its scabbard and sat down on the chair drawn up in front of the desk. "I'm quite overwhelmed," he said. Revere refilled the wine glasses and then took a seat opposite Arnold. Their eyes met, and both men smiled. "Perhaps we'd better talk about costs at this point," Arnold said.

Revere slid over a piece of paper with the itemized costs. "In addition to the silk hose, it is my pleasure to include the sword-knot at no additional cost to you."

Arnold read the figures. The uniform was at the highest end of the range that Revere had quoted to him before the work commenced. The sword was very expensive. "I already have two swords," he said uneasily.

"Be that as it may, General, it is entirely up to you. I want to say, however, that I have such high esteem for you as a soldier and your great achievements for the patriot cause, and I know of your renown as a merchant in earlier times, that I am quoting for you the lowest possible prices. My commission is but a token, but one honorably and honestly gained, as I know you will agree."

"I must say I am surprised at the variety of your interests."

Revere spread his hands. "With a family as large as mine, one must do what one can. The silver work takes a great deal of time, and the profit is not always commensurate. So I must do other things. Fixing teeth, engraving, printing money for the state, helping Ansart make his cannon, whatever might be needed. I always insist on the highest quality in whatever I do. I consider any other course a waste of time. As I've always said, and I know you will agree, General, the only bargain is to get what one pays for."

"I made one other request."

Revere nodded. "And I've succeeded. But I hesitate to even show you these goods."

Arnold stiffened. The implication was that if he could not afford the sword he would find the cost of the other goods absurdly out of reach. "I'm most serious about this," he said. "Very well," Revere said. He took a key from his desk drawer, got up, and went over to a varnished wooden chest that was set against the wall. Grabbing one end handle, he dragged it over near the desk and unlocked it. Arnold came around as Revere lifted the lid. A mingled aroma of camphor and perfume rose, pungent and pleasant. Revere began lifting out gowns and bolts of cloth and spreading them on the floor. It was a treasure trove of brocade, damask, silks, in a rainbow of colors, along with buckles of gold and silver, cloth-covered buttons, scarves, a quantity of lace, all elegant materials for a lady's wardrobe of a quality to be found in the finest shops in Paris and London, but absent in shops in North America for as long as two years.

"Amazing," Arnold said, on his knees, his eyes glistening as he caressed first one and then another of the precious cloths. "Just as I described. Even better!"

"You asked for a variety of materials and enough to fill a good-sized chest."

"I never dreamed—how did you do it? You really are extraordinary."

"I admit it." Revere smiled. "As you know, such fine European goods are just not available in any normal channels. And that means, alas, that—"

"I know, I know." Arnold sighed, getting up and resuming his chair. Revere also sat down again and passed another sheet of paper to Arnold who managed to study it without betraying any emotion. The sum was staggering.

"Perhaps you wish to select only a few of the items. That would be acceptable to me. I'll have no difficulty disposing of the rest. Then if you don't take the sword, you—"

"No, no," Arnold said. "I want it all. You've calculated only in English crowns."

"Not due to any affection for that currency, I assure you. Of course, I cannot accept paper money. I may print the stuff, but I can't use it."

"Of course." Arnold involuntarily jangled a fat pouch suspended beneath his coat at the waist line. "I have quite a mixture of coins—French, West Indian, Spanish, Dutch."

"No problem," Revere said, reaching into his desk for a parchment on which were inscribed his tables for converting various currencies.

Arnold brought his pouch of coins to the table, and calculations and conversation followed for another fifteen minutes. Through it all, Arnold's mind swirled. He had already laid out a small fortune for the cause, from buying supplies to impulsively handing out money to one or another of his soldiers who had done something exceptional. He could afford it—he still had plenty left. But he hated to be taken advantage of—when it came to business, he was a hard bargainer. In this case, however, Arnold was so overwhelmed by the accuracy of Revere's "arranging" and by the quality of the goods that the haggling was very polite indeed. Benedict Arnold had met his equal as a trader. He left Paul Revere's shop much poorer in coins but far richer in goods. He had gotten what he paid for.

Everything was in order for the pleasant task that awaited him. A small fire crackled in the grate. Outside, through the round window in his gabled room, Arnold could see snowflakes falling on North Square, swirling in the light of the street lamp below. There were two fine quill pens on the table before him, a bottle of ink, a sheaf of paper, envelopes, sealing wax, all illuminated by the glow of an oil lamp. All was in readiness for the letter he would write. Arnold was sure it would be the most important letter of his life.

He was near the end of his fifth trip to Boston since he had reported to General Spencer early in January. He wanted this letter to be finished and sent before he left the next morning to return to Providence.

On this visit to Boston, Arnold was enjoying private quarters thanks to the courtesy of Lucy Knox, the wife of the bulky chief of artillery of the Continental Army, who was on duty at Washington's headquarters in New Jersey. Lucy was due to leave herself in a few weeks, to join her husband at the Morristown camp. Along with many other Tories and Crown officers, her father, Thomas Flucker, the former Royal Secretary of Massachusets, had deemed it prudent to accompany the British to Halifax when they had evacuated Boston almost exactly a year earlier. Ironically, the main cause of the evacuation had been the heroic efforts of Henry Knox in transporting fifty-nine cannon overland from Fort Ticonderoga to Boston in the dead of winter. Their placement on Dorchester Heights made the British position untenable. Now Henry and Lucy shared the spacious house of her parents, along with Lucy's brother and his family.

Arnold leaned back, marshalling his thoughts, and he noted, first with surprise and then some degree of amusement, that he was uncommonly contented. It seemed that all of his life he had been agitated for one reason or another. He always seemed on fire to accomplish something, or he was angry at someone, or consumed with a spirit of rivalry or combativeness, whether in commerce or in war. But ever since he had returned home to New Haven at Christmastime he had been in a state of mild euphoria in which excitement was still present but subdued. He was famous and respected. Even here in Boston he had been welcomed into the homes of the wealthy where once he would have been looked at askance as a mere tradesman. He was progressing more swiftly in his career and toward his cherished goals than he had dared hope. In public and in private, his chief had praised him with genuine warmth. By now, Congress would have acted on the promotion list, and any day Arnold would receive official word of his advancement to the rank of major-general.

But most marvelous of all—Benedict Arnold was in love.

* * *

It had happened here, three floors below, in the drawing room of this very same house, in January during the first of his trips to Boston to seek help in recruiting troops for General Spencer's army to confront the British in Rhode Island. Lucy Knox and her brother had offered a reception in honor of General Arnold, and it seemed that all of the elite leadership of Boston—at least all those remaining after the most prominent Tories fled—had come to see this unlikely hero who had emerged from the wilderness. He remembered his surprise at seeing patriots mingling so easily with others who were either neutral or suspected of being favorable to the Crown. He knew that all of the guests were of the monied classes; inevitably, that meant that there would be a substantial proportion of British sympathizers among them. And Lucy Knox was in a position to bridge the factions gracefully, as the wife of a patriot general and the daughter of a former Royal Secretary. Still, it was a sight alien to Arnold's eyes, and he sought an explanation. Early in the evening he managed to draw aside a patriot leader, Colonel Israel Hampton, an elderly and wise man who served as chief military adviser to the local committee of safety.

Arnold sipped his glass of punch and asked his question: "I thought we were engaged in a war. Am I mistaken, or am I watching patriots and Tories in a most amicable relationship?"

Hampton arched his eyebrows and spoke in a small voice. "Tories?"

"Well—sympathizers, let us say."

"I wondered what you were thinking about that. Here you are, away fighting the war, where it's very clear who is the enemy and who is not, and you come back to find people acting in some respects as if nothing had happened."

"Exactly."

"I'm glad you spoke to me first," Hampton smiled. "The first thing you should know is that it's considered very bad form to raise any such political question in a gathering of this sort."

"Yes," Arnold said drily. "I've noticed that people seem a great deal more concerned about the price of flour and where to find eggs and how to get household help."

"It's understandable, really, when you stop to think about it. Since the British Army left a year ago, the war has not directly touched Boston—except for shortages in the shops, of course. Oh, people worry some about Clinton's army at Newport, but I agree with you—I don't think it's a threat to Boston. And, unless the threat is imminent, people tend to forget, *want* to forget, really. They hate the business of neighbors becoming enemies. They want to act as normally as they can under the circumstances. We have to live together, once this is over. Only the radicals on either side fail to understand that. The radicals on their side, the worst of the Tories, they all left with the British, and damned smart they were to do it or there would've been bloodletting in the streets of Boston." Hampton turned to Arnold with twinkling eyes. "Now, the radicals on *our* side—well, you won't find them here. You'll find them working down on the docks or roisting about in the taverns."

Arnold bristled. "I consider myself—"

"You certainly have nothing to prove, General. Please don't misunderstand me. I'm talking about *fanatics,* those who have no understanding of human nature, no sense of charity." Hampton glanced around at the assemblage of well-dressed people milling about the large drawing room. "There are many here, such as you and I, willing to die for our cause. At the same time, they are gentlemen, too, and they understand that one cannot remain at a fever pitch of enmity forever. One must be prepared to forgive and forget, in due course."

Arnold nodded. There was much to think about in Hampton's words, and Arnold decided that he basically agreed. Something in the elder man's calm expression of his views helped Arnold to relax. At first he had felt awkward, meeting so many new people, wondering what their true beliefs were, finding himself the object of intense curiosity, feeling self-conscious about his uniform, the best that he had with him, but somewhat threadbare and marked in places by ineradicable stains of battle. His uniform, his manners and speech, his weatherbeaten face and hard, calloused hands, all were in contrast to the elegance of the guests, their pale complexions, fine clothes, studied manners, and the aura of well-being and superiority they projected so effortlessly.

The idea of purchasing a new uniform, one more suited to elegant social occasions such as this, occupied Arnold's mind for a few moments. He felt more at ease. He believed he understood these people better, after listening to Hampton's remarks. By right, he was of their class. Soon that demonstrably would be the case. In fact, his accomplishments still to come in the war would place him on a plane above them, he was sure, a man to be honored and respected by all—and to be rewarded in that measure.

More newcomers arrived, including several attractive young ladies. The faces and names were a blur to Arnold as he was introduced, until he met Mrs. Gilbert DeBlois and her daughter, Elizabeth. The mother was a handsome woman, the daughter a beauty. She had a freshness and vivacity that appealed instantly to Arnold. He took her hand. It was like covering delicate ivory with rawhide. "Please" she cooed, "my name is Betsy. Everyone calls me Betsy." She had blond curls, merry eyes, a buxom figure, and a way of puckering her mouth that seemed to beg for it to be kissed. In one brief encounter, Arnold was conquered.

She was swept away by the crush of people. Arnold endeavored to follow her. In a few moments he found himself surrounded, virtually assailed by a bevy of young ladies, now including Betsy. They chattered and giggled and blushed, touching him lightly, speaking in high-pitched voices, very much in the manner of their sex and class, and Arnold was enthralled by the softness and colorful gowns and sweet smells of them, as he tried to respond to their inane questions about the wilderness and the war. Through it all his eyes were on Betsy. He tried to move toward her, but there seemed no way to break through the circle of bobbing faces. Then the loud voice of Lucy Knox from across the room called for everyone's attention. She introduced a musical interlude, a matron playing the harp, accompanied by a young man at the pianoforte. Betsy moved closer to the musicians, next to her mother, but several times she glanced coyly at Arnold. Their eyes met and his pulse quickened.

When the music mercifully ended to polite applause, Arnold found Hampton at his elbow. "I see you heeded my words," the older man said. To Arnold's puzzled expression, Hampton whispered: "All those beautiful young ladies are the daughters of Tories. I noticed that you were very pleasant to them. Some day I shall figure out why the most attractive young ladies are of the wrong party. The most fashionable ones at least."

"Do you know Miss Betsy DeBlois?"

"Oh, yes! Quite a charmer, our Betsy is. I hope you're not smitten. You'll never get past the dragon at the gates." Seeing Arnold's bewilderment, Hampton went on: "I'm talking about the mother, of course. Very protective. She's desperately afraid some rebel will win Betsy's heart. As far as Mrs. DeBlois is concerned, all of the eligible males have left for Halifax or London, some of them wearing red coats. In any case, Betsy's only sixteen."

Arnold's spirits flagged momentarily. He was nearly old enough to be Betsy's father. No matter. Such matches were made frequently. And the "dragon" did not worry Arnold. If he could fight the British Army and Navy, he could certainly devise a way to handle one old woman. Hampton was explaining to him that Betsy's father had gone on to London while Betsy and her mother had returned to Boston from Halifax to keep a claim on family property and valuables. Doubtless a wise choice by the father, Arnold thought, but also a rather cowardly one.

Arnold's attempts to pursue Betsy that first evening availed little. The drawing room was too crowded and too many people had demands on his attention. Had dancing been a part of the evening, he might have been alone with Betsy in a crowd, however fleetingly. He left the Knox home knowing that he was enormously attracted to her, and soon he confessed to himself that he was in love. And that suddenly made life seem very different. Every day was a joy to him, no matter what the irritations of the moment. Whether he was in Boston or Providence or traveling in between, his thoughts constantly were on Betsy, on the passions she stirred within him, on their future together as he imagined it.

It was as if a great burden had been lifted from Arnold, the easing away of a constant gnawing mood of anxiety and depression. Like many men of action and physical prowess, he had a strong sense of the erotic. Unlike most, he found he could rarely indulge it by wallowing in whatever flesh might be available. Sexual release was not fulfilling for him without a sense of oneness, of intimacy and sharing and security in another's love. As he watched his comrades whoring around, Arnold would wonder, in rare moments of introspection, whether his desire for a relationship with one woman, the love of his life, whoever she might be, was some sort of flaw in his character. Now he no longer thought of such things. He thought of Betsy.

Like a good soldier, Arnold planned his strategy to win Betsy's hand as if it were a military campaign. Lucy Knox was amused at first, writing to her husband how "Cupid's shaft" had found its mark in "our hero," but she soon became an ally, doing her best to create opportunities for Arnold and Betsy to be together. During his subsequent visits to Boston, which now occurred more often than strictly necessary, Arnold saw Betsy numerous times at balls and musicales and smaller social occasions. He had never spent much time on the dancing floor, but he was such an agile man of catlike grace that he performed well enough. At these affairs he pressed his sentiments with Betsy as best he could, and she was all smiles and charm in return. But Arnold noticed recently that he seemed to have a rival of sorts, a gangling young apothecary named Martin Brimmer, whom he observed exchanging meaningful glances with Betsy. Arnold had come a long way from his own apothecary days, and he felt confident that he could surpass this moon-eyed young man in Betsy's affections.

He soon intensified his campaign, sending small gifts to Betsy and her mother and calling at the DeBlois home whenever possible. The mother could scarcely bar entry to such a celebrated general of the Continental Army, but she kept a strict and watchful eye. Beneath her frigid politeness, Arnold was sure that she saw him as little better than a ruffian, a crude and unlettered rustic. She managed to convey this haughty tone in small ways. At one soiree Arnold chanced to overhear Mrs. DeBlois wondering to another matron what "the great he-bear from the wilderness" was doing with his "paws." The fact that Martin Brimmer also was not warmly received at the DeBlois home was of small solace. Indeed, for Arnold, the likelihood that his winning of Betsy's affection would cause severe pain to the "dragon" became an added incentive.

The flame of the oil lamp sputtered, sending up a wisp of black smoke. Arnold adjusted the wick. He picked up one of the quills and dipped it into the ink. In his plan to win Betsy's hand, it was time to wheel up the heavy artillery—the trunkful of European finery he had purchased from Paul Revere. Arnold had often heard the ladies of Boston prattle on incessantly about the terrible hardship the war had brought them—the virtual disappearance of fine clothing and material of every kind from the shops. In this situation, the contents of

Arnold's trunk would be the feminine equivalent of a hoard of pirate gold, a stunning gift for Betsy. Such a gift might even soften the adamantine features of her mother.

The accompanying letter should be just short of a proposal of marriage. That would come next, during the trip to Boston a few weeks hence that Arnold would arrange once he had delivered the contingent of new recruits to General Spencer. He began to write:

Dear Madam,

Twenty times have I taken my pen to write you, and as often has my trembling hand refused to obey the dictates of my heart. A heart which has often been calm and serene amidst the clashing of arms, and all the din and horrors of war, trembles with diffidence and the fear of giving offense when it attempts to address you on a subject so important to its happiness. Long have I struggled to efface your heavenly image from it. Neither time, absence, misfortunes, nor your cruel indifference, have been able to efface the deep impressions your charms have made.

Dear Betsy, suffer that heavenly bosom to expand with friendship at last, and let me know my fate . . .

Arnold went on in this flowery vein, quite proud of what he had written as he scanned it once again, so proud that he bent immediately to the laborious task of making a fair copy to keep for himself. He thought of Mrs. DeBlois reading the letter. This would show the old shrew that he was no unlettered rustic!

He had expressed his appreciation and said his farewells to his hosts at dinner that evening, to Lucy Knox and her brother and his wife. Arnold expected to be up and out of the house before they awoke in the morning. He and Hampton had finally succeeded in recruiting enough men to form the core of a new Massachusetts regiment. The men would form up on the common at seven o'clock in the morning. Arnold would be escorted there by two of the regiment's officers to lead the march to Providence. He had spoken to Lucy Knox about the trunk of gifts for Betsy, and she had agreed to superintend its delivery. He penned an explanatory note to Lucy to be placed on the trunk in the front hall, together with his letter to Betsy:

I have taken the liberty of enclosing a letter to the heavenly Miss DeBlois, which I beg the favor of your delivering with the trunk of gowns and materials. I hope she will make no objection to receiving it.

You know the fond anxiety, the glowing hopes, and chilling fears that alternately possess my heart. I trust you will have it in your power to give me favorable intelligence.

It was past midnight. He should have been in bed hours ago. Arnold felt good about what he had accomplished. He straightened out the writing materials on the table and placed the letters and copy in his dispatch case. He turned down the oil lamp and headed for the chamber pot and bed.

Arnold had finished breakfast the next morning when his escort arrived at six thirty. Accompanying them was Arnold's saddled horse and a team and wagon to take his baggage, which was stacked neatly in the front entrance hall. The wagon men began hauling it out, and Arnold watched to make sure they did not take the special trunk of gifts that he had placed in the opposite corner, exactly where he had told Lucy Knox it would be. Placed conspicuously on top of it were the two envelopes, one for Lucy and the other for Betsy.

The escort officers had brought a courier's pouch with them, and Arnold took it back to the breakfast table to scan its contents quickly. There was a dispatch from General Spencer and letters from Hannah, John Lamb, Gates, and Schuyler. Then Arnold spotted the letter from headquarters in Morristown. It was from the commander-in-chief. He tore it open and read eagerly, expecting news of his promotion to major-general. Halfway through the letter Arnold laid it down and stared blankly at the wall opposite him. He could not believe his eyes. He started reading at the beginning again, straining to understand. The paragraph that stunned him, written in the chief's bold, familiar hand, read as follows:

We have lately had several promotions to the rank of Major-General, and I am at a loss whether you had a preceding appointment, as the papers announce, or whether you have been omitted through some mistake. Should the latter be the case, I beg you will not take any hasty steps in consequence of it; but will allow time for reflection, which, I flatter myself, will remedy any error that may have been made. My endeavors to that end shall not be wanting.

Arnold read on. The list Washington had received showed five men promoted to the rank of major-general—William Alexander of New Jersey, who had taken the name of Lord Stirling, Thomas Mifflin and Arthur St. Clair of Pennsylvania, Adam Stephen of Virginia, and Benjamin Lincoln of Massachusetts.

It was preposterous. *Absurd!* Arnold was the senior brigadier-general in point of service and the only one who had become famous through his exploits in battle. Nothing was more certain than his promotion to major-general. The other men were all junior to him and none had half his experience, not even a tenth. Stephen was far down the seniority list—he had been promoted over eleven other brigadiers. Lincoln was a militia officer—he had been brought in from the outside and promoted over brigadiers of the Continental Army.

Arnold's head swam. How could this have happened? He thought of resentments he had repressed in recent months in his mood of well-being and concentration on Betsy. He had been upset at Washington for allowing him to proceed home and to Rhode Island just days before the brilliant attack on Trenton. He had asked to participate, but the chief had sent him on. Had the chief lost confidence in him? No—that was totally at odds with what he had said in their meeting that night. Had the slanderous charges of Hazen and Brown swayed enough delegates in Congress against him? It did not seem likely, but Arnold again cursed the fates that had prevented him from seeking out Congress in December.

If in fact he had *not* been promoted, that would change everything. He would be disgraced in the eyes of everyone. The charges of Hazen and Brown and anyone else against him would be believed whether they were true or not. It was a blatant slur on his honor. It was common for officers thus dealt with to resign. Not to do so would be to acquiesce in being dishonored.

Arnold suddenly was perspiring, despite the chill of the house. Pain gnawed at his stomach. He rose to go to his fourth-floor room to write immediately to the commander-in-chief. Who could he write to in Philadelphia? The troops could wait at the common. This was the first priority. Then he stopped. Before he would be able to finish any letters Lucy Knox would be awake and he would have to explain to her what had happened. The word would spread in Boston. Betsy would hear of it.

He realized that a courier bearing his letters would have to travel via Providence. He could get there nearly as quickly with the regiment, or he would forge ahead at a faster pace with a small escort. He would send his letters from Providence, keeping quiet about this business for the time being, until he learned more.

Arnold was in a wretched state, nearly trembling from the shock. He sat down again and reread the letter, his brow wrinkled. Apparently the newspapers in Philadelphia had carried a report that he had, in fact, been promoted. But the list Washington received had named just the five men. The chief's letter spoke only of the possibility of a mistake, Arnold now realized. It did not admit of the possibility that he had been passed over. Arnold looked up and chuckled at his state of near panic. Of course it was a mistake! There could be no other explanation. Or could there? Deep inside, Arnold feared some dark and evil design against him. He shook it off. It had to be a mistake.

Washington's letter urged him to take no hasty steps until he had firm knowledge. That was good advice. Arnold rose and pulled himself together. He walked out to the entrance hall. His baggage was gone. The two lieutenants who would escort him waited inside the front door.

"Well, gentlemen," Arnold said cheerfully, pulling on his greatcoat. "Let us be on our way."

Chapter 18

Morristown, New Jersey
March 30, 1777

The room resembled a countinghouse in a mercantile establishment. It was crammed with writing desks and tables, each one overflowing with documents. There were piles of papers on the floor, leaving scarcely enough space for a man to maneuver between the desks and chairs. In the fireplace, a small blaze did little to fight off the chill in the room, but it kept the tea kettle hot. Five men were at work, scratching away with quill pens.

"Here's good news, lads," said Colonel Robert Hanson Harrison, the eldest of the aides at thirty-two. "Dr. Shippen is coming to camp to see to inoculation against the pox for all."

"My God, he'll kill half of us," grumbled Lieutenant-Colonel John Fitzgerald, a broad-shouldered Irishman with a wry edge to his humor. Sniffling with a cold, he tightened the muffler wrapped around his neck.

"No, only one in ten," said Colonel Tench Tilghman. He was the senior aide in point of service, having joined the staff the previous summer. Three aides had left in January for regimental assignments, and another for a political career.

"I'd rather take my chances and get the disease the natural way," said Lieutenant-Colonel George Johnston, a January newcomer to the staff.

"Shippen says he's heard of a new method developed in London last year, a safer method, a special potion," Harrison said.

"Oh, well, there's no problem then. I'm sure the British are rushing a supply to us right at this moment, out of the goodness of their hearts." Fitzgerald rose and went to the tea kettle to freshen his cup, wriggling his hips to pass between the tables. He glanced at the slender figure of the fifth aide, who was bent over his work at a table in one corner of the room. "Hammie," he said, "give us a progress report on Fort Nonsense."

Lieutenant-Colonel Alexander Hamilton, at twenty-one the newest and youngest of the aides, looked out one of his corner windows in the direction of the fortification that was being built on the ridgeline of Kemble's Mountain, a modest hill a half mile away. It was intended merely to give the troops something to keep them busy during the winter months. Somehow the troops had come to realize that. Through the rippled distortion of the glass, Hamilton could see a few soldiers moving about as if in a trance.

"I've never seen such energetic labor in my life," he said, to the general mirth of his colleagues. "I hope we do a little better at West Point." Because of his knowledge of French, Hamilton had been assigned the job of analyzing recommendations for the site of a new fort to be built in the Hudson Highlands. It was a favored project of the commander-in-chief who wanted an "American Gibraltar" to protect the vital waterway that was the key to the north, supplying the entire Hudson Valley all the way to Ticonderoga.

"That's where it's going to be?" Johnston asked.

The recommendations Hamilton was sifting had been made by a team of French engineers, one of the few contributions of France to the American cause thus far. Hamilton said: "That's what du Portail, Laumoy, and Gouvion all say. Only Radiere seems unconvinced. It's a high bluff overlooking a point where the river narrows and bends sharply. There are some primitive fortifications near there now. I'm recommending that we get Kościuszko's opinion and then go ahead." His hand ached from writing, and he leaned back and flexed it. "Do you suppose I can get a pension for a crippled hand?" he asked the group in general.

"Not even for combat wounds, Hammie," Fitzgerald said. "Certainly nothing for the debilities of staff work. Poor Harrison."

Harrison shifted uncomfortably on the cushion ring he had arranged on his hard chair. He was so deskbound that he suffered from an acute case of hemorrhoids, and he failed to understand why this was a source of amusement to his colleagues. "Mind your own business, Fat Fitz," he said to the Irishman, who was not fat, but stocky and muscular. Fitzgerald just laughed.

Hamilton rested his hand and gazed out the other window at what he could see of Morristown. Even in the dreary overcast of a typical March day in northern New Jersey, it was a pretty little village, nestled amid hills and rolling countryside. Headquarters had been established in the Freeman Tavern on one side of the village square. On the opposite side was the Morris Hotel, which had been taken over as a military storehouse except for a few offices and a large room on the second floor that served alternately as a ballroom and a Masonic Lodge. Hamilton could see a number of civilians lined up at the entrance to the building. Citizens of New Jersey were still showing up to sign the oath of allegiance that General Washington had promulgated, even though it had become charged with controversy.

In addition to offices, Freeman Tavern provided enough rooms for three generals and their wives to sleep and dine, as well as the five aides who were quartered dormitory style. Most of the other officers were billeted with families of the village; the troops lived in log cabins and tents that stretched in neat rows away from the village square.

General Washington had come to rely heavily on the two generals who also lived at headquarters that winter, Henry Knox and Nathanael Greene. Their wives, together with Martha Washington and the wives of several brigadiers

and colonels in camp, had arrived recently to try to stimulate an agreeable social life in the community, proposing rides in the countryside on pleasant after-
noons and dancing in the evenings. They contributed a genteel touch to
dinner, which began about three o'clock and often was a long affair to which
officers of the day and civilian visitors to camp were invited. Washington had
the custom of not sitting at the head of the table; instead, his staff aides rotated
as host. One of Hamilton's nervous moments came the first time the responsibility fell on him, but two delegates to Congress were visiting that day and the
conversation had been lively.

Hamilton had been on the job almost a full month, and it was working out
much better than he had expected. That was due largely to the friendly spirit
among the staff aides, a camaraderie that Hamilton had experienced only fleetingly before during his year at Elizabethtown Academy and the following year
at King's College in New York. After his birth in Nevis, his childhood had been
a squalid and difficult one on the Danish island of Saint Croix. There, according to Danish law, he was officially labeled "an obscene child," meaning one of
illegitimate birth. His father was a roving and declassed Scottish aristocrat,
who had deserted his family when his two children were infants. Hamilton's
mother, Rachel, was regarded as a woman of loose virtue. She died when he
was eleven. The hardships of the early years bred in Hamilton a fierce desire to
achieve, to be independent and make his own way. He knew he had to leave the
island to advance his education, and so he seized the chance eagerly when several merchants on Saint Croix, recognizing the youngster's quick mind, put together a subscription to send him to school in America when he turned
sixteen.

Now, only five years later, Hamilton was an aide to the commander-in-chief
of the Continental Army. He was not overly impressed with that; he had not
sought it and had not been sure at all that he wanted it. The offer had come in a
strange way. Hamilton had fallen ill in January not long after his creditable performance in the action at Princeton, and his artillery battery had moved to winter quarters in Bucks County without him. A friend had brought him the
Pennsylvania Packet of January 25th, which had the following notice:

> Captain Alexander Hamilton of the New York Company of Artillery,
> by applying to the printer of this paper, may hear of something to his
> advantage.

The "something" turned out to be a message from General Washington
inviting Hamilton to an interview to discuss the possibility of his joining the
headquarters staff in Morristown. Hamilton had already turned down an offer
to join the military family of Lord Stirling, which was the name that William
Alexander, a Scot of aristocratic pretensions, had taken when he was commis-

sioned a brigadier-general in the Continental Army. One didn't turn down the commander-in-chief so easily. Hamilton knew that he would at least have to go to Morristown for the interview.

Hamilton felt a special warmth for the two Marylanders, Tilghman and Harrison. He expected a cool reception, but they proved to be modest and friendly men. They described to him the nature of the work and the habits of the chief, his sense of formality, his concern for secrecy, his occasional flashes of temper, which they saw as an understandable release for a man who was stoic most of the time in enduring a seemingly endless stream of bad news. The chief was an early riser, and the flow of work in the office was prodigious. Writing skill was essential for an aide, as was the ability to emulate the style of the chief. Washington would write some short letters himself and dictate others haltingly to an aide, but in most cases he would describe what he wanted and the aide would go off to do a draft for the chief's review. The aides handled a great deal of correspondence themselves; knowing what could be done without bothering the chief was a knack one soon picked up. Of course, one had to be wary of the mercurial temperaments of some of the army commanders and civilians who had business with headquarters and their sensitivities over dealing with an aide instead of the top man.

Tilghman told Hamilton he might find Washington slow moving and ponderous at times, but that usually was because he was either contemplating an insoluble problem or mentally balancing the pros and cons of a very difficult one. Sometimes he would carefully write the options down and study them. He sought counsel and was open to the views of his aides, but he made the decisions, and they almost always were very firm ones. The relationship was cordial, but also correct. Although Washington relaxed visibly after hours and could become quite an amiable companion—at dinner, in social repartee, with the ladies, while dancing in the evenings—there was always a sense of distance, a personal line that one did not cross. That was fine with Hamilton; the last thing he wanted was dependence on a patron.

In his first meeting with the two older aides, Hamilton wondered aloud how Washington, out of all the officers of the army, had happened to pick an artillery captain who had merely done his duty in the recent campaign but nothing special otherwise. Tilghman said that after the winter turnover with three aides departing, General Greene had commented to the chief that Hamilton "was a most extraordinary young man." Harrison pointed out that Washington had come to prefer younger aides, having had several unhappy experiences with older officers. Aside from Greene and Lord Stirling, Hamilton knew three other generals, having served under McDougall, Knox, and Wayne. While at Elizabethtown, he had come to know members of the powerful Livingston family who were prominent in both New Jersey and New York. William Livingston, brother by marriage of Lord Stirling, was now the first governor of the

State of New Jersey. Could any of these men have spoken well of him to Washington as Greene had? Hamilton discounted the fact that he had once met and conversed briefly with the commander-in-chief, the previous summer when the Americans were awaiting the British attack on New York. Washington was in the habit of frequently stopping to chat with the officers and men during troop reviews; he must have talked with dozens of young captains that day. Hamilton also thought it unlikely that the pamphlets he had written in support of the revolution while at King's College had ever come to Washington's attention.

When Tilghman ushered him into Washington's office, the physical presence of the man came back to Hamilton with an impact. Here he seemed to fill the room. At the age of forty-five, Washington was impressive in stature, over six feet tall and of strong build. From the encounter in New York, Hamilton remembered the penetrating grey eyes and well-modulated Virginia voice, the strong jaw and thin, bloodless lips. Washington's face was faintly pockmarked from a childhood bout with smallpox, and when he smiled he rarely parted his lips, so self-conscious was he of the poor condition of his teeth. Hamilton asked how his name had come up; Washington responded merely that he had heard well of Hamilton, including the fact that he spoke fluent French. No one else at headquarters could speak the language more than haltingly, he said, and having a competent French speaker and translator had become a necessity, what with increasing correspondence and the growing numbers of French officers in the service. Hamilton explained that he was not eager to get into staff work, that he wanted to advance himself in the combat line. With a trace of a smile, Washington commented that all of his staff aides said the same thing. A tour at headquarters gave a man a chance to see the war in its broadest perspective, to engage in matters of policy and decision. That was valuable in itself, but it also had enabled his aides to improve themselves when they returned to the line. As an aide, Hamilton would have the rank of lieutenant-colonel, quite a step up for a captain who had just turned twenty-one years of age. It would only be a brevet rank, Washington cautioned. Congress always seemed confused about military rank and structures, and it had made no provision for commissioning staff officers. The chance to influence policy appealed to Hamilton, and he was not concerned about rank. He suddenly felt that he belonged, and he knew he could help this man.

And indeed he had. Physically frail, Hamilton was not short, but so small-boned and slender that it seemed he was. He compensated with restless energy, intellectual brilliance, and an omnivorous appetite for work. Harrison dubbed him "the little lion," and the name stuck. In only a few weeks it was clear to everyone that Hamilton rapidly was becoming Washington's favorite aide. Most satisfying to Hamilton was that this produced no sign of backbiting or jealousy from his colleagues.

Tilghman was the aide responsible for what his colleagues liked to refer to as "the numbers"—keeping track of the strength of the army and its disposition. He had just completed a hand-drawn map showing the latest information. He moved to the front of the room and displayed the drawing as if he were a teacher about to lecture his pupils. "There it is, lads. Pretty, isn't it?"

"There are some things you're good at, Tilly," observed Fitzgerald, "but mapmaking isn't one of them."

Johnston was peering intently. "You've got everything on there. I wonder what General Howe would pay for that."

"Don't even joke about such a thing," Harrison said.

Hamilton could see boxes with numbers in them, representing the strength of various units, those of the Northern Department at Albany and Ticonderoga under General Schuyler, McDougall's command at Peekskill protecting the Hudson Highlands, the headquarters camp, Gates's command in Philadelphia, Putnam's command at Princeton, Wayne's group in Bucks County, and scattered small units.

"How many bodies altogether?" Hamilton asked, noticing that Tilghman did not show a total.

"Fifteen thousand."

This was met with a chorus of derision. "C'mon, give us the real number," Fitzgerald said. "Not more than ten thousands effectives, I'll bet."

"Oh, you want *effectives*!" Tilghman said. "That's a different matter." He grimaced. "Try eight thousand, five hundred."

Fitzgerald made a low whistle. The same thought was in everybody's mind: under Howe in New York and Carleton in Canada, the British were believed to have as many as forty thousand troops in North America, to say nothing of their navy and various detachments of Loyalist troops and Indians. "Where the hell are all the summer soldiers?" Fitzgerald asked no one in particular. "We'll take 'em."

Out of his window Hamilton could see tangible evidence of the problem. A large body of men was busy assembling gear, in a hurry to get home for spring planting. Their enlistment time was up at the end of March. "Did you subtract the Virginia Volunteers and the Cecil County militia?" he asked.

"For the chief I did," Tilghman said. The others understood. By tacit consent at headquarters, the numbers game consisted of shading the figures to the low side to anyone who could do anything about recruitment, in order to stir them to greater efforts. To most others, the strength of the army was exaggerated in varying degrees to help dispel the pervasive feeling that the cause was hopeless. No one thought seriously of this as deception—often the results depended on which category one selected for certain groups. In any case, it was difficult to know the exact truth. It was hard enough to keep track of the regulars, but the difficulties were compounded in the case of the state militia units called to short-term service with the Continental Army and other militia units active within the states. The problem was illustrated in Washington's characterization of the militia as "a mixed, motley crew" and as the "here today, gone tomorrow" troops.

The disastrous series of losses over the fall and winter had made it seem for a time that the cause indeed was lost. The only good news was that the British thrust in the north had been stalled without the loss of Ticonderoga. Then the surprise attacks at Trenton and Princeton boosted patriot morale and shattered General Howe's comfortable assumption that all he needed to do to hold New Jersey was to show the flag and spot garrisons at various key locations. Howe's withdrawal to the north left three fourths of the state open to Washington, who had settled on Morristown for winter quarters. The turnabout stirred hope that enlistments would rise to strengthen the Continental Army and lessen dependence on militia. Congress had authorized sixteen new regiments of infantry, four of artillery, and four of cavalry, and the recruitment levies had gone out to the thirteen States. There was optimistic talk of "the Army of 1777," but the results thus far were disappointing.

"Well, I'm off to make my report," Tilghman said, rolling up his map like a scroll. "Wish me luck," he tossed over his shoulder as he left the room to cross the landing to Washington's adjoining corner office. It was a reference to the fact that the chief had been out of sorts lately. He had been ill for nearly a week and had returned to find a huge backlog of work, most of it disturbing—reports on desertions, lack of supplies, corruption, bickering among his commanders, too many young French aristocrats being given commissions by Congress, good officers resigning, too few men taking the bounty to reenlist. Even the rare good news turned out to be bad. General Stephen's report of success in a skirmish with the British Forty-second Regiment near New Brunswick proved on investigation to be substantially exaggerated.

Hamilton found it difficult to return to the labored reports of the French engineers. *Let's just do it,* he thought. West Point sounds fine. He continued gazing out the window at the activity in the village square, and he spotted Captain Caleb Gibbs, whose laconic New England style masked an impish wit. Gibbs was commander of the Life Guard, the elite two-hundred-man force responsible for guarding the headquarters camp, most particularly the person of the commander-in-chief. Like Washington, the guards all had to be six feet tall or more. Ironically, they were also required to have clear, unpocked complexions and good teeth.

Gibbs and several of the men were helping to organize the line of oath signers. The oath had been a sore point, but it was an issue that fascinated Hamilton, typical of what made him glad that he had accepted the post of staff aide, that had set his mind spinning not only about how to win a war but how to build a nation out of thirteen independent and quarrelsome entities that now were emphatically known as states rather than colonies. With the central-izing bonds of king and aristocracy and parliament gone, how would these states function together in the future? Would they be thirteen little countries, jealous of one another and constantly warring in the fashion of the Greek city-states?

When the British overran New Jersey, General Howe had issued a bom-bastic proclamation, calling for New Jerseyans to sign an oath of loyalty to the King. Convinced that the rebellion had been crushed, thousands of citizens of all persuasions had flocked to sign. Then the startling reversal occurred, with the British all but withdrawing from New Jersey. Washington thought the Howe oath signers should be given a chance to change their minds, and so he had issued a counterproclamation calling for an oath of allegiance to the United States of America. To cancel their oath to the King, citizens were to re-port to the nearest officers of the Continental Army to sign the new oath. Those whose beliefs would not allow them to do so would be given safe con-duct to British lines. Those who remained and refused to change their oaths would be regarded as enemies.

The first denunciation came from the radical patriots who wanted to be much more punitive. But Washington, ever fair minded, believed that he could win more people to the cause by understanding their fears and respecting their opinions, while the British were losing them through pomposity and rough treatment. Many a Tory sympathizer or neutral had been converted to a patriot by abuse from the soldiers, especially the Hessians.

The more serious criticism came from the New Jersey Assembly and the state's delegates to Congress. They demanded to know by what right Washing-ton was requiring citizens of New Jersey to sign a loyalty oath to anything other than New Jersey itself. They argued that there was no such thing as the "United States of America" as a superior political power. In their anger, they used such words as "dictator" and "tyrant," and they wondered aloud whether Washington was contemplating some sort of "new monarchy." The furor had abated only when John Adams, who could hardly be outbid in radical creden-tials, finally arose in Congress to tell his colleagues that it was an honest mis-take and no harm done.

But the debacle of the oath was only one example; the troubles caused by factionalism and bickering went on. Congress was no longer the same noble body that had produced the Declaration of Independence the previous July. Of that group, only five individuals, including Adams, remained in office. The new men were much more parochial, deeply suspicious of Washington and the Continental Army as the only conceivable force of authority that could span more than one state. As a result, they were niggardly in providing material help but quick to set rules and create impediments to keep the army from becoming a threat to state sovereignty. It was exactly such problems that would be the subject of the meeting scheduled for the afternoon, including the headaches caused by the latest promotion list issued by Congress.

Hamilton believed in the cause and republican principles as much as he had when he had been a firebrand at King's College, but now he could see how such principles could be distorted and abused, how much they needed to be set within the framework of some new form of centralized authority. The problem of how to achieve that without curtailing basic freedoms fascinated him.

Tilghman opened the door and beckoned to Hamilton. "Let's go, Hammie. Knox and Greene are here."

"How did the chief react to your map?" Fitzgerald asked.

Tilghman shrugged. "He wasn't surprised. Seems much more worried about morality in camp. Too much drinking and gambling. He says they'll destroy a soldier's morale more than the enemy can. He wants stern orders to be drafted."

"Oh, Lord," Fitzgerald said.

"And he wants you to draft them."

"Me! Why me? I *like* drinking and gambling."

"That's why!" Tilghman laughed.

Over Tilghman's shoulder, Hamilton could see the bulk of Knox coming up on the landing. He scooped up his papers and joined Tilghman.

Chapter 19

Morristown
March 30, 1777

By the time Hamilton followed Tilghman into the chief's office, Knox and Greene were already there, peering over Washington's shoulders at Tilghman's map. The office, smaller than the staff room, was filled with large vigorous men. Knox weighed close to three hundred pounds, and Greene, a tall, gruff Rhode Islander, was a former ironmonger and looked the part. The room contained a half dozen spindle-backed chairs in a rough semicircle facing the escritoire and a larger chair that Washington used. Next to them was a long table laden with maps and papers where the three senior men now were gathered.

"A rather thin line," Greene commented.

"Yes," Washington murmured. "Perilously thin." He turned and sat down in his chair. Knox gave Hamilton a friendly wink as he began the process of settling his large body into one of the spindly chairs. As he watched Knox sit, Hamilton winced inwardly, half-expecting the chair to collapse into kindling. Greene also had difficulty settling himself because of his stiff leg, a boyhood injury that almost precluded a military career. His reputation had suffered as a result of the disaster at Fort Washington, though of course the chief had approved of Greene's decision to try to hold out against the British. This undoubtedly was why there had been no censure of Greene for the crippling loss and the capture of twenty-eight hundred American troops.

Like Tilghman, Hamilton took an end chair and pushed it back a few inches as if to denote his subordinate status. He sat primly, prepared to take notes.

Washington seemed unusually sober. "It's the end of March," he said softly. "Howe could begin to make a move at any time now. What are we going to stop him with?"

"Excellency, I don't think he'll try much for another month at least, perhaps two," Knox said, engaging in his habit of twisting a black handkerchief in his hands, the better to conceal the loss of two of his fingers. "He doesn't like the rain and the muddy roads. By that time—who knows? Perhaps recruitment will pick up."

Washington's gloom persisted. "We don't know what the British are planning for this season. Reinforcements might be on the way to Howe right now. He'll still outnumber us three to one—or more."

"He'll never get all of his strength to bear on us at once," Knox said.

"Ah, yes, our Fabian defense," Washington smiled, glancing at Hamilton. It was he, at a previous conference, who had likened Washington's strategy to that of the Roman general, Fabius, noted for always avoiding pitched battle with the Carthaginians, preferring instead limited engagements and hit-and-run raids in order to preserve his army.

"The only trouble with Hamilton's analogy," Greene said drily, "is what happened next." He had been checking up on his classical history. "The Roman politicians got tired of Fabius. They wanted the glory of victory. So they replaced him with another general."

There was an uncomfortable silence. At length Washington asked: "And what did the new general do?"

"He marched out and met the Carthaginians directly. And lost."

Again there was silence. Hamilton was beginning to wish that he had never heard of Fabius. Finally, Washington said: "Well, at least it shows what happens when politicians meddle too much. We may need to tell our politicians that story one of these days." Briskly he changed the subject. "What do you think of a general conference of war soon? We've got to try to anticipate Howe."

"You may not need one, Excellency. For a while, anyway. I can tell you what everybody in Philadelphia thinks," said Greene, who had just returned from a week in that city, trying to represent the chief's point of view in dealings with Congress. "Everyone I talked to—except Gates and Schuyler—is certain Howe will attack Philadelphia."

"Well, at least Gates and Schuyler agree on *something*. What do you think?"

Greene grimaced and was silent for a long moment. Then he leaned forward, an intense expression on his rugged, handsome face. "You see, Excellency, this is where that business about Fabius could come true. Howe knows that the real way to win the war is to eliminate this army." He glanced directly at Washington. "And *you,* sir. Once you're gone, morale will be destroyed. Howe can't catch us, as long as we stay in these highlands and stay prepared to move fast. So, he may reason that if he attacks Philadelphia you may be forced to make a stand. After all, they've taken lower New York, they still hold part of New Jersey and Rhode Island, and if they threaten Philadelphia, our largest city, the seat of Congress, then public morale, political pressure, could force you to defend the city to the last man. If you don't—well, look what happened to Fabius." He leaned back, triumphant in his logic.

It was an impressive argument, Hamilton thought. He saw Knox nodding. "Yes, Howe may think that he wins either way." Knox turned his great head and luminous eyes to gaze on his chief. "If you make a stand—one decisive battle—he expects to win. If you don't make a stand, then you'll be relieved of command, and Howe still wins."

"Besides," Greene added, "I think Howe was embarrassed by his failure to take Philadelphia last December. He'll want to rectify that."

If Washington was affected by the argument, he gave no sign. "What do Gates and Schuyler think?" he asked Greene.

"Well, no surprise, since they're squabbling over the northern command, they both think Howe will go north—to do what it seemed the British were about last season, to meet up with Carleton coming south."

Washington nodded. "That's what I fear the most. We'll know it's afoot if the British send their major reinforcements to Canada. If they'd succeeded last fall that might've been the end of us. Thank God we had Arnold up there."

"We may not have him anymore," Knox said.

"I know. And that brings us to our main subject. The officer corps. We can only wait until Howe commits himself, and there's not much more we can do about recruitment at this point. Either it begins to increase or it doesn't. But there must be something we can do about the officer corps. We've lost two brigadiers to battle, two to disease, three to resignations. We've lost a dozen good colonels. General Lee is a prisoner, and there seems no hope of an exchange."

"If I may interject, Excellency," said Knox, "we do have one great compensation. I'm referring to our present position. I freely admit that when you decided to make winter headquarters this far north in New Jersey I felt some trepidation. Now I see what a master stroke it was. We are ideally positioned for either eventuality. If Howe decides for Philadelphia, and goes by land, we'll quickly be in his way. Possibly he'll move his army by sea, given the huge fleet his brother has in New York harbor. If so, we'll have ample time to move south while the British are sailing down around Cape May and up the Delaware River estuary toward Philadelphia. On the other hand, if reinforcements come to Canada and Howe strikes north for a juncture with Carleton, we can move to defensive positions in the Hudson Highlands to intercept him, in only a day or two."

"Yes, we'll be in position to confront Howe either way. The northern prospect concerns me the most," Washington said. "We may be able to stop Howe or slow him down, but we also could be caught between two armies, with Carleton moving south. What could we possibly send to reinforce the Northern Department? It's truly ironic, but if we actually got the new regiments, we wouldn't have enough officers to lead them."

"John Adams thinks we have more than we need," Greene said. "The other day he spoke in Congress about our having too many superannuated officers from the days of the French and Indian War. Wooster, McDougall, Putnam, Schuyler. He'd like to see them all retire."

"He didn't mention me, did he?" Washington asked, with the trace of a smile.

"No, sir."

There was enough truth in the charge that some of the generals were getting too old for combat duty to forestall any violent reaction from the chief. "There are days when I wish Mr. Adams would retire," Washington said mildly. "Do you have any *good* news from Philadelphia?"

Very deliberately, Greene opened a pouch that had been resting on his lap and took out a sheaf of notes. He looked straight at Washington. "You know me, Excellency. One thing I'll never do is make it sound pretty when it isn't. First of all, there's the rivalry between Schuyler and Gates. I met with Gates three or four times. Then Schuyler arrived while I was still there—to defend himself, of course, and make his own try with Congress. I thought I could talk sense into one or the other. It's hopeless. They've each got their political backers, and the fight just keeps going on. Isn't there something you can do?"

"I tried redefining the Northern Department so they'd each have a command. That just made them both angry at me."

"If we don't get this settled," Knox said, "we'll be so demoralized up there that the British will be able to just walk on through."

"The problem would be solved if Gates would just agree to be adjutant general," Washington said, referring to the chief administrative post in the army. Vacancy in that position for months ever since Reed's departure was one of the reasons for the heavy workload at headquarters. "He's been avoiding me. Did you try to pin him down?"

"He won't do it," Greene said. "He says he's done that before and sees no reason why he should do it again. He says it would just diminish him in status and rank." *Despite the fact that it's apparently the perfect job for him,* Hamilton thought. Gates's reputation at headquarters was that of a superior if cantankerous administrator, good at details, but not a leader of men in the field.

Washington was visibly irritated by Gates's attitude. Hamilton knew that he intensely disliked the practice of some officers of repeatedly going over his head with Congress. Gates was by far the worst offender. Normally careful about swearing, Washington muttered an oath under his breath. "Well, let Gates stay where he is. Schuyler's been returned to the northern command. Congress can't change its mind again. That should end it."

"I wouldn't be too sure," Greene said. "Gates has an advantage being stationed in Philadelphia, while Schuyler can only visit. And Gates is relentless in stirring up the New England claque, keeps inflating their fears that Schuyler means to take over the Hampshire Grants for New York."

"That's got nothing to do with the problems we face now."

"They don't see it that way. And Adams is Gates's firm ally, as you know. Even arranged for Gates to address Congress. He harangued for close to two hours. Incredible! And I'm sorry to say my fellow New Englanders can get pretty vicious. Even so low as inferring that because Schuyler is a man of property he must be a Tory at heart."

Washington, who knew the same slander had been whispered about him, waved his hand as if to dismiss the affair. "I have to take the position that the Northern Department is the prerogative of Congress. I've done all I can. What else?"

"There's the matter of the French officers," Greene said. "Congress has already given Thomas Conway a commission. And I'm afraid they're about to do the same for du Coudray. Apparently, Silas Deane never learned how to say no."

Deane was one of the American representatives in Paris. Every French officer who showed up in Philadelphia claimed that Deane had promised a congressional commission. Conway was an Irishman with a long history of service in the army of His Most Catholic Majesty, Louis XVI. Philippe Charles Tronson du Coudray had arrived in Philadelphia with his personal entourage of ten sergeants and twenty soldiers. He wanted to be chief of the artillery and the engineers.

Washington rolled his eyes in frustration. "This is how Congress thinks it can help with the officer corps. The cheap way. A French *army* is what we need, not all these vanity-laden and glory-seeking aristocrats who cause more problems than they solve. Conway could be different. I was impressed with him. But du Coudray! That's impossible!"

All eyes turned to Knox, who spread his hands. "If du Coudray is commissioned, what can I do? It's a matter of honor then. I'll have to resign."

"Never!" Washington snapped. He glanced at Hamilton. "I'll write another letter immediately. As soon as we're finished here."

Greene shuffled his notes and cleared his throat. "Next subject. I've checked the February promotion list thoroughly. I'm sorry to report that it's accurate as you received it. And nothing I could say produced any hope of changing it."

There had been some confusion about the list, which had contained the names of ten new brigadiers and five new major-generals. Much of the list was at variance with Washington's recommendations. Deserving men had been skipped over, and Congress had not appointed the three lieutenant-generals Washington had urged. John Stark was a deserving man who had been neglected, and so he had resigned to return to his farm in New Hampshire. The worst omission was the name of Benedict Arnold. He remained a brigadier according to the list, but the *Pennsylvania Packet* had carried an item saying that Arnold had, in fact, been promoted.

"So much for newspapers," Knox said. "That editor probably couldn't believe that Arnold was passed over any more than we could, so he assumed it was a mistake."

Washington got up and began to pace. "I hoped so much it was true. Can you imagine how Arnold feels? Here he is, the senior brigadier, a man who's seen more action than anyone else. That winter march through Maine to Quebec will live in the annals of military history. He was wounded but continued to fight with great skill. He saved most of the northern army by the way he covered the retreat. Can you think of *anyone* else who could've done what Arnold did at Valcour Bay? His reputation is celebrated from Boston to Charleston. He's given everything he has to the cause. His brigantine was burned, his business wrecked. His wife died while he was on campaign. He has young children at home. He's given all of his personal finances. What else could a man do? How could they possibly pass him over?"

"He also seems to stir controversy wherever he goes," Knox said. "He has quite a knack for making enemies."

"You can't be a fighter like Arnold without making enemies. He has no patience for the foolish or the timid."

"As far as I could tell, there was nothing personal in it," Greene said. "It was all political. The delegates I talked to—and some were quite sympathetic to him—they said Arnold wasn't promoted because Connecticut already has two major-generals. As simple as that."

"Try explaining that to Arnold," Washington said. "We've had several exchanges of letters already. He wants a court of inquiry."

Greene shook his head. "Wouldn't do any good. Arnold thinks that if he got a court all the facts would come out and virtue would triumph. Believe me, it doesn't work that way in politics."

Washington grimaced. "After all the pleading I've done on these promotions. Why do they do this to us?"

"I'll tell you why," Greene said. "Politics again. Congress wants to make it painfully clear that the army is subordinate to the civilian authority."

"I accept that," Washington cried. "I'm the first to uphold that principle."

"Yes, but their way of doing it is to attack seniority in promotions and ignore half of your recommendations." Greene consulted his notes. "In the debate, Adams called seniority 'one of the most putrid corruptions of absolute monarchy.' He said seniority is 'merely a delicate point of honor that is incompatible with republican principles.' "

" 'Merely a delicate point of honor'! My God!" Knox snorted.

Washington was growing increasingly livid. The others began bracing for one of his herculean rages. Hamilton looked at Greene, wondering why he had to be so explicit, but that apparently was his way.

"Why does he twist it so?" Washington's voice grated. "If you don't promote by seniority and the recommendations of the commanding officer, what have you got left? Politics and favoritism, that's what. They'll destroy the army quicker than the British ever could."

"It's not so much seniority as it is your authority they want to limit," Greene said.

"Damnation!" Washington roared, slamming his fist on the map table. "Limit my authority all you want. But don't ruin the army!" He worked visibly for control. "Sometimes I think their view of me is so distorted that I become an impediment. And the only way I can think of dealing with that is to step aside myself."

This statement was met by a chorus of dissent. Hamilton, who thought for a moment that his tenure as a staff aide might be very brief indeed, listened with growing fascination as the others made their arguments as to why Washington should not resign. It was a one-sided argument because the chief made no further effort to defend the proposition that he *should* resign. He merely listened gloomily to the excited protests of Greene, Knox, and Tilghman, which, to Hamilton, began to border on sycophancy, although he credited Greene's argument as the best: that for Washington to resign would be to play into the hands of the critics, for that was what they wanted and it would also seem to prove their criticisms to be correct. Fortunately, Hamilton thought, no one reminded the chief that he could have made the promotions himself during the period in which Congress had given him full authority over all army matters, as one of its last acts before ignominiously fleeing for safety to Baltimore the previous December when the British seemed on the verge of taking Philadelphia. The chief had made very little use of his "dictatorial" powers during the time he possessed them, in line with his genuine belief in civilian authority. Inferring that he *should* have used them in the case of promotions might produce a full-blown rage on his part, Hamilton thought.

The crisis soon passed. It would take much more than a faulty promotion list to cause the man who had endured so much to take the ultimate step. Hamilton was amused by the thought that a meeting convened to discuss "the crisis of the generals" almost became a crisis of *the* general. At the moment, the need to end the meeting was most pressing; stomachs were growling and it was very near the three o'clock dinner hour.

As the group broke up, Washington seemed genuinely sad about Arnold. "Stay, Hamilton. I'll have to write Arnold again," he said bleakly. "What can I tell him? There's nothing I can do. He'll have to make his own choice."

"Maybe he won't resign," Greene said. "He's a warhorse if there ever was one."

Knox shook his head emphatically. "He'll have to resign. He has no choice."

PART V

Ridgefield

Chapter 20

New Haven
April 25, 1777

Benedict Arnold chewed unhappily on a piece of salt fish. He looked down at the boiled potatoes and mashed turnips that comprised the rest of his supper. "The fish are running," he grunted. "Why don't we have fresh fish?"

The question was addressed to his sister, who sat at the opposite end of the table. Hannah was a study in grey and black with her habitual black gown, her greying black hair drawn back tightly in a bun, and a complexion that remained a grey pallor even in the flickering candlelight.

"We would if you'd go fishing," she sniffed.

"That's very amusing. Why don't you *buy* some fresh fish?"

"I would if you'd give me a decent sum of money to run this household."

Her tone was neutral but the subject was ominous. Arnold decided to drop it. Perhaps it would be better to go back to having supper with the boys present. Their childish chatter had given him indigestion, and so he had taken to dining later in the evening, alone with Hannah. That was turning out to be worse. All of the disadvantages of a wife and none of the pleasures, he thought. Several times he had invited his cronies, John Lamb and Eleazer Oswald, to share the evening meal, but unaccountably Hannah had become a frigid hostess.

She had always been good-natured before, witty, likeable, willing to accommodate herself to her brother's needs. Lately, since Arnold had returned home from Providence at the beginning of the month, she had become tense and withdrawn, more inclined to complain. Arnold realized that his own troubles weighed heavily on her. And perhaps she was growing weary of the burden placed on her by the death of Peggy. Hannah had always been fond of

Peggy, closer to her in some ways than Arnold himself was. Perhaps it was the fact that Hannah now almost certainly would live out her days as a spinster.

Arnold rarely wasted time regretting past actions, but he was beginning to wonder in the case of the young French sailor he had sent fleeing for his life many years ago. His dislike of the French, to say nothing of "Papists" in general, went back to the French and Indian War and to several nasty encounters later on during his Caribbean trading days. No sister of his was going to marry a Frenchman. Twice he had thrown the young sailor out of the Arnold family home at Norwich, and when he found him with Hannah a third time, Arnold had fired his pistol at him, making sure to miss. The French sailor was never seen again in Connecticut, and from that moment on Hannah rebuffed all suitors and devoted herself to her brother's career. She came with him when he moved from Norwich to New Haven, making his household for him until he married Peggy Mansfield. Hannah might have had a better life, Arnold thought, but it was her own fault that she had not found a suitable man to marry. On the other hand, perhaps it was for the best. Without Hannah, he would have a difficult time finding someone reliable to maintain his household and care for his three young sons.

Ever since that fateful morning in Boston when he had read the startling news in Washington's letter that there was some question about his promotion, Arnold's state of mind had been one of continual anxiety and misery. There had been a flurry of letters exchanged among Arnold and Washington and several friends in Philadelphia. The news had gotten progressively worse. It turned out that the editor of the *Pennsylvania Packet*, like many other people, simply could not believe that Arnold hd been passed over, so he had included his name in the promotion list. So much for that thin reed of hope. Weeks passed while Arnold waited in vain for word that Washington's efforts to rectify the situation had succeeded.

Arnold had come home from Providence after it seemed fairly certain that there would be no action there. He and Spencer and Hampton had continued trying to raise troops to oppose General Clinton's force at Newport. But then Arnold learned that Clinton had been called to England for consultations. Then orders had come from Washington's headquarters in Morristown in March transferring most of the Continental troops at Providence to the Hudson Highlands under General Heath, following a damaging raid on that area by a Tory force commanded by William Tryon, Royal Governor of New York. Not only did this decision take much of Arnold's army out from under him, but there was no mention at all of a new assignment for him in the coming campaign season—it was as if Washington had given up on him, expecting him to resign.

And so Arnold had come home in a foul mood, grappling with the decision he knew he would have to make, procrastinating, hoping for a miracle. His problem was not yet widely known to the public, but it soon would be. Arnold threw himself into a frenzy of activity with Lamb and Oswald. The three men had agreed in correspondence earlier to go ahead with development of the Artillery Company of New Haven. Once Arnold was on the scene personally, he participated in training sessions and spent time and money searching out and buying cannon. He and Lamb and Oswald also took it upon themselves to harass the worst of the local Tories.

No amount of frenetic activity could work off Arnold's deep anger and disappointment. He had never been more depressed in his life. He stared down at his dinner plate, now seeing nothing. Then he heard a rush of footsteps and pealing laughter. His three sons burst into the dining room. Behind them in the doorway stood the Irish maid.

Arnold came out of his torpor. With a grin, he spread his powerful simian arms and scooped the three children to his chest, burying his face in the bobbing tousles of black and brown curls. The children were ready for bed, fresh and sweet-smelling, and their father clasped them tightly.

"Tell us a story, Papa," cried Benedict Jr.

"No more blood and gore," Hannah snapped, but her voice was lost in the chorus of appeals from Richard and Henry. Four-year-old Henry had already squirmed his way to a place on his father's lap.

"Not tonight, my lads," Arnold said, beginning to shepherd them away, patting their rumps. "Go to bed like good boys and tomorrow night I'll tell you about the bear I wrestled way up on the Dead River."

"Now, tell us now," they cried, but Arnold stilled them. "Say good night to your aunt Hannah." Dutifully, the boys filed out, each submitting to a peck from Hannah.

Arnold's brief sense of pleasure left the room with his sons. He felt a dull headache again and a tingling in the leg that had been twice injured. He feared the gout would come again, as it always seemed to do when he was inactive and depressed. Although healed, the leg had become something of a barometer. Without stepping out of doors, he knew there was a foul April chill and that rain would come soon.

"You should spend more time with them," Hannah said. "In two years you've been home only a few weeks. They hardly know their father."

"They know me," Arnold said. He could still see their beaming faces in the crowd that day on the green when the whole town of New Haven had turned out to honor him. That was only last Christmas week, and already it seemed so long ago! He could remember how he felt, that glow of inner pride and sense of well-being. Would he ever feel that way again?

Hannah's voice cut like a rasp through his thoughts. "Even when you're home, you spend all your time running around with those *friends* of yours, frightening people to death."

"It's important," Arnold growled. "Those *people* you refer to are the worst kind of Tories, the ones that'll shoot you in the back if ever the British come through here."

Hannah was only slightly subdued. "Why can't you let it be? You're on leave, for heaven's sake. How much money have you spent on those foolish guns?"

"That's important, too, dammit! I've told you. There isn't another artillery company in all of Connecticut." If Hannah only knew how much he'd spent! A good share of his remaining savings, to purchase a strange assortment of vintage field pieces. No matter what else happened, he'd get reimbursed from Congress eventually—or he'd end up shooting a few of the honorable delegates.

"Everything's important except your own home and your own children," Hannah muttered.

"That's enough!" Arnold barked, pushing his chair back and throwing his napkin on the table.

It *was* enough, Hannah decided. She knew her brother's temper all too well. Strange how differently they had turned out. They were the only survivors of the family. The other children had been taken in a yellow fever epidemic. Despite the illustrious background of the family, the father of Hannah and Benedict managed to die penniless, his health destroyed by alcohol. A sad life had made their mother all the more pious a soul. On Benedict's eighteenth birthday, she passed to the beyond she seemed to long for so much. For years she had lectured her children incessantly about God's will and how they must accept the burdens of this life in preparation for the next. Hannah was inclined to that thinking, but not her brother. His response to piety, caution, and the idea that one should accept whatever life brings was violent action and an effort to impose his will on every situation. In him, Hannah found the only source of strength and energy, short of the Almighty, that conceivably could hold the hostile forces of the world at bay. This was comforting to her because she feared the world, and because her brother was compassionate toward those who accepted his protection, who depended upon him. Now he was depressed and uncertain, and that frightened her.

"I'm sorry, Ben," she murmured.

He gestured, dismissing it. If anything, contrite women bothered him more than carping ones.

"Ben, what will you do now?"

"Go back into business, I suppose."

"I'd be happy for that, because I'd know you'd stay alive, then, for the sake of your boys." Arnold said nothing. She watched him as he brooded, eyes glittering under a gathered brow. "I know how much the other means to you," she said softly.

"Maybe I could get a privateer," Arnold said. "That's the way to make real money."

"That's so dangerous!"

"Good Christ, woman, there's nothing worthwhile that isn't dangerous!"

"Maybe you don't—he didn't say you *had* to resign. Perhaps he can still do something. Perhaps if you wait . . ."

Arnold looked at her as if she were a simpleton. "You still don't understand? My God, it's an unbreakable rule of every respectable army in the world—of every civilized country! But they broke it! They promoted five men over my head, men that were subordinate to me before. Now I'm subordinate to *them*. Not one of them has done a tenth of what I've done. So what do you conclude from that?" He leaped up from his chair, pulsating with anger, his powerful upper torso heaving in spasms. "I'll tell you what you conclude. It's an insult! A deliberate insult of the worse kind. My honor, my whole life, is at stake. If I don't resign, I'll be a laughingstock. All those people who were cheering me before will start wondering and whispering. 'There's something wrong with Benedict Arnold,' they'll say, 'there must be. All those stories about his courage at Ticonderoga and Quebec and Valcour Bay must be false. He must've done something terrible. Else why would Congress treat him with such contempt? Those people who are busy slandering him, Moses Hazen and John Brown and the others, they must be right,' they'll say. Don't you see? I have to resign. I have no choice."

"It's so unjust."

"You're damned right it's unjust! I'm out shedding blood on the battlefield to win their precious independence for them, and this is what Congress does to me." Arnold fumed for a few moments and then abruptly left the room.

Hannah dabbed at her moist eyes with her napkin. Despite her own troubles and fear of the world, she had basked in the glory of her brother-hero. She had found deep pleasure in the cleansing of his reputation. What constructive future could there be for the boy who picked fights with bigger boys and even once with the constable in Norwich, who ran away from home twice to try to fight in the French and Indian War, who was constantly involved in pranks and acts of bravado? What constructive future could there be for the young merchant who was so aggressive that many people found him offensive? The answer was now clear. The future for such a person would be as a "fighting general," a military hero. Benedict Arnold's destiny needed a war to make him whole, and it had happened. The qualities that some people once regarded as grievous faults were now considered to be virtues. Old-timers who would have fired buckshot at the rowdy young Arnold on sight now gleefully told stories of his youthful escapades, implying that they had known all along that he would become a famous general. Benjamin Franklin's slogan "Don't Tread on Me" seemed made to order for Benedict Arnold. He was seen as the quintessence of the fighting spirit of the Revolution, and citizens of Connecticut who once feared or disliked him now worshipped him.

Yet unknown men for unknown reasons many miles away could force him to relinquish it all, unfairly and under a cloud of suspicion. His reputation once again sullied, he would be reduced to starting all over again in business. All the hardship and suffering and sacrifice of the past few years would have been for nothing. Worst of all for Hannah, she was completely powerless to help or advise her brother in any useful way. In her confusion and fright, she could not even prevent herself from bickering with him at times.

Arnold reappeared, carrying with him the most recent letter from Washington, the one that seemed to end all doubts on the matter. Hannah shivered inwardly. The arrival of this letter had seemed to push Arnold over some edge of civility, away from rationality into an unfathomable rage. He had stalked through the house, clutching the letter, shaking his fist, raving and cursing. Now he almost seemed calm as he sat down and spread the letter out before him. "Listen to this. Listen to what he writes about Congress." His voice took on a sweet sarcasm as he read:

"Public bodies are not amenable for their actions. They place and displace at their pleasure, and all the satisfaction that an individual can obtain, when he is overlooked, is, if innocent, a consciousness that he has not deserved such treatment for his exertion."

Arnold looked up, feigning an air of amused perplexity. "That's supposed to make me feel better! That's as bad as King George and his Parliament ever were. Worse, by God! And what does he mean by *innocent,* for Christ's sake? I'm innocent all right, innocent of any brains in my head when I go out and risk my life for nothing."

"Washington is the one who should resign," Hannah said stiffly, "if he can't do better for those who are loyal to him."

"Oh, no, never. He's the great indispensable man."

Arnold crumpled the letter and threw it down on the table. "I don't want to think about it anymore. I'm going to bed." He got up and stalked out of the room again.

Hannah sat immobile for a long while. Then she smoothed out the letter and read the last sentence: *The point does not now admit of a doubt, and is of so delicate a nature that I would not even undertake to advise; your own feelings must be your guide.*

The "point" the letter referred to was the fact that Arnold had been passed over and that Congress would not rectify it. There had been no mistake. It had been intentional. Washington could not, or would not, do anything. Ben was right. There was no hope. He had to resign. Hannah dabbed at her eyes again.

Several hours later, Arnold was back downstairs, unable to sleep. He decided he had to finish his letter of resignation that night. Hannah apparently had expected him to come down. The letter from Washington lay on the dining room table along with a note from her saying that there was bread pudding if he wanted some dessert. "Jesus!" Arnold muttered, stifling a sour belch. He took the Washington letter and went through the parlor to the little room that he used as a study.

Rain hammered at the windows, as Arnold's "barometer" had predicted. He was dressed in a nightgown and cap, with woolen stockings and a jacket thrown over his shoulders to guard against the late April chill. Transferring the candle flame to an oil lamp, he sat down and riffled through the papers scattered on the desk, his previous attempts at a suitable draft. This time he was determined to finish the job. For a long while, he alternately examined drafts and scribbled away, jabbing his quill into the ink horn. He finally decided on the right approach to Congress, one that clearly registered his amazement at being ignored while men junior to him had been promoted, but yet was dignified and correct. There was always the possibility that Congress would recant and restore his seniority once it learned that he was actually resigning. He read the final paragraph again:

My commission was conferred unsolicited, received with pleasure only as a means of serving my country. With equal pleasure I resign it when I can no longer serve my country with honor. The person who, void of nice feelings of honor, will tamely condescend to give up his rights and hold a commission at the expense of his reputation, I hold as a disgrace to the army, and unworthy of the glorious cause in which we are engaged.

Satisfied, he signed it with a flourish. His letter to Washington was more discursive, but still constrained by a sense of future possibilities. So long as he could maintain his pride, there was no point in letting his anger alienate either Congress or the chief—not yet, at least. The final paragraph read:

When I entered the service of my country, my character was unimpeached. I have sacrificed my interest, ease, and happiness in her cause. Now I sensibly feel the unmerited injury my countrymen have done me. I cannot think of drawing my sword until my reputation, which is dearer than life, is cleared up, when I am willing to bleed for my country, if necessary.

With great effort, he had kept control. Now he had to unburden himself to somebody. He took up the pen again and began writing a letter to Gates, one of the few officers he felt he could confide in. Arnold wrote of the villains who had slandered him, of the malice and envy he had attracted because he was not content with merely doing his duty. He wrote bitterly of Congress as a body governed by whim and caprice, which made sport of honorable men without sufficient reason. He wrote darkly that no one who had wronged him would rest in safety, that he would have revenge for injured honor.

He laid down his pen and massaged his aching hand. He would make the copies in the morning and send the letters off. It was done. The satisfaction he felt in completing the letters so eloquently soon ebbed, replaced by the bleak reality of the future he faced. Incredible that the uniform he loved so much could be turned into a cloak of shame by a group of jabbering idiots who pontificated "in Congress assembled" while the real struggle was fought by others.

He had come close. With the promotion that rightfully should have been his, that he had earned more than any other man, he would have been ready for a major command during the coming campaigning season—and for new glory on the battlefield and new advancement. From the sense of deprivation that dominated his youth, Arnold would have climbed further toward the pinnacle of wealth and position that was his goal.

But now it was over. Barring some miracle, Arnold had to face the reality that his soldiering days were ended. It was back to the oppressive routine of commerce. The only hope he had left now was Betsy. How would the unmerited disgrace affect his chances with her? What would she think of a dishonored soldier?

The trunk of finery had not worked quite the magic Arnold had hoped. Betsy had been effusive in registering her gratitude, but also fashionably coy and there had been a hint that her battle-ax mother might refuse to allow Betsy to keep the gifts. Arnold had been so preoccupied by the inexplicable failure of his promotion that he had not pressed his campaign to win Betsy's hand. He had not followed up the gift with a letter of proposal, as originally planned. His last advice from Lucy Knox, in a letter from the headquarters camp, was to be prepared for a long siege—she thought it would take a courtship of at least a year or more for him to fight his way past the redoubtable Mrs. DeBlois and into Betsy's heart.

But Betsy was there, in his mind and in his dreams, to give him solace at this time of lowest ebb in his life. From a secret drawer in his desk he withdrew the copy of the letter he had written to accompany the gift, and he took it with him as he padded back into the parlor, settling himself in the easy chair. The sound of the rain was now a lulling hum and the clock ticked methodically. It was well past midnight. Arnold considered his letter to Betsy to be a masterpiece. He was not one for the studious life, but he prided himself that he had become an articulate man, refining his speech and writing by careful attention and effort. He adjusted the oil lamp and read the letter again with deep satisfaction. Betsy was his only solace now. He could not believe that she would reject him, too. He dozed and thought of her and felt a delicious glow in his loins.

It was nearly dawn when Arnold awoke to incessant pounding on the front door. He could hear a muffled voice calling his name. Groggy and disoriented, he went over and squinted through the peephole. He saw a strange apparition, a lean, bony face with a look of astonishment on it. Water ran down in rivulets and dripped from the end of the man's nose. He was wrapped in a huge cloak against the rain. One hand held the reins of his horse and the other continued pounding on the door. He kept calling Arnold's name.

Now fully awake, Arnold slipped the bolt, yanked the door open, and shouted: "Shut up, for God's sake, you want to wake the whole household?"

The man began stammering: "The British—the British—"

"Get hold of yourself. What are you saying?"

"The British have landed!"

"*What?* Where?"

"Compo Point, sir."

That was near Norwalk, thirty miles away. "I'll be damned. How many?"

"I don't—thousands. Big army."

"Who are they?"

The man gaped for a moment and then understood the question. "Reg'lars. Hessians. Loyalist brigade."

"Where are they headed?"

"North."

Arnold thought for a moment. "Danbury," he said. There was a supply depot of the Continental Army in Danbury. He saw Punch appear suddenly from around the corner of the house, club in hand. "Hold it, Punch." He spoke to the stranger again. "When did the British land?"

" 'Twas past noon, sir. Twenty-eight sail we seen comin' in. Please sir, General Wooster wants you. They need you."

Arnold felt a sudden maniacal impulse to laugh. It began as a deep chuckle and then became full-throated. "They need me, do they! That's too bad. I just resigned!" He roared with laughter. The laughter began to die when Arnold saw that his visitor's expression was unchanged. Arnold decided that the man's look of astonishment had remained fixed ever since he had first seen the British coming in.

"What's your name, soldier?"

The man drew himself into a semblance of attention. "Sergeant Ashbel Grayson, sir. Fairfield County militia."

"All right, Sergeant Grayson. Listen carefully. And you, too, Punch. Here's what I want you to do."

Chapter 21

Western Connecticut
April 26–28, 1777

Arnold took the stairs three at a time. At the top he saw Hannah's terror-stricken face peering out from behind her bedroom door.

"Ben, what is it?"

"We just had a visitor."

"I *know* that—who was it, scaring a body to death?"

A wide grin on his face, Arnold said: "Opportunity just came and knocked on the door!"

"What?"

"The British have invaded."

"Oh my God!"

"Don't worry, they're going to Danbury, not here."

"Ben, you don't have to—you're going to resign!"

"Not at the moment!" Arnold shouted over his shoulder as he dashed into his bedroom. He studied the uniforms hanging in his wardrobe, passing over the elegant dress uniform with the gold sword-knot and epaulettes he had purchased from Paul Revere. That was for glory days; now he needed something for dirty work. He selected an older uniform and dressed hurriedly. He pulled on the knee-length boots and then hung his sword and a tin of cartridges from his belt. The last thing he took, from its velvet-lined box, was his Scottish pistol. He shoved it into his belt for the moment; it was heavy and would rest in the special holster built into his saddle.

He emerged from his room to find that Hannah had the three boys lined up. They were drowsy eyed, but began blinking with awe at the sight of their warrior-father all girded for battle. Arnold knew that Hannah always prepared for the worst. She would want his sons to see their father one last time. He drew erect, brought his heels together smartly, threw his cloak over one arm, and methodically fitted the battered campaign hat to his head, its wide brim fastened back on one side with a blue cockade. All the while his eyes locked with his sons', each in turn. Then he saluted them, knelt, and kissed each boy, from the eldest to the youngest.

"Forget about that bear," he told them. "I think I'll have a better story for you." He rose and gave Hannah an affectionate kiss on the cheek. He looked straight into her eyes and said: "I'll be back."

His saddled horse was waiting for him; Punch and Grayson had gone off as instructed to alert the others. By the time Arnold reached the rendezvous, Grimsby's Tavern on the Post Road west of town, the sky was growing bright and the rain had stopped. It was a damp and sparkling spring morning. He could see that Punch and Sergeant Grayson had done well—nearly a dozen men of the Artillery Company of New Haven were gathered on the veranda. A few more were inside; the proprietor had been roused and had opened up. Arnold now regretted that his largesse for the new battery had not extended to providing uniforms. That would have been good for morale. The men wore the usual miscellaneous oddments of clothing, with homespun and fringed jackets predominating.

Cheers and applause greeted Arnold as he rode up. He dismounted and handed the reins to one of the men. "You thought this was all for fun," he shouted to the group in general, grinning broadly. "Now we've got business!"

They cheered again and clustered around him as he entered the tavern. Arnold was known for his way with militia. He spoke their language, clapped them on the shoulders, eased their fears with banter—and demanded the utmost from them. Often unreliable under fire, they would follow Arnold farther and longer than any other officer.

Arnold saw Punch standing off to the side. From his expression, Arnold knew that Punch wanted to come on the expedition. He walked over and said in a soft voice: "Not this time, Punch. You're needed at home . . . to guard the family." With a half smile, Punch touched his forefinger to the floppy brim of his hat.

Arnold stopped to talk to one young private, a new father: "How's your new son, lad?"

"Fine, sir, thankee."

"You'd best stay home with your wife and babe," Arnold said in a serious voice, guessing that this particular young man would never do that.

"Oh, no, sir, I be with you."

"Good lad," Arnold said, turning to the others. "There's a soldier for you." He shouted to the proprietor who was in the process of handing over mugs to several of the men. "Hold that grog! We've got some talking to do first."

Arnold selected the largest of the round tables in the public room and took a chair. He motioned to Grayson to do the same. No longer looking astonished but merely dead tired, Grayson slid appreciatively into a seat. The two officers of the battery, John Lamb and Eleazer Oswald, sat down on either side of Arnold.

"Where are the maps?" Arnold asked.

Lamb produced an oilskin packet and extracted his best map of western Connecticut, spreading it flat on the table. Men clustered around, peering over the shoulders of the officers. Arnold traced his finger along the Saugatuck River.

"They landed at Compo Point, right?" He glanced at Grayson, who nodded. "Who's in command?"

"Of the British?" Grayson asked dully.

"Of course. We know who's in command of our side," Arnold said with a half smile and a glance at Oswald.

"Yes," Oswald said, returning the smile. "That would be General Wooster, I believe." The sixty-seven-year old Wooster had been a colonel as far back as the French and Indian War. From his pinnacle as top commander in Canada, Wooster's incompetence had caused him to be reduced to commanding the Connecticut militia. Oswald and Lamb exchanged knowing glances. Not for long would Arnold be held back by Wooster.

"I don't know who's in command of the British, sir," Grayson said.

"Think hard now. How many troops do they have?"

Grayson squirmed and shook his head. "I couldn't count 'em, sir. But it looked like thousands, I swear."

Arnold knew that such estimates were almost always exaggerated. Still, Grayson had been specific about the number of ships. "Twenty-eight sail you said. You're sure?"

"Yes, sir."

Arnold looked around. "Well, if it's one hundred men per ship, that's twenty-eight hundred."

There were several low whistles. The ardor of the men was palpably diminishing. "Yes, it's bad," Arnold said. "No use fooling ourselves. They're almost certainly going to Danbury. That's a rich prize—they can do a lot of damage there. And we haven't got much to throw against them. Two of the Connecticut militia units are with Heath at Peekskill. Wooster's been trying to get them back." A successful British raid on the Hudson Highlands late in March had prompted Washington to replace McDougall with Heath as commander there and to reinforce him with the Connecticut units, as well as with Arnold's former command at Providence.

"Peekskill is closer to Danbury than we are," Lamb said, adjusting his black eye patch. "Maybe Heath should get over to help out. Has Heath been alerted?" he asked Grayson.

"I dunno, sir."

Lamb turned to Arnold. "This man is a real fountain of information."

"No, he's done well. He's the only man among us deserves a shot yet." He snapped his fingers at the proprietor, who began drawing a mug for Grayson. "Makes no difference, anyway. Heath's a cautious man and that's rough country between Peekskill and Danbury. He'll be afraid this is a feint to draw him out so the British can attack the Highlands again. It's true he has more troops than he needs and we won't have enough, but it makes no difference. We're on our own."

"What about the countryside?" Oswald asked. "Will they turn out?"

Arnold shrugged. "You know as well as I do. You'd think so now that the British are invading their own towns and farms. I hope Wooster is doing everything to stir 'em up."

More men had drifted in, stilling their conversation as they saw the anxious group surrounding Arnold. He now returned his attention to the map and studied it a long time before speaking again.

"All right," he announced, "here's what we're going to do. I'll take two men and go find Wooster. We'll see what kind of an instant army we've got. I'll take Ozzie with me, too—we'll be short of officers. You can manage without him, John, as well trained as our lads are. Whatever we've got, we'll give the British as rough a time as we can, every step of the way. When they get back down to Compo Point, if they do, I want the Artillery Company of New Haven in position to give them a nice warm welcome."

Lamb was skeptical. "How do we know they'll leave by Compo Point?"

"Obviously, we don't. You just watch the ships. Go wherever they go. Nine times out of ten they'll leave the same way they came in."

Lamb shook his head. "Moving those pieces thirty miles? Jesus!"

"You can't expect the British to be nice enough to come to you. You've got to go where they are, for Christ's sake! Besides, you've got good roads all the way." Arnold pointed to the map again. "Now listen carefully. I want you to cross the Saugatuck and set up on the other side—the *west* bank. Position yourself *south* of the bridge, toward the sound. I'll keep them on the *other* side of the river from you, the *east* side. That way they can't attack you when they come down, but they have to pass right in front of you, between the river and Compo Hill. You open fire once enough of them are past the bridge. They won't take the time to back up and cross the river to stop you—they'll run for it. And that should give you some good shooting."

Lamb nodded. It was a good plan. "How will you do that—keep 'em on the east bank?"

Arnold slapped Lamb's shoulder as he rose. "Don't worry about it! Just get your men and guns there in time."

"And when is that? How much time do we have?"

"If they're going to do anything in Danbury," Arnold mused, "they can't possibly get back down to the water until late tomorrow at the earliest. With some opposition to deal with—it'll be some time on Monday."

"We'll be ready."

"Good. One round for everybody and then let's move."

That night at ten o'clock, Arnold stood on a hill in Bethel with Major-General David Wooster and watched the red glow in the sky that meant that Danbury, two miles distant, had been put to the torch. The Americans had sniped at the British flanks during the waning hours of daylight, but with fewer than five hundred men assembled, including the one remaining regiment of militia, they had been powerless to do more. Agents were scouring the countryside throughout the night to drum up more volunteers.

"What a sad sight," said Wooster in his gravelly voice. "If I had all my regiments, we'd give 'em some real trouble."

Arnold nodded, but he knew that even if the Connecticut regiments at Peekskill were on hand he and Wooster still would not be able to match the British force. From a few captured soldiers, they had learned that the enemy numbered in excess of two thousand men, all light infantry except for one artillery company to handle the train of small brass cannon they had with them. The commander was William Tryon, one of the most hated of the enemy, the former Royal Governor of North Carolina, now the Governor of New York. With the onset of the war, it had become a nominal office; the British governed only where their army was, making it literally a military government. So Tryon, who thought of himself as a military man more than a politician, passed his time dreaming up raids on lightly defended areas. It was he who had raided the Hudson Highlands earlier in April.

"Too bad we couldn't save the stores," Arnold said.

"Yes," Wooster said. "This will be a terrible blow to the commander-in-chief. Damn it all, he shouldn't have taken my troops!" In his sudden, crisp way, he turned to Arnold and offered his hand. "Strange that you and I should be comrades. I want you to know I'm glad you're here."

Arnold shook his hand and said, "Thank you, General."

He knew that Wooster thought of him as an impudent upstart. He thought of Wooster as a tired old has-been. But the two men now had grudges against Congress in common: Wooster for his reduction to militia commander and Arnold for being passed over unfairly for promotion.

"Any ideas?" Wooster asked.

"We can't stop them. All we can do is make them pay as much as possible and delay them as long as we can. The longer we keep them inland, the more men we'll get and the more damage we'll do. Let's divide our men. One force to circle around and harass them from the rear once they leave Danbury. The other to stay in front of them, setting up a roadblock wherever possible."

"Divide our force in the face of a superior enemy?"

"It doesn't very often make sense," Arnold said, looking at Wooster with a penetrating gaze. "In this case, it does."

Wooster thought about that for a moment. "Yes, I see what you mean. I'll give you your choice, General."

Arnold had no fear of being overruled. He wanted the tougher job—getting in the enemy's way instead of pecking at him from the rear. "I'll stay in front."

"Done." Wooster nodded.

*   *   *

Early the next morning Arnold took up a position at Ridgefield, far enough south of Danbury to allow time to build a roadblock. He chose a spot on the road that was flanked by broken country with a large outcropping of rock on the left and a farmhouse on the right. Beyond the farmhouse was a small open field that quickly became a swamp. Beyond that was more rocky ground and dense forest.

The ranks had swelled during the night, but the turnout was not even remotely comparable to the "minutemen" of Massachusetts two years earlier. Arnold now had five hundred volunteers and Wooster had another hundred plus his last militia regiment of three hundred Fairfield County men, the First Connecticut, under the command of Colonel Jedediah Huntington. Arnold's men were as varied as the populace of Connecticut, their garb ranging from frock coats to homespun; their privately owned weapons ranging from pikes and antique pistols to Pennsylvania rifles. All morning they had toiled to barricade the road between the rocks on the left and the farmhouse on the right, using wagons, furniture, logs, stone, and earth. Finally, they could do no more. Arnold sent Oswald and a hundred men to disperse into the broken country to the left, to the slope and the top of the rock escarpment. It was all he could do against the obvious British flanking maneuver. He had another hundred men inside the farmhouse and outbuildings and grouped behind them to cover the small field on the right. Another hundred were set back in reserve, ready to move to either flank. That left two hundred at the barricade, arranged in firing lines. Arnold was at the center on horseback.

By eleven o'clock the last patches of morning fog were lifting under a weak sun. It was quiet except for an occasional muffled conversation and nervous cough. Then Arnold's scouts appeared, running back from another wooded area several hundred yards to the north, waving to indicate that the British were nearing. Soon the British advance party came into view where the road curved out of the woods. The advance party halted when they spotted the barricade, awaiting their officers and the main body. Then a rustling sound could be heard, the eerie noise of thousands of footfalls. The mounted officers came into view followed by the column, ten abreast, that seemed to stretch endlessly. Arnold could feel the chill running through his men as the column halted and the silence returned.

"All right, lads, easy does it," he said.

He could see the enemy officers conferring. They would be wondering how much of a force was behind the barricade, whether they should just forge ahead or try to go around it. Then the distant sound of musket fire could be heard, followed by the booming of cannon. The scale of the sound could mean only one thing—Wooster was attacking from the rear. Arnold cursed. The plan was that Wooster would limit himself to harassing the enemy until he was sure that Arnold was fully engaged. Now it seemed he had attacked. Arnold tried to think of something he could do to help Wooster. He knew that to leave his position to attack would be suicidal.

Among all the men he had found exactly twenty-three who owned Pennsylvania rifles. He had grouped them into a sharpshooter's platoon. He called over to them now. "You sharpshooters. Commence firing. Everyone else, hold your fire." It was all he could do.

The rifles were much more accurate than the muskets, but took longer to load. The muskets had a smooth bore and took a ball smaller than the caliber of the barrel. This allowed the weapon to be used even as it was fouled by ash and grime, but it meant that the direction of the ball was affected by whichever side of the barrel it last happened to touch as it was propelled from the muzzle. And that meant that accuracy was only a sometime thing. On the other hand, the rifle barrel was striated and the ball was wedged in tightly by means of a greased cloth patch wrapped around it. In the hands of a veteran who knew how to compensate for drift, that meant accuracy over distances of two hundreds yards and more.

The sharpshooters were having an effect. Some of them were as good turkey shooters as Morgan's Virginia Riflemen, Arnold thought. He let out a whoop of joy when he saw an officer tumble off his horse. He hoped it was Tryon. With wounded men suddenly on the ground, the British drew back a bit with the front ranks taking cover. "Cease firing," Arnold shouted. Soon the distant sound of musket and cannon fire ceased as well, and the eerie silence returned. A long time passed. Arnold was content to wait all day if it meant keeping the British from their escape via Long Island Sound. Then he saw them bringing up the brass cannon.

"Take cover, lads," he cried. "This can't hurt us much."

For an hour the British tried to blast the barricade out of the way, but for the most part the cannonade only helped to solidify it. Only a few men were wounded, one with a huge wood splinter sticking out of his chest like a spear.

The calm returned. And then Arnold sensed the attack coming. He carefully loaded and primed his Scottish pistol. "Get ready!" he shouted. Five minutes later, the British troops spread out as much as they could and began moving forward on the double, straight ahead, but then a large contingent veered toward Arnold's left flank across the broken country, a smaller party to the right.

"Fire at will!" Arnold commanded, and the air was filled with the resounding clatter of musket fire, acrid smoke rising in swirls. Arnold wheeled about to shout and shove his reserve off to the left. He watched them run and wondered how many would simply run away. Turning around, he cantered back and forth, shouting encouragement.

The enemy was coming in a rush, some redcoats and German jaegers in their coats of forest green, but mostly the hated Loyalists in their coats of

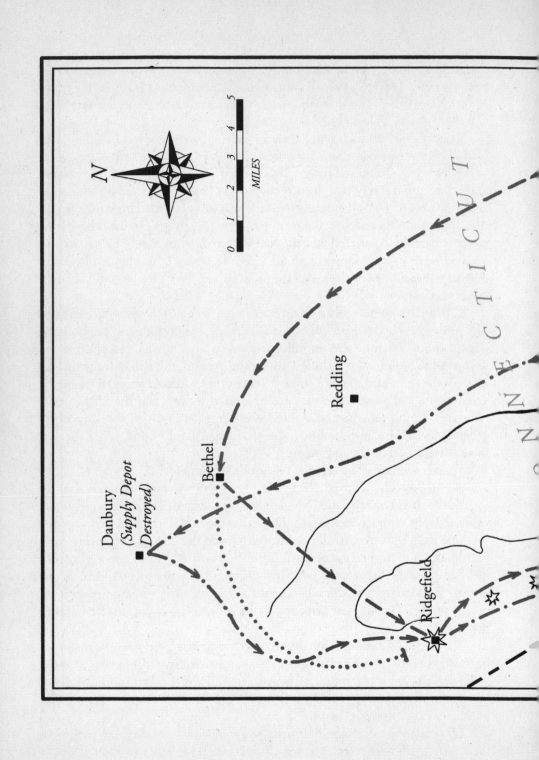

N

MILES
0 1 2 3 4 5

Danbury
(Supply Depot
Destroyed)

Bethel

Redding

Ridgefield

CONNECTICUT

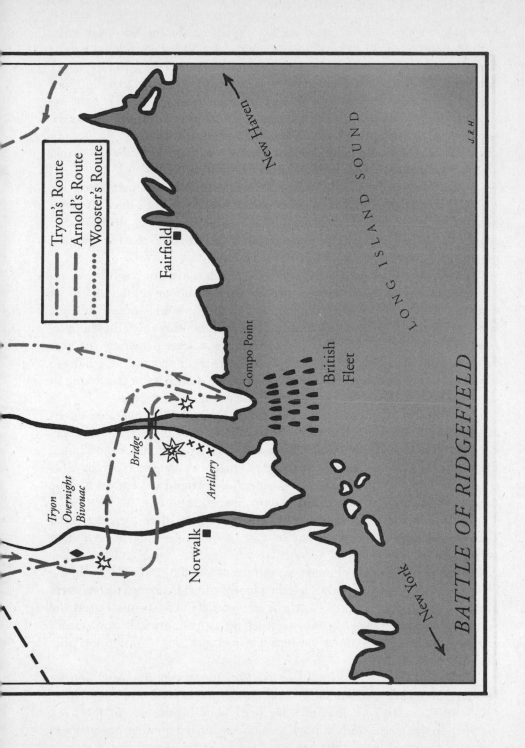

Tryon's Route
Arnold's Route
Wooster's Route

New Haven

LONG ISLAND SOUND

J.R.H.

Fairfield

Compo Point

British
Fleet

Bridge

Tryon
Overnight
Bivouac

Artillery

Norwalk

New York

BATTLE OF RIDGEFIELD

bright apple green. Arnold could see that they were coming European style, with bayonets fixed. The British loved that; the Americans considered it to be barbarous and they feared it. The British casualties were heavy, and the attack sputtered, fell back, and then came on again with renewed strength. Once again the enemy faltered under withering fire, then surged forward. For one exultant moment, Arnold thought he might hold, that concentrated fire in the bottleneck of a road might be too much for the British. But out of the periphery of his vision, Arnold could see that dozens of his men had fallen, too, that the dirt road behind the barricade was becoming slimy with blood.

Every time Arnold spotted a man turning, blanched and panic stricken, throwing his weapon down and beginning to flee, he charged after him with sword waving. He chased one man and whacked him so hard on the shoulders that he drew blood and sent the man sprawling. "Get back in that line, you son of a bitch!" he roared.

There comes a moment in any such attack when the calculations of battle—numbers of men fallen, men running, men shooting, the intensity of noise, the distance remaining—begin to bring the knife edge of terror to the bravest defender. The fear is a physical thing, concentrating along the shoulder blades and the back of the neck the moment one attacker penetrates the line, for now there is confusion and the defender fears an unseen enemy, a blow to the back of the head, a bayonet in the back. The defenders began fleeing in droves. Enemy soldiers were scrabbling at the top of the barricade.

For the moment, the right appeared to be holding, but only because the attackers on that side, seeing their comrades surmounting the barricade, veered back toward the road. Arnold rode back and forth, trying to block the flight of his men with his horse, screaming at them to hold a bit longer, to continue firing as they fell back. But the panic was general and Arnold suddenly was alone except for the dead and wounded and onrushing enemy.

At that moment more than twenty Hessians appeared on the crest of the rock escarpment thirty yards to the left of the barricade. Like an enlarged firing squad, they all took aim at Arnold. He wheeled his horse and the volley crashed down. The horse plummeted, and Arnold hit the ground hard, sliding along his face and shoulder through the bloody grime, his sword thrown free. He felt a sharp pain in his right ankle; it was twisted in the stirrup. Dazed, the wind knocked out of him, he pushed himself up with one arm. He saw a green-coated Loyalist bearing down on him, bayonet gleaming. "You're my prisoner," he shouted.

Arnold gulped air. He felt his foot free from the stirrup. In one motion, he snatched his pistol, rolled on the ground, and leaped to his feet in a crouch.

"Not yet, you Tory bastard!" He fired point-blank and hit the Tory squarely in the chest. With a quick motion he dodged another bayonet and slammed the metal pistol sideways into the face of the second man, breaking his jaw. He darted off to the right, running low and zig-zagging, plunging into the swamp as bullets whined around him, ripping his hat off, tearing through an epaulette.

Less than hour later Arnold had rounded up more than a hundred of his volunteers. They were resting in a glade in the forest, waiting for more to straggle in. Arnold sat with his back to a tree, no longer panting but still clutching his pistol. He was uninjured aside from the sprained ankle and painful shoulder. His face was smeared, his uniform torn in a dozen places, one whole side stained in blood, though not his own. Arnold was certain that the ankle was not broken, though it was swollen to nearly twice its normal size; he wondered how he had been able to run so swiftly.

Huntington had survived the attack at the rear and he soon joined Arnold with more than a hundred men of his regiment. He explained that Wooster had insisted on attacking. The British cannon had been located toward the rear of their march so that they were soon used against Wooster. At the cannon bursts, the men began to flee, leaving Wooster standing there trying to rally them. Grapeshot had broken his spine, killing him instantly.

"Damn," Arnold said. "I didn't much care for the old man, but he had guts."

Arnold had sent men to round up more of his fighters, and small groups began arriving. Soon Oswald showed up with more than forty of his men. The overjoyed Arnold rose and embraced his friend. "Damn my eyes," he cried, "you're too crazy to kill!"

Oswald began explaining how he had been overwhelmed on the left, but Arnold shut him up. "I know, I know, don't worry. We did as much as ever I thought we could, even more." The pain from his ankle caused him to sag back to the ground.

"Oh, you've got a nice one," Oswald said, kneeling to examine the ankle. He had experience in treating wounded men. "I don't think it's broken," he said. He rummaged in his haversack and pulled out a long roll of linen.

"The best thing would be cold compresses," Arnold said, "but we don't have time for that. I've got to find a horse soon. Just bind it up, Ozzie, best you can."

Oswald wrapped the linen around the ankle, and he and Huntington helped Arnold to his feet. He took a few tentative steps.

"How is it?" Huntington asked.

"At least it's not the same leg that was hit at Quebec," Arnold said. "Now I feel equalized." He consulted his pocket watch. "We held 'em up for a half a day and we hurt 'em, by God we did!" He spoke to the group in general. "All right, let's get organized. We've got a long afternoon ahead of us."

*   *   *

The next day at noon, Arnold watched the British column approach from his position on the west bank of the Saugatuck River, half a mile above the bridge. The more than twenty miles from Danbury to the sea had been a torment for the invaders. Arnold had not been able to assemble enough mass to effect another blockade, but the harassment had been almost constant, with so many skirmishes that he had lost count. He had soon borrowed the indispensable tools of command in battle, a horse and a sword. When Tryon learned that Arnold was back in action, he tried to increase his pace, but instead had been slowed by the almost constant need to redeploy in the face of American raids. The invaders had spent an uncomfortable night encamped, crouched behind a heavy picket line. Now they were poised for their last dash to safety. The British fleet was clearly visible on the sparkling waters of Long Island Sound, anchored as close as possible to where the east bank of the Saugatuck became Compo Point.

Committed to forcing the British to the east bank before the bridge, Arnold tried to make his force of nearly six hundred men appear as formidable as possible. He knew the British could overwhelm him—even with their losses they still outnumbered him at least three to one. But Tryon might not know that with certainty, possibly having in mind the stories of how thousands of farmers had appeared in '75 as if by magic to threaten the British column's return to Boston from Lexington and Concord. Arnold was gambling that Tryon would have little stomach for what looked like another encounter with a barricaded force, not with safety plainly in sight. He was right; the enemy began fording the river beyond his range. He moved some men up to snipe at them and continued peppering as the British returned fire and moved along the opposite shore at double time.

As soon as the bulk of the enemy passed the bridge, Arnold assembled his men and crossed to fall in on their rear. The British fought a rearguard action as the main body moved along comfortably, safety now very near. And then the Artillery Company of New Haven opened up, five cannon booming grapeshot across the river, enfilading the main enemy force.

Lamb and his men worked furiously, keeping the bombardment going. The enemy panicked. Dozens of men fell. Others began scrabbling up the slope of Compo Hill. Those who still had loot from Danbury dropped it and ran pell-mell for the sea. Arnold threw back his head and screamed a wild, piercing battle cry. On foot now, he led the attack, sword waving in the air, the pain of his ankle once again forgotten. The Americans fell on the shrinking enemy rear guard in hand-to-hand fighting. And then the longboats began pulling in, filled with Royal Marines coming to the rescue. The artillery fire began petering out as the guns fouled and the ammunition ran low.

Arnold's men stopped advancing. The British stopped their flight; they formed a solid line and began firing in orderly fashion. The Americans began to flee. Arnold exhorted them to stay and keep firing; the British wouldn't attack now. But soon he faced the enemy virtually alone, only Oswald and a handful of men with him. Arnold cursed the fates, fervently wishing for a few hundred soldiers of the kind who wouldn't flee under fire, the kind he'd had with him at Quebec.

The battle was over. The expedition had succeeded in destroying the military stores of the Continental Army at Danbury but had cost the British much more dearly than expected in casualties, nearly four hundred troops. The Americans, with their hit-and-run tactics, had lost fewer than one hundred, though several hundred had fled after the hot action at Ridgefield.

Arnold finally turned his back on the British and began to limp toward the bridge. His eyes glowed with a demonic fury. Some of the men who had fled and taken cover shrank away as he passed. He came upon the brass cannon that the British had abandoned in their flight to safety, and the sight suddenly struck him as comical. How much effort and money it had taken to round up five vintage cannon, and now the Artillery Company of New Haven would have some shiny new brass pieces, free of cost! Tryon would be a very unhappy man! Arnold laughed, looked across the river at Lamb and his men, and shook his fist in a victory signal. A rousing cheer echoed back.

Arnold and Oswald walked across the bridge to where Arnold retrieved his horse, and then they moved down to greet the others. Arnold came up to Lamb and shook his hand. "They'll think twice before they come back here. Good work, John." He shook the hand of every man of the Artillery Company of New Haven.

Chapter 22

Morristown
May 13, 1777

For once, the bad news that came into headquarters at Morristown turned out to be good—for a while at least. And then it turned bad again.

The first report on the British raid at Danbury was dismal. There were two salient facts: the supply depot had been totally destroyed and General Wooster was dead. There were polite lamentations about Wooster, but it did not require great perception to recognize that as far as headquarters was concerned the real disaster was the loss of the supplies. General Washington seemed obsessed by the fact that three thousand tents had been burned.

There was an admixture of guilt, too, although it was not discussed at the higher echelons. Everyone knew that the order sending the Connecticut militia units to the defense of the Hudson Highlands, leaving Danbury exposed, had come straight from headquarters.

The gloom eased the next day when reports came in that two privateers had run the British blockade, one arriving at Philadelphia and the other at Little Egg Harbor, New Jersey. Both were loaded with supplies from France, including tents, cloth for uniforms, leather, flintlocks, and powder. The good feelings occasioned by this intelligence turned into jubilation when confirmed reports arrived from Connecticut to the effect that the British raiders had taken a severe mauling and that it had been largely due to the heroic leadership of Benedict Arnold.

Hamilton was treated to the rare sight of Washington almost beside himself with glee. The chief kept slapping his writing table and chortling.

"That Arnold!" he laughed, wiping tears from his eyes. "I knew he'd find a way! Now they'll *have* to promote him!"

Later, Hamilton commented wryly to Tilghman: "You'd think Arnold *planned* the whole affair, just to get promoted."

"I know," Tilghman said. "But you do have to give the man credit. He's remarkable. I didn't even know we *had* an Artillery Company of New Haven, and it's my job to keep track of these things. Apparently Arnold created it all by himself."

To no one's surprise, word arrived a few days later that Congress had belatedly commissioned Arnold a major-general. This was followed a day later by a copy of another resolution that read:

That the Quarter-Master General be directed to procure a horse and present the same, properly caparisoned, to Major-General Arnold in the name of this Congress, as a token of their approbation of his gallant conduct in the action against the enemy in their late enterprise to Danbury, in which General Arnold had one horse killed and another wounded.

These actions were discussed with relish at the staff meeting the next day until Greene, puzzling over the text of the first resolution, pointed out that something was missing. Congress had promoted Arnold to the next highest rank, but had failed to restore his *seniority*. Although he now was of the same rank, the five men who had been promoted over his head were still senior to him, because their promotions were dated earlier.

At first, Hamilton thought it was rather a nice point that could be glossed over, but he soon saw the significance as the older officers discussed it. The fact that Congress, in the act of promoting Arnold, had still kept him subordinate to *his* former subordinates, men of much less experience and renown than he, could be regarded as the verification of an insult instead of a reward, especially in the light of yet another example of Arnold's initiative and courage in action and his ability as a commander. In this context, the gift of the horse, apparent afterthought that it was, became a mere sop—a "token" as the citation itself said. The good news had turned bad.

Greene tried to keep alive some hope. "After all, Arnold *is* a major-general now," he mused. "Maybe he can ignore the business about seniority. We should try to persuade him."

Knox shook his leonine head. "What would you do?"

"What do you mean?"

"If you were in his shoes, if this happened to you?"

Greene's exasperated expression was answer enough. "Of course," Knox said. "You'd resign. Trying to persuade Arnold to ignore this only insults him further."

"Why does Congress do this?" Washington asked. "If they're going to reward him why not do it properly? They must know he can't accept unless his seniority is restored as well."

Greene, who had become something of the group's expert on the fallibility of Congress, had an explanation. "They want it both ways. They feel they have to reward Arnold for his obvious heroism, and yet they don't want to admit they made a mistake in passing him over in the first place. Some of these fools probably won't even understand why Arnold can't accept this."

"He'll have to petition Congress," Washington said. "It's his only recourse. Perhaps they can be persuaded on the matter of seniority. It does seem a small thing once they've gone this far."

That afternoon the chief summoned Hamilton for dictation. In a somewhat plaintive letter to Congress, Washington expressed his pleasure over Arnold's promotion, but asked: *What will be done about his rank? He will not act most probably under those he commanded but a few weeks ago.* Then he wrote to Arnold approving his request to come to headquarters for a meeting, knowing full well that Arnold would ask for help and for permission to go to Philadelphia to seek vindication.

On the day that Arnold arrived in camp, less than three weeks after the action in Ridgefield, Hamilton was an amused witness to some of the trappings and mysteries of fame. Washington ordered a detachment of his own Life Guards to escort Arnold from the picket line, an honor reserved for unusually distinguished visitors. The word had spread throughout the encampment, and there could be no doubt of Arnold's popularity with the rank and file. For an army badly in need of reasons to cheer, his presence was like a tonic. The men poured out in droves to shout and wave as the "fighting general" rode by, and he returned their fervor with a huge grin. Even Caleb Gibbs and his Life Guards, normally among the most laconic of men, seemed imbued with a sense of honor in escorting the hero, riding bolt upright and with a verve that reflected their pride. A large welcoming delegation spilled out of the headquarters building, led by Knox and Greene and most of Washington's aides.

To Hamilton, it all seemed a bit out of proportion to the minor affair at Ridgefield, but then one had to consider that that followed Ticonderoga, Quebec, and Valcour Bay, to mention only the most famous of Arnold's exploits. And one also had to consider that he had risked his life without hesitation at Ridgefield despite his ill treatment at the hands of Congress, something that perhaps few men would have done. Indeed, Arnold's current situation made him a champion of another kind, a test case in upholding the military code against unwarranted and ignorant civilian intrusions. Despite himself, Hamilton felt excitement at the prospect of meeting a man who rapidly was becoming a living legend.

Arnold himself was clearly charged by the stir he had created in camp. He seemed to radiate energy as he reined up smartly and dismounted with athletic grace. Hamilton got an impression of virility, of a powerful torso for a man of medium height, and of strong white teeth set off by a somewhat swarthy complexion. Arnold gave the assembled group a precise salute, and then flashed a brilliant smile. There was a babble of comradely greetings as Knox and Greene led the surge forward to shake Arnold's hand and clap him on the back.

Arnold disappeared in the crowd about him, but soon Greene was able to start introducing him to the new men. Hamilton suddenly felt his hand clasped in a firm grip and had a sense of being raked over quickly by pale blue eyes.

Knox shouted over the din: "Hey, Ben, this your new horse?"

Arnold laughed. "Hell, no! The new one's coming from Congress. That means I'll get it—well, maybe by Christmas! This here's the last of my own nags. I'll tell you something, though." He went to his horse and lifted a fat leather pouch that was suspended by a drawstring from the pommel of his saddle. "The day after Ridgefield an old tanner went out to skin my dead horse. He got nine musket balls out of the carcass. You imagine that? Nine! And those were only the ones he could find." He jangled the pouch. "Came all the way to New Haven to give 'em to me as a souvenir. By God, if those Hessians were sharpshooters, I'd be weighted down a bit!" He gave an exaggerated impression of a man with posture tilted way over to one side, to the mirth of the group.

"You lead a charmed life, Ben!" Greene said.

Arnold nodded emphatically as he hung the pouch back on the saddle. "Damn their eyes, they'll never get me."

Washington appeared on the porch, and the group made way for him as he came down the steps into the courtyard. Arnold stepped forward and saluted. Washington returned the salute and held out his hands. "Well done, *Major-*

General Arnold, well done indeed!" he said, emphasizing the new rank as he clasped Arnold's hands in his.

"Excellency, I'd rather hear that from you than any other reward I could possibly imagine."

"Well, I could think of something else—if it were in my power," Washington murmured, with the hint of a smile. It was an obvious reference to the problem of Arnold's lost seniority. "Come." The chief led the way up the steps and into the building.

On the stairs to the second floor, Hamilton overheard Arnold asking Knox about his wife's health and wondering when it might be possible for him to see Lucy. On the landing Hamilton watched as the chief escorted Arnold into his office and closed the door behind them. Hamilton's curiosity began to mount as it always did on the rare occasions when the chief was closeted alone with someone. As he hoped, it was not long before he was summoned. He was motioned to a seat as soon as he entered Washington's office.

"I've agreed to assign General Arnold temporarily to Philadelphia so that he can make his representations to Congress," the chief explained. "So we need orders and we need to draft a letter in his support."

Hamilton moved his chair closer to the gate-legged table on one side of the room and spread out his paper on the green baize to take notes. Arnold leaned forward and spoke with intensity. "There are three issues, Hamilton," he began. "One, I want my seniority restored. Two, I want an investigation of these wild charges that have been made against me by irresponsible people, the past year and more. Three, I want a full and fair settlement of my accounts."

"Yes, well, I shan't go into details," Washington said in a monotone. He rose. "It'll be a strong letter, you can be sure of that. Colonel Hamilton will see that you receive a true copy before you leave camp."

Hamilton noted that Arnold was quick to read the signals sent out by the chief. When Washington rose, it meant that the meeting was over. Arnold rose, too, and prepared to leave. "Thank you, Excellency."

Washington now seemed lost in thought, gazing past Arnold and Hamilton. Then he made a hesitant motion with his hand. "No, stay a moment." He resumed his seat, as did Arnold. Hamilton stood there awkwardly, not sure whether to go or to stay, until Washington motioned him to sit.

The chief began: "I hope your business in Philadelphia is successful. And soon. We're short of officers. We're going to need you badly, General Arnold."

Arnold expressed his appreciation again, but Washington seemed oblivious. He droned on.

"I tell you in obvious confidence that we've received some disturbing news. It's not general or public knowledge yet, but it will be soon enough. You know the northern territory as well as any man, perhaps better than anyone else. I'd like your assessment. We have confirmation of earlier reports that reinforcements have been sent to Canada once again from England. It seems certain the British again will have a very large army in Canada this season. A major force, possibly twelve thousand men or more. And it is confirmed that the intention once again is to drive down and secure the line of the Hudson River, thus severing New England from the rest of the states."

Arnold's response was a sardonic half smile. He nodded. "I knew they'd try it again. I never doubted it for a moment. They'll get off to a much faster start this year—because now they control Lake Champlain. Most of it, anyway. We have nothing north of Fort Ticonderoga. Will Carleton remain in command? Or will it be Burgoyne?"

"Our most authoritative source—in London—says that the plan was devised by Burgoyne. And that he'll be in command."

"Makes sense," Arnold said. "They'll blame last year's failure on Carleton. We had word last summer that Burgoyne was anxious to attack us, but that Carleton was being cautious. So, now it's Burgoyne's turn. He'll be more aggressive. Any word about General Howe? Will he attempt to go north from New York to join Burgoyne?"

"Uncertainty there. Some reports say that Howe's army will go north, and others say he has a free hand—to go north if Burgoyne needs help or to attack elsewhere. Indeed one informant maintains that his design is Philadelphia. And to add to the confusion, we have one quite recent report—from Canada— that speaks of the possibility of a *third* army. To swing around to Lake Ontario and then cross New York eastwardly down the Mohawk River Valley to a junction with Burgoyne at the Hudson, above Albany. I hardly know whether to credit this."

This last clearly intrigued Arnold. "I would," he said. "General Schuyler suspected they might try that last year. It sounds to me like the kind of stew Burgoyne would cook up for us. That third army—the point there would be to stir up the Indians further and take advantage of Loyalist sentiment in the valley. And secure an easy source of food for his main army instead of depending on Canada. Altogether, it's a mean threat. They really are bastards, the British. How soon do you think Burgoyne will be ready to begin?"

Hamilton winced, but Washington took no notice of Arnold's language. "There's reason to believe that Burgoyne may already have arrived in Quebec by now," the chief said. "I'm expecting confirmation any day. Half of his army is already in Montreal. Give him time to organize, provision, consolidate his forces, and then march to St. Jean to come down to the lake. A month perhaps. We think he could be investing Ticonderoga some time after the middle of June."

"How will you position yourself, Excellency?"

Washington rose and walked over to his map table, staring down, as if he could find the right answer somewhere in the disarray of papers. "I am certain of only two things," he said in a low voice. "First, my chief concern must be the main enemy force under General Howe. I'll do what I can to help the Northern Department. But my resolve must be to counter Howe. Wherever he goes—to the north, to Philadelphia, wherever—I must go. Recently he's been demonstrating in New Jersey, trying to draw us out. We'll wait until he reveals his hand."

After a long silence, Arnold asked: "And the second thing, Excellency?"

Washington managed a smile. "Yes, the second thing I'm sure of—I'm going to need you very much. All of this is why I hope your affairs in Philadelphia go well—and swiftly."

Arnold's mind was racing. Perhaps Schuyler and Gates could cancel each other out in their struggle to control the Northern Department. And that could mean that if Congress restored his seniority, Arnold would be in a position to—no, it would be too much to expect this season. The realistic goal for Arnold was to be second-in-command in the Northern Department to whichever of the two adversaries prevailed. Then the following year, depending on what happened in battle, he could be in command—and perhaps second only to Washington in the entire Continental Army. And then—but he realized that Washington would say nothing about a specific assignment until the current problem of Arnold's seniority was cleared up.

He made ready to leave, fortified by the knowledge that the chief very badly wanted him in a key role in the north. He mumbled the conventional sentiments, ready to be of service wherever and whenever the chief needed him, and so on, and left, anxious first to see Lucy Knox and learn if there was any word from Betsy DeBlois—and then to get on to Philadelphia.

After Arnold left, Washington fell silent again, staring out the window. Finally, he began to dictate. It was one of the strongest letters to Congress that Washington had written, endorsing Arnold without reservation and insisting that he be fully heard. The final paragraph stated:

It is needless to say anything of this gentleman's military character. It is universally known that he has always distinguished himself as a judicious, brave officer, of great activity, enterprise, and perserverance.

PART VI

The Road to Saratoga

From the narrative of Sir Thomas Stanley, KB

The weather in the North Atlantic, as our armada of troop ships and supply vessels sailed to Canada, was a good omen for the exciting campaign that lay before us. It was the best of his three crossings, my uncle said. The winds were even favorable for proceeding up the broad Saint Lawrence estuary to Quebec, and the ice had already disappeared by the time we arrived on May 6th, the result of the mildest winter any Canadian could remember.

Another good omen occurred in the first meeting my uncle held, the one he had been dreading—with Sir Guy Carleton, in his austere office in Quebec's Recollet Convent. A hostile governor-general would have been serious trouble for the expedition, because so much depended on supply lines and other support from Canada. Sir Guy clearly was not happy at being superseded by General Burgoyne as commander of the invasion force, but his anger was directed mainly at Lord Germain. Carleton's basic decency showed when, to my uncle's vast relief, he pledged to do everything within his power to support the expedition.

Montreal was the assembly point for the invasion army, and the five thousand troops that had come from England with us proceeded to that destination to join those that had wintered in Canada. My uncle and I stopped at the halfway point, Trois Rivieres, to meet with the Baron von Riedesel, commander of the German troops. He was unhappy because War Office rules specified that British officers could command German troops, but not the other way around. Burgoyne said he would petition on the matter and in the meantime see that the Germans operated in self-contained units as much as possible. Somewhat mollified, von Riedesel's anger disappeared when my uncle told him he had approved the request of the Baroness to come to Canada.

Then it was on to Montreal, to a jubilant reunion with General Phillips, to endless days of hard work to solve problems and prepare the army—and to a grand review on June 4th in honor of the King's birthday and the arrival of the commanding officer.

Chapter 23

Montreal and St. Jean, Canada
June 4–16, 1777

"Truly," Sir Guy Carleton said, "this is the most splendid army I have ever seen."

But certainly not the largest, Burgoyne mused, standing next to Carleton on the wooden platform erected on the heights above the Faubourg des Recollets in Montreal. He was still unhappy over the fact that the twelve-thousand-man army he had called for in his plan had shrunk to less than ten thousand. But yes, if one speaks of quality rather than quantity—appearance, perfection in drill, morale, military experience, caliber of the officer corps—it was indeed the most splendid army *he* had ever seen as well.

On the reviewing stand, Carleton and Burgoyne were in the company of Major-General Will Phillips, Major-General Baron Friedrich Adolf von Riedesel, and a score of aides and civilian leaders The parade ground was a sea of motion and color, as eight British regiments marched by in their brilliant scarlet uniforms, flags and pennants snapping in the breeze. Next came nearly four thousand German troops divided among grenadiers, light infantry, and Prince Ludwig's dragoons. To their disgust, the dragoons were dismounted and would remain so throughout the campaign, unless suitable horses could be captured in the Colonies. None could be transported from Europe and none were to be had in Canada.

In position at one end of the parade ground were forty-two of General Phillips's artillery pieces, manned by nearly five hundred artillerymen in their dark blue coats with red facing. Ninety-six more guns had already been moved to St. Jean to be loaded aboard the transport ships for the invasion.

Tonight the town of Montreal would be illumined and special festivities, including a "grand publick ball," would take place in honor of the King. Above the reviewers fluttered the Royal Standard, a flag normally raised only when the sovereign himself was physically present but lately used to show dominion on special occasions, the symbolic presence of the British monarchy. The flag bore the three golden lions of England, the red lion of Scotland, the harp of Ireland, and the fleur-de-lis of France, the last because George III still adhered to the fifteenth-century notion that the British monarch also ruled France.

So stirring was the sound of drums and bugles and the pageant of marching men that Burgoyne for a time could forget the nagging problems of supply, of making baggage carts out of green wood and trying to find draft animals to haul them, of the shortfalls in the irregular components of his invasion force—Canadians, Indians, and Loyalists. Instead, Burgoyne's spirits soared. There was certainly nothing wrong with the *regulars* of his army—the experienced British and German troops, and, above all, the superb cadre of officers that commanded them. Nothing could stop so fine an army.

There was one jarring note later when Phillips reported to Burgoyne that he had suddenly become aware that the details of the invasion plan were common knowledge in Montreal.

"I don't understand," Burgoyne said. "Obviously, with all of our troops converging on Montreal, everyone knows we're planning an invasion."

"No, I mean the entire plan in detail," Phillips said. "A paper was circulating in the city with a description of the size and makeup of the army, the plan for St. Leger's expedition, three armies converging on Albany, everything."

"How the devil could that happen?"

"Carleton is investigating. No answer yet. Meanwhile, I've ordered the taverns closed, to stop this rumor-mongering. It's a good idea, with all the troops coming here."

"All right. For the time being, anyway. We've got to get to the bottom of this. We'll hang whoever's responsible."

Over the next several days, Phillips arranged a series of meetings for Burgoyne with principal figures in the invasion plan. The first session was with Colonel Barry St. Leger—Phillips pronounced the name "Silliger" as did everyone—to discuss the Mohawk Valley expedition. St. Leger, a beefy, red-faced nephew of an Irish viscount, had been recommended by Germain. He had a reputation for being a harsh disciplinarian and having too much fondness for spirits, but as a veteran of warfare in Canada and the wilderness he seemed a good choice. With him came Sir John Johnson, commander of the Loyalist ranger corps known as the Royal Greens. As the only son, he had inherited his father's vast estate north of the Mohawk but had barely escaped when a rebel mob attacked the mansion. He made an arduous seventeen-day trek through the wilderness to reach Montreal, accompanied by nearly a hundred of his followers, the men who now were the nucleus of the regiment. Johnson seemed commendably eager to return to his native territory to teach his former neighbors a lesson.

"What's the size of your ranger corps now?" Burgoyne asked Johnson.

"It's already doubled, sir, to more than two hundred. Once we reach the valley," he said, "that number will double again. I'm sure of it. And Colonel Butler is making good progress with his regiment, now near two hundred strong, and his son, Walter, will go to the Mohawk Valley ahead of us to recruit more men."

"And what do you know of the Indian forces?" Phillips asked.

St. Leger was smugly confident. "Joseph Brant has been very busy. We are now certain that he will meet us at Fort Oswego with at least a thousand braves. By the time we get there"—St. Leger shrugged—"who knows? He may have twice that number."

Burgoyne was doing mental arithmetic. The Loyalists, the German jaegers, and three companies of St. Leger's own former regiment, the Thirty-fourth Foot, would total as many as a thousand white men. Adding at least a thousand Indians meant that the Mohawk Valley expedition would meet the target he had set, a sufficient force to deal with any opposition that could possibly arise in the valley so long as the Americans had to deploy most of their troops to defend Ticonderoga and Albany.

When the two men left, Burgoyne turned to Phillips: "We need Joseph Brant here. Or his counterpart. Someone who can stir up Indian recruitment for us. I'm disappointed that we can't get more of the northern Indians for the main army, the Ottawas and Hurons and Abnekis."

Phillips looked shrewdly at Burgoyne. "We *do* have Brant's counterpart now, at least if you approve." He went on: "We need someone who truly knows the Indians, who's worked with them and speaks their languages, whom they respect and will follow. We simply haven't had anyone like that." He paused for effect. "We do now. If you approve."

"All right," Burgoyne said, "let's have it. What are you talking about?"

"I've managed to find La Corne St. Luc."

"My God," Burgoyne said, "I thought he was dead."

"No, he's very much alive. And he's willing to work with us. For a price."

Burgoyne shuddered. St. Luc was of the rare breed of men that it seemed only the French could produce—the Jesuit priest, the fur trapper, the Indian agent, the explorer, men who could forsake civilization and spend their entire adult lives in the wilderness, living and working with the Indians until they seemed to be Indians themselves. St. Luc was particularly notorious, having been one of the chief organizers of the tribes in fighting the British and the Colonials in the French and Indian War. Stories were told of how he calmly watched as the Indians tortured their captives and slaughtered civilians.

"If we traffic with St. Luc, Carleton would clap us in irons." Burgoyne sighed, aware of Carleton's hearty dislike for employing Indians as warriors. "St. Luc must be over sixty by now."

"He's still active. If you want the best Indian fighters, this is the way to do it."

Burgoyne puffed his cheeks. "Well, Sir Guy doesn't necessarily have to know about it right away. If we use St. Luc, I want to make sure he understands my policy. No brutality. I'll meet with him and then we'll decide."

It was soon clear to Burgoyne that Phillips had prearranged everything when he produced St. Luc for an interview the very next day. It was an eerie experience for Burgoyne to see the legendary Frenchman, whose skin was like sandpaper, mottled blue and red. Burgoyne met the piercing gaze from St.

Luc's one good eye and wondered what horrors that eye had seen. St. Luc was always attired completely in black and wore a black eye patch to heighten the sinister effect of his facial expression and reputation.

The conversation was in English because of Phillips's very limited French. Burgoyne explained his views carefully, that his policy was to maximize the advantages of having Indian warriors and scouts in his force and minimize the disadvantages. That meant, above all, *no* atrocities. Burgoyne said he recognized that the Indians must be allowed to take scalps, but only from the dead they had honorably slain in arms.

St. Luc listened patiently, eyebrows raised and lips pursed. At length he spoke slowly in his heavily accented English: "I unnastan' you, m'sieu. We will do our bes'. But zere come a time when ze bus'ness mos' be brutalize." To Burgoyne's puzzled expression, he said: "Ze settlers fear z'Indians—ver' mosh. Zat is to your advantage. It means zey will not come *near* z'army. You will have ver' few raids, ver' few en'my scouts so brave to come near. Ze people will give you zair corn, zair cattle. Ze fear, m'sieu. Ze fear is ver' importante."

It seemed a good statement of the harsh policy George III favored, euphemistically referred to as "distressing" the American settlers until they obeyed out of sheer terror. But Burgoyne would not have it. Considerably more labored conversation was required back and forth before he was convinced that St. Luc understood *his* policy: the Americans' fear of the Indians would be exploited, but actual atrocities would be rigorously avoided.

"I will do my bes' to convey zis to my Indian frans," St. Luc said, "but I also t'ink you mos' do so as well. Zey will be impress by you and your brilliant uniform as z'incarnation of ze Great White Father beyond ze waters." St. Luc explained that, because of Carleton's presence, he should not be visible in Montreal in connection with any Indian recruitment. He was sure he could send as many as one hundred Ottawa and Abneki braves to Montreal, but that he personally would lead the main force he would recruit—as many as five hundred Ottawa and Huron braves—to join the army en route, somewhere along the shores of Lake Champlain. At that point, Burgoyne could address all of the assembled Indians in the name of the Great White Father. An agreement was forged, a bounty was agreed upon, and the rendezvous set for June 20th or thereabouts at the place where the Little Bouquet River flowed into Lake Champlain on its western shore.

The following day, Phillips had another decision for Burgoyne to make. "We need a commissary-general," he said. "Sir Guy has a candidate for us, a civilian named Felix Loescher. He used to be storekeeper at Ticonderoga."

"Well, since we depend on Sir Guy for a steady flow of supplies, perhaps we'd better take his man. Set up a meeting, will you?"

Ironically, it was only when Burgoyne met Felix Loescher that he decided that the dozen or so wives of high-ranking officers who were present in Canada could come along on the invasion instead of staying behind in Montreal. When

Loescher arrived at the Château Ramezay for his appointment, Burgoyne found it curious that he brought his wife with him. He was enchanted. Fanny Loescher was a statuesque, raven-haired, full-bosomed beauty, probably half her husband's age. Burgoyne scarcely paid any attention to Loescher, but once he thought he caught a meaningful look from him. Loescher clearly wanted the job. Was he offering something? Fanny was demure, but her eyes sparkled. She seemed thrilled at meeting such an august personage as a lieutenant-general of the British Army in his radiant uniform, and in such luxurious surroundings. Some of the army wives, Harriet Acland and Frederika von Riedesel in particular, were attractive women, but obviously unavailable. If they were allowed to come with the invasion force, Fanny could come, too. And Burgoyne felt that he was getting a message that Fanny *would* be available—during the trips back to Montreal that Burgoyne would make sure her husband took in order to keep the supplies coming.

Several days later, Burgoyne and Phillips strolled down the corridor of the château toward the ballroom for a meeting with the full officer corps. Phillips was complaining that the American Loyalists he was relying on to recruit troops from the Hudson River Valley area for the main army were not producing anything like Sir John Johnson's results for the Mohawk Valley expedition.

"They've only a handful," he said. "But they're promising wonders once we get down to Ticonderoga. They say men will flock to us then."

"Well, you can't expect much until they get down to their own region," Burgoyne said. "What do you think of Major Skene?"

Phillips frowned. The founder of Skenesboro had signed on as Burgoyne's political adviser. Phillips thought the advice given by Skene so far was not very good. "He's promising wonders, too. Loyalists coming to us in droves, ample fresh provender from the territory of the Hampshire Grants, and so on. He also thinks there are good horses for cavalry to be found there and in New Hampshire as well. I only hope he turns out to be right and half as good as he thinks he is."

Phillips was also concerned about the discontent among the other officers over the fact that he, an artillery officer, had been designated second-in-command of the entire expedition. In some ways, Phillips was the opposite of his suave and mannered chief. A blunt man, little given to small talk and social niceties, Phillips was a grizzled veteran of many campaigns, and somewhere on his body there was a scar as a badge of almost every one of them. On campaign he lived like a scout, prepared, if necessary, to take nothing with him that he could not carry himself. He was totally devoted to the army and to Burgoyne.

"I'd rather withdraw than let this cause rancor and dissension," Phillips said as they strode along.

"Absolutely not," Burgoyne snapped. "I'll take care of it."

Sentries came to attention as the three men arrived at the double doors leading to the ballroom. Burgoyne paused and spoke to Phillips. "As soon as we're finished here, I want you to begin drafting a line of march for Chambly and St. Jean."

"Righto."

"And you can open up the taverns."

"Hold on." Phillips clutched Burgoyne's arm as he was about to enter the ballroom. "I don't think that's a good idea."

"Why not, for the few more days we'll be here? Let the men enjoy themselves, give the tavern keepers and whores some business."

"That's fine. It's those new Indians St. Luc has sent to us that I'm worried about. They've been paid their bounty. If we make liquor available, then we—"

"If our men can drink, so can they."

"Jack!"

Burgoyne vanished through the double doors leaving Phillips to shake his head in dismay. He went along with most of the liberal policies that made Burgoyne the most popular commander in the British Army, but some he regarded as bordering on foolishness.

The hum of conversation in the cavernous room was cut short by a booming voice: *"Tenshun!"* More than one hundred British and German officers leaped to their feet as if released by a single giant spring. Burgoyne strode to the dais and said: "At your ease, gentlemen. Please be seated."

He paced back and forth, surveying his officer corps. There were his two mainstays, Simon Fraser and Baron von Riedesel. Flanking von Riedesel were his three top commanders, Brigadier Von Specht, Colonel Baume, and Colonel Breymann, all known as excellent soldiers. His eyes roved further over the assemblage. He saw Brigadier Hamilton, Brigadier Powell, Colonel Money, Colonel Kingston, and the younger men, Major the Earl of Balcarres and Major Acland, whose wife, the Lady Harriet, was the daughter of an earl. Further back were even younger men, Lord Petersham, the Earl of Harrington, the impetuous Sir Francis Clarke. It was an amazing cross-section of British and German nobility and professional soldiery, the best officer corps that could have been assembled for this or any campaign, in Burgoyne's eyes.

"Gentlemen," Burgoyne began, "before I discuss our plans with you, there is one matter I must dispose of immediately. It has come to my attention—not from the gentleman in question, I might add—that some of you have complained because I have appointed an artillery officer as my second-in-command of the army."

Burgoyne paused as he watched men shift uneasily in their seats. "The nature of warfare is constantly changing," he resumed, "and nowhere is this more true than in the North American wilderness. This is a subject I shall discuss with you frequently. I recognize there is a custom which holds that infantry and cavalry should be commanded only by their own. I consider this an outworn prejudice. I have appointed General Phillips my deputy because he is senior, because he is able and experienced in North American duty, and because he has my complete confidence."

Burgoyne paused again for dramatic effect. "I also respect your views. Therefore, any officer who cannot accept this decision I ask to step forward now and resign from this campaign. I guarantee that this will be done without prejudice."

Phillips's craggy features did not change expression. Inwardly he glowed with a fierce pride and love for Burgoyne.

After a heavy silence, Burgoyne said: "Please understand that any officer who does not resign now will be expected to obey General Phillips's orders as if they were my own. The slightest insubordination to him will be dealt with most severely."

Again Burgoyne waited. No one stirred. After a long interval, he said: "I congratulate you. You have chosen well. You are now the leaders of an expeditionary force that will make history, that will win a campaign and end a war victoriously." He broke into a broad smile "Welcome to the Army of the North!"

The scene at the restored fort and shipyard of St. Jean on June 16th was a festive one. Thousands of soldiers milled about in their colorful uniforms, though many of them had their coattails and hat brims clipped—commissary-general Felix Loescher's solution to the problem of getting material for spare uniforms. The officers agreed that the clipped soldiers would be better off in the wilderness, anyway; the soldiers weren't so sure. Captain Skeffington Luttwidge of the Royal Navy had proudly bedecked his fleet with pennants and banners, and the Royal Standard had been raised once again, this time from the topmast of the newly built large ship, the *Royal George*. The fleet included three captured and repaired American vessels, two of the row galleys and a gundelo.

There had been only one sour note in the final days at Montreal. After the taverns had been opened at Burgoyne's order, there had been a riot of drunken Indians, and, in trying to help put it down, Major Stanley had suffered a broken collarbone and various cuts and contusions. Burgoyne's chief staff aide was lost to him for weeks.

Burgoyne had hosted a gala dinner the evening before in honor of Sir Guy Carleton. Now, as the first columns of troops began boarding their transports for the movement down the chain of outposts to Lake Champlain and American territory, Carleton was preparing to return to Montreal with his escort of dragoons. He and Burgoyne found a secluded spot on the northern docks for a last few minutes of conversation.

"I think I've found out how everyone learned the details of your invasion plan, Jack," Carleton said.

"Oh?"

"It seems that Lord Germain has Canadian partners in land speculation. A prudent businessman, he thought they should know what is likely to be happening in this part of the world. So he wrote to them. And these esteemed *seigneurs* apparently felt no constraints at all in talking about it."

Burgoyne shook his head. "I could think of some things to say"—his voice grated—"but I'd better not."

"I know what you mean," Carleton said. "Ever since Minden, everyone's assumed that Germain's problem is cowardice. It's not. It's slothfulness and stupidity. If not outright corruption."

"The difficulty is that if everyone in Canada knows our design, the Americans will know it, too."

Carleton pursed his lips and surveyed Burgoyne's troubled expression. "I wouldn't worry overly much about it, old boy. Your western expedition is first rate. Your British and German troops in the main army are the best in the world. You have a truly excellent officer corps. Look on the bright side!"

"What's your latest word on the Americans?"

"Well, that's it, you see. Nothing! They've done nothing, as far as I can tell. Ticonderoga is your only real obstacle. A fellow named Anthony Wayne, a Pennsylvanian, has been in command there, and he's done nothing to improve the situation there at all. The garrison virtually disappeared over the winter They're trying to rebuild an army in the north, but with little success so far. Schuyler is still commander, and Gates may have given up trying to unseat him. He's no longer in the north."

"Too bad. The more that Schuyler and Gates fight, the better for us." Burgoyne laughed. "I was hoping to teach Horatio a lesson, some things he never learned when he was on our side. What of Benedict Arnold?"

"Ah, our bête noire, the fiery Mr. Arnold. A curious thing there. He's apparently in disfavor of some sort. Passed over in promotions. I don't know where he is or what command he has, but he's not in the north. Last word was that he's expected to resign."

"The devil you say! He's clearly the best of a rather mediocre lot. A worthy opponent. I can't believe they'd let him go."

"Yes, extraordinary. One suspects they have a counterpart of Lord Germain somewhere, making decisions."

"I must say," Burgoyne mused with a smile, "I'm feeling better already."

"Of course you are, Jack. We really have only these supply problems to worry about. We'll do our best to surmount them. Tomorrow you'll embark on your great adventure, and I give you great joy of it. You may not need Sir William Howe to come north. Though I'm sure by now he has his instructions from London. Three armies will meet at Albany. If I were a betting man, which of course I am not, I would wager on John Burgoyne being there first. Now, I must leave, and I say to you, Godspeed!"

Chapter 24

Philadelphia
July 4, 1777

The dress uniform purchased from Paul Revere was resplendent when Arnold donned it in the morning. Now it was marred by damp patches of sweat, rivulets trickling down his spine and groin. Even so, his excellent physique and relative youth enabled him to withstand the blazing heat better than the other general officers of the Continental Army, who stood shoulder to shoulder on the wobbly reviewing stand, along with a host of congressmen and local leaders.

Some of the reviewers were visibly wilting, but Arnold feared that the overweight Gates, standing next to him, would keel over from heatstroke. Gates's coarse, ugly features were bright red, and he was bathed in sweat. This attracted flies, which the general combated ineffectually, muttering curses under his breath all the while.

Music for the first American anniversary celebration of the Fourth of July was being provided by a Hessian army band, captured intact at Trenton the previous December, a note of irony that Arnold found amusing. The mustachioed Germans were tootling their way through their limited repertoire of American songs, happy to earn their keep by this small service and stoically enduring the clouds of dust raised by curious youngsters, yapping dogs, and the parade of the Philadelphia militia battalions tromping by.

There had been some confusion over the date to be selected for formal recognition of Independence Day. John Adams thought it should be July 2, the date in 1776 when Congress, with New York abstaining, had taken the crucial vote for independence. Adams called for a great celebration every anniversary of that achievement with bells and bonfires. Others thought a more proper date would be July 4th, when Congress attended to the details by adopting the specific text of the Declaration of Independence, after considerable amending of Thomas Jefferson's original prose. A few thought it should be July 8th, anniversary of the day in 1776 when Colonel John Nixon of the Philadelphia militia read the document aloud to the public in this very same spot. Still others thought the right anniversary day should be July 9th, when General Washington had the Declaration read aloud to every brigade of the Continental Army, as the troops waited in New York for the imminent British attack.

Despite the oppressive heat of the day there was a genuine spirit of celebration in the air. A surprisingly large crowd had turned out for the afternoon ceremony in the State House Yard behind the imposing red-brick building where the Congress held its sessions. All morning, bells had pealed through-out the city, though once again the great State House bell remained silent, not because of its famous crack, but because nothing had been done to shore up the rotting wood of the steeple in which the bell rested. So sure were Philadel-phians that their city would be the object of General Howe's expected summer offensive that a resolution had been passed the previous month to remove the State House bell and all major church bells to a place of safety, in order to deny the metal to the British to melt down for armaments—but the work of removal had not yet started.

A slight breeze stirred occasionally, bringing with it a fetid smell from the overworked public privy in one of the Walnut Street corners of the brick-walled yard. No one seemed to mind. A liberty pole had been erected, flags of every description were waved, and the crowd cheered the passing militia parade and the efforts of the perspiring German musicians. More than thirty dignitaries were clustered on the American Philosophical Society's twenty-foot-high circular wood platform, now eight years old, with more dignitaries in reserved seats below the stand, surrounded by the enthusiastic crowd.

One reason for the large turnout was the organizing ability of the radical patriots, led by Joseph Reed and the Supreme Executive Council of Pennsylva-nia. Philadelphia was now in the firm grip of the puritanical patriots who were suspicious of anyone they regarded as less pure than themselves. This seemed to extend even to matters of dress and social behavior. The atmosphere now was grim and egalitarian, though strictures were somewhat loosened for this festive day. Even Congress, having returned to Philadelphia from Baltimore early in March, seemed to defer to the radicals; the Fourth of July celebration was being staged and managed by Reed and his colleagues. The delegates to Congress on the stand seemed as uncomfortable as the generals.

Arnold disliked the ultraradicals instinctively, their dour appearance and holier-than-thou attitude. To him, the real test of patriotism was whether or not a man showed up on the battlefield with a gun in his hands. Those who did not had better have good reason for staying at home, finding some genuinely useful way to support the war effort and doing it in a modest manner, with due appreciation of those engaged in the real work. Service in Congress or on the Supreme Executive Council of Pennsylvania did not quite measure up, as far as Arnold was concerned.

He reserved special dislike for Reed, who, of course, *had* served in the army and was known as a particularly able officer, but who had left his post as adjutant general the previous winter at the low ebb of the Revolution. Wash-ington had counted on Reed, and yet the man had resigned to claim his politi-cal position back home, and this was contemptible in Arnold's eyes.

Now Reed was mounting the podium for the main event, the reading of the Declaration of Independence. He wore the plain broadcloth coat affected by the radicals and a satisfied smile on his lips. His lean face was so clean-shaven it appeared waxen, yet it still had a bluish cast to it. The German band finished making "Yankee Doodle" sound like a Bavarian folk dance, and the crowd cheered lustily.

Reed set his text down and gripped both sides of the podium. He surveyed the crowd intently, eyes darting, the familiar stance of the confident orator asserting his mastery over the audience by waiting patiently for silence. The sounds died down. Soon it was deathly quiet. Even the dogs, struck by the sudden calm, stopped yapping. Still the speaker did not begin.

Reed's mood-setting technique irritated Arnold. He began to wish that Gates, a man of legendary flatulence, would break the silence with one of his shattering farts, but the wind seemed to have already gone out of the sagging figure next to him. It was just as well, Arnold thought. The reviewing stand was showing signs of its age; it probably would collapse under such a strain.

Finally, Reed began. His sonorous voice and the majestic words of the preamble seemed to weave a spell over the audience. It was as if a religious ceremony were taking place. Murmurs of assent rose and fell as Reed gave voice to the "self-evident" truths. Then, when he came to the "long train of abuses and usurpations," to the bill of particulars against the King of Great Britain, his voice shifted to a staccato bark. The crowd soon picked up the rhythm and greeted each incisive charge with a sort of huzzah, a deep rumbling sound of affirmation.

"He has refused to assent to laws most wholesome and necessary for the public good . . ."

Huzzah!

"He has dissolved representative houses repeatedly . . ."

Huzzah!

"He has affected to render the military independent of, and superior to, the civilian power . . ."

Huzzah!

"For quartering large bodies of armed troops among us . . ."

Huzzah!

"For cutting off our trade with all parts of the world . . ."

Huzzah!

"For imposing taxes on us without our consent . . ."

Huzzah!

"He has plundered our seas, ravaged our coasts, burned our towns, destroyed the lives of our people . . ."

Huzzah!

"He is at this time transporting large bodies of foreign mercenaries to complete the works of death, desolation, and tyranny already begun . . ."

Huzzah!

"He has excited domestic insurrections among us, and has endeavored to bring on the inhabitants of our frontiers the merciless Indian savages . . ."

Huzzah!

On and on it went until Arnold began to feel, in a mood of deep sarcasm, that the lowest place in hell surely was reserved for George III. Each indictment was a shaft in the side of the British Lion. Reed was winning the war, right here, with his own spittle and bursting passion and Jefferson's words. Any suspected Tory would be well advised to stay behind locked doors this night. The crowd was whipping itself into a frenzy. Now, Arnold thought, if each man among them would grab his musket and report to the nearest recruiting agent, all would be well.

Reed swung into the finale, to the declaration that the Colonies are free and independent States with the full powers of such States, and each power he enumerated was greeted by a cheer. Then a pause, and, in the most solemn of tones, came the final pledge of "our lives, our fortunes, and our sacred honor." This was met with a shuddering whisper, and then a mighty cheer that outdid all the rest. Despite his dislike of Reed, Arnold found, to his surprise, that he was cheering, too, such was the power of the words and Reed's skill in uttering them.

At last, it was over. The crowd milled about, people dancing and shouting. The foreign mercenaries in the German band, not aware that their kind had been pictured as villains in Reed's text, joined in the cheering, too. Whatever was going on, they seemed to be saying, it must be good to make all these people so happy.

Arnold felt a sudden weight on his shoulders. It was Gates clutching him in a comradely embrace that was really a desperate bid for physical support.

"Ale, ale," he croaked in Arnold's ear. "Let's get out of here."

After carefully descending from the rickety platform, the two generals began threading their way through the crowd, heading for the Indian Queen tavern two blocks distant at the corner of Fourth and High Streets. Fortunately, Arnold thought, the patriots have not taken to closing the taverns for the moral uplifting of the people. Not yet, at least. He had grown weary of his drinking bouts with Gates, but he was thirsty and had nothing else to do. Anything was better than returning too early to his lodgings in the home of Dr. Benjamin Rush. Initially, Arnold had been grateful for free bed and board, but lately he had begun to feel that too high a price of another kind was being exacted from him. Often, he had been trapped and had to listen to the endless moralizing and intellectualizing of Rush, who considered himself to be an expert on everything, especially the art of war. The two men had nothing in common except a shared dislike of Reed—and a growing dislike for each other.

After the bright sunlight, the Indian Queen was a cave. The air was stale with the sour smell of ale, but it was a few degrees cooler inside. Gates and Arnold flopped into chairs at a corner table, and Gates consumed two tankards of ale as soon as the waiter could fetch them. Eyes glazed, he leaned back and belched loudly. He slowed his pace with the third ale, sipping slowly.

The two men had become nearly desperate with frustration. Gates was certain that the main arena of action would be the north and was now passing him by. He had spent a long time promoting himself for the command of the Northern Department, had finally received it a few months ago, and then a surge by the New York delegates and their supporters had reversed Congress's ruling and restored Schuyler to the command. Gates's New England support was as strong as ever, but he had alienated other delegates, especially the New Yorkers. There was no overriding reason for the rest of Congress to succumb to the blatantly political will of the New Englanders and depose Schuyler once again in favor of Gates. And so Gates was stalemated.

"Burgoyne must be at Ticonderoga by now," Gates observed mournfully.

Arnold nodded and said: "And St. Clair is in command there." Arthur St. Clair, one of the five men who had been promoted over Arnold's head, had succeeded Anthony Wayne as commander of the fort.

"Yes, by God, if I had the Northern Department I'd have *you* at Ticonderoga. Wouldn't want anyone else." In reality, Gates was not so sure. Arnold's act of disobeying Gates's order to stay on the defensive on Lake Champlain last fall still rankled. Gates suspected that if Arnold were at Ticonderoga he would march out and meet Burgoyne head on, never mind the fact that Burgoyne's army must surely outnumber St. Clair's garrison by a considerable margin.

"Arthur will give a good account of himself," Gates grumbled. "There'll be a lot of blood shed at Old Ty."

Arnold merely grunted in response. Normally the thought that such a battle might be taking place even now—and that he was missing it—would have agitated him severely. But he feared there would be no more battles for him. He was preoccupied with the mental process of composing another letter of resignation, having been successful in only one of his three issues with Congress. The Board of War had reviewed the charges brought against him by Hazen and Brown and others during the Canadian campaign, in which those malcontents had alleged everything from stealing to treason, and the board had dismissed all of them as "wicked lies." Based on the board's report, Congress had passed a resolution denouncing Arnold's critics for "cruelly and groundlessly aspersing" his good character.

It was sweet justification, but when it came to settling his accounts, Arnold found that men responsible for such matters were interested only in pieces of paper, not the claimant's good character. He had several stormy sessions with the investigating committee appointed by Congress. His claims were voluminous, extending all the way through the Canadian campaign and Valcour Island right up to the money Arnold had laid out for the Artillery Company of New Haven. The most difficult problem was the long, drawn-out Canadian campaign, because of the loss of Arnold's documentation. He had used personal credit with old trading sources in Canada to equip his expedition when his own funds ran low. He also wanted reimbursement for a trading ship he owned that had been burned by American units. True, it was flying a Canadian flag, but Arnold explained that that was just a ruse.

At one point Arnold exploded, asking the committee members if they had any idea what it was like to be commanding officer, quartermaster, paymaster, and financier of an expedition all rolled into one. When they kept asking for documentation, Arnold explained how he had witnessed the destruction of the ship that contained his personal effects, including all of his papers. He inquired scathingly whether the committee expected Sir Guy Carleton to call a temporary halt to the battle so that Arnold could retrieve his papers for the benefit of the money-grubbing clerks of the American Congress.

Finally, the committee offered a settlement of more than Arnold could prove, but considerably less than he was demanding. He dismissed the offer contemptuously. Arnold now had come to believe that this issue colored the third one, that of his seniority. Here he was met with soothing words but endless delay. He nearly lost his temper again when one delegate fatuously explained to him that it was "a matter of republican or monarchical principles at a crucial time." Arnold wondered what he was supposed to conclude—that monarchical principles were better?

He continued to find sympathy from fellow officers, but that gave him little solace, for, in his eyes, Congress insisted on besmirching his honor on two counts. On the financial matter, the delegates would not accept his word of honor; by refusing to restore his seniority, they were in effect registering the belief that Arnold had so small a sense of honor that he would accept the slur. It was an infuriating combination of insults. Once again, Arnold had become acutely self-conscious of his uniform, convinced that every person who gave him more than a passing glance was secretly deriding him.

To cap it all, Arnold had learned that the lovely Miss Betsy DeBlois of Boston had announced her engagement to young Martin Brimmer. Now Arnold had not even the hope of a woman's love for comfort. After so long a time of waiting and hoping, it was a bitter blow. Betsy's poor judgment in choosing Brimmer over him caused her charms to plummet in Arnold's estimation. The news had come to him through the medium of Lucy Knox, who had the bad taste of coupling it with a broad hint that she and other ladies of Boston would dearly love to have items from the trunkful of European finery that Arnold had assembled for Betsy. But he was intent now on somehow retrieving it for himself, hoping that Betsy would have the good grace to return it or that the earlier suggestion that her mother would not allow her to keep it was true. Like a good soldier, Arnold now wanted to save his ammunition for a possible future conquest.

All the while that Arnold had been mentally reviewing his problems, Gates, now recovered from his near case of heat prostration, had been prattling on about *his* problems. Increasingly, the meetings between the two men had taken on the character of dual monologues. They took turns running through the litany of their complaints, neither paying much heed to the other. Arnold still avoided joining in Gates's frequent denunciations of Schuyler, believing as before that he wanted to avoid taking sides in their struggle for control of the Northern Department, to stay on the good side of the two rivals.

The tavern had become crowded and noisy with revelers seeking relief from the heat. Across the room Arnold spotted Thomas Conway, the Irishman from France who had been commissioned a brigadier in the Continental Army. When Conway had joined Arnold and Gates in previous gripe sessions, the conversation had taken a turn that Arnold did not care for—excessive criticism of Washington. This theme seemed to animate Conway and Gates to an astonishing degree. Arnold had his own mixed feelings about the commander-in-chief, but Washington had supported him strongly, clearly holding Arnold in high esteem. There was a certain permissible level in the old army game of griping, but beyond that Arnold refused to participate. He rose, threw some money down on the table, and hastily made excuses as Conway came over to join them.

Outside, the heat was still oppressive, and the sky had the yellowish overcast that often portended one of Philadelphia's violent summer thunderstorms. The sounds of revelry were less than Arnold expected and seemed concentrated over by the river, where more of the taverns were located. That suited him; his mood was so low that he wanted to avoid the celebrants as much as he did Benjamin Rush, and so, trying to clear his mind, he began to walk in a direction where few people now were to be seen, south on Fourth Street. If it began to rain, he would cut over one block to the Rush house on Third Street at the corner of Walnut. Perhaps Rush would not be at home, occupied somewhere with Fourth of July festivities. A happy thought! In any case, there were fine houses down this way, and if the rain held off, Arnold would keep strolling to the southern limits where there were several elegant estates to stimulate his dreams of future wealth and position.

Except for a few weeks when he had been on temporary duty commanding the troops west of the Delaware River in Bucks County to help guard against the maneuverings of General Howe, Arnold had been confined to Philadelphia. Now so much time had passed that he was forced to the point of fateful decision again, and he suddenly had become profoundly weary of Philadelphia, of wrangling with Congress, of the posturing of Rush and Gates, of the smothering heat that blanketed the city.

His most difficult struggle now was to achieve self-restraint. He was eager to lash out at Congress—he dreamed of having some thirty-five consecutive duels to settle scores with those congressmen who either opposed him outright or did not support him, sparing only the dozen or so whom he had identified as friendly. First on his list would be John Adams. He knew that the only intelligent course was to write a temperate letter of resignation once again. In his present mood, forcing himself to yield to prudence was very nearly maddening. He *had* to resign, but with Washington's support there was at least a slim possibility of future reinstatement under honorable conditions. His mind was so weighted down with the prospect of returning to New Haven as a civilian, back to Hannah and the boys and life as a merchant, that he failed to notice the knot of people and carriages drawn up before the house at No. 98 South Fourth Street. He was almost upon them before he realized they were blocking his way. It seemed to be a bevy of women, finely dressed young ladies, with servants busily unloading chests and boxes from two carriages and a wagon.

And then Arnold saw a man, a thin, spry gentleman in his fifties, prancing about and giving instructions. He saw that one of the women was older than the rest. This was obviously a man and his wife and their daughters—no fewer than four of them—returning from a trip. The man saw Arnold, and a look of fear appeared on his face.

Arnold started to cross the street to avoid this family group but then he stopped. He was too close; it would have been awkward, even impolite. He drew himself up, touched his hat, and said: "Good day to you."

His thoughts had been so gloomy that this came out in an unintended harsh tone. From the perspective of Judge Edward Shippen and his wife, they had suddenly been confronted by a major-general of the Continental Army in full dress uniform with a stern, foreboding look on his face and a menacing edge to his voice. This immediately brought one of Judge Shippen's perennial fears to the surface—that an officer had been sent to arrest him and commandeer his house.

From Arnold's perspective, all of these staring eyes were more proof that everyone knew of the shame of his treatment by Congress. Instead of being hostile, he was merely embarrassed.

Judge Shippen finally found his voice, a tremulous one. "Good day to you, sir," he quavered.

Making small talk as he began figuring out how to pass on his way, Arnold touched his hat, bowed slightly, and asked: "Have you been enjoying the celebration?"

"The . . . uh . . . celebration?"

"Yes, Independence Day—the Fourth of July."

"Oh, no. Oh, *yes!* Of course. We . . . ah . . . I've just brought my family back from our country home. Near the Falls of the Schuylkill. I've been here all along, of course." Having nothing better to do and feeling that his family was safe, Judge Shippen took pains to return to the city on most days to exert a presence, on the theory that an occupied house would be less easily commandeered. Now he had wearied in the course of waiting for a British attack on

Philadelphia that never seemed to materialize and had decided to bring his family back from the place of refuge in the country—for the time being at least.

The picture began to come clear to Arnold. While strolling by on several previous occasions he had noticed this gentlemen airing out his house and flapping the shutters in a curiously energetic way, drawing attention to the fact that he was there. Arnold now recognized the family from the description given by Dr. William Shippen, assistant chief of the medical department of the Continental Army, who lived only a few doors south at the corner of Locust Street. Arnold liked Dr. Shippen because he was a critic of both Benjamin Rush and Joseph Reed. At tea one day at Dr. Shippen's home, when the conversation had drifted to factionalism and whether Reed's ultraradicals or the staunch Tories were the worst, Arnold had listened to Dr. Shippen opine that the hardest lot of all was to be neutral for then one tended to be afraid of everything. As a case in point, he described the constant nervous tension of his cousin, Judge Edward Shippen, who feared that the city would be attacked, that his four beautiful daughters would be raped, that his house would be commandeered or burned, that he would be arrested and tried for treason by one side or the other, or possibly both.

For reasons he did not fully comprehend, Arnold felt compelled to ease the older man's tension. "Of course, you must be Judge Shippen," he said. "I've met your cousin, Dr. William Shippen. He speaks most warmly of you." Arnold smiled broadly and extended his hand. "Major-General Benedict Arnold, at your service, sir."

Judge Shippen took Arnold's hand and pumped it gratefully, as words cascaded forth. "Really? How very nice of him. Thank you, sir. I, of course, know who you are, sir. Everyone knows you. Everyone knows of your fame. I wonder if you remember, sir, that we did meet once before, in seventy-four I believe it was, September, at the time of the First Congress. You were in the company of Mr. Silas Deane, Colonel Dyer, and others of the Connecticut and New York delegations."

Arnold began to recall the occasion, one of many social events he had attended at the homes of Philadelphia's more noted families.

The Judge kept babbling on. "May I present my family? You may remember them from seventy-four. Mrs. Shippen; my daughters—Elizabeth, we call her 'Betsy'; Sarah; Mary, she's 'Molly'; and my youngest, Margaret. We call her 'Peggy.' My son, Edward Junior, is away visiting friends."

Arnold felt himself surrounded by a delicious confusion, a treasure trove of feminine riches, hazel eyes, green eyes, auburn hair, brunette hair, coquettish smiles, intriguing scents, lovely bonnets, dainty curtsies. He kept smiling, murmuring niceties, trying to bow without knocking heads. When Dr. Shippen referred to his cousin's four beautiful daughters, he had not exaggerated in the slightest. The youngest, Peggy, stood slightly apart, looking at Arnold with a level gaze, a hint of amusement in her grey eyes. Arnold felt that sudden pang again, the sense that he was being mocked. He caught himself. This was a very young girl. Despite her comely figure, she could not be more than sixteen or seventeen years old. What could she know? She was prettier than any girl had a right to be, with thick, lustrous blond curls framing the soft curve of her cheek. It was her penetrating look that drew Arnold, the faint air of condescension and the enigmatic smile as she offered her hand. He took her hand and met her gaze—and then he *remembered* her, remembered being entranced with her as everyone else had been when he had visited at the Shippen home in '74, despite the fact that she was just a child then, but one so vivacious and charming that she was unforgettable. Now, for a long moment, their hands remained clasped and their eyes locked, and Arnold suddenly felt very strange. And then the first big soft raindrops splashed down, breaking the spell.

The Shippen girls squealed and fled for the doorway. Judge Shippen hesitated and seemed about to say something, but Arnold waved and moved on, and then cursed himself inwardly. Perhaps the man had been about to invite him inside out of the rain. Now it was too late. If Arnold took the shortest route to the Rush house, crossing the street to cut down Willing's Alley, it would make him look foolish by revealing that he had been strolling with nowhere to go. The rain now was coming down in sheets. Better to look foolish than be totally soaked. As he hurried across the street he glanced back and his heart took a leap. Peggy Shippen was still standing in the doorway, still gazing at him. Their eyes met again for an instant, and then she entered the house. Arnold turned and dashed on. What had he ever seen in Betsy DeBlois?

Chapter 25

Fort Ticonderoga
July 7, 1777

Lieutenant-General John Burgoyne stood naked before his full-length mirror. He liked what he saw. The old sense of fitness was back. No sign of a double chin now. He stroked himself lightly with the special oil the surgeon had given him to ward off mosquitoes. It smelled faintly of roses. Much better than using the sticky cedar sap. He donned a silk robe and sat down at his campaign desk, anxious to finish his letter to Charles James Fox before his special guest for the evening arrived.

Burgoyne was not yet aware of the significance the Americans had attached to the Fourth of July. He had his own reasons for celebrating. On that date he made the decision that delivered Fort Ticonderoga into his hands. Before dawn on the 5th, General Arthur St. Clair and his entire garrison had evacuated the fort, fleeing to the southeast. Burgoyne had taken the strongest American position in the north, where he had expected the bloodiest battle of the campaign, without a single casualty. He owed it to Lieutenant Twiss of the artillery and General Will Phillips, who had done what Horatio Gates had decided was impossible. They'd had cannon hauled up the steep northern slope of Sugar Loaf Hill, also known as Mount Defiance, from whence their fire could make kindling of Fort Ticonderoga and slaughter its defenders. The cannon looked right down on the fort. Because of Gates's opinion, expressed when he commanded the fort the previous autumn, the Americans had never fortified the hill, even though Benedict Arnold pleaded with Gates to do so. Arnold, despite his weakened leg, had managed to climb the eight-hundred-foot-high mountain to prove that a gun could be hauled to the summit, but still Gates refused to believe it. Now, as Phillips told Burgoyne: "Where a goat can go, a man can go. And where a man can go he can haul up a gun." Burgoyne gave his approval to the effort and the fate of the fort was decided.

Burgoyne's only regret now was that just one of the three escape routes for the rebel defenders had been sealed off in time. British troops had cut off the portage to Lake George, but von Riedesel's troops had been bogged down in the swamps on the eastern shore of Lake Champlain, leaving open the south branch of the lake to Skenesboro. And that also left unblocked the log bridge crossing the narrowest portion of the lake and leading around Mount Independence to the road toward Hubbard Town in the Vermont territory. Two blunders had alerted St. Clair to the danger from Mount Defiance and caused him abruptly to make the decision to evacuate—a party of Indians lit bonfires on the summit and an overzealous gun crew fired a premature volley, aiming at an American boat, but at the same time telling the Americans that the summit was manned and that cannon were there. That very night, St. Clair began his evacuation, sending his sick and wounded in bateaux down the south branch of the lake toward Skenesboro with a guard of six hundred troops. Before dawn, he led the remainder of his command, some three thousand troops, on the road to Hubbard Town, meaning to pass through and loop around to Fort Ann to meet the other group and proceed on to General Schuyler's base camp near Fort Edward.

General Simon Fraser hurried off in pursuit, though his advance corps was only half the size of St. Clair's retreating army. In the hot fight at Hubbard Town, Fraser had been badly mauled, and Burgoyne had to send a force led by Baron von Riedesel to support him. Meanwhile, the smaller American party heading for Fort Ann via Skenesboro had been caught and dealt a severe blow. After Hubbard Town, St. Clair and his main body were forced to take a much longer route through Vermont before they could safely turn back toward the Hudson River.

Several hundred American troops had been killed or captured and the others had fled for their lives; above all, the capture of the fort was a great victory. Once again, Burgoyne mused, these actions demonstrated the superiority of a trained army of European professionals over the American amateurs. So he felt exceptionally good, fresh from a celebratory dinner with the officers still present at Ticonderoga. He was now thoroughly relaxed, having this day made the only difficult decision that confronted him after the sudden fall of the fort—which of two possible routes to take for the crucial next stage of his advance, the fifty or so miles to Fort Edward on the east bank of the Hudson River. Well before he reached Fort Edward, Burgoyne was certain, Schuyler would have retreated southward. This would allow Burgoyne to rest his troops at Fort Edward and decide on the best place to cross to the east bank of the Hudson to pursue Schuyler.

Of the two routes to Fort Edward, the western one was generally regarded as easier, because most of the travel would be by water—down Lake George's thirty-mile length by bateaux, arriving at Fort George at the foot of the lake. Then a formidable portage was required—south from Fort George and then east and south again to loop around the big bend of the Hudson River, fifteen miles in all, to Fort Edward on the east bank.

Then there was the eastern route, regarded as more difficult because it required the army to traverse a wilderness, the area known as the Drown'd Lands. The first leg, down the narrow, southernmost finger of Lake Champlain from Ticonderoga to Skenesboro, would be easy. Next was a ten-mile trek through rough country to Fort Ann, and there the wilderness thickened, twelve miles of streams and swamps and dense forests that brought one out to the east bank of the Hudson in the vicinity of Fort Edward.

Burgoyne decided to move the bulk supplies and heavy ordnance down the western route, where maximum advantage could be taken of the waterways. But he would march the army down the supposedly more difficult eastern route. For one thing, much of the army, under Fraser and von Riedesel, was already a considerable distance in that direction, chasing the Ticonderoga garrison. Major Skene had also urged that choice. It was easy to see that Skene wanted the army to move through his own territory to reclaim it and build a road through the Drown'd Lands. But he was persuasive that in this direction lay greater prospects of Loyalist recruits and horses that could be captured for the dragoons. And Burgoyne was also interested in seeing the place where Benedict Arnold had built his doomed fleet just a year ago.

After the fall of Ticonderoga, Burgoyne had decided against moving to the dank interior of the fort or his cabin on the *Royal George,* preferring instead to remain in his capacious tent with its double-lined walls of silk and luxurious furnishings. He wanted to rest, catch up on his reading and writing, and await the results of the pursuit of the fleeing Americans. His personal baggage on the expedition required forty-seven carts, including the one he'd had specially made with double springs to cushion its precious cargo of fine wines.

There was a rustling sound at the entrance to the tent. Burgoyne said, "Come!" An orderly entered bearing a bottle of champagne and two crystal glasses on a silver tray. The bottle had been cooling for several hours in the swift-flowing waters of a nearby brook. Burgoyne checked his watch. Good, the orderly was right on time. Burgoyne had fifteen minutes to finish his letter before his guest was due to arrive. He snapped his fingers, and the orderly removed the cork with a soft popping sound. He wiped the bottle, reinserted the cork, bowed, and left.

Burgoyne sifted the papers before him. One was a report to Lord Germain on the Ticonderoga victory, completed and ready for the fair copy to be made. Another was the almost-finished letter to Fox. All of the frustrations and blunders of the campaign thus far, even the two stupid mistakes that had warned the Americans prematurely of the peril from Mount Defiance, now seemed minor and almost inevitable in the afterglow of the Ticonderoga success. Burgoyne was enjoying himself as he wrote about them to Fox.

He could write candidly about the problems encountered thus far, because most of them were solved or under control, and the remaining ones seemed manageable. He could report honestly that the elusive miracle of campaigning that he had known before was becoming manifest. A palpable spirit had arisen among the men. They were lean and seasoned and ready for action. The leaders of the pincer movement from the west along the Mohawk Valley, St. Leger and Johnson, had impressed Burgoyne with their eagerness, and they had left for Lake Ontario with a confident air. The stunning success at Ticonderoga had capped it all. Nothing could stop the Army of the North on its victorious course now. It amused Burgoyne to tell Fox that his Christmas wager was in jeopardy.

There was only one serious matter to address, one that Fox had raised in his letter in Burgoyne. He had expressed shock and disbelief at hearing that Burgoyne planned to use Indians against the Colonials. Burgoyne was confident that his policy for managing the Indians made perfect sense, but trying to explain it convincingly to Fox was not easy. He decided to focus on the two steps he had taken to advance his tricky combination of terrorizing the enemy and yet restraining the Indians from committing atrocities. One was the issuance of a proclamation to be widely disseminated to the American settlers of the region. The second was the rules for the Indians he had set down when he had delivered a personal address to them, as St. Luc had proposed.

Burgoyne made the threat of terror central to his proclamation, the first of several literary efforts drafted on the campaign by the man who had written plays, who considered himself a master of the pen. He began by condemning "the present unnatural rebellion," terming it the "completest system of Tyranny that ever God in his displeasure suffer'd for a time to be exercised over a stubborn and froward generation." He then told the Colonials how he expected them to act:

Animated by these considerations; at the head of Troops in full powers of health, discipline, and Valour; determined to strike where necessary, and anxious to spare where possible, I by these presents invite and exhort all persons, in all places where the progress of this Army may point—and by the blessings of God I will extend it far—to maintain such a conduct as will justify me in protecting their lands, habitations, and families. . . . The domestick, the industrious, the infirm, and even the timid inhabitants I am desirous to protect provided they remain quietly at their Houses, that they do not suffer their Cattle to be removed, nor their corn or forage to be secreted or destroyed, that they do not break up their Bridges or roads; nor by any other acts directly or indirectly endeavor to obstruct the operations of the Kings troops, or supply or assist those of the enemy.

After vowing that all manner of provisions brought to his camp would be paid for "at an equitable rate and in solid coin," Burgoyne delivered the threat of terror to those who would not obey:

I have but to give stretch to the Indian Forces under my direction, and they amount to thousands, to overtake the harden'd enemies of Great Britain and America (I consider them the same) wherever they may lurk. . . . I trust I shall stand acquitted in the Eyes of God and Man in . . . executing the vengeance of the state against the willful outcasts.

He concluded with the dire warning that the Indians would visit "devastation, famine, and every concomitant horror" upon all who opposed his will.

The proclamation was released on June 20th at the Little Bouquet River, forty miles north of Ticonderoga, when Burgoyne and his highest-ranking officers put ashore to greet St. Luc and the Ottawa and Huron braves he had brought with him to join the invasion force. The sight gladdened Burgoyne's heart—more than four hundred warriors and scouts had come at St. Luc's call, giving the army an Indian complement of more than five hundred. Though not the "thousands" he had referred to in his proclamation (unless one counted the Indians in St. Leger's army), Burgoyne decided that the number was probably just about right—a larger Indian force might border on the unmanageable.

The Little Bouquet River encampment was an enchanting scene of cascading water and deep ravines. Standing on a tree stump on a mossy knoll created by an abandoned redoubt, Burgoyne addressed the assembled Indian chiefs and sachems, pausing occasionally to allow St. Luc to translate. Having issued his threat of Indian terror to the Colonials in his proclamation, Burgoyne now was intent on driving home the *other* side of his policy—that the Indians must conduct themselves in a restrained manner.

He began by paying flowery compliments to the Indians as "sagacious and too faithful to be deluded or corrupted," and made many references to "the great King, our common father." He was at pains to make it clear that this was a "new" kind of war for the Indians, one in which not everyone was an enemy. "The King has many faithful subjects dispersed in the provinces," he said, "consequently you have many brothers there, and these people are more to be pitied." He said it was the responsibility of himself and his officers, speaking from the principles of religion and warfare and policy, to "regulate your passions when they overbear, to point out where it is nobler to spare than to revenge, to discriminate degrees of guilt, to suspend the uplifted stroke, to chastise and not to destroy." He asked for their attention to "the rules which I hereby proclaim for your invariable observation during the campaign."

The Indians seemed to be listening eagerly and they occasionally shouted "Etow! Etow!" by way of applause as Burgoyne held up a copy of the proclamation of rules that he had drafted, reading it to them in his best parliamentarian voice:

PROCLAMATION AND NOTICE
TO OUR NOBLE INDIAN ALLIES
IN THE EXPEDITION FROM CANADA

By John Burgoyne, Esq.
Lieutenant-General and Commander of His Majesty's
Armies of the
Expedition from Canada

Chiefs and braves of all Indian forces joining us in our glorious undertaking are advised that there are certain laws of God and nature, as well as customs of civilized warfare, which all men serving under my banner must obey.

I positively forbid bloodshed when you are not actively opposed in arms.

Aged men, women, children, and prisoners must be held sacred from the knife and hatchet, even in the time of actual conflict. I will punish any man who breaks this rule, no matter what excuse for conduct otherwise that he may offer.

You shall receive compensation for the prisoners you take, but you shall be called into account for scalps.

In conformity and indulgence to your customs, which have affixed an idea of honour to such badges of victory, you shall be allowed to take the scalps of the dead, when killed by your fire, and in fair opposition; but on no account, or pretence, or subtlety, or prevarication, are they to be taken from the wounded, or even dying; and still less pardonable, if possible, will it be held to kill men in that condition, on purpose, and upon a supposition that this protection would be thereby evaded.

Burgoyne grunted in satisfaction as he held up a true copy of the proclamation, which he planned to enclose in his letter to Fox. It was an eloquent and precise statement. He glowed in appreciation of the grace and power of his own words, once they had passed through the fine creative mesh of his mind to appear on paper. Yet there was a nagging doubt. Burgoyne had been so sure of the necessity of using the Indians and of his ability to control them, but there had been continuing trouble.

Once again, he recalled the day he had read the proclamation. The chiefs and sachems were ignorant savages to be sure, and yet they were dignified in their own way, as they stood there in colorful raiments and decorations, listening carefully to every word, nodding gravely at times and then applauding with shouted "Etows!" He just was no longer sure of the Indians, of their language or languages—how many did they have? It seemed to Burgoyne that they spoke mainly in grunts and signs, interspersed with an occasional mispronounced word or phrase in French or English. Could their dialects comprehend thoughts of subtlety and complexity? How good was the translation? Would the Indians understand the phrase "be held sacred from the knife and the hatchet?" Burgoyne remembered the expression of cynicism and mirth he caught in an unguarded moment on the face of St. Luc—not an encouraging sign.

He read his last paragraph again, realizing it was all one sentence. A masterpiece of literary construction! Though perhaps too complicated for the Indians. It would have been better broken into a series of short sentences. But Burgoyne felt he *had* communicated, remembering how carefully he had intoned and emphasized each phrase. They could not have missed his meaning. Even St. Luc said afterward that the Indians had understood, and while Burgoyne was not sure he could trust this French mercenary, he could not imagine any reason why St. Luc would lie.

Burgoyne had been reassured when the Indian leaders conferred and an aged chief stood up to respond to the proclamation, making frequent use of such phrases as "great white father" and *"les Anglais"* and *"les Bostonnais,"* the last being the term by which the Indians referred to American troops. The old man seemed to understand everything Burgoyne had said perfectly well. There had been a celebration afterward, as Burgoyne ordered a tot of rum issued to every Indian as a reward, making sure, of course, that the supply was then locked and guarded. A contingent of braves held a war dance to the rhythmic sound of drums, an unforgettable sight as they contorted and twisted, their bodies smeared with bear grease and painted in garish colors. Some were naked and others wore breech-cloths and war bonnets or helmets made of animal skins with horns or feathers flapping, an eerie and oddly disturbing spectacle.

Burgoyne laid the copy of the proclamation down and picked up his quill again, searching for the right words to convince Fox of the necessity of his Indian policy and his determination to handle it properly. The air was close in the tent, and Burgoyne felt damp with perspiration. He heard the sentries come to attention, and he rose as the flap parted and Fanny Loescher entered.

She wore a simple blouse and long skirt and a shawl that almost completely covered her face. She removed the shawl and brushed back her long black hair with one hand. The movement caused her unrestrained breasts to ripple against the sheer fabric of the blouse, and Burgoyne felt a sudden clutch at his groin.

"Good evening, my General." Fanny smiled. Their liaison was new enough that both were still a bit awkward. It was Fanny's custom to act becomingly modest at first, almost embarrassed, but soon that would melt into a hearty lust that fascinated and consumed Burgoyne. He came up to her. "My dear Fanny, what a delight it is to see you." He glanced at the entrance to make sure no curious sentries were lingering

"Thank you, General."

"My darling," Burgoyne whispered, "as I've told you, in our private sanctuary you may call me John." He put his hands on her waist and drew her to him, burying his face in her rich hair, drinking in the musky scent. Then he kissed her on her full, warm lips.

"Now," he said briskly. "I have some champagne for us. But first, I need just a few moments to finish a letter—I want it to go with the first courier in the morning. Forgive me."

Fanny slapped at a mosquito. Burgoyne saw several welts on her arm. He darted over to get the jar of rose oil. "I have just the thing for you. My surgeon gave it to me. Very nice and very effective."

He returned to his desk as Fanny began applying the oil to her arms. Burgoyne tried to concentrate, but it was not easy to explain the Indian policy in a manner that would be convincing to Fox. He thought of the time when two Huron braves had been caught breaking into the rum supply. Burgoyne had them lashed, but the next morning it was discovered that they and a score of their relatives and friends had melted silently into the forest, taking their British-issued muskets with them. To avoid this, Burgoyne had been forced to forgo punishment for a series of later infractions, which was certainly an unsatisfactory course. Hardly instructive for the white soldiers to see that an Indian could break a rule and not be punished because the commander was afraid the miscreant and his friends would simply desert. There seemed no answer to the dilemma. At least there had been no outright atrocities. Perhaps it would all work out—the Indians *were* indispensable as the eyes of the army. Burgoyne sighed and leaned back. Then he glanced up and saw a sight that transfixed him.

Fanny sat very erectly on the edge of the feather bed, naked to the waist.

She was applying the oil gently with one hand. She caught Burgoyne's gaze, and a smile played at her lips. Her breasts were extraordinary, large and full and pendulous. The red-brown nipples were hard. She poured more oil and then, with great deliberate care, she cupped and manipulated each breast in turn, her gaze flickering back and forth to watch Burgoyne's fascination with approval. In the amber glow of the candlelight, Burgoyne could see that her swaying breasts were filmy and slippery with oil, and he heard sweet sounds of suction.

He found his voice. "My dear, I see that you need assistance." He laid down his quill. Fox would understand.

Chapter 26

Morristown, New Jersey
July 16, 1777

Major-General Nathanael Greene sat in a rocking chair on the porch of the Freeman Tavern and watched a civilian approach on horseback. Greene's stiff leg always bothered him in hot weather, and he shifted uncomfortably in the chair. The sun blazed down on the parched scrub grass. The civilian and his escort of two horsemen from the picket line reined up, and the man dismounted. Greene hauled himself up and returned the salutes of the escorts. He waved them away and signaled an orderly to take charge of the visitor's horse. Then he put his hands on his hips and glared. The civilian was Benedict Arnold, late of the Continental Army.

Greene shook his head. "I never thought I'd see such a sorry sight."

Arnold looked down at his new civilian suit and brushed some dust from it. "Feels worse than it looks," he said.

"You look like a goddamned merchant or congressman or something worse."

"The hell with you, too," Arnold said.

Greene guffawed. He beckoned Arnold to the porch. "C'mon, Ben, get in the shade and rest your bones. It's good to see you."

Arnold slid into an adjoining rocker and sighed. "I can't say it's so good to see you. Under these circumstances, at least. It seems to me the reception was a bit different the last time I came to headquarters."

Greene raised his eyebrows. "Well—you're a civilian now."

"I'm very conscious of my new status, thank you. I had a hell of a time getting through your picket line. I got so angry I reached for my sword to smack your sentries on the ass. But I didn't have a sword!"

Greene laughed. "Before you came, I was thinking what would happen if you were stopped by a British patrol. They'd ask your name and you'd say 'Benedict Arnold' and they'd fall over in shock."

"That's no joke. Could be dangerous. They'd think I was a spy."

"You better come back in." Greene glanced at Arnold slyly. "It's safer."

"The hell you say!"

"There aren't any British patrols around here. They're all gone." Seeing Arnold about to ask a question, Greene asked one of his own: "So where you headed? Back home to New Haven?"

Arnold nodded. "I sent my trunks ahead. I'll catch up with them tonight in Paramus."

The two men rocked silently for a while. Arnold glanced around. "Where is everybody? Place looks deserted."

"Damn near is. Only my division is still here. And we're spread out a bit. Anybody with any sense has found hisself some shade."

"Where's the chief? The other divisions?"

"They've . . ." Greene gave Arnold a cool glance, and a smile played at the corner of his mouth. "You're a civilian now. I shouldn't be tellin' you 'bout the army."

Arnold was offended, his voice icy. "I don't give a damn. I'm out of it."

"No sense getting bitter about it, Ben."

Arnold flared. "Don't tell me that. What do *you* know about it? You have no—"

"Easy," Greene interrupted. "I was just joking. Too damned hot to get excited, anyway. Here, cool off with this." He removed the lid from a stoneware jar next to his rocker and ladled out a glass of cider. He passed it to Arnold and ladled one for himself. "Still nice and cool."

After a long silence, Arnold spoke. "I got your message just as I was leaving Philadelphia. I was surprised to hear the army was back in Morristown."

"Yeah, we were surprised to be back. We broke camp here at the end of May. We moved around a lot when Howe was trying to draw us out for a fight."

"I know. I was over the Delaware, in Bucks County, watching your flank."

"I remember. We were at Middlebrook quite a while. A good camp. Only eight miles from New Brunswick, but great high land. Like a fortress. There's this high cliff right near it that the chief loved. You could see twenty, thirty miles easy on a clear day with a spyglass. He was watching the British fleet in New York Bay. You've never seen so many ships! He couldn't take his eyes off it. Never say very much. Dreamin' about what we could do with half that many ships."

"I'll take just one. I'd like to talk to him about that. He might be able to help me get a privateer."

Greene seemed not to have heard Arnold. "Then we get reports from Schuyler and St. Clair that Burgoyne was advancing on Ticonderoga. This was the beginning of July. All of a sudden the British got very busy in New York. They began loading their ships in a big hurry. Horses, fodder, supplies, cannon, and twelve, fifteen thousand effectives. After looking at that going on for a couple of days, the chief decided it meant that Howe was going north, up the river to meet Burgoyne, maybe another wing to Providence to move north from there. He decided we'd better get ourselves in position to defend the passes in the Hudson Highlands. If Howe took them, that could be the beginning of the end. There'd be no way we could stop Howe and Burgoyne from joining up. So we came back here to Morristown. A good position to move quickly to the Highlands if it turned out Howe was really going that way— and yet not so far that we couldn't get down to Philadelphia if Howe went that way."

"So what happened?"

"Around here? Nothing. We kept Sheldon's dragoons moving around constantly, as far down as Elizabethtown, keeping an eye on the British. But they haven't budged."

"How the hell long can they sit there, crammed on those ships?"

"I don't know. I think Howe just can't make up his mind what to do. It's got to be hard on his men, all cooped up. It's hard on us! You realize how long we been tryin' to figure out whether Howe is going north? Ever since we heard about Burgoyne's new army in Canada. Nearly three months! It's drivin' the chief to distraction."

"When I was here before—in May—he told me the best intelligence reports said Howe would go north. But everyone in Philadelphia thinks he'll attack there, especially after all his maneuvering around in New Jersey."

"I know, but now that he's pulled back and boarded his ships, it looks like all that was a feint. If he wants Philadelphia, he'd move by land, wouldn't he?"

"Not necessarily," Arnold said. "He could sail around, come up Delaware Bay, trying to flank us. Better way to move all the artillery, too."

"Well, I think it means he's headed north. But he just sits there. What's he waiting for? When we got confirmation that Burgoyne had taken Ticonderoga, we figured that's it. Howe will certainly move now. That was six days ago. The next day the chief and three divisions pulled out, headin' for the Highlands. They were so sure there'd be a fight they cooked three days' rations before they left. Now they're squatting there, just like Howe, doin' nothing."

"Where are they, exactly?"

"Smith's Clove." Out of sensitivity for Arnold's feelings, Greene did not mention the fact that each of the three divisions was commanded by one of the men promoted over Arnold's head on the February list—Adam Stephen, Benjamin Lincoln, and Lord Stirling.

"On the other hand," Arnold said, "Howe might figure he's not needed in the north. Not after Ticonderoga fell so easy."

"Could be. I still think he's going north."

"How'd the chief take the news about Ticonderoga?"

Greene made a sour face. "I just can't tell you how bad it was. We didn't believe the early reports. Then when we were certain—it was awful. I've never seen the chief so angry and dejected."

It was the same everywhere. The loss of the symbolic fortress in the north without any struggle sent waves of anger and embarrassment throughout the thirteen States. Arnold said: "In Philadelphia they're marching through the streets calling St. Clair and Schuyler traitors. I've never seen anything like it. Gates will probably get the northern command after all."

"I suppose. As you've learned, Ben, there's no justice. Schuyler didn't tell St. Clair to run, but he's getting blamed for it. You know what St. Clair said?" Greene's voice took on an edge of derision.

"What?"

"He said, 'We've lost a fort, but saved a province.' "

Arnold thought about that for a moment. "You know, he may well be right."

Greene was genuinely astonished. "Jesus, you're the last man in the world I'd expect to be defending—"

"Why do you say that?"

"Well, you never would've pulled foot at Ty. You would've fought to the last man."

"How do you know that?"

"After what you did at Valcour Bay?"

"I attacked at Valcour Bay for very good reasons."

Greene looked point-blank at Arnold. "You are the only commander in the entire world who would have attacked in that situation."

"Goddammit, I'm telling you I sat down and figured it out. I did it for very deliberate reasons. You want me to explain it to you?"

"No, no, I understand."

"If I attacked there for good reasons, I might withdraw somewhere else for good reasons. I'm tired of people thinking I'm some sort of madman because—"

"Hold it, I get your point. It turned out you were right, Ben, and I understand. Here, have some more cider." Greene took Arnold's glass and ladled more cider into it, and then refilled his own.

Arnold sipped, his face still glowering. "I don't know why I even talk about it. I'm through with it."

Greene was quiet for a long interval, rotating his glass and staring at the amber liquid as if seeking inspiration. "Ben, I appreciate your coming to see me, under the circumstances. I mean, I have some idea of how you feel. You've been dealt with very badly. It's incredible, what's happened to you. We all know that. Now, there's something I want to say to you, and I'd appreciate it if you'd hear me out and not get excited again until I've finished."

"If it's what I think it is, you can save your breath."

Greene spread a hand, palm up, in exasperation. "Will you just listen?"

"When you asked me to stop at camp on my way, I had some idea what you wanted. But I want something, too, so I decided to stop. The chief could use his influence to help me get a privateer."

"You're crazy! Forget about a goddamned privateer. The chief can't help you with that. In the first place, he has no authority for that. You'd still have to deal with Congress or a state, and get yourself financed somehow. In the second place, the chief would have no interest in it. You'd be out at sea somewhere. Maybe it would help the cause and maybe it wouldn't. We'd never know it. When you're here, he knows how to use you, he knows what he's got."

"He's got nothing. I'm a civilian, remember? I resigned."

Greene contemplated his glass again, and spoke softly. "You're still in the army, Ben."

"Like hell! I resigned!"

"We know you sent a letter of resignation to Congress. Did they accept it? Until they do, you're still in the army."

"Why you bastard! If you think—"

"Hold it! I'm not trying to play games with you. All I'm saying is that it's still not too late to change your mind. Now listen to me. The chief wants you to go north to help Schuyler. He wrote a letter to Congress. I've got a copy. I'll show it to you. He asked Congress not to accept your resignation, instead to order you to go north, especially to take care of the militia. We're stuck with mostly militia up there. He told Congress he needs you. He said, and I'm quoting him directly here, he said he had no doubt you would add to the honors you've already acquired."

Arnold was shaking his head. "Nat, do you have any idea what I've been through?"

"Answer just one question. Did Congress turn you down?"

"What do you mean?"

"You asked for your seniority to be restored. They didn't refuse, did they? They just haven't acted."

Arnold's color was rising. "So what? You're not defending those pompous bastards, are you?"

"Of course not. But they didn't turn you down, did they?"

"What is today? July sixteenth? For nearly two months all I've asked is to be fairly treated. And I got nothing."

"You did the right thing. Only thing you *could* do. I understand that, we all do. Same thing happened to John Stark, and he resigned, too. He's back on his farm in New Hampshire. Knox says if Congress commissions Coudray chief of artillery, he'll resign, too. I'm just making the point, first, that you're still in the army, second, they didn't actually turn you down. Hold it!" Greene raised both hands to quell Arnold's protests. "Now, look at our situation. It's desperate, I don't have to tell you. We have to send help north, but we can't really afford it. I mean, Howe outnumbers us two or three to one or more, as it is. So what does the chief do? He says, we can't send large numbers, so we'll just have to send the best. Do you hear that, Ben? The *best*, he says! What does that mean? He says we'll ask Arnold to go—and if possible, maybe we can send Morgan's riflemen later."

He finished with a triumphant smile. Arnold was impressed about sending Morgan's Virginia Riflemen to the north. He'd had them with him at Quebec. Without any question in his mind, they were the most valuable infantry outfit, man for man, in either army. But had Washington really called him the best commander?

"You see, Ben," Greene resumed, "the chief would never say directly to you what I just said. You know that."

"What do you mean? How do I know that?"

"Dammit, you know what I mean! He'd be afraid you'd think he was just flattering you. So he'd never say that, I mean about you being the best. When you see him, he'll just ask you to go, say he needs you, nothing more. He said it to all of us, at the staff meeting."

Arnold was still skeptical. "How do I know he really said it?"

"For Christ's sake!" Greene glared at Arnold.

"All right, all right. If you say he said it, then he said it." Arnold fell silent, gazing off into the distance as he tried to quell the excitement he felt rising within him. He tried to sort the whole business out in his mind. He had taken the honorable course. He had resigned. Now Congress has refused to accept— or had they? He turned to Greene. "How do you know they'll do what the chief asks? Ask me to go north?"

"Don't worry about it. Believe me. A courier is going to arrive any minute from Philadelphia with your orders from Congress. All that counts is what you want to do. Are you with us, Ben?"

Arnold's mind was still churning. If what Greene said was true—then he could serve with honor. On a temporary basis, to be sure. Just for this one campaign, because both Congress and the chief were pleading with him, saying they needed him. But wait—there *was* a problem.

"What if I run into one of the others—those that were jumped over me. How can I take orders from them?"

"Look, that's very unlikely. The only one that's up there is St. Clair and he's in trouble. He'll be lucky to survive a court-martial. The others are all down here. But if it should happen—well, the chief would expect you to be man enough to follow proper procedure. On the other hand, I think you'll find that those five men will defer to you. None of them wanted what happened. They still see you as their senior. I know that Lincoln and Stephen and Stirling all feel that way. I talked to them."

Greene eyed Arnold shrewdly, sensing he almost had his man. "Something else, Ben. I've got the perfect fellow to recommend to you for your staff."

"Who's that?"

"Young Matthew Clarkson. Very bright boy, nineteen years old. Well connected. His uncle is Governor William Livingston of New Jersey. That means he's connected to both the Schuyler and the Livingston families. He's volunteered and he'd love to be your aide."

"Where is he now?"

"He's at headquarters in the Highlands, at Smith's Clove. Look here, let's go up and see the chief. I've got to go, anyway. We can get to Paramus tonight and get your things, and we'll be at headquarters before noon tomorrow. The chief would like to see you. And you can look young Clarkson over. And let the chief tell you himself what he wants you to do. How about it?"

Arnold drained his glass of cider. He felt the same way he had when Sergeant Ashbel Grayson pounded on his door almost three months ago. Opportunity beckoned again, and what Greene had told him *did* make a difference. "All right," he said to Greene, "let's go see the chief."

Chapter 27

New York Bay
July 21, 1777

The surface of New York's upper bay was uncommonly smooth, rippled only occasionally by a light breeze. Captain John André leaned against the railing of HMS *Cerebrus* and shaded his eyes as he looked west through the forest of masts to the New Jersey shoreline, the Kill van Kull, and Staten Island, not much more than a mile across from where the great ship lay anchored in the midst of the British armada. The land beyond, lush with greenery and fertile farms, looked deceptively peaceful, but it was an area in constant fear and turmoil, a veritable no-man's-land where the rule of the British Army was sporadic at best and one could not distinguish between Loyalist and rebel by appearance alone. Scanning the horizon, André imagined he could see the smoky ridgeline of the Watchung Mountains, the modest range some ten miles from the shore that was widely referred to as "the short hills." Behind them lay the Great Swamp, a rolling valley, and the gradually rising hills of Morristown, a good defensive position for George Washington and his rebel army.

"You get the feeling that they're out there watching us," André said to the husky young officer standing next to him. "Probably laughing at us. It really galls me."

Captain Oliver DeLancey, Jr., shifted slightly. He had been standing as still as possible, trying to minimize the flow of sweat that itched inside his tunic. "Why should they be laughing?"

"Why not? We wear ourselves out chasing them, with nothing to show for it. And then we board ship and sit here for weeks like prisoners. My God, the season's half over!"

DeLancey was a brash, outspoken young man, one of the few Loyalists allowed to purchase a commission in the British Army. That had been due largely to the powerful influence of his family, the wealthiest in New York City, and the fact that young DeLancey had distinguished himself in the flanking movement that had won the Battle of Long Island, at the head of one of the Loyalist DeLancey battalions that his father had raised. He curled his lip. "I don't think they're laughing. They're frightened to death. Besides, we'll have our orders by tonight."

André turned away from the shoreline. "I hope so," he sighed.

The *Cerebrus* was no ordinary seventy-four-gun ship of the line. She was the flagship of Admiral Richard Lord Howe, and as such she was spendidly immaculate, her brightwork gleaming in the sun and her decks scrubbed until they were bone white. A host of barges clustered around her, one for each of the high-ranking officers who had been summoned. There were several conversational groups on the main deck, composed of staff aides of the visiting brass and junior officers of the *Cerebrus*. Thirty feet away from where André and DeLancey stood were the beautifully varnished slatted double doors, framed in gold leaf, which led to Admiral Howe's private quarters. That was where the conference was taking place, a conference that seemed unusually significant because all of the commanders had been assembled and all the staff aides excluded. There was enough gold braid in there to sink the *Cerebrus,* André thought. Admiral Howe, General Howe, Lord Cornwallis, Sir Henry Clinton, the Baron von Knyphausen, Sir Charles Grey, a dozen others.

"Why do you think they kept us out?" DeLancey asked. He had been assigned temporarily to the staff of Sir Henry Clinton, who had returned from consultation in London less than a fortnight earlier.

"Because it's too damned hot in there."

"It's not is if we don't know what's happening. Why do they spend so much time talking? We're going north. Clinton's very clear about that."

"He may be the only one who is."

DeLancey was perplexed. "But it seems so obvious! What does Grey think?"

"He doesn't confide in me the way Clinton apparently does in you," André said sarcastically, but it was lost on the irrepressible DeLancey. The truth was that Grey kept little from his staff aide, but he genuinely had no idea what General Howe would decide to do.

"What do you think, John?" DeLancey asked.

"I'm just tired of all the waiting and the rumors and the guessing games. I'm beginning to think I made a mistake." The last was a reference to André's decision to remain behind in North America when his regiment was transferred home. It was a difficult decision, because it meant not only forgoing a return home, but also the loss of André's commission and seniority until he found and purchased a new commission. Fortunately, André had found a way to bring his military journal, complete with illustrations and carefully drawn maps, to General Howe's attention. In the two interviews that followed, Howe also like André's engaging personality, his apparent fortitude about the war, his ability in German among the four languages he spoke, and so he had found a commission for André to purchase and recommended him as an aide-de-camp to the newly arrived Major-General Grey. With his newfound status, André soon was able to enter Neddy Burd's name on an exchange list, and by now Neddy was safe at home on parole.

André had found it much more difficult to explain his decision to stay in North America to his mother and sisters than he had to Despard. When they expressed bewilderment in their letters, he knew he could not adequately explain his change of attitude. He was honest enough to himself to recognize that he had been a dilettante as a younger man and had purchased his original commission only for lack of something better to do. How to tell those tender beings at home that he had been converted, that he was now imbued with the warrior spirit? They could never understand what the miserable months in Carlisle as a prisoner had done to him.

He also knew that the decision was in part based on his discovery of ambition, the realization that the army offered a context for advancement and prestige in a kind of game that he now knew he could play very well. He knew he was pleasing to older officers because of his appearance, his manners, and his many talents. To those he added a calculated style that was so skillful that it was not seen as ingratiating, but rather as a combination of candor and quick competence.

It was thus somewhat natural that some of André's peers found reason to resent him, more or less openly, but this was part of the game, too, one that he could handle in his stride. However, to DeLancey, André was fascinating. They were the same age, twenty-seven, and DeLancey's family was so prominent in New York that George Washington had intervened personally in a vain attempt to persuade the father to lead his clan to the rebel cause. Young

DeLancey had spent several years in London, but his education and experience did not approach those of André, with the result that at times there was an air of master and pupil about their relationship, André taking pains to acquaint his new friend with some of the finer things of life. André was careful as always not to appear arrogant or snobbish. But it was only DeLancey's natural assertiveness that kept him from feeling like a provincial clod in the presence of André.

Neither man was in a mood to discuss things cultural during the long wait for the conference to end. DeLancey had difficulty restraining his impatience, but after a while the heat and inactivity made André drowsy. A sharp jab from DeLancey alerted him. He saw the ensigns stationed at the admiral's quarters come to attention as the double doors parted and officers began to stream on deck, blinking in the bright sunlight.

"Oh my God, here they come," DeLancey said, his voice rising in excitement. "I can't wait!"

Grey was one of the first to appear, and he walked toward André and DeLancey.

"Here comes Grey," DeLancey whispered hoarsely. "Ask him what they decided."

"Certainly not."

The two young officers stood erect as Grey came over and leaned against the railing wearily. In the pecking order of command, he would have a considerable wait before his barge would have its turn at the debarking ladder.

"Thank God that's over," Grey said, wiping a film of perspiration from his forehead. He had a thin, vulpine face with heavy dark brows. His reputation was that of a ruthless commander with a killer instinct, and that suited André's new punitive mood perfectly. Their relationship had ripened as Grey recognized that his new aide was not only extraordinarily competent, but also had an intense desire for battle.

DeLancey could contain himself no longer. "Are we going north, Sir Charles?" he ventured.

Grey glared at DeLancey. "What the hell," he snarled. "How dare you ask a question like that?"

That was enough, even for DeLancey. He spotted Clinton emerging on deck, muttered an apology, and hastily withdrew.

"A cheeky sort, that," Grey said, leaning back against the railing again. "That's what comes of giving these provincials commissions. You should teach him some manners." After a while, he glanced at André. "I don't suppose you're curious about the meeting, are you?"

André smiled. "I am literally consumed with curiosity, sir."

Grey smiled back. "I prize honesty—and tact—above all on my staff. Therefore, let me see what I can tell you." He glanced at the growing crowd of high-ranking officers milling about and began speaking in a monotone, barely

above a whisper. "We have an interesting alignment here. Consider our esteemed second-in-command, for example." André looked at the stocky figure
of Clinton, whose often peevish nature was now reflected by a frown and puckered lips. He was listening to excited words from von Knyphausen, DeLancey
hovering at his elbow.

"Sir Henry comes to us from London with information that Lord Germain
expects us to go north to a juncture with Burgoyne. He says there is no question that this is the understanding in London. He brings no written orders to
that effect. General Howe says that his latest written communication from Germain leaves the choice to him, that he has a clear hand to use his own judgment
as to whether Burgoyne needs help or whether we can go elsewhere."

André watched the tall, well-proportioned figure of General Howe as he
leaned over to chat with his older brother who was nearly a head shorter than
he. Both were considerate commanders, well liked by their officers and men.
The admiral's nickname of "Black Dick" had nothing to do with an evil temperament, but merely a somewhat swarthy complexion.

Grey resumed: "General Howe makes much of the fact that Burgoyne has
taken Ticonderoga easily and continues to move southward with apparently
little opposition. Therefore, he may not need help. He invites the opinions of
everyone and every option is discussed at great length. Clinton, of course, is
very strong that we should go north. Von Knyphausen agrees, and so do I. It
just seems to make more military sense to me. I really don't care as long as we
go *somewhere*. However, it is becoming clear that General Howe really would
prefer to attack Pennsylvania, to outflank Washington and finish what was not
finished last December. Admiral Howe likes that course, but chiefly, I believe,
because he sees greater use for the fleet in that direction, maneuvering in open
waters and wide estuaries rather than the narrower confines of Hudson's river.
Cornwallis is on fire to go directly after Washington, wherever that might lead
us. I think he's still smarting from that business at Princeton last January. I
understand he'd practically set foot on his transport bound for England when
word came of Washington's foray at Trenton. Charles had to turn around and
go back down there only to be outmaneuvered at Princeton. Yes indeed, he
wants revenge."

Grey fell silent, thinking that he had hardly depicted the true intensity
of the debate. Clinton had scoffed at Howe's thought that he could go after
Washington and still have time to turn about and assist Burgoyne, if that were
necessary. Or that Clinton, left behind to command New York City, could
demonstrate up the Hudson in support of Burgoyne. Clinton complained that
he would be left with far too small an occupying force to both protect New
York City and do anything useful to the north. In one aside, Clinton had whispered that Cornwallis was "the evil genius" who was influencing Howe to go in
the wrong direction.

After waiting patiently for a time, André finally asked his commander: "And the result, sir?"

"Eh?"

"What decision, sir—or is it premature of me to ask?"

"Decision! Surely you jest! There's no decision. We're going to meet again in a few days And then probably again. And again." He turned and spat disgustedly over the side.

From the narrative of Richard Varick

The arrival in the north of Benedict Arnold, the man who had saved us the year before, was a boost to morale. But it was short lived as we realized he had been sent alone, not at the head of an army of reinforcements. Having already lost Ticonderoga, we were in much more perilous condition than the year before. Even with most of St. Clair's garrison finally joining us at Fort Edward, General Schuyler still had fewer than five thousand men, only half of them Continentals.

With characteristic vigor, Arnold took over the job that Schuyler had started—making the Drown'd Lands even more difficult for Burgoyne's army to pass through. Work gangs destroyed bridges and causeways, felled huge trees to block the trail in numerous places, and cut channels and dammed ponds and streams to spread water as widely as possible. It was effective—in moving his army from Skenesboro down to Fort Ann and then to Fort Edward, Burgoyne was able to progress no faster than one mile per day over the twenty-three-mile stretch. By that time, we had begun our steady retreat.

In August, we learned that St. Leger had completed his long journey to the eastern shore of Lake Ontario, where he moved inland to surround Fort Stanwix at the western end of the Mohawk Valley. It was defended by only 600 soldiers and settlers, against an enemy of 2,000 men. A force of 850 Tryon County militia under General Herkimer attempted to relieve Stanwix, but on August 6th they were caught in an ambush six miles from the fort, at a place called Oriskany, and suffered terrible losses.

It was an excruciating dilemma for General Schuyler. Now, only he could help the Stanwix garrison. But it was one hundred miles to the west. As pleas came from the valley for help, he finally called a council of his officers on August 12th. It was a painful meeting, as the officers derided the idea of splitting our army in the face of a superior enemy, and for a hopeless cause. All manner of objections were made. The New England officers behaved the worst, with jeers and catcalls.

Finally, a New England officer stood up and volunteered to lead an expedition to relieve Fort Stanwix. It was Benedict Arnold.

Chapter 28

German Flats and Fort Stanwix
August 16–26, 1777

Hon Yost Schuyler was going to die.

He knew that with certainty as he sat with his back to one side of the exercise pen, his knees hunched up to his chest, his matted yellow hair nearly concealing his dirt-stained face. Across from him, four Mohawk Indians stood sullenly in a group, three of them wearing only breech-cloths and moccasins, their skin burnished to a darker bronze than usual where the sun beat down on shoulders and on heads that were shaved except for one narrow strip down the center. The fourth Indian wore a faded red coat with a brass gorget hung from his neck. At the other end of the compound stood the lone white man, pacing back and forth methodically, his expression managing to convey both contempt and concern.

The six men had been caught at a wilderness tavern several miles away where they had been trying to organize a Tory uprising in the valley. A number of the plotters had escaped, as many as ten, the captors thought.

The exercise pen was located in one corner of the small parade ground of Fort Dayton, the outpost at the dusty settlement of German Flats on the south bank of the Mohawk River, some thirty miles east of the besieged Fort Stanwix. Colonel James Weston, commander of the small garrison, had refused to act as judge at the trial of the six men, saying that he must defer to his superior, Major-General Benedict Arnold, who was expected to arrive momentarily with a brigade of nine hundred troops of the New York Line.

This had left the council of safety in something of a quandary. The members had no difficulty with sentences for five of the men, though they would ask General Arnold for affirmation. The four Mohawks would be given fifty lashes each and released. Hon Yost would be hung, the reason being that he was officially on the rolls of the Tryon County militia and therefore was guilty of treason for participating in the Loyalist cabal. The problem arose in the case of the white man, Walter Butler, a scion of one of the most noted families of the valley. Though a Tory, who the council believed had been conspiring to foment an uprising and recruit men for St. Leger's army, Butler had argued eloquently in his defense, saying that he had come to the region under a flag of truce. The council members thought he should be hanged, but they wanted the sentence to come from a military court rather than a civil one of local people, out of fear of reprisals and some lingering respect for the status of the

Butler family. They had deferred Butler's case, hoping that General Arnold would agree to try him.

No one cared what happened to Hon Yost. He was a half-breed and widely regarded as a half-wit. His claim to be distantly related to General Philip Schuyler was greeted with guffaws, though such a thing was entirely possible, given the decades during which "black sheep" members of the Schuyler clan might have intermarried and disappeared into the wilderness. Even the late Sir William Johnson, who had been more powerful than Philip Schuyler and nearly as wealthy, had taken an Indian woman, the sister of Joseph Brant, as his second wife. But the contrast between the filthy, addle-brained Hon Yost and General Schuyler, the wealthiest patroon of upper New York, was just too great for anyone to take the idea of a relationship seriously.

Through the fog of his mind, Hon Yost understood his sentence, and his bowels had turned watery with fear at the thought of hanging from the end of a rope. He had spent the better part of the morning exercise hour arguing with the teenage militia guards to take him to the "necessary" to relieve himself, but, imbued with the power of the muskets in their hands, the guards had disdained him, one very nearly clubbing Hon Yost on the side of the head.

The Mohawks stayed clear of Hon Yost, fearful that his death sentence would rub off on them. He was, after all, a strange being of the kind the Indians thought might have a special connection to the Great Spirit. The Indians generally were ambivalent about Hon Yost, at times dismissing him as merely a half-breed fool, at other times wary that his eccentricities might have some magical roots. Better to play it safe, and that was enough to enable Hon Yost to live and survive among the Indians on the frontier without losing his tangled tresses.

To Walter Butler, Hon Yost was invisible, beneath contempt. He had been included in the cabal only because someone thought he might have influence over the local Indians, the Oneidas. It was doubtful that Hon Yost had even understood the purpose of the meeting. Butler strode back and forth, conscious of his body odor and his itching five-day growth of beard. When captured, he had quickly discarded the apple-green uniform tunic of his Loyalist regiment, knowing that it was an object of intense hatred for all those who called themselves "patriots." A friend had brought him old and mildewed civilian clothes to wear during his imprisonment. Butler suddenly stopped pacing. He could hear some faint sounds, a rhythmic beat, then the trill of fifes. The Mohawks heard the sounds, too, and began jabbering. Civilians in the fort began moving excitedly to the gates to join settlers now streaming from the seventy-plus homes that constituted the settlement of German Flats. Despite himself, Butler moved to the edge of the pen to stare out of the open gates of the fort. He was curious to see the man who controlled his fate, the man the Indians called "Dark Eagle" and "Heap Fighting Chief."

The music had a different effect on Hon Yost. Whimpering, he had to let go. Fortunately, the guard who had threatened to shoot him if he did so had left to go to the gate. Hon Yost thought wildly of escape now that everyone was distracted, but the stinking burden in his pants prevented him from moving.

Outside the stockade, Lieutenant-Colonel Marinus Willett and scout Levi Stockwell moved toward the sound of the fife and drums. They had arrived at Fort Dayton only the day before, the latest couriers from Stanwix to make the perilous journey through enemy lines to plead for help. The fact that Willett, second-in-command at Stanwix, had come only underscored the desperation of the defenders. Fearing that his mission was hopeless, Willett had been stunned with joy by the news that a relief column under Benedict Arnold was on the way.

Arnold had brought the column along at the quickest possible pace without prematurely exhausting the men. The musicians followed the vanguard, then came the party of mounted officers followed by the wagon train, the bulk of the troops, and the rear guard, in all stretching for nearly half a mile. After Arnold had volunteered for the mission out of anger at the way General Schuyler was being treated, he was amused when Schuyler later showed him a dispatch from Washington, in which the chief wrote that Arnold might be the one "to operate with good effect against St. Leger."

Arnold's act of volunteering had deflated the tension of the council of war. Schuyler's gratitude was so deep that it brought tears to his eyes. The shame-faced officers had promptly voted to approve the mission. In the changed circumstances, it was not necessary for Schuyler to have to ask for troops to volunteer as well. He simply assigned Brigadier-General Ebenezer Learned's Continental Brigade of Yorkers.

Arnold was not yet sure how he would handle St. Leger—much depended on how many of the once-beaten survivors of the Tryon County militia could be reassembled to augment the nine-hundred-man Continental Brigade and whether the friendly Oneidas would cooperate. Since he would have to take the offensive, Arnold wanted his total force, including the six-hundred-man Stanwix garrison, to at least equal St. Leger's army. But he was confident, for the moment contenting himself with thoughts of double glory—saving Fort Stanwix by vanquishing St. Leger and then returning to the Hudson just in time to save Schuyler's army from Burgoyne's onslaught. That would show the bastards in Congress something! Arnold's earlier anger had subsided, confident as he was that any day a message would reach Schuyler's headquarters with word that Congress had voted to restore his seniority out of gratitude for his magnanimous act of continuing to serve despite his attempt to resign.

Whenever settlers streamed out to cheer the column as it passed along the King's Road, the fifers and drummers had performed. This had happened at the hamlet of Little Falls, close to General Nicholas Herkimer's impressive stone house on the opposite bank. Though badly wounded at Oriskany, Herkimer still lived. Arnold halted the column and summoned the brigade surgeon, a young doctor named John Simmons. Arnold told Learned to proceed with the column after a rest break, that he and Simmons and Matthew Clarkson, his new aide, would catch up after paying their respects to Herkimer and seeing if they could be of any assistance.

After their horses picked their way across the shallow river below the falls, the trio was greeted by a pale and haggard-looking Maria Herkimer. She told them that her beloved "Honnikol" was gravely ill from his wound. The doctor from German Flats had dressed the wound and said there was nothing else to be done except change the dressing daily. There was a smell of rotting flesh as the men entered the parlor that had become Herkimer's sickroom. The gruff old man lay on his bed, head and shoulders raised enough by pillows so that he could puff on his pipe.

Tears filled Herkimer's eyes, so grateful was he that Arnold would come to visit him. Clarkson stood back, nearly gagging from the odor, while Arnold chatted with Herkimer, and Simmons gingerly examined the wound.

Arnold's understanding of the gallant fight at Oriskany grew as he talked with Herkimer who, it was clear, suffered from the thought that he could have done better, that his neighbors in the valley would think he had let them down. "Ach, Gott!" he said several times. "I lost zo many of mein poys." He told Arnold how he had feared an ambush and tried to get the militia to proceed more cautiously. Half of the men disliked him, thought that he might be a Tory at heart because he had done well in life and because his brother served with Sir John Johnson's Tory outfit. Herkimer had been forced to yield to the demands of the impetuous ones to proceed forthwith, and so the militia had marched right into the trap. Seeing the parallel to the abuse General Schuyler had to endure, Arnold tried his best to comfort the old man, saying that everyone back at Schuyler's camp knew of his valor and how badly he had hurt the enemy.

After a while, Herkimer dozed and Arnold conferred with his aides in one corner of the room. "What do you think?" he asked Simmons.

"It's very bad," the young doctor said. "The leg is mortified. Gangrene. It should have been amputated immediately. He was wounded more than a week ago."

"I can understand why he would want to try to save it," Arnold said.

Simmons shook his head. "Even if by some miracle the wound had healed without infection, the leg would've been useless. The knee joint is shattered. The bones would never knit."

"Can you cut off the leg now?"

Simmons blanched and shrugged. "It'd probably kill him."

"And if you don't? If we just leave him?"

"He might last another day or two. He has no chance. None at all."

"So let's amputate."

"I'd have to go so high—to try to get beyond the rot. I . . . I'd need help. I . . ."

"You have Mrs. Herkimer and her Negress here. And her farm hands. Plenty of linen and water and your medicine kit." Arnold looked at Simmons intently. "You've never done this before, have you? Cut off a limb?"

"No. No, sir. I've been present, but I've never done it myself."

"Well, I'm afraid it's time you started. A small chance is better than none."

Herkimer now was awake, his spirits clearly revived by Arnold's visit and his words of praise. He knew what must be done. "Ja, ve mus' do it," he said, clutching his wife's hand. "Maria, brink me meine brandy und anozzer pipe, ja?"

After the celebration of his arrival at Fort Dayton and a series of earnest conferences with Willett, Stockwell, and the council of safety, Arnold was well briefed on the urgency of the situation of Stanwix. He was impressed by Willett and Stockwell, who were anxious to march immediately out of concern for their comrades at Stanwix. Willett described how St. Leger had threatened to turn the Indians loose on the settlers when the fort was taken, and how his men were now digging trenches to bring explosives closer to the ancient walls.

An unexpected delay arose when the local commanders sent the call out to the populated areas of Tryon County for militia to report. The results were meager, so paralyzed by the loss were the settlers, with virtually every household in mourning. So Arnold immediately turned all of his energies to recruiting, waving aside such distractions as serving as judge of the six prisoners. He made numerous speeches to the settlers in German Flats and other settlements, trying to get them to see that they would face St. Leger's army sooner or later. Better to rally around and do it sooner, with the aid of the Continentals. Although morale had improved with the capture of the conspirators—a general Tory uprising was no longer an imminent danger in the valley—it was clear that the shock of what had happened at Oriskany would not be overcome soon or easily. To Arnold's disgust, only twenty or so men had stepped forth, and the Oneidas, as before, would volunteer only as scouts, not as warriors.

Arnold continued to meet with his brigade officers in the largest room of the blockhouse, which had been set aside for his use. Weston, Willett, Stockwell, and several officers of the Tryon County militia were invariably present as well. Arnold laid out the plan for them. They would use the caution that Herkimer had been denied, splitting the army, one wing to move straight ahead, the other to flank the dangerous area of the ravines around Oriskany so that a potential ambush would itself be ambushed. Better use would be made of the Oneida scouts. Willett and Stockwell would attempt a return to the fort in advance of the relief column in order to alert the garrison, doubling their chances of making it by going separately, each with an Oneida scout. They would make sure that the commander at the fort, Colonel Gansevoort, was prepared to launch a full attack to fall on the enemy's rear when the cannon signal was heard or when St. Leger moved his army to meet Arnold's advance.

After two days of very limited success in raising militia, Willett and Stockwell were consumed by anxiety. Learned and all the other officers except Arnold voted against any action until more militia could be assembled to even the odds. Arnold growled that he would allow two more days for recruiting, and then he was marching for Stanwix if he and Willett and Stockwell had to go alone.

Several times the arrival of news interrupted the tedious wait. The first news was sad. An ashen-faced John Simmons arrived at the fort on August 17th to report that Nicholas Herkimer was dead. "I amputated the leg," Simmons said. "I got all the mortified part. But the bleeding. I couldn't stop the bleeding."

"Couldn't you sew or clamp the artery? Or use a tourniquet?" Arnold asked.

Simmons shook his head. "I had to cut off too much. I couldn't quench the blood. There was no place a tourniquet would hold."

Arnold thought there must have been something more the doctor could have done, perhaps the old method of cauterizing the wound, a horrid procedure. He recognized that in any case Herkimer was probably already too far gone from infection to save him. Arnold reached over and patted the anguished surgeon on the shoulder. "It's all right. You did what you could. He's with God now."

Arnold had sent off a routine request to Schuyler for reinforcements, knowing it was hopeless. A returning courier brought joyous news of another kind. A major side expedition composed of Hessian troops sent by Burgoyne to secure forage and horses in Vermont and New Hampshire had been soundly defeated at a place called Bennington. Though details were scant, there apparently had been a hot fight, with Burgoyne losing nearly a thousand of his troops. Schuyler's army had not been involved. It was all the New Englanders, who finally had been roused, but only by the threat to their own territory. The leader had been the noted frontier fighter, John Stark of New Hampshire, who, in the footsteps of Arnold, had finally overcome his anger at being passed over in promotions to return to the fighting.

"By God!" Arnold shouted at Clarkson. "That'll show 'em. Two men insulted by the goddamned Congress! One cuts off Burgoyne's arms and legs *east* of the Hudson. And *this* one"—he pounded on his chest—"is gonna cut 'em off *west* of the Hudson! There *is* some justice in the world."

The next bit of news was not so favorably received. The word came that Horatio Gates had been appointed by Congress on August 4th to succeed Schuyler as commander of the Northern Department. Two weeks later Gates still had not reported to his new post. Arnold was sorry to see Schuyler mistreated again. He knew there was no objective reason for sacking him. He had done everything right with what little he had. But Arnold had been expecting this development ever since the fall of Ticonderoga. The only surprise was that it had taken so long. Emotion and ignorance ruled the day.

Meanwhile, Arnold's patrician young aide was beside himself with anger. "How could they *do* this to Cousin Phil?" Clarkson wailed. "The tide is turning. That business at Bennington proves it. And now they do this! It's so unfair."

"Life is unfair. It's a lesson we all have to learn, my boy," said Arnold, a man who would never abide anything he regarded as unfair to him in his own life. He began chuckling at the memory of how long Gates had been striving to achieve what he now had, how many hours Arnold had been forced to listen to Gates's denunciations of Schuyler. At least he had kept his skirts clean with Gates, Arnold mused. The change in command should make little difference to him. Arnold chuckled again at the thought of Gates taking his sweet time to arrive. Typical! Gates was dallying so that if a disaster were to occur, it would happen before he got there.

A letter that also came in the courier's pouch brought a smile to Arnold's face. It was from Lucy Knox, reporting that Betsy DeBlois's engagement to Martin Brimmer had been scotched, apparently due to the heavy hand of her overly protective mother. Lucy wanted to know if she should continue her efforts to retrieve the trunk of fine goods that Arnold had given to Betsy. Arnold's mind went immediately to thoughts of an ardent letter he might write to rekindle his interrupted courtship. The more he thought of Betsy, however, the more the image of Peggy Shippen came to his mind. The two young ladies were of a similar age, but, in comparison, Peggy's slim figure made Betsy's curvaceousness seem of the type that would produce considerable plumpness in a mature woman. And Peggy seemed more alert and intelligent, though Arnold barely knew her. He resolved to rectify that if he ever got to Philadelphia again. In the meantime, he had *two* beautiful young ladies to dream about.

The day before Arnold's ultimatum expired, he decided to deal with the six prisoners, both to break the boredom and to distract the locals who grumbled that the relief column should have already left, though they personally were not ready to join it. A makeshift court was convened in the general store. Arnold appointed Willett as judge-advocate. The first prisoner brought in for judgment was Hon Yost Schuyler, a pathetic figure in his oddments of Indian garb covered by a blue jacket.

After a few questions, Arnold turned to Willett and Clarkson. "This poor soul is half-crazed," he whispered. "It'd be cruel to hang him."

Willett leaned over: "I agree. Besides, he's held in awe by some of the Indians. As if he were a shaman. If we let him be executed, they might see it as bad medicine."

As Arnold digested this information, a commotion arose near the door where a number of chairs had been placed for the public. All were filled and no one else was allowed to enter. A bedraggled crone with stringy hair, dressed in a variety of dirty, colorful cloths, had left her seat to come rushing up. She threw herself at Arnold's feet and clutched his legs, babbling incomprehensibly all the while. With her, a tall young man in buckskin clothes, his face a mask of stone, came forward. This animated Hon Yost, who began twitching and shouting as well.

As Clarkson hauled the woman away from Arnold's legs, some sense of what she was shrieking began to filter through. She was Hon Yost's mother and the silent young man was his brother. Arnold slammed the flat of his hand on the table and roared, *"Shut up!"*

Cowed, the woman shrunk back. "Madam"—Arnold now addressed her calmly—"you will be quiet or I will arrest you and your son." He turned to Hon Yost. "Are you a shaman?"

Hon Yost began rolling his eyes and then his head, with a silly grin on his face. Arnold watched this for a while and decided that it was the shaman's way of saying yes. An idea was ticking at his brain. He leaned over and whispered to Willett, who nodded and stood up to address the room. "We need to interview this prisoner and his family in private," he said. "This court is adjourned until this afternoon. At two o'clock."

After all the members of the public had filed out, Arnold resumed his questions. "You, Hon Yost. Do you know who I am?"

Hon Yost nodded emphatically.

"What do the Indians call me?"

"You are Heap Fighting Chief," Hon Yost said in solemn awe and perfect English.

Arnold gave an admonishing glance sideways at Willett and Clarkson, who were concealing their grins.

"You are correct," Arnold told Hon Yost in a very serious tone. "I *am* Heap Fighting Chief. And there is another name your brothers have given me. Do you know that name as well?"

"You are Dark Eagle," Hon Yost said.

"You are correct again," Arnold said. "Now, what is the meaning of these names your brothers have given me?"

Hon Yost's expression was blank. Then he began nodding slowly.

"Yes," Arnold said, "they mean that all who oppose me will die."

At the look of fright on the prisoner's face, Arnold said: "Don't worry, Hon Yost. I won't let them hang you. In fact, if you do what I ask, and you do it well, I will set you free. Will you do what I ask?"

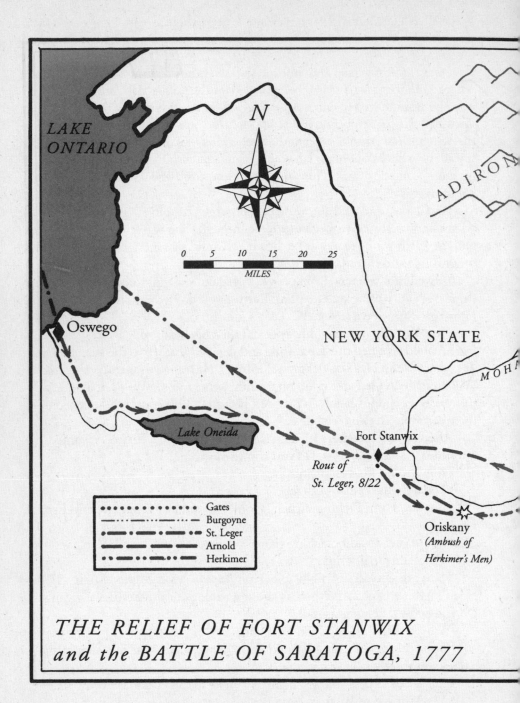

LAKE ONTARIO

ADIROM

N

0 5 10 15 20 25
MILES

NEW YORK STATE

MOH

Oswego

Lake Oneida

Fort Stanwix

Rout of
St. Leger, 8/22

Oriskany
(Ambush of
Herkimer's Men)

•••••••••••• Gates
———·——— Burgoyne
—·—·—·— St. Leger
— — — — Arnold
▬▬▬▬ Herkimer

THE RELIEF OF FORT STANWIX
and the BATTLE OF SARATOGA, 1777

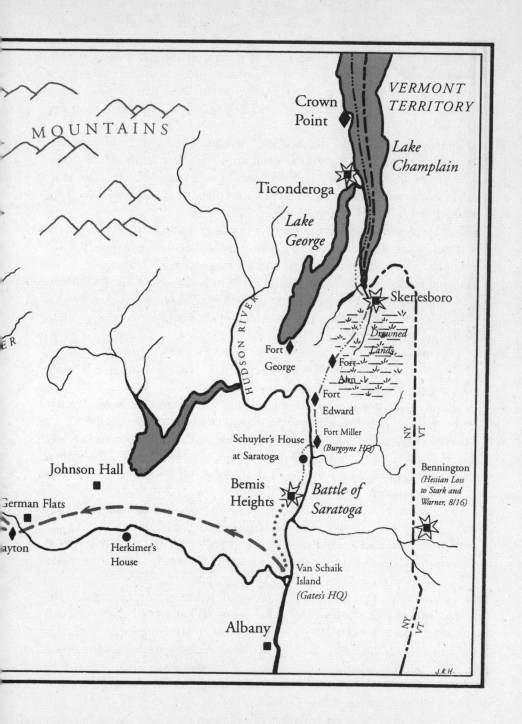

MOUNTAINS

VERMONT
TERRITORY

Crown
Point

Lake
Champlain

Ticonderoga

Lake
George

Skenesboro

Drowned
Lands

Fort
George

Fort
Ann

Fort
Edward

Fort Miller
(Burgoyne HQ)

Schuyler's House
at Saratoga

Johnson Hall

Bemis
Heights

Battle of
Saratoga

NY
VT

Bennington
(Hessian Loss
to Stark and
Warner, 8/16)

German Flats

ayton

Herkimer's
House

Van Schaik
Island
(Gates's HQ)

Albany

NY
VT

HUDSON RIVER

J.R.H.

Hon Yost again nodded. Arnold explained that he wanted Hon Yost to run to the campfires of the Mohawk and Seneca with St. Leger's army to tell them that he had escaped and had come to warn them that Dark Eagle was on the warpath with a huge army. He would punish only the white soldiers, not the Indians if they would leave their camp peacefully. As Arnold spoke, Hon Yost's face took on a look of cunning, and he began jumping about, shouting, "Yes, yes!"

Arnold then addressed the mother: "Madam, would you and your son agree to be my guests here at Fort Dayton until Hon Yost returns?" She nodded, and Arnold turned back to Hon Yost. "I will certainly not harm your mother. Your brother will be a prisoner in your place until you return and I am satisfied that you have done what I ask."

Hon Yost seemed not to have heard. He was grinning and clutching at his blue jacket, pointing his fingers and clicking as if he were firing a gun. "I make bullet holes! They will think I escape and my magic save me."

Arnold smiled. "Good idea," he said. He turned to Clarkson: "Matthew, take Hon Yost outside and make some bullet holes." As they left, Arnold said to Willett: "Can you find me a trustworthy Oneida scout? Preferably a young man of some intelligence?"

"I'm sure I can."

"Bring him to me. I want him to follow Hon Yost at some distance. He can leap in and confirm what Hon Yost is saying."

Half an hour later the three men and the young Oneida, Sacandagawa, watched as the wiry figure of Hon Yost disappeared to the west on the King's Road, his jacket powder-stained and riddled with holes, moving at an easy trot that it seemed he could maintain all day. As soon as he was out of sight, Willett slapped Sacandagawa on the shoulders, and he took off at a similar pace, carrying a belt of wampum.

As they watched the scout running away effortlessly, Clarkson shook his head and asked: "Sir, do you really think this is going to work?"

"You never know," Arnold said as he and Willett smiled at each other. "It can't hurt to try. I couldn't hang the poor bastard, anyway."

That afternoon, Arnold ruled that the four Mohawks would be released the next day without being lashed. He explained to Willett and Clarkson that this act would confirm that Dark Eagle had come not to take vengeance on the Indians, but only on the British and Tories. Arnold also gave Walter Butler the choice of death by hanging or freedom after another week of detention if he would sign a parole not to bear arms or recruit soldiers for one year. Not surprisingly, Butler made the prudent choice.

The three men emerged from the store late in the afternoon to find that recruitment had spurted. Apparently, the combination of passing time,

Herkimer's death, the lure of revenge, and the knowledge that Arnold would march alone if necessary had returned some backbone to the men of Tryon County. Willett's eyes glowed when he learned that more than two hundred men had signed up.

Arnold summoned Learned and his colonels and issued orders for three days' rations to be assembled, gear to be inspected, and a forced march to commence at dawn. A short time later, Willett and Stockwell left on horseback. They and their scouts would ride into the wilderness as far as they dared and then sneak on foot though enemy lines to Fort Stanwix before first light.

That evening Arnold wrote a letter congratulating Gates on his new appointment and concluded: "You will hear of my being victorious or no more."

By late morning the next day the column had passed the burned-out village of Deerfield and had just crossed the ford to the south bank of the Mohawk when a party of horsemen was observed in the distance. Soon Willett could be identified out in front, a huge grin on his face, followed by Stockwell, Hon Yost, Sacandagawa, another Indian, and three officers.

A joyous reunion commenced as men dismounted and began hugging each other, Willett and Stockwell shouting that the fort was saved, that St. Leger was gone. Everyone finally calmed down while Willett told the incredible story. Hon Yost had leaped into the Indian encampment late the night before, dancing about the campfire and screaming gibberish. All the Mohawk and Seneca chiefs except Joseph Brant were present for a council meeting. The Indians were angry with St. Leger because once again he had assigned them the hazardous duty of going out to ambush a relief column. Hon Yost began shouting that Dark Eagle was near. Moments later Sacandagawa leaped into the circle to confirm the danger, saying that Dark Eagle's quarrel was only with the white soldiers, not the Indians. He gave the belt of wampum to the chiefs as Arnold's token of good will. The Mohawks milled about, confused, and then one asked how many soldiers Dark Eagle had. Solemnly, Hon Yost pointed up to the leaves of the trees overhead. Then still another Oneida, one whom Sacandagawa had recruited on the way, came into the circle chanting, "Dark Eagle! Dark Eagle!" He said that a talking bird had told him the Indians should flee before it was too late.

The chiefs ran to St. Leger's tent to tell him to retreat. Befuddled with drink and drowsiness, the commander waved them away. This infuriated the Indians, who immediately went on a rampage, seizing the rum supply and as many weapons of the white soldiers as they could gather up. When the commotion brought British, Loyalist, and German soldiers pouring from their tents, the Indians began attacking them. The unarmed and outnumbered soldiers began to flee in panic. The Indians pursued them, killing and scalping stragglers. St. Leger and his guard wisely joined the flight, and by now he and his survivors might have reached Fort Oswego and their bateaux, moored on the shores of Lake Ontario.

Willett said that when he and Stockwell arrived at Stanwix at dawn, the garrison and settlers were streaming from the fort, stunned and overjoyed at their deliverance, having overcome their disbelief when Hon Yost and the two Oneidas had approached the stockade shouting that St. Leger was gone. Impulsively, Willett seized Arnold by the shoulders and cried: "Your reputation, sir, is worth precious gold!"

The next morning at Stanwix, Arnold was the center of praise and gratitude, along with Hon Yost and Sacandagawa and his Oneida friend, who were bedecked with flowers and grinning from ear to ear over the unaccustomed praise they were receiving from white people. Scouts reported that all of St. Leger's Indians had fled to their home villages, taking with them the loot they had seized from their erstwhile white comrades. St. Leger had only a few hundred survivors, climbing on board their bateaux at Lake Ontario. Originally intending to finish them off, Arnold gave it up as heavy rains began falling.

That afternoon, during a lull in the rain, the Fort Stanwix garrison formed up on the parade ground. The men of the relief column and the settlers became the spectators, cramming every available space in the fort and along its catwalks, to watch as Arnold mounted a platform to address the heroic men of the garrison. From the flagpole atop one of the blockhouses fluttered the tattered homemade version of the Stars and Stripes, the flag design authorized by Congress on June 14th. Its presence throughout the siege marked the first appearance of the new design on any American installation. Arnold spoke eloquently in praise of the valor of the defenders. When he finished, a mighty cheer arose that shook the walls of the old fort more than St. Leger and his army had been able to do.

Afterward, Arnold asked Learned to arrange a rotation in order to furlough the Stanwix garrison and to draft a line of march for the return to the Hudson, to leave at dawn the next day, August 26th. He wrote a note to Gates to be sent ahead. As was his custom when he knew he had accomplished something that would speak far louder than any words, it was a masterful understatement: "There is nothing to fear from this quarter." He had left Schuyler's camp with nine hundred Continentals. He was returning to Gates not only having vanquished an enemy force of two thousand, but also without the loss of a man, with his full complement of Continentals and with the addition of Tryon County recruits, now three hundred strong and growing.

PART VII

"The Very Genius of War"

Chapter 29

With Burgoyne's Army
September, 1777

The invaders from the north had been encamped for more than two weeks at
Fort Miller, waiting to accumulate supplies before crossing the Hudson and
continuing their advance southward, when news of the latest stroke of ill fortune reached them. Word had come from half a dozen Loyalist refugees of the
complete defeat and dispersal of St. Leger's command at Fort Stanwix. Most
credible were two who had participated in the rout of St. Leger's army. They
had come eastward from Stanwix all the way to Fort Miller, staying north of the
Mohawk River to avoid the enemy.

"I couldn't credit it at first," sighed Simon Fraser, blinking in the sunlight
as he stood on one of the ramparts of the fort with General Burgoyne, surveying the sprawling British camp, which occupied all of the open ground spread
out before them. "But those two fellows—they brought back such intimate detail that there's no doubt it's true."

"That damned Arnold," Burgoyne muttered. "Who would've thought it
possible? His mere presence panics the Indians."

"Well, at least you can say that we're not relying on the Indians anymore,"
Fraser commented. The Indians had been deserting steadily, ever since Burgoyne's policy of no atrocities had been violated horribly more than a month
earlier by the slaughter of an entire family of settlers and then the murder and
scalping of a beautiful young American girl, Jane McCrea. Even the Indian
agent, La Corne St. Luc, had disappeared. Only a small number of scouts remained with the army.

"Don't remind me of that," Burgoyne said. How wrong he had been! It
was not easy for Burgoyne to absorb the devastating truth that the Indians

would not respond to his policies. It seemed that the French way of managing the Indians was the one that worked—give them full release to engage in slaughter. And then came the Bennington disaster. A complete surprise and a terrible loss of a thousand men to a band of frontier fighters. Now this latest blow from Fort Stanwix. Wholly incomprehensible.

"Looks like more supplies are coming," said Fraser, staring upriver. Burgoyne's gaze followed his, and he could make out a large flotilla of boats.

"This should be the one that Tom Stanley is bringing. It'll be good to see him," Burgoyne said, happy to have the subject changed to something more pleasant than the train of bad news that had afflicted his expedition.

Stanley indeed had been co-opted to command the supply train from Montreal, having sufficiently recovered from his injuries in the Indian riot. After two months of enforced idleness, he was jubilant to rejoin the expedition and his commander. He devoted several hours to supervising the unloading of the barges and then came to Burgoyne's quarters in the late afternoon. There was not much to tell his uncle of events in Montreal, though Stanley did confirm the demise of St. Leger's expedition from reports he had heard at Fort George, where he had tarried to transload his supplies for the portage to the Hudson River. A number of refugees from the disaster at Stanwix had turned up there. This news had the effect of returning Burgoyne back to his fitful, annoyed state.

"After that glorious success at Ticonderoga, how could anyone figure that everything would begin to go wrong? That damned march through the swamps. The Indians deserting. Bennington. Stanwix."

"With such a run of bad luck, it's bound to change, sir," Stanley offered.

"One would certainly think so."

"We heard of the scalping of the young girl," Stanley said. "A terrible thing. But I couldn't understand why that would make the Indians desert the expedition."

"It just went all wrong," Burgoyne said dejectedly. "The problem of punishing them, for example." He remembered the day, July 27th, when he had observed three Indians riding into the camp at the edge of the Drown'd Lands. They were returning from scouting Fort Edward, some five miles to the south. Leading the trio was a particularly unruly brave named Wyandot Panther. A proud leer on his face, he held up an astonishing fall of beautiful dark hair, nearly five feet long, but mangled and matted at the top with blood. With a shock, Burgoyne realized that it was a scalp, and that was confirmed when the young Loyalist lieutenant David Jones moaned and fell to his knees. Everyone knew that he was anticipating a reunion with Jane McCrea, his betrothed, who had been awaiting the British advance to Fort Edward. Everyone was anticipating their wedding.

"I went down to the Indian encampment and argued with everyone in sight, chiefs, sachems, even La Corne St. Luc," Burgoyne told Stanley. "I wanted to hang Wyandot Panther. In the end I agreed with St. Luc. Let his chiefs try him. But he was gone. And every day we've lost more Indians. Just a week ago, St. Luc finally pulled out."

A long silence prevailed. And then Stanley asked: "What about General Howe?"

Burgoyne turned and fastened an expressionless gaze on young Stanley. "I have no idea where he is. Whether he's coming north or has gone to Philadelphia. No message at all."

Stanley digested this information for a minute. "It's really not possible that he would disregard the plan. Perhaps his couriers have been captured—it must not be easy to communicate from New York to here."

"Yes, of course you're right," Burgoyne said. He leaned back and gazed at the ceiling, heaving a big sigh. "Fort Miller is the crucial point. When we cross the river here, we'll all but cut our supply lines to Canada." He turned to face Stanley, all brusque soldier now. "I have confidence in the British soldiers. And confidence in Howe. As soon as we accumulate twenty-five days of supplies for the army, we're crossing and catching Horatio Gates. The British troops haven't been engaged yet. They're spoiling for a fight. Haven't you noticed their spirit? We're less than forty miles from Albany. I'm going to give them their chance."

Ten days later, the army crossed the Hudson on a bridge of boats near Battenkill, a few miles south of Fort Miller. Then, as if symbolically burning their bridges behind them, all the boats were pulled over to the western side. Burgoyne did not want to leave troops to guard them, and the boats were needed in any case for transporting supplies.

Burgoyne's mood was infectious, and the morale of the army was high. Whatever the travails, the men realized that they were near their primary objective. Brothers-in-arms from New York City would be pressing northward to join with the northern army. Burgoyne rode up and down the line of march, nodding to the men, stopping here and there to make conversation. He came upon Baroness von Riedesel, riding in a large calash that had been made by the troops for her, with seats for her two children and two women servants.

"General, it is such a beautiful day," she cried. "We have boundless forests and magnificent tracts of country." She smiled wickedly. "All the farms are deserted. No one is here."

Burgoyne smiled at the tiny curvaceous figure. "Yes, they've decided to be elsewhere as we come through. But never fear, they'll be back some day soon— and under our rule!" He touched his finger to his brow and reined off, shouting, "The English never lose ground, you know!"

For the first encampment after crossing the river, Burgoyne pressed on to Saratoga. He was anxious to see and make use of General Schuyler's country house. He found the village to be a pleasant place, with a number of smaller dwellings, apparently for the families of his workers dotting the hillsides. Schuyler's house, though not to be compared to English country houses, was nevertheless a handsome structure, well situated on a peninsula formed by the river and a stream known as Fish Kill. Surprisingly, Schuyler's crops had only been partially destroyed, and the army gladly reaped the harvest of fruit from his orchard and the corn, potatoes, beans, and grain from his garden and farm. General Burgoyne and his staff occupied the house, and a sumptuous dinner was held that night for the top officers and the ladies, fortified by cured hams and a goodly supply of wine, brandy, and rum. Best of all, a substantial cache of coffee beans was discovered, a rarity to the army indeed. The officers lifted a merry and somewhat sarcastic toast to the vanquished General Schuyler and his unintended largesse.

Once the ladies retired, a sort of impromptu council of war began in place of the usual resort to card games and carousing. Some of the officers were concerned that so important a step as crossing the river had been taken without general discussion.

In the growing conversation that evening, all of the elements of the situation were voiced by one man or another and analyzed back and forth. The bright side was emphasized—that the army had come more than three fourths of the way toward its objective and that the core was not only intact but actually hardened by the rigors of the march and spoiling for combat. And the dark side: the losses at Bennington and Stanwix; the need to siphon fighting men away to garrison Ticonderoga and Fort George and Edward (Carleton had sent too few troops for that purpose); the weakening of the auxiliary forces with the loss of most of the Indians and only about six hundred Loyalists still present; the lengthening of the supply lines.

Despite the spirits that had been imbibed, all of this was said soberly, without any trace of defeatism. Although scouting was severely curtailed, the occasional deserter or prisoner or Loyalist materialized, and so the army was aware that the Jane McCrea incident had stimulated recruitment to Gates's force. He now was nearly equal to the British Army with more than six thousand men, and his growth was continuing.

Yet, no one believed that the farmers and shopkeepers flocking to Gates could withstand such a superbly trained and led corps of professional soldiers. Burgoyne decided the moment was auspicious for sharing his concern over General Howe's intentions.

"Gentlemen, I must tell you that I have been waiting for weeks for confirmation that General Howe will come north to join us, as our plan calls for. There has been no word, none at all. And I remind you that he earlier voiced an interest in taking Philadelphia, and he may have been encouraged in that by our success at Ticonderoga."

There was a marked increase in excited conversation among the men. Then Simon Fraser rose and spoke: "Gentlemen, I for one believe there is no chance that General Howe will ignore the plan and desert us. Word will come soon. In a sense, it really makes no difference. This army we lead has not yet directly confronted the enemy. That confrontation is very close. The men are eager for the fight. What would they think if we were to fall back now? What would history think of us? I say we have no choice but to forge ahead and seek battle!"

The men were cheering and applauding Fraser's statement. Burgoyne decided there was no need to mention the last point he had intended to share—that his orders gave no liberty for any course but striking for Albany, no matter what the circumstances.

Burgoyne believed that the enemy was encamped at Stillwater or perhaps a few miles north of that place—meaning that no more than fifteen miles separated the two armies. With the new consensus forged in the impromptu council of war, the army was ready to advance to the clash of arms. But indications of wariness were contained in the general orders for Sunday, September 14, which called for a standing order for the rest of the campaign for all pickets and guards to be "under Arms an hour before daylight every morning and remain so 'til it is compleately light."

The army advanced only three miles on the 16th, camping at the village of Dovecote, where there was evidence of a recent rebel outpost. The enemy clearly were very near. Progress the next day was also painfully slow because bridges over the tributary streams of the Hudson had been destroyed and the latitude for marching began to narrow as rocky bluffs appeared on the right. One could picture enemy marksmen and perhaps even artillery arrayed on top of the bluffs to rain fire down on the crowded ranks, circumscribed as they were on the left by the river.

That night, at a place called Sword's Farm, the general decided that the bulk of the army must ascend the high ground, where he suspected the enemy was located. Orders for the 18th divided the army into three columns. The left column, led by von Riedesel, accompanied by General Phillips, would continue on the river road; the other two to seek the high ground over a rutted road that led westward. This was facilitated when it was discovered that the rebels had neglected to destroy a bridge over a large ravine that bisected the area ahead. The center column under Burgoyne crossed the bridge and ascended to the plateau, while the right under General Fraser followed the wagon trail up to the west to cross the ravine at its smallest depth in the woods.

That afternoon a group of some forty soldiers and women from among the

camp followers wandered out to the first farm on the high ground to search for
potatoes. They were surprised by an enemy reconnaissance party and a number were killed and some twenty taken prisoner. This brought forth an angry
reproach from General Burgoyne:

> *The Lieut. Genl. will no longer bear to lose Men, for the pitiful considera-
> tion of Potatoes, or Forage. The life of the Soldier is the property of the King, and
> since neither friendly admonitions, repeated injunctions, nor corporal punish-
> ments have effect, after what has happened, ye Army is now to be informed, and
> it is not doubted that commanding Officers will do it solemnly, that the first Sol-
> dier caught beyond the advance Sentries of the Army will be instantly hanged.*

As angry as Burgoyne was, he also realized that this episode had brought
him confirmation of what he suspected. He now knew that the enemy was also
occupying a position on the heights overlooking the river. That night he met
with Generals Phillips, Fraser, and von Riedesel to plan a cautious advance the
next day, to make contact with the enemy. Burgoyne said he did not necessarily
seek battle unless conditions clearly indicated it. He would begin the advance
at the center when the morning mist burned off, and by a signal of three guns
would tell the two wings when to advance.

Chapter 30

Gates's Headquarters Camp
September, 1777

The tale of Arnold's stunning achievement at Fort Stanwix cascaded eastward
throughout the Mohawk Valley. On September 2nd the hero himself arrived at
Van Schaik Island at the head of his column of nearly thirteen hundred men, all
looking trim and ready for action, their spirits justifiably high after their amazing victory. The story of the victory was told and retold a thousand times, with
all the officers and men applauding Arnold, especially the New Yorkers who
revered him as the angel of deliverance for the entire Mohawk Valley. Even the
New Englanders cheered—after all, Arnold himself was a New Englander. It
seemed hardly possible, but his reputation had soared even higher than before.

General Gates had emerged from his quarters to greet Arnold and congratulate him. He told Arnold that he was in command of the left wing of the
army. When he had left for the Mohawk Valley, Arnold had been second-in-
command to Schuyler for the entire army. Was this a demotion? But the army
had grown, and command of the left was the "position of honor," whose occu-

pant often *was* second-in-command. Arnold was so busy fielding statements of pleasure and confidence from all sides that he failed to ask the question.

That evening, after the celebration had died down, Colonel Varick made a call at Arnold's tent. He was welcomed by the general, who had been having a conversation with his aide, young Matthew Clarkson.

"I'm surprised you're here, Varick," Arnold said, "after General Schuyler is gone."

Varick smiled grimly. "I was all prepared to leave, but General Schuyler insisted that I stay. I would no longer be his aide, of course, but I would remain as muster-master and report to whoever is commanding general." He didn't volunteer that he still would be reporting secretly to General Schuyler. "I'm not surprised to find myself being somewhat frozen out at General Gates's headquarters."

"Damned shame to let Schuyler go," Arnold said. "He did everything right with what he had."

"It was Ticonderoga."

"I know," said Arnold. "I've been expecting it every moment since then."

Varick thought of what had happened, the retreats from Fort Edward, Fort Miller, Saratoga, Stillwater, and now all the way down to Van Schaik Island, where the Mohawk flowed into the Hudson, only a dozen miles north of Albany. That was the end of it, Schuyler had said. Now we'll go north. And then news of Gates's appointment arrived.

Arnold spoke: "Things are different here now. Gates is different. He's much colder than before. And he has that damned Wilkinson as his chief aide."

"Gates fears you," Varick said. "He sees you as a rival to him, now that he's disposed of General Schuyler."

"Nonsense," Arnold scoffed, even though he knew there was truth in what Varick had said. He decided to change the subject. "What can you tell me of the late Sir William Johnson's land? It's been confiscated by the state, yes?"

While Varick tried to readjust his thinking, Clarkson continued the thought: "We made a little detour on the way back from Stanwix," he said. "It's an impressive property, but rather run down now."

"Yes," Varick said. "It's called Kingsborough. Over a hundred thousand acres, I believe."

"When the war is over, there'll have to be some disposition of these Tory estates," Arnold said. "Skenesboro is another one. Over thirty thousand acres, I'm told, and definitely confiscated. There might be grants to officers of the army who've done well in the cause, by Congress or New York State. Or at least an opportunity to purchase land at nominal cost."

"Yes, I suppose so," Varick said. "If anything like that is to happen up here, I'm sure General Schuyler would be the first to know of it."

"Yes," Clarkson said eagerly, "that's what I've told General Arnold, too."

He turned to Arnold. "If you wish, Dirk and I can open the subject with General Schuyler. Find out more and see what the possibilities are. Then you can broach the subject with him."

"Yes, very good," Arnold said, "when the time is right. It's a bit early now. We'll have to see what happens here."

Two days later, Daniel Morgan arrived in camp with his regiment, at least two weeks overdue. Morgan, like Arnold, was a walking legend, a bear of a man, his fringed buckskin garb bleached white, his hair also burned nearly white by the sun. To say that he was tough would be an understatement indeed. While serving as a wagon driver in the French and Indian War, Morgan had struck a British officer who had prodded him along with his sword. The penalty was five hundred lashes, which Morgan somehow survived. Whenever anyone mentioned that ordeal, Morgan would laugh and say: "The drummer miscounted. There was only four hundred and ninety-nine strokes."

Because of the way he was treated, Morgan hated the British. Whenever there was an opportunity to fight them, he would be there. He had been among the first to arrive at Cambridge in '75, and he was with Arnold at Quebec, with a scar to show for it where a cannonball had brushed the side of his face.

After his year's parole, the condition of his release from captivity at Quebec, he had been busy reconstituting his regiment, known as Morgan's Virginia Riflemen, though many of his recruits came from Pennsylvania. They were tall and rangy, the very image of the American frontiersmen with their fringed buckskin clothes, coonskin caps, and deadly Pennsylvania rifles.

Arnold and Morgan rushed to embrace each other, the huge Morgan almost lifting Arnold off the ground. The troops cheered. Clearly, morale in camp was on the rise. But Morgan's troops were not in very good shape, they having traveled by boat from Esopus against headwinds and the river current, with sickness running through their ranks. Barely more than three hundred of his five-hundred-man regiment were fit for duty.

By the next day, the obvious thought had occurred to Arnold. Why had not Gates sent an officer to notify Washington and Congress of the victory at Stanwix, just as Schuyler had sent off his aide Henry Livingston after Bennington? Gates was having tea in the late morning when Arnold arrived to pose his question. James Wilkinson sat at the table with the commander, the better to serve his role of passing papers back and forth.

After Arnold was seated and had asked his question, Gates was momentarily flustered, looking at Wilkinson for guidance. "It was just too late, General," Wilkinson said. "Yes, of course," Gates picked up, "we weren't sure at all where we'd find Congress. Or Washington, for that matter."

Arnold thought for a moment. Then he said: "I eliminated two thousand men from the forces opposing us. At Bennington, Stark eliminated one thousand."

"Word went off in the regular channels, you may be sure of that," Gates said. "But with things so unsettled down there—it wasn't right to send an esteemed colleague."

"What 'esteemed colleague' would you have sent?"

Gates again was flustered. "I think we never thought of it," he said. "You do have only one aide."

"Well," Arnold said. "I need another one or two."

"Yes, I'm aware," Gates said, eyes hooded.

Arnold decided there was nothing to be gained. He glanced out the window as he rose. "Some recruits are straggling in," he said. "But none from New England."

Despite Gates's boastfulness, the New Englanders were joining John Stark's camp. And Stark was being as difficult as ever, despite much flattering and pleading from General Benjamin Lincoln, a Massachusetts man who had joined the northern command after Arnold had left for Stanwix. Schuyler had sent Lincoln to the east to help prepare the area for possible offensives by Burgoyne's column. He was still there, but Stark was an independent operator, and he simply sat with his army east of Bennington, ignoring Gates. Arnold was aware that Stark was as indifferent to Gates as he had been to Schuyler.

Gates was miffed by Arnold's comment, and his expression showed it. "They'll be here, when they're needed. Never you fear, sir."

On September 8th, General Gates decided the time had come for the army to seek a better defensive ground than Van Schaik Island. He felt that enough time had passed since General Schuyler had recommended Stillwater to him, a hamlet across the Mohawk River and some dozen miles up the western side of the Hudson, opposite where the Hoosic River came in on the other side. Stillwater was abandoned and fields of crops were destroyed between the bluffs and the river.

One of the first arrivals at the new campsite was a surprise. It was Henry Livingston, returning from his mission of bearing the news of Bennington to Congress. He being Schuyler's aide, Varick had thought Livingston would stop at Albany and would be seen no more. But he had come to camp specifically to see Varick. He had indeed reported to Schuyler, but the general had sent him on to query Varick about the possibility of Livingston joining Matthew Clarkson, his cousin, as an aide to Arnold.

Varick thought it was a capital idea. He liked Henry and Matthew a great deal—they were the finest sort of young men, both around twenty. They were intelligent and well placed, Henry the son and Matthew the nephew of Governor William Livingston of New Jersey, and both related at several removes to General Schuyler.

Varick knew Arnold would find Livingston appealing, and Clarkson would be overjoyed as well. So it turned out when the three men visited

Arnold in his tent that evening. He readily agreed and told Clarkson to break open several bottles of wine in celebration. It was a lively conversation, because Livingston was full of news of what was happening in the south.

Following proper protocol, he had gone first to Washington's headquarters, which on August 22nd he located on the southwest branch of the Neshaminy River at the intersection of the York and Bristol Roads. The Continental Army had been encamped there for ten days, awaiting firm information as to General Howe's whereabouts. Livingston said he had found the place a beehive of activity, with the army breaking camp to march southward. Word had arrived only that morning that Howe's armada had been sighted coming up Chesapeake Bay with the apparent intent of landing his army at the head of the bay to march on Philadelphia. Despite the frenetic activity on all sides, General Washington and several of his aides welcomed Livingston in the drawing room of the Moland House, where his news of Bennington was gladly received. There were congratulations all around and a joyous toast. Washington immediately assigned an aide to draft a special order in commemoration of the victory. He then gave Livingston the expected honor of carrying the news to the Congress.

Once in Philadelphia, Livingston found the city in a state of alarm. Confirmation had arrived that General Howe had indeed come up the Chesapeake Bay with the intent of landing his army of eighteen thousand troops at Head of Elk, some forty miles southwest of Philadelphia.

It was the custom for the Congress to award a promotion to a military officer who brought official news of a great victory. Indeed, that was why General Schuyler had chosen Livingston to be the bearer of good tidings. But he did not become a lieutenant-colonel. A resolution was offered in Congress, but it failed to receive a majority of votes, the New England bloc voting in the negative to a man. Livingston was left to ponder the reason. Was it because he was an aide to a general who no longer held a command? Or because the New England delegates thought that one of their own should have had the honor?

On the 24th, Livingston witnessed the march of the Continental Army, coming down the Yorktown Pike to parade through the streets of Philadelphia before crossing the Schuylkill River to stand between the city and Howe's army. Livingston thought the American troops looked quite formidable, though, as usual, with infinite variety of dress, headwear, weapons, and style of marching. General Washington was cheered as he rode past, surrounded by other generals and his aides.

Livingston described a new face in that coterie, one that he had noticed in the gathering at the Moland House: "He was an odd-looking fellow, with a great slanty forehead and nose and spokes of red hair sticking out. He looked quite young, possibly in his early twenties. I soon learned that he was a Frenchman named Lafayette, the Marquis de Lafayette—and that only days earlier, he had been commissioned a major-general by the Congress!"

This brought forth howls of derision from the small group, aided considerably by the spirits they had imbibed, with particular scorn directed at Congress—for its ill treatment of Arnold, Schuyler, and now Livingston, all compounded by the insult of giving such high rank to a callow aristocrat from France, while ignoring deserving Americans.

After all the laughter and sneers died down, Livingston said: "In truth, I met the gentleman that very same night, at a dinner given in honor of General Washington, and I must say I found him to be a very likeable person." Livingston explained that his uncle Robert, a delegate to Congress from New York, had taken him along to the affair. To his delight, he discovered that Alexander Hamilton was there, an old friend of the Livingston family. "When I asked him about the new French officer," Livingston said, "he merely raised his eyebrows. He told me that Congress at first had treated young Lafayette quite rudely, but Washington had warmed to him. I asked Hamilton about the state of the army in general. He told me that Washington had some eleven thousand effectives, but was concerned that so few men of the area had turned out to help. He said there had been some debate on the matter, but Washington was committed to the defense of Philadelphia."

"There was no fighting before you left?" Arnold asked.

"No. I left on the last day of August, and I stayed several days with my parents on my way."

"Well, today is the eighth. There must have been a fight by now," Arnold said. "I'd give my left arm to know what happened. Did Hamilton have any explanation of Howe's madness?"

"Sir?"

"Why is Howe down there instead of coming up here? And why didn't he simply go up the Delaware, to land at Wilmington or someplace near? Only twenty miles from Philadelphia. Instead, he takes weeks to sail hundreds of miles to go all the way around and come up Chesapeake Bay!"

Livingston shook his head. "I asked just such questions, but Hamilton was as mystified as we are. He said that he and his colleagues always thought Howe would go north, but that perhaps Ticonderoga convinced him Burgoyne didn't need his help."

"It's a damned sight different now, isn't it?"

"And his best guess on the other is that they found contrary winds and strong tides in Delaware Bay. And that Admiral Howe feared the mudflats on the upper river and the forts south of Philadelphia."

"Well, it's in our favor, I guess," Arnold said. "But I fear that once Burgoyne knows this, he'll pull foot and head back to Canada. We'll lose our chance."

"Hamilton did tell me something quite amusing," Livingston said. "I asked him about the military plan he had carried to Congress before I arrived at Moland House. He laughed and revealed that the council of war at Neshaminy made a decision based on the belief that Howe was headed for Charleston to attack the southern states. They knew they couldn't do anything about that, so they agreed to march *north* to attack Clinton and retake New York City—and then to march up here to help against Burgoyne! And Congress approved it! Of course, everything changed when word came that Howe was already well up the Chesapeake."

That story brought much guffawing and Clarkson broke open more bottles, as the group caroused late into the night.

It seemed that the day before Livingston arrived in camp, Gates had asked Arnold to make assignments for two new militia regiments. To please Gates, and also because these were raw troops, Arnold assigned them to the center, the most heavily defended part of the line. The center of the army was under Gates's direct control. The day *after* Henry's arrival and the boisterous party in Arnold's tent, new orders came from Gates, signed by Wilkinson, which assigned the two regiments to Glover's brigade in the right wing of the army. Accompanied by Livingston and Clarkson, Arnold strode angrily to confront Gates. He demanded to know why his orders had been contradicted without consulting him, putting him in a "ridiculous light" before the army. Sharp words were exchanged before Gates said it was an honest mistake that would be corrected. It never was—and Arnold continued to resent it.

Arnold promptly proclaimed Stillwater a poor place to make a stand. The river plain was quite broad and much cleared for farming, a good area for European maneuvers and artillery, but not for the Americans. The Polish engineer, Tadeusz Kościuszko, who had been assigned to the Northern Department a year earlier, was of the same opinion. A taciturn person with a passable command of English, he was competent and well liked by the other officers, who referred to him as "Kos."

A farmer named Neilson had come into camp to tell that the area around his farm, some six or seven miles to the north, consisted of high ground overlooking a narrow strip along the river, bordered on the other side by densely wooded broken country and crossed by a series of ravines. The next day, September 11th, a party rode out in the morning mist to inspect, including Neilson, Wilkinson, Kościuszko, his two young surveyors, and Arnold and his two aides.

The group soon reached the area known as Bemis Heights, named for a tavern once owned by Samuel Bemis, a Loyalist, who of course was nowhere to be seen. At this point, the main north-south road, which led along the riverbank, was cramped up against a narrow defile by a westerward bend of the river. For several miles to the north, the road was flanked by the river and by cliffs that rose over a hundred feet to an undulating plateau. The tavern, situation on a side road that ran up the defile to the high ground, was pretty much wrecked. Neilson's small log cabin and clearing were a little over a half mile to the west of the tavern. A few other cabins dotted the area. The party rode slowly along the plateau to the north, Arnold and Kościuszko in the lead, occasionally exchanging brief comments. They encountered heavy woods and underbrush for the most part. Every so often a ravine cut through the plateau and the cliffs, one of them the passageway for Mill Creek, with an offshoot for its northern branch. The ravines were rocky and bottomed by sticky clay, with cool, dank air in contrast to the bright colors and fresh air of the highlands, where the sandy soil made a degree of farming possible.

After a mile and a half, the riders came upon a deserted farm owned by a Loyalist named Freeman, which, like Neilson's farm, was located on the western edge of the plateau, snug up against the wilderness. Half a mile north of Freeman's farm was the largest ravine, which promptly was dubbed "the Great Ravine." The clearings offered areas for open fire and artillery, but there were few of them. Along the entire western edge of the area that had been traversed, the ground was rocky and densely wooded and rose steadily to more than three hundred feet above the river. In general, the area was more suitable for frontier fighting than European-style maneuverings.

The party rode back to Neilson's farm, and Arnold and Kościuszko stopped to dismount and confer, as the others crowded around. Arnold looked once again to the north and said: "This is where we should fight."

Kościuszko had said little during the ride, but his darting eyes had taken in everything. Now he stroked his giant mustache and said: "Ja, this is good. Very good. This is the most narrow place between the edge of the cliffs and where the land goes higher. This is good ground."

Arnold, the man of instinct and experience, and Kościuszko, the man of training and reading, exchanged ideas about the type of defense to be built.

"Ja, we can build good defense here," Kościuszko said, taking out some paper to begin sketching. "In U-shape, open to the south. We go from cliff here across to farm house with log and earth breastworks. Closed redoubts at corners for artillery. We barricade road below along river. They will not pass. I need a thousand workers."

Arnold spoke to Wilkinson: "Do you think General Gates will approve?"

Wilkinson nodded. "Yes, I do think so. Though he'll want to see for himself."

"Our chief engineer will make an excellent guide for the general," Arnold said. He turned to Kościuszko. "You'll have your work party by this afternoon." He took another long look around. "We'd best not waste any time. The enemy is near. This is where we're going to fight. And it will happen soon."

Chapter 31

Freeman's Farm
September 19, 1777

The day dawned bright and beautiful, the sun slanting down from a cloudless sky on the white ground fog that covered most of the area. It was cold, the grass in the meadows and the tree limbs in the forest glinting with hoarfrost. The colors of autumn were already appearing, hints of scarlet and gold mixed with many shades of green.

The soldiers in the British picket lines suffered grievously from the chill. Like the Baroness von Riedesel, the troops had left behind their heavier clothing, expecting that this would be entirely a summer campaign. The main British camp was stirring as the center column under Burgoyne began to form, consisting of four regiments—the Ninth, Twentieth, Twenty-first, and Sixty-second—some twelve hundred rank and file known collectively as the British line. Burgoyne had already sent Captain Thomas Jones's artillery battalion forward to position six six-pounders along the line where the forest gave way to the clearing of Freeman's farm.

Considerably to the right of Burgoyne, Simon Fraser commanded the elite of the British Army, the Grenadier Battalion and the Light Infantry Battalion, along with the Twenty-fourth Regiment, and Breymann's German Brigade. They had ascended more than a hundred feet along the rise to the forest west of Freeman's farm where they bivouacked for the night beneath the trees.

On the river road, von Riedesel's Germans also maintained the position they had reached the day before. The area between the bottom of the cliffs and the river was crowded for a mile to the rear with soldiers, cannon, and carts loaded with provisions. The boats, many of them still laden, were tied up to the bank all along the way. Several hundred yards to the south, von Riedesel could see through the thinning mist to the first American blockade across the road just beyond Mill Creek. He surmised it could be blown away by a sustained cannonade, but the time for that had not yet come. He knew there was a second blockade half a mile beyond the first that was out of his line of sight. Using a spyglass now, he could barely discern the outline of the bridge of boats the Americans had put in place to the east bank of the Hudson. Across the river, American scouting parties sometimes came into view, posted there to give the alert in case the British tried to recross the river at any point. And then, out of the mist, von Riedesel saw a large body of marching men gradually appear, headed toward the American pontoon bridge. They kept coming until von Riedesel was sure there were many hundreds of soldiers. *Mein Gott!* he thought to himself. *More reinforcements for Gates!* He called back to General Phillips to come witness this distressing sight.

Behind the American fortifications, Benedict Arnold paced back and forth, every nerve tingling. He was itching for battle, having drawn first blood the afternoon before when his reconnaissance party surprised the potato foragers on the open ground of Freeman's farm. Livingston and Clarkson had wanted Arnold to order an attack, but it was already late afternoon, not enough time to persuade Gates to bring up sufficient force. "You'll see plenty of lead tomorrow, lads," Arnold told his two eager aides.

On this morning, he had been engaging in a running argument with Gates over the tactics for the day, when Gates abruptly moved away to confer with his aides and a courier who had just arrived. Gates had chosen a cabin to the rear for his headquarters and residence. It was one of several small structures in the area, some old and some newly built by the engineers. The Americans had greatly enlarged the cleared area of Neilson's farm to nearly a hundred acres, and Colonel Kościuszko had outdone himself in bordering the field on three sides with an impressive line of earthen and log breastworks, a double line at the northeastern point. The breastworks stretched northwestward from the cliffs across to Neilson's house and then turned southward along the line of the forest. The house was now called Fort Neilson, having become a fortified redoubt bristling with cannon. An abbatis of sharpened logs pointed to the enemy beyond the frontal breastworks. Kościuszko's men had labored nearly a week to build these strong barriers, behind which a sprawling armed camp burgeoned, thousands of soldiers milling about, with many more in reserve to the rear in a large park of carts and draft animals that stretched so far it was lost to view.

The argument between Arnold and Gates was entirely predictable, putting the aggressor versus the conservative, the attacker versus the defender, the daring man versus the cautious one. Gates was very pleased that his army had grown to more than seven thousand men and that he stood behind a formidable defensive position. Every day that passed he grew stronger, he was certain, and Burgoyne weaker. There was no need to risk an attack.

Arnold conceded the strength of the position. He was not calling for an all-out offensive. He argued that it was better to choose the time and place of battle than to let the enemy do so. Burgoyne's army was very dangerous. Better to keep him off balance, to goad him into attacking when he was least prepared for it, to do this by lightning American thrusts at his flanks.

As Gates dispatched his aides and turned, Arnold came up to him to resume the argument.

"We heard they had more than a hundred cannon when they left St. Jean," he said to Gates.

"They don't have nearly that now."

"No, but they have enough. If they bring them up in range, they can batter down these breastworks."

Gates frowned and Arnold rushed on: "We have nearly two miles of good fighting ground between our lines and the enemy. We should fight them out there, not here. If we do that they'll never get all their cannon lined up this side of the Great Ravine."

Gates still frowned and said nothing. "Look at it this way," Arnold said. "If we fight out there and we break, we've got these fortifications to fall back on. If we wait for them to attack us here and we break, we have no place to go. Think of it as two lines of defense."

To Gates, it was Lake Champlain all over again, the last time he had heard talk of two lines of defense. Arnold's fleet and Fort Ticonderoga. And what had happened? Arnold had disobeyed orders and gone on the offensive. On the other hand, the fort had survived. Gates recalled that he had always thought that Arnold would have his uses. Perhaps this was the time. Let the crazy bastard go out and get himself killed.

"All right, listen to me," Gates said. "You can operate on the left. We'll stay here and see what happens. Send out a scouting party in force and see if we make contact."

"Good," Arnold said. "And if it gets hot we can support them, right?"

"That depends. I want it clear that I do *not* seek a full-scale battle today. Do you understand that? Can I make it more clear to you?"

"I understand." Arnold began to leave.

"Wait a minute," Gates said, a smug smile on his face. "You saw that courier? He tells us that Stark is on the way with his entire brigade! Nearly two thousand men!"

"My God, I thought he was lost. He's taken his sweet time, hasn't he?"

"He's been quite ill, I understand. I knew the New Englanders would come to me. They're on the bridge now. They'll be here momentarily." Gates was delighted that his army was on the verge of sudden growth.

"Good! All the more reason to poke Johnny Burgoyne in the ribs." Arnold strode over to where Livingston and Clarkson were standing, holding the reins of their mounts. Clarkson also held the reins of Arnold's grey horse. The three men mounted and Arnold said: "Let's go talk to Dan Morgan."

It was now past nine o'clock. Morgan was standing to the left of the compound, chatting with three of his officers, Colonel Butler, Major Morris, and Captain Van Swearingham. Arnold reined up, dismounted, and began explaining what he had in mind. "I want you to advance slowly and carefully and spread out as much as you think is safe, the better to make contact at some point. When we hear serious gunfire, we'll come up immediately in support."

"Not till then?" Morgan asked.

"No. I'm not allowed. Gates thinks of this as a large scouting party. He doesn't want to fight today and I wouldn't want to give him apoplexy."

As a look of disgust passed over Morgan's face, Arnold said, "Don't worry about support. We'll be up on the double. I've got a lot of regiments on the left. Poor's brigade of New Hampshire Continentals, Dearborn's sharpshooters, the Connecticut militia, Learned's brigade, Van Cortlandt's Second New York, the Massachusetts Line. I'll send them all if I have to."

Livingston's eyebrows went up. "General Gates approved that?"

"Not quite," Arnold said. "But he will."

Morgan spoke to his officers: "All right, you heard. Let's get organized." He then puffed three turkey calls on a small instrument slung around his neck, the signal for his men to come to him.

Arnold clutched Morgan's sleeve. "Listen, Daniel. You can take your time. Let the mist burn off. Doesn't help a sharpshooter to have to aim through fog. I'd say at least another hour."

"Good, gives us time to make sure everybody knows what he's doing." Morgan watched the men streaming toward him, more than four hundred of them.

"Daniel," Arnold said. "Be careful."

Morgan laughed. "Don't worry. We're ready to give Burgoyne hell. By God, that's what we're here for. You just be sure to come up at the right time." Morgan frowned. "Damn, I don't know why I said that. You're the one man I *don't* have to say that to!"

Now it was Arnold's turn to smile, as Morgan touched his finger to his forehead and moved off.

It was just past noon by the time Morgan's stretched-out line reached the southern edge of Freeman's farm, a large oblong-shaped clearing. He was behind the center on horseback, Butler in charge of the left and Morris of the right. Some of the men on the right entered an abandoned log cabin at the southeastern corner of the farm and others crouched down along a split-rail fence leading to the west.

They could clearly see an enemy party of fifty or so lolling in front of another cabin directly across the field, something over two hundred yards away, enjoying the warmth of the sun now that the fog had completely disappeared. The group included several officers.

Major Morris whispered hoarsely to his left and right. "All right. On my command. Space your shots from left to right so we don't all hit the same man." Twenty of the nearby sharpshooters took careful aim and Morris yelled: "Fire!" The crash reverberated, and, as the smoke cleared, Morgan's men saw that a dozen of the enemy were down, including the officers. The rest fled in panic, wounded men trying to crawl after them.

Morgan galloped over at the sound of fire and blew the signal for attack when he saw what had happened. All across the southern edge of Freeman's farm, the Virginia Riflemen poured out of the woods on the run, howling their battle cry. Before they reached the other side of the clearing, they saw that the

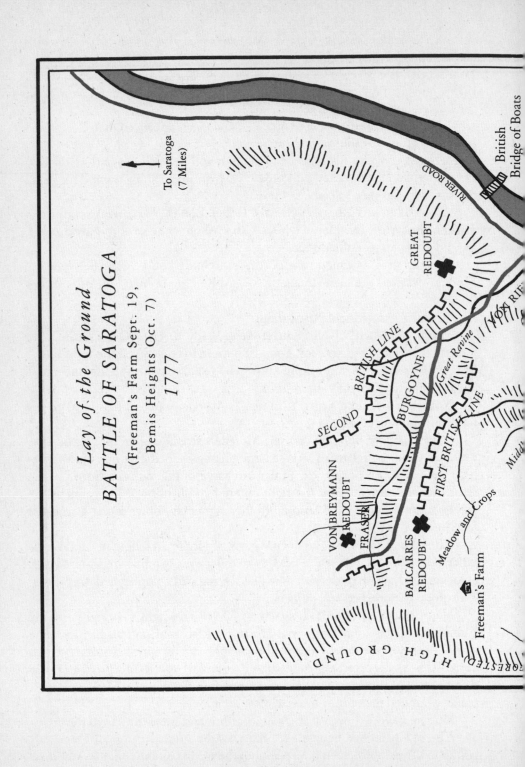

Lay of the Ground
BATTLE OF SARATOGA
(Freeman's Farm Sept. 19,
Bemis Heights Oct. 7)
1777

To Saratoga
(7 Miles)

RIVER ROAD

British
Bridge of Boats

GREAT
REDOUBT

BRITISH LINE

SECOND

BURGOYNE

Great Ravine

FIRST BRITISH LINE

VON BREYMANN
REDOUBT

FRASER

BALCARRES
REDOUBT

Meadow and Crops

Freeman's Farm

HIGH GROUND

(FORESTED)

Middle

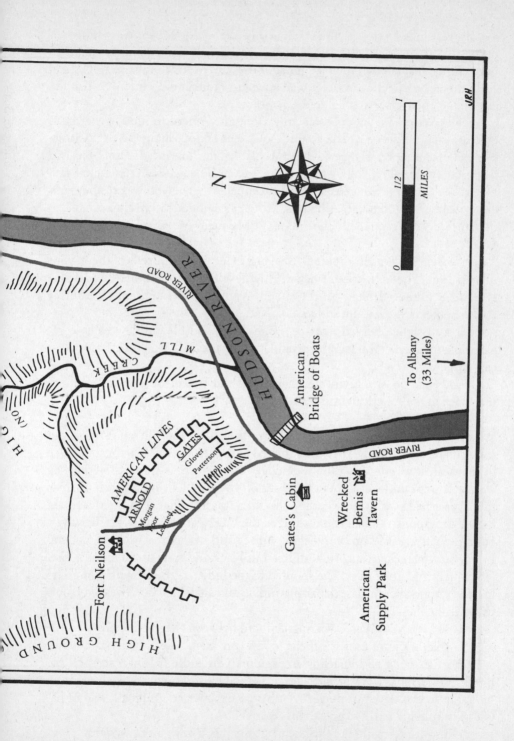

N

MILES

1/2

0   1

To Albany
(33 Miles)

HUDSON RIVER

RIVER ROAD

RIVER ROAD

MILL CREEK

HIGH (GROUND)

HIGH GROUND

American
Bridge of Boats

Gate's Cabin

Wrecked
Bemis
Tavern

American
Supply Park

Fort Neilson

AMERICAN LINES

ARNOLD

GATES

Morgan

Poor

Learned

Glover

Patterson

Lincoln

JRH

woods were full of redcoats, the oncoming center of the British Army. The red-coats were as surprised as Morgan's men, and it took them some moments to begin firing, just enough time for most of the Americans to reverse tracks and scatter in every direction at redoubled speed. A number were hit by British fire out on the open space and fell to the ground.

James Wilkinson galloped laterally along the American line, having been able to reach the scene by the simple expedient of not asking Gates's permission. He came upon Henry Livingston also riding toward the line. He had been sent by Arnold to follow Morgan's advance. The two men reined to a halt when they encountered the dismounted Daniel Morgan, who was sobbing uncontrollably. Big and tough as he was, Morgan's emotions were always close to the surface. "We're ruined," he sobbed. "My men—we're ruined, for God's sake."

"No, no," Wilkinson shouted, "I've just come past hundreds of them, your officers, too. The losses aren't heavy." Livingston confirmed that he had also seen many of the riflemen. "And General Arnold has already sent Dearborn's sharpshooters this way," he added.

Morgan sighed, wiped his face, remounted, and blew turkey calls to re-assemble his men. "You lads be careful," Morgan said. "Man on a horse is an easy target."

"And you, too, sir," Livingston said, as he and Wilkinson wheeled about to race back to the American fortifications.

Wilkinson had exaggerated slightly. From the left of the riflemen's line, Van Swearingham and a large party had rushed to the attack and then turned to flee to the nearest woods along the west edge of the clearing. They thought they were safe until thirteen of them were cut off by two Light Infantry companies that Fraser had sent to see what the shooting was all about. Van Swearingham lay on the ground with a flesh wound as the other captives were herded away. Four Indians sneaked up brandishing knives and began to strip him. General Fraser's batman came into view, dressed in black and swinging a club. " 'Ere, 'ere, you buggers, get away!" he shouted to the Indians. "Be off with you." The batman darted after the last departing Indian and snatched Van Swearingham's wallet from him.

"God bless you," Van Swearingham said between clenched teeth.

"I wouldn't want those 'eathens to 'ave any man," the batman said, handing over the wallet and kneeling to examine where the ball had scraped the thigh. "Oh, it looks awright, sir! The surgeon'll fix you up in two shakes."

"I'm sorry I have no specie," Van Swearingham said, pulling a wad of paper bills from his wallet to give to his rescuer.

"Oh, no, sir! I couldn't. Thankee, but I'm just 'appy you're awright."

At that moment a resplendent British officer on an iron-grey charger rode up. It was Simon Fraser, followed by a lieutenant and several soldiers on foot. "You there! How many men were in that attack?"

Van Swearingham raised up on his elbows. "Our army is commanded by General Gates and General Arnold, sir."

"I asked you, how many men in that attack!" Fraser voice was louder and harsher. "Are there any more coming up?"

"Our army is commanded by General Gates and General Arnold, sir."

"Damn it man, you'll tell me this moment or I'll hang you!"

Van Swearingham looked directly into Fraser's eyes and said firmly: "You may if you please."

Fraser cursed, wheeled about, rode away, and then abruptly reined up. "Will," he called to the batman. "Come here." The batman hustled over. "It looks like he's *your* prisoner, Will. Get him to the surgeon. And see that he's not ill treated." As he rode off, the batman smiled.

Back at the compound, Arnold had not waited for Livingston to begin sending reinforcements. Colonel Cilley's First New Hampshire and Scammel's Third were pouring through the passageway adjacent to Fort Neilson at double time, led by Brigadier Enoch Poor, as Wilkinson and Livingston galloped in and dismounted.

Arnold was ordering up the last New Hampshire regiment and the three Connecticut militia regiments to go next when Gates rushed over in an agitated state. "What are you doing?" he yelled.

"Sending support for Morgan," Arnold said. "He's under fire."

"I don't want a battle!"

"Morgan's in trouble, sir," Wilkinson said.

"Yes. Well. All right," Gates said. Then he glared at Wilkinson: "Where the hell have you been when I need you?" Before Wilkinson could say anything, Gates began wailing: "They're gone! They're gone! I can't stop them."

"Who's gone?" Arnold asked.

"Stark and all his men!"

"They just got here this morning."

"I know. But they say their enlistment time is up. Every last man!"

"What the hell!" Arnold exploded. "We've got a fight going on here. They can hear the gunfire. And they're leaving? Why did they come all this way if they're quitting?"

"Only God and John Stark know. And I haven't seen Stark at all. He didn't report to me. Only he can stop it. I've got to find him. C'mon," Gates beckoned to Wilkinson as he headed off to his horse.

Arnold heard three measured cannon shots in the distance. "That must be Burgoyne's signal for an attack," Arnold said to Livingston. "We've got to hurry." He paused only long enough to tell Van Cortlandt to have his New

York regiment in readiness. Either Livingston or Clarkson would return to tell him when to move out.

It was after two o'clock before Arnold satisfied himself that Poor's brigade was well positioned, with the Connecticut troops coming up to form a second line behind them. The entire northern edge of Freeman's farm was lined with redcoats, who were firing across the open field at the Americans spread across the southern edge. Some of Morgan's and Dearborn's marksmen had climbed well up into trees for a better shooting angle. Because of them, the Americans were having much the best of the volleying back and forth. Particularly hard hit were the British artillerymen, targeted successfully to keep them from bringing their cannon into play.

Answering a general command, the entire British line, stung by the sniper fire, began pulling back deeper into the woods for cover. Arnold, stationed at the center with the First New Hampshire, sent Livingston to his left and Clarkson to the right to alert unit commanders for an attack. He gave them a few minutes and then shouted, "Forward!" Fifteen hundred American troops began pouring across the field. Arnold guided them toward the right, hoping to turn Burgoyne's left flank.

The Sixty-second, anchoring Burgoyne's left where the ground began to fall away to a ravine, took the brunt of the charge. Americans troops overran the cannon positions and began turning the guns around to fire at their owners, but the fleeing British had taken the linstock and the Americans had none. Burgoyne ordered his reserve unit, the Twenty-first, to counterattack, and after a hot engagement at point-blank range, the Americans began falling back across the field. The British started to chase them but stopped and fell back after a withering barrage from the marksmen.

At three o'clock, Arnold ordered another charge, with the same result. The Americans had initial success, crossing the field to reach the woods and force the British back. The Sixty-second nearly broke, but General Phillips, having heard the sound of the battle from the river road, had come up to lead the Twentieth and Twenty-first in a counterattack, and once again the Americans fell back.

Burgoyne was convinced that the attacks were feints and that the main danger was that the Americans would try to turn his right flank, and so he ordered Fraser to stay in position there. After a hurried conference with Phillips, Burgoyne sent orders down to von Riedesel to bring up reinforcements from the river road to help the Sixty-second hold the left portion of his center position. It was a dangerous move, leaving the army's left flank considerably weakened and vulnerable to American attack, but Burgoyne decided to take the chance.

Lieutenant James Hadden was the only surviving artillerist of the thirty-two who initially had manned the guns, so Phillips ordered up another artillery company. The Sixty-second had lost half of its men, and the top two officers, Colonel John Anstruther and Major Henry Harnage, were both down with wounds. Harnage was by far the worst off with a ball in his abdomen. Next to him, leaning against a tree, was sixteen-year-old Second-Lieutenant Stephen Hervey, nephew of the adjutant general of the British Army, who had been wounded three times but kept returning to the fighting until a ball shattered his thigh. As he was being carried off, another shot penetrated a lung. Colonel Anstruther lay next to him, the surgeon off to his right.

"You understand, it's mortal, my boy," the surgeon spoke softly. "I'm afraid there's nothing that can be done." Hervey, his face a greenish pallor and blood trickling from his mouth, nodded. "Except," the surgeon continued, "I can give you a powerful dose of opium. That way you'll pass soon and quite peacefully. Otherwise, it would be a long and terrible time for you."

The boy nodded again and the surgeon prepared the draught. Colonel Anstruther leaned forward: "Anything we can do for you? Any affairs to settle?"

With a weak smile, Hervey said: "I'm too young, I guess. Everything's adjusted." He swallowed the draught. "Please, sir, just tell my uncle I died like a soldier."

"Amen to that," Anstruther said, as Hervey went unconscious and, within a few minutes, died. The surgeon glanced at Major Harnage with raised eyebrows. Did he wish to partake? "No, thank you," Harnage groaned. "I'm going to survive this. I've too much to do in life." The surgeon nodded, knowing that the gut-shot almost always died.

Tim Murphy was an ace among marksmen, the frequent winner in friendly competitions among Morgan's men. He had found a fine fork halfway up a giant oak tree, with a smaller limb branching off on which to rest his double-barreled rifle and a view of the field through a break in the foliage. Sure that he had notched eight victims so far, he was looking for a ninth. He had in mind a particularly handsome officer who had been dashing back and forth on horseback. Murphy believed it was Burgoyne himself. Who else would have such a splendid uniform and such a richly embroidered and laced saddle cloth?

He saw his target cantering across the British line again. Murphy moistened his thumb and wiped it across the muzzle of his piece. He took aim, following the rider until he reined up. He fired and saw the man blown right off his horse.

The news raced through the American camp that Burgoyne was down. But the victim was a wealthy young man, Captain Charles Green, one of Burgoyne's aides. It *could* have been Burgoyne: he recklessly exposed himself to fire all afternoon.

The fire never slackened, even when one side or the other pulled back.

The six-pound guns, joining in concert like peals of thunder, assisted by the echoes of the woods, almost deafened the combatants with the noise. The different battalions moved to relieve each other, some being pressed and almost broken by superior numbers. For four hours a constant blaze of fire was kept up, and both armies seemed to be determined on death or victory.

When his blood was up, General von Riedesel was anything but the stolid German; despite his portly frame he moved quickly. He selected his own von Riedesel Regiment, half of the Rhetz Regiment, and two six-pounders from Captain Pausch's Hesse-Hanau artillery. The Germans struggled along the ravine and began to ascend toward the eastern edge of the battleground, where the Sixty-second was on the verge of breaking in the fourth close-quarters engagement of the afternoon. If it collapsed, Burgoyne's entire center column could be rolled up and the battle won by the Americans.

British soldiers saw the Germans coming and cheered, many of them skidding down to grab the drag-ropes and help bring the cannon to the top. Beating their drums and grunting their battle cry, the Brunswickers poured over the top and enfiladed the American attackers, who had expected no enemy troops from that quarter. Pausch set up his guns and began firing grapeshot at the Americans. The British troops rallied, and together with the Germans began a bayonet attack, forcing the Americans back.

Seeing this, Arnold was certain that with one more set of reinforcements he could win the day, either the Massachusetts regiments or Learned's brigade, nearly one thousand strong. Arnold figured his advantage of the sharpshooters was balanced by the British cannon. The struggle was an equal one. With only one more incursion of fresh troops, a decisive victory could be won. He turned and galloped back to persuade Gates.

During his ride down to the river road and the bridge, in his unavailing effort to bring Stark's troops back, Gates had his first good look at the British position on the road, a half mile to the north. It looked formidable and something was stirring there. He became convinced that Burgoyne was on the verge of ordering an attack along the road to encircle the American fortified position. He rode quickly up to the compound to order the Massachusetts regiments down to reinforce the blockades on the road.

As the regiments streamed down the defile to the road, Arnold galloped into the compound, dismounted, and breathlessly began telling Gates what he needed.

"No, no," Gates said. "They're going to attack along the road."

"No, they're not!" Arnold shouted. "Von Riedesel is already in the fighting. He brought two regiments up the ravine. That's why we need help. Learned's brigade is ready. Let me have them."

"We're low on ammunition. Only forty rounds reserve per man."

"That's plenty. We'll win the day with that. Besides, Schuyler is sending more ammunition from Albany. Varick should be here any minute with the train." Arnold was referring to Schuyler's all-out effort to keep the army supplied, even stripping lead from the window panes of the town.

"I can't jeopardize this camp. Suppose Burgoyne breaks through?"

"No chance of that, believe me. Besides, only my troops of the left are engaged. You've got the right and center still here. Give me Learned."

Gates clenched and unclenched his fists. "All right, give the orders. That's the last of it. Not one more man."

Arnold was already gone to find Learned. After a quick consultation, Learned's troops began to move forward.

At that point, Colonel Morgan Lewis, Gates's deputy quartermaster, galloped in. Arnold rode over to hear the news. "The fighting is extremely hot," Lewis reported. "The issue is still undecided."

"By God, that's going to change," Arnold said, putting his spurs to his horse and galloping forward.

Watching him disappear, Lewis, who knew of Gates's attitude toward Arnold, changed his story slightly. "It's really going quite well," he told Gates. "I'm afraid he'll do something crazy."

"Go after him," Gates snapped. "Give him my direct order to come back here."

Lewis caught up with Arnold halfway to the front and delivered the command. Arnold felt like telling him to go to hell, but he decided he had irritated Gates enough for one day. He reluctantly turned back.

As the dusk deepened, the firing gradually ceased. The Americans had no intention of camping on the spot but began withdrawing back to the fortifications, carrying their wounded comrades and as many of the dead as they could bear away. British soldiers staggered onto the field, many of them sinking to their knees in exhaustion, too tired to carry away all the wounded and bury their dead. That would have to wait for morning. Later that night, in pitch darkness, the field was left to the ghoulish scavengers from among the camp followers, searching every corpse and even the wounded for anything of value.

Because the British occupied the field, they could claim victory. Captain Anburey expressed the truth of it to a fellow soldier that night. "The only apparent benefit gained is that we kept possession of the ground. But they came out and attacked us. I thought they'd stay behind their works. I thought they were incapable of standing a regular engagement."

That night the Baron von Riedesel worked at a campaign desk in the small log cabin he occupied with his wife and children. He was laboriously writing a third-person account of the participation of his German soldiers in the battle, barely containing his glowing pride at the maneuver that had brought German troops to the salvation of the Sixty-second Regiment and the left of the British line. The German troops were praised by the British commanders, but von Riedesel sourly commented on that in his conclusion: "British pride did not desire the acknowledgment of bravery other than their own."

The baroness was more concerned about the trauma she saw all about her. Several wounded British officers had been brought to her cabin, including Major Harnage and Ensign Henry Young of the Sixty-second, whose thigh had been broken by a bullet. While her husband labored away over his document, oblivious to everything around him, the baroness saw to events. The wounded men were laid in the next room, complete with blankets and a mattress her women servants had located. All through the night she heard the details of treatment through the thin partition. Around midnight, the doctors finally secured permission from the wounded young man to take off his leg, but the bleeding remained stubborn. By dawn, she could hear Young's last groans.

Late the night of the battle, Burgoyne conferred with Fraser, after Colonel Kingston brought in the final returns from the regiments. The British Army had lost 556 men, including an unusually high proportion of officers. "Those damned sharpshooters," Burgoyne muttered. Some regiments had been especially hard hit, notably the Sixty-second, which had fewer than ten men per company still standing.

Burgoyne suggested an all-out attack the next day, on the theory that the enemy troops would be tired and confused and not expecting another battle. Fraser demurred, saying they could hardly be more tired and confused than the British troops, who would scarcely sleep a wink this night after the battle. Burgoyne agreed to wait a few days. "But then we'd better start digging in to a good defensive line. Who knows? If Arnold has his way, they may be the ones who attack."

The man they were talking about indeed wanted to attack the next day, but he was so bitterly angry at Gates that he couldn't bear to be in his presence, for fear that he would lose control and physically assault his commander. Varick came to Arnold's cabin that night with the returns from the American units that had fought in the battle. The army had lost 313 men.

Arnold was angry at the stupidity and obstinacy of Gates. Although Gates had acquiesced in ordering Learned's brigade out, he had left them without the guidance they needed when he had called Arnold back. Learned led his brigade to the forest on the left where the only result was a light skirmish with Fraser's troops. Arnold would have led the reinforcements exactly where they were needed, to the right where the Americans had punched the British all afternoon and where he was convinced that fresh troops would have broken through. Gates had left the troops without an overall commander at the scene of action.

"What could you do?" Varick asked. "It was a direct order."
"It's an order I should have ignored—or disobeyed," Arnold said.

Chapter 32

Philadelphia
September 26, 1777

At Lord Cornwallis's command, the column moved out at precisely half past eight in the morning. Three companies of the Light Horse comprised the van, followed by the British band, which soon struck up "God Save the King." Next came Cornwallis and a large party of officers and flag-bearers, leading three British regiments of foot and the artillery company with its four horse-drawn six-pounders. The rest of the column of three thousand was made up of three German regiments, the German band, and the usual assortment of followers— sutlers, soldier's wives, whores, and opportunists of various stripes.

A distinguishing feature of this particular march was the presence of three civilian Loyalist leaders—Joseph Galloway, Phineas Bond, Jr., and Enoch Story—who rode up front with the Light Horse. They were guiding the triumphal march of the British troops into the largest American city, taking them down the Germantown Pike and across to Second Street for the grand entry— a distance of six miles to the center of town. At the moment, there was no civilian government in Philadelphia, the Congress having fled days earlier, as well as a very large number of pro-independence citizens, including all of the radical patriot leaders of the city. One of Cornwallis's duties for the day would be to approve a governing committee of Loyalists headed by Galloway, although law and order and true control of the city would remain with British arms.

It was precisely the problem of growing anarchy that had caused General Howe to yield to the pleas of Galloway to send in a force to restore order. Howe preferred to remain with the main army in Germantown, giving his most experienced battlefield commander the honor of leading the first contingent of the British Army into Philadelphia. One reason Howe stayed behind was the fact that George Washington's army was still intact after the bruising battle twenty miles west of Philadelphia at Brandywine Creek on September 11th. Howe had played a cat-and-mouse game with Washington ever since, pursuing northward as far as Phoenixville, before abruptly turning about and moving back south so that his army could cross the Schuylkill River to Germantown without interference. Washington had been forced to deploy on a wide front north of Valley Forge and Phoenixville to protect his forges and munitions and supply depots at Reading, Warwick, and Lancaster, and thus had been in no position to molest Howe's crossing.

Philadelphia, unscarred by battle thus far, was there for the taking, like a ripe plum. Howe was not concerned about detaching Cornwallis's force to begin the occupation; his main army still had numerical superiority over the Continentals, who, in any case, seemed disorganized and scattered to the north.

Another reason that Howe agreed to Galloway's plea for what seemed to some a premature move into the city was the need to prepare it for full-scale occupation. The agenda for Cornwallis's meetings on this day with the Loyalist leaders concerned the myriad problems of arranging housing, supply, hospital care, and defense lines for an occupation army that, with all its auxiliary forces and needs, would add very substantially to Philadelphia's population.

Captain John André rode with the staff aides behind Cornwallis and the other top-ranking officers. André was most pleased with himself, having adroitly managed to manufacture reasons for his chief, General Grey, to second him to Cornwallis's staff for a few days. André had been in Philadelphia three times before and claimed to know the city well—including many of its leading citizens and the more handsome residences that might be commandeered for use by the top British and German officers. This had become André's assignment—riding throughout the city to make a list of the most promising homes (and thereby avoiding all the boring meetings). Grey, realizing that André thus would be able to spot a choice place for *his* commander and staff, had been glad to detail his aide to Cornwallis.

André rode alongside Lord Rawdon, Cornwallis's chief of staff, a young noble whose upbringing had conditioned him for the most haughty and supercilious airs of the British gentleman. Rawdon was totally insensitive to how his bearing affected others; in contrast, André had always found it easy and useful to vary his conduct and style according to whatever situation he found himself in.

After a heavy downpour the day before, the sky was overcast early, but the sun began to break through as the column rested at the halfway point. It was cool, an excellent day for marching in contrast to the burning heat of recent weeks, and the morale of the men seemed high. When the march resumed, spirits were enlivened even more by the throngs of people who turned out along the way, increasing in numbers as the outskirts of the city neared. Most of the parade watchers were women and children, and most of them cheered as the column passed. The little boys were enthralled by the cavalry, a resplendent sight with scarlet coats and jet-black horses, helmets and sword hilts glittering in the sun, pennants and plumes waving in the breeze.

Rawdon sniffed, his eyes sweeping the crowd. "A scruffy lot these people are," he said. "Quite peasantlike."

Yes, André thought, just like a crowd that might turn out in any English market town. He changed the subject. "That heavy rain yesterday was certainly providential."

"Indeed," Rawdon said. "I hope we'll be in time to prevent these wretches from their act of madness."

He was referring to the fear that Philadelphia would be set ablaze, just as New York City had burned when the British were occupying it, making everything considerably more difficult for everyone, not only the troops but the civilian population as well. Having endured that trauma, Howe and Cornwallis were determined that Philadelphia would not share the same fate, especially when they learned that a conspiracy to torch the city did in fact exist. One attempt had been foiled the day before by the heavy rainfall that André had mentioned.

For Rawdon, the chief danger appeared to be that a fire would ruin chances of finding a suitable residence for Lord Cornwallis and his staff. The prime location, of course, would go to General Howe, but if Rawdon had any say about it, the house for Cornwallis would be just as good. He, in fact, had much to say as he began telling André for the fourth time what His Lordship's requirements were: "It should be of brick, of course, with an imposing facade, three floors, and at least half a dozen bedchambers, a good central location near to where General Howe will be, elegantly furnished, with outbuildings sufficient for the servants, a pleasant garden, a goodly stable for at least six horses. I hope the owners will be absent. If not, they may have to move—although His Lordship can be tender-hearted about such things." Rawdon heaved a deep sigh. "I fear there will be nothing of this nature in this provincial place."

"On the contrary," André said, "I assure you there are some very fine residences." Rawdon's description was eerily close to the Shippen and Chew homes, André realized. One reason for this self-satisfied mood was that the assignment he had wrangled might enable him to fulfill the promise he had once made to protect the homes of his friends.

"Well, do your best to find a suitable place," Rawdon said. "His Lordship's pleasure will depend upon it. I wish I could go myself, but I judge we shall be mired in these sticky meetings for hours. As soon as you find the right house, come and fetch me and I shall go inspect it. Ideally, we'll be able to lodge in the dwelling this very night."

"Of course," André said, edging his horse away from the insufferable Rawdon to a more kindred spirit, Captain John Montresor, the chief engineer, a man who would be extraordinarily busy for weeks trying to arrange everything needed for an army of eighteen thousand to occupy a city of thirty-five thousand. Montresor was a sober, earnest individual, not of the artistic temperament of André, but the two men shared a passion for drawing maps. Montresor was a superb draftsman, and more than once he had profited from information, sketches, and maps that André provided.

For the next half hour, André was treated to a dissertation on the countless tasks that Montresor faced. Several times André was able to interject, telling Montresor of buildings that should be useful, such as the Bettering House, the Academy, Carpenter's Hall, the State House, and City Hall. He said that the new Walnut Street jail would serve well for American prisoners and the old north barracks might accommodate as many as two thousand British soldiers.

"Good," Montresor said wryly, "we only need to find a place for fifteen thousand more! Fortunately, tents will suffice for another month or so, but we've got to get the troops under roof by the time the cold season comes. And then there's the matter of finding suitable quarters for hundreds of officers."

"So many rebels have fled the city. There must be plenty of empty houses."

"Yes, fortunately, that is so. We think as many as ten thousand citizens of the city have already left. Of course we have hundreds of Loyalists returning with us and they'll want to reclaim their former homes. And those are likely to be the nicer places. You say there are many churches in the city?"

"Yes."

"Are there large ones?"

"Some of them are quite imposing."

"Good. We can use them for hospitals. And as stables and riding academies for the officers."

"Good heavens," André murmured.

As concerned as he was about logistical matters, Montresor seemed obsessed by the problem of providing defensive works for the occupied city. He lamented the fact that the rebels still had a choke hold on the Delaware River in their forts on both banks and the river islands and the cheval-de-frise to the south. Until these were subdued, the Royal Navy would not be able to bring up many of the supplies that Montresor needed. As he chatted on about the defensive line he envisioned building a mile or so north of the city—a series of redoubts and demi-lunes, stretching from the Delaware to the Schuylkill—André's mind began to wander.

His sense that he had become a warrior had been put to the test in the only other major engagement of the campaign thus far, aside from Brandywine Creek—General Grey's surprise midnight attack on Anthony Wayne's force of fifteen hundred American troops near the Paoli Tavern. Already the British were aware that the Americans referred to the action as "the Paoli massacre" and had coined a name for the British commander—"No Flint Grey."

André's sleep had been tormented every one of the five nights since the battle occurred. He had nightmares of men screaming in agony and rivers of blood flowing. One of his most chilling memories was of Grey's lean countenance as he gave his officers their instructions only an hour before the charge. One side of his face was carmine from the glow of a campfire, the other in darkness except for glittering eyes, his voice almost trembling from excitement and anticipation. "No, no," he said, answering an officer's question. "This will be the night of the long knives! Bayonets and swords only. No gunfire at all." And then he made a remarkable decision. Concerned that some soldier might fire his weapon in the panic of attack, he ordered the officers to see to it that the flints were removed from every single gun of his three-thousand-man army. "We will be merciless, gentlemen. Merciless!"

Washington's main army had crossed the Schuylkill, leaving Wayne's contingent on the west side to exert a presence and harass British supply lines. They were camped on the night of September 20th in a meadow surrounded by forest. Grey's men poured from the woods, overwhelming the pickets in an instant, though two managed to fire their muskets in warning before being cut to pieces. The alarm did Wayne no good, however; almost all of his men were drugged either with sleep or drink. They staggered to their feet only to be cut down by bayonet and sword. The Americans were illuminated by the embers of their campfires, the oncoming British almost unseen against the blackness of the forest. In the space of minutes, more than three hundred Americans were stabbed and hacked. The wounded who could not flee were bayoneted to death. But seventy-five men had been taken alive, the British rejoinder to the charge that they had given no quarter. Wayne managed to escape with more than a thousand of his men, fighting a rearguard action for two miles before crossing the Schuylkill to safety. The British lost one officer and two enlisted men, five men wounded.

André had been in the thick of the charge, swinging his sword violently, more than once striking the flesh of an enemy soldier. Then he had stopped abruptly, sickened by the slaughter. That fact and his tormented dreams made him wonder just how much of a warrior he really was. He was also unnerved by Grey's bloodthirstiness, the way he continued to rub his hands and wallow in pleasure at the memory of how many screaming men had been slaughtered. For the first time, André had begun to think of the possibilities of transferring to another general's staff.

Reflecting on that macabre night brought a sudden thought to André. Once the parade was over, he would be riding about the city alone, bent on a mission that some local citizens might strongly resent, if they knew what it was. He maneuvered over to Rawdon's side again. "I say, Major, has the general any anticipation at all that there might yet be some resistance in the city?"

"What, what?"

"Any possibility of fighting? Snipers, armed gangs, whatever?"

"Don't be ridiculous," Rawdon sneered. "All the rebels are gone, cowards that they are. If were any chance of resistance, I assure you we'd be entering the city in quite a different manner."

At that moment, the loud boom of a cannon was heard. It came from some distance, perhaps from the river, and the ball landed far from the advancing column. Two more loud reports quickly followed.

Rawdon immediately rode to Cornwallis's side, got his orders, and dashed forward to dispatch the Light Horse. They raised an enormous clatter as they galloped down the cobblestone street. Cornwallis spoke urgently to other officers. André saw Brigadier Samuel Cleaveland, chief of artillery, turn to ride back to his battery. As orders were barked, the band merged to one side of the street and the infantry regiments divided to allow the horse-drawn guns to come charging forward.

Chapter 33

Philadelphia
September 26, 1777

At breakfast that morning, Judge Shippen began tapping his three-minute egg and then paused. He raised his eyes to the ceiling and offered several silent prayers of thanks. One was to General Washington, a man to whom he already felt the utmost gratitude for his kindness the previous January in setting the foolish Edward III free after his capture at Trenton. The Judge had heard often that Washington had vowed to defend Philadelphia to the last man against the current threat from the British, which would have meant fighting from street to street, house to house, with cannon fire laying the city waste. That had not happened. Washington had met the British a good distance from the city and now the two armies had maneuvered each other to the north. Philadelphia, apparently, was to be spared. The Judge supposed that the radical patriots would denounce Washington for failing to live up to the letter of his vow. But he had done the wise thing. He had made a show of defending the city, but in fact had spared it, and had survived himself to fight another day.

The second prayer of thanks was to the Almighty for sending down that lovely drenching rain of yesterday. That had saved the city from burning, and enabled a posse of Loyalists and patriots, forgetting their mutual hatred for the moment, to apprehend a number of the perpetrators, catching some of them red-handed as they tried vainly to ignite the tarred faggots they had hidden in outhouses strategically located about the city.

Ever since the British landed their army at Head of Elk, the Judge had lived a life of torment. The city had been in turmoil for weeks, no longer a safe place to walk about. Patriots harassed Loyalists, and another oath was promulgated, which the Judge was happy to sign since it was not a pledge of allegiance, but rather a pledge to avoid political activity and any assistance to the British. Those who did not sign, mainly devout Quakers, were sent to imprisonment in Virginia. Now, as the tide changed, Loyalists were harassing patriots, even those who had helped in apprehending the gang of would-be arsonists, filling up the Walnut Street jail. Thousands of people fled the city, using every sort of conveyance for personal property, and the rattling of wagons, the cries of children, and the galloping of horses could be heard all through the night. The bells were removed from almost all of the churches and public buildings, including the State House, and together with public records and other valuables were transported to Bethlehem and Allentown. All of the decked vessels on the waterfront were dispatched either north to Bordentown or south to Fort Mifflin.

Through it all, the Judge had wrestled with the question of whether to remove his family once again from danger's path. But where would a safe haven be? The New Jersey farm? The cottage up toward Germantown? A house at Kennett Square that the Judge owned? Mired in indecision, the Judge did nothing. In his misery, he rationalized that to leave the city in the face of a British occupation would brand him a rebel. Just as to flee *to* the British would have branded him a Tory. He was neither—he was a neutral! He would stay put, right where he was, and damn the consequences. And, *mirabile dictu,* it had worked! The city had been spared and nothing dire had happened. At least not yet. For the first time in two years, the Judge felt somewhat feisty and confident in his avowed neutrality.

Wait. There was a problem yet. The British would be seeking the more attractive houses to commandeer for their officers. The Shippen house was not among the most splendid in the city and environs, but it was undoubtedly highly attractive. With a sinking heart, the Judge feared there would be an ominous knock on his door very soon.

As the Shippen children watched the Judge's expression change from the beatific, eyebrows raised heavenward, to one of deep gloom, brow furrowed, they decided it was safe to begin their chatter again. This morning the unified theme was to gain permission to witness the British entry into the city. The Judge had tried sweet reason, and now he became adamant.

"No, I say, no!" he shouted. "There is still anarchy and danger in the streets."

Edward III piped up in a petulant voice: "Certainly there's no reason why *I* shouldn't go."

"For you especially," the Judge spoke drily, "there's every reason *not* to go." His son's escapade that had led to his capture at Trenton had been the most dangerous threat so far to the Judge's ability to walk the tightrope of neutrality.

"But Papa—" Mary and Peggy began wailing.

"No, I say! Only the lower sorts will turn out for this. None of you wanted to see the Continental Army when it marched through the city. Why the British Army now? If it's British officers that stir you, I daresay you'll be seeing all too many of them before long."

"But, Papa," Peggy cried, "Lieutenant André may be among them. We owe him so much."

"Indeed," the Judge said. It appeared that it had been André's good offices that had placed Neddy Burd on an exchange list. He had returned in April and now lived in Lancaster, devoting himself to his law books instead of more soldiering. "My dear, if Lieutenant André is with General Howe's army at all, I warrant we shall see him very soon and will be able to offer our appreciation in person. Until then, you'll just have to be patient."

After the British column reached the State House, the regiments were dispersed to different quarters of the city to take up positions and bivouac for the night. The cannon fire had turned out to be a somewhat farcical episode. Two sloops of the Pennsylvania Navy had come up from the river forts to begin firing at the docks. No one could understand the reason, unless the captains thought the British were already installing batteries along the waterfront. The captains had misjudged the tide and one of the vessels became stuck on a mud-flat, where General Cleaveland's artillery made good sport of her until she surrendered. The other, smaller ship made it safely across to the New Jersey shore. Thus ended the only sign of resistance to the British occupation.

Refreshments were set out for the British officers on the lawn behind the State House. After a light repast, André discreetly withdrew and mounted his horse to begin his round of the city, the ubiquitous leather carrying case in place in his saddle pouch so that he could take notes. His plan was simple—to work from the top down. Howe first, Cornwallis second, von Knyphausen third—and then Grey, of course! After that, his list contained ten more names of British and German general officers. With luck, this afternoon and tomorrow would suffice to finish the scouting, and the third day could be devoted to completing any necessary formalities, such as arrangements for compensation or eviction.

Recalling the descriptions offered by the little Tory shopkeeper, Joseph Stansbury, as they had ridden across Philadelphia in the post coach last December, André had a good idea of the right place for General Howe, the one that Stansbury had called the Penn-Masters house. It was very near the State House. André loped up Sixth to High Street and immediately remembered the house on the southeast corner as belonging to Joseph Galloway, who, of course, would be reclaiming it. As André turned the corner to head eastward, he saw a garden behind a brick wall, between the Galloway house and the next one, which he realized with satisfaction was the Penn-Masters house. It was an imposing residence, built right up to the brick walkway in the Georgian fashion, with two windows on either side of the front entrance, five evenly spaced windows across the fronts of the upper two floors, and two dormer windows for illuminating the attic. André jotted down the address, 190 High Street, and wondered whether such close proximity to Galloway was a good idea or not. He shrugged as he dismounted to look around, tying his horse to a brass post. Howe had plenty of people to keep unwanted visitors away, and the house fit the bill in every other respect, including nearness to the State House. A charming gate between two pedestals was open to the rear of the house, and André walked in, noting the extensive back buildings and the substantially larger garden stretching to the east. He came upon a group of stone masons at work, being watched by a slim gentleman dressed in the black coat and wide-brimmed hat affected by the Quakers.

"Good day to thee, sir," the Quaker said. "I am John Quimby, agent and caretaker for this residence. May I be of service?"

Quimby had betrayed no surprise or anxiety at the sudden appearance of a British officer. André introduced himself and explained his mission, the need of General Howe for a suitable residence in Philadelphia. Quimby told him that the owners of the house, Richard Penn and his lady, were in London, and were not likely to return, at least not until the current unpleasantness had ended. "Is the house vacant at present?" André asked.

"It is, sir," Quimby responded. "The most recent tenant left quite without ceremony several days ago."

"Mr. Penn does rent the house out then?"

"Yes, indeed. And I'm sure he would be quite pleased to have General Howe take up residence here. Doubtless, an arrangement could be made to pay the rental fee directly to Mr. Penn in London."

"Yes, quite," André said. Very wise. British currency for the Penns, instead of local paper money. What about Quimby's commission? Let Quimby worry about that.

"Would thee care to inspect the interior, sir?"

"If I may return the day after tomorrow for that. And to sign any paper of agreement you may wish to draw up? I daresay the rent will remain the same as for the previous party."

"Very good, sir. I shall be on the premises."

As André rode away, he wished devoutly that all his coming transactions would be so easy. Not a chance, he thought. His need now was to find a place very much like the Shippens'—but not their house, of course—that would serve for Lord Cornwallis. He decided to explore the neighborhood around the Shippens' for several blocks in each direction, recalling many fine structures he had seen before in that area. As he rode along taking notes, André became accustomed to the stares of the citizens and wore a pleasant expression on his face, nodding and smiling from time to time. Passersby tended to freeze at the sight of a lone British officer riding down the street, but then relaxed as they perceived he was not bent on a hostile mission, some returning a smile, others nodding or just staring.

André had listed half a dozen houses as candidates but was drawn back to the first one he had noticed, because it was very close to the State House and to the Penn-Masters house. It was located on the south side of Chestnut, near Fifth Street, and thus but a short walk to the State House. He knocked on the door, which opened to reveal a pretty young maiden. André introduced himself and the girl gave her name, Deborah Logan.

"Oh, is it the same Logan family that owns the house known as Stenton, near Germantown? That is where General Howe is currently staying."

"No, sir, that is the James Logan branch of the family."

André then explained his mission and was pained by the look of fear that crossed the girl's face.

After an awkward silence, André spoke: "May I ask, who is in residence aside from yourself?"

"Only my mother and grandmother. She is ailing."

The girl had not invited André inside and he decided not to impose. Let Rawdon do that, he thought. He's good at it. "Well, good day to you, Mistress Logan. If there is any further interest, we shall let you know." Three women could share one room, he thought, and the rest of the house would be ample for Cornwallis's retinue. Or the women could be easily relocated.

As he rode away, André was depressed by the reality of invading people's homes. He tried hard to think of places for von Knyphausen and Grey that would be trouble free. Then the idea came to him. He knew of at least one prominent American who was away from the city, far away, in Paris—Benjamin Franklin. At his advanced age, he doubtless would not have a large family remaining behind in his residence, André thought. Perhaps none at all. It could be a delightful place, full of the great man's scientific gadgets and paraphernalia. André knew the house was on High Street—Stansbury had mentioned it. But André could not remember exactly where. It would not do to ask directions. Then he grinned as he thought of one place where he might find the answer. Before riding east toward the Delaware River and Black Horse Alley, André penned a note to Rawdon with the Logans' Chestnut Street address and left it for him at the State House.

Joseph Stansbury worked industriously, removing fine china pieces from packing cases, dusting them, and placing them on display shelves. He was not yet open for business but had not locked his door since going out to witness the passing British troops.

He whistled one of his own tunes happily. His wish to see the Crown's authority restored to his adopted city had finally come true. He heard the bell jangle and turned to see a British officer entering the shop. He peered through his thick glasses and instantly recognized his caller.

"Lieutenant André! What a wonderful surprise! My word!"

"You remember me, do you!"

"Of course! A fellow poet never forgets! Oh, this is quite wonderful."

"It's Captain André now. I was afraid I wouldn't find you here."

"I came back only yesterday to reopen my shop. It's been closed for six months. Hardly any business at all with the rebels in charge. I found myself a hidey-hole in New Jersey. But now I believe trade will be good with your army occupying the city."

"I suppose so, in due course," André said. He explained his mission to Stansbury and asked about the Franklin house.

"You know, the house was built while the old man was abroad," Stansbury said. "When he came back, his wife had died and he lived there less than two years with his daughter and her family before he went to Paris, late in seventy-six I believe it was. She stayed on. She's married to a man named Bache and they had some kids. Who knows, they may have fled the city." In answer to André's query, Stansbury began listing other houses he thought might suit officers' needs. Then he stopped. "Oh, dear. It's almost like informing on people. I'm not sure I like that."

"My dear friend. It's going to happen anyway. I only need a dozen or so, all for high-ranking people. That's all I've promised to do. I don't want to get involved at all with ejecting people for all the other officers who'll be looking for a nice house"

"Yes, I see what you mean." Stansbury soon was able to come up with a number of dwellings whose occupants were likely to be absent from the city, including those owned by John Cadwalader, Elias Boudinot, Robert Morris, and the like.

Twenty minutes later, equipped with Stansbury's final list and the directions to Benjamin Franklin's house, André extricated himself from the shopkeeper's nonstop talking and left the shop.

There was joy in the Shippen household when André arrived, he having found no one present at the homes of both Peggy Chew and Rebecca Franks, after his inspection of Benjamin Franklin's three-story brick residence set back from High Street in a little enclave of its own. A perfect place, and André was glad to find a caretaker to deal with, the Bache family having indeed left the city for a relative's farm in New Jersey.

Peggy and Mary hurried downstairs as the Judge greeted André, Peggy barely able to restrain herself from rushing to embrace him. Heartfelt thanks were expressed for André's aid to Neddy Burd.

"Is he well?" André asked.

"Quite recovered, thank you," the Judge said. "He brought his prison pallor here for several months and then went home to Lancaster. I see you have been promoted."

"Yes. I'm an aide to General Grey now."

"Is Lieutenant Despard with you?" Mary asked demurely. André thought how wonderful Despard would feel if he knew that Mary had remembered him.

"No. Our regiment left for England in January. I decided to stay behind."

Peggy's heart raced at the thought that perhaps André had stayed because of her. "Father, can Molly and I entertain Captain André in the garden? It's such a pleasant day." Peggy was certain that Mary would discreetly withdraw, leaving her alone with André.

"If he wishes. First I must have a word." The Judge led André into his library and poured two glasses of sack from his last good bottle. "What a delightful surprise!" he said, settling into his wing chair. "I hoped we would see you, but I never fancied it would be so soon."

"As a matter of fact, it took a little arranging for me to come into the city with this first column." André explained his mission to find suitable quarters for the highest-ranking officers. Then he saw that the Judge's expression was frozen, his eyes round.

"Oh, please don't misunderstand," André said. "I'm not here for that reason! I sought this assignment precisely to make sure that your house is *not* on the list. I came to reassure you of that. Remember, I promised to do what I could."

The Judge shook his head. "You are an astonishing fellow. A true friend. My gratitude is—"

"I can protect you from general officers. But there may be brigade colonels or others poking around. I've thought of something that may help there, too. Before I leave I shall write out an order saying that this house is reserved. That it can be commandeered only with General Howe's express permission. You can show it to anyone who comes here. That should work!"

It took some time, but André finally quelled the Judge's effusions of gratitude. "I was afraid that I wouldn't find you here, sir. That you might have taken your family elsewhere, as you did before. I gather that both the Chew and Franks families are gone."

"I expect that both families will be returning now that your army is here," the Judge said. "I was strong tempted to remove to my house at Kennett Square or the cottage, but I finally decided to remain. Many of those who fled the city will live to repent it, I am sure."

"A wise choice." André smiled. "If you'd gone to Kennett Square, you'd have been precisely where the Brandywine Creek battle began. And if you'd gone to the Northern Liberties, you'd be close to Germantown where General Howe is encamped with our entire main army."

"Were you in battle?"

"At Brandywine, our division was held in reserve. We did fight at Paoli."

"Oh. I hear that was a massacre."

"A victory. A bloody one, yes, but not a massacre. We took many prisoners, quite alive and unharmed."

"Will there be another battle? So much time has passed since Brandywine. And we've heard that General Washington's army has survived."

"A few days after Brandywine, I thought we would have the climàctic battle. Washington seemed prepared to meet us. Both armies were lined up on the field, ready for Armageddon. And then it rained, a veritable cloudburst, with strong winds and fog. I think every cartridge in both armies was ruined. No one could fire a gun. We couldn't even make a bayonet charge in the teeth of that wind and rain. Some people called it the Battle of the Clouds. It wasn't a battle at all. Then Washington decamped to the north, wisely I think. So, yes, there almost certainly will be another battle. But not in the city. Somewhere to the north, I suspect."

"It seems you are winning the war," the Judge said.

André demurred. He wasn't sure of that at all. "Not unless we eliminate Washington's army," he said. "And until we learn the fate of General Burgoyne in the north. I'm afraid he's been left quite alone. In any case, we shall spend the winter here at least, and life may return to some degree of normality."

"Thank God for that."

André found Peggy seated on a wrought-iron bench in the charming rose garden to the south of the house. It was a lovely sight, Peggy's pink bonnet and gauzy dress complementing the still-blooming roses, bright yellow chrysanthemums, and the grey-green of a small weeping willow. "An enchanting sight," André murmured, sitting down next to Peggy. "It calls for the skills of a great painter."

"Such as you." Peggy smiled.

"Not I!" André laughed. "This lovely scene is beyond my poor skills. Besides, I scarcely have the time. I can only stay a moment. I still have so much to do." He explained his mission to Peggy and told her of his conversation with her father. "I stopped at the homes of the Chews and the Franks down on Third Street. No one there."

Peggy felt a little pang of jealously that André had not come to her home first. "Becky Franks is my best friend. And Peggy, too, of course. Perhaps Becky is already returned to Woodford. That's their country mansion, in the Northern Liberties."

"I know it," André said. "I was there once."

"And the Chews are at their country house, Cliveden, in Germantown."

"Goodness. They both could be in harm's way. Your father made a very wise decision."

"Can't you stay for supper as least?"

"Thank you, no. I cannot. I have so much to do."

"It's just as before," Peggy pouted. "We don't have time to talk."

"Oh, we'll have time. Our army will be in Philadelphia at least until the next campaigning season, perhaps much longer."

"If you need quarters, why don't you stay with us?"

André laughed. "I think all your bedrooms are accounted for."

"We could send Edward to Lancaster. He's such a pest, anyway."

"I would love it, but it wouldn't do. I'd have to bring my general with me. A captain doesn't rate quarters in such a fine house by himself. I'd have to be a colonel at least."

Peggy giggled. "Hurry and get promoted again," she teased.

"I'd have to stay with my general in any case."

"Where will that be?"

André smiled. "Unless I completely misunderstand General Grey's tastes, it very likely will be the home of Benjamin Franklin."

"Oh, that is quite near."

"Yes. And I shall be able to call on you and your sisters, as I promised. I think we'll have a very gay season in Philadelphia, once everything settles down. I have ideas for putting on a play or two. There'll be balls and musicales. You'll see."

"How exciting!" Peggy's lower lip trembled as she moved closer to André.

He gazed at the uncommonly lovely face of this seventeen-year-old girl. With only a slight movement, he could kiss her. "I can't attempt a fine painting, but I promised to make a sketch of you. Remember?"

"Yes," Peggy breathed.

André rose abruptly. "We shall do it soon. Now I must go. I'm sorry, but I really must."

Lord Cornwallis's retinue, led by Lord Rawdon, had taken possession of the Logan house at four o'clock in the afternoon. A guard was posted at every door and the yard to the side was filled with soldiers and baggage. Several ordinary soldiers were beginning to erect tents in the yard. Deborah and her mother were in the grandmother's sickroom, Deborah weeping and the mother shaking with anger. Rawdon stood at the doorway.

"My dear ladies, this room is ample to accommodate the three of you."

Mrs. Logan was appalled at Rawdon's haughty manner. "This cannot do! This is quite impossible. You have no right."

"If you wish, we can find quarters for you in another house."

"Never. This is *my* house! I shall never leave it."

"Madam, we are not *taking* your house. Merely using it for a time. You will be recompensed handsomely."

"No. I wish to see Lord Cornwallis. This instant!"

"That is quite impossible. His Lordship is—"

"I insist. I shall not rest until I see him."

Rawdon sighed. "I will see if he has yet arrived. Come down to the sitting room."

Cornwallis received Mrs. Logan graciously, ushering her to a chair. With speech both rapid and halting, she explained her distress, clenching and unclenching her handkerchief, her eyes filled with tears. She spoke of her ailing mother. She said that with so many strange men she and her mother and daughter could not stay in her own house. And they could not leave.

Cornwallis rose and took Mrs. Logan's hand. "My dear madam, I am truly sorry to give you such trouble. Be assured we shall find another house this very afternoon and leave you in peace."

Rawdon turned to face the door so that His Lordship would not see the look of disapproval and disgust that passed over his face. Where the hell was John André?

Chapter 34

Bemis Heights
September 20–October 6, 1777

The day after the Battle of Freeman's Farm, Arnold's resentment boiled over. He went to Gates's cabin, brushing past Wilkinson to go into Gates's office and confront him. "You see what's happened, don't you?" he shouted. "We had victory in our grasp—and you called me back from the battle! Learned went the wrong way. I wasn't there to tell him. We could have won!"

Gates rose up. "By God, sir, watch what you say to me!" He fumed for a moment, seeing Wilkinson and Livingston at the door. "Get out!" he shouted to them, striding over to slam the door. He turned to Arnold and snarled: "You disobeyed my orders again, and by God, it's the last time! I didn't want a battle. We've got them bottled up. Let them rot!"

"We almost defeated them!" Arnold shouted back. "Don't you understand? One more attack will do it. You can take Burgoyne's sword by suppertime tonight. My division is ready to roll. Give the word and I'll be off!"

With a tremendous effort, Gates controlled his temper. He picked up papers from his desk and coolly walked over to the door to the next room. His hand on the knob, he spoke to Arnold: "I am in command here, sir. We will do what I say. And that does not include an attack until I say so. Good day."

Arnold was not present among the officers at Gates's dinner table that evening, which allowed Gates to begin ridiculing Arnold's claim that a victory had been lost and his demand to lead a new attack. Varick was among the guests, and he began chafing as Gates made more snide remarks. Varick stood up, exploded in fury at Gates, shouted his resignation as muster-master, and left.

He went to Arnold's tent to tell him what had happened. Arnold, still in a sour mood from his morning exchange with Gates, immediately asked Varick to join his staff so that he could stay in camp. Varick agreed and wrote to General Schuyler that night, saying that he would rather be drawn and quartered than continue to serve Gates in any capacity.

For Arnold to take Varick on after his outburst was tantamount to insulting and defying Gates publicly. He now had three aides who were intensely partisan to Schuyler and contemptuous of Gates. It did not take long for the other side to make telling counterthrusts. The first came when Wilkinson, quite deliberately, showed Henry Livingston a copy of Gates's official report on the Battle of Freeman's Farm. It made no mention whatsoever of Arnold's key role in the battle.

Livingston immediately shared this with Varick and Clarkson. After their initial consternation, the three aides decided to spread that news throughout the camp, knowing that every officer and soldier of the army would recognize it to be a ludicrously false report. They pounded each other's backs in glee, scribbled their notes to Schuyler, and kept feeding the fires of rumor and innuendo.

Meanwhile, Gates taunted Arnold by paying conspicuous attention to two men Arnold heartily disliked. These were Benjamin Lincoln and John Brown, the first being one of the five officers promoted over Arnold's head and the second, one of Arnold's long-term enemies who never rested in trying to assassinate his character. Brown had been specifically overruled and censured by the Congress for his defamation of Arnold, but that failed to stop him.

Lincoln, who had become a sycophant to Gates, was in command of three thousand militia that patrolled east of the Hudson, and Brown was an officer under him. Wilkinson began spreading rumors that Lincoln was to be moved back to the main army with a major command, perhaps displacing Arnold at the left. Brown was given a brevet promotion to colonel. And then he was chosen to lead a thousand men to harass the British garrisons at various points in the north. Brown made successful raids against Fort George, Mount Independence, and Ticonderoga, bringing back several score prisoners of the British Fifty-third Regiment and destroying some of the bateaux and armed naval vessels the British had amassed at Ticonderoga. Brown's action did not cut the British supply line to Canada, but clearly demonstrated how vulnerable and tenuous it was. When Brown returned, Gates made sure there was a loud celebration in camp, while Arnold sulked in his cabin.

Gates began trying to seduce Daniel Morgan, Arnold's staunch friend and comrade-in-arms. From his Canadian experience, Wilkinson knew how far back the association between Arnold and Morgan went. And, from the Freeman's Farm engagement, Gates certainly had come to realize how valuable Morgan's regiment was. He had, in fact, mentioned Morgan in his account of the battle. The blow came on September 22nd when orders were issued placing Morgan's regiment under Gates's direct control in the center, moving him from Arnold's command of the left. Militarily, the move made no sense. Everything about Morgan's regiment made it ideal for a flank position—rapid movement under maximum forest coverage, scouting duty, raiding thrusts, closer range at the flank for sharpshooters to enfilade the enemy, and so on. It was clear from his demeanor that Morgan did not care for this reassignment at all. The only sense of the move was to further goad Arnold.

It succeeded admirably. The cumulative effect of all the insults was to send Arnold into a towering rage, and he descended upon Gates's office in a foul mood. The danger of physical assault brought Livingston running after Arnold and put Wilkinson on the alert, both of them hovering at the door while their chiefs raged at each other. Gates discarded his mask of coolness and indifference and became just as vituperative as Arnold, who railed against Gates for the move of Morgan's regiment without even the courtesy of consultation. He was caustic in critizing Gates for failing in his report to mention Arnold and the fact that the entire offensive had been carried out by the troops under Arnold's command. Gates icily responded that he was not aware that Arnold was in fact a major-general who rated a divisional command. He said he had learned from friends in Congress that Arnold had resigned on July 11th and although he had suspended his resignation, he had not withdrawn it. Gates said he had ordered Lincoln to return to camp to assume a divisional command, and that Arnold therefore was no longer needed. Stunned with outrage, Arnold stalked away.

He immediately wrote a long letter to Gates, citing all the slights and abuses he had endured, and closed with a request for a pass to leave camp with his aides to go to Philadelphia "to join General Washington."

Gates's response was simply a one-paragraph unsealed letter to John Hancock, president of Congress, stating that he had agreed to General Arnold's request to leave camp. Arnold angrily responded:

In Camp, Sept. 23, 1777

Sir:

When I wrote you yesterday, I thought myself entitled to an answer, and that you would at least have condescended to acquaint me with the reasons which have induced you to treat me with affront and indignity, in public manner which I mentioned and which has been observed by many gentlemen of the army; I am conscious of none, but if I have been guilty of any crimes deserving such *treatment, I wish to have them pointed out, that I may have an opportunity of vindicating my conduct. I know of no reason for your conduct unless I have been traduced by some designing <u>villain</u>.*

I requested permission for myself and aides to go to Philadelphia, instead of which you have sent me a letter to John Hancock, esq. which I have returned. If you have any letters for that gentleman which you think proper to send sealed, I will take charge of them. I once more request your permission for myself and aides to pass to Philadelphia.

> *I am, Sir,*
> *Your obedient servant,*
> *B. Arnold*

Gates replied mildly, enclosing a simple pass, and saying that he would discuss the affair no more. Lincoln's troops arrived in camp, the portly Lincoln making an unsoldierly sight aboard a small ancient nag, his feet nearly touching the ground. Gates admitted Lincoln and Brown to his conferences but excluded Arnold. And then Gates appointed Lincoln to command of the right, taking the left and center wings himself. In effect, Arnold was stripped of command, though no formal notice of that was posted.

As word spread that the feud had reached the point that Arnold might be leaving camp, there was a great deal of uneasiness among the officers at the prospect of losing the most experienced combat general of the Continental Army. Varick wrote to Schuyler, saying he had "the fullest assurance that General Arnold will quit the Northern Department in a day or two." Livingston wrote on the same day, stressing Arnold's importance "as the life and soul of the troops" who "would, to a man, follow him to conquest or death." He concluded: "The reason for the present disagreement between two old cronies is simply this—*Arnold is your friend.*" To these missives, Schuyler responded that Gates "will probably be indebted to General Arnold for the glory he may acquire by a victory, but perhaps he is so very sure of himself that he does not wish the other to come in for a share of it."

Indeed, it had become apparent that Gates had tolerated Arnold at first, had even supported his actions in the battle of the 19th, though not nearly enough, because he was not sure at all of victory and wanted this intrepid fighter to be at his disposal. Gates was a man who kept the supply wagons constantly loaded to facilitate an escape if necessary. But, as the days passed, recruits kept flocking to the camp, and Gates thought that he no longer needed Arnold to persevere.

Restiveness over the affair among his officers was another matter entirely for Gates. Trying to resolve the dispute, Brigadier Enoch Poor drew up a petition praising Arnold for the action of the 19th and requesting him to stay. As Varick informed Schuyler, many officers signed but others declined, such as

Brigadier Dearborn, out of fear of giving umbrage to Gates. And then, Arnold's three aides were suddenly taken aback by Schuyler's vigorous response, saying that he took no pleasure in the squabble and expressing concern over what might happen if the army were deprived of the services of Arnold, "that gallant officer," on the eve of battle.

Arnold's aides suddenly realized that they had overreached, that in striving to denigrate Gates they had not served Arnold well. They proposed to Poor a modification of his petition, dropping the praise of Arnold and asking only that he stay. This Poor did, and every line officer of the army signed it except Gates and Lincoln.

This gave Gates pause, and he sought to lay the quarrel to rest, but in a clumsy way that only angered Arnold the more. Through intermediaries, he repeatedly conveyed the idea that Arnold should consider making some overtures, the first of which would be dismissal of Livingston. Varick wrote to Schuyler: "When this was told to Arnold he could scarcely contain himself." Livingston wrote: "It has several times been insinuated by Gates to General Arnold that his mind has been poisoned and prejudiced by some of his family, and I have been pointed out as the person who had undue influence over him. But General Arnold would not sacrifice a friend to please the Face of Clay."

Nevertheless, the aides agreed that it was time to deflate the tension. Livingston said he would retire to Albany, and Varick told him he would join him there shortly. Arnold disagreed and then begged Livingston to stay another day so that it would not seem as if he had left at the wish of Gates. Schuyler agreed that the aides had overstepped the boundaries. He asked that Clarkson come to Albany as well. But he told Varick to stay and hold his temper, not as Arnold's aide but once again as muster-master, since Gates had not acted on his resignation.

This act of conciliation changed nothing. Gates continued to ignore Arnold. One day Arnold saw Lincoln giving orders to units of the left wing. Arnold confronted him angrily and Lincoln withdrew. As Varick wrote to Schuyler: "Arnold is determined not to suffer anyone to interfere with his division and says it will be certain death to any officer who does it in action, if it be not settled before." It was clear that Arnold was thinking of challenging Gates or Lincoln or both to a resolution on the field of honor once the enemy was vanquished.

Gates then showed how low he could stoop in insulting Arnold. Having run out of ready cash, Arnold had written out a chit for a fifty dollar reward to a soldier for meritorious conduct. Gates rescinded that order, even though it had been made back before Gates had even arrived in camp to take command.

Arnold, of course, did not really want to leave camp before the enemy was defeated. He had never before left the field of battle. The petition made it possible for him to stay, though he had become a lonely figure, bereft of command

and staff, uninvited to any meetings. He tried to satisfy his anger by continuing to send letters to Gates. On October 1st, he wrote:

Notwithstanding the ill treatment I have met with, and continued daily to receive, treated only as a cypher in the army, never consulted or acquainted with one occurrence in the army, which I know only by accident, while I have every reason to think your treatment proceeds from a spirit of jealousy, and that I have every thing to fear from the malice of my enemies, conscious of my own innocence and integrity, I am determined to sacrifice my feelings, present peace and quiet, to the public good, and continue in the army at this critical juncture, when my country needs my every support.

Arnold then urged Gates to take the offensive, saying that the army was restive from drill and camp work and wanted to meet the enemy and defeat him. He said that if inaction persisted, as many as four thousand men, militia in particular, would desert and Burgoyne would be able to escape. He said there was danger of a threat from the south. Though he did not mention the source, Arnold had received intelligence from Schuyler that an enemy courier had been caught. Though he swallowed the silver bullet containing the message, the courier was given tartar emetic, and when the bullet was retrieved, he was hanged. The message was from Clinton to Burgoyne, stating that he was preparing to lead an attack on the Hudson Highlands in an effort to relieve the pressure on Burgoyne.

Arnold concluded his letter to Gates:

I hope you will not impute this hint to a wish to command the army, or outshine you, when I assure you it proceeds from my zeal for the cause of my country in which I expect to rise or fall.

This letter, as well as others Arnold wrote, was simply ignored. Arnold was wrong about desertions. The army continued to grow, now nearing ten thousand men. The new arrivals included a band of Oneida Indians, who behaved well, scalping only the dead as they harassed the flanks of the enemy, almost daily bringing in prisoners. Gates was gleeful over giving Burgoyne a taste of his own Indian medicine. British and Hessian captives were put in the prison camp, but Loyalists were given by Gates to the Indians "to buffet," meaning that the poor wretches had to run the gauntlet.

This may have entertained some in camp, but Arnold was right about General Clinton's intentions and about restiveness setting in among the troops. Two and a half weeks had passed since the action of the 19th. It was well into October and the chill and blazing colors of fall were increasingly manifest. The men were wondering. Was Gates simply trying to starve the enemy into submission? Was he waiting until winter came? If he waited long enough, would Clinton lead a force out of New York City to attack from the south? Would Howe finally be able to send a large army all the way from Philadelphia to succor Burgoyne?

Gates knew Burgoyne as a gambler. He was waiting for him to make some rash move. As for Arnold's three aides, their role was over. They had made the mistake of being insensitive to the damage they unintentionally were doing to Arnold in their zeal to create turmoil for Gates. They were left to wonder as well. When would the final battle occur? And what role, if any, would Benedict Arnold play?

While the American camp was riven through the weeks of the stalemate by internal dissension, some three miles northward another issue entirely taunted the British leadership—would help come in time from the south?

General Burgoyne was filled with nervous anticipation after being awakened at four in the morning by news of the arrival of a courier from General Clinton. This occurred just three days after the Battle of Freeman's Farm; Burgoyne had been praying that a message would get through from his fellow commander in New York City. The exhausted courier said he knew that two other messengers had been sent by Clinton and must be presumed to have been captured en route by the rebels.

There was momentary panic when neither Burgoyne nor his hastily summoned secretary Thomas Stanley could find the hourglass template that was needed to screen out all the irrelevant words, leaving only the real "message within a message" to be seen.

"Goddammit!" Burgoyne roared at Stanley. "After all I've been through, we can't even decode the most important message of my life?'"

Stanley frantically worked to recreate the hourglass figure from memory, cutting out various sizes to place over the message, until at last he isolated the crucial words:

Sept. 12

You know my good will and are not ignorant of my poverty. If you think 2000 men can assist you effectually, I will make a push at Montgomery in about ten days. But ever jealous of my flanks if they make a move in force on either of them I must return to save this important post. I expect reinforcements every day. Let me know what you wish.

Stanley quickly procured the right map and Burgoyne refreshed his memory as to just where in the Hudson Highlands Fort Montgomery was located. Tracing a finger, he saw that it was more than forty miles north of New York City at a sharp double bend of the Hudson River. That would leave

Clinton still far south of Albany, more than a hundred miles. Nevertheless, Burgoyne reasoned, the pressure would soon be felt and should serve to draw off some of Gates's army. He wrote a response urging Clinton to act: "Do it my dear friend directly."

Burgoyne walked to the entrance of his marquee tent, its double-lined walls of silk stained and torn in places after the rigors of the march but still serviceable. Dawn was just breaking and the camp was stirring. It was ten days since Clinton had written the message. That meant that his assault on the Highlands could be getting under way at any moment. Burgoyne was now glad that Fraser had talked him out of an immediate counterattack the day after the September 19th action. Much better to preserve his force and wait until Clinton's pressure had its effect. The men had already made a good start in building defensive works. Before long, Burgoyne told himself, the position will be every bit as strong as the rebel one at the other end of the heights.

As the days passed and the autumn colors reached their brilliant peak, Burgoyne became increasingly restive. There was a monotonous stalemate in effect, with little significant military action. Nearly two weeks passed before Burgoyne decided that the deadlock must end. There had been no further communication from Clinton and no evidence that his pressure affected Gates, indeed if there were any pressure at all. Gates clearly was content to wait while Burgoyne's supplies vanished, limiting himself to harassing Burgoyne's flanks and scouting parties, but not attempting a general attack.

Burgoyne had already cut the army to one-third rations, and he knew that rebel units were accumulating to his rear, endangering the avenue of escape to Canada. It was nearing the season when Carleton had pulled out the year before, out of fear of the winter snows. Burgoyne shuddered; he was positively phobic about winter cold. Desertions were increasing. The defensive works were complete, a series of redoubts defending a line well more than a mile long, running between Mill Creek and the Great Ravine, from the cliff westward to the dense forest and high ground. North of Freeman's farm, the line made a half turn where a redoubt facing south and southwest was entrusted to Lord Balcarres and his Light Infantry. The anchor redoubt to the northwest was manned by Germans under Colonel Breymann. A second and shorter line was built on the north edge of the Great Ravine, dominated by a citadel known as the Great Redoubt.

Venturing south of the defensive works to the no-man's-land between the two armies was extremely dangerous—most scouting or foraging parties took losses from the rebel outposts and roaming Indians. Confined to the camp proper, the horse and cattle had grazed the ground bare. Now the animals were dying of starvation, giving the whole area a putrid smell.

It was time to take action, Burgoyne knew. His instinct was somehow to find a way to attack. He needed a plan and he needed the opinions of others. At his order, his two aides, Stanley and Sir Francis Clarke, went off to summon Generals von Riedesel, Fraser, and Phillips to a conference in Burgoyne's tent.

The four generals reviewed their situation, every aspect tinged with gloom except the fact that the morale of the regular troops, despite all hardships, still seemed high. Burgoyne expressed confidence that Clinton was on his way. Fraser frowned, pointing out that Clinton's message was not a strong one, mentioning only two thousand troops, as well as his "poverty" and readiness to withdraw if his flanks were threatened. Burgoyne countered by citing Clinton's expectation of reinforcements. Von Riedesel was concerned that almost nothing was known of the American fortifications, aside from meager information obtained from the rare deserter or captive. Only along the river road could the works be seen at a distance, and they looked formidable.

"There's one way to find out," Burgoyne said. "By attacking."

A plan grew in Burgoyne's mind. He proposed leaving a thousand men to man the defensive line while he led more than four thousand troops in an all-out effort to turn the enemy's left flank, marching up the rise and looping around through the woods.

Von Riedesel's reaction was highly negative. He thought it would take two or three days to complete such a maneuver through dense woods, even if opposition were light at first, leaving Gates plenty of time to attack frontally and overwhelm the thousand-man defense of the main camp. Instead of flanking the enemy, Burgoyne's attacking force itself would be flanked and all the stores captured.

"Gates is a coward," Burgoyne said. "And lethargic. He won't attack."

"He has Benedict Arnold," Fraser pointed out.

"Yes," Burgoyne murmured.

The meeting broke up without any resolution, and the four men walked the ground, including the second line dominated by the Great Redoubt, to see if a thousand men could possibly hold there. They decided it was impractical in either position and agreed to reconvene the next day, Sunday, October 5th.

Von Riedesel opened the second meeting by making the case for retreat, the first time the idea had been seriously discussed in conference. He proposed abandoning some of the materiel to pull back quickly and recross the river at Batten Kill and Fort Miller, before enemy forces to the north and west became any stronger. There the army would be able to withdraw to Canada safely, if necessary, or resume the offensive if Clinton or Howe came up in force.

Fraser broke the silence after von Riedesel had finished. "I have to say," Fraser said quietly, "this seems the wisest course."

Burgoyne looked at Phillips, who shook his head and said: "I give no opinion."

"Can you imagine the shock and scandal in London if a British Army re-treated before ever being fully tested in battle?" Burgoyne asked.

"It's not our fault," von Riedesel rejoined. "Why didn't General Howe come north, as the plan intended? We'd be in Albany now, victorious."

"I don't know why," Burgoyne said. "Perhaps some day we shall find out. We must deal with the situation as we find it. We have our orders. And I do be-lieve Sir Henry Clinton is coming north." Burgoyne ruefully thought of his ca-reer and reputation shattered if he ordered a retreat without doing battle. He thought for a long moment, and then proposed a plan almost the opposite of the one he had suggested the day before. On October 7th, he would leave the bulk of the army in its defensive positions and lead out a reconnaissance in force, some fifteen hundred regulars plus the six hundred Canadians and Loyalists. They would test the American left, and meanwhile protect foragers who would scoop up any potatoes, corn, wheat, and grass that could be found. If the American left seemed at all approachable, an all-out attack would be made on the 8th. If not, Burgoyne said, he would order a retreat for Octo-ber 11th, one day before he had told Clinton, in his last message, that he could hold out.

There was no reaction, other than uneasy glances. Von Riedesel finally nodded. At least a retreat was in the plan, though too late, he feared. The next day, to encourage the men, Burgoyne ordered a double ration of beef and rum. Before eleven in the morning on the 7th, the reconnaissance party moved out in three columns, Light Infantry on the right, Grenadiers on the left, Germans in the center, and the auxiliaries and ten cannon following. Behind them came officer's servants and camp followers with wagons for forage. The lead party pressed forward three quarters of a mile, past Freeman's farm, and halted along the line of Mill Creek.

Chapter 35

Bemis Heights
October 7, 1777

Benedict Arnold walked back and forth nervously in the American compound. The alarm had been sounded by scouts and now the beat of drums called sol-diers to order. Gunfire could be heard. Wilkinson rode into camp, having been sent forward by Gates to reconnoiter. Arnold watched the messengers coming and going about Gates. He came close enough to hear Wilkinson's report and Gates's somewhat theatrical response: "Well, then, order Morgan out to begin the game."

Morgan came over to suggest that he attempt to turn the British right by making a circuit through the woods and high ground to the left. Gates nodded. A plan was forming in his mind. He wanted to emulate what he thought had happened in the battle of the 19th—firing at the exposed British from protected positions in the woods but not attempting a further attack. He passed the word for Dearborn's sharpshooters to follow Morgan and for Enoch Poor to lead his brigade to the right to preoccupy the British left. As Morgan's men loped out of camp and Poor and Dearborn were forming up their units, Gates called Ebenezer Learned over and instructed him to position his brigade in the center, not to attack but to make sure the British could not advance.

Arnold was dismayed as he watched all of these troops moving out and preparing to move. All of them were units that had been under his command on the 19th. It was especially difficult for him to watch Learned's brigade depart for the front. It included the New York regiments that had been with him at Stanwix and the Connecticut regiments he knew from home. Many of the men looked at him as they passed by, wondering why he was not leading them.

At two in the afternoon, Poor's units were the first to reach their position, lining up on the right opposite the British Grenadiers, who occupied the rise of land beyond Mill Creek at the far left of Burgoyne's lines. British cannon fired at the Americans concealed in the woods but did little damage. Poor's orders were not to fire before receiving the first volley from the enemy, giving Morgan time to reach his position on the left.

Major Acland, commander of the Grenadiers, was frustrated by the lack of action. He ordered his troops to fire. They made the common mistake of men firing downward from an elevated position—shooting too high. Acland shouted: "Fix bayonets and charge the damned rebels!" The Grenadiers poured down the slope, whereupon Cilley and Scammell shouted defiance and ordered their New Hampshire regiments to charge. Acland had not realized that Poor's seasoned Continentals outnumbered his Grenadiers two to one. Scores of redcoats fell in the first murderous volley from the Americans. Acland was hit in the leg and fell in the angle of a split-rail fence. As he rolled in agony, another bullet struck his other leg.

The Grenadiers fled. An American surgeon, bandaging the wounds of a captured British officer, held his bloodied hands high, shouting, "I've dipped my hands in British blood!" Colonel Cilley leaped astride an abandoned brass twelve-pounder, waving his sword and dedicating the cannon to the patriot cause. Then he jumped off and ordered the gun turned to be used against the fleeing enemy.

Meanwhile, Morgan had engaged far at the other end of the line, coming down on the flank of Lord Balcarres and the Light Infantry. Driven back, Balcarres managed to stabilize his line behind a rail fence and traded fire with Morgan.

From his position behind the center, Burgoyne saw that both flanks were endangered. He sent Sir Francis Clarke forward to order the whole line to pull back. Before he could deliver the order, Clarke pitched from his horse, a bullet in his side.

Benedict Arnold still stalked back and forth, building up a furious rage. He heard the massed firing of a British line and then the irregular shots of American troops. He heard the thrilling roar of cannon fire. No one spoke to Arnold. Gates was the center of attention, as couriers mingled around the entrance of a tent Gates had for his use nearer to the breastworks than his cabin. Arnold's pulse quickened when he thought Gates was looking in his direction, but Gates was just lost in thought and looked away. Arnold abruptly mounted his horse and rode restlessly back and forth. Ranks of soldiers stood in line nervously, waiting to be ordered out. They looked at Arnold as if they expected him to give them orders. He waved his sword and rode on. Finally he guided the horse to the top of the breastworks where he could see flashes of fire in the distance and swirls of white smoke. His nostrils caught the acrid smell of gunpowder. Wounded men were being carried back. They looked at Arnold. Why was he there? Why wasn't he in the battle?

Arnold rode back down to the camp level. Compounding his fury was a complete lack of knowledge of exactly what was happening at the battle line. A courier dashed in from the woods. Arnold tried to stop him, but the man dodged and ran to Gates. Arnold could take it no longer. Those were *his* men who were fighting and dying!

"Goddammit to hell!" Arnold screamed. "Victory or death!" He put his spurs to the big horse and it darted forward and leaped over a sally port, galloping toward the battle.

Gates saw him leave and was appalled. Arnold's presence would ruin the plan, changing the battle drastically, dangerously. He clutched the arm of his nearest aide, Major John Armstrong. "Go after him!" Gates cried. "Stop him! A direct order. Bring him back here."

Armstrong mounted and took off, choosing the wagon opening rather than attempting a leap over the sally port. Arnold was far ahead of him, unconscious of any danger, while Armstrong proceeded much more cautiously.

Stragglers saw Arnold riding swiftly to the front and turned around to follow him. He reined up among the familiar faces of Learned's men at the center of the line. No one was firing. Arnold could see Hessian ranks in a wheat field beyond the creek, also with guns at rest. He shouted; "C'mon, boys, let's get 'em. Charge!" He rose toward the Hessians, the ranks following him. The Hessians opened fire and Arnold realized he was alone. He rode back and rallied the men and charged again. This time the Hessians broke, running back in disorder. Learned rode over in dismay, conscious that his orders had been not to attack. The enemy was scrambling to retire behind their fortifications. According to Gates's plan, that meant the battle was over. But he was not present. Arnold was in de facto command.

Arnold rode back and forth, ordering every unit he came upon to attack. Far to the left, he saw that Simon Fraser, aboard his iron-grey charger, had rallied several regiments to cover the retreat back to the fortifications. Arnold dug in his spurs and began to gallop across the entire length of Freeman's farm, exposed to cross fire from both sides. Watching soldiers expected him to fall at any moment, but he miraculously came through the thick fire to reach Morgan's position. He grabbed the surprised Morgan by the arm. "On the horse, there," Arnold gasped, and pointed. "That's Simon Fraser. If we can get him, they'll break."

Morgan nodded and shouted instructions to Tim Murphy, who climbed a small tree overlooking a copse of bushes, carrying his double-barreled rifle.

Fraser rode back and forth, shouting instructions. The first shot cut the crupper of his horse. The second passed through the horse's mane. Fraser's aide shouted for him to draw back. Fraser ignored him. The third shot struck him in the abdomen.

The troops ran pell-mell for the fortified line, as Fraser slumped in the saddle, then fell to the ground. His aide grabbed some fleeing soldiers, who carried Fraser to camp, one of the few wounded British soldiers to be brought back.

Lord Balcarres had done the best in holding his position, but now he was flanked. His men fell back to the redoubt named after Balcarres, a vital post in the defensive works, which other fugitives from the reconnaissance expedition had already reached. Arnold rode back and led the Connecticut troops in an assault on the redoubt. They carried the abatis of sharpened logs and stormed up the breastworks, but were checked by heavy fire from the fortified position. The Americans took cover behind trees, felled logs, and stumps, and kept up a steady fire.

Arnold rode back to the west toward Breymann's redoubt, which sat on a knoll sloping steeply on three sides. On the fourth side, a gentler slope to the southwest, Breymann had erected a log barrier. Arnold noticed two fortified log cabins defending the ground between Breymann and Balcarres, and rallied units of Learned's brigade for an attack. The Canadian defenders fled in panic and the cabins were taken. Breymann was now flanked to the east, as well as receiving heavy fire from the south and west.

Rather than leave the encampment to take any part in the battle, General Gates retreated—from the tent to his cabin a quarter of a mile further back. He had given Dr. Townsend and several orderlies permission to take the wounded Sir Francis Clarke to the cot in his office and to have his maidservant attend him.

For the better part of an hour, Gates engaged Sir Francis in a debate over the merits of the American Revolution. Despite his very serious wound, Clarke remained an impetuous and lively person. He took umbrage at Gates's attempts to persuade him that he was wrong, that he had come to this sorry pass in a misguided effort to quell the liberties of free men. He said that he had originally sympathized with all the grievances of the Americans, but opposed the Declaration of Independence. He had then come to believe that the idea of disunion was a premeditated one, that the Colonists were the dupes of the Puritans of New England, and therefore he felt justified in taking arms against them. Gates argued that the idea of separation had never entered the head of any American until the repeated oppressions of the British government left a choice only between vassalage or freedom. Wilkinson arrived to hear part of the debate, and Gates soon became so agitated that he left the cabin when Dr. Townsend returned for another look at his patient.

"Have you ever heard of such a damned impudent son of a bitch?" Gates asked Wilkinson, who had followed him outside.

"Well, sir, since he's probably dying, a little allowance might be made."

"You think the wound is mortal?"

"Yes, sir, I would think so. The surgeon would know."

The two men returned inside where they heard Clarke chiding the surgeon. "Doctor, why do you pause? Do you think I'm afraid to die?"

Townsend hesitated, and then said: "As a matter of prudence, sir, you might wish to arrange your private affairs."

Clarke nodded. "I understand. When I—when it's over, perhaps you'll be kind enough to write to General Burgoyne. As for my private affairs, my father settled them for me. I have just a few legacies." Clarke turned to Gates. "May I have paper, sir?"

As Clarke laboriously wrote out a bequest of twenty guineas to Jenny, the maidservant who had tended him so well, Gates whispered to Wilkinson: "He's the seventh baronet of Hitcham in Buckinghamshire. Only twenty-three, he is." Though he disliked and often derided the peerage, Gates was still somewhat in awe of them. As Townsend left, Gates followed him outside to ask what Clark's chances were.

"It's certainly mortal," the doctor said. "The ball entered his right flank and struck the last two of the false ribs. It penetrated the abdomen and seems to run toward the spine. The muscular tension, the involuntary discharge of urine, these are bad signs. I think his best friend in the last hours will be young Jenny."

Inside the strong redoubt, Colonel Breymann verged on panic. Having loaned two hundred of his men to the ill-fated reconnaissance expedition—they were either dead or fled elsewhere—he had only nearly three hundred left. There was a pause in the shooting, but Breymann could see that it was only because the rebels were massing on two sides. If the redoubt fell, the rebels would succeed in turning the corner of the entire line of fortifications. Breymann knew that the officer on the grey horse shouting instructions, Benedict Arnold, was too close for a cannon shot. At Breymann's order, three of his soldiers took aim at Arnold and fired their muskets, but all missed.

With a fearsome howl, the rebels charged, led by Arnold. Breymann yelled orders, but then fell with a bullet in his back. A despised tyrant to his men, Breymann had already sabered four of them who tried to flee. A fifth one shot him from behind just as the charge gained momentum.

The Hessian soldiers fired their weapons and then began to run, climbing over the low barrier to the rear. Rebel soldiers were scaling two other sides of the redoubt, scrabbling over the wall. Arnold's great stallion leaped through a broken portion. A last volley from the rear of the redoubt brought Arnold's horse crashing down, pinning his rider's leg. A wounded Hessian soldier, slumped against the rear wall, raised his musket and fired. The ball shattered the femur of Arnold's free leg.

One of Morgan's men began to rush forward to bayonet the German, but Arnold grabbed his ankle. "No, no!" he shouted. "Leave him be. He was just— he was doing his duty."

In moments the redoubt was cleared of Germans, except dead and wounded, and American troops pursued the others with a hot fire but soon fell exhausted to the ground. A knot of men gathered around Arnold and with great exertion freed his other leg from beneath the horse. Someone found a blanket to place over him. Dearborn came in, followed by Morgan. Soon Learned was there, too. Major Armstrong arrived and dismounted. Not entirely aware of what had happened, he tugged Dearborn's sleeve. "General Gates wants General Arnold to return to camp. It's a direct order."

Dearborn wearily said: "Really. Well, I think you can tell General Gates he'll be along soon."

Morgan was cradling Arnold's head. In shock, Arnold now was lapsing in and out of consciousness. Dearborn leaned over and whispered: "How bad is it, General?"

"It's my leg," Arnold said. "He managed a wan smile. "The same one. Wounded three times. Only this time, it's bad. Very bad." He looked up at Morgan. "I wish it had been my heart."

It was growing dark when two surgeons arrived. The troops were so tired that there was no chance of organized pursuit. And then a debate arose between Learned and Dearborn. The cautious Learned wanted to pull out and leave the redoubt, for fear of a counterattack. Dearborn argued heatedly that the place must be held. While the surgeons examined Arnold's wound and soldiers worked at making a litter to carry him back, Wilkinson arrived with an order from Gates to hold the redoubt at all costs. Learned said to Dearborn: "Well, it's *your* post. You can have it."

The surgeons conferred, and one leaned over to speak to Arnold: "There's nothing for it, General. We'll have to amputate. Immediately."

"No! I forbid it."

"But, General," the other surgeon said, "morbidity will set in. You'll die."

"I'd rather die than lose my limb. I forbid it." Arnold lapsed into unconsciousness again.

Burgoyne soon learned that his right flank had been turned. He immediately realized that this made his whole position untenable and gave orders for a withdrawal of the entire camp across the Great Ravine to the second line. He closed his eyes and shuddered at the thought of the brave officers and men he had lost on that day. Fraser, Acland, Clarke, the list seemed endless. For a moment, he wished that he had joined them. It was not for want of exposure— three times enemy bullets had torn through his uniform and hat. He hoped the rebels would be decent enough to tend the British wounded and bury the dead. There was no dispensation by anyone to talk about what to do next, only a slow, miserable exodus across the ravine to wait for what the next day would bring.

Baroness von Riedesel had been planning a small party that day as a break against the monotony and anxiety of the camp. She had hummed a tune that morning as she supervised her maid in setting the table. She and her husband would be entertaining Burgoyne and Fraser for dinner at their cabin near the Great Redoubt. Later that morning she became aware that there would be military action that day. Her husband stopped by briefly to say that he was joining Burgoyne and Fraser in a reconnaissance.

Late in the afternoon, men arrived at the cabin bearing the wounded Simon Fraser in a litter. They dismantled the dining table, putting away all the glasses and fine china, and set it up as a bed for the general. The baroness watched the process with fear, thinking of her husband still out somewhere in the battle.

The baroness also concerned herself with another refugee in her cabin, Lady Harriet Acland, who was wretched after being told that her husband had been mortally wounded and left on the field of battle. After much effort, the baroness found a grenadier officer who told her that Acland had been wounded in the legs, twice, and probably would survive, because the Americans had carried him away. She brought this news to Lady Acland and urged her to seek Burgoyne's permission to go to enemy lines and nurse him herself.

As the evening wore on, the Baron von Riedesel returned, unhurt, but with a faraway look in his eyes. The baroness whispered thanks to God for hearing her prayers. He came up to embrace her and spoke closely to her ear: "Keep yourself in constant readiness to go. By no means give anyone else the least inkling of what you are doing."

Throughout the night, General Fraser occasionally groaned but often sent notice to the baroness in the next room to ask forgiveness for causing her so much trouble. She was constantly afraid that her children might wake and disturb the poor dying man. At one point, Fraser laboriously penned a note to General Burgoyne, asking that he be buried on a hill near the Great Redoubt. At eight the next morning, he was pronounced dead by the surgeon. Two corpsmen washed the corpse and wrapped it in a sheet where the general had spent his last night. The baroness then came into the room with the children. The sad sight was before them the entire day.

The day after the battle was marked by no significant military action. There was some sporadic cannon fire and sniping from the American side, and General Lincoln managed to get himself shot. Misunderstanding an order from Gates, he was leading a militia unit up the river road when a British sniper knocked him from his miniature horse with a shot through the calf of his leg. The fact that both Arnold and Lincoln were down left Gates with no officers above the rank of brigadier.

Burgoyne and his remaining officers agreed that the army should retreat to Saratoga to regroup and see if any viable course of action was open. But Burgoyne took the chance of delaying the movement for a day in order to fulfill Simon Fraser's dying wish. The grave was dug and the burial party assembled on the hill at six o'clock. Chaplain Edward Burdenell solemnly read the service, paying no heed to the cannonballs that came from the American side, occasionally throwing a spray of dirt across his visage. Later, Gates said that if he knew a funeral service was going on, he would have ceased all fire.

That same evening, the chaplain escorted Lady Harriet to a skiff manned by two men. Lady Harriet carried a letter from Burgoyne to Gates, requesting that she be shown all courtesies. Despite the chaplain's arguments, however, the American sentries detained the party at the sentry post until daybreak, leading to a cold and unpleasant night with very little sleep to be had. Once taken to Gates in the morning, Lady Harriet was graciously received and conducted to her husband in the American hospital camp.

In this same camp, Benedict Arnold lay on his litter alternately slipping into and out of consciousness as the surgeons tried repeatedly to convince him that he must have his leg amputated, if he were to survive. Arnold adamantly refused each time. Finally, the surgeons did their best to cleanse the wound, remove the musket ball, and push and maneuver the broken femur into something resembling the correct position. They dressed the wound with oils and powder and wrapped the leg in oil-soaked linen. Then they placed Arnold on a firm bedstead and fitted the leg into a fracture box.

The surgeons agreed that Arnold must be taken to the military hospital in Albany, where Dr. James Thacher might be able to persuade him to undergo what they firmly believed was his only chance for survival. Arnold was placed in a closed wagon for one of the most terrible ordeals of his life, the rough, jolting twenty-two-mile trip to Albany.

Chapter 36

Military Hospital, Albany
October 14, 1777

The patient was pinned to his bed like the man on the cross, his leg encased in the cumbrous fracture box. His hair was unkempt, his face unshaven, his bedclothes and sheets wrinkled and damp. The fracture box was a wooden, three-sided affair, open at the top, anchored by bolts to the end and side frames of the bed. Linen strips with soft cotton pads on the underside bound his leg the length of the box. Midway on the thigh was a dressing of soft flannel soaked in oil to facilitate the draining of the fluids. An uneven, aureate stain spread across the bandage. Beneath it was the wound with its fearsome eye, the entry point of the musket ball that had shattered the femur. The thigh was mottled and purplish, swollen and hot with infection.

Benedict Arnold gritted his teeth and groaned. The pain was a constant companion when he was awake or nearly awake. He opened his eyes, blinking, and surveyed the room, his vision blurry. Whitewashed walls. A door. Where in God's name was he? He closed his eyes and groaned, and soon was back into a form of half sleep, the pain still there.

A short while later something woke him up, and he found that he was staring at the ceiling. He moved his head slightly, and the images of men swam into his vision. The man closest to him looked familiar. Arnold spoke, his voice a nasal rasp. "No. I said no." He tried his best to focus on the figure. "Who are you? Where's the young man?" A less distinct figure next to the tall man stepped forward. He sat in the chair by the bedside.

"Don't worry, General, I'm here," whispered David Franks.

The tall man withdrew to the corner of the room where four other men stood. It was a large room with a second bed but had been kept exclusively for General Arnold by General Schuyler's order. Schuyler spoke to Dr. James Thacher: "It's been exactly a week since he was wounded."

"Yes," Thacher said. "And the infection has spread."

"There's no point amputating now," Schuyler said, making a statement rather than asking a question.

"No."

"Has he been sober at all?"

"I suppose he has been," Dr. Thacher said. "Always angry. He was angry at this young man"—he waved a hand in the direction of Franks—"until he perceived him as an ally."

"Major Franks will be staying with General Arnold throughout his illness," Schuyler said. He indicated the other three men: "These men will be going home."

Thacher nodded. "Major Franks may not have to stay very long," he said.

"We realize that," Schuyler said. "The general has made a very difficult decision. But it's entirely his decision to make. We have to understand that."

"It would be easier to accept if I knew he was fully awake and able to balance the considerations," Thacher snapped.

Young Franks turned. "He's fully awake now."

Schuyler came over to the bed again. Arnold's eyes flitted over him. "General Schuyler," he said, his voice rasping just above a whisper.

Schuyler sat in the chair from which Franks had risen and took Arnold's hand in both of his. "General Arnold, I'm so glad to be able to talk with you. I just—"

Arnold's head moved back and forth. "Don't let them take my leg," he whispered. His head continued to move, as if propelled by nervous tension.

"Don't worry. We're past that now. They won't take it."

"What happened? The British?"

"They're surrounded. At Saratoga. There are negotiators going back and forth. They'll surrender very soon. I'm confident of it. Your charge turned their line."

Arnold's mouth contorted into a grin. "Gates won't agree."

"Ben, Varick and Livingston and Clarkson are here. They'll all be going home. David Franks will be staying with you. And me, of course."

The three men crowded over and, one by one, reached down to touch Arnold's hand and say something. Before they were through, Arnold dozed off again.

"It's too much for him," Varick said. "God bless him."

"Yes," Schuyler said. "What a tragedy! This man you see before you. He's the very genius of war. We won't be seeing his kind again."

PART VIII

The Decadent Season

Chapter 37

Philadelphia
December 9, 1777

Captain John André clutched his greatcoat tightly about him as he rode down Second Street toward Loxley Hall, where Lydia Darragh awaited him. This would be his last interview of the day before writing his report to General Howe. Although the case at hand was a baffling and tedious one, André was still excited in the knowledge that he had finally found the specialty in the army that he believed made the best use of his skills.

Despite his youth, André had been selected for a temporary appointment to fill an important vacancy created by illness—he was acting as the new intelligence officer on General Howe's staff. The opportunity came about through André's new friendship with Major Robert McKenzie, General Howe's personal secretary, who had reminded the supreme commander of André's special talents in languages, the arts, and military sciences.

Once again, General Grey had been obliging in allowing his prized staff aide to take a temporary assignment elsewhere, in the belief that nothing new was in store except a boring winter occupation of the city. Then Grey's division was ordered out as a key element of the force that General Howe was amassing for a winter offensive on the night of December 4th against Washington's army, which was ensconced on the heights at Whitemarsh, some twelve miles due north of Philadelphia. For Howe, the maneuver was his last chance in this season to gain total victory by destroying the enemy army.

The British troops, unaccustomed to winter action, had endured three miserable days of hiking back and forth across the frozen terrain north of the city, to no avail. Washington clearly had ample warning and was well prepared. There had been numerous skirmishes across a five-mile front, but Washington's position was unassailable, and he could not be lured out for a general confrontation. The British soldiers suffered much more from frostbite than bullet wounds. André was glad he had been spared the fruitless ordeal; now his task was to find out how Washington had been alerted.

Though he had spent the day interviewing prisoners and Tories from the north of the city, he had learned precious little. The damned city is like a sieve, he thought, farmers and citizens and spies crossing the lines without much difficulty. Now he was going back to the beginning, to the room where the winter attack had been planned. Had Lydia found a way to eavesdrop? Was she the informer?

Averting his face from the cold wind, André could see the Delaware River to his left and ample evidence that the stubborn American defense of the river forts had finally been broken in mid-November, just in time to open the water route to the sea and avert mass starvation in the occupied city. André could see the British warships anchored out in the middle of the river to allow the merchantmen room at the docks to unload their cargoes of food and supplies. It had taken an unbelievable six weeks for the British to subdue Forts Mercer and Mifflin and break open the cheval-de-frise that had blocked the narrow channels threading through the mudflats south of Philadelphia.

Loxley Hall was in the center of a neighborhood that teemed with high-ranking British officers. Across the street was the house owned by the American general John Cadwalader, which André had located as a residence for Lord Cornwallis and his staff, after Cornwallis had given up on the Logan home. A block away was the building occupied by the top Hessian commander, Lieutenant-General Wilhelm von Knyphausen. Further on was the so-called slate-roof house, once occupied by William Penn, now a boardinghouse filled with British officers.

This proximity had caused the British commanders to take over a large room on the second floor of Loxley Hall for their conferences. For the Darragh family—husband, wife, and two of their five children—it was a small price to pay in order to keep the rest of the house for themselves. Initially, they had feared they would lose it all when André came knocking on the door in his earlier role as real estate scout for the top commanders. But a small miracle occurred when Lydia went to General Howe's headquarters to appeal. The polite young captain on duty there introduced himself as William Barrington. That had been Lydia's maiden name back in Dublin, and the two soon found that they were second cousins. The captain made sure that the Darragh family was not inconvenienced beyond giving up the one large room on the second floor.

The Barrington connection and the fact that the Darraghs were Quakers made them seem harmless to the British officers. In fact, they were staunch patriots. Unknown to the British, Lydia's eldest son, Charles, was an ensign in the Pennsylvania Second Regiment, on duty at Whitemarsh in Washington's army. And her two youngest children were staying on a relative's farm near Frankford, not far from Whitemarsh. Several times, Lydia had already conveyed information to the American camp by obtaining passes to send her fourteen-year-old son, John, to visit his siblings in Frankford—and secretly to see his eldest brother in the American camp.

On the evening of December 2nd, the conference to plan the winter offensive had taken place. André had come early to advise Lydia of the meeting and to ask that she and her husband lay up a fire in the room, see that no visitors were about, and retire to their bedroom early. He would return after the conference to knock on Lydia's door to let her know that she could now lock the front door of the house.

For the interrogation a week later, André met with Lydia in the same conference room, where a number of tables had been pushed together and surrounded by straight-backed chairs to serve the room's purpose. André told her that General Howe was convinced that someone had betrayed the plans to the Americans, and he described the interviews he had held during the day.

Lydia was a petite woman in her mid-forties, though still retaining the prettiness of youth, with large blue eyes and sandy hair neatly in place. One look at her in her somber Quaker garb gave André the feeling that he was wasting his time. But one must try.

"I have to tell you, Lydia, that some suspicion has fallen on you," he said.

Her face took on a look of utter astonishment. "Me, sir! Oh, no, sir. It never could be me. Even if I had the inclination—which I certainly do not—I would never have the courage for it!"

"Well, we know that you came to General Howe's headquarters on December third to seek a pass through the lines to Frankford. Captain Barrington issued the pass."

"Yes, sir, that is true. The reason was to get flour. We had none at all. And to see my two youngest at their great-uncle's farm."

André thought for a moment. It was not unusual for Philadelphia women to get passes for such purposes. Did Quakers lie? Probably, André thought. They're human despite being Quakers.

"When did you make the journey?"

"The next morning, it was. Thursday, the fourth."

"How much flour did you get?"

"Twenty-five pounds, sir." Lydia's expression was the picture of innocence, though she was trembling inwardly.

"That's a large amount for a—forgive me—for a slight woman to carry so far in such cold weather."

"Indeed it is, sir. But I managed."

"Why didn't your husband go? Or your son?"

"William had his classes to teach. And it was too much for a child. I wouldn't send Johnny on such a cold day. And I wanted so bad to see little Susie and William Junior."

"Of course," André murmured. "By the way, I poked around and took a good look at that closet out in the hall. There are some cracks in the wall. You can actually see light from this room. You're sure you didn't overhear anything of our meeting?"

"Oh, no, sir!" Lydia remembered how frightened she had been that night in the closet, her ear pressed to the wall.

"One other thing," André said. "One of the people I interviewed today, a Loyal person from up north, told me of an incident he witnessed at the Rising Sun Tavern, about midday on the fourth. It's a place near the York Road where the rebels congregate. He saw what he called 'a rather poor-looking old woman in a shawl' come in and seek out Colonel Boudinot. She spoke to him and passed over a message. He immediately left with an urgent air about him. Were you there, Lydia?"

A small smile. "Not I, sir. I don't think I'm an old woman. Not yet."

André smiled back. "No, that's true."

"I know of that tavern. It's a long way from Frankford."

"Not so far. Three miles perhaps. A detour for you?"

"No, sir."

André thought of the night of the conference when he had gone to rap on Lydia's bedroom door to tell her she could lock up. He had tapped on the door five times before she finally came to open it. She had appeared quite drowsy, as if she had been awakened. Lydia was thinking about the same event. She had hesitated out of pure fear that she had been caught, going to the door only when her husband began to stir.

"Well," André said, rising and offering his hand. "I hope you take no offense. You understand that I must ask these questions."

"Of course, sir."

André left feeling for the first time that Lydia might really be the culprit. Her answers were just a bit too quick and cool. Anyone could feign drowsiness. And, with the benefit of cold weather and a shawl, Lydia could make herself appear to be "a poor-looking old woman." What was he going to do? Put her on the rack? Ruin her life and that of her family, with nothing more than a hunch? Hardly.

It was nearly eight o'clock when André passed through the archway to the inner court where the Benjamin Franklin house was located. General Grey was out for the evening, and André was not surprised to find that several friends had congregated for supper and some cardplaying with his fellow aide, Oliver DeLancey, the young Loyalist officer from the wealthy New York family.

Despite Grey's dislike of "provincials," he had acceded to André's request that DeLancey be taken on as another aide.

DeLancey was seated at the card table in the parlor, engaged in a game of whist. His partner was the engineer John Montresor. The opposing pair were two of General Howe's aides, Major McKenzie and Captain Barrington. Over recent weeks, these officers and several others had gravitated together, partly as a defense against being drawn to the chief amusements of most other officers— drunken carousing and heavy gambling in the many taverns in the area.

Small stakes were permissible, however. DeLancey was totting up the score of a rubber when André entered, sinking into a chair and tossing his greatcoat aside. With a smug smile, DeLancey said to McKenzie and Barrington: "Seven shillings apiece, if you please." He turned to André: "Ah, the intelligence officer returns. And not in a good humor. No luck, John?"

André shook his head. "Damned little. And I don't look forward to telling General Howe that I've been unsuccessful." He glanced at Barrington. "Will, I do suspect one person. Your cousin."

"What? Poor little Lydia? Mother of five children? A spy? You're daft, man."

"She had the opportunity to eavesdrop. And she was up north *before* the attack—with the pass you gave her."

"So were hundreds of other people," Barrington said. "You wouldn't indict Mistress Darragh just to have something to say in your report, would you?"

André snorted. "Did you hungry beasts leave me any food?"

DeLancey waved a hand toward the dining room and began shuffling the cards.

"I wouldn't worry about it, John," McKenzie called as André got up and went into the dining room. "I don't think the general really expects you to apprehend a master spy. He was just venting his frustration."

"Of course," Montresor said. "At least fifty people must have warned Washington we were after him. How can you move an army of fifteen thousand through an area swarming with rebels and their sympathizers and not expect the enemy to know about it? It's ridiculous to think you're going to find one spy that did it."

André returned with a plateful from the cold buffet the servant had set out—ham, smoked tongue, cheese, bread, and best of all, fruit from the Caribbean, courtesy of one of Admiral Howe's transports. He had poured a glass of claret rather than dip into the pails of evil-looking beer that DeLancey had ordered from the Indian Queen tavern around the corner. "That's fine, Monty. Maybe I'll just say that in my report."

"Well—it would do our leader good to hear some plain talk," Montresor muttered, casting a sideways glance at McKenzie. Ever since the agonizing effort to subdue the river forts, which had nearly killed Montresor from exhaustion and frustration, he had become a caustic critic of Howe, leading more than once to a verbal fight with McKenzie, who, as much as he might agree with some of Montresor's complaints, did not want to hear or talk about them. For weeks on end, Montresor had waded through mud and icy river water, trying to set up gun emplacements and barricades, waiting for men and supplies that never arrived in sufficient quantity, all the while with Washington reinforcing the forts from the Jersey side. Despite Montresor's pleas, Howe failed for a long time to see the forts as a difficult obstacle to overcome, leading to the loss of scores of men in undermanned attacks and two warships blown apart by rebel cannon after going aground on the mudflats. Finally, Howe had come personally to the scene to mount an overwhelming offensive.

"C'mon, let's play cards," DeLancey said, trying to avert another argument. He spread the cards on the table. "Cut for partners."

"Sit in for me, John," Montresor said wearily to André.

"No, go ahead and play another rubber. I'm still eating."

While play progressed, André gazed up at the oil portrait of Benjamin Franklin on the wall above the players. It had been painted in 1759 by an artist named Benjamin Wilson. André like the picture, though he found it of no help in trying to fathom the character of the great man. Strange that the Bache family had left the painting behind when they obviously had cleared out so many of Franklin's personal possessions before fleeing from Philadelphia.

André enjoyed thinking about Franklin, a man who apparently was curious about everything. He guessed that Franklin by now was nearly as famous in Europe as he was at home. Certainly he had many admirers in London, and now he was in France, trying to seduce Louis XVI to join the war on the American side. André was aware of many of Franklin's accomplishments—his career as a printer and journalist, his electricity experiments, his many inventions, the origination of postal service, a public library, the American Philosophical Society, and the idea and practice of fire insurance. In Franklin's cellar workshop, André had seen scattered papers and artifacts left behind— Leyden jars, armonica glasses, a printing press, foundry matrices and molds.

André took his plate back to the dining room and walked through to Franklin's study and library. Disappointingly, most of the bookshelves were bare. André coveted one of the sets of books that remained behind, treatises in French on the arts and sciences. Franklin must be able to speak French. Of course, why else would the Americans send him to Paris? André thought that Franklin might now be the most dangerous man on the American side if he were able to bring the French into the war, aided enormously by the debacle in the north, the humiliating loss of Burgoyne's entire army.

Sitting down at Franklin's desk, André reflected on the evidence of several lesser-known interests of the great doctor. He had found papers indicating that Franklin was attempting a catalog of marine animals. Then there was the evidence of a musical turn—the notes for a composition that André had found, as well as the pianoforte and viola de gamba in the parlor. In the kitchen, also located in the cellar, were the ingenious baking oven and the special contrivances to carry off smoke and steam that Franklin had apparently designed. The house, of course, was equipped with lightning rods and Franklin stoves.

How did such a man arise on a remote continent barren of any history in the arts and sciences—no great universities or libraries or museums, no great writers or poets or painters? Perhaps it was simply the dearth of such things that made Franklin stand out. No, André thought, he is truly the product of the Renaissance and the new rationalism in Europe, a free thinker whose mind and abilities stretched in every direction. Among André's colleagues, only the scientific-minded Montresor and, surprisingly, General Grey seemed to have anything like the appreciation of Dr. Franklin's career that André had.

Part of that fascination was that André saw in himself a range of abilities that could lead to a career somewhat in the path and eminence of Franklin. André had even excelled in mathematics and the military sciences at Goettingen, in addition to his linguistic and artistic abilities and interests. But he recognized that he simply lacked the motivation to dabble in science and practical inventions. His forte was the arts, the strong desire to write poems and plays, to enjoy music and possibly compose, to engage in design, and perhaps even painting. It was time to begin stretching in those directions. The winter occupation of Philadelphia could offer the need, the opportunity, and the time to do something important. It would take initiative on his part and help from like-minded people.

André's thoughts were broken by loud voices coming from the parlor. Apparently, cardplaying had proved no barrier to argument. He walked to the parlor to see what was going on just in time to witness the red-faced McKenzie slam his hand on the table and shout: "Damn it, Monty, you go too far sometimes!"

"What are you going to do?" Montresor rejoined. "Tell General Howe that his engineer thinks he's a fool?"

"Of course not! You'll get in trouble all by yourself. I just hope you haven't been spouting off like this in other quarters. What's the point? You can't change anything."

"Maybe if somebody had spouted off before, as you put it, we wouldn't be in the mess we're in now."

"What mess?" DeLancey challenged. "We've thrashed them three times. At Brandywine, Paoli, and—"

"My God, you just don't see it, do you?"

"What?"

"We've thrashed them three times, but not badly enough. And we tried a fourth time and failed. The point is, laddie, we haven't *defeated* them. They're still there. They control the countryside and we're penned up in this city with a thousand problems every day. They'll harass our lines all winter, keep us constantly on edge. They're already intimidating the farmers so they don't dare come into the city with their food. So we have to feed everybody, not just the troops, but the civilians, too. The American prisoners are dying by the score because they're last in line so they're starving. The hospitals are overflowing. The streets aren't safe at night. We have floggings and hangings of our soldiers every day, trying to control plunder and crime. There isn't a fence post or rail left in the city, they've all been burned for fuel. We have no—"

"But the river's open and the transports are unloading every day," De-Lancey protested. "There'll be plenty—"

"Right. And who does it benefit? The profiteers down at the docks setting up their vendues. Charging ten times what coffee and tea and molasses and flour and everything else used to cost. There's no natural market here any-more. We've destroyed it. And we're going to pay the price."

"What *price* are you talking about?" Barrington asked. "Things are getting better every day. The army is safe and civilian life will return to normal in time."

"The price, my dear optimistic friend, is that we've lost another year and gained nothing," Montresor said. "Occupying this city while the rebels control the countryside gains *nothing*! The real question is—how did we get into this mess? And why? What in the hell are we doing here? We lost an entire army up north because we didn't go up there, according to what everyone thought was the plan. Everyone except General Howe, that is." Montresor shook his head. "The news about Burgoyne's army has probably reached London by now. Can you imagine the reaction there? Do you think they'll care that we occupied Philadelphia?"

"They will when we march out next spring and destroy Washington and his army," DeLancey said.

"That's what everyone was saying last year," Montresor observed drily.

McKenzie spoke quietly: "You know the answers to your questions as well as any of us, Monty. The general made a military judgment. It hasn't turned out as well as it might have, we'll all agree, including General Howe himself. But he had his reasons. He thought Burgoyne could take care of himself and that the most direct way to end the war would be to destroy Washington's army."

"Right!" Montresor said. "Now Burgoyne's army has vanished, Washington's is still intact, morale in London will plummet, and we're trapped into something we should have avoided like the plague—spending our time and energy running another damned city."

"There are more Loyalists in this city than anywhere else in the Colonies," McKenzie said.

"I think I heard someone say that about New York," Montresor said.

"Maybe you're right, but what good does it do us? The Loyalists are a problem, too. They depend entirely on us. They can't form regiments successfully. We can't recruit enough workmen to help build the defenses. We can't even find civilians to serve as night watchmen."

McKenzie raised a hand as if to pursue the argument, but subsided. DeLancey, who might have been expected to defend his fellow Loyalists, had a low opinion of the Philadelphia Tories and so did not break the silence that ensued.

Finally, André spoke for the first time. "A lot of us have thought about the things Monty's talking about. I say the time for that is really past. It's done. We're here. I agree with Will. Things will settle down, and we might as well make the best of our time here. Nothing in a military way will happen till next spring. That means we have four months or so to do something."

"Like what?" Montresor asked sarcastically.

"Well, for one thing, I'd like to see us form a theater company. To put on a series of plays over the winter."

"Oh, that'll solve everything," Montresor said.

"The Quakers will frown on that," Barrington added.

"They don't have any influence anymore," André said.

"The other sects are even nuttier." Barrington sighed. "Sometimes I think they believe that if they smile they won't go to heaven."

"It'd be done *by* us and *for* us—for morale," André continued. "Something to do other than drink and gamble and go whoring about. This city has a reputation for tolerance. That's the reason they're so many sects here in the first place. Even Jews and Catholics. They've put on plays here before. There's a theater down on Cedar Street, the Southwark Theater. Unless Monty has made it into a stable or something."

"No, no, it's being used as a hospital now," Montresor said. "The only way to keep it from being torn down for firewood."

"Who's going to do all this?" DeLancey asked.

"We are!" André laughed. "We start the company and bring our other friends in. We'll plan the plays, maybe write one or two, make the scenery, recruit the actors, manage the whole enterprise. There's a lot of talent. I know several naval chaps who are wonderful actors."

"Where do we get the money to do all these things?" DeLancey asked.

"It pays for itself. We charge admission! The only thing—will General Howe support this?"

It was Barrington who responded. "Of course he will! He loves the theater." He continued in a somewhat defensive tone, glancing at Montresor. "Sir William is a very decent man. Highly principled. No commander is more solicitous of his men. He's even respectful toward the Americans, so we can live with them after the war."

"I agree with all of that," Montresor said mildly. "It's the military judgment that concerns me."

"We can recruit civilians, too," André said. "All my little friends of Third and Fourth Street. The pretty Loyalist girls. They can paint scenery and copy scripts if nothing else. Peggy Chew and her sister. Becky Franks. The Shippen girls, three of them at least. The two Willing girls."

"Oh, I like this idea more and more," Barrington said, his eyes glistening. "How do we proceed?"

"We form the nucleus of the company right here tonight," André said eagerly. "We'll bring in a dozen of our friends. The whole group will meet again in a week or two, and by that time I'll have a plan prepared, a list of possible plays and actors, drafts of some public announcements, a budget, and ideas for selling tickets. Monty, can the Southwark Theater be cleared out for us? Say within a few weeks?"

Shaking his head, with a wry smile, Montresor said: "Anything can be done—if General Howe wants it to happen."

"Mac, will you get General Howe's approval?"

"Of course."

"Good! We'll have our first play on the boards by the end of January!" André lifted his glass of wine. "A toast to Howe's Thespians!"

Chapter 38

Military Hospital, Albany
Winter, 1777–1778

The first phase of Arnold's agony lasted for several weeks after Schuyler and his aides had come to visit him, an occasion he scarcely remembered. The infection set in, the wound putrefied, and the leg became discolored, as Arnold lapsed in and out of consciousness. When he was out, Arnold would either be glacially still as if he were indeed dead, or thrashing about with some horrible nightmare, prevented from tearing the wound or moving the broken bones only by the fracture box. When he was awake, he was in constant pain, which he endured with a grim rigor, jaw clenched and eyes smoking, fingernails scraping the bedsheets.

He was delirious at times, as well, rambling on incoherently, reliving times of battle or some episode in his youth or castigating his enemies, who seemed to be legion. Dr. Thacher did everything he could to help Arnold. He drained the wound and changed the dressing daily, and occasionally removed specks of bone that had migrated to the surface. He administered a bewildering variety of medicines and potions to combat the infection, both applied to the wound and taken orally, though Arnold vomited much of the time. He could keep little down and he began to waste away fearfully.

Before the third week was out, Arnold looked so bad that his aide, David Franks, began discussing funeral plans with General Schuyler. Arnold, of course, would not touch on this subject at all. And then he suddenly took a turn for the better. The pain was always there, but it seemed to have lost its ferocity. There was no more delirium, and Arnold began to take food successfully. The color of the leg looked better, and each day Arnold seemed to become a bit more alert and lucid.

Franks discussed this amazing development with Thacher: "Is this the result of sheer wizardry on your part, or is it sheer willpower on Arnold's part?" For the first time, he saw the dour Thacher smile. "Probably both," he said, "but the general won't think so. He'll think he did it all on his own." Thacher still refused to be optimistic. "The infection is not gone," he said. "It could come back at any time."

If he did progress in a positive way, Arnold still faced months of recovery, Thacher pointed out. "I'm not sure just how those bones will knit, if at all," he said. "At best, the leg will be weak and painful for the rest of his life. It may be as much as two inches shorter than the other one. I don't think he'll ever sit in a saddle again. But no point telling him that. The real test will come about six weeks from now—when he tries to put weight on the leg. When we see if the muscles and blood flow come back at all. When he tries to learn to walk again. If he just can't do it—we may still have to amputate."

Franks was smart enough to keep this conjecture to himself and tried to be as cheerful as he could with Arnold. Gradually Arnold's color returned and he became quite talkative. He enjoyed letters from his sister and her reports of the progress of his sons. He began to have a stream of visitors, some of them very interesting and educational for Major Franks, who, having come down from Canada, had little history of the Continental Army.

One of the first was Major-General Benjamin Lincoln, who had been in a room down the hall recovering from his own leg wound. It was entirely a flesh wound and therefore not to be compared to Arnold's. On the day of his release from the hospital, Lincoln entered Arnold's room. Franks was taken aback at seeing the pudgy, bland-looking Lincoln, because he had been given to understand that he and Arnold were enemies for some reason.

Lincoln said he had come to wish Arnold well and to apologize for not being more attentive to him during the actions at Saratoga. "I thought you hated me because I was promoted over your head," Lincoln said.

His visit was a decent gesture, and Franks kept his fingers crossed that Arnold would be gracious about it. He indeed was. "No," Arnold said. "If it seemed that way it was only the situation at the time. It wasn't your fault. I hated Congress."

Lincoln laughed at that and then turned serious again. "I've changed my opinion of General Gates," he said.

"How so?"

"He didn't mention you in any of the reports of the battles. Nor did he mention Daniel Morgan in the last report. A dastardly thing to do."

Arnold nodded. "That's the God's truth."

"It'll do Gates no good," Lincoln said. "Everyone will know what really happened. They'll hear the truth from me as well."

"You're still senior to me," Arnold said.

"I'm ashamed to hear it. Surely Congress will act now."

Arnold shrugged. Lincoln examined Arnold's wound, shaking his head and audibly sucking in breath. Then he noticed the earlier wound from Quebec on the lower portion of the same leg, and realized it was virtually identical to his own injury. The two men were quite taken with this coincidence as Lincoln displayed the similar scar on his calf.

"Thacher told me how fortunate I was to have all my wounds in the same leg," Arnold said. "Fortunate! I wish *you* had three wounds in the same leg, I told him!"

Arnold's most enjoyable moment came later when Franks described a dinner party at General Schuyler's mansion. There were prominent people there from the Albany area, and Generals Burgoyne and Gates were both in attendance. Inevitably, the battles were rehashed for the benefit of the civilian guests, and Burgoyne was unstinting in his praise of Arnold and Morgan. There was no question in his mind about who had won the battle. Gates was bitterly crestfallen at this.

At no time did Arnold think that Gates would have the grace to visit his fallen comrade. Word did arrive from the Schuyler household that Burgoyne was coming. That morning Franks shaved Arnold and made sure that his linens were changed and the room freshened. He even had some special scent that he pumped into the air, to Arnold's disgust.

There was quite a stir in the hospital when Burgoyne came. He could be heard greeting several of his own officers down the hall who were also recuperating from wounds. Preceded into the room by his principal aide, Major Thomas Stanley, Burgoyne could not have been warmer and more solicitous in greeting Arnold. He clucked over Arnold's wound and praised not only his military valor but also his physical strength and endurance in taking such a terrible injury. In turn, Arnold repeatedly praised Burgoyne for his courage and the British troops for their fighting spirit and skill.

"I've wanted to meet you for a long time," Burgoyne said, sitting in a chair at Arnold's bedside while Stanley and Franks stood together at a respectful distance from the two generals. "I soon realized that you were our most formidable opponent."

"Thank you for that," Arnold said. "We did meet once—at a considerable distance."

Burgoyne laughed. "Oh, yes! When you tempted us so audaciously at St. Jean. I thought we would capture you then."

"I was sure it was you."

"And then I thought we'd have you again, at Valcour Bay."

They went on in this vein for some time, recalling their encounters and analyzing the battles. And then Arnold asked: "What will happen when you return to London?"

Burgoyne mused and said: "I'll have quite a rough go, I'm afraid. Everyone will be covering their backsides. They'll want to blame it all on me."

"That's an outrage," Arnold said. "We knew what your plan was. Despite it, you were left quite alone up here. None of us could understand why that happened."

"Nor could I. And I mean to find out."

"If you want a witness to the valor of you and your army, I shall always be ready to testify."

"Thank you, General," Burgoyne said, shaking hands with Arnold. "And London shall hear about the bravery and military skill of Benedict Arnold."

A sure sign that Arnold's recovery was progressing well came when he displayed a sense of humor, crude as it was. This occurred on the day when two British officers, Lord Acland of the Grenadiers and Major Harnage of the Sixty-second, visited him to bid farewell. They were to join Burgoyne's entourage the next day for the trip to Boston to await transport to England for the defeated army. Acland, whose leg wounds involved only one simple fracture, was still using crutches, while Harnage, who had been gut-shot in the first battle, seemed perfectly fit. His recovery, along with Arnold's, was regarded as a miracle in the hospital. The two men, who had visited Arnold several times before, brought along a bottle of brandy to celebrate Acland's release from the hospital. Arnold was persuaded to take a glass, and it seemed to elevate his spirits, given the level of bantering that went on.

Dr. Thacher stuck his head in the room on his afternoon rounds. "Come in, Thacher," Arnold shouted. "Have a brandy with us!"

"Never touch it," Thacher snapped.

Arnold looked very serious. "I now realize I've wronged you, Thacher. I've made my decision. You can do it now."

Thacher was wary. He never knew what form Arnold's abuse would take. "Do what?"

"Why, cut off my leg, of course! C'mon, bring in your saw."

Disgusted, Thacher withdrew and slammed the door, as Arnold burst into laughter, joined by Acland and Harnage.

Tears rolling down his cheeks, Arnold sputtered: "Oh, how he wanted that limb! I think he wanted to stuff it and put it over his mantelpiece, boot and all! Can't you see it? He'd have a plaque saying 'Left leg of Major-General Benedict Arnold, Captured at Saratoga by Doctor James Thacher.' "

"Really, sir," Acland laughed, "you're too hard on him. He's a decent sort and a damned good doctor, judging by the three of us. A man of parts, actually. Did you know he's a poet?"

Acland had not intended a pun, but Arnold picked up on it. "He's a man of parts, all right. Other people's parts! Arms and legs and God knows what all!"

Everyone dissolved in laughter. "Did you say he's a poet?" Arnold asked, through spasms of mirth.

"Yes, truly!"

"I *knew* there was a reason I distrusted him so!"

The most interesting visitor by far was Lieutenant-Colonel Alexander Hamilton, one of General Washington's staff aides. He arrived in Albany in mid-November on a mission to find out why General Gates had not responded to Washington's pleas to send troops to him now that the threat in the north was over. He came to the hospital to extend the greetings of his chief and himself to Arnold. Although the two men did not know each other well, Arnold eagerly anticipated the visit, so hungry was he for news from Washington's camp. Also, Arnold was resentful over the fact that he had not heard officially from anyone in the south, not the Congress nor even Washington.

Arnold told Franks that Hamilton was widely regarded as the most brilliant man in Washington's circle. A slight, fit person with blond hair and sharp-featured good looks, Hamilton was affable and yet quite direct and candid in his remarks.

After the usual preliminaries of compliments and comments, Hamilton responded to Arnold's queries with an insider's detailed description of all that had been happening since Howe's army first appeared to menace Philadelphia. From his narrative, it was plain why Arnold had not yet heard from Washington, though it was not enough to satisfy him. The chief clearly was under enormous stress and had time only for the daily problems immediately at hand.

"I'm surprised that you were constantly outnumbered," Arnold said. "Why didn't the citizens of the region come forth? As they did at Boston in seventy-five, and even up here, once it was clear that the tide turned in our favor."

"Well, that's it, you see," Hamilton responded. "Everyone thought we had no chance against Howe's superior strength, backed up at close hand by a powerful naval armada. So few volunteered. More than that, the Philadelphia region has a very large proportion of Tories and neutrals, such as most of the Quakers, for example."

"So you had to come up here to get troops from Gates. Good luck!"

Hamilton smiled wryly. "Yes, Gates failed to respond to the chief's request. And we need the troops. We're still hanging on to the river forts, which gives Howe fits because he needs the channel to the sea. He can't supply his army and the city overland. But the forts can't last, and once Howe takes them, we expect he'll come after us for a major battle."

"In the winter?"

"We think so. Unless Howe truly defeats our army, it's an empty victory for him to have Philadelphia."

"So is Gates cooperating?

"Hardly! I had to exercise the chief's order to recall the troops we sent up here, including Morgan's regiment. And several other Continental regiments as well."

Arnold nodded, and then Hamilton began a discourse that amounted to an education for Franks in the internecine warfare of the cause—the jealousies, fears, conceits, and power-seeking that were rampant among the States, between the Congress and the army, within the army itself. It was a shock to hear how much the greed and venality and wrong-headedness of human beings at their worst will make their mark even within the noblest of causes.

"We know how Gates treated you," Hamilton said at one point. "And it was no surprise to us. He's always been a problem. Refusing assignments, going to Congress, always going to Congress, instead of to his commander. I don't want to seem overly suspicious, but there are some ominous signs. Gates succeeded in cutting down Schuyler. Now, I fully believe, he's intent on cutting down General Washington."

"I've suspected so for a long time," Arnold grumbled. "He'll never succeed. I have no love for Congress, but they'd never allow it."

"I'm not so sure," Hamilton said. "Congress is not the same noble body that created the Declaration of Independence. They meet up at York with never more than twenty-five in attendance, sometimes as few as nine. There's a very strong pro-Gates faction—John Adams, Samuel Adams, Richard Henry Lee, Benjamin Rush, James Duane. They're revising the Board of War to make it more powerful, and there's a rumor they might put Gates in charge. The malignant faction is much larger than just the Congress, of course. Everywhere we hear the contrast drawn between Gates's brilliant victory up here, for which he of course claims all the credit, and Washington's alleged failures as a commander. There are different motives. The Pennsylvanians, for example, Thomas Mifflin, Joseph Reed, they're indignant because Washington didn't sacrifice every soldier of the army to defend Philadelphia. Others, such as Rush, have reluctantly concluded that Washington is simply incompetent as a general and that we need a new man. And then, of course, there's naked ambition in the persons of Thomas Conway and Gates."

"There may be some comfort in the nature of your enemies," Arnold grunted. "Mifflin is the worst product of vain, arrogant Philadelphia society. Rush may be a good doctor, but otherwise he's a pompous know-it-all. Conway is the most arrogant man I ever met. As long as a year and a half ago, I heard him criticizing Washington. And Gates—I won't even talk of Gates for fear of bringing on a stroke."

"Yes, Conway regards himself as a military genius, and he's not shy about telling everyone that. Nor is he shy in criticizing General Washington—except in person, of course. Now he's up at York agitating with the Congress to make him a major-general."

"Speaking of major-generals, what can you tell me of this new Frenchman, Lafayette?"

Hamilton smiled. "He's intensely loyal to Washington. Something about him has totally charmed the chief. It's not his title, his wealth, the fact that he takes no pay, his sincerity about fighting for freedom—it's all that and more. It's something about his personality. Engaging, yet reserved. He's like a puppy dog to the chief, who treats him like a son. There are those who think I might be jealous about that, but I'm not. I cannot dislike the marquis. Now he wants to fight. He wants a field command."

Arnold was visibly tiring, and Hamilton made ready to leave. Arnold put his hand on Hamilton's arm and asked: "Isn't there some direct action you can take? To put a stop to Gates's conspiracy?"

"I don't think so. Not yet. It's all in the shadows. If there truly is a conspiracy, it will come out in time and we'll deal with it."

Arnold shook his head. "It's all too incredible."

"I thought so, too. Until I talked to Morgan." Hamilton proceeded to relate Morgan's story of how Gates had attempted to turn him to his side and against Washington.

"It's what I was saying earlier," Arnold muttered. "They're all fools. Gates is a fool to attempt to seduce Dan Morgan. Of all people! Not a chance."

Hamilton had risen. "Well, your only concern now is to regain your health. I needn't tell you that the chief is praying that you'll be able to return to us and take a command next spring."

"Where are you wintering?"

"We were at Whitemarsh when I left. North of the city, but too close. We'll end up somewhere else."

"I'll find you. God willing, I'll be able to join you in a few months. I'll be there as soon as I'm fit to travel."

Any notion of rejoining the army in a few months was pure wishful thinking on Arnold's part. For nearly that length of time, he remained flat on his back, crucified on his bed, praying that the bones would knit sufficiently to enable him to walk again. Dr. Thacher began a regimen of having Arnold's leg muscles manipulated and massaged to prevent total atrophy. This was always painful, excruciatingly so at first.

In some ways, this long idleness was worse for Arnold than the raging fever and infection had been. After Hamilton left, there were very few visitors. The hospital slowly emptied as its patients either died or were discharged. For the quintessential man of action, it was a lonely and maddening ordeal to be pinned down helplessly.

He lapsed into severe depression, which reached its nadir on the day that the news came that Congress had awarded a gold medal to Gates for the victory at Saratoga. He also heard that Gates had been made president of the Board of War, that Conway indeed was promoted by Congress and named inspector general, and that James Wilkinson had been promoted to brigadier-general and named secretary of the Board of War. Arnold and Franks couldn't tell what the import of this news might be. A gradual takeover by Gates? Or just more maneuvering?

News that at another time might have cheered Arnold also arrived. Congress finally acted to restore his seniority, so that he now outranked the five men who had been promoted over his head and all others promoted since. Arnold really didn't seem to care anymore. And then a letter of apology and praise and prayers for Arnold's health finally arrived from General Washington, together with a gift of a gold sword-knot and epaulettes. Arnold studiously counted the days before replying, allowing nearly as much time to pass as he had waited to hear from the chief.

This was an indication of the deep bitterness that gradually replaced the depression. There were days when Arnold railed constantly at his enemies, and even those he had thought of as friends, who ignored him at this lowest point in his life.

The last prominent visitor was none other than the Marquis de Lafayette himself. He called to introduce himself to Arnold and bring greetings from General Washington. Franks feared for this meeting, not only because Arnold was in such low spirits but also because of his strong dislike of Frenchmen and Papists in general. Franks found Lafayette to be every bit as amiable and gracious as Hamilton had described, and he had a decent command of English. Fortunately, Arnold was polite and subdued. It turned out that Lafayette was in the north on what he described as "a fool's errand." Dissatisfied because Washington would not attempt a winter assault on the British in Philadelphia, the Congress had authorized an "irruption" into Canada at the urging of Conway and Gates. Although Washington disliked the plan, he agreed to Lafayette's plea to command the invasion. An army of five thousand seasoned troops had been promised at Albany by Gates and Conway. But of course, like Gates, most of the troops who were victorious at Saratoga were gone, most of the Continentals to the south, the volunteers to their homes, and the militia back to their home states. The two veterans of Canada, Arnold and Franks, tried to control their mirth at this ridiculous "irruption," out of deference to Lafayette's sad demeanor at the loss of his opportunity.

Not until well into January did Dr. Thacher begin the process of testing the usefulness of Arnold's poor, scarred, atrophied leg. At first, the doctor merely got him upright where he could gingerly touch the floor with his toe. It was sheer agony for him. Thacher determined the degree of bone loss and had a special boot made with a riser. With the doctor and Franks supporting him on either side, Arnold attempted to place weight on the leg. After days of attempting a bit more each time, Thacher was satisfied that the bones had knit well enough so that they would not snap. Arnold worked on this therapy for weeks until he reached the point that he could take a few tentative steps with crutches before starting to collapse.

Late in February, Thacher finally pronounced that Arnold was fit to travel, and that his wish to be released from the hospital to go home and convalesce in New Haven could be fulfilled. Matthew Clarkson, who had returned from home leave, and Franks received detailed instructions from Thacher on how to proceed with the therapy. General Schuyler was as solicitous as ever, providing a carriage fitted out with extra cushions and springs to ease the trip, as well as a stretcher that could be used to transport the patient at their various stops. Clarkson and Franks had their horses, though most of the time one of them would ride in the carriage with Arnold. On the day they left, Clarkson and Franks were gratified that Arnold apologized to Dr. Thacher for being such a trying patient. He said his behavior was his way of avoiding madness.

The stretcher was useful because Arnold had retrogressed and could not take a step. His two aides had to remove a door jamb at the house of Dr. John Quihot in Kinderhook, New York, in order to carry the stretcher through. By the time the group reached Middletown on the Connecticut River, Arnold could take no more. He stayed there for several weeks in the home of an old friend from his trading days, General Comfort Sage. This stop was enlivened by a hero's welcome to Arnold by the citizens of Middletown and by the fact that two of Arnold's sons were in school there.

At Middletown, he was only a day's ride from New Haven, but Arnold just seemed to lack the will to go on, even to reach his home. Franks wondered if they would ever get to New Haven, much less Valley Forge, 150 miles further on, the place where they now knew the Continental Army was in winter quarters.

Chapter 39

Valley Forge
Winter, 1777–1778

When Alexander Hamilton returned to headquarters after his mission to the north, he found the situation of the army even worse than he had feared. The systems for logistical support, always inadequate at best, had now collapsed, resulting in extreme hardship for the troops. Criticism of Washington had spread to an astonishing degree, with evidence mounting that Conway and Mifflin and others were working assiduously behind the scenes to promote Gates over Washington. The stoic and resolute chief never complained or faltered, but even he was heard several times in staff meetings to voice the fear the army might simply dissolve, so wretched were its conditions.

In the midst of it all, two events in particular agitated Hamilton, events that to his mind were supreme indignities. One produced a rage of anger within him; the irony of the other brought forth tears of laughter.

The first concerned the winter quarters of the Continental Army. The places earnestly discussed in numerous meetings were all towns—Wilmington, Trenton, Reading, York, Lancaster, Bethlehem. Any of these would offer at least a modicum of housing and amenities against a severe winter, though they were already overcrowded with refugees from Philadelphia. Then Joseph Reed, erstwhile comrade-in-arms and now an arrogant politician, delivered an ultimatum—either the army would stay within twenty-five miles of Philadelphia *or* the Supreme Executive Council of Pennsylvania would no longer supply any troops or provisions or wagons. His declaration was preemptive: Washington had given no indication that he would leave the area, and, in fact, was already considering Valley Forge. Hamilton and the other aides were furious at Reed's attempt at coercion, but Washington ignored it and made the decision to go to Valley Forge.

The site was an abandoned forge eighteen miles northwest of Philadelphia, not a valley at all, but high ground bordered by the Schuylkill River and Valley Creek. Although it was only fifteen miles west of Whitemarsh, it took the army nine days to reach it by a torturous, zigzag route, due to harsh weather, difficulties in crossing the Schuylkill, and clashes with British foraging parties. The weather was the worst in local memory for mid-December—snow and sleet almost every day, turning to slush in the afternoon and then freezing into sharp ridges of ice at dusk. Having engaged in hard campaigning for four months, the troops were exhausted, their clothing nearly worn out. Only near-starvation rations were to be had. There were *no* new supplies. For all practical purposes, the quartermaster-general, Thomas Mifflin, had all but abandoned his post, possibly in anger at Washington for not saving Philadelphia from the British.

Once at the bleak, windswept ridge and undulating plateau of Valley Forge, the men pitched their tents and huddled together as best they could for warmth. Washington issued orders for the troops to build log cabins, each to accommodate a maximum of ten men, according to a design drawn up with the aid of the French engineer General Louis du Portail. Simultaneously, du Portail began surveying the entire area and drawing up plans for the construction of defensive lines and redoubts.

The cabins were to be rectangular, fourteen by sixteen feet, six and a half feet high, with a roof sloping to the sides from a centered ridge pole. The fireplace and chimney were to be placed at the rear and lined with clay. Meanwhile, Washington had his tent pitched next to the John Potts house, the most substantial structure among the few in the Valley Forge area, a two-and-a-half-story stone farmhouse built twenty years earlier. Although he used the house to meet visitors and transact other business, Washington refused to live in it until his men were sheltered.

Within three weeks, the vista of Valley Forge was transformed. It was almost denuded of trees, and, in their place, in neat rows, stretched nearly one thousand identical huts, organized in groups by brigade. Accompanying the chief, Hamilton visited a number of the rude structures. Wind whistled through chinks and crannies, and the interiors were filled with noxious smoke from inadequate chimneys, but the men were protected from the worst of the elements. *To hell with you, Joseph Reed,* Hamilton thought. These indomitable troops have made themselves a city in the wilderness. But they suffer even more from the lack of decent clothing and food. *Where are the provisions, Joseph Reed?*

The second event that animated Hamilton occurred not long after Washington moved into the Potts house. The two men had spent an arduous morning preparing a number of communications. One was a message to Congress in which Washington said to those urging an attack on the British in Philadelphia that it was much easier for "gentlemen" to contemplate such a thing "in a comfortable room by a good fire than to occupy a bleak hill and sleep under frost and snow without clothes or blankets." Another message was a proclamation to be widely distributed throughout eastern Pennsylvania warning farmers to hold half of their grain stores for sale to the army or lose it all without recompense. There also were plans and orders that Washington and du Portail had compiled for the building of a new hospital at Yellow Springs, a spa located ten miles west of Valley Forge. It was meant to be large, well ventilated, and specifically designed as a hospital, to replace dozens of miserable hovels and huts and barns where the sick now lay dying.

Hamilton retired to an alcove he used for writing final drafts for the chief's signature, prepared for a "session of the aching hand," as he called it. He had filled the last remaining pages of his own notebook with "headings" and notes for the various communications. He set up his inkwell and quill pens and reached into the box where he kept his supply of writing paper. There was none there. Hamilton knew that a number of sheets had remained after his last writing session the previous morning. Who had stolen his paper?

He rushed down to the foyer to accost his fellow aides. Only Fitzgerald and Harrison were in the building. Fitzgerald said: "I'll bet it was Tilghman. He was looking all over for paper yesterday afternoon"

"Where is he?"

"Gone to Stirling's headquarters," Harrison said, referring to a farmhouse several miles beyond the camp "It's no use. He used up all the paper he got from you."

"Do you have any?" Hamilton asked.

Both men shook their heads.

"How can we all run out of paper at the same time? Let's search the house. Maybe the family—"

"I've already searched," Fitzgerald said. "Nothing."

In exasperation, Hamilton sank to a bench. "Who's going to tell the chief that he can't send any letters out? Letters he wanted out yesterday."

"I guess you are," Harrison said.

"You're senior."

"You're the one with letters to write."

Hamilton began chuckling. Soon he was roaring with laughter. "No paper! How can you run an army without writing paper? No food, maybe. No clothing. No medicine. But no *paper*? That's impossible!"

Despite themselves, the other two laughed as well. "With no paper, the chief doesn't need us!" Fitzgerald said. "We can go home."

"Why don't you try the painter?" Harrison asked. "He must have paper." "Who?"

"Peale. He's painting Knox. In there." Harrison indicated a small parlor off the entrance hall that was used for receiving visitors.

The three men burst into the room, startling the young artist Charles Willson Peale, who lifted his pleasant, angular face and said: "Oh dear, you've ruined his eyebrow." General Henry Knox sat impassively on a straight-backed chair, then raised a real eyebrow at the intrusion. Peale had been a much-liked militia captain, but his enlistment term had expired. His usual good spirits had returned after his painting hand recovered from being nearly frozen when it dangled down between the floorboards of a barn where Peale had fallen asleep on a foraging expedition. Now he lived in a refugee house with his family near

Reading but returned often to camp to earn money by exercising his amazing skill in painting miniature portraits of the officers.

When the intruders explained their need, Peale said: "I don't use paper at all. Pasteboard or canvas, if I can get it. Look what I'm reduced to now." He lay down his brush and held up a bundle of blue-and-white bed ticking. In his other hand, he held an oval, either of wood or stone, about twice the size of an egg. A small piece of the bed ticking was stretched over the oval, on which the leonine head of Knox was taking shape.

Fitzgerald leaned over. "Very good," he murmured.

Knox, perhaps embarrassed at engaging in what some might see as a frivolous activity at a dire time, felt a need to explain: "I want to send it to my wife, to encourage her to come to camp." Peale smiled at this, anticipating more commissions when the ladies reached camp.

"This won't serve," Harrison said. "Look, I'll send couriers to the nearest towns, Reading and Lancaster and Pottstown. They should find some paper to buy there."

"That won't help me now," Hamilton said.

"No. You'd better start scrounging in camp. Somebody must have some paper."

"The diarists," Peale exclaimed.

"What?"

"A number of people are keeping diaries. They've got to have paper for that. Dr. Waldo, for example. He scribbles every night."

"Right," Hamilton said, going off in search of his greatcoat.

Within a half hour, Hamilton reached the large hospital hut that served Anthony Wayne's brigade, at the southwest corner of the camp. When he entered the hut, the putrid stench was almost like a physical blow. The room was crammed with men, far more than it was meant to accommodate, most of them lying on straw mats, others sitting on their haunches with bleak expressions. The twenty-seven-year-old Dr. Albigence Waldo, wearing a blood-stained apron, was directing the igniting of pitch-tar in the fireplace. He turned and held out his hand. "Ah, Hamilton. You've come at a bad time. We're just starting to fumigate."

"And none too soon," Hamilton murmured. Even burning pitch-tar smelled better than blood and decaying flesh. He explained his need.

"You have no writing paper? Why, that's just terrible," Dr. Waldo said sarcastically. "Imagine that!" He put his hands on his hips. "*I* have no opium. No decent material for bandages, no clean straw, no—"

"Please. I understand that. All I—"

"Look at these men." Dr. Waldo waved his arm around. "We have every ailment here known to mankind. The worst is the putrid fever," he said, referring to typhus. "Nine out of ten die," he whispered in an aside to Hamilton. Then he resumed his litany: "We have the pox, of course. Those with the red swollen limbs, that's erysipelas. We have dysentery, rheumatism, diarrhea, consumption, mumps, scurvy, gout, whooping cough, scrofula, lumbago, asthma—"

"How do you treat them?" Hamilton interrupted.

"We bleed 'em," the loquacious doctor responded. "We cut the fingers and toes off those who are frostbitten. We give them calomel, Peruvian bark, snakeroot, whatever we can come by. We need limes to stop the scurvy. You find me some limes, I'll find you some paper. Or get me some clean straw. That might be easier. These poor wretches come in here wearing the same tattered clothes they've worn for five months, infested with vermin, and we lay 'em down on the same dirty straw where four or five men have already died."

Hamilton was feeling sick himself. But he had an idea. He began explaining to Dr. Waldo about the orders and plans for the new hospital at Yellow Springs, about how urgent it was to get all that down on paper to start the project.

"The spa with the mineral water?"

"Yes."

"That'll take months. All these fellows, they'll be dead by then."

"The sooner we start, the sooner it'll be finished."

"It would be a blessing. We're told to send our worst cases up to Dr. Shippen in Bethlehem. That's forty miles, in wagons without springs, in this weather. Of course, we don't have any wagons—or horses to pull 'em. So our patients die here instead of up there. All right, come with me." Waldo discarded his apron and slipped into his coat, Hamilton following him out the door.

In the hut he shared with several other surgeons and aides, Waldo sat on his cot and reached into a trunk to pull out a wad of paper. He apparently felt a need to say more before handing it over. Looking at Hamilton with glistening eyes, perhaps from tears or the lingering smoke in the hut, he said: "We've got to help these men. Has God forsaken us? Yesterday their dinner was half a gill of rice and a tablespoon of vinegar. That was a good day. Now we're back to firecakes and water. I saw one poor fellow this morning on sentry duty. He was standing on his hat so his bare feet wouldn't freeze. He was wrapped in a blanket so tattered you could see he had almost nothing on beneath. But he still clung to his musket. Yes, I keep a diary. I don't ever want to forget what's happening here. I want others to know." He rummaged again and produced a sheet with handwriting on it. "Here, read this. I try to capture the reality."

Hamilton took the sheet and began to read:

I am sick—discontented—and out of humor. Poor food—hard lodging— Cold weather—fatigue—Nasty Clothes—nasty Cookery—Vomit half my time— smok'd out of my senses—the Devil's in't—I can't Endure it—Why have we been sent here to starve and freeze—What sweet Felicities have I left at home; A charming wife—pretty children—Good beds—good food—good Cookery—all agreeable—all harmonious. Here all Confusion—smoke & Cold—hunger and filthyness—A pox on my bad luck. There comes a bowl of beef soup—full of burnt leaves and dirt, sickish enough to make a Hestor spue—away with it Boys—I'll live like a Chameleon upon air.

Hamilton started to make some response to this astonishing monologue, but Dr. Waldo abruptly handed over his writing paper: "Give us that hospital as soon as you can."

"Thank you. And I'll replenish your supply as soon as I can."

"Bring me some limes then, too."

Hamilton smiled as he left the hut. "I'll try my best."

For the high-ranking officers, February brought some relief from relentless misery when the ladies began to arrive. First was sweet, unaffected, motherly Martha Washington, who had vowed to spend every winter of the war with her "old man." Others soon followed—Lucy Knox, Rachel Greene, Lady Stirling and her daughter Kitty, Mrs. Clement Biddle, and a half dozen others. With Colonel Tilghman's aid, Martha rounded up a gang of carpenters from among the troops to build an addition to the Potts house extending out from the back door, a sizeable wooden room to serve as a mess and a social center.

One of the first events Martha arranged was a party for her husband's forty-sixth birthday. She paid fifteen shillings to a band composed of soldiers so that there would be music and dancing. Several evenings a week Martha had social gatherings. She enjoyed inviting some of the younger officers, particularly two young Virginians she had become fond of, James Monroe and John Marshall. She often included the French officers on her list of invitees, so that Rachel Greene, who had been studying French, could improve her speaking ability. The best American conversationalists in French, however, were Hamilton and a new aide, John Laurens of South Carolina, whose father was one of the small band of staunch Washington supporters in the Congress. The evenings featured storytelling and singing, though not cardplaying. Washington enjoyed cards, but he had banned gambling in the entire camp as an evil influence on the troops.

Every weekday, Martha and the other ladies convened in the social center to make and patch clothing, and every afternoon she would visit a hospital cabin with a servant bearing a basket of clothing and any other provisions she could find.

In one sense, the pleasing presence of the ladies was agonizing for Washington and his senior officers and aides—they were all too aware of the contrast with the dismal daily life of the soldiers. February was the lowest month for the army. Only a trickle of provisions reached camp from foraging parties sent widely throughout the region. By now, merchants adamantly refused to accept paper money in payment for their goods. Weeks passed while Washington tried to arrange a replacement for Thomas Mifflin as quartermaster-general. Congress would not accept Philip Schuyler for the colossal and thankless task, so Washington reluctantly turned to General Nathanael Greene, the man he regarded as his right arm. In the worst way, Greene did not want the job, but his loyalty to Washington came first. Now there were delays in getting Congress to appoint Greene and to agree to new conditions for the provisioning of the army.

The only bright note in February was that the pressure to replace Washington with Gates began to deflate. The unraveling could be traced back to November when Lord Stirling sent a note to Washington in which he reported that James Wilkinson, on his dilatory way to report the victory at Saratoga to Congress, had stopped at Stirling's camp. Over too many drinks that night, Wilkinson told Stirling's aide about a letter that General Conway had written to Gates. Stirling had only one direct quotation from the letter: *"Heaven has been determined to save your country; or a weak General and bad Councellors would have ruined it."*

It was easy to see that what was heaven-sent, in Conway's judgment, was Gates and his victory at Saratoga, in enough time to save the country from Washington's ineptitude. Washington conveyed the quotation to Conway in a short note saying merely that it had come to him "in a letter received last night." Conway wrote to protest his innocence in a letter best summarized on Washington's staff by John Laurens, who termed it full of "flattery" and "evident insincerity." Gates learned of the exchange from Conway and was mortified and then truculent, denouncing the quotation as "a wicked forgery" in a letter to Washington that he also sent to Congress. At one point, he intimated that "a spy" had riffled through his personal papers in Albany. Since Hamilton had been in Albany at the time in question, he exploded in anger and was ready to challenge Gates to a duel, but Washington squelched that impulse.

The fact that Gates had sent a copy of his letter to Congress opened the matter to a much wider audience, in a burgeoning network of communication that included civilian leaders and other officers of the army. Washington responded to Gates, also sending a copy of his letter to Congress, detailing exactly how the quotation had reached him, including naming Wilkinson. Two more letters from Gates arrived protesting innocence, again calling the quotation a "fabrication," and trying to dismiss the affair as "harmless." Gates also included a defense of Conway, realizing that Washington had not seen anything else in the Conway letter other than the now infamous quotation.

On February 9th, Washington spent the entire morning closeted with Hamilton to devise a final letter to Gates on the matter. Though neither Gates nor Conway ever made the full text of the original Conway letter available, Washington had learned that it was in the main a scathing criticism of his abilities as a commander, including the detailing of no fewer than thirteen mistakes Conway alleged the chief had made in losing the Battle of Brandywine Creek. With Hamilton's aid, Washington's response was brilliant and tough, denouncing Conway in no uncertain terms:

Were it necessary, more instances than one might be adduced, from his behaviour and conversation, to manifest that he is capable of all the malignity of detraction, and all the meanness of intrigue, to gratify the absurd resentment of disappointed vanity, or to answer the purposes of personal aggrandizement, and promote the interests of faction.

Hamilton was proud that his chief for once had risen above his usual imperturbability to display very human emotions in the February 9th letter that marked the beginning of the end for the conspiracy against him. Washington's detestation of Conway was long-standing and deeply felt. When Conway had arrived at headquarters to take up duty as inspector-general, he was treated by Washington with such icy cordiality that he was unnerved. In one of his letters to Washington, Conway wrote in a way that was eerily reminiscent of the disputed quotation:

My opinion of you, Sir, without flattery or envy, is as follows: You are a brave man, an honest man, a patriot and a man of good sense. Your modesty is such that although your advice is commonly sound and proper you have often been influenced by men who were not equal to you in point of experience, knowledge or judgment.

Washington and his aides interpreted this as saying that although he was a good man he made the mistake of appointing inferior people to his staff and then made the even more stupid mistake of listening to them. This was not popular with the staff. At one point in February, Washington summoned all six of his aides to tell them that he was very disturbed at a report that they were being referred to in some quarters as "the pistol squad"—because of the frequency which with they had threatened to use dueling pistols to deal with critics of Washington. He angrily forbade any such talk.

The question of affairs of honor arose again at another staff meeting late in February. General Greene reported he had heard that Mifflin had said of Greene's pending appointment as quartermaster-general that he wanted the job only to be out of range of bullets on the battlefield. Greene said to Washington: "Would you not agree, Excellency, that the only way to respond to such a charge would be with bullets—in an affair of honor?"

With a grim expression, Washington said: "No, it is *not* the only way. The only way is to ignore it. Do not lower yourself. I said it before and I say it again. I positively forbid such talk in my military family."

Washington reported yet another communication from a congressman who wanted a winter attack on the British. Hamilton knew that Washington constantly pondered ways to execute a coup such as the victory at Trenton a year earlier that had wrought a miraculous reversal of fortunes. Surprising a Hessian garrison was one thing; a British army of fifteen thousand men was something quite different. Of the American army of ten thousand that had departed from Whitemarsh, fewer than seven thousand were left, and of those, half were unfit for duty. There were days when the army was hard put to man its picket line, much less mount an offensive. There had been so many resignations of officers that a critical shortage loomed once again.

"What are the prospects for General Arnold?" Washington asked Hamilton, who had been in correspondence with Arnold's aide.

"Major Franks reports that General Arnold will probably arrive here before the end of April," Hamilton reported. "He is very doubtful that the general will have recovered sufficiently to take a field command."

Washington shook his head. "A sad business. We need Arnold more than ever before. We must think ahead. We've got to restore the army and the officer corps by the time the campaigning season begins."

First the army will have to *survive*, Hamilton thought to himself. It was a miracle that desertions still did not exceed an average of twenty per day. There had been only one incipient revolt among the troops, which was forcefully put down by Major Aaron Burr.

"This is why I have asked Colonel Boudinot to join us," Washington said. Boudinot was chief of intelligence, whose responsibilities included negotiating prisoner exchanges. Turning to him, Washington said: "We must have General Lee back. Nothing you could accomplish would gratify me more."

Uneasy glances were exchanged among the men in the room. Hamilton found it hard to believe that Washington would welcome Lee back. He had been nearly as unstinting as Conway and Gates in criticisms of Washington, and was frequently mentioned along with Gates as a likely successor to the chief.

No one disliked the idea more than Boudinot, who knew that Lee lived in splendor in New York and was remarkably cozy with his British captors. "I can certainly try, sir," Boudinot said. "Perhaps if we offer as many as six British officers in exchange."

"Don't let any trifle stand in your way," Washington said.

"Perhaps Prescott alone would suffice." General Richard Prescott had been taken by an American patrol in Rhode Island in a manner similar to Lee's own capture.

As the conversation shifted to other officers, Knox asked: "What of the new fellow, the German, von Steuben?" He was referring to a recent arrival in camp who had been recommended by Benjamin Franklin and Silas Deane in Paris. Friedrich Wilhelm Ludolf Gerhard Augustin, Baron von Steuben, represented himself as "a former lieutenant-general in the service of the King of Prussia." Hamilton had been present to provide French translation when the German had his audience with the chief. Von Steuben had few words of English and Washington few of German. Hamilton knew, as did the chief, that von Steuben in reality was neither a baron nor a lieutenant-general, but an out-of-work captain, as a former staff aide to Frederick the Great. But he seemed to know his business and had a delightful personality.

"I am impressed by him," Washington said. "He says he wants no pay, merely expenses. He brought only two aides with him. He does not demand a field command. He seems interested in training and discipline for our troops in the Prussian style. I have it in mind to create a special hundred-man detachment to be assigned to him for training. We'll see what he can do."

"Sounds like he would make a better inspector-general than our present officeholder," Greene murmured, referring to Conway, who had not taken up his duties after his cold reception at headquarters. Now that he had his rank of major-general, he was demanding a divisional command instead.

"Indeed," said Washington. "We shall see."

By the middle of March, conditions for the army had started to change perceptibly. Greene had received his appointment as quartermaster-general on March 2nd, and had tackled the job with characteristic energy and efficiency. For the first time since November, supplies started to flow more or less steadily to the army. Hamilton was sure that Greene was hell-bent for success so that he could return to the line for a field command in the coming season. On the day that Greene miraculously produced two barrels of limes at headquarters, Hamilton jubilantly filled a sack and ran all the way to Dr. Albigence Waldo's hospital hut.

Colonel Boudinot reported a likely success in trading Prescott for Lee and expected that Lee would reach camp sometime in April. Also, Baron von Steuben was remarkably successful in training his hundred-man detachment. In drill and maneuver, they now performed as well as any British or Prussian counterpart. These men would now be used to assist von Steuben, as his training authority was extended to the entire army. Hamilton and Laurens were happy that they would no longer be needed for translation duty with the Prussian drillmaster, particularly since translating his usually good-natured stream of profanity from German to French to English was not easy. Two men were found who spoke fluent German and were surprised and happy to find themselves suddenly promoted to von Steuben's staff.

At the same time, the animus against Washington had waned still more. Gates, whose letters to Washington now were becoming obsequious, resigned as president of the Board of War. Conway once again had threatened to resign from the army if he did not receive a divisional command. He had used the threat of resignation twice before in pushing Congress to give him the rank of major-general. This time, there were rumblings in Congress. It was conceivable that Conway's resignation might be accepted. Even Conway's former advocates had tired of his importunings. In general, there were increasing signs that the vocal critics of Washington were now themselves being discredited.

Hamilton thought that his chief had behaved with remarkable patience through the entire, drawn-out campaign against him and had shown appropriate anger at just the right time. Washington had written to his cousin that he would be pleased to return to Mount Vernon if he were convinced that "the public" wanted him replaced with another man. But he would not yield to mere "factionalism," the self-serving yearnings of malcontents. Such a dispute also needed to evolve over a period of time, Hamilton realized. Critics and detractors would always speak out first, and it would take time for supporters to realize what was happening and to rally vocally to Washington's defense. The cause was aided by the near revolt of American officers who were angered by the promotions of Wilkinson and Conway. A number of American brigadiers supported the protest of forty-seven colonels over the elevation of the boyish Wilkinson to their rank. Above all, Hamilton thought, the troops had never faltered in their respect and admiration for their commander-in-chief. If what came to be known as the "Conway cabal" had succeeded in ousting Washington, the army would have truly dissolved. Only Washington could have kept the army together through this winter, Hamilton thought. And, in turn, it was the troops who helped save him.

Chapter 40

Philadelphia
Winter and Spring, 1778

Readers of the *Pennsylvania Packet* of December 24th, 1777, might have noticed the following unusual call for help:

Wanted for the Play-house, a person who writes a quick, and a legible hand; also a Person well-versed in accounts, to act as Clerk and Vice-Treasurer. Any people that have ever been employed about the Play-house, as carpenters or scene-shifters, may get employment by applying to the Printer of this Newspaper.

All positions were filled within a week. With General Howe's enthusiastic support, the "Play-house" was emptied of its patients, despite the shortage of hospital space in Philadelphia. A thorough airing and a burst of hard work restored the Southwark Theater to usefulness for its original purpose, ready for the selecting of plays and for casting and rehearsals. John André and his colleagues of the Society of the Gentlemen of the Army and Navy, as the new theater company was formally known, were overjoyed when tickets for the January 19th premiere performance, for sale in half a dozen locations in the city, quickly disappeared.

Peggy Shippen and her friends of "the little Society of Third and Fourth Streets," as André liked to call them, did not need to respond to the advertisement nor did they need to purchase tickets. In advance of the premiere, they were invited to spend a day with André and several of his friends at the theater to help in scenery painting and script copying. The group included Peggy and her sister Molly, Becky Franks, Peggy Chew, and several other friends—Janet Craig and Becky and Nancy Redmond. André's colleagues were stunned at the beauty of this bevy of young ladies, with the result that many a friendship was formed, marking the beginning of a lively social season for all concerned.

After the girls left that day, the young officers were treated to a grim warning by Major McKenzie, who said they could delight in the company of the beautiful young Tory women but must treat them with great circumspection. He told them of the quick and decisive way in which General Howe had disposed of the case of young Lord Cathcart. He had been ordered to marry the Tory girl from New York whom he had gotten with child. Howe would be adamant on this score, McKenzie stressed. Therefore, he said, be prepared to *marry* a Tory girl whom you violate—or stay celibate or seek sexual release elsewhere. After all, there were plenty of choices—the whores who already had begun to loiter around the theater, common soldiers offering their wives to officers, lower-class American women, mulattos, and so on.

Given this background, André had been pleasantly surprised when he had called to seek Judge Shippen's permission to invite the Shippen girls for a day of helping at the theater. He was ushered into the library, where he found the Judge holding a book in one hand, his thumb hooked into it to keep his place, his reading glasses positioned at the tip of the long blade of his nose.

"Ah, Captain André, please, seat yourself," the Judge said. He held the book aloft. "Milton. The *Areopagitica.* About freedom of the press, as you doubtless know. Given scribblers like Tom Paine, Milton may have been somewhat amiss in his conviction against censorship. Do you agree?"

"A fitting treatise for a gentleman of the law," André smiled. "The title taken, if I am correct, from the supréme tribunal of Athens."

"Indeed," the Judge said. "But this is no time for philosophy. The young ladies will be down shortly. You wished to see me?"

André described plans for the theater company and explained the opportunity for the Shippen girls to be involved in a minimal way. Would the Judge permit it?

"Sometimes I wonder about books," the Judge responded. "There are those that can fill the minds of the young with wrongful prejudices. I do approve of amateur theatricals! I think there is no method so useful in teaching young people the grace and power of speech."

And that was all it took—although the Judge turned grave and wagged his finger at André. "You have been a most decent and helpful young man to us. I believe in your good character. I trust you in the company of my daughters, that you will not suffer them to be traduced or compromised in any way."

"Believe me, sir," André said fervently, "on my honor, they will be entirely safe with me."

With similar sessions at other households, a day of participation was soon arranged for the "little society." And its members were then invited by André's group of young officers to attend the opening performance and a party afterward. The theater accommodated an audience of six hundred. Admission was one dollar for boxes or the pit and a half dollar for the gallery. Doors were opened at five P.M. and the first play was to start at precisely seven P.M. On opening night *No One's Enemy but His Own* and a farce entitled *The Deuce Is in Him* were the featured plays.

The girls had their own box and were enchanted by the sight of the darkened theater, the chief illumination being the long row of oil lamps along the apron of the stage. Tremors ran through Peggy, not entirely from the chill of the interior, now gradually being warmed by the throng. It was the first time she had ever attended a real theater, and she was wide-eyed at the sights and sounds all about her.

General Howe was greeted with standing applause when he made his grand entrance, escorting his paramour, Elizabeth Loring, wife of the commissioner of prisoners. Howe had no qualms about consorting with her publicly, thereby, to the Quakers and other moralists, setting a tone of debauchery in the occupied city. Sitting in a box on the opposite side of the theater from the girls, Howe smiled, nodded, and waved his hand at individuals he recognized below.

Peggy was thrilled when the first person to step from behind the curtain was Captain John André. He greeted the audience and announced that the "laudable" purpose of the theater was "to raise a supply for the widows and orphans of those who have lost their lives in His Majesty's service, as well as for such other generous charities as their funds may enable them to perform."

André then introduced Major Robert Crewe, the director of the theater, to deliver a prologue, not just to the evening, but to the entire season. Once again Peggy was thrilled. She knew the prologue had been written by André, he having tried it out on her during the day of work at the theater. Bewigged and heavily made up, Crewe bowed deeply and began to recite the couplets:

> *Once more ambitious of theatric glory,*
> *Howe's strolling company appears before ye,*
> *O'er hills, and dales, and bogs, thro' wind and weather,*
> *And many a hair-breadth 'scape we've scrambled hither—*
> *For we, true vagrants of the Thespian race,*
> *Whilst summer lasts, ne'er known a settled place;*
> *Anxious to prove the merit of our band,*
> *A chosen squadron wander throughout the land,*
> *How beats each Yankee bosom at our drum,*
> *"Hark! Jonathan, zounds, here's the strollers come."*

Cheers and laughter greeted the references to "Howe's strolling company" and the fearful Yankee "bosom." Crewe bowed and withdrew and, in a few moments, the curtain rose for the first play—and for a season of success beyond the dreams of André and his colleagues. Every Monday evening's offering of two plays was sold out for sixteen weeks. Notices had to be published admonishing officers against trying to bribe their way into the theater. A collective groan was heard when two evenings had to be canceled, one due to the illness of an actress and the other because the planners had erred by scheduling a performance during Passion Week in April. The repertoire grew to fifteen plays, including works by Garrick, Cibber, and Fielding, and Shakespeare's *Henry IV, Part I*.

The great success of the theater, and General Howe's obvious delight in taking pleasure in any way he could, spawned a wide range of other social activities. Another group of officers came together to sponsor a series of balls at Daniel Smith's popular City Tavern. Tickets to these glittering Thursday night affairs were sold at half a guinea to pay for refreshments and music, with no more than three hundred persons allowed to enter. Unlike balls held previously in Philadelphia, where ladies were expected to dance only with their escort, the British practice at the City Tavern was for them to have as many partners as possible, dancing with any one man no more than twice. British officers regularly called at Philadelphia's finest homes to fill up their dance cards in advance. For Peggy and her circle of friends, every Monday and Thursday night was checked off on the calendar throughout the entire gay season.

Every kind of amusement occurred, from sleigh riding when snow was on the ground to boating on both rivers and horseback riding as the season warmed. The sports-minded officers engaged in cricket, cockfighting, foot races, and horse races. Groups of officers established their own dining clubs for long evenings of drinking and gambling, with new taverns being opened to accommodate the demand. The Indian Queen was reopened and renamed the British Tavern. Holidays were celebrated with festivals and fireworks. A surge of deserters from the American camp appeared in time for St. Patrick's Day, men of Irish descent who wore shamrocks in their caps when they were brought into town. A procession wound through the city on St. George's Day with a replica of the saint. When the marchers passed 190 High Street, General Howe appeared to offer a tot of rum to all.

Older and more serious-minded officers found their amusements as well, many establishing friendships with Philadelphia families for pleasant evenings of conversation and cardplaying. Bookstores flourished. Lectures and courses on natural philosophy, music, and foreign languages were oversubscribed.

For Peggy and her friends and many other Tory belles, the true pleasure was their immersion in the constant social whirl, on the arms of handsome young officers. Every regiment of the army and ship of the navy seemed to be competing in offering a bewildering round of dinner parties and dances and masquerades and comedies. The lights often blazed late into the night at the Penn-Masters house as if General Howe were enjoying the summer season at Hampton Court instead of the third winter of a bitter war on another continent.

The young ladies of fine families vied with each other in imitating the latest hair styles from London and Paris, seeking the newest perfumes and finest laces, demanding the most brilliant colors in silk and damask and brocade for their ball gowns, in a frantic quest for all the finery that miraculously had appeared in shops with the advent of the British and the opening of the Delaware.

Gone were the grim days of spartan simplicity before the occupation when the radical patriots had held sway. Many of the sisters and daughters of the rebels remained behind, their hair drawn back tightly in buns, dressed in plain cottons and ginghams, their features disapproving and dour as they watched the haughty young belles of the new society lining up at the doors of hairdressers and seamstresses.

Just as John André was attentive to other girls, particularly dark-haired, beautiful Peggy Chew, so was Peggy Shippen squired about by other officers. Lord Rawdon was one of those smitten by her, confiding one day to André that she was "the handsomest woman in Philadelphia." Among nearly two hundred invitees, she was the particular guest of Captain A. S. Hammond for a dinner-dance on the warship HMS *Roebuck,* where she was piped aboard with honors. It was a calm evening so that lanterns could be strung in the lower rigging, casting a mellow glow over the convivial throng. Peggy was the center of attention as she took a different partner for every dance. Captain Hammond commented wryly to another officer: "Everyone is in love with her!"

Was this true of John André? That was the question that agonized Peggy in rare moments of lonely introspection. She was growing up fast in the social whirlwind. More than once she had fended off advances from half-drunken officers. She knew the power of her beauty, sensing lust in the many glances directed at her. The only officer who never took liberties, whose glances were warm and affectionate but hardly lustful, was the only one, she knew in her heart, from whom she would welcome advances. She told herself many times that either she was in love with John André or else she had no idea what love was really like.

She saw him often enough, at balls and parties, in her own drawing room where they talked about plays for hours or when André played his flute, forming a delightful trio with Captain Ridsdale and his violin and Molly at the pianoforte. Peggy was alone with André at times, too, huddled beneath a fur robe on sleigh rides, in a carriage riding about town, or in the garden or at the theater when they took time aside for André to sketch her. It was always a joy to be with him—but nothing of a truly intimate nature ever happened.

Peggy knew that she could have almost any man she wanted. If a glance or a slight movement by her attracted lustful eyes in every social setting, why was John André immune? She wanted to talk to someone, to probe the mysteries of life and love. She glanced at her mother, sitting in her favorite chair, knitting deftly. Impossible. Poor, dear mother! She loved physical activity, long walks, gardening, flitting about the household doing things. But on intimate matters, she had never gone beyond whispering to her daughters that they must preserve their virginity until they married—and she never would, Peggy was convinced. Her glance turned to her father, sitting across the room and scowling into the pages of the latest *Pennsylvania Packet*. Totally impossible! Peggy could not imagine broaching any subject of intimacy or passion with him. In any case, his euphoria when Philadelphia changed hands without being destroyed had lapsed back into grouchiness over the cost of maintaining his household, so greatly exacerbated by the expense of keeping his daughters equipped for the social whirl.

Peggy suddenly thought: What are older sisters for? She'd had lively exchanges with them before about men and love and life, but never any deeper than a certain level of teasing and jesting. She ruled out Betsy, who already seemed like an old married woman, though her marriage to Neddy Burd had been indefinitely postponed until the world had settled down. Sarah could be very cutting and sarcastic. Sweet Molly could be the one for a serious conversation. Peggy abruptly went upstairs to Molly's bedroom, where she knew her sister was fussing over her gown for the evening.

She found Molly sitting on her knees on the bed, a scowl on her face, a hand to her forehead.

"What's the matter?"

"It's terrible! Look!" Molly removed her hand to reveal a tiny red dot, a virginal pimple, smack in the middle of her forehead. "It's awful," Molly shrieked, as if she were afflicted with some monstrous, festering carbuncle.

"It's nothing," Peggy said. "A little powder and nobody will notice."

"But I have a new escort tonight. I don't want to make a terrible impression."

"I thought you were in love with Captain DeLancey."

"Love! With *him*? Are you mad? He's a brute. He only wants *one* thing," Molly said with a knowing look. "I have to fight to keep his paws off of me. No, I'll never be with him again. Captain Ridsdale is my escort tonight. A man who plays the violin like he does must have a sensitive nature." She sighed. "In the end I think they're all brutes."

"Not Captain André."

"Well, consider yourself fortunate. Oh, what shall I do about this," she cried, hand once again to her forehead.

Peggy realized there was no possibility of a sensitive, intimate conversation here. "Just keep your hand on your forehead all evening," she tossed over her shoulder as she left.

In desperation, Peggy decided to unburden herself to her closest friend. At nineteen, Becky Franks was nearly two years older than Peggy, but she seemed much older in wisdom of the world. Even more than Peggy, she was the undisputed belle of the social season, seen everywhere, gay, charming, gregarious, and so outspokenly pro-British that she had often embarrassed her father in the days before the British occupation. Peggy discounted the fact that Becky was seen with André on occasion. She was seen with everybody! Her relationship with André, Peggy knew, was a friendship that dated back to André's early visits to Philadelphia. She sensed that her real rival was Peggy Chew.

Peggy found Becky in her boudoir, seated at her writing table, the bed and other furniture covered with gowns and accessories, waiting to be chosen. Becky, clad in a robe of oriental silk, with a gauzy fabric protecting her newly dressed hair that was piled high on her head, greeted her friend effusively. After an exchange of pleasantries, Becky indicated the letter she had been writing. "I so want to entice Anne Paca for a visit. She's so charming, yet life must be so grim for her." Because Anne was the wife of a delegate to Congress, she was forced to live out in the countryside. "I'm telling her just what life is like here," Becky chattered on. "Here, see for yourself."

Peggy took the letter and began to read:

You can have no idea of the life of continued amusement I live in. I can scarce have a moment to myself. I have just come from under the hands of the hairdresser, Mr. J. Black, and most elegantly am I dressed for a ball this evening at Smith's where we have one every Thursday. You would not know the room 'tis so much improved.

I spent Tuesday evening at Sir William Howe's where we had a concert and a dance.

The dress is more ridiculous and pretty than ever I saw—great quantity of different colored feathers on the head at a time besides a thousand other things. The hair dressed very high . . . though I assure you I go less in fashion than most of the ladies. There's no being dressed without a hoop.

No loss for partners. Even I am engaged to seven different gentlemen for this evening, for you must know 'tis now a fixed rule never to dance but two dances with the same person. Oh, how I wish Mr. P. would let you come in for a week or two—tell him I'll answer for your being let return. I know you are as fond of a gay life as myself—you'd have an opportunity of raking as much as you choose either at plays, balls, concerts, or assemblies. I've been but three evenings alone since we moved back to town. I begin now to be almost tired.

I must go finish dressing as I'm engaged out to tea.

"There, you see? Am I not accurate?" Becky asked. "Even restrained?"

"Nothing's restrained these days," Peggy laughed, handing back the letter. "But Mrs. Paca could not come here. Wouldn't she be arrested? Held as a hostage?"

"No, no. I have more influence than you can imagine."

Perhaps, Peggy thought, but it was still such a bad idea that she began to doubt the wisdom of her friend. If Mrs. Paca came to Philadelphia to enjoy the giddy society the British had fostered, her husband's standing with the rebels obviously would be destroyed. Mr. Paca might as well come himself, confess his sins, and become a Loyalist.

"You have to dress for tea," Peggy said. "I've come at a bad time."

"No, no, stay a while."

"I . . . I just wanted to talk to someone."

"Good." Becky waited, but Peggy just fidgeted, then looked up with tears in her eyes. "What on earth is the matter?" Becky asked in an anxious tone. Still Peggy just shook her head, a tear rolling down her cheek. *Oh my God,* Becky thought. *Could she be with child? She looks wretched enough.* Becky took Peggy's hands. "What *is* it?"

"I'm in love. With Captain André."

Becky placed her hand on her bosom, almost dizzy with relief. "Oh, is that all? So is everybody else."

"No, I mean *truly* in love." Peggy burst into tears. "And he doesn't love me!"

Becky put her arms about Peggy. "Oh, poor, pretty Peggy! Of course he does. He's told me so."

"No! You don't understand. He's never even tried to kiss me."

Becky drew back, a knowing look coming into her eyes. "You're really serious, aren't you?"

"Of course I am."

"Our good friend, the other Peggy, she has the same problem."

"I know. I think she's the one he loves. And I'm dying. I don't know what to do."

"He loves you both, in his way. As very dear friends. Peggy Chew understands that. And you should, too. Have you ever been in love before?"

"No."

"No, of course not. I really don't know what to say to you—without sounding like your old maiden aunt. If I must, I must. Peggy, you're just too young to be so serious."

A look of anger crossed Peggy's face. "Haven't *you* ever been in love?"

"Of course. Several times. I recommend at least three times before you dare get too serious about it. Then you might know what you're doing."

"You're trifling with me."

"No, I'm not. I'm very serious. Let me tell you what you should do. You should fall on your knees and thank the Lord that you're alive at this particular time, in this particular place, at your age, with your beauty—and just enjoy this fairy tale we're living. It can't last. It will end, perhaps soon. And there'll never be another time like it in your life."

Peggy remained stubbornly silent.

"Consider this," Becky said. "Have you ever thought about how lax our parents have suddenly become? We're out to all hours of the night, with different men. If this were Paris, we'd have chaperones with us. Our parents want to be nice to the British officers, they want us to have a good time, but they're worried. They don't know what to do. They try to keep an eye on *which* particular gentlemen we go out with, whether they seem honorable or not. They fret and worry, but they're swept away by it, too. What I'm trying to say is that, for a time at least, we somehow are free to enjoy ourselves as never before. Your fate is to be seen constantly in the company of the handsomest, most charming, most talented, most popular officer in the British army—and all you can do is worry and moon about."

"I *do* enjoy it! Can I help it if I'm in love with him? I want him to myself. I want it to last."

Becky sighed. "All right, let's talk about that. You say he's never even kissed you. Of course he hasn't!" She told Peggy about the rigid policy of General Howe that had been communicated to the young officers.

"According to Molly, Captain DeLancey pays that no heed."

"Well, he's just a crude New Yorker. John André is an honorable man." Seeing that this was of small solace to Peggy, Becky went on. "Let's say that you truly are in love with John—"

"I am!"

"—and that he loves you just as deeply. What happens then? If you were to know each other in a carnal way you might become with child. If he were forced to marry you, your life would be miserable."

Peggy just shook her head.

"All right, let's say that doesn't happen. You both are still madly in love. What *does* happen? Does there come a time when you marry him?"

"I—yes, I would think—"

"You'd *better* think about it. He's a soldier. The war isn't over. There'll be more battles this summer. He could be killed. Aside from that, he's not a casual soldier. It's his career, his life. Do you really want to spend *your* life in lonely military outposts around the world? Or in England, never to see your family and friends again? Because that's where you'd be, not here."

"That doesn't matter."

There was a long pause before Becky spoke again. "That serious, is it? Well, I have one more thing to say to you, though I hesitate. But—what for it? Do you know that there are men—and for that matter, women—who are partial only to their own sex?"

Peggy glared. "If you think that John—"

"I don't think anything. I don't know. It's possible. Such a thing is not uncommon in the army. Think of Grecian and Roman times, too. Such men often display certain characteristics. They're charming, easy in the company of women because there's no future responsibility involved, and women like them because they're good company and *safe*. They tend to be artistic, effeminate, very handsomely dressed, partial to—"

"Becky!"

"I'm describing John André to you. He's the best hairstylist and milliner in town. Not that he does these things, but everyone goes to him for advice. I'm just saying this is possible, and it could explain a lot. There are all kinds of people in the world. There are men who like *both* sexes—and I do mean as sexual partners. I don't know what they call themselves, but it's something to think about."

Peggy was silent, wanting to say that such things had never entered her head, but that was not entirely the case. Although she truly *had* never heard of the last. Could that really be true?

"None of this says anything about whether you *like* such a person or not," Becky continued. "At least it doesn't for me. So my advice to you is to just relax, continue to enjoy John's company, let some time pass, and then see where you are. Don't press and ruin a wonderful relationship. Speaking of that, you might want to talk to Peggy Chew about it."

"Oh, I couldn't."

"Why not? You have something in common, but not something that should make you rivals or ruin your friendship."

"You won't say anything to her, or to anybody, will you?"

"Really! I may be a chatterbox, but I know a confidence when I hear it. That's one thing you *don't* have to worry about."

Near the end of April, John André was confirmed in his appointment as chief of intelligence for General Howe and given a brevet promotion to major. He was thrilled by this and wondered how it had come about. He soon learned from Major McKenzie, who informed him confidentially that General Howe would be relinquishing his command and returning to London. It appeared that Howe was methodically clearing up loose ends before his departure, which probably would not occur until June.

"Why is he leaving?" André asked in an anguished voice. He had become uncommonly devoted to Howe.

McKenzie just shrugged his shoulders. "It's not clear. I don't think London is recalling him. He wrote to Lord Germain, asking permission to return to England. And an affirmative reply has just come back."

"Who'll take his place?"

"General Clinton will be coming down from New York. When he arrives, probably late in May, then everybody will know. In the meantime, keep this quiet. The Tories will be very upset to know it."

"Do you think the peace commission has anything to do with it?" André asked, referring to a five-man commission appointed by George III to make one last effort to negotiate an end to the war.

"Not really. Since the general and his brother are two of the members, he'll surely want to see if the commission can succeed before he leaves. The other three members are on their way from London now. Lord Carlisle is the chairman."

"Any chance?"

"Anyone's guess. The rumor is they'll offer the rebels everything but independence."

"They should take it."

"Yes, but if the French come into the war, they probably won't." Rumors had been flying through Philadelphia for weeks that Benjamin Franklin had succeeded in Paris, that His Most Catholic Majesty, Louis XVI, would recognize America as a sovereign nation, which would be tantamount to declaring war on Britain.

André brooded over this news for a while, recognizing that Howe's departure and French entry into the war, if it happened, would change everything. The consequences were certainly unknown and could be quite serious for British arms. He could do nothing about that, but he quickly became convinced that the army must find some unique and truly impressive way to say farewell to General Howe. He found that his friends and other officers were of a like mind. In many planning sessions, an idea began to take shape, very much influenced by John André.

It was that subject that brought him to the Shippen household on a sunny Sunday afternoon, May 3rd. Once again, he was seeking participation and support for a grand scheme. He had arranged through Peggy to be invited for tea, along with Captain DeLancey and Captain Barrington, both very active in planning the event. The three took chairs in the elegant Shippen parlor with the Judge, Mrs. Shippen, Peggy, Sarah, and Molly, the last presiding over the tea service.

There was brief discussion of the prospects for the peace commission, and then the group lapsed into social banter. The Judge began to feel left out as he heard references to people he did not know and events he had not attended. He became drowsy and decided he had better excuse himself, when he became aware that André was addressing him.

"And I wanted so much to have your opinion, sir."

"Eh, what? Yes. Of course." Opinion on *what*?

"You see, we want to get the opinions of some of the fine families of Philadelphia. It should be a tribute, not only from the army and the navy, but from leading citizens, too."

"Oh, yes, to be sure. Yes, indeed." Tribute? What had he missed?

With a nod to DeLancey and Barrington, André said: "We've been talking about it for weeks. We've got a plan now and a committee has been established. We're raising a subscription to cover the costs. You see, sir, no commander in all of history has been more loved by his army than Sir William Howe. I can't tell you how much affection we hold for him. And I hope that civilian leaders will feel the same way and will support us. It's been a wonderful season, with such marvelous hospitality."

"What exactly is your plan?"

"To have a great occasion as a climax to the season, at the end of this month. A very special occasion—dedicated to General Howe."

My God, another party, the Judge thought. Is that all! The girls were gushing with excitement. André continued to develop the concept, drawing pictures in the air with his hands and speaking with fervor.

"It would be a great event, the greatest ever held on this continent. All of the officer corps of the army and navy would be there, and a delegation of civilian leaders. It would be a grand masquerade, with all the rich and dazzling colors and costumes and scenery, with the best of music and food and wine. The theme would be "The Age of Chivalry." Officers would be chosen to be knights, attended by squires and escorting their ladies. There we will need the gracious young ladies of Philadelphia. Your daughters, for example, would each be escorted by a knight."

The girls thrilled palpably at this.

"Tell him about the name," DeLancey urged.

"The knights would hold a symbolic joust. We'd have noble steeds and jongleurs and unicorns, all the orders of knighthood and offices of heraldry. We've been doing research for weeks, ransacking every bookstore. Perhaps you might have a useful book or two in your fine library."

"Mmm, perhaps, but I don't know that I have anything of medieval times that would serve."

"Tell him about the name!" DeLancey insisted.

"Yes, the name. We'd call it the '*Meshianza.*' "

"The Meshi—what?"

"The *Meshianza.* It's an Italian word, or perhaps Portuguese. I'm not sure. It's a grand conceit on the Continent now. It means a medley of entertainment, a grand festival."

"Fancy that," the Judge said. "But—why don't you just call it 'Grand Festival'? Then everyone would know what it is."

André was nonplussed. Peggy broke in. "Oh, no, it *should* be the *Meshianza.*" Her eyes sparkled and she accented the word with a charming lilt to her voice. "That has a hint of mystery to it, and elegance and beauty. That makes it special. People will never forget that. I think it's a wonderful idea!"

She received a grateful glance from André, who thought she expressed the idea beautifully. To the Judge, it all sounded decadent, like an orgy. "There's just one thing," he said. "What about the war?"

"The war, sir?"

"Yes. Forgive me, but it does strike me that if you apply all this ingenuity and effort to the war rather than social affairs, there might be a speedier end to the conflict."

This was met with a chorus of protest from Mrs. Shippen and her two daughters. Again, André was not sure what to say. He had never thought of the *Meshianza* as somehow competing with the conduct of the war. After all, it would be a tribute to Sir William.

The Judge wagged his head. "My views may not be popular, but it does strike me as a distraction. For example, General Washington will certainly know about your great festival, well in advance. With all your officers so engaged, would it not be an opportune time for him to attack the city?"

DeLancey barely restrained a guffaw and Barrington politely hid his smile behind his hand. "Now I see what you mean, sir," André said. "Let me put your mind at rest. As you know, it was a terribly cold winter. Washington's army practically vanished before his eyes. The poor devils were freezing and ill supplied. No, they cannot attack us."

The Judge started to say something about Saratoga or the need for a peace commission, but thought better of it. "Well, perhaps you're right. Spring is here and it always brings new life. And they're hoping that France will join on their side."

André shrugged. "They're stubborn to be sure. But banish any thought of them disturbing our plans to honor Sir William." He smiled: "That's just not possible."

Chapter 41

Valley Forge
Spring, 1778

Alexander Hamilton had developed a theory to explain the noticeable improvement in the morale of the American troops. To be sure, he credited the onset of spring and slightly better rations. The main reason, he believed, was the perception the men had of how their British counterparts had been passing their time throughout the grim winter. Every soldier at Valley Forge, from the commander-in-chief to the most wretched soldier, was aware of the enormous contrast between their lot and the conditions of life for the British Army in Philadelphia. The news seeped constantly through the sieve between the two camps—descriptions brought by deserters, spies, newspapers, and letters such as the one Rebecca Franks had written to Anne Paca.

The men knew that the British had an entire city at their disposal instead of a rude camp in a wilderness scoured clean of almost everything useful to survival. The enemy had good housing, food and supplies brought in constantly by their navy, generous aid and friendship from the hated Tories—in all, so well situated that they were engaging *en masse* in the pursuit of pleasure to an extent never before known in North America.

It was a bitter contrast for the American troops who supposedly represented the Congress and the citizenry, those who did so little to succor the army in its time of direst need. Hamilton wondered why desertions were not many times greater than they actually were, why the army did not simply *dissolve*, as had been discussed and feared in Washington's councils. Nearly two thousand men died during the blackest weeks of the winter, and, as far as Hamilton was concerned, the cause was starvation—either directly or in so weakening the men that they could not resist the myriad ailments waiting to afflict them.

Somehow the army survived, and, as conditions slowly improved, the attitude toward the cushy life of the British in Philadelphia was hardening into a positive morale factor for the American troops. Just walking through the camp, Hamilton could sense the determination of the men to make the British officers and troops and their Tory collaborators pay in the end. The new attitude was reflected in greater aggressiveness in raiding British outposts. It could be seen in the alacrity with which the men responded to Baron von Steuben's training regimen, marching and maneuvering with spirit and dash, responding crisply to shouted commands and hand signals, for the first time really beginning to *look* like an army.

Truly, Hamilton thought, Shakespeare was right—*Sweet are the uses of adversity*. But was it necessary that adversity be quite so awful? So much of it was manmade. And the basic conditions that caused it were not likely to change. Hamilton had evidence of that in the papers that lay before him on his writing table—a copy of the Articles of Confederation, the document intended to create a degree of national authority to overcome the weaknesses and ills of the present arrangement. After more than a year of wrangling, the draft had been approved by Congress the previous November and sent to the States for ratification. But it took a while for a reliable copy to make its way to Valley Forge, so uninterested were the delegates in any opinion that might come from the army.

Hamilton was depressed as he studied the text. There were a few useful powers given to the Congress, minor ones, such as a provision for the extradition of criminals. In all important respects, the Articles improved nothing. Each State remained supremely powerful in its own domain. No national currency, no banks, no power of taxation to support the war effort, no power to regulate commerce for the general good, no national executive authority such as a chairman or president or prime minister, no judicial system, no way to maintain order within the States, no way to control western lands—only the lamentable Congress, functioning as before with a few added and inconsequential powers.

Hamilton thought back to the time when he had joined Washington's service, when it had been immediately apparent to him that some meaningful form of national authority for certain specified purposes had to come eventually if there ever were to be any effective unity among the thirteen States. Since that time, Congress had labored mightily and brought forth a mouse. All of the critical weaknesses that Hamilton had noted back then had worsened—jealousy, parochial viewpoints, dislike of almost any kind of government authority, fear of taxation, fear of the army, and the consequent lack of will and ability to organize effectively for the conduct of the war. Hamilton saw a very good model for what was needed—the British government, *without* the monarchy, but instead functioning as a republic under its great unwritten constitution.

Hamilton was wise enough not to express this view in intellectual discussions with his colleagues. There *was* a King and there *was* a war, and that's what counted. Everyone agreed that Congress and the near anarchical system it wallowed in were hopeless. The prevailing attitude was simply that this was a burden that must be borne—there was nothing anyone could do about it. Thus, the arrival of a copy of the Articles produced no significant reaction at Washington's headquarters, as if to say that one could expect no more of such a Congress. Most of Hamilton's colleagues simply dismissed the document because all thirteen States would have to ratify it to make it effective. Already it was known that the five States referred to as "landlocked"—because they were cut off from claims to western lands by neighboring states—strongly opposed the Articles unless all western claims were given up to the Congress, which seemed very unlikely.

In his attitude toward all of this, George Washington was, to Hamilton, both a puzzle and a power to be admired. The chief's belief in civilian authority over the army was so strong that he never made a single suggestion to Congress about what the Articles should contain. He believed that politics was the business of Congress and winning a war was *his* business. Although politics relentlessly interfered with his business, he never seriously questioned the authority of Congress. With a chuckle, Hamilton recalled Benedict Arnold's excellent characterization of General Gates as the "Face of Clay." In contrast, Washington was the "Mask of Stone"—indomitable, persevering, with principles and beliefs so deep-rooted that they could not be shaken by any person or adverse circumstance. It was ludicrous that the busybody politicians feared Washington so much, feared that he might become some modern-day Julius Caesar or Oliver Cromwell who would use his army to wipe out the maddening obstacles and shortcomings of the civilian authority. There were times that Hamilton almost wished he *would* do so, or at least threaten to, but it would never happen. In Hamilton's judgment, Washington was not a great intellect. He could be aggravating at times in his seeming slowness and his imperturbability But there was no question of where he stood and what he represented— he was the rock who kept the army and the cause in existence and aimed in the right direction, despite all the unknowing and malicious men who mocked and hindered him and even schemed against him.

How incredible that there were those who wanted to send Washington back to Mount Vernon and replace him with Gates or Lee! How could people be so stupid? At least the most serious attempt had totally collapsed in a series of fiascoes, beginning with the disillusionment of James Wilkinson. In his anger at Wilkinson for revealing the "weak general" quotation and his repeated insistence that the statement had never been made, Gates seemed to be saying that Wilkinson had fabricated the whole thing. Wilkinson thereupon challenged his commander to a duel. The two men met with dueling pistols behind the Anglican Church in York, but Gates took Wilkinson aside, broke into tears, and said he would as soon shoot his own son. Wilkinson relented and called off the duel, but Gates coldly ignored him from that moment on. Later, dismayed by the reaction against his promotion, Wilkinson vowed to resign from the army—but did not.

As for Conway, Congress had finally done something right by accepting his third threat of resignation, much to that individual's surprise and distress.

He then managed to insult General John Cadwalader, who challenged him to a duel. Conway fired and missed, and Cadwalader carefully took aim and shot his opponent through the mouth, the ball passing through Conway's cheek. The Frenchman survived and soon returned to France.

Having managed to avoid a duel, Gates now suffered a damaged reputation and his influence was diminished. He commuted between his country estate in western Virginia and the Congress at York. Congress simply left him to languish in his command of the Northern Department, which had virtually ceased to exist in the wake of Saratoga.

Hamilton's respect for Washington was based on his chief's character and principles, more than his judgment. In Hamilton's eyes, Washington's saving grace was that he was candid and secure enough to admit that he made mistakes just like every other human being. But rarely could one convince him in advance that a mistake was looming. A perfect case in point to Hamilton was the new hope the chief was investing in Charles Lee. Washington arranged a reception for Lee's arrival at Valley Forge in early April that Hamilton thought would be more fitting for an Oriental potentate.

Accompanied by his mounted Life Guard, Washington rode out on the road to Philadelphia to greet Lee. The two men dismounted and hugged as if they were long-lost brothers. They then reviewed the entire army to martial music provided by a hastily assembled band. The troops greeted Lee with loud cheers. That evening he was entertained at a lavish feast, followed by chamber music and singing. Because Lee's exchange would not officially begin for another two weeks, he would be in camp only one night before proceeding to York for a consultation with Congress. Accordingly, he was Washington's personal guest and assigned a bedchamber behind Martha's sitting room.

The disgusted Elias Boudinot later told Hamilton what transpired the next morning: "Lee overslept and was late for breakfast. When he appeared he was dirty as if he had been in the street all night. Soon I discovered that he had brought a miserable dirty hussy with him from Philadelphia, a British sergeant's wife. He had taken her into his room by a back door and slept with her all night."

This abuse of hospitality did not go over well. Even worse, Boudinot later informed Hamilton what happened when he had accompanied Lee to York to present him to Congress. "The bastard's mouth can't stop running," Boudinot said. "He told me that General Washington was not fit to command a sergeant's guard."

No one had the courage or heart to relay this to Washington. Though the chief was disturbed by Lee's appearance and manner, he continued to think that the scrawny eccentric would be a valuable man in the coming campaign.

That campaign was the subject of a staff meeting in mid-April, a gathering of Washington's inner circle—Greene, Knox, Lafayette, and all six aides—as a prelude to a much larger council of war to be held later, at the suggestion of Congress. The meeting room was enlivened by the continuing rumors that France would come in on the American side. And there was good news from Congress, which now seemed to be trying to atone for the general neglect over the winter and the Conway fiasco. It had quickly accepted Washington's recommendation that Baron von Steuben be rewarded with the rank of major-general and the post of inspector-general. Congress also authorized bounty money for reenlistments and new recruits, and strongly backed Greene's efforts as quartermaster-general. The result was that supplies increased and new uniforms began to arrive. New troops trickled in as well, though not nearly enough to suggest that the army would soon regain its former strength of ten thousand effectives.

The discussion of strategy was desultory—there simply were too many imponderables. The situation reminded Hamilton of similar discussions the previous year at Morristown, which in the end were meaningless because Washington simply had no choice but to wait to see what Howe would do and react to it. It seemed that the same Fabian strategy would have to be operative again. Although various ideas for taking the offensive were earnestly discussed, it was clear to everyone that the strategy had to be reactive, for the foreseeable future at least. The Americans were still outnumbered and the British still had their powerful fleet at their backs. The more likely event, everyone agreed, was that the British Army would move out to attack the Americans. It was obvious to everyone that unless the enemy destroyed the Continental Army in battle, their occupation of Philadelphia would have achieved nothing of strategic value.

The news that Howe would be returning to England and be replaced by Clinton was known in camp, but no one could muster a convincing argument to attach any significance to it. It was simply another imponderable on a long list. In the end, everyone agreed that the burning question was: would France enter the war on America's side? If so, what effect would this have on British strategy and how soon would an alliance be manifested in tangible assistance?

French aid could not come soon enough. Despite the improved conditions for the army, there was a growing sense of war weariness in the air, even stronger among civilian leaders and the populace than in the army. That was why Washington was concerned over the five-man Carlisle Commission, established by George III to try to negotiate peace terms. Even now, the Earl of Carlisle was on the high seas, bound for America. Everyone expected that the commission would offer everything the Americans wanted except independence. Washington feared that this would be seductive and would lead to divisiveness or complacency. He missed no opportunity to urge that the commission be turned down flat, that the Congress never agree to giving up independence.

In the end, the only decision the chief made at the meeting was to authorize a reconnaissance in force before the end of May, led by the Marquis de Lafayette, to move east of the Schuylkill with about a third of the army to test the British response. Lafayette had been chafing for a field command since his expedition to Canada had turned out to be illusory.

Despite the concerns and inconclusiveness of the meeting, there soon followed, in rapid succession, three reasons to celebrate.

The first, before the end of April, was the annual shad run, the migration of the fish up the Schuylkill River to spawn. The British tried mightily to thwart the will of nature, throwing obstructions in the river and bombarding it with cannon, but the fish were indomitable. This produced a scene of unparalleled joy in the American camp, as virtually the entire army waded in the river for days, using sharpened sticks and every manner of homemade net. The troops gorged themselves on shad and filled hundreds of barrels with fish to be pickled for future needs.

If possible, even greater joy erupted on May 4th when affirmation arrived that in February Louis XVI had formally recognized the United States as an independent nation and entered into an alliance with the nascent country. In effect, this meant that a state of war existed between France and England, and that tangible help to the rebel forces in America would certainly be forthcoming. A massive *feu de joie* swept the camp, with every weapon, from pistols to cannon, being fired into the air, soldiers dancing as if they were intoxicated, great bonfires being ignited, and French flags waving everywhere along with the American.

And then the soldiers had reason to celebrate again—to welcome Benedict Arnold into camp, the fighting general whom they now all recognized as the true hero of Saratoga, the great victory that had convinced France to join the American fight against Great Britain.

David Franks rode with Arnold in the open, four-wheeled chaise as it entered camp, with Arnold's West Indian manservant, Punch, at the reins of the two horses. Matthew Clarkson, who had rejoined Arnold while Livingston had left the army, was sent ahead to double-check on the housing that would be provided for the party. Also in the chaise were Mrs. Lucy Knox and her infant son, who had traveled the entire distance with Arnold.

They arrived on May 21st after a six-day trip from New Haven, most of it in the closed, well-sprung carriage that General Schuyler had provided to Arnold in Albany. The chaise was brought along for the possibility of a nice, sunny day en route and to grace the entrance to camp. The small caravan also included a baggage wagon. Arnold's intention was to sell both carriages and several of the horses later on.

A contingent of the commander-in-chief's Life Guard escorted the caravan into camp, where thousands of soldiers were lined up to cheer. Progress was slow because many of the men had served under Arnold in one or both of the battles in the north that had brought the Saratoga victory. They pressed close to clasp his hand, and Arnold recognized many by name.

A poignant moment came when Punch spied Colonel Daniel Morgan standing in the pathway ahead of the chaise. Punch reined to a halt, and Morgan came around to hoist himself up on the step, lean over, and embrace Arnold. There was silence while this happened and then a mighty cheer. The episode was especially touching because Arnold later learned that Morgan was weary and ill and had resigned to return to his home, expecting never to bear arms again. He had delayed his departure from camp in order to greet Arnold in person.

For the previous month, Arnold's convalescence had gone well. Several doctors in New Haven trained Punch in the various massages and exercises, and he became quite expert. The therapy included immersion in warm water and mineral salts in a copper tub twice daily. The strapping young man from Tortola lifted his master in his arms for these sessions. Punch did more than this—he was the most effective person in nudging Arnold to exercise and walk. Before long, Arnold could walk a hundred paces or more with the aid of a cane and the riser in his boot. Even more, he was able to stay aboard a horse for a while. By standing on a stool and with the aid of Punch, Arnold could mount and dismount a horse, somewhat awkwardly, and the entire process was still extremely painful for him.

As the procession neared the headquarters house where all the generals were lined up, including the chief, Arnold was hoping to be able to walk unaided to greet them, but it was not to be. The immobility of the carriage ride and fixed position of his leg temporarily robbed him of the ability. Franks and Punch flanked him and caught him as the leg gave way, serving as his crutches as the generals crowded forward to greet and congratulate him. Their expressions of welcome certainly were heartfelt, but the judgment could be seen in their eyes—there was no possibility that a man in this condition, no matter how courageous and talented, could ride a charger and lead a division in battle, at least not for a long time. Franks thought he had caught a glint of a tear in Washington's eye as he embraced Arnold.

The group was led inside for a reception of wine and other refreshments, Arnold taking a comfortable chair with his leg extended on a stool before him. Clarkson by now had joined the assemblage, and he was known by all present. Franks was dazzled and struck almost mute by the great honor of meeting General Washington and his lady. The two persons he had known from before, Mrs. Knox and Alexander Hamilton, were very kind in seeing that he was introduced to everyone. There was an air of gaiety and many toasts were proposed, but before long it was clear that Arnold needed to rest.

The house provided for Arnold, ironically, was the one that Generals Mifflin and Gates had used earlier when they were in camp. It was the Coates house, at the far end of the camp, an attractive sight, for it obviously had been tidied up. A number of cherry trees, which miraculously had been spared the ax, abutted the house and were in full bloom.

There were bedrooms upstairs for the aides and a shed outside for Punch where he could sleep and tend the horses. Adjoining Arnold's bedroom on the ground floor was a small room that he could use as an office and another small room that Punch quickly set up for the continuing therapy. The camp was an awesome sight, extending beyond view in several directions, quite neat and orderly now in contrast to the hellhole it had been in the winter months. Dr. John Cochrane, the camp's chief surgeon, wasted no time in calling to examine Arnold and review his treatment.

In truth, there was little for Arnold to do at first. He attended several of Martha Washington's soirees and was present at headquarters for several meetings with the chief and his staff. He was able to demonstrate his ability to walk aided only by a cane and to ride a horse, followed of course by Punch mounted on another horse and carrying the stool. In these ways and other times by using the chaise, Arnold was able to visit and converse with other officers in their quarters and to witness several of von Steuben's drill and parade sessions, which were quite impressive.

A week after his arrival, Arnold attempted to repay the generous reception he had received by drawing on the commissary for an elegant outdoor feast and party in the cherry grove. There were twenty-one attendees, including Greene, Knox, Lincoln, Stirling, and other generals and the ladies. Hamilton and Lafayette only came by late to sip a glass of wine, and Washington sent a short note excusing himself. Arnold caught a whiff of a feeling that it was unseemly to dine so luxuriously, given the terrible hardships the army had endured. If this were true, he thought it a rather foolish sentiment. That was then, this was now. There were plenty of elegant meals at Washington's table.

The pattern of wide swings in mood for Arnold continued. He rejoiced in the comeuppance that Conway and Wilkinson had been dealt, and in the diminishment of Gates's reputation. His long-standing dislike of the French caused him to curse the new alliance. Of course, he could see the advantages, but he regarded it as a crime to have to embrace a Papist and monarchical regime. He kept this pretty much to himself, though, aware that everyone else regarded the alliance as salvation. At other times, he brooded and seemed deeply depressed. He wanted so much to be of value, to be able to employ his military skills and daring once again, but he knew the prospects were dim.

He swore allegiance in a new oath administered by General Knox out in his artillery park. Every general officer was required to take the oath that spring. Benedict Arnold solemnly swore that he would "renounce, refute and abjure any allegiance or obedience to George the Third, King of Great Britain" and that he would "to the utmost of my power, support, maintain and defend the said United States against the said King George the Third, his heirs and successors, and his or their abettors, assistants, and adherents, and will serve the said United States in the office of Major General, which I now hold, with fidelity, according to the best of my skill and understanding."

Early in June, the camp became abuzz with rumors that the British occupiers of Philadelphia intended to withdraw from the city under their new commander, General Clinton. Arnold came from a meeting at headquarters to tell his aides that it was apparently true. Clarkson and Franks were chuckling over how this made the entire strategy of General Howe—taking Philadelphia instead of driving north to join with Burgoyne—into an embarrassing farce, a complete waste and failure. Arnold agreed but said that the reason for the decision to evacuate probably had to do with French entry into the war. The British ministry in London and General Clinton apparently were in agreement that their forces must be consolidated and that New York was a better base for operations. The British could not afford a divided navy in American waters should a French fleet appear, and much of the action might now shift to defense of the valuable Caribbean islands, over which the British and French had been contesting out of memory.

Word had also arrived that Congress had totally rebuffed the Carlisle peace commission, saying that it would agree to meet only if the commission recognized American independence in advance. *That* the Earl of Carlisle, now in Philadelphia, could not do, and so he faced a long sea voyage for nothing— and there would be no pause in hostilities.

Arnold said the meeting was dominated by discussion of how best to attack the British as they evacuated, assuming that a substantial portion of their army would march overland across New Jersey. This had overshadowed another bit of news at the meeting, which, Arnold said, could affect him— Congress had passed a resolution creating a large new military district centered on Philadelphia. In anticipation of a British withdrawal, the resolution created the post of military governor and contained instructions for the person who would fill that role.

"It was not discussed directly," Arnold said in a monotone, "but from several glances from the chief I formed the distinct impression that he will offer that command to me. I am to call on him tomorrow morning." Then his voice turned bitter: "He has no faith that I can take a field command. Only days ago, he talked about how, if I were able, he would give me command of the left."

That was regarded as the position of honor in the army—and a wonderful tribute by the chief in recognition of Arnold's military skill. But it was plain to see that such an assignment was just not yet possible. Arnold knew it, but it was hard for him to accept, and that evening he was depressed and consoled himself with a bottle of brandy.

When Arnold met the next morning with Washington and Hamilton, he accepted the command of the Philadelphia district. Hamilton had prepared a set of instructions, which he had rewritten from those set forth by the Congress. He and Arnold scrutinized and discussed each of the main provisions. An important one called for Arnold "to take every prudent step in your power to preserve tranquillity and order in the city and give security to individuals of every class and description, restraining as far as possible, until the restoration of civil government, every species of persecution, insult, or abuse, either from the soldiery to the inhabitants or among each other."

Washington explained that while the most notorious Tories would almost certainly leave the city with the British, as had happened at both New York and Boston, there was still danger of wanton bloodletting as soldiers and civilian patriots poured into the city with some form of revenge in mind. People would try to settle scores by making accusations, Washington pointed out. Not only Tories, but also the large number of neutral persons in Philadelphia, such as the Quakers, might be vulnerable to attack by overly zealous patriots.

"There well may be Tories who should be punished, but this must be done without frenzy or malice, but calmly and judiciously," Washington said. "Your authority may be the only protection that innocent people have."

Washington was equally forceful on the matter of looting and plundering. "From all reports, the city is loaded with goods of every description, brought in by the enemy before their decision to evacuate was made," he said. "They have no chance of getting more than a fraction of those supplies out of the city, not with an entire army and its provisions and hundreds of Tories to move to safety. As it is, they won't be able to take much more than the Tories and their artillery by sea. I'm now certain that the main part of the army will have to march to New York, and that will give us an opportunity to strike them. Without a firm hand by you, I fear the city could descend into an orgy of looting."

Hamilton interjected a comment: "Pennsylvania has the most radical government of any of the States, with its Supreme Executive Council. They had power only a short time before the British took over the city. Now they'll be back and eager to make up for lost time, to show how righteous and pure—and dangerous—they can be."

It was clear that the chief regarded the assignment as a highly important one that required a man of the stature and reputation of Benedict Arnold. He would have to maintain law and order and at the same time deal diplomatically with the radical civilian authority which would be sharing the city with the Congress. The city would be more important than ever before, with a minister arriving to represent the French government.

Later, Clarkson and Franks discussed the challenge that had become much more complex and bewildering than they had imagined. Physically, it was a behind-the-scenes assignment that Arnold could handle until he was healed enough to move to a field command. Could he handle it mentally or in terms of his forceful personalty? Franks had been with Arnold long enough to know that he was a man who had very little patience for fools or, for that matter, anyone who disagreed with him. Given the radical civilian leadership, the Congress, the populace, and the interests of the army, there were enormous possibilities for disagreements of all kinds. In some ways, the stress could be greater than on the battlefield, he imagined. Was Arnold "diplomatic" enough to survive this potential maelstrom? Only time would tell.

As soon as Arnold's appointment became known, he began to receive visitors who voiced concerns of one kind or another having to do with the city. One was a merchant named Robert Shewell who owned an interest in the seventy-five-ton schooner *Charming Nancy,* then lying at Philadelphia with a valuable cargo. Without a valid pass, such a vessel would not get very far before being attacked by American privateers. Shewell was not a man of good repute, having been physically expelled from camp only days earlier by Baron von Steuben. Nevertheless, on the day that he was serving as Officer of the Day for the Valley Forge camp, Arnold issued a pass to Shewell for safe conduct to any American port—where the ship's cargo would bring a fancy profit.

Franks raised his eyebrows at this but understood later when he learned that Arnold was entering into a business agreement with Shewell and his two New York partners. He learned even more when he told Arnold that, as interested as he was in his assignment in Philadelphia, he thought he should resign from the service in order to pursue business interests. The money he had brought out of Canada had been loaned for the support of the army at Bemis Heights and probably would never be seen again. Thus, Franks was financially destitute, having learned that pay in the Continental Army was always in arrears. Arnold himself had not been paid for nearly three years.

Arnold replied that staying in his service was probably the best way for Franks to recoup his fortune. For example, he said, he was planning to provide Franks with money and send him into Philadelphia a day ahead of his own arrival to buy up all the European and East Indian goods he could lay his hands on. Franks would hide these goods until they could be sold at a profit, and he would not tell anyone that he was acting on Arnold's behalf.

That was intriguing! Franks decided to stay in the army, thinking that the role in Philadelphia was going to be quite interesting. Little could he have foreseen just *how* bizarre and fateful it was going to be.

Chapter 42

Philadelphia
May 18, 1778

Judge Shippen was amazed at how quickly the mood within a household could plummet from joy and eager anticipation to despair and bitter recrimination. The transition was abrupt, as if a bomb had exploded in the Shippen parlor.

The bearers of the bomb seemed harmless enough. Three somberly clad Quakers came to call on Judge Shippen two days before the *Meshianza* was scheduled to occur. The Judge had not been in the circle of Friends since boyhood, when his father had left to convert to Presbyterianism and move to Lancaster. The Judge eventually had drifted to the Anglican Church, the faith favored by his aristocratic friends. But he had always respected the Quakers, as quaint and old-fashioned as they now seemed to him. They, after all, had *founded* Pennsylvania. They were scholarly, peaceful, tolerant, and moralistic, the last too much so at times, though the Judge credited their influence with elevating Philadelphia above the vulgarity and turpitude of London, New York, and even Puritan Boston.

He could not imagine why the Quaker delegation wanted to see him on Saturday afternoon, May 16th. From his legal career and prominence in civic affairs in the past, he knew all of the Quaker leaders but had never been really close to any of them. They surely would not be calling to try to persuade him to return to the circle; that was not their way. A rainstorm was looming and the sky had grown dark. Lights had not been lit yet within the Shippen household, so the Quakers had an almost sinister air about them, their dark clothing and angular features almost fading into the gloom as they took their seats in the parlor. The Judge offered refreshments, which were declined. Samuel Allwyn, leader of the trio, cleared his throat and began to speak—and curiosity was soon replaced by shock.

Allwyn was very polite, saying that the delegation had presumed to ask for the Judge's time only because they knew so well his high moral standing in the community, his fair-mindedness, and his willingness to listen. Their concern was what they regarded as the decadence and immortality of the extravaganza the British were planning, the *Meshianza,* which would play its way out on the coming Monday afternoon and evening. The more the three visitors talked of the event, the more stern their features and words became.

They could not hope to influence the British, they said, but they felt it their duty to appeal to leading citizens of Philadelphia to set an example for all by not allowing their daughters to participate in such an unseemly spectacle. Specifically, they were concerned over the appearance of sixteen young women of Philadelphia society in the most elaborate set-piece planned for the evening, a mock duel between two teams of eight "knights" each—the "Knights of the Blended Rose" and the "Knights of the Burning Mountain." Each knight—a British officer dressed in medieval costume—would be attended by a squire and a fair lady. The last were to be, in John André's words, "ladies selected from the foremost in youth, beauty, and fashion." Attired in Turkish costumes, they were to play the part of heathen girls attached to knights of the Crusades.

Most of the members of "the little society of Third and Fourth Streets" were among the sixteen young women chosen for the prestigious roles— including no fewer than three of the Shippen daughters. The Judge had worried about that, although in truth his concern initially had been the cost of making the three Turkish costumes, a considerable addition to the small fortune he had already laid out to enable his daughters to participate in the gay season. Then he had some misgivings over the nature of the event, feeling that somehow it was excessive, just pushing a bit too far. His girls had already been given great liberty for the social scene, more than the Judge was comfortable with, but the argument always had been that "the other girls were doing it." He had almost made up his mind to ban their participation in the *Meshianza*, but Mrs. Shippen had persuaded him otherwise. The girls had been fully involved in the social season, she pointed out, and nothing dire had happened. To deny them now, for the greatest and climactic event, would bring tremendous resentment. They would feel cheated and would mourn their father's decision the rest of their lives. Better to let them have this one last joy, to finish a glittering season in full glory. The Judge, always ready to be talked out of a confrontation, acquiesced.

Now the Quakers had come to shatter his complacency and pillory him in his own parlor. After bidding them farewell and saying he would consider their views very carefully, the Judge retired to his library and poured a glass of Madeira. He sat in his wing chair and brooded in the gathering darkness. The Quakers had no hold over him. They could not even threaten to expel him from the circle of Friends. His resentment toward them quickly faded. They had not couched their appeal in any way as a demand, nor had they made any reference to the fact that the Judge was once of their faith. They were simply doing their duty as they saw it, just as the Judge realized he should have done his duty as a parent long before. The Quakers had appealed to him as a man of known moral rectitude and a leader in the community. And, what was more, they were right—their appeal had merit and moral force.

The decision involved only Mary and Peggy, Sarah having already withdrawn from the *Meshianza* a week earlier, not for any moral concern, the Judge was convinced, but something to do with a dispute regarding the officer she had been paired with. She was too old for this sort of thing, the Judge thought. None of the other girls was over twenty, and Peggy, three weeks shy of her eighteenth birthday, was the youngest. He feared the reactions of Mary and Peggy—they had been moving dreamily about the house in a glow of ecstasy for days, clutching their Turkish costumes to their bosoms as if they were childhood fetishes.

The Judge dreaded telling them. But it would have to be done. First, he would write a note to Major John André, chief designer of the extravagance, telling him that Mary and Peggy were forced to withdraw. This would make the decision a fait accompli, an aid in withstanding the hysterical remonstrances he was certain would come from the two girls—and possibly from Mrs. Shippen as well. The Judge was saddened by the wave of anger he felt against André, the man whom everyone in the family admired so much. But he remembered how fervently André had pledged not to allow Peggy to be traduced in any way. How could he not have seen that such a nonsensical farce would inevitably damage her reputation? Thank God that André at least had dropped the notion of leading citizens playing a part in the affair. The Judge had already begun to fear that the high visibility of his daughters in the British social whirl was seriously eroding his cherished stance of neutrality. For him to play a part personally in the tribute to General Howe would surely have branded him a Tory in the eyes of everyone.

He studied the note he had written and then added words to the effect that a servant could be sent to fetch the two Turkish costumes in the event that young ladies were found to substitute for Mary and Peggy. Perhaps someone—André?—would be decent enough to recompense the Judge for the cost of the costumes. The Judge immediately dismissed that as a petty and unworthy thought. His mind turned to the much more pressing matter of just how he was going to tell his daughters of a decision that they would certainly regard as catastrophic.

It was pouring rain by the time Ernst returned from delivering the note for John André to the Benjamin Franklin house. All afternoon and evening the Judge's stomach threatened to revolt. He could eat only a few bites of supper. Afterward, he asked to see Mary and Peggy in the parlor. Mrs. Shippen, naturally, followed them in, a puzzled expression on her face. When the older children hovered about, the Judge shooed them upstairs.

He knew that the members of his household had been curious about the unusual delegation that had visited him that morning. He thought the girls might have divined the purpose, given the looks of foreboding on their faces now. After clearing his throat several times, the Judge decided that the only way to do it was to do it. He plunged right in, beginning with his own previous misgivings about the *Meshianza,* and then relating the moral concerns the Quaker elders had so ardently presented. They were right, he said. It was unseemly. He had made up his mind. None of the Shippen girls could participate.

The silence that followed was ghastly, broken only by the guttering of a candle flame. Mrs. Shippen cast her eyes upward, shaking her head slightly. Mary and Peggy stared incredulously at the Judge, their faces drained of color.

"Father, you can't be serious!" Peggy gasped. Mary batted her eyes at her father, hoping against hope.

"I most certainly am."

"Oh, Papa, no, no!" Mary wailed.

Peggy had almost withdrawn from the *Meshianza* herself when she learned that her rival, Peggy Chew, would be escorted by John André, while she was relegated to a Lieutenant Sloper of the Seventeenth Dragoons, a mere stripling of eighteen. André had told her it meant nothing, that the pairings for the two teams of knights had been made on the basis of rank and age, and that he would dance with her more than anyone else throughout the night. But to Peggy it meant everything, to the point that she almost emulated Sarah's decision to withdraw. Then her mood became defiant and her determination had steeled: she vowed to go and be more radiant and beautiful than ever, to be the center of men's eyes so that Major André would be jealous. Now came the astonishing news that she might not be able to go after all. She gathered her wits to take on her father in argument. "I'm sure the gentlemen who called on you are sincere," she said forthrightly. "They're wrong. Very wrong. There is nothing immoral about the *Meshianza*. We are merely playing a role. As if on the stage. You love the theater, Father. Think of it as a play and nothing more."

"On the stage? In the heathen costumes of a Turkish harem? Never!"

"That's not true!" Peggy cried. "They're *not* harem costumes. We're portraying Turkish ladies of—of good birth," she finished lamely.

"The whole thing is decadent," the Judge said. "I positively forbid it."

Peggy was nearing desperation. Mary already seemed submissive, head bowed, eyes closed, tears trickling down her cheek. "Father, try to understand," Peggy said. "The gentlemen protest on religious grounds. But Lord Cathcart—he's the Chief Knight of the Blended Rose—he's escorting Miss Auchmuty of New York." She managed *not* to say "his pregnant wife." "Her father is rector of Trinity Church. And *he* has no objection."

"We speak only for ourselves. No, I say!"

Peggy burst into tears. Her eyes grew red and her cheeks puffy. "You can't mean it! I'll never forgive you, Father, *never*!" She sank to her knees, turning to her mother. "Mother, Mother, *please.*"

"I can do nothing," Mrs. Shippen said. "You know I will not cross Mr. Shippen. You'll have to face it, my dears." She dabbed at her eyes and moved away.

At that moment there was a sharp rap at the front door. Judge Shippen moved to the entryway as Reuben opened the door to admit a British sergeant, who carried a large silk bag over one arm. Thank God André had not come, the Judge thought.

"Suh!" the sergeant clicked his heels and bowed slightly to the Judge. "Sergeant Orcross at your service, suh!" the sergeant said in an unnecessarily loud voice. "Compliments of Major André, and I've been sent to fetch two garments."

The sergeant was startled by a loud shriek coming from the parlor. He could not avoid seeing a beautiful blond young lady on her knees, who shrieked again as if in mortal agony, her hands pressed against her temples.

The Judge shivered. It was Peggy going into one of her terrible fits.

John André and Oliver DeLancey had been forced by the driving rain inside the Wharton mansion, where they worked on one of the walls, painting a beautiful sky over a verdant and fertile plain. Other workers had come to join those inside, so that the decorating of the house proper was proceeding apace, aided by the fact that most of the furniture had been removed. André hoped to be finished with everything by tomorrow afternoon so that there still would be time for rehearsals of several of the more intricate events. Then on Monday morning, he would be able to inspect the coiffures and turbans and hair ornamentation of the fourteen maidens (two had withdrawn), the most beautiful young ladies of Philadelphia. André joked that he was becoming the premier hairdresser and milliner of the city, the arbiter of taste.

DeLancey was working on painting clouds, giving them an edge of grey as André had shown him. Across the ballroom, made huge by the folded doors of two adjoining rooms, was a long row of French doors facing toward the river. These would all be opened on Monday evening, to allow passage of the more than four hundred guests from the outside events to dinner and dancing inside. The house and grounds, known as Walnut Grove, had been confiscated from Joseph Wharton, a wealthy Quaker merchant who now lay dying in exile in Virginia. The mansion commanded a stunning view, across more than two hundred yards of beautiful lawn and gardens, stretching gracefully down to the Delaware River. The guests would be brought downriver from the main docks of Philadelphia in gaily decorated barges, to disembark at the Wharton property.

DeLancey followed André's glance at the closed French doors and said: "We'd better pray it doesn't rain like this on Monday."

"Call it André's luck. This storm is passing through now. We should be fine on Monday."

The two friends were among the twenty-two officers who had subscribed more than 3,300 guineas to pay the costs of the extravaganza. Older officers were in charge of the tribute to General Howe, but André was clearly the artistic director, planning events, designing costumes, writing verse, decorating the buildings and grounds.

"The rain is slacking," DeLancey said. "We'd better go. We've been here since dawn."

"Righto," André said, stretching wearily. "We'll have to come back tomorrow." Dressed in a paint-smeared smock, he smiled at himself as he walked toward the French doors, watching his image appear successively in the mirrors that lined the walls. Eighty-five full-length mirrors had been rented from shops and borrowed from families to provide multiple reflections of the gorgeous colors of the bunting and pendants and wreaths that decked the hall.

Once outside, the two officers made an inspection tour on the way to their wagon. They stopped to watch the carpenters who had resumed work on the amphitheater adjoining the jousting field. The banquet hall, built next to one side of the ballroom, was all but complete. André chatted with the chief engineer, John Montresor, who was in charge of the fireworks. He assured André that only rain at the wrong moment could spoil a "jolly good show" on Monday evening. André and DeLancey walked the length of the 180-foot pavilion leading up from the gardens. Made of wood and stretched canvas, it was gaily painted and featured the niches on either side where the statues would stand on display as the guests moved forward. The previous day, André had inspected the regiment of Grenadier Guards, which included the finest specimens of manhood in the army. He had picked thirty handsome men who stood six feet tall. Clad in Roman togas, they would be the "statues." Beyond the outer end of the pavilion, the guests would pass through two Doric arches, nearly a hundred yards apart, which were complete except for the garlands of flowers that would be woven into the structures on Monday morning. The arch nearest the river was intended as a salute to Admiral Howe, featuring at the top a statue of Neptune with his trident and inscriptions on the side supports extolling the virtues of the god of the sea. Workers were bringing up hundreds of boxes and barrels from the river dock, containing china and tableware and goblets. Admiral Howe's transport vessels had reached Philadelphia in time, bringing food, spirits, and rare fruit from the Caribbean. These goods would be brought up to the greatly enlarged kitchen area, starting tomorrow afternoon.

Back near the road, André and DeLancey took one of the empty work wagons for the trip back to their quarters, now that the rain had stopped. They moved along the waterfront on their way in order to inspect progress in decorating the houses and taverns that faced the river. Passing Knight's Wharf, where the regatta would embark at three thirty Monday afternoon, they saw an inspiring sight—the warships and thirty barges clustered along the riverbank with workers swarming about to decorate them. Several of the military bands had taken up positions on Water Street to practice, surrounded by crowds of applauding civilians.

Once inside the Franklin house, André and DeLancey threw off their smocks and collapsed onto sofas, bone-tired, but with the kind of weariness that is pleasurable in the glow of much good work accomplished. For the first time, André believed that everything would actually be ready in time and that all would go well. A servant brought in a note that had arrived earlier for André. He tore it open and his face fell.

"Good God!"

"What is it?"

"A note from Judge Shippen. Mary and Peggy are withdrawing! The old man thinks the event is not proper for his precious daughters."

"The devil you say! I'd like to punch the old bastard. They're the two prettiest girls of the lot. Peggy, anyway. Lord Cathcart is still in love with her. I'm afraid he'd much rather have her than his new wife. What do we do now?"

"Nothing we *can* do. Except try to get substitutes. It's awfully late for that. Two of the knights are already lacking ladies as it is." He sighed: "I guess two more absences won't ruin it."

"Perhaps if you go see the old man yourself. He's always been partial to you."

"I was just thinking of that. But I can tell he's angry. The note is rather curt. Probably thinks I shouldn't have included his daughters in the first place. And he says to send someone to get the costumes if we wish. That has an air of finality about it. I'd probably just make it worse if I went there to plead with him."

"I suppose. Damned shame."

"Yes." André grimaced. "I know Peggy's heart will be broken."

When Peggy did not appear for supper Saturday night, her mother brought up a tray and tried to speak to her through the closed door, to no avail. The next morning, to the Judge's consternation, Peggy left the house before anyone else was up. She did not appear at church and did not come home until nearly dark. Mary had surrendered to her father's will and was not carrying on in any way, other than being more subdued and paler than usual. She told her mother she had seen Peggy carrying her paint smock all rolled up when she entered the house and went directly to her room. Mrs. Shippen, of course, conveyed this to her husband and also that she had learned, by speaking again through a closed door, that Peggy was not feeling well and would not be down for supper.

All of this put the Judge in a foul mood. He was irritated that Peggy apparently had spent the Sabbath working with others in preparation for the *Meshianza*. He wondered if she had spoken to John André and what had transpired. He almost went to pound on her door but checked himself. Better to let the matter sit. Peggy obviously was submitting the family to the old silent treatment. She would get over that in time.

Yet the whole business pained him sorely. His cool, level-headed Peggy, his darling, the one child more than any other who had followed him around as she grew up, learned from him, who was content to spend hours conversing with him, who seemed to love him so much. They had had their differences before and he could scarcely bear them, but this seemed the worst by far, as trivial as the Judge might think it was in the great scheme of things. What was it Mrs. Shippen had said? That the girls would never forget being denied the *Meshianza*? And Peggy—she said she would never forgive him. It couldn't possibly be. Nothing so transient could breach the love that father and daughter held for each other. Peggy would see that, the Judge was sure.

Up in her darkening room, Peggy was not ill and not hungry, having eaten sufficiently of the food laid out for the workers at Walnut Grove. She was weary from stress and her day of work, however, and wanted nothing more than a good, long night's sleep. She fingered her formal invitation to the *Meshianza*, an elaborate parchment emblazoned with the Howe family crest and bearing the motto *"Vive, Vale"* and the inscription: "The Favor of Your meeting the Subscribers to the *Meshianza* at Knight's Wharf near Poole's Bridge at half past three." The enclosed ticket showed a sun setting in the sea with a Latin motto on a streamer that translated: "He is shining as he sets. But he shall rise again in greater splendor." The background of the ticket showed every kind of military equipment, from cannon and flags to shields and drums, and a large laurel wreath that symbolized General Howe's military accomplishments.

As she lay on her bed, Peggy closed her eyes and envisioned her costume, the most beautiful garment she had ever seen, designed by none other than John André. It was enchanting, from the gauze turban to be fastened to her high, stylish hair, spangled and edged in gold and silver, enriched on one side with pearls and tassels of gold and a crested feather, decorated on the other with a mantua that descended to her waist; to the dress itself in the polonaise style, sashes about the waist and a huge bow hung very low, all in the colors of her knight, white and pink, with feathers and other decorations in red and black.

Peggy's eyes brimmed with tears, but her jaw was set. She had made up her mind. She knew what she was going to do.

The day of the *Meshianza* was bright and mild, with only occasional gusts of wind for worry. Peggy waited until she saw her father leave the house on his morning constitutional and then fled down the stairs and out the front door, paying no heed to the muffled call of her mother from the dining room. She returned three hours later, to the stares of her mother and sisters as she entered the house. Although she was attired in plain, everyday dress, her hair was coifed high in the continental style, as if she were leaving imminently for a fashionable party. She marched directly into her father's library where she found him reading a book. Her voice trembled with fear and excitement as she addressed the astonished Judge.

"Father, I was going to be a coward and not come back here at all, but I couldn't do that. I had to tell you my reasons, though I know you will not accept them."

"What on earth are you talking about? And what—"

"I am going to the *Meshianza.*"

"No, you are *not!*" The Judge half rose from his chair.

"I am going because of all that you have taught me about what is right and what is wrong."

The Judge sank back, sputtering in anger. "What preposterous nonsense!"

"Please hear me out, Father. You and the Quaker gentlemen think I should not go for some reason of principle that I cannot fathom. They can only say that it is immoral. I reject that. It is *not* immoral! It is merely the brilliant end of a wonderful season. I have been privileged with a special invitation. I have committed myself to be there. I will disappoint others if I am *not* there. You taught me never to do that. You taught me to keep my word. And that is what I am going to do."

"No!"

"Will you restrain me by force? Summon Ernst and Reuben to tie me up like an Indian squaw or a slave?"

With that she turned on her heel and ran from the room and out the front door, heading for Becky Franks's house, where her costume awaited her. Enraged, the Judge tried to follow. On his doorstep he saw Peggy disappearing down Willing's Alley. He saw neighbors walking along the street. He clenched and unclenched his fists. What could he do? Run after her to drag her screaming back into the house? He stood there a long minute, his breath coming in gasps. Then he turned and entered the house, deflated, shoulders sagging.

One had only to join the growing throng at Knight's Wharf to begin a magical transformation to another world. The galley *Ferret,* with several general officers and their ladies aboard, led the first flotilla of passenger barges. Next came the galley *Hussar* and its cluster of gaily decorated craft bearing the guest of honor, General Howe, and Mrs. Loring, accompanied by Admiral Howe and the newly arrived Sir Henry Clinton. The third flotilla was led by the *Cornwallis,* with General von Knyphausen aboard, bringing up the rear of the grand water pageant. The boats maneuvered easily now that the wind had calmed.

The frigates *Vigilant* and *Roebuck,* clad from waterline to mast top with streamers and flags and pennants of every color, were stationed near the Market Street Wharf, where a huge throng had gathered to watch the three flotillas as they moved upstream to turn and take their proper places. Six armed barges patrolled the perimeter of the flotillas to keep order among a horde of small boats. Never had the Delaware River been so laden with festive craft.

Three large barges, carrying more than one hundred musicians from half a dozen British and German regiments, drew up close to the *Hussar,* where the massed band played "God Save the King" to General Howe's salute. This was followed by a thunderous roar from the crowd and a nineteen-gun salute from the *Roebuck.* Cheering citizens crowded every wharf and rooftop along the one-mile route, as the three flotillas slowly moved downstream to the strains of Handel's "Water Music."

It was past six o'clock by the time the revelers debarked and passed through the first arch to the field that had been marked off for the mock joust. Becky and Peggy and the other twelve maidens were escorted by the squires to divan pillows that had been set within the curve of the small amphitheater, open to the one side that adjoined the field. Peggy's pangs of conscience over her defiant act had long since vanished in the mood and wonder of all that was happening about her. She lay demurely on her cushion, playing the part of the temptress to the hilt, and smiled in joy when she saw the eight Knights of the Blended Rose lining up on their white horses. Their crest displayed two roses with stems intertwined and the motto "We Droop When Separate." Because armor would prohibit dancing, the jousters wore costumes modeled after those of the court of Henry IV. Peggy quickly identified Major André in his pink blouse and white satin vest, his scarf, hat brim, sword belt, and wide buff leather boots edged and trimmed in black, red, and silver, with pink bows at the knees and red and black plumes jutting from his high-crowned satin hat.

Trumpeters from the massed band stepped forward to blare the opening of the "Ceremony of the Carousel" as the hundreds of guests surrounded the field of honor to watch the joust. The herald of the Blended Rose entered the quadrangle, the eight knights and squires behind him, and proclaimed:

The Knights of the Blended Rose, by me their herald proclaim and assert, that the ladies of the Blended Rose excel in wit, beauty, and every accomplishment, those of the whole world, and, should any knight, or knights, be so hardy as to dispute or deny it, they are ready to enter the lists with them and maintain their assertions, by deeds of arms, according to the laws of ancient chivalry.

The herald of the Knights of the Burning Mountain, bearing the motto "I Burn Forever," then entered to proclaim his response, the eight knights behind him mounted on black steeds and wearing orange and black costumes in contrast to the pink and white of their foes:

The Knights of the Burning Mountain enter these lists not to contend with words, but to disprove with deeds of arms the vainglorious assertions of the Knights of the Blended Rose and to show that the ladies of the Burning Mountain as far excel all others in charms as the knights themselves surpass all others in prowess.

The rituals were performed almost as a dance, the teams of knights circling around the field and then saluting the audience, the maidens, and one another. A trumpeter blared for a parley and the teams faced each other in the center. Lord Cathcart threw his gauntlet to the ground, and a black knight's squire picked it up and returned it to accept the challenge. The teams lined up at either end and charged, each managing to splinter his wooden lance against a foe's shield. There followed another charge with each knight firing a pistol into the air, and a third of combat with wooden swords that soon broke, followed by mock hand-to-hand battle. The blare of trumpets ceased combat and a judge came forth or declare that "with ladies so fair and knights so brave it would be impious to decide in favor of either side."

Each knight went to claim a favor from his lady and the two entire retinues lined up on each side of the path from the second arch to the pavilion to bow and smile and accept the cheers and congratulations of the guests as they filed through into the garden and up the stairs to enter the ballroom via the French doors. Temporary tables had been set up, covered with green baize, bearing a light repast of coffee, tea, lemonade, wine, and punch, and a wide variety of cakes. The guests munched and socialized for an hour before being called back outside just past nine o'clock to witness Captain Montresor's fireworks display.

Two miles away, Captain Allen McLane and his hundred-man cavalry unit, supported by Major Clough's dragoons, sat silently aboard their horses staring at the British defensive works just ahead of them on the northern edge of the city. McLane had divided his force into four groups of twenty-five men, each accompanied by two wagons bearing kettles full of whale oil. Soon the red, white, and blue showers of sparks from the rockets, Chinese fountains, and fire pots of Montresor's display could be seen in the sky, followed by the steady rumble of the explosions. With hand signals, McLane directed his men, who dismounted and carried the kettles up to pour the oil on the dry wooden abbatis of the British lines. They ignited the fuel and ran back to their horses, as the works began blazing for a distance of more than a hundred yards. As British troops rushed out to stem the blaze, McLane's men fired their weapons as rapidly as they could. It was fifteen minutes of confusion before the British amassed a sizeable enough force to sally out and attack McLane's position. More than twenty officers who had rushed on horseback from Walnut Grove appeared on the scene. McLane's force rode away, pursued for nearly five miles.

The officers from Walnut Grove cursed the Americans for their pathetic attempt at an "annoyance" to disrupt a night of pleasure and joy. They did not know until the next day that the intent was not an annoyance, but a diversion to coincide with a planned break from the Walnut Street prison by captive American troops. Seventy-three men escaped that night.

* * *

At Walnut Grove, General Howe rose to quiet the tremor that ran through the throng, saying that the noises that were heard were merely a distant extension of the brilliant fireworks display. The tables were moved to the perimeter of the huge room and laden with the heavier spirits, rum, gin, and various liqueurs. An orchestra selected from the massed band, augmented by a hired civilian string section, began to play music for the dance. The couples formed and began their graceful pirouettes, swirling faster and faster as the hours passed. True to his word, John André danced four times with the ecstatic Peggy Shippen to only two with Peggy Chew. André was giddy with joy at the great success of his planning, and his dances with Peggy were nearly exercises in complete abandon.

It was past midnight before the elaborate feast was served in the newly built banquet hall, over two hundred feet long and forty feet wide. Fifty-six pier looking-glasses were set around the perimeter, dressed in green silk and flowers, and eighteen chandeliers were suspended overhead, each bearing twenty-four spermaceti candles. The servers, thirty black men dressed in white shirts, black pantaloons, blue sashes, and silk turbans, bowed to the waist as the guests entered. Settings for 430 guests had been laid on two long tables. Several varieties of hot soup were served from large silver tureens, and a cold collation followed, of chicken, lamb, ham, Yorkshire pies, veal, puddings, and fruits. On small tables lining the walls were pyramids of cheeses, jellies, syllabub, cakes, and sweetmeats, as well as heavy silver servers of coffee and tea.

Toward the end of the banquet, the herald of the Blended Rose and his trumpeters appeared to proclaim the health of George III. The entire assembly stood and sang as the orchestra again played "God Save the King." A long series of toasts followed, each accompanied by three cheers and a musical salute—toasts to the King, the Queen, the royal family, General Howe, the army, the navy, the commanders, the knights and their ladies. For a finale, a quartet of Hessian officers rose and shouted, "God save the King, and success to His Majesty's arms!"

The evening became even more dreamlike for Peggy, as most couples returned to the ballroom to resume dancing, while others strolled about the grounds. In one corner, a Hessian officer had established a faro bank and customers lined up to lose their money trying to break it. Many guests sat at the small tables, conversing and drinking, some of them nodding off into the arms of Bacchus. Other couples slipped up to the second floor for amorous dalliances.

As dawn neared, Peggy was near to fainting from drink and dancing and the exertions of fending off the sloppy advances of the pimple-faced Lieutenant Sloper and more than a few other gentlemen. She had not seen John André for hours. She managed to climb the majestic stairway to the second floor in search of him. It was a mistake. The party had turned orgiastic in some corners, and she was assailed by a drunken Lord Cathcart, who had taken his exhausted and pregnant wife home hours earlier and then returned to the party. He suddenly appeared from a second-floor room onto the broad corridor to grab Peggy and begin pawing her.

John André miraculously appeared at that moment but hesitated over the dilemma of whether he should try to physically restrain the man who was both his superior officer and his Chief Knight of the Blended Rose. He was spared the decision when Peggy twisted free and Cathcart collapsed to the floor, unconscious in a drunken stupor.

Peggy sank onto an emerald-colored sofa, dizzy and nearly unconscious herself. André sat beside her and began to console and stroke her. She opened her eyes and saw him as if in a dream.

"There, there, Peggy, my sweet, you'll be all right now," André crooned. "I'm sorry for this—but I'm so glad your father relented and allowed you to come. You *are* the most beautiful girl of all."

Peggy had her wits about her enough to know that this was not the time to tell him that she had brazenly defied her father. She felt a pang at the sudden memory of that.

"Why couldn't Mary come, too?"

"She—she was not well."

"Oh, too bad." André continued to gaze at Peggy with open admiration, his face only inches from hers. Then he leaned down and kissed her, softly, sweetly, upon the lips. She returned the kiss ardently.

André drew back and said: "Please forgive me, Peggy dearest. I'm sorry. I couldn't help it."

"Please don't say that," Peggy whispered, placing a finger on his lips. "I've dreamed of this." She put her arm around his neck and drew him to her for a long, sweet kiss.

Chapter 43

Philadelphia
June, 1778

The *Meshianza* was the last gasp of British hedonism in Philadelphia. The theater closed and the parties, balls, and games ceased, as preparations for the evacuation slowly began. The Tories were so unnerved by news of the planned departure that even genteel entertaining of military guests by Philadelphia families now rarely occurred.

General Howe's last military effort briefly held high promise of a miraculous turnaround but then fell flat. By dint of good intelligence work, Howe had Lord Cornwallis and a large force in position north of the city when the Marquis de Lafayette brought fully one third of Washington's army east of the Schuylkill River. Cornwallis almost closed the trap at a place called Barren Hill, but at the last moment the marquis barely escaped by crossing his army back to safety at a little-used ford that the British knew nothing about.

After that, Howe seemed thoroughly deflated, left only to commiserate with his Tory friends and certain officers who were disconsolate over the planned evacuation, as Sir Henry Clinton took command. Erskine and Grey, among other generals, were appalled at the decision to withdraw, seeing it as a blow to British honor to retreat in the face of what they regarded as an inferior enemy.

Trying to move his ablest aides to Clinton's staff, Howe succeeded in the case of Major McKenzie, but not John André. It was Howe himself who, with regret, informed André that he would have to return to General Grey's staff. "General Clinton has his own man as adjutant general, who takes care of the intelligence function," Sir William told André.

"My only regret is to lose the brevet rank of major," André later said to McKenzie. "Otherwise, I'm just as happy, to tell you the truth. Although I enjoy the work, I don't know that I'd enjoy it under General Clinton. He seems so sour and acerbic."

McKenzie's raised eyebrows and shrug conveyed that he did not disagree entirely with André's assessment. "Yes, he was very sour on the *Meshianza* and perhaps disapproves of you on account of it. He's not a bad fellow underneath that veneer of toughness. You'll see. The truth is, as you probably know, our two generals do not care for each other very much. In fact, it's much worse than that. They're bitter rivals, have been for years."

Thus forewarned, André could see the covert hostility between Howe and Clinton in the meetings he attended before Howe's departure. Clinton was peevish for good reason. Although he had strongly opposed the expedition to Philadelphia, he now was being asked to clean up the mess while Howe sailed blithely away. The dislike was evident when the head of the peace commission, Frederick Howard, the thirty-year-old fourth Earl of Carlisle, arrived with his two colleagues from London just before General Howe was due to leave. Joined by the two Howes, the five-man commission held a stormy meeting with General Clinton. The earl was unhappy because he arrived to find that the American Congress had declared it would not agree to meet with the commission unless it conceded American independence beforehand. The two other recently arrived members, George Johnstone, former governor of West Florida, and William Eden, member of the Board of Trade, argued that holding on to Philadelphia was the only bargaining chip the commission had. The earl cursed loudly when General Clinton informed him that his orders to evacuate were specific and unbreakable. The commissioners would have to come to New York with the rest of the British and await developments here.

André was present when a delegation of prominent Tories, led by Joseph Galloway, came to plead with Howe for help. They, of course, were devastated by the British plan to withdraw. For them, it meant economic ruin. The leaders would have to flee with the British, the husbands at least, or face unspeakable abuse and humiliation, or even the gallows, from the oncoming radical patriots. Howe was only able to give them the unsatisfactory advice to "make peace with the States, who I suppose will not treat you harshly." His brother, Admiral Howe, gave similarly bland counsel, recommending that the Tories petition the American Congress for a general amnesty. As far as Galloway was concerned, this would be "like having a rope around my neck and my property confiscated." He had formed a deep dislike for General Howe and waited until his departure before trying again with General Clinton.

Howe left on May 24th aboard the *Andromeda* from Market Street Wharf. André was there along with hundreds of other officers, mostly of the middle and junior ranks, for Howe was no longer popular with some of the senior men. Nevertheless, André paid him the ultimate compliment in remarking to DeLancey that the rousing cheer as the vessel drifted away from the dock was even greater evidence of the love of the army for General Howe "than all the pomp and splendor of the *Meshianza*."

Now Galloway renewed his petition, this time with Clinton. He nearly broke down when Clinton told him that his orders direct from the ministry in London were firm—he *had* to evacuate. Galloway then asked permission to send a delegation to York to petition the Congress for a general amnesty. Clinton refused, saying he could not consent to treating with the rebels, and that a flag of truce would be tantamount to his condoning a treaty. He added that he could not be a party to seeking more advantageous treatment for the Loyalists of Philadelphia than for those of New York, since half the garrison in New York was composed of Loyalist troops. As the depressed Galloway left the room, he told a fellow Loyalist, "My fate shall be that of Cain, a homeless and despised person roaming the earth." He soon recovered enough to send out notices that all persons desiring to leave Philadelphia with the British Army should come to his office to register, inasmuch as space would be limited.

Bereft of information after Howe's departure, André invited his friends McKenzie and Montresor to join him and DeLancey for dinner at the Benjamin Franklin house in the expectation of finding out what was going on from reliable sources. The quartet was lamenting the failure of Howe's near success in trapping Lafayette, which could have changed everything, perhaps even leading to the rout of Washington's army.

"That would've made it all worthwhile," Montresor said. "At least General Clinton is doing rather well in keeping Washington off balance."

"How so?" André asked.

"He wants Washington to stay where he is so we can get a long start in marching across the Jerseys to New York. So he keeps feinting to the north, and he's even got some of my boys out building new redoubts. Fake ones, of course. So far it seems to be working. Washington shows no signs of moving."

"We may have a secret weapon," McKenzie laughed. "You know, Washington has General Lee back, and he's made him second-in-command. Which means that Lee will be leading any attack on us in New Jersey. Now, just this morning, a letter from Lee addressed to Clinton arrived. I was so astonished that I made a copy. Listen to this. He writes: '*General Lee presents his most sincere and humble respects to General Clinton. He wishes him all possible happiness and health and begs, whatever may be the event of the present unfortunate contest, that he will believe General Lee to be his most respectful and humble servant.*' "

"That must be a hoax!" DeLancey laughed.

"No, it isn't. It's real. I think we could give him an idea on how he might serve General Clinton!"

"What concerns me," André said, "is the terrible mess we're leaving in this city. Whole houses torn down for firewood. Huge piles of rubbish on every street. Almost every church has terrible damage from the stables or hospitals we put in. Every house used by the troops is nearly ruined. Most of them just cut a hole in the floor for their wastes." He turned to Montresor. "Shouldn't we at least make some effort to clean up?"

"Still the idealist, are you, John?" was the response. "We'll be lucky to get out with our skins. And they'll be lucky if the city isn't burned down. You can scarcely fathom what a gigantic job this move is. Just getting the heavy ordnance on the transports is like building the great pyramids of Egypt in a week. We simply have no time to tidy up. The fortunes of war. And the order to move out could come any day now."

"I guess I'd better get around to say good-bye to my friends," André said gloomily.

Like most Philadelphia families, the Shippens had taken on something of a fortress mentality in the days following the *Meshianza*. The city was visibly deteriorating around them, and it was no longer safe to wander about the streets. Peggy was particularly unhappy with each passing day. She could not bring herself to regret what she had done in disobeying her father, but she knew she had hurt him deeply. He seemed older and spiritless. There were no recriminations, just deadening silence.

Finally, Peggy could stand it no longer and sought counsel from her mother. "I want so to make it up, Mother," she said. "I don't know what to do."

"This is a very trying time for your father," Mrs. Shippen said. "He's desolate over the breach with you. At the same time he's worried to death for all of us. He now thinks it was a mistake to stay here with the British. He's afraid there'll be false accusations and retributions once the patriots return."

"What can I do?" Peggy's voice was agonized.

"He'll never speak of it. Unless you do first. You think he wronged you, and in a way he did. But you wronged him far more seriously. Honor thy father. Read your Bible, child. Go speak to him. You know how much he's always loved you. Let your heart be your guide."

Peggy found her father once again in his library, a book in his lap. This time he had nodded off. She stole in, sank to the floor next to him, embraced his legs, and lay her head down on his lap next to the book. The Judge stirred and gradually woke. Through shade-drawn eyes, he discerned the lovely blond head of his daughter. It seemed like a dream as he reached out and stroked her hair.

Peggy turned up to him, her eyes glistening. "Oh, Father, I'm so sorry. I'm so sorry." She dropped her head again and the tears flowed.

"There, there, child," the Judge murmured, stroking her again.

"I never wanted to disobey you. I never wanted to hurt you. I'll never do it again. I swear! *Never!*"

The Judge's eyes moistened. "It's in the past now. We'll put it behind us."

"I love you, Father."

"And I love you."

On June 12th, Benedict Arnold was one of fifteen generals who filed into the log structure that Martha Washington had had built onto the Potts house. Following the council of war and accompanied by Punch, Arnold rode back to the Coates house where David Franks was eagerly awaiting the news. Clarkson was off to Reading to try to arrange a trade of two of Arnold's wagons for a four-horse coach.

Arnold was exhausted and in pain from the ride. Franks and Punch helped him down and to the bench on the front porch where he sat for a long while, breathing heavily. Finally, he began to speak: "We've got to be ready to move any day now. The British are definitely leaving. And we can't let the city be more than one day without authority. They're afraid of massive looting. The town is apparently even more crammed with goods than we thought." Arnold barked a hoarse laugh. "They were building up supplies for the spring campaign! Now they've got to move it all or lose it. The British are already trying to destroy what they can, dumping barrels into the river, breaking up field pieces, burning boats along the Delaware. It'll be a wonder if they don't burn the city down—by accident if nothing else."

"You still want me to go in early?"

"Yes. The way I figure, the last British troops will leave at night. You'll want to go in with McLane's cavalry at first light the next day. I'll come in with the troops the next morning. Forget what I told you about buying up goods, though."

"Why?" Franks's expression was pained.

"I have a directive from Congress to immediately close all shops. To prevent looting."

"Damn!"

"Don't worry. We'll have our opportunities. I'll have proclamations and orders for you to bring in. And you've got to find decent housing before I get there."

"Why not where General Howe was living?"

Arnold smiled. "Why not? Take a look. But make sure it's adequate. We'll have a household staff of about ten. Two or three carriages. Ten or so horses."

"Right. What else happened?"

Arnold shifted and grimaced with pain. "A lot. Washington is very unhappy with Congress because they won't respond to his request for a provisional amnesty for the Tories."

"Why does he care about them so much?"

Arnold smiled again. "First, because he's a humane gentleman. And there are a lot of bloodthirsty people looking for revenge. Gouverneur Morris thinks the thousand leading Tories should be jailed and forced to contribute one hundred thousand pounds to the Revolution. Joseph Reed—he's the one we'll be dealing with the most—he thinks the five hundred top Tories should be hanged."

"He can't be serious!"

"Oh, but he is. We'll have our problems with Mr. Reed. There's another reason why Washington is concerned, others, too, Laurens and Boudinot. It seems that a whole lot of Philadelphia mechanics and artisans did some work for the British here and there over the winter. These people are afraid they'll be branded as Loyalists and punished. So a lot of them might leave with the British because they don't know what will happen. We don't want them to do that. We want to keep them. So Washington thinks it's important to ease their fears."

"Well, that makes sense."

"Yes, it does."

Franks raised his eyebrows. "This is going to be a messy job, isn't it?"

"Yes, it is." Arnold was sweating now, his leg throbbing. "Damn this leg. I'd much rather be leading the troops across the Delaware than going into Philadelphia."

"What do you mean?"

"Everyone's pretty well convinced by now that Clinton will be marching his army across New Jersey. He doesn't have nearly enough ships to move everything. Half of Admiral Howe's fleet is in the Caribbean now. So there'll be a large British army with a huge baggage train strung out in New Jersey. A wonderful target. Washington has ordered six brigades to cross the Delaware at Coryell's Ferry and Bordentown, ready to strike south and intercept the British line."

"And you want to lead them."

"Damn right. Lee will be in command, Lafayette his number two. A fool and a boy sent to do a man's job. But I have this leg that won't let me go. It's killing me right now." Arnold leaned forward and gently rubbed the leg. "I'm out of laudanum. Go find Dr. Cochrane. First tell Punch to prepare the tub. I've got to soak my leg—or just die, sitting right here."

The 17th of June dawned hot and humid, presaging one of Philadelphia's blistering summers. Captain John André was trying to finish his packing. He would leave the city that night with General Grey. And this afternoon would be his last chance to pay a final visit to the Shippen household.

André was sweating profusely as he worked on packing the last three wooden crates to be loaded on the army wagon outside in the courtyard. Sitting on a fourth case, his legs swinging, was André's Swiss friend from their days together in Geneva, Pierre Eugene du Simitiére, who had come to say good-bye. The two had taken drawing lessons from the same master. Du Simitiére had built a reputation as a brilliant miniaturist and had come to America as a civilian with the idea of settling. His ambition was to create the first museum of the arts in America.

"So you're really going to stay here?" André said.

"Yes."

André shook his head. "Why anyone from Geneva, on the shores of beautiful Lac Leman, would come to Philadelphia to live is quite beyond me."

"Well, I may not stay forever," du Simitiére said. "Only if I can make a success of my plans."

"When the radicals arrive, they'll probably think you're a British spy and hang you," André said.

Du Simitiére smiled. "Not a chance. They know who I am. Now listen, John, you promised."

André straightened up to stretch his back. "I know, I know. Time just ran out." His promise was to provide several of his sketches and paintings for du Simitiére's collection, and he had been flattered that his friend thought him talented enough to be worth saving. He reached over to pick up his thick military journal from a nearby table. He also grabbed a stack of papers and handed the lot to du Simitiére. "Here, look through my journal. It has a lot of sketches. And here are some more recent things. Maybe you'll find something that will serve."

Du Simitiére riffled through the material as André resumed packing. The recent material consisted of drawings of well-dressed young ladies and black silhouettes cut out by scissors, a particular skill that André had. From the journal, du Simitiére held up the watercolor of the Indian brave that André had done at Fort Chambly. "How about this?"

"Oh, that's one of my favorites."

"It's the best thing in here."

"All right. And take one of the ladies. They're all from the *Meshianza*. I wanted to capture the various hairstyles and gowns. I designed most of them. Take the one of Peggy Shippen. The most beautiful girl there."

"Won't she want it?"

"I already gave her a better one." André smiled.

Du Simitiére put the two works in his own folder. "These will serve well, John. And also give me a way to meet Miss Shippen."

"Leave her alone, you rascal. I'm going over to say good-bye to Peggy and her family as soon as I've finished here and cleaned myself up. I'll warn her about you."

Du Simitiére smiled and then focused for the first time on exactly what André was packing—electrical gear, armonica glasses, and a set of foundry matrices. "John, what are you doing? Aren't those Dr. Franklin's things?"

"Yes, indeed."

"You can't take them. That would be stealing."

"Hardly. They're souvenirs. I'll spread the word of the doctor's greatness by showing them off."

"That set of books, too? Are they souvenirs?" Du Simitiére was pointing to the stack of French books on the arts and sciences.

"Well, no. Those are for me. Think of it as retribution for the doctor's evil genius in bringing the French into the war."

"And the painting, too?" Du Simitiére pointed to the Benjamin Wilson portrait of Franklin, leaning up against one of the wooden crates.

"That? I want to give it as a gift to General Grey. He has much admiration for Dr. Franklin's scientific accomplishments, if not his statecraft."

"I see. You're giving a portrait of Franklin that *he* owns as *your* gift to your general. Interesting logic. John, this is all beneath you. This is looting."

André flared for a moment. "Look around this house. See what fine condition it's in? Nary a speck of damage. You should see the wrecks that some of our men have made of other houses."

"You think that justifies it?"

"Yes, I do. I would think the good doctor would want to give us these tokens for taking such good care of his house."

"I think what the good doctor would want would be for you to leave his things alone and pay him rent for occupying the house."

*   *   *

André was received cordially at the Shippen household, chatting with the entire family in the foyer. Then the Judge drew him into the library, beckoning Peggy to follow.

"So this is farewell, is it?" the Judge said.

"Yes, sir, I'm afraid so. I'll be leaving tonight for New York. Tomorrow the first of the rebels will be entering the city. I do hope they have the orders and the will to keep the city calm."

"The entire army will be gone by tonight?"

"Just a rear guard left behind, I believe. Most of the troops are already across the river."

"Has Lord Carlisle gone?"

"He left yesterday."

The Judge sniffed. Carlisle had taken his quarters in the home of the Judge's close friend, Samuel Powel, the most recent mayor of the city. He and his wife, Elizabeth, were childless but were forced to move to the servants' quarters of their handsome home, only a block from the Shippens, while Carlisle occupied the house proper. Even so, Powel was lucky to have a British boarder for less than a month. And the Judge knew how fortunate he had been in that regard, thanks to the handsome young man sitting before him.

"How many civilians are leaving with your fleet?" he asked.

"I'm told something over three thousand," André replied. He smiled. "Not including the Shippen family, I see."

"No. I've agonized over it. But as I told you once before, I've learned that those who leave end up regretting it."

"It's truly a sad and sorry sight to see so many people leaving everything behind. Most of them very unhappy. Again, I think you've made the right choice."

"I hope so. I'm more concerned now than ever before. I'm afraid there'll be vengeance in the air and many innocent people will suffer. Especially with General Arnold as military governor. By all accounts, he's a ferocious warrior. Possibly a bloodthirsty type, don't you think?"

"I certainly hope not. I know him only by reputation."

"I can't say we know him," the Judge said. "We did have him for dinner, back in seventy-four. And we had a chance encounter, just last summer. He was most cordial on both occasions."

Peggy remembered the meeting on the sidewalk the year before. She had sensed an aura of power around the strongly built figure of Arnold, so resplendent in his uniform. And she remembered the penetrating gaze he had leveled at her.

André looked up, his face brightening, and addressed the Judge: "By the way, before I forget, I want to thank you for changing your mind and allowing Peggy to come to the *Meshianza*. You saved the entire event. She was definitely the belle of the ball!"

The Judge glanced at Peggy, who wore an air of innocence as she shrugged slightly. "Mmm, yes. Really," he said drily. Then he rose. "I know you two wish to say farewell in private." He clasped André's hand. "To you, sir, I say heartfelt thanks for all your kindnesses. We'll never forget you."

"Nor shall I forget you and your wonderful family. Thank you for everything, sir."

Out in the garden, Peggy turned before sitting down on the wrought iron bench and said in a jocular tone: "I think my father just gave us permission to marry."

André flushed and then smiled. "Oh, I don't think so. He'll be very particular when that decision comes along, you can count on it."

"Well"—she smiled—"at least I wish he'd decided to take us to New York. Then I could see you again."

"No, you don't wish that, believe me. You've never seen such wretched people."

"Will I ever see you again?"

"I just don't know. The fortunes of war. It's possible. Perhaps we'll be able to correspond in some way."

"Oh, I hope so."

"Right now, Peggy, I must leave. I have some more packing to do before my rendezvous with General Grey."

"Must you go so soon?"

"Yes. Or risk leaving some of my baggage behind."

"How—where will you depart tonight?"

"Knight's Wharf," André said, as he rose from the bench. "At six o'clock. To cross the river and join the main army."

Peggy stood up, too, and put her hands on his shoulders. "I dream about the *Meshianza*—what happened late that night." Eyes closed, she leaned forward. André put his arms around her waist and kissed her, and she returned the embrace fervently. He smiled, turned, and left, waving good-bye. "Farewell, Peggy my sweet," he said over his shoulder. "I predict it will not be the last time you'll see John André."

Back in the house, the Judge gave Peggy a small smile and asked: "What was that about me changing my mind?"

"He just assumed that, Father. I never told him anything of what happened."

"Just as well, I suppose."

"He's leaving tonight at six at Knight's Wharf. Can I go and say good-bye?"

The Judge met her gaze and shook his head. "No. It's much too dangerous to be out, on this of all days."

"Yes, Father."

*　　*　　*

On the morning of the 18th, McLane's hundred horsemen dashed through the city waving their sabers, looking for British stragglers and terrifying everyone. They fought a sharp skirmish on Water Street with the last of the British rear guard, capturing thirty soldiers. Two British officers, tarrying overly long with their mistresses, were also taken. A trickle of people appeared on the roads leading to the city, anxious to reclaim their houses. As the day wore on, the trickle threatened to become a flood.

David Franks was a more pleasing sight to Philadelphia citizens. Very nattily dressed, he was all geniality as he rode about on his errands. The next morning, Franks rode out on the Germantown Pike to meet Arnold's procession into the city. A company of the Philadelphia Light Horse led the way, followed by Arnold riding alone in the four-wheel chaise, Punch at the reins. Matthew Clarkson rode alongside. Behind marched a regiment of the Massachusetts Line, attached to Arnold's command as the garrison for Philadelphia.

Franks found Arnold in an expansive mood and feeling no pain, he having been supplied with laudanum by Dr. Cochrane. Franks made his report and Arnold nodded genially. The new commander of the city wore his best uniform, complete with the gold epaulettes and sword-knot that General Washington had given him. Franks took up his position on the other side of the chaise as the procession continued, with more and more people lining the way, cheering the arrival of the American commander and his troops. By the time the caravan began to cross the city on High Street, thousands of onlookers had gathered to wave flags and cheer. Arnold looked every bit the part of a conquering hero as he smiled and waved.

PART IX

"One Shining Stroke"

From the narrative of David Franks

Almost from the moment General Arnold and I entered Philadelphia, his prediction that this would be a turbulent and difficult time began to come true.

I secured the handsome house at 190 High Street for the general, but found that the interior was not in good shape, with well more than half of the furniture gone. I couldn't imagine what General Howe had done to it, but it was necessary to take temporary quarters for General Arnold in the Slate-Roof House, the one that William Penn once occupied and then became a boarding-house.

Our first visitor was Joseph Reed, who was vice president of the Supreme Executive Council and the member responsible for the Loyalists. He was most anxious to have General Arnold promulgate the orders he had drawn up for the shops to be closed. The two men did not like each other at all, but General Arnold finally complied with Reed's request, knowing as he did that the Congress had also passed a resolution calling for the closure. It was one of the very few times that he did what Reed asked—the hostility between the two was intense. And in this case, Arnold lost—the shopkeepers all blamed him instead of Reed, until the shops were open again.

We finally occupied 190 High Street, Arnold having gone to the expense of buying furniture for it from the shop of Mr. Joseph Stansbury, a tradesman in ceramics and glassware. I remember wondering how it was that Stansbury happened to have this one load of furniture that fit perfectly into the house—but Arnold had no time to focus on that strange episode. He was too busy getting the city cleaned up, setting law and order in place, battling with Mr. Reed, and becoming the social leader and great host in a city that was struggling to be restored.

He took upon himself the responsibility for the Fourth of July dance at the City Tavern, and it was at this venue that the first signs of the battle between the adherents of General Arnold and Mr. Reed took place—signs seen in dress and fashion that were a precursor of much worse to come.

And it was at this venue that Benedict Arnold fell in love.

Chapter 44

Philadelphia
July, 1778

General Benedict Arnold had become expert each day in conserving the small amount of strength in his damaged left leg. He sat at the top of the stairway leading to the cellar of the handsome house he now lived in, only one block from the Pennsylvania State House. By leaning forward and craning his neck, he could make out the figure of Major David Franks below. Franks was instructing a group of workmen who were carrying household goods of all kinds through the large cellar doors to the rear of the house.

"Franks, make sure you know where everything is," Arnold bellowed down the stairway.

"Not to worry, sir. It's all in good order," came the reply.

"Are we getting everything we asked for?"

"Indeed we are, sir."

"All right. Come see me as soon as you're finished."

"Aye, sir."

With difficulty, Arnold pulled himself to his feet, grasped his cane, and began his tentative path around to the central hall stairs to the second floor. He was prideful of his new house, which was repainted, recarpeted, and refurnished in several of the major rooms, after having endured ten months of the ducal reign of Sir William Howe, the commanding general of the British Army. In the central hall, Arnold encountered Punch, the chief butler and his personal manservant.

"May I assist you, sir?" Punch asked.

"No, thank you, Punch," Arnold replied, regarding the climb to the second floor as part of his minimal daily exercise. He began to shuffle his way up the stairs, one step at a time. It was an extremely difficult passage for him, and he stood at the top, clutching the corner post and gasping for breath. Wearily, he addressed Punch, who was still standing below: "I think I'll have the mineral bath this evening."

"Yes, sir," said Punch.

Arnold had taken over two adjoining rooms facing High Street for his personal use, one as the bedchamber, the other as his office. Across the hall was the doorway providing second-floor access to the wooden back buildings—the kitchen, privy, smokehouse, servants' quarters, bathhouse, and other facilities. It was in a small room next to the bathhouse that Punch had rigged up treatment facilities for Arnold's leg, including the copper bathtub.

Owned by the former governor of Pennsylvania, Richard Penn, the house was one of the best in Philadelphia, and was rent free to Arnold, since it was in the process of being confiscated by the State. In addition, Arnold had been promised funds from the State to manage his household and office as military governor, in addition to his salary and rations—which had not been paid for nearly three years.

He continued to be sought after for interviews, with the result that they now were restricted to a two-hour period beginning at noon at 190 High Street. Some of the callers were individuals with whom deals could be made, which is why Franks served as Arnold's business assistant instead of Clarkson, who was given more outside duties to perform. Though the son of a mercantile family in New York, Clarkson had the defect of frequently seeing things through rather disapproving eyes.

Most prominent among the visitors was the clothier-general of the army, James Mease, and his assistant, William West, who had the assignment of taking or purchasing at very low prices items that the army needed from the vast quantities of goods in the city that had belonged to the British Army or fleeing Loyalists. These goods would soon be appropriated by the State. Mease, who had come to see Arnold in the Slate-Roof House only four days after he had entered Philadelphia, reported that a substantial portion of the goods he could acquire were not really needed by the army. So he made a secret deal with General Arnold for the sale of these items at very depressed prices. This was the source of the quantities of food, wine, medical supplies, and gifts that were now flowing into the 190 High Street cellar.

Arnold was scanning the lists for invitees to the Fourth of July dinner dance at the City Tavern when Franks arrived upstairs from the cellar, looking as fashionable as he always did.

"Who gave you this list?" Arnold asked his aide, holding up a sheet of paper with very distinctive feminine handwriting.

"That's from my cousin, Becky Franks, sir. You remember, you wanted to make sure that we had plenty of good-looking young girls at the party. So I asked her to help."

Arnold had already noticed the name of Peggy Shippen on the list. "It looks as if she knows what she's doing. Good work, Franks."

"Thank you, sir. Do you know any of the people on her list?"

"None of your damned business."

Unperturbed, Franks had taken a seat next to the desk. "We really can't take any more goods, General," he said. "We have enough stuff in the cellar to last us a year."

"You're unloading the last wagon now."

"I know, but I'm afraid it's too much."

Arnold gave him a disgusted look, to which Franks replied with a hint of a smile and a shake of the head. "I think it could be quite embarrassing, sir."

"What?"

"Taking these goods at such low prices. From the clothier-general."

"My dear Franks. I have pointed this out to you before. I am only doing what any commanding officer would do in my situation. I have not been paid in nearly three years. I have not been compensated for the rations due to me. If I were to be paid, it would be in depressed continentals. Congress has refused to settle my accounts fairly. And I have not yet received anything from Pennsylvania to support me as military governor. Furthermore, I am acquiring these products for my own personal use, not for resale. Now, just answer one question. Do you want to do without these things?"

Franks was smiling now. "No, sir, I do not. But if you'll forgive me, it is an unusual and secret channel. And the army could sell these very same items for ten times the price."

Arnold regarded his aide bleakly. "I'm glad you want to stay. Because if you don't want to consume these rations, you'd be someplace else. Now I'm tired of explaining this to you. Perhaps I should switch you with Clarkson."

"Oh, no, sir!" Franks said. "I understand completely and you will hear from me no more on this subject."

Arnold had bypassed Franks and was looking to the doorway, where Punch stood. "What is it, Punch?"

"Beggin' your pardon, sir. There's a visitor here."

"Not until noon, dammit!"

"It's Captain Peale, sir. About the business next door."

Arnold fixed Franks with a stare. "Who's Captain Peale?"

"Oh, he's that artist fellow. A nice man, but a little strange. He works for Reed. In the patriot guard."

Arnold thought for a moment, and then said: "Punch, go tell Peale to be seated. Major Franks will be down in a moment." He turned to Franks as Punch left. "Go see what he wants, will you? And try to settle it."

Arnold watched Franks leave. He suspected that Peale's business had to do with Grace Galloway, who lived next door in the house on the corner of Sixth and High Streets. She had been left behind when her husband, Joseph, the leading Tory in Philadelphia, had fled with the British. Joseph Reed was now trying to evict her from the house, which was in the process of being formally confiscated by the State. Only a few days previously, Reed's troops had padlocked her parlor. Arnold had responded by putting sentries at various doors, thus allowing Mrs. Galloway to sleep soundly. Now what?

He soon found out when Franks returned a few minutes later. "I couldn't solve it myself," he said. "Peale very politely asks to borrow your chariot, so he can remove Mrs. Galloway in decent fashion. Instead of the chair he'll have to get if you don't cooperate."

"That Reed really is a bastard," Arnold said in disgust. "Go tell Peale—

very politely—that I can't cooperate with the State in this matter. So, he cannot use my chariot. Then come back and get the letter I'm going to write to Mrs. Galloway right now."

Arnold took a sheet of paper, dipped his quill, and wrote his offer to Mrs. Galloway to use his carriage at any time that she wished, for any purpose. But he also offered his housekeeper to help Mrs. Galloway pack, and apologized that he had no authority to change the course of events.

The second Fourth of July was to be celebrated enthusiastically, not only as Independence Day but also to commemorate the liberation and recovery of Philadelphia. The year before, the only official event had been the public reading of the Declaration of Independence by Joseph Reed. This year, the State authorities organized the giant parade in the afternoon, and General Arnold was in charge of the ball to take place in City Tavern in the evening.

The line of march, across High Street and north on Broad to the Bush Hill estate of lawyer Andrew Hamilton, just outside the city limits in the Northern Liberties, was watched by what surely was the largest crowd of people ever assembled in Philadelphia. Joseph Reed was prominent, leading his light horse troop. The military governor contributed his Massachusetts regiment, with its fife and drum corps. There were floats and decorations from each of the thirteen States and from the various guilds in the city—the bankers, vintners, seamen, butchers, carpenters, masons, and so on. Much in evidence was the flag of the United States, with its thirteen stars on a blue field and thirteen red and white bars. At the Bush Hill grounds, many toasts were drunk, the main oration was delivered by James Wilson, signer of the Declaration and the most prominent lawyer in town, and fireworks were set off to complement the thirteen-gun salute delivered by the frigate *Rising Sun,* anchored in the Delaware River. Adding to the joyous din were the booming sounds of the great bells that had been returned to the State House and Christ Church from their exile in Allentown.

Arnold had begged off participating in the parade because of his leg and watched for a while from his office at 190 High Street, as the marchers passed. In truth, Arnold's leg *was* fatigued, and he was suffering from a painful stomach ailment, the cause of which he did not know. Nevertheless, he was at City Tavern in the evening to welcome the ball guests, including those who came back across town from Bush Hill after the fireworks. The room was tastefully decorated in patriotic fashion, the music was elegant, and the refreshments and spirits were excellent.

The most fascinating feature of the party was the mix of guests, many of whom were well-known patriots, including some of the radical variety, and others composed of the more conservative classes, some even suspect of having Tory sympathies. This was the result of Arnold's policies as military governor and the work of his aides on the invitation list. Arnold was determined not to discriminate, to treat everyone even-handedly, and to try to bring people together instead of allowing bitterness and enmity to flourish. The pretty young ladies on Becky Franks's list were the very ones who had so brightened the British social scene during the occupation—the Chew sisters, the Shippen sisters, the Redmond sisters, and so many more. They certainly were pretty, and very fashionable, with elegant ball gowns and high hairstyles, all in contrast to the more old-fashioned hair and gowns of the patriot women. Things were a bit awkward at first, and before the evening was too far advanced, Joseph Reed and several other radicals shepherded their families out in silent protest. But Arnold was such a genial host, despite his ailments, and the spirits flowed so freely, that in the end a good time was had by all who remained.

This was particularly true of Arnold, though he was unable to dance. He sat comfortably in an alcove adjacent to the dancing floor, his bad leg propped on a cushion, and enjoyed the goings-on with great interest. Frequently, dignitaries and couples would stop by to chat with him. At one point, Becky Franks had managed to surround Arnold with a bevy of the beautiful young ladies of fashion, who laughed gaily, crooned over him, and incessantly asked questions about his famous exploits. Arnold enjoyed it all immensely and noted that one of the young ladies—Peggy Shippen—only smiled on the outer edge of the circle and said nothing.

The dancing was to resume, and the group broke up, the young ladies going to their partners for the next dance. Arnold managed to take Peggy Shippen's hand and held it tightly for a moment. "My dear Miss Shippen," he said, "I recall that we met exactly one year ago—to the day."

Peggy was radiantly lovely and her smile charming, as she said: "Yes, indeed, I remember it well. We first met four years ago, when you dined at our house."

Arnold smiled and nodded, and then said: "I realize you must go to your dance partner. At the next intermission, will you come see me again by yourself?"

It was the better part of an hour before Peggy was able to return, and this time Arnold had Clarkson and Franks lined up to delicately screen off other guests. Arnold rose somewhat unsteadily and took Peggy's hand for the obligatory kiss. "Please sit here, my dear. I'm so glad that you returned."

"Your leg must have been truly injured," Peggy said.

"Well, it was. It's healing now. Very slowly, I'm afraid."

"I thought it was an emblem of the battlefield. One that you brought back with you to impress the young ladies." She smiled demurely.

Arnold stiffened at the import of what Peggy was saying. "No, it was quite badly injured. Otherwise, I would not be here. I'd be off somewhere on a field command."

"I suspect you'd be happier if you were," Peggy said. "I see you've been losing some of your guests."

Arnold surveyed the young lady for a moment. She was talking at a level entirely different from what he had imagined. Not necessarily offensive, but sharp and to the point. He looked at her cool, level, grey-eyed gaze, at the smile that played at her lips. He then said: "Yes, we have lost some. The party seems to be getting better."

"You've lost quite a few," Peggy said. "Tell me, why did you invite some of the most noted citizens in town, the conservatives, the higher classes? I was surprised to receive an invitation."

Arnold was taken aback. "Really, Miss Shippen, I was expecting to have a nice conversation with you, a 'making your acquaintance' kind of conversation. Instead, I find I'm being grilled about who I invited to this party." He held up his hand to screen away Clarkson, who was advancing with a couple to introduce to him.

"I'm sorry," Peggy said, beginning to rise. "Sometimes I talk too much. It's not important."

"Oh, but it is," Arnold said. "Don't withdraw from me. I just want to tell you that it's my own disposition, and General Washington's as well, to be open to all people of this city, and not to discriminate on the basis of rumor and innuendo. We're trying to bridge the factions."

It was no longer possible to hold off people crowding nearby. Peggy was now standing. She said: "I don't know that it can be done."

Arnold took her hand and held on to it for a few seconds. "May I call upon you?"

Peggy was silent for a moment. "As you wish," she murmured as she withdrew.

Two days later, Peggy came downstairs in answer to a call from her father. He was standing in the central hall with Reuben, the houseman, and a tall, dark, well-attired man who was holding a bouquet of flowers. A box was sitting on the floor next to him, and through the side windows of the doorway Peggy could see his carriage parked outside.

"I believe this young man has something for you, my dear," Judge Shippen said.

"Please accept this, my lady, from Major-General Benedict Arnold," Punch said. He handed over the bouquet. "And this message, if you would be so kind."

Peggy took the flowers and opened the note. It was from General Arnold and said that he would call on her at the Shippen household in two days' time, unless there was some reason he should not do so.

"And for you, sir," Punch continued, turning to Judge Shippen. "Please accept this gift as a token of General Arnold's respect." He leaned over and picked up the box. "May I place it somewhere for you, sir?"

"Uh—just on that table, if you will," the Judge said, indicating a large coffee table in the parlor. The young man carried the box over and then withdrew, touching his forehead as he spoke: "Thank you very much. And a most pleasant day to you both." And then he was gone.

Peggy and the Judge looked at each other. "Well, this is very interesting," he said.

Reuben's wife, Lucille, had come into the room. "Do you think you could find a vase, please?" Peggy asked, as she handed the flowers to her.

"Oh, how lovely," Lucille said. She took the flowers and left.

The Judge said to Reuben: "That's all for now, Reuben. I'll call you later." He then went over to sit on the sofa and gaze at the box. "Let's see what we have here. Come sit with me, my dear." Fishing out his penknife, he opened the top of the box to reveal six bottles of claret. He withdrew one and examined it carefully.

"My goodness," he said, "I haven't seen wine this elegant in years." He set the bottle down and gazed at Peggy. "To what do we owe this? The Fourth of July dance?"

"I'm afraid so," Peggy said.

"Well, tell me."

Peggy shook her head slowly. "It was nothing. This man is an invalid. He can't dance. I spoke to him on two occasions. Very briefly." Peggy looked up at her father. "When I left he was telling me that he was trying to bridge the factions in the city. He asked if he could call on me. I just said something and then left. 'As you wish,' I said. Or something like that."

Judge Shippen was feeling very good. For weeks he had been haunted by fears that there would be a backlash against him for the active role his daughters had played in the British social season. Now, suddenly, his youngest daughter was being pursued by none other than Benedict Arnold!

"I think we should give him some excuse as to why he should not come here," Peggy suggested.

"Nonsense!" her father replied. "I should be delighted to know him. He's the best general they have. Let him come to see us, several times. I wouldn't worry about it, if I were you. After all, he must be more than twice your age."

Benedict Arnold was a man of wide-ranging experience for Mr. and Mrs. Shippen and their daughters to probe when he called at teatime two days hence. He was, of course, on his best behavior, even speaking in neutral tones of people he detested, such as Horatio Gates and Joseph Reed, and a spellbinder in talking about remote and unknown venues—the high seas, the deep wilderness, battles in the far north.

Betsy and Sarah joined their parents and Peggy in having tea with the distinguished general and were quite fascinated by him, as Peggy sat silent for the most part, watching the performance of the man who had come to see her. Both Betsy and her father urged General Arnold to come again when Neddy Burd would be present, the former soldier and future husband of Betsy, who was so intrigued by the battles in the north.

For a time, Arnold responded to questions about the administration of the city and discussed his relationship with the Supreme Executive Council, pointing to differences with the radical leaders of the city and his hopes to prevent undue vengeance taking. This was of very real interest to Judge Shippen, but the two men did not allow the subject to dominate, both conscious that there would be an occasion in the future when they could talk of such matters.

Nearly two hours of conversation passed before Judge Shippen reluctantly moved to terminate the meeting by rising to take Mrs. Shippen's arm. With effusions of gratitude and hopes that there would be another such occasion soon, they left the room, followed by Betsy and Sarah, to allow Peggy to say good-bye to the guest.

She came out on the doorstep with Arnold and said: "You're very good, you know. They all loved you."

Arnold looked at her quizzically. "There you go again, Miss Shippen. I never know exactly what you mean." As Peggy started to reply, Arnold held up his hand and said: "Let us sit for a moment, there in the garden. I find it hard to stand up for very long as the day lengthens. Just a few moments." He led Peggy toward the wrought iron furniture in the side garden as Punch, already expecting Arnold to do what he did, remained seated quietly in the driver's chair of the parked chaise.

As soon as they were seated, Arnold said: "Forgive me for saying it, my dear, but though we've had very little time speaking alone, almost everything you say has a possible double meaning to it. In fact, it's a quality I thought I noticed in you when we met a year ago, just by your expression, for we said very little."

"It must have been imaginary then, for it is certainly so now."

Arnold smiled. "I would certainly accept your denial. But our conversations are not at all as I imagined they would be. For example, just now I thought I heard you saying that I was not entirely truthful with your family."

Peggy laughed. "Oh, no, sir, you were fascinating. I only meant that a man who fights in war and has no enemies is passing strange."

"Ah, I see." Arnold smiled. "You have caught me. Yes, I must confess there were gentlemen whom I would speak of quite differently, were I talking to comrades. I think it's a pardonable offense in a first conversation with a family."

"I agree," said Peggy. "Now, I must go in, sir. My parents will wonder what is detaining me." She rose.

Sensing that he had only a few seconds in which to make a final point, Arnold stood up and took Peggy's hand. "Of course, my dear. Just let me say, in parting, that I truly am trying to bridge the factions in this city. I know that you have doubts about the Revolution. I see that as no reason why we cannot get to know each other better. I shall call again."

Peggy nodded and said, "As you wish, sir," and then she was gone.

Arnold watched her enter the house and then began to walk painfully toward his carriage as Punch came down to assist him. Arnold's mind was flowing with thoughts of young Peggy Shippen. A much smarter lady than he had had any reason to assume. She made Betsy DeBlois of Boston suddenly seem very ordinary. Thank God for the quirks of fate that had saved him from her and presented him with Peggy Shippen. For very different reasons, this would not be easy. He was deliciously excited by the challenge. In all, a satisfactory beginning, he thought.

Chapter 45

Philadelphia
Summer and Fall, 1778

A story told to Benedict Arnold by one of his long-term guests at 190 High Street confirmed for him something he already knew instinctively—that he was considered an enemy by Congressman Joseph Reed and his radical allies in the Supreme Executive Council of Pennsylvania.

Silas Deane, an old friend from Connecticut, had arrived with a French fleet of twenty-one warships at Delaware Bay on July 9th. He and Conrad Alexandre Gerard, the first French minister plenipotentiary to the United States, had accepted Arnold's invitation to be his guests, after Arnold had hosted an elaborate welcoming party on July 11th for the French dignitaries. Deane, one of the first American emissaries to France, had come home to deal with charges of mishandling of funds in Paris. He took Arnold aside one evening to tell him of his encounter with Joseph Reed.

After pouring a brandy for Arnold and sitting next to him in a leather chair in the small downstairs drawing room, Deane said: "I want to tell you in confidence, Ben, that before I accepted your kind invitation to stay here with you, I was accosted on the street by Joseph Reed. You know him, of course. The Pennsylvania congressman who's affiliated with the radical leadership of the state."

"Indeed I do," Arnold responded, leaning forward. "What did he want?"

"Well, he warned me not to stay here with you. Said it would greatly endanger my own reputation as a patriot. What the devil does he mean by that?"

Arnold grimaced, as a draft of brandy hit his stomach. He shook his head, and then replied: "It means that he dislikes me. He's a radical, as you say. And I am a moderate. I'm trying to appeal to all elements of Philadelphia society, and he doesn't like it one bit. He wants to hang some five hundred suspected Tories, and the trials of some twenty-five or so are starting soon."

"I know he's a troublemaker."

"I don't think you're in any danger here," Arnold said.

"No, I don't think so," Deane said, as he roared with laughter.

Arnold's days were busy, as he carried out the functions of the military governor in public and looked for profitable deals to make in private, just as he was certain any self-respecting commander would do. Increasingly, he began to run into the opposition of the State of Pennsylvania, not always at first, but gradually, as Joseph Reed and his colleagues focused their sights on him.

A good example of the disputes between them was the private use of public wagons. Arnold used his authority to send twelve Pennsylvania wagons to the port of Chestnut Neck in New Jersey to bring back to Philadelphia a portion of the cargo of the *Charming Nancy,* which had been sequestered there by an American privateer. Arnold cleared 7,500 pounds in the deal with Robert Shewell—but in time the use of the wagons for private gain became a celebrated issue.

In another case, Arnold took up the cause of Gideon Olmstead and his men, who, as prisoners aboard the British vessel *Active,* had overpowered the crew and brought the ship into Chestnut Neck. Arnold advanced money to Olmstead for a congressional appeal after the court in the coastal town, headed by Joseph Reed's cousin, awarded Olmstead only one fourth the value of the ship. The appeal was won on September 15th, giving Olmstead the full value, which meant a secret prize to Arnold of 15,000 pounds. But, ignoring the will of Congress, Pennsylvania refused to pay, causing a loss to Arnold.

And so the wins and losses went through the summer and fall of 1778, as Arnold pursued his interests and Joseph Reed increasingly became annoyed by him. On August 25th, Arnold marked the birthday of the French King, Louis XVI, with a ball at 190 High Street, inviting once again political opponents, Reed's friends who were coalescing into a loose party know as the Constitutional Society, and old-line Philadelphians, who were forming a group known as the Republicans. By this time, the radicals could no longer tolerate neutrality or dissent. For Reed, the August 25th party was a declaration of war. In September, Reed accepted a bid from the Supreme Executive Council to become president of the State of Pennsylvania and also special counsel to prosecute suspected Loyalists, at a salary of two thousand pounds and the use of a confiscated house, horses, and carriages. Reed resigned from Congress to take the new position. And he selected the Grace Galloway house, next door to Benedict Arnold, as his private residence.

Reed redoubled his efforts to hang Loyalists, pressing dozens of cases in the courts. The noted lawyer James Wilson defended almost all of the accused people and saved all of them except two—John Roberts and Abram Carlisle, both Quakers. They were scheduled to hang in early November, and the contest between Reed and Arnold intensified as the date drew near. Most prominent was the vitriolic commentary in the local newspapers against Arnold, as Reed consolidated his control.

Nothing in Benedict Arnold's daily life could restrict his attention to Miss Peggy Shippen. The warrior had truly fallen in love, seeing Peggy as more than a beautiful face and figure, but also as a person of remarkable qualities. The prospect of life without her had become an unimaginable void in his mind.

Peggy's progress came more slowly. In one of their early encounters, she had tried to put a stop to their growing courtship by apologizing for her remarks at their first meeting and drawing out the marked contrast between an eighteen-year-old young lady who had hardly ever been outside of Philadelphia and a thirty-six-year-old general of the army, with a long and fascinating and wordly career as merchant and soldier already behind him.

Arnold responded that her earlier remarks had revealed some wit and spirit. As for their present roles, he believed that age was not important, that what really counted was the interest they had for each other.

In truth, Peggy was still in the shadow of the British social season and the gaiety of John André. And so, she reasoned, after listening to Arnold, why not let herself be entertained by the most prominent and unusual man in Philadelphia, instead of sitting home alone, absorbed in memories of something that would never happen to her again in her lifetime? The courtship had continued, with Peggy appearing at dinners at 190 High Street, on Arnold's arm at the same Southwark Theater that she had attended with John André, and at other balls and musicales in the city. They made frequent use of the parlor in the Morris household, Mrs. Robert Morris acting as the indispensable third party in a budding romance.

Soon Peggy learned that Arnold's talk of trying to bridge factions in the city was not nonsense, as she first had believed, and that intrigued her deeply. What could motivate a man with Arnold's history to be so conscious of the need to heal wounds? She became more interested in him, more happy to be with him and to learn from him.

She also took comfort in the thought that her family liked General Arnold and regarded the burgeoning romance as something good and proper—until she had a conversation with her father one evening in mid-September. He took her arm after supper and guided her into his study.

"Peggy, my dear," he began, after seating her on the small sofa, "I want to talk to you about the growing attention General Arnold has been paying to you. I'm wondering whether or not it's time when you might want to consider ending it."

Peggy was astonished. "But, Father—how can you say that? I thought everyone in the family was so pleased—except for Edward, of course. I never doubted *you*—I wanted to stop it right at the outset, but you wouldn't hear of it."

"I know, I know." The Judge shook his head wearily. "I never thought it would go anywhere. I certainly do not wish to offend the gentleman. I'm very approving of his attitude toward the radicals. But we've seen so much of him recently. He's quite serious, you know. There's no mistaking that. I'm sure he has it in mind to marry you if he can possibly find a way to do it."

"Oh, Father. I don't think so."

"He's so much older than you. He has three young children. Just think of some way of slowing it down. You can never be sure."

"What about General Arnold's friendship with our family serving as a kind of . . . of protection for us? For you especially. Peggy Chew's father is in prison. Becky Franks and her parents are being banished from the city. There are people on trial for their lives—only because they served the British in some way. You could be in danger, Father."

"Perhaps," the Judge said, taking his daughter's hands in his. "But I don't think that's a problem. We've survived through years of hardships, without a disaster befalling us. Except for the steady disappearance of money." The Judge rolled his eyes upward.

Peggy thought of the poor fare that had been served to General Arnold in her house, the worn rugs, the patched chairs in the dining room—all in contrast to the elegance of his surroundings at 190 High Street.

"Besides, I'm not talking of a complete break with the general," the Judge continued. "We'd still be friends, of sorts. I just don't see myself as a man who's trading his safety for the hand of his lovely young daughter. I'm thinking of you, of your future."

"I don't think there's any concern there," Peggy said.

On a bright Thursday in September, Arnold and Peggy had planned a day together, a carriage ride out of the city for a picnic lunch at John Bartram's Botanical Garden on the opposite shore of the Schuylkill River. It was a beautiful, sunny day, perfect for a picnic, and Arnold's housekeeper had prepared a delectable basket of cold chicken, ham, fruits, cheese, bread, and wine. With Punch at the reins, the carriage had called for Peggy at home at ten and then loped its way southwestward toward Grey's Ferry. It was a relaxed, restful ride through the thinning city, to the outskirts, to the ferry, Arnold and Peggy bantering lazily with small talk on the way.

After crossing the river, Punch turned south a mile and a half along the Schuylkill to the arched entrance to the garden, which was the enchanted wonderland of Bartram's wide-ranging botanical travels. The old man had died a few years earlier, after a lifetime of travel and exploration in botany, which had come to the attention of Linnaeus of Sweden and other great European botanists. Now his gardens were owned by his son William, who was following his father's direction.

With frequent rest stops for Arnold, he and Peggy strolled through various clusters of plantings, with little placards in the ground revealing what was being seen, some strange and others familiar. As soon as Arnold discerned that his arm about Peggy's waist had become a bid for support to supplement his gold-headed cane, he turned back toward the central area and the sight of Punch and the wagon. He waved and indicated a large flat rock down the bank toward the Schuylkill River.

Punch set up the luncheon from the basket and retired to the carriage. Peggy and Arnold ate slowly at first, and then ravenously, passing the delicacies back and forth and sipping wine. After they were sated, they leaned back and drank in the beautiful day, beset for the moment with their own thoughts. Peggy glanced at the man lying next to her, his eyes now to the sky. There was none of the ferociousness of the warrior that she had expected. Despite his familiarity with war, Arnold had always been gentle with her, had been gentle with everyone she knew. His prominent nose and firm chin precluded handsomeness, yet his face now stirred her more than any other, more than the perfect features of John André. She realized, with a sinking feeling, that she had come to accept Becky Franks's judgment, that André's sexual orientation was strange, and with that, the memories of those days seemed dim, seemed idealistic. In Benedict Arnold, she had found a man of great strength, in whose arms she could imagine safety and security, and yet she was still not certain. What could she bring, a woman barely adult, who had scarcely traveled outside of her home? What of the great differences between them? What of her father's judgment? Her eyes crested with tears.

Arnold saw her filmy eyes and sat up abruptly, putting his arm around her shoulder. "What is it, Peggy? What's the matter?"

Peggy dabbed at her eyes. "Oh, it's nothing. It's just—" Peggy had not meant to tell Arnold of her father's views. It came out impulsively. "My father—he knew of our plans for today, of course. And something stirred within him. The other evening he suggested I consider ending our relationship."

Arnold was genuinely surprised. He'd enjoyed his conversations with the old man, who always seemed happy to see him, to talk about the war and the city and Joseph Reed. "Did he say why?" he asked.

"It was nothing personal," Peggy hastened to say. "I mean with you, personally. He very much approves what you're trying to do in the city. He values your friendship. It's just the differences between us—age, experience."

Arnold thought for a moment. Suddenly he had a "dragon" at the gates, just as he had with Betsy DeBlois. But this situation was very different. "And how do you feel?" he finally asked Peggy.

Her eyes dry now, with a small smile, Peggy said: "I know that I'm no longer Peggy Shippen in the city. Now I'm 'the general's lady.' " She stopped short of mentioning the subject of marriage, as her father had. It was in the air, but she did not want to bring it up. "I certainly don't want to stop seeing you."

"Good," Arnold said. "Your father's concerns are quite natural, when you really think about it. Let's just keep on as we are. Give him time to change his mind. Something will happen soon."

"Please don't say I told you. I hadn't meant to. It's just came out." She tossed her hair. "I can't keep anything from you."

"I won't. I suspect I'll hear about it from his own lips, sooner or later. And I'll be prepared. Thank you for your confidence."

The two fell silent for a while. Arnold leaned back on both of his hands on his layers of blankets, his legs straight ahead of him on the rock, staring at the river. It was wider here as it neared its junction with the Delaware, several hundred yards wide, and skimpy compared to the great river on the other side of the city. His mind was churning. Peggy could keep nothing from him. And he knew he could keep nothing from her.

He began speaking: "This is a very difficult situation. I'm the military commander in this area, but my options are very limited. I have an implacable foe in Joseph Reed, who's just accepted the presidency of the State. He's selecting the house right next door to me to move into," Arnold said, with a bitter laugh. "I work for General Washington, who works for the Congress. Those are my two bases, the Congress and the army. And I have to say, I don't think much of the Congress. For several years now, they've been unable to reimburse me for money I've laid out for the campaign. They haven't paid my salary. I can survive, because of money I earned before the war. But it's unfair. It's dishonest. Now Reed—he works for the sovereign State of Pennsylvania. He's very powerful. He's not above threatening General Washington to get his way. Just a small slice of the population put Reed in power. I think most people in the city would support what I'm trying to do. But Reed has the power. There's a revolution within the Revolution. Reed and his radical supporters against the lawyers and merchants and tradesmen of the city. I'm the only leader they have. And the power's stacked against me. I'm not afraid of him. I'll fight him to the end, if I have to. But it's very difficult."

Arnold looked out at the river again, now silent. Peggy sat very still, not sure what to say. At length, Arnold began again. "When the war started, I leaped into it. I'd done very well in my trading business. But I was bored. The war was a heaven-sent opportunity for me. A chance to show what I could do. Just excel on the battlefield, I told myself, and you'll be rewarded by your grateful countrymen. And so I plunged in with everything I had. And it worked—up to a point. A year and a half ago, I wasn't promoted to major-general by the Congress. Five others were promoted over me, and I had done more than all five of them put together. I tried to resign, but they had sent me north and I was victorious—at Stanwix and Saratoga. And my trouble worsened. I got this." He laid his hand along his injured left thigh. "And my former friend, Horatio Gates, failed to mention me in any of his dispatches. So I came back here, to civilization."

He leaned down, taking Peggy in his arms. He said: "And I found you. And I wouldn't have it any other way." His face turned somber again, and he looked off into the distance. "As for civilization—I find it wanting. Very wanting. It's more an anarchy than anything else. No standards. No appreciation. A crude society. Thirteen little countries and an army that's continually starved. And individuals treated like dirt." He paused for a moment, then spoke somberly: "I really think we've made a mistake."

Peggy looked at him closely. "What do you mean?"

"I think we made a mistake," he repeated. "We never should've gone to war against Great Britain." Her face was very close to his, her eyes staring at him. He leaned down and brushed her lips with his. And then he kissed her deeply.

A hundred yards away, Punch stood in the shade of Bartram's house, leaning against the carriage. He watched the two lovers kiss. He smiled, thinking that his employer was doing very well.

What was said at the picnic turned in Arnold's mind for several days. He finally decided that it would be best to get the issue of his future with Peggy firmly on the table. He decided to write a letter to Peggy that was just short of a proposal of marriage, and a letter to her father to request his approval. For several evenings he toiled with pen and paper, trying to find the right words. He took out the letter he had written to Betsy DeBlois two years earlier and scanned it. He could do no better than that. He wrote down the opening:

Dear Madame—

Twenty times have I taken up my pen to write to you, and as often has my trembling hand refused to obey the dictates of my heart—a heart which, though calm and serene amidst the clashing of arms and all the din and horrors of war, trembles with diffidence and the fear of giving offense when it attempts to address you on a subject so important to its happiness. . . .

He continued with the extravagant language of love, but varied the text here and there to more contemporary times. At last satisfied, he turned to the task of writing to the Judge. He wanted no dowry, just Peggy:

My fortune is not large, though sufficient (not to depend upon my expecta-
tions) to make us both happy. I neither expect nor wish a dowry with Miss Ship-
pen. . . . Our difference in political sentiments will, I hope, be no bar to my
happiness. I flatter myself that the time is at hand when our unhappy contests
will be at an end, and peace and domestic happiness will be restored to everyone.

He dispatched both letters to the Shippen home on September 25th. Only
a little more than a week passed before Arnold found himself seated in Judge
Shippen's library, sharing a glass of wine with him.

"I hope you understand, General," the Judge said, "that my objection is
not personal at all, but answers to the more practical factors. The age and experience difference, that fact that you were already married and have three children from that state. I am deeply sorry, of course, to know the death of your
wife, but these are difficult times we live in."

"I take your point, sir, but in truth I must say that your opposition can only
be seen by me as a personal blow, of another kind perhaps, but one that could
affect me personally throughout my life."

"Yes, well, let us shift our attention away from you and on Peggy herself.
She is only now midway in her eighteenth year. Less than six months ago she
was completely immersed in the social net of the British occupation. Three of
my girls were among the favorites and they were busy every week. We could do
nothing to stop it. I hope you understand that. Toward the end, Peggy was very
much enamored of a most glamorous young officer. I lived in fear that I would
hear talk of matrimony. Fortunately, the British left, sooner than they expected
to, I warrant, and the problem was solved. I daresay she will never see or talk
again to this young man, but she was in a deplorable state. And now—only a
few months later!"

"Who was the young man?" Arnold asked, feeling a strange pang of jealousy. He had, of course, known of the gay British social life in Philadelphia, but
had never fixed Peggy with a particular male.

"Well, it hardly makes a difference, does it? She was swept away by a handsome young man who suddenly disappeared. A first case of childish love. And
now, only a few months later!" The Judge fell silent for a moment, his brow
knitted in thought. "Yet—I have heard Peggy say nothing of a permanent life
together."

Arnold thought quickly. He did not want to press again on the question of
the other man. He would have to talk to Peggy. And Shippen had narrowed his
objections down, on this occasion at least, to one that Arnold felt secure about.
He needed time.

He rose and said: "I am content to let this rest for a while. We both need to
see what Peggy herself wants. May I suggest that we talk again—perhaps a
month or more in the future?"

*   *   *

Relations with Peggy were strained for a while, as Arnold pressed her on the point of the unknown young Briton. Finally, Peggy realized that it was foolish of her to try to hide it. She had a perfectly good point, though not entirely an accurate one. And Arnold himself obviously had been in love before. His sister, Hannah, and his youngest son, Henry, were now in residence at 190 High Street to prove it. The two older boys were still at school in Middleton. These three children all manifested his love for his wife. Yes, Peggy thought, she was younger, but did that mean that she would be denied ever having felt the taste of love?

She told him one cold night in October about John André, on the way home from Southwark Theater in the carriage. "He's a very handsome and talented young man. Everyone loved him. He was the designer of the *Meshianza*. We seemed very close, and I thought I could spend my life with him. I was wrong." She paused, and tried to think of how she could make her point to Arnold in a way that he could understand. "He liked me very much. But he didn't love me. He couldn't love me." Her eyes turned to Arnold, appealing.

"I don't understand. There's *no* one who could not love you," he said.

"No, you don't see what I'm trying to say." Peggy fought back a sob and tried again. "He's a man who cannot love *any* woman." It wasn't enough. What else could she say? "It's the only explanation for his behavior."

Arnold stared quietly at Peggy. He tried very hard to understand what she was saying—and then suddenly he thought he could. It was not what he had expected to hear. Finally he spoke: "That is either the truth—or the most fanciful story I've ever heard."

"Well, it's the truth. Frankly, I don't care what you think it is."

The issue was getting dangerous. Arnold had other questions, but they could wait. He decided it was time to make amends. "My dear sweet Peggy," he said, taking her hand, "I love you so much I can't bear the thought of someone else. It's a fault I fully own up to. Please forgive me, and we'll say no more of this."

The date for the execution of the two Quakers, Abram Carlisle and John Roberts, was set for November 4th. Lawyer James Wilson had done all that he could, as had Arnold, but now Reed was set for his triumph. Arnold had heard the tales from the court, of Roberts's ten children on their knees, begging for their father's life.

As far as Arnold was concerned, the two men had certainly served the British, but so had thousands of others. What Arnold was against was the death penalty, and he gave Philadelphians a chance to express themselves on the evening before the execution by hosting a reception at the City Tavern for those in favor of commuting the sentence. The place was mobbed by people from the majority of Philadelphians who called themselves "Republicans," who came in an effort to save the lives of Carlisle and Roberts. It was to no avail.

The next day, Carlisle and Roberts were marched through the streets from the Walnut Street prison to the Centre Court of the city where the gallows awaited, their hands and legs cuffed. The crowds lining the streets and the Centre were huge, and were mostly somber. The war was commencing.

From the Narrative of David Franks

I look back now upon that season in Philadelphia as if it had occurred in a different life, in another country. Benedict Arnold had become military governor of the place at the precise time that the most radical government of any of the thirteen States now had its first chance to assert its full power. Arnold came in to uphold the standards of the Revolution of the United States, and found himself threatened by the new and incipient radical revolution of Pennsylvania, led by the New Light Presbyterian from New Jersey, the puritanical Joseph Reed, and his fanatical followers.

The leaders of the real *Revolution—the American one—did not want to be distracted by what was happening in Pennsylvania. And the majority of citizens in Philadelphia—the merchants, the lawyers, the shopkeepers, the professional men—were too confused and uncertain on how to act for too long. That left Arnold exposed in his opposition to the Supreme Executive Council, and he paid the price.*

Everyone knows Benedict Arnold today. No one knows of Joseph Reed and the Supreme Executive Authority. But they were real, not in another country, but in Philadelphia at that time, the dark underside of the American Revolution that could have become very bloody indeed. I know. Because I was there. And I know that two of the most minor actions of mine were inflated into major charges against Arnold by Reed. One was Arnold's issuance of a pass to go to New York for Hannah Levy, daughter of the partner of my uncle in their firm that was destroyed by Reed, the mercantile firm of Levy and Franks. This led Congress, pressed by Philadelphia, to take from Arnold the authority to issue passes. My other great mistake was in sending a militia sergeant on duty with us to fetch my barber to help me rearrange my hair. After a series of errors, the sergeant ran home to tell his father what had happened—and his father turned out to be Timothy Matlack, Reed's right-hand man! "Misuse of militia" became a charge against Arnold and even worse, led to the outbreak of newspaper criticism of the general, as vile and scurrilous an attack as I've ever seen.

The hanging of the two Quakers and Arnold's opposition set the war into motion. From that moment on, Reed and his cohorts concentrated on bringing Arnold down.

Chapter 46

Middlebrook and Philadelphia
February–April, 1779

The closed carriage lurched along the wintry road. Having left Trenton behind, Punch, in the driver's box, was heading northeast for Washington's headquarters in Middlebrook for the second night of a journey to Esopus, New York. Arnold had left Philadelphia on furlough for talks with New York State officials in Esopus regarding the disposition of large estates to the north. Encouraged by Philip Schuyler and the New York congressional delegation, he had been in correspondence with Governor Clinton and other officials over his candidacy to acquire either the vast William Johnson estate north of the Mohawk or the Skenesboro estate of nearly forty thousand acres east of the Hudson, as a reward for his services in protecting New York for the three previous years. Arnold liked Skenesboro, a better area for mills and other manufacturing enterprises. Besides, he *had* captured Skenesboro.

Details were not yet set. Arnold would have to purchase the estate, but at a privileged person's price, a fraction of the real value. The exact amount still had to be settled. The idea was that Arnold could then sell off plots of his land to former comrades-in-arms, creating a rural community, and some day a city. A dividend for the State would be that the growing community would be a hedge against incursions by hostile Indians or Britons from the north. Peggy had agreed that Arnold should proceed, despite her reservations about taking land that had been confiscated from Loyalists. She was toying with the vision of being the lady of a very large estate, starting life anew in the fresh woods of the wilderness and leaving the toils of Philadelphia. Arnold was enchanted by the opportunity to take advantage now and leave the army and Philadelphia thoroughly behind him. He was sure he could pay for the land. It would be a small amount, and he could deposit something up front and defray the rest through his sales.

The subject had been an animated one between Peggy and Arnold for several weeks. They were planning for the future because they were now secretly engaged to be married. No date had been set. They were still waiting for the conversion of Judge Shippen.

Arnold's mind was filled with images of Peggy in recent weeks, their breathless betrothal to one another, the lure of the vast land deal ahead of them that would dominate their future. He sat back in the chilly interior, a huge robe spread across his legs and midsection, his head lolling in the corner of the cab as he dreamed of the future. After a time, his mind began to ricochet between such endearing thoughts and the visage of his enemy, Joseph Reed, and the abuses he and his henchman had set for the military governor.

For more than two months there had been a steady stream of charges of misconduct directed at Arnold's establishment and withering coverage in several Philadelphia newspapers. Arnold wrote rebuttal notes to the newspapers, but they invariably opened a new and more dangerous response. Timothy Matlack, as editor of the *Packet,* had taken the ridiculous criticism of David Franks's sending his militia sergeant in search of his barber and escalated it to new heights. Arnold had written temperate letters to Matlack, only to have them misconstrued and taken advantage of. Most recently, Matlack had unearthed the mound of John Brown's criticism from the Canadian campaign of several years ago and reprinted it. When Arnold protested that the whole issue had been settled in his favor by Congress, Matlack wrote that the congressional decision was in default because Brown had never been brought to Philadelphia to testify. And he continued to use material from that file, most recently writing:

When I meet your carriage in the streets, and think of the splendor in which you live and revel, of the settlement which it is said you have proposed in a certain case, and of the decent frugality necessarily used by other officers of the army, it is impossible to avoid the question, "From whence have these riches flowed if you did not plunder Montreal?"

Arnold's angry reply was lost in the shuffle, as the charges continued. Far better to contemplate the future with Peggy than to lose one's temper with the hostilities of the moment. His mind turned to the night in December at the Shippen home when Betsy and Neddy Burd had been married, an obvious precursor to another similar moment that should occur soon. Arnold had liked Burd very much, a fine young man with a good record in the army, once having been captured by the British, and now completing his law studies with Judge Shippen's father in Lancaster. Burd had been excited by Arnold's presence, so near to the family circle, and so he had become an ally in promoting the marriage of Peggy and Arnold.

Arnold became drowsy in his corner as the carriage rolled along, a lulling melody in its repetitive sounds and movements. He thought he heard faint sounds of a horseman, and then woke with a start as the rider pulled up next to his doorway. Arnold began to search for his pistol in his belongings when he heard the familiar voice of Matthew Clarkson calling to him. The carriage stopped and Arnold pulled the window down.

"I'm sorry to overtake you, sir," Clarkson shouted. "But there's important news. Reed and the council—they've preferred formal charges against you. Here's today's paper." Clarkson handed over the rolled-up newspaper.

Arnold took the *Packet* and unfolded it to see the story of the charges against him on the front page. There was also a story about Arnold leaving town to avoid prosecution. A third story listed benefits, such as use of militia, that would now be denied to the military governor. A stream of invective flowed from Arnold as he slapped the paper down. With an effort, he got control and said to Clarkson: "We need to talk about this. We'll stop at the next tavern or inn."

After supper that evening at the Middlebrook camp, Arnold found himself alone with Washington in the commander-in-chief's office. The room was dimly lit by candles, but the chief was reading the *Packet,* as Arnold sat there waiting.

"Illegal pass for the *Charming Nancy,*" Washington murmured. "Closing the shops so that you could purchase illegal goods. Degrading services imposed on militiamen. What was that?"

"My aide asked his sergeant to fetch the barber. And then he—"

"Oh, yes, I remember. How trivial!" Washington resumed reading. "Interference in a prize case. The sloop *Active,* I believe. An illegal pass to an improper person, Hannah Levy. And these last two charges are just critical of your attitude toward the State." Washington looked up at Arnold. "It's really absurd to let this go to a civil court. Yet you can't ignore it."

"All of these charges are either inaccurate or trivial," Arnold said.

"They must be answered," Washington said. "Pennsylvania has been enough of a problem for us."

"I wouldn't be comfortable in Reed's own court," Arnold said. "I'd much rather deal with a court-martial composed of my fellow officers."

"Yes," the chief said. "You might want to try a congressional committee first. Say that your authority goes that way. It's a perfectly supportable course."

The officers at camp were all supportive. They told Arnold to go on to Esopus. Reed could wait. The weather was frigid and snow threatened, so Arnold decided to return to Philadelphia, to be with Peggy again and to seek relief from Congress. Late that night, in the small cabin he had been allotted, Arnold wrote three letters. One was to Philip Schuyler, explaining how bad the weather was, the reason for calling off the trip. The second was to the Philadelphia newspapers, criticizing the widespread distribution of the charges and declaring that he would ask Congress to hear them, to prove the council's allegations "as gross a prostitution of power as ever disgraced a weak and divided administration." Finally, he wrote to Peggy:

My dearest life,
   Never did I so long to see or hear from you as at this instant. I am all impatience and anxiety to know how you do. Six days' absence from my dear Peggy is

intolerable. . . . I am heartily tired with my journey and almost so with human nature. I daily discover so much baseness and ingratitude among mankind that I almost blush at being of the same species, and could quit the stage without regret were it not for some few gentle, generous souls like my dear Peggy who still retain the lively expression of their Maker's image, and who with smiles of benignity and goodness make all happy around them. Let me beg of you not to suffer the rude attacks on me to give one moment's uneasiness; they can do me no injury. I am treated with the greatest politeness by General Washington and the officers of the army, who bitterly execrate Mr. Reed and the Council for their villainous attempt to injure me. . . . The day after tomorrow I leave this, and hope to be made happy by your smiles on Friday evening. . . . Please present my best respects to our Mama and the family. . . .

Arnold returned to a Philadelphia in turmoil over the charges made against him. In Congress, Reed's men presented a motion to remove Arnold from command. It lost, with only Pennsylvania having a majority favoring it. Again, every State but Pennsylvania voted to refer Reed's charges to a committee headed by William Paca, a rich planter from Maryland whose wife was one of Peggy Shippen's friends. It became clear to Arnold that the State was not ready for prosecution, lacking evidence for most of the charges and not trusting the auspices of Congress. For two weeks the council criticized the committee, sending no representatives to confer with Paca and providing evidence only on the misuse of wagons. Reed forbade the committee to consider any other charge and threatened the committee "if any misstep should be taken." Paca calmly replied that the council would have nothing "to fear from our report."

On March 5th, Arnold's carriage took him the two blocks to Independence Hall for his hearing before the Paca Committee. The State sent no representative. Arnold was alone and calmly ticked off the facts to each of the eight charges, though not mentioning his financial interest in several of the issues. He concluded: "The president and council of the State will excuse me if I cannot divest myself of humanity to my enemies and common civility to all mankind in general, merely out of compliance to them."

The committee's report made March a happy month for Arnold. He was acquitted of six of the eight charges that the committee felt came within their power. The other two—misuse of militia and using wagons—should be considered by General Washington and a court-martial convened at headquarters, the committee proposed. Arnold was joyous. Washington would make short work of these two trivial charges. He told Peggy that the way was now clear for him to resign as military governor and prepare for a new life with her.

*   *   *

A few days later, Arnold's carriage rolled through Philadelphia's streets on its way to the Northern Liberties. It was an unusually warm day for early March, the sun streaming through the windows. Peggy was bright-eyed and cheerful, and kept badgering Arnold for clues to the "surprise" they were going to see.

"Darling, you've told me *nothing*! Give me a clue, at least!"

Arnold smiled broadly. "You'll see for yourself soon!"

"Oh, pshaw!"

Arnold was enjoying himself immensely. For weeks he had worked on the deal, paying seven thousand pounds, putting five thousand pounds down, and placing his New Haven house on the market to come up with the balance. He was riding in his carriage with the most beautiful woman in Philadelphia, soon to be his, and on their way to see something that would surely gladden her heart. And gladden the heart of the stubborn old Judge, her father.

"I'll give you a clue," Arnold announced.

Peggy turned to him in anticipation, looking impossibly beautiful with her wide-open eyes and smile.

"What we're going to see," Arnold said, "may influence your father. He's been weakening. We may be able to make definite plans soon."

"That's not a clue!"

"No, you're right. It's not a clue. That's not why I did it. You get no clues!"

The carriage soon was passing northward though woodland trails abutting the Schuylkill River, occasionally open to the parklike grounds of an estate. Peggy glanced back and forth from the window to the benign face of Benedict Arnold, her eyes questioning. When the carriage came to a halt in another space of manicured grounds, Peggy could see a mansion to the west, a beautiful, perfectly symmetrical four-story house with twin chimneys on either side and flanked by two large identical outbuildings. Peggy turned to Arnold, a stunned look in her face and her eyes misting. Punch had alighted and opened the carriage door. Peggy stepped down, followed by Arnold, who placed his arm around her waist.

"There it is, Peggy," he said. "Mount Pleasant. The future home of General and Mrs. Benedict Arnold!"

She shuddered and began to cry. "It's so beautiful," she said. "But how did you—did you rent it? What—"

"No. I've purchased it. We own it! I should say, *you* own it. It's in your name." Peggy gaped at him, her features bordering on incredulity. How could it be? She was not yet nineteen years of age, and yet she was the mistress of this beautiful house.

The two stood transfixed, taking in the dimensions of the house, the white stone with redbrick borders, the tall windows, the pediments and porticos, the front doorway directly in the center with wide stone steps leading up, the Georgian perfectness of the place.

"I don't often agree with him," Arnold murmured, "but John Adams called it 'the most elegant seat in Pennsylvania.' Ninety-six acres. We won't be able to live here for a while. The house is under lease to the Spanish mission. But it's owned by you and we'll live here some day soon." After a pause, he said: "Come, my darling. Let's go inside. Ambassador Miralles knows that we'll be here at this hour."

Mount Pleasant was persuasive for Judge Shippen, too. Several evenings later, he gave his blessing for the wedding, wisely not mentioning again the several points he had against Arnold. It would be a ceremony very similar to the one held in December for Neddy and Betsy, quiet, modest, with only family and very few friends invited. The date was set for April 8th, the earliest date that the assistant rector of St. Paul's Church would be available.

Arnold had talked earlier with Washington about resigning as military governor, but only when events were positive for him so that he would not seem to be running from pressure. That time was now. Arnold wrote to his commander-in-chief, saying: "A committee of Congress having voted in my favor, that objection ceases." He added that as soon as his leg was healed, he would take a field command in the army. But Arnold miscalculated the single-minded venom that Joseph Reed directed at him. The Supreme Executive Council besieged Congress with maximum pressure, Reed hurling accusations and threats at William Paca, and Paca more than holding his own. Reed threatened to withhold wagons and supplies and militia from the Continental Army. In the end, it was Congress that backed down. On April 3rd the Congress voted to order the commander-in-chief to court-martial Arnold on four of the charges, saying that it was "highly sensible of the importance and services of the State of Pennsylvania" and unwilling to allow "disrespectful and indecent behavior of any officer of any rank . . . to the civil authority of any State in the union."

Judge Shippen muttered, "Double jeopardy." Arnold was stunned into silence. The wedding was only a few days away.

On the early evening of April 8th, members of the extended Shippen family from Lancaster, Germantown, and elsewhere in Philadelphia came to 98 South Fourth Street for the wedding of Major-General Arnold and Miss Peggy Shippen. There were not more than fifty in the crowd, with only a handful from General Arnold's side—his sister, Hannah, and his military family of Clarkson and Franks.

Peggy was brilliantly beautiful in a white gown, and Arnold was resplendent in his best blue-and-bluff uniform with an elegant sash and gold epaulettes from George Washington. Neddy Burd watched Arnold appreciatively, noting that only rarely did he need physical support from Major Clarkson, the man who stood closest to him all evening. "This is a great night for the Shippen family," he whispered to his own recent bride, Betsy. Molly played appropriately on the pianoforte. At the climax of the ceremony, Arnold took his bride in his arms and delivered a fervent kiss, as everyone stood and applauded.

Food and drink followed, as the wedding reception played on. At a relatively early hour, a tired general and his ecstatic bride mounted up a few stairs and turned to wave good night to everyone. They were going all the way to the third floor, where Edward III's rooms were their honeymoon suite for the next several days.

Chapter 47

Philadelphia and New York
April–May, 1779

The three days of honeymoon at 98 South Fourth Street were blissful. Arnold made love to Peggy, almost unconscious of the time of day or night. Several times a day the lovers would come downstairs to greet friends who had called. As they left for 190 High Street, the nagging problem of the charges against Arnold soon reasserted itself. He ruminated bitterly over the reversal by Congress, with Peggy trying to soothe him. Finally, he decided that there was no point in venting his spleen. He wrote to the president of Congress regarding the vote against Paca's conclusions, saying that "if Congress have been induced to this measure for the public good and to avoid a breach with this State, however hard my case may be, and however I am injured as an individual, I will suffer with pleasure until a court-martial can have an opportunity of doing me justice by acquitting me of these charges a second time."

He then wrote to Washington to ask for a court-martial as soon as possible, conscious of the fact that Reed was still culling for evidence. Immediately after the wedding, Arnold had sent Clarkson and Franks south to Charleston for the ostensible purpose of buying a privateer, but in reality to remove them from the scene of evidence-gathering efforts.

Washington wrote to both Reed and Arnold, setting the court-martial date for May 1st. Reed immediately responded to Washington, demanding that the court-martial be indefinitely postponed while he gathered evidence, threatening that Pennsylvania would never again supply the army with Conestoga wagons. Unaware of this letter, Arnold took advantage of a movement in Congress to do justice for him by asking it to dismiss the charges that had not been forwarded to Washington. Reed's representatives notified him, and he quickly wrote to Congress that if it accepted Arnold's request the American people faced "a melancholy prospect of permanent disunion between this and the other United States." Congress backed down, fearful that Pennsylvania would secede.

Meanwhile, Washington had no choice. As he had before, he acceded to Reed's request, writing to Arnold:

Dear Sir,

I find myself under a necessity of postponing your trial until a later period than that for which I notified your attendance. I send this information in a hurry, lest you set out before it might arrive, if delayed to an hour or more leisure. In a future letter, I shall communicate my reasons, and inform you of the time which shall be finally appointed.

Back at 190 High Street, Arnold and Peggy gave up thoughts of an extended honeymoon out of town because of the May 1st court-martial date. He had arranged for his two older boys to resume their schooling at the Hardwood School near Hagerstown, Maryland, run by a Loyalist Anglican, the Reverend Bartholomew Booth, writing that "this city is a bad school, and my situation has prevented me paying attention to them."

Sitting in his office chair on April 27th, Arnold saw evidence of what had distracted him from his sons—and everyone and everything else, except Peggy. He held in his hand the curt note from Washington, giving in to the demands of Reed. On his desk lay another message that had arrived that morning from the Congress, announcing that the matter of his financial accounts had been turned over by the Board of War to the treasury committee. It meant a delay of at least a year, added to the three years and seven months since he had started out from Cambridge to lead his army across the Maine wilderness to Quebec.

They had all deserted him. He had been left to fend for himself. The Congress had sacrificed him to the power of Joseph Reed. He had turned to Washington. And now, it was clear, Washington had deserted him, too.

That night, as he lit more candles in the bedroom, Arnold prepared to turn himself over to the only person whom he trusted completely. Peggy, clad in a long white peignoir, lay on the bed, her back propped up by mounds of pillows. Arnold had just come from the mineral waters of Punch's copper tub, a large towel wrapped around his midsection. His chest and shoulders and arms seemed more powerful than ever, as a compensation for his shriveled leg that could be seen in the slit of his towel as he limped about the room. In the midst of his troubles, his mind turned to rehabilitating his leg more than ever. Some day he would need it strengthened to take revenge against those who persecuted him and those who turned away from him in time of need.

He faced Peggy. "Congress has deserted me. Washington has deserted me. I turn to the only one who never will, and ask: what should I do? Should I let myself be victimized by my tormentors? Or should I take some decisive action?"

Arnold had shown Peggy the two letters earlier in the day, and they had discussed them hurriedly. Now was the first time that they were thoroughly alone with each other. Peggy temporized. "I don't understand Joseph Reed," she said. "Did you know, he's married to a distant in-law of mine? Esther Reed. She's not in good favor in our family."

"I should hope not," Arnold responded wearily. With a sigh, he said: "My affair has become central for him. He sees signs of his own weakness. They're forming political parties in Philadelphia. Our friends, the conservatives, have created the Republican Society. It's a menace to Reed, because he got in by a minority, but it'll take a long time to develop. Congressmen are afraid of parties developing there, too. Several delegates have talked about moving Congress to another city. I never thought such things could happen. But they have."

Peggy said: "I think you know what you should do."

"What?"

"Take decisive action."

Arnold nodded. "Yes. I have done so all my life. I've always known what to do. Until now. I'm not sure now." He realized that he was just talking, postponing the moment. He had thought of this so many times in recent months. The image of it ran through his head repeatedly, playing out various triumphant scenarios. He was convinced that Peggy would understand, would applaud. She was, perhaps, experiencing a similar dilemma. But no, she had married a prominent American officer. How could she live with his change to a British officer? But she was a Loyalist—she believed in King and country. Once this idea were mentioned between them, life would never be the same. He sat on the edge of the bed and placed his hand on Peggy's. Their eyes met and locked for a long instant. Then he said: "There's only one decisive action I can even think of now."

Peggy's mind raced. In his desperate search for action, her husband had proposed several naval plans, which were turned down, and he had started an effort to get lands in the north. What could he be thinking of now? Nothing had worked. And then her intuition rose. He could be thinking the thought that had turned in her mind countless times, and that she dared not mention. She slowly began nodding.

Arnold spoke: "I've wanted to say this to you for some time. It's not easy. In fact, it's very dangerous. What I'm saying, Peggy, is—I could change my allegiance. I could fight for the right side."

There was a long silence, as Peggy stayed immobile, masking the churning feelings Arnold's statement had erupted in her. At last! He had said it! It must come from him, she believed. Now it *had* come from him.

"Yes," she said, in a small voice with no change in expression. "I can think of no other way."

Arnold turned from her and looked at the wall, but saw nothing. His mind reeled with the powerful thoughts of what he could do at the head of a British army, the revenge he would take of those who had tormented him—Reed, Matlack, Brown, Gates, Wilkinson, so many others. The peace he would bring to this terribly unsettled countryside. What of his men, his colleagues, those who had fought with him, followed his leadership even to the death? But they had been fooled as much as he had. They had fought, as he had, for something called freedom, only to find that it was a nasty, squalid anarchy. Even the French had made no difference. There was no French army in America, no French navy in American waters. France was a reason for taking the other side, to beat back the despotic monarchy and Papist aristocracy. Everyone was tired of the war. Arnold had heard Philadelphia socialites refer to it as "the tired old cause." But both sides persisted. Would the British continue to do so?

Arnold's mind stopped reeling as he looked back at Peggy. "What do they call it?" he asked her.

After a long silence, Peggy said: "It depends on who wins."

"What do they call it until someone wins?" Arnold asked.

Peggy's expression did not change. "They call it treason."

"Yes, they call it treason. A terrible word. But it can't mask the reality of why it happens. Think of General Monk. He was Oliver Cromwell's best general. But he turned against Cromwell's cause to help restore the monarchy and welcome back the King. None dare call that treason."

"It's a dangerous game," Peggy said.

"Yes, that's the truth of it. There's only one penalty for what they would call a traitor. Death by hanging. We'd have to be more careful than we ever have before in our lives. You especially. If it were uncovered they would come for me immediately and I would be gone. But you—you must be able to deny."

They were silent for a long time, looking at each other, searching out each other's face. "Could you do it?" Arnold asked. "Could you join with me in this greatest quest?"

She pulled him to her. "Yes," she breathed as she embraced and kissed him.

Over the following days, Peggy and Arnold spent a great deal of time alone together. Clarkson and Franks had not returned from Charleston, so it was possible for them to cloister themselves with no difficulty. Hannah would take young Henry out for walks, and Peggy and Arnold would meet and talk.

Arnold had backtracked. He thought perhaps he should undergo the court-martial before committing himself. But it wouldn't hurt to talk about it while he waited for the promised letter from Washington. He and Peggy explored the subject of secrecy exhaustively. No one should be permitted the slightest clue to what they were thinking. No one in the Shippen family. Not Hannah, nor Clarkson, nor Franks, nor even the devotedly loyal Punch. Only they would know—and whomever they would have to use for a courier.

This last thought caused anguish and long discussions. Going over to the other side was a simple idea—but an extraordinarily difficult one to execute, as Peggy and Arnold soon found out. The more they discussed it, the more that Arnold could see his move to the British to be a magnificent stroke, one that would cause thousands of American soldiers to waver and begin to rethink what they were doing. He had immediately vetoed the notion of a straight-forward flight to British lines to offer one's services. He must have an under-standing from the other side in advance, to make sure that the British intended to stay the course, to make sure that they understood the rare quality of the of-ficer who would come to them and be prepared to use him and compensate him in the right way. This required negotiations, and therefore a courier to British headquarters in New York to establish methods and a channel of safe communication.

Peggy knew many more British officers personally than did Arnold. She talked about all of the young officers who had been so prominent in the glitter-ing social season in Philadelphia—John André, Lord Cathcart, Lord Rawdon, McKenzie, Barrington, Ridsdale, Montresor, so many others. Many of the young Philadelphia ladies kept up a correspondence with them, some even do-ing long-distance shopping by ordering from them in New York. But it did not answer the problem—most of these officers, formerly attached to Howe, were at a cold distance from General Clinton. The problem remained: how to find the right way to convey a message to the right officer in New York, either Clin-ton himself or his chief of intelligence.

Peggy and Arnold spent time going over names of suspected Tories in Philadelphia who had a legal way of addressing communications to New York or going there on some sort of business. Finally Peggy came up with the perfect name.

"Joseph Stansbury!" she shouted.

"Who?" Arnold looked up from papers he was scanning.

"You know him, I'm sure. Joseph Stansbury, who has the little glassware market at Black Horse Lane. He's suddenly become anonymous with the Americans back in the city. But before—he was quite prominent. He was Gen-eral Howe's poet laureate!"

"I think I know him," Arnold said. "Unless I'm mistaken, he's the mer-chant we dealt with last year to get the furniture you're sitting in." Peggy looked at her hardwood chair. "We got a good price, but it seemed strange. A glass-ware merchant with furniture—and all he had fit in perfectly. But I don't really know him."

"He's perfect," Peggy said. "I understand he still gets away with the occa-sional trip to New York—for merchandise purposes. You could talk to him."

"I have no basis for trusting the man." Arnold shook his head.

"Stansbury would not go to the Americans and turn you in. He's a true

Loyalist, believe me. You should see some of the poems he wrote for General Howe. How he's survived so far is a mystery to me. Even so, you hold the power of life or death over him, as long as you deal with only one courier. If he turns you in, you say it was a test, and he's really the guilty one."

Arnold frowned. "It's a murky area," he said. "Let me give it some thought."

Nine days after the letter arrived from Washington promising to write Arnold again about a date for the court-martial, Arnold finally lost his patience. He wrote a bitter and unrestrained letter to the commander-in-chief:

If your Excellency thinks me criminal, for heaven's sake let me be tried and, if found guilty, executed. I want no favor; I ask only justice. . . . Having made every sacrifice of fortune and blood, and become a cripple in the service of my country, I little expected to meet the ungrateful returns I have received from my countrymen; but as Congress have stamped ingratitude as a current coin, I must take it. I wish, your Excellency, for your long and eminent services, may not be paid in the same coin. I have nothing left but the little reputation I have made in the army. Delay in the present case is worse than death.

As soon as he dispatched this letter, Arnold wrote a note to Joseph Stansbury. He summoned Punch and sent him off to the address in Black Horse Alley.

When Punch presented Stansbury in Arnold's office the following day, the little merchant was caught up in a tremor of fear. He assumed that his profitable enterprise in Philadelphia, which already operated under a cloud, would be in jeopardy. He was quite mistaken. Arnold greeted him warmly and settled him in a chair next to the desk.

"Thank you for coming, sir," Arnold said, most pleasantly, as the two men exchanged greetings. Then Arnold fell silent, leaning back in his chair and staring intently at Stansbury, his hands clasped before him. Stansbury shifted uncomfortably. At last Arnold spoke.

"Mr. Stansbury, I asked you to come here so that I could get to know you a little better. I had it in mind to establish a particular relationship between us. I wanted to see if my choice has been a good one."

Stansbury's mind was swirling. What kind of relationship was General Arnold talking about? What could there be about it that would be good and free of unwanted attention? He realized that he was expected to say something. "Yes, sir," he managed to mumble.

"I am told that while you greatly used to enjoy reading your poems in public and doing a great deal of gossiping, you are remarkably close to your chest in revealing information that you know is important. You are a man to be trusted. That is very important to me. Is it true, sir?"

Stansbury was very guarded. "Yes, sir. I believe what you say is true, sir."

"All right. I've asked you here, Mr. Stansbury, because I want you to perform a special mission for me."

"I would be happy to serve you in any way I could, sir. But I'm just a tradesman. With no special qualifications I could imagine you want." Stansbury was beginning to fidget even more. This sounded ominous. Was Arnold trying to get at him for selling to him the furniture he had purchased from Sir William Howe?

"Oh, but you do have special qualifications," Arnold said. "I understand you are able to travel to New York."

"Yes, sir, I have done so, several times over the past year. But it's all of record. I go for special merchandising purposes with the full knowledge of—"

"Please don't be alarmed," Arnold said. "I mean you no harm at all. I simply want you to take a secret message from me to a certain officer in New York."

"To a . . . to a certain officer. What officer would that be, sir?"

"A British officer."

Stansbury was stunned into silence. Arnold spoke: "I said I mean you no harm. I mean that. So long as you do exactly what I tell you and you do it in extreme confidence."

Stansbury gulped in silence. Arnold spoke again: "On the other hand, if you ever speak to anyone else, if you even hint at or whisper anything of what I am going to tell you—I will destroy you." Arnold gazed at the ridiculous little man sitting before him, trying to gauge his qualities, his reliability.

Stansbury squirmed in his seat in deeper fear than before. What on earth could the man be talking about? "Sir, may I say once again that I'm nothing more than a merchant. I'm sure you must have the wrong man."

"No. I believe I have the right man. Listen to me very carefully. I am going to offer my services to General Clinton."

With a sharp intake of breath, Stansbury sat back in his chair. Such a thought had never entered his head, so thoroughly was he schooled in Arnold's fame as a battlefield commander for the Americans. Was this at all possible? It could be a conspiracy to ferret him out as one of the hundred or so undercover spies that the British had left behind in Philadelphia. Yet, General Arnold had married Peggy Shippen, that lovely girl that Stansbury knew well and knew to be a Loyalist at heart. General Arnold had locked horns with Joseph Reed and presently was in serious trouble from charges that Reed had pressed. It *was* possible. And it was also extremely dangerous.

"I beg of you, sir. Do not involve me in something I should not be in. I've signed the new oath of loyalty to the Americans. I'm minding my own business. I'm just a—"

"Damn your oath of loyalty. You're already involved, sir."

Stansbury's mouth worked, as he thought for a moment. What could he do? Finally, he said: "Do I understand that you want me to take a letter to Sir Henry Clinton in New York offering to change sides in the war? I must say, sir, the moment I know *that*—my life is in danger. If anyone—"

"You already know it," Arnold said with a half smile.

"Yes, sir, I see what you mean," Stansbury said. "Let me also say, Sir Henry is next to impossible to reach. He's always surrounded by staff men."

"I anticipated that," Arnold said. "One of those staff men must be his chief of intelligence. Once I have written the letter and you are on your way, I must leave all to your ability and discretion. I'm sure you can find out who Sir Henry's intelligence chief is." Arnold stopped as he noted Stansbury's expression. "Do you know who it is?"

"I was told quite recently that John André has been promoted to major and is the new intelligence chief."

Arnold scowled. "I understood he was Howe's man, put out to pasture with a host of young officers. By General Clinton."

"That is very true, sir. But somehow he has managed to come back and is now a confidant of the general."

Arnold raised his eyebrows. The circle was growing tighter. Peggy would be very interested to hear this. At least there was the advantage that she knew a lot about John André. "Are you certain of this?" he asked Stansbury.

"I am not certain, sir. I was only told by someone recently, someone I trust, I might say."

"All right, Mr. Stansbury, you may return to your shop and carry on as ever before. As soon as I write the letter, I will notify you to come here again. And you'd better do whatever you do to prepare the way for a trip to New York."

"As a matter of fact, I have already done so, sir. I am planning a trip there within the week."

"Excellent," Arnold said. "You'll hear from me shortly. By the way, just one point. I am persuaded not to say that it is I, General Arnold, who is writing. My letter will refer only to an important, high-ranking American general for now. Do you understand?"

"Yes, sir."

"And also, Mr. Stansbury," Arnold said, "someone may have observed you coming to this residence. You will have to come again, at least once more. We need to have a reason. Let us say that we are discussing the order of a new set of china. Agreed?"

"Yes, sir."

Chapter 48

New York
May, 1779

André was one point from winning the match. General Clinton bounced the ball several times and then tried his high serve to carom off the right-hand wall. But his aim was off and André was able to smash the ball with power, aiming for a cross-court low shot. But *his* aim was off, too. The ball clunked off the metal, and Clinton was now only one point behind. A stout man considerably older than his opponent, Clinton was an ardent pursuer of exercise. Breathing heavily, he served again, a harder serve, and André barely was able to scoop the ball with his left hand, but he recovered to engage in a spirited rally. Finally, he caught a medium-high return and fired a shot into the corner, hitting the wall only an inch above the barricade. Clinton was exhausted, and stood there panting for a full minute.

"Good shot, John," he said between deep breaths, slapping André on the buttocks. "Your game, your match."

"Come, let's sit for a moment," André said. "You're too tough a match for me," he said as he sank onto a bench off the floor of play.

Clinton collapsed next to him and laughed. "If I thought you'd let me win, I'd have you back out on Long Island again, at some dreary post."

"Of course," André said, "why else do you think I win?"

Clinton put his arm around his new adjutant general. "Let's take a nice, easy ride for a while and work off the aches." The two men exited the court and sat on a bench outside.

After a few more minutes of silent recovery until the sweat stopped coming, they rose wearily, toweled off as best they could, and walked to their mounts. They were in the gaming and prostitution section of New York City, which had arisen west of Broadway near the Trinity Church ruins. It was well past lunchtime, and any number of British officers were in the area, to play handball or billiards, to bowl, or to visit a lady. The commanding general of the British Army and his new chief of intelligence had no such interest in the last pastime. They mounted and rode out north on Broadway until the street became a mere trail.

For months an outcast at a remote post on Long Island, André had finally come to know General Clinton through the aid of his mentor, General Grey. Clinton had despised Howe and his sycophants, and most of them had gone in other directions. He had his own aides and comrades in the army. But the persuasions of General Grey and the fine talents of André gradually worked their way through to the haughty, morose, and distant General Clinton. Grey left for home, and André stayed to be taken on as a member of Clinton's military family.

André progressed rapidly, using even his theatrical talents to enliven the general's dinner parties, when he performed songs or poems to ridicule the rebels, and, on one occasion, even General Howe, to Clinton's huge enjoyment. Only a few weeks ago, Clinton had appointed André as his chief of intelligence. That had happened after André had abandoned his normal reserve and became Clinton's lover. He much preferred younger men, even boys, but the reward of advancement was so obvious.

As he rode through the New York countryside on a warm day in May, André could reflect that he had regained all that he held exactly a year before, when he was Howe's chief of intelligence. Only this time, he was much closer to his general and he was rewarded with a larger title, that of Deputy Adjutant General, with the next post up vacant. The appointment was still a temporary one. As he had been in Philadelphia, he was darling of New York's Loyalist hostesses, and he was also working with his friend, Oliver DeLancey, and others to put on performances of Shakespeare at the Theater Royal on John Street.

Most surprising in the new relationship was the way that the friendship of Clinton and André grew. Clinton was not a popular leader in any sense. He was widely thought of as an overly cautious general, with oldtime New York Loyalists and British officers alike regarding him as vain, deceitful, and remote. André thought he saw behind the facade of General Clinton, reasons why he acted the way he did, while Clinton saw André as a new and exciting force in his life.

Joseph Stansbury had decided to violate his understanding with Benedict Arnold. He was on the verge of becoming a nervous wreck when he arrived in New York, but he headed directly to the residence of the Reverend Jonathan Odell, a physician, poet, and Anglican priest, who had a long history in dedicated spying for the British. Stansbury's fear of broadening his mandate from Arnold did not quite equal his fear of bearing his terrible secret alone.

When the war began, Odell was pastor of the Anglican church in Burlington, New Jersey, and an intimate of Governor William Franklin, son of the most dynamic star in the American firmament. As the war deepened, both men became vociferous Loyalists. Odell was censured and arrested twice, finally giving his word to remain silent. He broke it on the King's birthday in 1776, delivering an ode calling on support for the King to a group of paroled British prisoners on an island in the Delaware River, close to Philadelphia. Leaving his wife and young children, Odell fled and spent months hiding in a windowless space in Franklin's home. He emerged to become the chaplain to a Pennsylvania Loyalist regiment stationed on Staten Island.

Meanwhile, Franklin was arrested and spent a miserable year in solitary confinement in Connecticut before his release was negotiated. Nearly dead, he was finally paroled to New York. With the aid of Odell, he worked tirelessly for a more prominent role in the British scheme of things for the American Loyalists.

Stansbury was fortunate to find Odell at home in the tiny flat he had rented with his much-decreased income. He was disbelieving when Stansbury told him why he was in New York, now breaking his second limitation with Arnold by identifying the author of the letter he carried to Sir Henry.

"I agree that it's hard to believe," Stansbury said. "It seems totally at cross-purposes. But the more you know about what's happened to Arnold since his wound at Saratoga, the more one can understand it."

Stansbury watched as Odell slowly began to smile, his lean, parched face gradually taking on the visage of excitement. He abruptly got up and began to pace. "My God! What a godsend! This is exactly what William Franklin needs!"

He sat down and explained to the puzzled Stansbury. "He's being stalled by Clinton. What Franklin needs is a famous American general to lead the Loyalists in battle. Benedict Arnold is perfect! This could turn Clinton's mind, if anything could. Like all British commanders, Clinton doesn't trust the Loyalists much. That's why we're losing the damned war. To Clinton, the Loyalists are 'merely' Americans. This could change everything!"

"You're going to *tell* Franklin about this?"

"Of course!"

"Please, Jonathan, if you do so, it's entirely on your own choice. I'm already violating my agreement with Arnold by telling you. I don't want to see or talk to Franklin about this."

"I understand," Odell said. "We must protect you. If my name comes up at all, just tell Arnold that André involved me. He would in any case, I am most sure. And *I* will talk to Franklin instead of you—for the present at least. André is sympathetic to Franklin's mission, but he's become so close to Clinton that he protects him, no matter what the issue is. He helps us in various subtle ways. He *is* the right person to see, you know."

"Yes, I do," Stansbury said. As much as he dreaded the interview, he feared staying overly long in New York. "When can I see him?"

"We'll go tomorrow morning," Odell said, consulting his pocket watch. "Too late today. The British have a very confortable schedule. They work in their offices at One Broadway all morning, and then they disappear all afternoon to seek amusements. André should be there in the morning and I will take you to him."

*   *   *

Major André entered his office by the rear door the next morning, and in a moment his secretary appeared from the other doorway, bearing a sheaf of papers that he placed on the desk. "You have two very interesting callers this morning, sir," the young man said. "Two poets, Jonathan Odell, of course, and a man named Stansbury, Joseph Stansbury."

"The devil you say!" André looked up. "I know Stansbury quite well. He's from Philadelphia. Send them in. Give me about ten minutes first."

When the two visitors entered André's office, there were effusive greetings, as André rose and came around his desk to embrace Stansbury. "My word, Joseph," he exclaimed, "it's been a long time. Ten months at least since I've seen you. And now—in New York?"

"Yes, Major André." Stansbury smiled as he sat in one of the two chairs facing the desk, Odell taking the other. "I've been here several times before, but I didn't know where to find you."

"And a formal call at my office? Well, it must be important, if you've come in the company of my friend, Mr. Odell."

"Indeed it is, sir," said Odell, smiling smugly. "We've come to acquaint you with a new Loyalist. An American general!"

"Really. And who might that be?"

Odell proudly turned to Stansbury, who did not look very happy at all. "Several days ago, sir," Stansbury said, "I was summoned to the home of an American general. It was a secret meeting. He told me that he wanted to offer his services to Sir Henry Clinton, and that I must bear that news to Sir Henry or his chief of intelligence, to open up a channel of communication. I had heard that you were appointed to that post, sir, but I was not certain until I arrived in the city yesterday."

"Of course," André said. "And—who is this American general?"

Stansbury sighed and then reached into his inner pocket. "I have a letter from him, sir. To be opened by either you or Sir Henry. He doesn't give his name. It's not even his handwriting, but mine. He ordered me not to reveal his name on this first contact. But I cannot keep it in, sir. It is Major-General Benedict Arnold."

In the act of taking the envelope, André stopped dead, his jaw dropped. He recovered. "That's just not possible," he said.

"I know, sir. I thought so, too. But it's true."

"Benedict Arnold is by far the best general the Americans have. How do you know it's him, for sure? Did you see him?"

"Indeed I did, sir. I might say, he's been in a bad way since his wound at Saratoga. Even before that, I gather. Has not been appreciated."

André seemed not to hear, overcome by a nervous excitement and energy. Rising, he said: "I must talk to Sir Henry. It'll be more comfortable for you in the waiting room. I don't know how long I'll be."

More than an hour later, André reconvened with Odell and Stansbury in his office, and was now all business. "We have blanket approval to proceed from Sir Henry," he said. "We'll use the easiest of our our three systems for coding. This will be familiar to you, Mr. Odell." André glanced up at the poet. "Blackstone's *Commentary on the Laws of England* with three numbers for each of our words. The first one a page number, the second a line, the third a word in that line." Odell nodded sagely. "We'll also give our correspondent the method of invisible ink, written between the lines of an otherwise ordinary letter, so that he will be doubly protected."

"Excellent!" Odell interjected.

"Is Mrs. Arnold a party to her husband's maneuver?" André shot at Stansbury.

"I did not see her and did not ask the question, sir. I assume so."

"So do I," André said, "and that's very good. She's a very sensible woman. One thing General Arnold had better not do, Mr. Stansbury, is attempt to correspond through the letters of the young ladies of Society Hill, his wife's friends. You know who I mean, don't you?"

"Yes, sir, I do."

André held up Arnold's missive. "He raised the question of whether his defection should occur at once or should be part of some specific plan to end the war. Sir Henry and I both opt for the latter. If it is true, and I am persuaded it is, this is a very important opportunity for us. I'm sure you understand." As both men nodded, André continued: "At the same time, we must be able to find out much more." André mused: "He does not sign his name and does not use his own handwriting. We must act cautiously." Then André broke out into a smile. "Yet, the name he uses is very interesting. 'Monk.' Do you know who he's referring to?"

Both men nodded and smiled. "Yes," André said. "George Monk. The Cromwellian general who saved the monarchy. A very important man. And well rewarded by the King. By his choice of this name, our correspondent identifies his own prominence, and, I'm afraid, what he will want for his services."

"That is only correct, is it not, sir?" Odell asked. "He stands to lose everything."

"Of course," André said, "but there must also be real return. Now, down to business. I am going to write a letter to Mr. Monk, to be encoded and taken to him in Philadelphia by you, Mr. Stansbury. Once it is ready, I will want to brief you on various subjects on which we would like to hear intelligence from Mr. Monk. You can report this to him orally. And finally, I will arrange transportation for you to Perth Amboy, this very evening. That will put you there after dark and you will be met by a man who will ride with you out into the countryside. From there, you'll have a relatively unsettled portion of New Jersey to cross."

*   *   *

By mid-May, Arnold had André's letter and Stansbury's information in hand, and he and Peggy met in his study in a mood of calm excitement. The British had responded. The contact was made. They wanted him. Arnold saw himself embarked on a major new direction in his life. At the same time, he expressed caution to Peggy: "It's only the first exchange. André says there is no thought of abandoning the war. That's good, very good. Beyond that, there's nothing specific. He talks of the 'liberality' of Sir Henry, if information received should lead 'to the seizing of an obnoxious band of men.' Who is that? The Congress? The Supreme Executive Council?"

Peggy smiled at her husband's attempt at humor. "He also guarantees that they will indemnify you if the worst side occurs."

"Yes, that's nice, but it's still vague. For the moment, I should give him a good response, give him more information, and expect that some will come back from him this time. I'll dictate it to Stansbury. It'll be in his handwriting again."

Arnold had Stansbury in his office within a week. He substituted *Bailey's Dictionary,* 21st edition, for the cumbersome Blackstone as the codebook. He reported that Washington would move up the Hudson as soon as forage was obtained, which meant mid-June. Congress had given up Charleston, the most important city in the south: "They are in want of arms, ammunition, and men to defend it." He reported information obtained from a congressman: "No measure taken to prevent the depreciation of money, no foreign loan obtained, France refused to become surety, no encouragement from Spain." He referred to payment: "I will expect some certainty: my property here secure and a revenue equivalent to the risk and service done."

He concluded with what he knew was a preposterous note, asking for "a mutual confidence" with Sir Henry, one in which the British chief would reveal his plans for the campaign season and would "never be at a loss for intelligence." He wanted Clinton to understand just who he was dealing with.

He added a postscript: "Madam Arnold presents her particular compliments." Peggy wanted André to know that she was part of the planning from the beginning.

Arnold was surprised when a letter came from Washington, notifying him that the court-martial was now set for June 1st with July 1st as a fallback date. He was experiencing severe gout in his good right leg, which only made the left leg feel much worse. He was lifted into his carriage for the trip to Washington's headquarters at Middlebrook, at the end of May. Arnold was the guest of General Nathanael Greene in his quarters at the site and was happy to find that Greene was very much on his side.

The court-martial lasted only one preliminary day. Representing himself,

Arnold successfully challenged the number of Pennsylvanians on the fourteen-member court, and changes were made. That evening, word came that the British had launched an attack on the Hudson forts and particularly the crossing at Stony Point. The court-martial adjourned as the officers hastened to the north, Washington leaving word that it might resume fairly soon. Arnold went on to Washington's headquarters at Morristown, suspecting ruefully that it was his intelligence to Sir Henry Clinton that had forewarned him of an opportunity to attack in the north before Washington sent up extra troops. Arnold spent three weeks at Morristown, collecting intelligence to forward to New York, and then went home, convinced that the court-martial would not occur for months, now that the campaign season was in full sway.

In July Arnold heard from André. His message said that General Clinton would not reveal any advance plans—and, since Arnold had initiated the correspondence, it was up to him to deliver services. "Join the army," André urged, "accept a command, be surprised, be cut off." For services of such a nature that led to the capture of five or six thousand men, Sir Henry would pay "twice as many thousand guineas."

Arnold disliked the tone of this letter, but he continued to send André intelligence reports. He received nothing in return. On July 19th, word came that Continental troops under Anthony Wayne had recaptured Stony Point, and Philadelphia erupted in celebration. Finally, in August, Arnold heard from André, who had two new points to suggest. First, he said that if he could see Arnold, a conversation of a few minutes might satisfy him entirely. Second, he asked for an accurate plan of West Point and an account of what vessels were in the river near the fortress.

Arnold replied that he had nothing specific on West Point, but was planning a trip to Connecticut in a few weeks. He would visit West Point then, and make drawings of what he saw. He would also try to "contrive" an interview with André.

With that, the correspondence fell into an impasse. André seemed to have changed. At first, his prominence in the British victory at Stony Point seemed to play a role. Then it appeared that he had gotten a good picture of Arnold from other officers, seeing him as without any command, in a state of arrest for a court-martial, and physically handicapped. What good could he be? And by August, André was already engrossed in Sir Henry's plans for a British attack on Charleston later in the year, another target provided by Arnold's intelligence.

Arnold was disgusted. Sir Henry would deal with him on *his* terms—or not at all.

Chapter 49

Philadelphia and Morristown
Winter, 1779–1780

As the days shortened and the fall season arrived, Continental currency sank to a new all-time low, and grumbling over food shortages and high prices in Philadelphia began to give way to protests and outbreaks of rioting. Talk of the war as the "tired old cause" had grown. People were fond of saying that five years of warfare had gained nothing except a ruined economy and unbearable hardships. Radical thugs roamed the streets of the city, eager to punish any Loyalist they came across.

Early in October, Joseph Reed was at home, ill with a fever. He was called to his second-floor front window late in the afternoon by his wife, Esther. She stood at the window, prim and scowling, and pointed out a number of men who were loitering nearby.

"Who are they?" she demanded. "Are they your men? They're dangerous. What are they doing here?" Several indeed were carrying muskets and others held clubs.

Reed sighed and clutched the flannel more tightly about his throat. "I know who they are. I'll get them to disperse," he said, as he began opening the window.

At that moment, Benedict Arnold's closed carriage rolled up to his house next door, and Arnold opened the door as his driver leaped to the ground to assist him. The men closed in on him, shouting menacingly. Now on the ground, Arnold drew out his pistol and handed his heavy cane to Punch.

Reed opened his window and shouted: "You men, go home! Stop it, I say."

Arnold looked up at him and shouted back: "Thank you, neighbor! You'd better do something about these fools or there'll be real trouble."

Reed ignored him and shouted again: "Go on home, I say. This is no way to act."

He closed the window, as the men slowly began to move off. Esther drew herself up and said: "That insufferable Arnold! You should have let the men have at him."

"No, my dear," Reed said. "We *have* Arnold. Just where we want him."

There *was* real trouble several nights later, at the southeast corner of Third and Walnut, the home of noted lawyer James Wilson, who had become a target for his leadership in organizing ever larger groups of anti-Reed citizens under the

Republican banner. On Monday morning, October 4th, the street rowdies and militiamen called a meeting at the Paddy Byrne Tavern on Tenth Street, drinking and carousing as they tried to organize their plans. Their general objective was to round up Republicans and expel them from the city before some of them could stand for election to the assembly a week later. The conclave of radicals grew steadily until it numbered more than two hundred men, including some Pennsylvania German militia who had two small cannon with them. Finally the boiling point was reached. The men emerged from the tavern and began marching across town, stopping at several places to seize suspected Republicans from their homes, their drummers beating "The Rogue's March." Their quarry: James Wilson.

Across town, word filtered through. Benedict Arnold joined Wilson and General Thomas Mifflin as they were drilling about thirty Republicans, and the group quickly moved to the home they had dubbed Fort Wilson, entering the sturdy brick house and barricading the doors and windows. The thirty defenders were reinforced by members of the City Troop, a socially elite dismounted regiment. As time passed and nothing happened, the City Troop members went home for lunch at noontime. And then the attackers arrived at Fort Wilson.

Reed, who was home in bed, received a messenger from the Supreme Executive Council telling him what was happening. He hurriedly dressed and rushed to try to reconvene the City Troop. At Fort Wilson, the first shot came from a third-story window, as one of the defenders fired his pistol at the mob below. He received a return blast from the street and fell to the floor dead.

As the most experienced military officer on the scene, Benedict Arnold quickly took charge of the defense. He stationed himself on the upper floors and put Mifflin in charge of the first. A full-scale battle began. Arnold threw open third-floor windows and began firing both of his pistols. He saw Captain Peale down below and shouted: "Your president has raised a mob and now he can't quell it!"

One of the German militiamen smashed the front door down with a sledgehammer, and his comrades poured in. Colonel Stephen Chambers was rushing down the stairs and fired his pistol at them, wounding a man. Then a militiaman grabbed his hair, pulled him down, and thrust a bayonet through him. A barrage from the two upper floors drove the attackers back, giving Wilson and several of his men the chance to barricade the door again. Outnumbering the defenders seven to one, the attackers rallied and assaulted the front of the house a second time, and again they broke through the restored barricade. At that moment, Reed arrived with only a few of the City Troopers. His shouts were of no avail in slowing down the rioters, but then two companies of Baylor's Virginia Regiment galloped to the scene, swinging their deadly sabers and forcing the rioters together and surrounding them. Reed ordered everybody in and out of the house arrested.

The Republicans were able to post property bail and were immediately released, but the militiamen spent the night in the Walnut Street jail. The German regiments outside of town learned of their comrades' plight and marched the next day to free them. Reed appeared before the Pennsylvania Assembly and won amnesty for the militiamen, saying the bloodshed at Fort Wilson was one of the "casual overflowings of liberty." It was an overflowing that cost ten lives and dozens of wounded.

Wilson and other Republican leaders decided it was a good time to leave town for a few weeks, but Arnold boasted that he would stay forever and barricaded his house and armed his servants. Within days, a guard was finally posted in front of his door, but soon disappeared as the elections occurred and the fervor died down. After his initial joy at the battle, Arnold soon descended again to the gloom that prevailed at 190 High Street. He was left to think about the sad state of life in Philadelphia—and the fact that no one in the militia respected him.

Life had become a sort of purgatory for Arnold. The war seemed almost dead, yet he was forced to wait for a court-martial. His romance with the enemy had come to naught, as he was seen as a discredited major-general, with no assignment. He worked daily on rehabilitating his leg. He had several frustrating meetings with the Treasury Board on his finances, with no outcome. He worked on keeping the peace between his new bride and his old, faithful sister. And he sent an intended final message for André, delivered orally by Joseph Stansbury, saying that he was sincere in desiring to "accelerate the settlement of this unhappy conflict," but that he could not simply "hazard his all" and "part with a certainty for an uncertainty."

To give stiffness to his "certainty," he needed to be acquitted of all charges by the court-martial. The campaigning season, which had led to little in the way of campaigns, was dying. Arnold worked daily on preparing to represent himself, and in November the word came: the court would convene in the Dickerson Tavern in Morristown on December 23rd.

As he and Peggy rehearsed the charges, Arnold began to feel himself once again, ready to clear his name totally, and then find some way to take on the future. His only lapse as he left for Morristown, accompanied by Franks and Punch, was the inability to find John Mitchell, the Pennsylvania wagon master who was scheduled to testify. Arnold left Peggy in charge of trying to find Mitchell, and took off for Morristown.

As he entered the low-ceilinged public room in Dickerson's Tavern, reconfigured to serve as a courtroom, he surveyed the thirteen-member court with satisfaction, until he came upon the face of Moses Hazen, who had first accused him of plundering in Canada. Arnold rose with a protest, and Hazen was excused, replaced by another officer. Unknown to Arnold, however, was the fact that four other members had served on the court in Ticonderoga.

He was pleased with the court, with General Robert Howe as its president, and the fact that John Laurence, judge advocate general of the Continental Army, was the prosecutor. Reed had not come to Morristown, sending only Timothy Matlack and his son, who, along with Franks and the missing John Mitchell, were to be among the few people to testify.

Arnold was in his full form as he began his defense, his leg stronger than it had been since his wound nearly nearly two years earlier. He established himself as an "active, judicious, and brave officer" from the earliest day of troubles until the present moment. He cited numerous sources, including Washington's letters to Congress recommending him for promotion, and then paused dramatically before asking: "Is it probable that such a man should all at once sink into a course of conduct equally unworthy of a patriot and soldier?"

With that in the air, he switched to a denunciation of his persecutors in Pennsylvania, criticizing them particularly as the source of endless delay for the trial. He hit them again and again as he preceded to speak of all eight charges against him, having insisted that the court review them all instead of only the four that he had been indicted for by the Congress. In the charge of misusing militia, Arnold so persevered in his cross-examination of Sergeant Matlack that the young man ended up contradicting himself and floundering helplessly. On the charge that he favored and protected Loyalists, Arnold rose to full-throated oratory in denouncing Joseph Reed for his treatment of General Washington when he resigned from the army at the hour of maximum peril: "I can say I never basked in the sunshine of my general's favor and courted him to his face, when I was at the same time treating him with the greatest disrespect and villifying his character. . . . This is more than a ruling member of the Council of the State of Pennsylvania can say." Directly on the charge, he said: "The president and the Council of Pennsylvania will pardon me if I cannot divest myself of humanity. It is enough for me, Mr. President, to contend with men in the field. I have not yet learned to carry on warfare against *women,* or consider every man disaffected to the cause who, from opposition to those in power in Pennsylvania, may, *by the clamor of party,* be styled a Tory. This odious appellation has been applied indiscriminately to several of illustrious characters."

Arnold's oratorical flights ended when it came to the charge of using Pennsylvania's wagons to bring his goods to safety in Philadelphia. Peggy had no luck in lining up Mitchell to testify. She wrote: "You mention Sunday for your return. I will not flatter myself I will see you even then if you wait for Colonel Mitchell. . . . I never wanted to see you half so much . . . Farewell, I need not say how affectionately." The trial was held in abeyance while Arnold returned to Philadelphia, carrying with him Washington's order for Mitchell to appear. He had a few glorious days with Peggy, but then returned to Morristown bringing the reluctant Mitchell with him.

By mid-January, the weather was already being pronounced by everyone as the coldest within memory, much worse than the winter of Valley Forge. The conditions affecting the troops were similar. Though their housing was better for their third winter encampment in Morristown, supplies of food, clothing, and medical supplies were almost nonexistent. French aid had been much too small to make a difference. Near flashes of mutiny ran through the camp of the depleted army, the entire scene feeding Arnold's visions of a declining American cause.

John Mitchell managed to confuse the issue in his testimony, saying that Arnold had requested the wagons, not ordered them, but that he still felt obligated to comply. Arnold left the matter on the point that he had never made a secret of his use of the wagons and that it was in the public interest to prevent property from falling into enemy hands.

Arnold was at his brilliant best in his closing statement, his confidence raised by the fact that the prosecution had introduced no new evidence. He touched on every point, and, regarding the charge of speculation while the shops were closed, nearly went overboard. If he had done this, he said, he would "stand confessed, in the presence of this honorable court, the vilest of men. I stand stigmatized with indelible disgrace, the disgrace of having abused an appointment of high trust and importance to accomplish the meanest and most unworthy purposes; the blood I have spent in the defense of my country will be insufficient to obliterate the stain."

On January 26th, Arnold entered the public room of Dickerson's Tavern for the last time, ready to hear the verdict of the court. He was expecting to be completely cleared of all eight charges. The court exonerated him of everything except the issuance of the pass for the *Charming Nancy,* characterizing it as an illegal act. On the misuse of wagons, the court absolved Arnold of any fraudulent intent, but said that "considering the delicacy attending the high station in which the general acted . . . that requests from him might operate as command." The recommended sentence: an official public reprimand from the commander-in-chief.

Arnold was shocked, though to everyone else the finding of the court was lenient. Arnold went home to the arms of Peggy, the one person he knew would sympathize with him totally. Within a matter of two weeks, the verdict had been delivered to Congress and approved there, with only three negative votes. Now only Washington needed to act, to issue his reprimand.

Arnold and Peggy secretly vowed to move ahead on their plans to go over to the British side, if a way could be found consistent with Arnold's position. Meanwhile, he was a busy man. He had the entire 179-page transcript of the trial printed in English and French and distributed it as widely as he could. He renewed his request to take over leadership of a naval expedition, arguing once again that he could function well on a quarterdeck, if not yet on horseback. Again he met with negative reactions from Congress and the Board of Admiralty. He met several times with the Treasury Board on his accounts, and again made no progress. And he wrote again to Major André, offering to arrange the capture of a major military prize for ten thousand pounds and command of a battalion in the British Army. But André was away on the attack on Charleston with General Clinton, so the only response was a polite reply from André's assistant, saying that the letter would be held for André's return.

On March 19th, Peggy had her first child, Edward Shippen Arnold, named after her father. Her husband proudly wrote the news to Washington. But the family now needed to face up to the fact of diminishing income. No new funds had come in and Arnold's wealth was both greatly diminished and tied up in real estate. They let most of the servants go, and then Arnold agreed to Clarkson's desire to return to civilian life and bid him farewell. The family left 190 High Street and moved to a small house on Eighth Street that Judge Shippen owned in his real estate business. Now on indefinite leave of absence, the major-general kept Franks on his staff. He had become indispensable, especially to Peggy. The only other residents of the new household were Hannah and Henry, the youngest of Arnold's previous sons, as well as the baby, Punch, and a maid.

Arnold needed money. He made an appointment to see Caesar La Luzerne, the new French minister, to ask for a loan. If the British would not buy his services, perhaps the French would. He told the diplomat that his finances had run so low that he would have to leave the army if he could not find help. A French loan would allow him to stay in to pursue the common cause and also to seek every chance to favor the French interest. In as easy and polite a way as he could, the French minister declined the request. Arnold came home in humiliation, blasting the monarchists and Papists.

By the end of March, Washington wrote a letter to the Arnolds, warmly congratulating them on their new son. Then, only a week later, came Washington's reprimand. Striving to write as gentle a letter as circumstances would permit, Washington said:

The Commander-in-Chief would have been much happier in an occasion of bestowing commendations on an officer who had rendered such distinguished services to his country as Major-General Arnold; but in the present case, a sense of duty and a regard to candor oblige him to declare that he considers his conduct in the instance of the permit as particularly reprehensible, both in a civil and military view, and in the affair of the wagons as imprudent and improper.

It was a light touch. Say nothing about it and let it drift into the mists of history. But not for Arnold. From this moment on, Washington was his personal enemy. His planning now began to be informed by a burning desire to get even with the chief, in any way that he could.

This became the main subject in Arnold's late-night sessions with Peggy. How best to improve his attractiveness to the British and to serve his goal of diminishing Washington? Arnold reviewed his correspondence with André, seeking an answer. He remembered that at one time the British officer had urged him to find an important command—"one shining stroke," André had called it—that he could turn over to the British.

What could it be? And then Arnold remembered that André had once expressed an interest in West Point. Arnold had planned to stop there on a trip to Connecticut to get more information, but had not done so as the correspondence with the British lapsed. That would be the perfect answer, Arnold thought. Washington had been building the great fortress for three years as an "American Gibraltar," sitting athwart the vital river to the north. Delivery of West Point and its garrison to the British would certainly be a "shining stroke"—and it was also a defensive assignment, one that Arnold could lay claim to in his injured state.

Arnold knew that Philip Schuyler, now a congressman from New York State, would be leaving soon for a meeting with General Washington at the Morristown camp. He had just been elected chairman of a committee to confer with Washington on the reorganization of the army and cooperation with the French. Arnold decided to write, asking Schuyler to recommend him to Washington as the commander of West Point. He knew that Schuyler, to whom West Point was especially important, would be happy to do so.

Arnold's spirits rose as he worked on his note to Schuyler. This was the perfect answer. West Point would be his shining stroke.

PART X

West Point

Chapter 50

New Jersey and New York
Summer, 1780

Several times, while waiting to hear from Philip Schuyler, Benedict Arnold took from the hidden place in his desk the well-worn copy of a letter he had received from Colonel Beverly Robinson, back before he had broached with Peggy the subject of changing sides. Now serving with General Clinton in New York, Robinson had been an outstanding man, a good friend of General Washington's, who had stayed neutral at first during the war. Eventually he had taken up arms with the British. He had written an appeal to Arnold to come over to his side. Arnold had regarded the letter as insulting at first, but he had not thrown it away. And lately, he had reread it numerous times.

Robinson reviewed the new American government that could arise under the concessions that Britain was now willing to make, granting every desire except complete independence from the King—a two-house Parliament with only native-born American members, a viceroy appointed by the King, all the powers and citizenship rights of Britons at home: "They will enjoy, in every sense of the phrase, the blessings of good government. They shall be sustained, in times of need, by all the power necessary to uphold them." Robinson's appeal was to Arnold to come over and serve as the leader of all the Loyalists:

> It is necessary that a decisive advantage should put Britain in a condition to dictate the terms of reconciliation. . . . There is no one but General Arnold who can surmount obstacles so great as these. A man of so much courage will never despair of the Republic, even when every door to a reconciliation seems sealed. Render then, brave General, this important service to your country. . . . Let us

put an end to so many calamities. You and ourselves have the same origin, the same language, the same laws. . . . Beware, then, of forever breaking the links and ties of a friendship whose benefits are proven.

It was exactly the role that Arnold now saw for himself. He had kept the letter and had reviewed it often. He was determined to fulfill it. He wrote again to André in New York, specifying his terms in money and command, stating that were it not for his family he would have no terms at all, and asking for a small sum of money to aid in communication. He told of his itinerary for the next few weeks. Stansbury brought back a reply from General Wilhelm von Knyphausen, the German commander who was standing in while Clinton was in the south. He sent Arnold two hundred pounds, a dictionary to be used in decoding, and a small ring, keeping an identical ring to be given to an officer who would later meet with Arnold.

Arnold wrote to Schuyler to say he had not heard from him and broadened his request, saying that the coming campaign season looked to be more active than he had thought and that he was determined to rejoin the army. A letter then arrived from Schuyler in early June, saying that Washington could not have been more welcoming in bringing Arnold back to active service and promised that a suitable command would await him. Schuyler said he believed that Washington would have alternative proposals for Arnold, including West Point.

By this time, Arnold had heard secret intelligence that Washington was planning an American invasion of Canada, in coordination with the French army due to arrive in North America soon. The American forces would go north up the Hudson and Connecticut River Valleys while the French would attack along the line of the Saint Lawrence. It seemed a dubious proposition to Arnold, but he immediately sent off a report to von Knyphausen in New York.

Now he was ready for his trip north—to Washington's headquarters to try to pin down the West Point assignment, to West Point to assess its condition for the British, and to Connecticut to begin the process of transferring assets to London.

He arrived in Morristown on June 12th and found that Washington had already gone north. Arnold stayed for a number of days, picking up as much intelligence as he could. Before leaving, Arnold wrote to New York to revise his last letter. The French were headed for Rhode Island instead of the Saint Lawrence and had just been sighted off the Virginia coast. If Clinton could move swiftly, he could intercept them. He added a postmortem, telling Clinton that he was now commander of West Point, even though he had not yet seen General Washington.

He reached West Point on June 16th and rode over the grounds in the company of the commander, General Robert Howe, who had presided over his court-martial. As far as Howe was concerned, that was in the past. He was all cordiality as he showed Arnold the layout of the post. West Point was actually ten forts, built at different levels and sizes and for different purposes. The main station had a satisfying name for Arnold. It was called Fort Arnold and was built on the center of a bluff at the first ninety-degree bend of the river. It was modeled somewhat after Ticonderoga, with four triangular ramparts. Behind it was the equivalent of a small town with sutlers, barracks, storehouses, a hospital, a jail, and a powder magazine. Across the river, on the east side, was the first defensive position built at the site, on Constitution Island. The array of heavy guns between Fort Arnold and Constitution Island made the river deadly at this location for any ship attempting to pass. A vessel would have to come about when under fire and then face a short distance to another ninety-degree turn back to the north. Stretching more than a thousand feet between the two positions was a heavy chain, each link weighing more than one hundred pounds and floating on log pontoons below the surface to block passage.

As formidable as this area was to ships on the river, Fort Arnold was exposed to land attack, situated as it was on a relatively low elevation and flanked on the west by a bowl of high ground rising hundreds of feet into the air. Artillery on these heights could destroy Fort Arnold and Constitution Island. Tadeusz Kościuszko was assigned to West Point after Saratoga and given the challenge of strengthening it as the "American Gibraltar" that Washington imagined. He succeeded admirably by building more forts and chains of redoubts on the heights, all within a mile of one another and all mutually reinforcing.

West Point, to a large extent, was the product of the British invasions from Canada in 1776 and 1777. It flowed from Washington's imagination as the stranglehold on the river, now assuring free traffic between New England and the rest of the states. It was at the center of Washington's military planning.

As pretty and formidable an asset as West Point was, Arnold could see defects as he rode about, barely hearing the idle chatter of General Howe. Only fifteen hundred men, who had the look of invalids about them, were at the post, which required a garrison of nearly double that amount, though Howe assured Arnold that twelve hundred more men from Albany were due to join the West Point force soon. Arnold kept careful note of what he saw, and that night, at Fishkill, he wrote down a detailed report for the British.

In Hartford, Arnold hired a lawyer to look after his interests as the state moved toward indemnifying soldiers for the depreciation in value of their back pay. In New Haven he worked on selling his estate, retaining another lawyer. He wanted payment in hard currency, not Continental dollars, so that he could have the funds deposited in London.

Unknown to him, British operatives were watching his movements on the orders of John André, who had returned to New York on June 18th with General Clinton. They had been successful in the southern campaign, having captured Charleston along with General Benjamin Lincoln and his 4,500-man army. They wanted to complete their invasion of the south but were forced to return by the pressure of the grumpy and near senile Admiral Marriott Arbuthnot. He feared the arrival of French ships, so the main British army was forced to withdraw, leaving Cornwallis on land in command of diminished operations.

André and General Clinton had reversed roles. Clinton was now very taken with Arnold's latest messages regarding West Point and was ready to contemplate an operation to the north. But André was concerned with veracity. Neither man had certain proof that the person they had been corresponding with was actually Benedict Arnold, despite the word of Joseph Stansbury. André wanted to press for the personal meeting that had been mentioned several times in their correspondence, and Clinton agreed.

Meanwhile, Arnold had returned to Morristown, where he was able to see Washington briefly. The commander had received a letter from a New York delegate to Congress, Robert Livingston, urging that West Point be given to Arnold. Arnold knew that this was the result of advances made by Peggy, but he backed off when Washington nearly scorned the idea. Impressed by Arnold's use of his injured leg, Washington had other hopes for him. He pointed out that West Point would not be suitable for an energetic general, "as I should leave none in his garrison but invalids, because it would be entirely covered by the main army." Arnold left for Philadelphia, now worrying that he could not get West Point, even though the British would think he was already in command.

Back home in Philadelphia after nearly a month's absence, Arnold had a joyous reunion with Peggy, but then was disappointed to find that there had been no replies to his letters to the British. He began to be assailed by doubts. For the first time, he agonized over a letter to be sent to André. Finally he summoned Stansbury late at night and gave him an oral message to deliver. He wanted some specific response to his requests on payment. He wanted to arrange a conference with a British officer. And he reported that the idea of an invasion of Canada had been a ruse—the real target was New York.

That night he tossed fitfully, wondering whether he had been duped by Stansbury. Several days later, on July 11th, he summoned another Loyalist, Quaker businessman Samuel Wallis of Philadelphia, not aware that Wallis already worked with Stansbury and Odell. He repeated material he had sent with Stansbury but couched his letter in strong terms, saying that if "a mutual confidence between us is wanting" then the correspondence ought to end. If not, then the abuses ought to cease and "a stricter attention" to the interests of both parties "may remedy the misfortune." He added: "It is now necessary for me to know the risk that I run in case of a loss." He slipped in another note, keyed to the dictionary von Knyphausen had sent him, making his offer to betray West Point more specific. The sum of "twenty thousand pounds I think will be a cheap purchase for an object of such importance."

Finally, Arnold assured General Clinton that the populace was disheartened and could not take another year of war: "The mass of the people are heartily tired of the war, and wish to be on their former footing. They are promised great events from this year's exertion. If disappointed, you have only to persevere and the contest will soon be at an end. The present struggles are like the pangs of a dying man, violent but of a short duration."

When this missive arrived, André and Clinton finally met to focus on the use of Benedict Arnold. Clinton wanted to take West Point whenever Arnold was fully in position and prepared. André conveyed this to Arnold in Philadelphia, accepting all of Arnold's demands except indemnification, covering that only by the statement that Arnold would not "be left a victim." He also suggested that he would be the officer to meet with Arnold at a place to be agreed upon. André wanted a personal triumph, having become aware that his assignment and rank would last only as long as Sir Henry Clinton stayed as commander-in-chief. He knew that Sir Henry was anxious to go home to his rose gardens in Bath, and that others were being considered for the top command in America.

Before this letter arrived, Arnold left Philadelphia to find Washington and nail down the West Point assignment, having become aware that a crisis was brewing. The French had landed safely at Newport, and the British embarked on an armada down the Long Island Sound with six thousand troops to attack them. Washington countered by moving his army down toward Dobbs Ferry to menace New York. But he knew the dismal truth. The American army was probably too weak to sustain an attack on New York, even with Clinton and a substantial portion of his army absent.

By the time Arnold found Washington, the crisis was over. Admiral Arbuthnot responded to rumors of an incoming French fleet by breaking off the expedition, and Clinton and André and their army returned to New York.

On July 31st, a hot, sweltering day, Washington had ridden to the top of a crest south of Peekskill to observe the movement of the American army across the Hudson to the west, their concentrated position near Dobbs Ferry now being menaced with the British return to the city. Arnold saw Tench Tilghman, Washington's chief of staff, at headquarters, who told him where to find the commander-in-chief.

Washington was near desperation over the weakened state of his army, just as his French allies had finally arrived in America. While commissaries were driving cattle to the French camp, to be paid in gold, the Americans were slowly starving. In a letter to his brother, Washington bitterly lamented the fact that the army had gone five or six days without meat, then as many without bread, and then "two or three times without either." No wonder there had been no new enlistments. Below he could see the long lines of the Continentals trudging under a hot sun with shouldered muskets, down to the dock at Fort Lafayette, ready to board the barges of King's Ferry to cross over to Stony Point. There they faced a sharp climb and then a twenty-five-mile march to the main American camp at Tappan, hard on the New Jersey border.

Washington was also short of battle-seasoned generals: Lincoln had been captured, and Greene had been sent to the south to take over from Gates, who had been embarrassed by Cornwallis at Camden to the point that he was due for a court-martial. But approaching Washington now was his best field general, who had been denied to him for more than two years, ever since Saratoga, by his terrible wound. Now he seemed fit and ready for action, indeed was riding his horse again. Benedict Arnold reined up and saluted.

Washington smiled, as the discouraging thoughts left his mind temporarily. It was good to see Arnold looking so fit. After an exchange of pleasantries, the two men sat in silence for a moment, looking down at the long, undulating line of troops in movement. And then Arnold asked: "Do you have something for me, sir?"

"Yes, I do," Washington replied, beaming at Arnold. "I'm going to give you the position of honor!"

Arnold nodded, though his mind was a bit uncertain. Was the chief referring to West Point?

"Now that you're well enough again, I want you in command of a brigade—and positioned on my left!"

It was the classic military post of honor—command of the left wing of an army. Such an assignment would wipe away all the humiliation of the court-martial in the eyes of everyone. But it was not what Arnold wanted. He was far past that. His heart sank and his face colored as he looked down. "I don't think my health will allow it," he said.

"You look very good, General Arnold," Washington said. "It's been well more than two years since your wound. Surely you're ready now."

Arnold said nothing, as Washington looked at him, perplexed. Several other officers were riding over to join them. "Go on down to my headquarters. I'll be there in a few moments. And we'll settle this." He watched Arnold ride away dejectedly.

On his own way down the hill half an hour later, Washington was intercepted by Tilghman, who reported that Arnold was limping back and forth in the staff room, complaining that his leg hurt him grievously. Tilghman was concerned because the orders for August 1st were already distributed. In them was the announcement that Arnold had been put in command of the left of the army. He told Washington that Arnold was muttering that only a stationary command like West Point would suit him.

Washington took Arnold into his office alone with him. "General Arnold," he said, "you seem too fit, and obviously too high-ranking, for the command at West Point. I need a man of your rank—and your abilities—in the field. We're short of good major-generals."

"I'm sorry, sir," Arnold said. "I just can't do it. This wound is still very painful. I can only stay on a horse a short while. I'm only suited for a rear-area assignment."

Washington kept trying for a while, gravely and courteously, trying to embarrass Arnold into joining him on the line. As Arnold resisted, Washington began to fear that the years of recovery, the wound itself, and too much political wrangling had robbed Arnold of his martial spirit. It was a depressing thought, added to those Washington already had—and one not expected. He finally broke off the interview, still loathe to give in. He told Arnold he would think the whole matter over.

In Philadelphia, Peggy Arnold had been the shining light at a dinner party at the Robert Morris home. Her special friend, Robert Livingston of the Congress, was there, along with other leaders of the city's elite society. After the meal, a group of men nearly surrounded the beautiful lady when a newcomer came up, bowed, and congratulated her. She ceased fanning herself and smiled and asked, "What for?"

"Why, the promotion of your husband by General Washington. To the post of honor! To command the left wing of the army!"

Peggy digested this for a moment and then understood it. She fainted. The onlookers took her to the nearest couch as one ran to get the smelling salts. Peggy awoke and began sobbing and felt herself lapsing into the hysterical fits that came upon her at times of severe stress, which seemed to leap outward when one of the men would try to console her by pointing out that command of the left was much more important than West Point. As someone whispered the comment that the poor woman only feared that her husband would now be exposed to grave danger, her mind took control and she began to enourage this thought with more discreet weeping.

The general orders of August 3rd contained a correction. Major-General Benedict Arnold was the new commander of West Point and an enlarged military district that ran from Albany to New York City. After Arnold had left him, Washington had agonized briefly over the matter and then decided that he had no other choice. Arnold could have West Point, and that probably was the future limit of his military activities. To make the command somewhat larger for a major-general, Washington redrew the New York military districts.

The moment that Arnold heard the news, he moved with grim satisfaction and renewed energy to take command of West Point. He stopped first at the large house of Joshua Hett Smith, which overlooked the wide expanse of

Haverstraw Bay, some five miles south of King's Ferry on the river. Though the younger brother of the chief justice of New York, Smith was a key man in Robert Howe's espionage network, but there were also rumors that Smith told secrets to the British in New York. Arnold could scarcely credit Smith with enough intelligence and quickness to serve both sides. His attitudes seemed to bespeak a Tory, but the most important fact about Smith was that he was not very bright. And Arnold liked Smith's house very much as a possible site for a conference with a British officer. It was in American-held territory, but loosely held.

Arnold greeted the affable, thirty-five-year-old country squire on the wide terrace of his house. Predictably, Smith was all effusive jollity in the presence of a high-ranking officer. Arnold stayed for dinner with Smith and his young wife and two children. After the meal, he took Smith out on the terrace. He explained that he was riding north nearly twenty miles to Beverly. It was the former home of none other than Colonel Beverly Robinson, the Tory who last year had written the invitation to him to change sides. The home was situated on the east side of the Hudson only a few miles south of West Point and had been used as a residence by General Robert Howe. Arnold was following in Howe's footsteps.

He invited Smith to stop and see him at Beverly whenever he was in the region. Then, in a lowered tone, he whispered some mumbo-jumbo about his extensive command and the special events that might be occurring. He might want Squire Smith's help for one or another of these occasions. Smith was all eager interest and assent.

The next morning, Arnold started out on the ride north to Beverly. Along the way, he thought of enlarging his military family, now that he had such a large territory to control. The foppish David Franks could be very useful, and was a special aid to Peggy, but Arnold had tired of him. Who could he get on short notice, somebody that he knew so that he wouldn't have to develop an entirely new relationship? Clarkson and Livingston came immediately to mind, but Arnold remembered how happy both were to return to civilian status. Then he thought of Dirk Varick, who had been helpful at Saratoga. Varick had left the army to read the law at his parents' home in Hackensack. Perhaps he would serve as Arnold's secretary now. He would write to Varick as soon as he reached Beverly, and to Philip Schuyler as well, asking him to write a note of encouragement to his former devoted aide.

When he arrived at Beverly, Arnold found that Colonel John Lamb, second-in-command at West Point and an old friend, was there to greet him and make sure that he was comfortably settled in his new command residence. The one-eyed Lamb, with the terrible scar on one side of his face from the cannon blast at Quebec, was an invalid and therefore suitable for West Point, although, as Arnold knew well, he was an extremely able man.

Beverly was a spacious, two-story frame house, with a commanding view of the Hudson River, although screened from West Point by a heavily wooded bluff of land to the north. There was a barn and other outbuildings and plenty of level land with orchards and space to bivouac the special Life Guard that Arnold planned to assemble. It was a lonely place—there were no other buildings in sight. Except for a trail off to the southeast, the only road was the River Road, which passed in front of the house and ran through wooded country to Fishkill in the north and Peekskill to the south. Between the road and the river was a fairly steep, overgrown stretch of more than two hundred yards.

After Colonel Lamb and General Arnold had traded greetings, Lamb queried Arnold about choosing to live at Beverly instead of West Point. Arnold responded that he planned to have his wife and child with him. After a good meal, Arnold watched Lamb descend the difficult path to the dock on the river, where his barge awaited. Now his planning could begin in earnest.

From the narrative of Richard Varick

After two years of living at home with my parents and reading for the law, I was, frankly, bored. Initially, I had been concerned about their safety in the no-man's-land of northern New Jersey, but by 1780 the problems had died down somewhat. When the call came from Generals Schuyler and Arnold, asking if I would be interested in reenlisting to serve as Arnold's secretary at West Point, I was intrigued. I had tried to follow Arnold's career through the newspapers ever since our sad parting at Albany, and was happy to see him revived and back into action.

There were some inducements in the offer. Arnold wrote that I would be able to have some time for continuing to read my law books. And the matter of rank was easily established. I knew that David Franks was still with Arnold, in fact was his only military aide. I would outrank David. But Arnold pointed out that our assignments would be different, Franks to continue to serve as a sort of general aide, while I would be a secretary to handle correspondence and much of the accounts of West Point.

It was too good an opportunity for me to miss, and before mid-August I had arrived with my gear at Beverly to resume my military activity.

I soon learned that Arnold had changed. There was little of the camaraderie we had experienced at Valcour Bay and Saratoga. He placed me at the far end of a large ground-floor working space in Beverly and loaded me up with paperwork. He spent most of his time in his smaller inner office, which he made clear was to be kept inviolate.

Franks and I soon became good friends, and we complained to each other of Arnold's personal withdrawal from us, and the many letters he tried to send into New York. But never once did we think of the real conspiracy that was unfolding around us. We came to think of Arnold as an avaricious man who was trying to line his own pockets.

In particular, we were dismayed at Arnold's apparent friendship with a man who seemed to be a Tory, Joshua Hett Smith. Franks disliked Smith greatly, and I soon came to share his view. Even the arrival of Mrs. Arnold and her baby, in early September, only temporarily relieved the pressure that was growing—for whatever reasons, Franks and I were unable to comprehend until too late.

Chapter 51

Robinson House
August–September, 1780

Once in residence at the Robinson House, Arnold set to work zealously to implement his plan. At West Point, he selected two men from each company for a Life Guard to live at Beverly in tents erected on the acreage. Eleven of them were detailed to serve as the ten oarsmen and coxswain for the barge that was given over exclusively to Arnold's service. It was an elegant thirty-foot boat, complete with awnings and seats, and also sported a sail that could sometimes be used on the river.

Arnold began inspecting West Point for his secret purpose of preparing it for a British takeover. It was not an easy task, because he had to weaken the fort by strengthening it. Sir Henry Clinton's terms had specified delivering the fort and three thousand troops—there were less than fifteen hundred currently on duty there. The twelve hundred troops from Albany that Howe had spoken of, in true army fashion, turned out to be fewer than five hundred, and came down to West Point only after repeated orders by Arnold. He ransacked his large command for small bands of troops here and there, and gradually began to augment the garrison. He then planned to break these men up into work groups to be sent out to nearby locations where they could be surrounded and captured. This was inventive work, and Colonel Lamb began to grow concerned over the detachments scheduled to be sent out from West Point on construction details or to cut down trees for winter wood.

The chain across the Hudson served Arnold's purpose through neglect. The engineers had identified important repairs that were needed, and Lamb was anxious to get the work done. Here he ran into confusing delays by his commanding officer, who secretly was satisfied that a good-sized ship would easily break the chain.

Back at Robinson House, Arnold greeted Varick when he arrived on August 13th. The new aide was so full of energy that Arnold soon began to regret the decision to bring him on board. Given his large area of command, Arnold needed at least two full-time staff aides to look sufficiently proper, but he really wanted two quiet and relaxed aides. Varick was anything but that, and his enthusiasm soon perked up Franks, who had begun to gripe and complain about the new distance between himself and Arnold.

Arnold was anxious to find safe channels for communicating with the British in New York, only fifty miles away. He was still waiting for a response to his offer to deliver West Point for twenty thousand pounds. In answer to a query, Joshua Smith wrote Arnold a note saying that his predecessor, on his own authority, had given passes to civilians to go through the lines. Arnold thought he was in business until Varick looked at the note over his shoulder and reacted.

"Smith is a damned Tory," Varick exploded. "That's a civilian affair!" At Arnold's visible irritation, Varick was puzzled. "What's the matter? Ask the governor, if you don't believe me."

Arnold wrote a note to the governor, and back came the predictable reply: only the civilian authority could issue such passes. For the present, his only way to communicate a fifty-mile distance was to use a three-hundred-mile distance—via Peggy in Philadelphia and then back to New York via Stansbury. Even that route became constrained when Stansbury abruptly quit as a courier, his nerves strained by all the trips he had made to New York.

August became a lonely ordeal for Arnold. He put Varick to work with a load of West Point accounts and kept Franks busy on errands, irritating both of them. Squire Smith came to visit several times, and the two aides barely concealed their hostility for the young man, who seemed so at ease with their oddly distant chief. Arnold's leg began to ache again, and he longed for the presence of Peggy, the one person in the world to whom he could unburden his innermost thoughts. He filled the void with letters to Peggy, showing his nervousness and depression.

Late in the month, a letter from her revealed that she had received a message from André—Sir Henry had accepted Arnold's terms for West Point. Arnold's heart leaped—it was the first time he had heard from André in a month. And then there was the postscript from Peggy—she wanted to come to West Point to be there with her husband. It was a decision the Arnolds had postponed. Arnold was concerned that a successful capture of West Point by the enemy would put him squarely with the British. If Peggy were at Robinson House it would be very difficult—probably impossible—to find a way to include her on the right side of the lines. But Arnold was past such concerns now. Peggy could feign innocence in Robinson House as easily as she could in Philadelphia. He only wanted to see her.

The news that Peggy would be coming enlivened the household. There was a dividend for Arnold in getting rid of the troublesome, griping Franks for a while. He sent him off to Philadelphia to escort the lady he admired so much, and with him sent a nervous, excited letter of instructions. He worked out an itinerary for Peggy based on stopping over on six nights along the way and suggested specific places for her to stay. He cautioned her to send Punch ahead to check on each place every day, and to order her dinner. He urged her not to hurry: "Let me beg you not to make your stages so long as to fatigue you or the dear boy, even if you should be much longer in coming." He suggested she ride in the open wagon with extra cushions, which would be more comfortable in the hot weather of September than the closed carriage. At each ferry or bridge crossing, she should alight from the wagon to be safe from accidents. She should carry with her some ham or tongue and her own wine.

At Robinson House, preparations were also under way. Arnold wanted to barter some of the stack of rations owed to him for actual produce, in order to set as fine a table as possible when Peggy arrived, but Varick had objected to previous attempts. He was given an assignment to find a new mattress for the master bed, which sent him away from the property for a while, allowing Arnold to proceed in his bargaining with local farmers.

A disagreeable letter from Hannah arrived, which put Arnold out of sorts. A year her famous brother's junior, Hannah had remained a spinster to serve him, caring for his children and handling his business accounts. Now she lived in perpetual unease in a household dominated by Peggy, half her age, beautiful, socially active, even too much so in Hannah's view. Hannah had plenty to be concerned about—the grinding heat that made her want to die, the two older boys away at a strange school where she feared they were desperately unhappy, her pervasive loneliness—almost ignored by Peggy and "socially cut" by old friends in the city. Arnold did not want Hannah and eight-year-old Harry at Robinson House, and he had made the point in a series of letters to Hannah. These were "diatribes," in Hannah's view: "Ill nature I leave to you, as you have discovered yourself to be a perfect master of it." Hannah's instincts and intuition told her something was terribly wrong, but she couldn't identify what it was. She vacillated between grim, lonely bitterness to outpourings of sugary love for the infant Edward Shippen Arnold. She was aggravated by the many visits of Congressman Robert Livingston to see Peggy: "I could tell you of frequent private assignations and of numberless billets doux, if I had an inclination to make mischief. But as I am of a very peaceable temper, I'll not mention a syllable of the matter." Hannah's veiled implication of Peggy's infidelity did not disturb Arnold. Cultivating Livingston had been part of the plan.

Arnold was past caring about Hannah, about old comrades such as John Lamb—they had been deluded as he had. He was setting about to make it right, and they soon would understand. Meanwhile, the need to find new ways to communicate with New York was essential, now that Peggy was to leave

Philadelphia. Fortunately two travelers appeared in the same week at Robinson House to obtain passes from Arnold, based on letters of authorization from the governor. William Heron, a member of the Connecticut Assembly, wanted to go to the north end of Manhattan to collect a debt. Arnold invited him to stay overnight while he worked laboriously on a letter to André in mercantile language and disguised handwriting. He sealed the letter and then broke the seal, telling Heron it had been left with him for delivery to New York and he had examined it. Heron went to New York for his real business—offering his services to the British as a spy—and never delivered Arnold's letter, which he thought was unimportant.

Arnold had better luck with the next person, a woman named Mary McCarthy, wife of a British prisoner of war, who was traveling with her two small children. Arnold included Varick in this attempt, telling him that he was corresponding with an American secret agent in New York. He dictated a letter to Varick for Mrs. McCarthy to deliver to James Osborne, the code name for Jonathan Odell. Once again in the phony language of trade, Arnold asked "John Anderson" (John André) to meet him at the most forward American outpost, posing as an American agent. This was the post at Lower Salem in Westchester County under the command of Colonel Elisha Sheldon of the dragoons. Mrs. McCarthy left for British lines aboard Arnold's barge. Arnold then wrote to Sheldon to begin to prepare him for the visit of a secret agent to his post to meet with General Arnold on September 11th.

"The tide of the war has changed drastically," Sir Henry Clinton said to the men who had joined him for tea in his office at One Broadway. He allowed himself a small smile, his lips twitching, and glanced at Admiral George Rodney. "Thanks to you, sir."

Rodney graciously bowed his head. He had arrived from the Caribbean with ten ships of the line, giving the British naval superiority in North American waters. The French fleet that had worried Admiral Arbuthnot so much was blockaded at Brest. "I thank you, sir," Rodney said. "And I would add the loss of the American southern army in South Carolina. By Jove, Cornwallis gave Horatio Gates a good roasting!"

John André, Wilhelm von Knyphausen, and Beverly Robinson joined in the general laughter over the fate of Gates, who had not only lost his entire army in the battle at Camden but also fled the scene for 180 miles. "So much for the hero of Saratoga!" André expostulated.

Sir Henry smiled. "Yes, indeed. And we have the real hero of Saratoga, Benedict Arnold, at our disposal. That's why I wanted to meet with you, gentlemen. Everything is favorable to our cause now. The enemy, which was threatening us not too long ago, now can do nothing this season. The French army in Providence is cowering out of concern for the loss of their naval support. If we don't bag them beforehand, they'll spend the winter there. And be ready to leave for home as soon as they can in the spring, I'll warrant."

Rodney said: "We should certainly let them go unmolested—until they get out to sea!"

There was easy laughter at this among the gathering of men. Colonel Robinson, dressed in the green uniform of a Loyalist officer, refilled cups of tea for himself and General von Knyphausen.

"The Americans are in dismal shape," Sir Henry resumed. "We have reliable word that Washington is turning away the few recruits who show up at his headquarters in Tappan. He can't feed them, by God!"

André said: "It's literally true. The farms are bursting with produce, and Washington can't feed his men because he has no money. It's really quite pathetic."

"What all of this means for us," Sir Henry said, "is that it's the perfect time to seek a major victory. If we take West Point and bring Arnold to our side, it will be a catastrophic blow to the Americans. The French will leave the war. Washington's army will dwindle away. We'll be victorious. I tell you, ever since I heard that Arnold had taken command at West Point, I've been eager for this."

"We'll be ready," Rodney said. "As soon as you give the word, I'll cancel shore leave and have the vessels loaded and ready for the dash up the Hudson."

"I know I can count on you, Admiral," Sir Henry said, once again thankful for the fates that had delivered this cooperative person from the other service in place of the irascible and unhelpful Arbuthnot. "But first we need to work on the plan and the timing. And before that, we've got to make certain that we're really dealing with Arnold."

"How so?" Rodney was shocked. "I thought you'd been in touch with him for well over a year."

"We have. At least we think we have. A very difficult communication. He's never used his own name nor his own handwriting. It's been an off-and-on business. It's warm again, now that Arnold is at West Point. Our intermediaries say that it *is* indeed Arnold—but we've got to make certain."

"Yes, of course you must," Rodney said. "How do you propose to do that?"

Sir Henry grimaced. "There's really no other way than a face-to-face meeting. One of our own officers meeting with Arnold, somewhere, under some guise. He wants a meeting as much as we do—to settle the plan. And make sure he'll get his demands. We've just received his letter, signed 'Gustavus.' He proposes a meeting at an American outpost at Lower Salem. But the gall of it! He wants Major André to come to the meeting *disguised* as an American agent!"

General von Knyphausen, Clinton's deputy commander, shook his head and spoke in German: "That cannot be. If something goes wrong, André would be in danger. Arrested without his uniform. As a spy."

"Exactly," Sir Henry said after André had translated. "We can't allow that. In fact, I don't think Major André should be involved in this at all."

"But, sir—"

"John, I don't think this is appropriate for you. That's why I invited Colonel Robinson to join the meeting. We understand that Arnold is living in the colonel's house, a few miles south of West Point, amazingly enough. There are matters to discuss, furniture, I believe." Robinson nodded. "He'll make an excellent officer to meet with Arnold. *In* uniform! And at a different place. Lower Salem is too far inland. I suggest Dobbs Ferry. Our lines come up that far and our ships control the river. The time is right, September 11th, if we get our message off to Arnold right away. What say you?"

André was nervously fidgeting. He was badly in need of this assignment, the one that could end the war, so that he could become well known, so that his rank of major would not lapse to the lowest captain in his regiment, once Clinton went home and André again was left adrift, subject to the whims of a new commander.

"Sir, I think Colonel Robinson is an excellent choice as well. But I beg you to consider that it is I who has been corresponding with Arnold all this time. He expects to meet with me. I'm the chief of intelligence and—"

"Yes, John," Clinton said in a kindly tone, "but that's why you probably shouldn't go." Watching the disappointment cloud André's face, Clinton relented. "Well, you could *go,* of course, as a member of the escort. But Colonel Robinson should do the negotiating."

When Arnold received André's latest letter from Sheldon, he was horrified. He had identified John Anderson as a civilian spy, while André identified him as a British officer! He immediately wrote to Sheldon to disclaim the letter, saying that something had interrupted his correspondence. There was not enough time to correspond with the British again. Arnold bitterly decided he would have to take the risk of going to the vicinity of Dobbs Ferry and try it the British way. Sir Henry was insisting on it.

Two days later, Arnold sat in his boat for the grueling eighteen-mile ride down the Hudson to Belmont, Joshua Smith's mansion on the plateau overlooking the town of Haverstraw and wide Haverstraw Bay. He stayed the night and left the following morning, down the steaming river past Teller's Point, heading for the Dobbs Ferry area. At last the docks came in sight, across the river from the American blockhouses on the western shore. Arnold was unhappy with the thought of having to meet a British officer under flag of truce to discuss devious business while patriots watched from a distance. Then, suddenly, a British gunboat darted out from the shore and began firing its cannon at Arnold's barge. Obviously, André had not remembered to alert the gunboats, Arnold thought, as his oarsmen pulled strongly for the American shore and cannonballs hit the water on either side of the boat. An American blockhouse on the shore opened up on the gunboat, which then pulled back a distance, but continued to row up and down like a terrier before a rat hole. Nothing to do but wait, Arnold concluded, and see if André makes an appearance and calls off his gunboats. He passed the time chatting with the blockhouse commander.

André and Robinson had ridden up from Kingsbridge. They came into Dobbs Ferry, keeping back away from the shoreline. Unaware of the gunboat attack, they waited, too, hoping that Arnold would soon show up. Hours passed. As dusk neared, André and Robinson gave up and turned their horses around. On the opposite shore, a boat bearing a very disgruntled Benedict Arnold pulled quietly away from the blockhouse and headed north up the river.

Three days later, on the 14th, Arnold was on the river again, making the eighteen-mile trip to Belmont, where he expected to meet Peggy. He was still trying to figure out how to meet with John André after the abortive effort of the 11th. It was now clear to him that André, under Sir Henry's direct orders, would insist on wearing his uniform. Arnold was working on a draft of a letter to New York that would contain the final elements of a plan for the meeting. The location: Belmont, or a spot very near to it.

On the terrace at Belmont, Arnold rushed forward to embrace Peggy. They clung to each other for a long minute, Squire Smith and his wife beaming at them from a distance. As the two gradually relinquished their embrace, Arnold was able to whisper to Peggy that she should keep Franks with her and engage Mrs. Smith in conversation so that Arnold could have some vital words with Mr. Smith.

While she and Franks chatted over tea with Mrs. Smith in the parlor, Arnold drew her husband aside on the terrace. He found the gullible country squire anxious to cooperate. Arnold said he planned to bring his secret agent from New York City ashore at Haverstraw Bay five nights from now, possibly on the 20th. Smith needed to be sure that his house was free of family and servants. He would be obliged to row out to Dobbs Ferry to fetch the agent. It developed that Smith had no rowboat. Arnold fumed but said he would requisition one at Stony Point to serve the purpose. Smith said he had two farm hands who could row the boat for him. Arnold would come to Belmont once the agent were safely on shore. Despite the prospect of a long nighttime pull on the river, all the way to Dobbs Ferry and back, Smith was all eager agreement.

The next morning, Peggy marveled at the scenery of the Hudson River and Highlands, the steep hills already showing the first tinges of autumn, as Arnold's barge proceeded northward, past Fort Montgomery until Robinson House came in sight, gleaming white on its plateau on the right bank. At Beverly, Peggy's personality was at its enchanting best, as the entire compound turned out and excitement reigned. Varick greeted her most enthusiastically; Franks stood nearby, wryly amused.

A confidential letter from Washington awaited Arnold. The chief was undertaking a rare journey away from his army, traveling to Providence to meet with the French commanders: "I shall be at Peekskill on Sunday evening, on my way to Hartford to meet with the French admiral and general. You will be pleased to send down a guard of a captain and fifty at that time, and direct the quartermaster to have a night's forage for about forty horses. You will keep this to yourself, as I want to make my journey a secret."

Traveling with the chief would be Knox, Lafayette, Hamilton, other aides, and twenty of his own Life Guard. It was a perfect opportunity for the British to capture the lot of them, though there probably was not enough time to get organized. But Arnold hastily wrote to André anyway.

On the day he was to leave for his evening meeting at King's Ferry with Washington, Arnold was the host of an enlarged midday meal, Peggy's first Sunday dinner in the new house. There was tension in the air, because Franks and Varick were so unhappy at the presence of Smith and his family. Joshua Smith was taking his family upriver to Fishkill for a week's stay with relatives, thus getting them out of Arnold's way. Colonel John Lamb and other West Point officers completed the table in the spacious dining room of the house. No sooner had everyone sat down when a courier arrived from a sloop in the river to deliver a message to Arnold from Beverly Robinson. The sloop had been sent by Colonel James Livingston, American commander at King's Ferry, who had received the message from HMS *Vulture*, now anchored off of Teller's Point. Arnold opened the letter in front of everyone and read that Robinson wanted to meet him to discuss the disposition of his furniture. The letter contained references known only to Arnold, verifying that Robinson was part of the conspiracy.

Colonel Lamb reacted energetically. "How dare he propose a meeting with you?" He advised writing Robinson to contact the governor or, better yet, for Arnold to show the letter to General Washington later in the day. Arnold agreed to do the latter.

After lunch, Arnold and Franks set out for King's Ferry, riding horse this time instead of taking the barge down. The situation at the important river crossing was peaceful in the late-afternoon autumnal haze. Arnold was not surprised—his message to André could not have arrived in time to mount an action. He and Franks were waiting at Verplanck's Point when Washington's party of less than forty men arrived across the river from Stony Point, where they met with the additional guard of fifty men that Arnold had ordered Colonel Livingston to provide.

On the ride to the house in Peekskill, where Arnold was to join Washington and his party to spend the night, Arnold conversed with the chief. Washington was appalled at Beverly Robinson's request to meet with Arnold. Refer him to the governor, the chief said. Then he told Arnold confidentially to expect him at Robinson House in perhaps five days' time on his return from his meeting with the French in Hartford. Washington wanted to inspect West Point. He would stay the night with the Arnolds, probably the following Saturday or Sunday, September 23rd or 24th. Would that be acceptable?

Chapter 52

The Hudson River Valley
September 17–22, 1780

Arnold was intent on forging the final plan when he returned from seeing Washington. He found his household quiet but soon learned it was the quiet between the storms. Peggy told him how enraged Varick had become at Smith, soon after Arnold and Franks had left on their trip. She had tried everything to separate the two, and finally calmed Varick down by complimenting him as "a warm, staunch Whig," after Smith and his family left for Fishkill. Then the storm returned after Arnold and Franks came back, Franks losing his poise over some exchange that Arnold couldn't even remember. Franks petulantly cried that Arnold had repeatedly insulted him on their trip. He shouted that he would resign and fled to his room. That disturbed Peggy, and Arnold had to calm her by saying that it was just a nervous outburst from Franks. He wouldn't resign.

By late evening, past ten o'clock, all was blessedly quiet as Arnold sat with Peggy at a round table before the windows and door in the master bedroom that led out to the balustraded porch on the second floor of Beverly. The room was dark except for the glow of a single candle on the table before them, which had been cleared for their work. Arnold had listed all of the decisions he had made and would make to weaken West Point. With that completed, he leaned back and looked at his lovely young wife. She had noted everything he had said about West Point. And she was wrenchingly beautiful, her eyes piercing and her face limned by the candlelight.

"Now let me tell you about the plan," Arnold said, keeping his voice low— one could never know who might be eavesdropping. "Washington said I couldn't agree to meet with Robinson. It's a civilian affair. But I have to *tell* him that!" he smiled smugly. "That means that tomorrow I can write to Robinson. I'll send a captain of my own Life Guard with the message, under a flag of truce, directly to Robinson, on the *Vulture* or at Dobbs Ferry."

He paused as he saw the nervous strain return to Peggy's face. He took her hand. "That's what frightens me so much," she said. "The uncertainty."

"What uncertainty?"

"Dobbs Ferry is so far from Belmont."

"If the *Vulture* is in the river, that's where Robinson will be. I have to include Dobbs Ferry, just in case he's gone back. I wouldn't worry about it." He patted her hand.

"You keep saying 'Robinson.' I thought it was André you wanted."

"I do. But Robinson is the excuse—and the channel to André."

"It's so confusing," Peggy said. "How can we be sure of anything?"

"It's only the timing that's delicate. Washington said he'd be here in five or six days' time. That's next weekend. I've got to see André before that, soon, and let him get back to New York. If the British can organize and move in time, they could take Washington as well as West Point!"

Peggy shuddered. "That's a terrible business. Besides, if Washington is with you at West Point when the British attack, won't he be the one giving the orders?"

Arnold thought for a moment. "Yes, that's a good point." He seized Peggy by the arms, smiling. "I knew there was a reason I included you in this!"

Peggy smiled nervously. Arnold kissed her and then leaned back and said: "But, think of it, Peggy! Capturing Washington! *And* West Point! The war would be over. In one stroke. We'd make a fortune!" He sighed heavily as he watched her anguish return. "Don't worry. It'll be Clinton's decision."

"How soon can you see André?" Peggy asked.

"I'm going to try for Thursday. I'll tell Robinson that my man will come for André on Wednesday night, to bring him to Belmont. I'll be there Thursday morning for our meeting."

"What shall I do while you're gone?"

"Just continue to be yourself. Continue to run the household. Start preparing for Washington's arrival next weekend. And remember, you know nothing of what I'm doing, no matter what happens."

She nodded, but her expression was bleak. Arnold studied her face. She had been a source of strength through all of the planning. Now it was upon them, and the tension was palpable. Would she be able to hold up and see it through?

The next morning, Monday the 18th, Arnold found Varick to be in an obnoxious mood, glowering as if he were ready to resign, too. He had become uncommonly troublesome. Even Arnold's unalloyed glee at the humbling of Horatio Gates in South Carolina had been muted when Varick said it was, after all, an American defeat. Varick, of all people! Sighing, Arnold handed Varick a draft of the letter to Robinson.

"My God," Varick expostulated. "Sounds as if it's written to a friend rather than an enemy!"

"Oh, really?" Arnold asked mildly. "Why don't you rewrite it then? Put it in proper language." Varick stalked off to do the rewriting. The letter was irrelevant, anyway. What would count was whatever Arnold put in the envelope with it. Arnold wrote:

I shall send a person to Dobbs Ferry, or on board the Vulture, Wednesday night the 20th, and furnish him with a boat and a flag of truce. You may depend on his secrecy and honor, and that your business, of whatever nature, shall be kept a profound secret. . . . I have enclosed a letter for a gentleman in New York from one in the country on private business, which I beg the favor of you to forward, and make no doubt he will be permitted to come at the time mentioned.

The "gentleman in New York" would be understood by Robinson to be André. Arnold was being as clear as he could about who he expected to come ashore with Smith. He then wrote a second note to André with Washington's itinerary, including his plan to stay at Robinson House the following weekend. Later, he inserted his two additional notes into the envelope that Varick provided him, wondering just how Varick would feel if he knew what was really going to Robinson. He carefully sealed the envelope with hot wax and called for Captain Archibald of his Life Guard.

Two days later, as expected, Smith passed by Robinson House on his way home after leaving his family at Fishkill. He managed to see Arnold without being observed by Varick. Arnold brought him up to date. That very night, his "American spy" would be ready to come ashore near Belmont. He gave Smith a pass that would cover "John Anderson," the only name he was to know.

"Will you be ready?" Arnold queried.

"I will." Smith was glad that the long pull to Dobbs Ferry was probably out. He was tired, having already come twenty miles, and he had twenty to go to get home.

"All right," Arnold said, "bring him ashore to your house tonight. I'll be there tomorrow morning early."

On the late morning of the same day, Sir Henry Clinton held Arnold's letter before his eyes. Then he laid it down and picked up the note to André. His eyes glinted as he addressed the two men sitting before him, André and General von Knyphausen. "Arnold says Washington will be staying at Robinson

House this weekend, possibly Saturday night. With a corporal's guard! What an incredible opportunity. If we were to take Washington *and* West Point, the war would be over!" His smile faded and he shook his head. "But I don't see any way of doing it. That's only three or four days from now."

"If we begin organizing immediately"—von Knyphausen shrugged his shoulders—"perhaps we could."

"We just don't know enough. It could be a trap, after all. Remember, we're not completely certain that the man we've been corresponding with is really Benedict Arnold." As usual, André translated for him.

"It must be him," von Knyphausen said. "He told us that Washington would be at Peekskill last Sunday night. And he was there."

Sir Henry's conservative nature dominated. "Yes, but the message arrived on Monday," he said drily. "This could all be a very clever ruse. Very clever, indeed." He fell silent, his brow knitted in thought.

"We must have the meeting with Arnold first," André said. "According to his note, it's set for tonight. If we can see him and get back here tomorrow, then—"

"Yes," Clinton mused, "he's insisting on seeing you, John. He's dictating to us."

His two visitors said nothing, André fidgeting a bit. Clinton watched him, somewhat concerned over André's eagerness to go on the mission. Over the last few days, he had been working on completing his latest poem, *The Cow Chace*. It was a mock epic, lampooning General Anthony Wayne, who had been beaten off in an attack and had captured a herd of cows on his retreat. The night before, André had recited the last quatrains at a party at Baroness Frederika von Riedesel's house. Now he was aching to go on a dangerous mission. Clinton remembered the ending of the poem: *And now I've closed my epic strain / I tremble as I show it / Lest this same warrior-drover Wayne / Should ever catch the poet*. That could be the problem, Clinton thought. André was a born romantic. That was his charm—and he was a very competent romantic.

"You'll have to go, John," Clinton said at last. "Go up river and join Robinson and Sutherland on the *Vulture*. You'll have to leave soon so you'll be there by dusk. There are a few things I want to say to you." He ticked off the points on his fingers. "First, wear your uniform at all times. Do *not* discard your uniform for any reason. Second, if it is you who goes ashore to meet Arnold, make certain that you are are under a flag of truce and that you are in territory held by the King's arms. Or in disputed territory. A no-man's-land. *Not* American-held territory. Finally, do not carry away any incriminating papers. Is all of this clear to you, John?"

"Yes, sir."

"I hope so. Because if you violate any one of these instructions and are captured, you'd be rightfully charged as a spy. And be hanged." The last word was heavy in the air for a moment. Then Clinton said: "As for Washington, we'll wait to see what you can tell us, as you say. The baron and I will start organizing the army while you're gone—and I'll alert Admiral Rodney. Perhaps we can move out fast enough. Or we'll give up on Washington and postpone it a week. We'll see. We'll need to know what you can learn."

Brilliant in his red regimentals, André rode all the way to Dobbs Ferry, arriving there in the late afternoon. A sloop was awaiting him and, with a good wind, it reached the *Vulture* before dark. He was welcomed by Captain Sutherland and Colonel Robinson, the only two men aboard the *Vulture* who knew of the mission. They were delighted that the meeting was scheduled for that night. The three men retired to the captain's cabin for a drink and dinner, and then André rested until nearly midnight.

On the bluff at Teller's Point, a long peninsula arcing into the bay almost exactly opposite Squire Smith's mansion, Colonel James Livingston put down his spy glass. He had come down from King's Ferry to see the *Vulture,* nettled by its comfortable anchorage off the shore he commanded. "All right, my beauty," he whispered, "just stay here a day or two longer and we'll get you." He turned to Captain Asa Pittman, in charge of the emplacement, who had lodged the complaint that his small guns were unable to reach the *Vulture*. "With any luck," he told Pittman, "the six-pounders I asked Colonel Lamb to send down from West Point will be here sometime tomorrow. He's a reliable man. Then you'll have some good shooting."

Joshua Smith was relying on two tenant farmers to do the rowing to and from the *Vulture*. Their name was Colquohon, but they were known to each other and everyone else as "Cahoon." They were large, stupid, and slow-moving men. When he finally arrived home after dark, exhausted, Smith summoned Samuel Cahoon to tell him that he would be rowing out to the *Vulture* at midnight.

"We don't have no boat," Cahoon said.

"Damn!" Smith had forgotten about the letter Arnold had left with him requisitioning a rowboat at Stony Point. "We can't go tonight, then. You'll have to take a message to General Arnold at Robinson House, up near the West Point, on the other side. You'll have to get there before breakfast. And get me Joseph before you go. I'll send him to fetch the boat in the morning."

Before midnight, John André emerged on the deck of the *Vulture* and cast his eye toward Belmont. Although the day had started out grey and rainy, it now was a clear night with good starlight, but no moon. He could see a fair distance. Nothing was disturbing the water. He waited several hours, pulling the huge cloak about him against the chill. Nothing. There would be no meeting that night. He went below, bitterly disappointed.

That same night, Arnold retired thinking that everything was all set. Archibald had brought back a communication from Robinson, saying he was sorry that Arnold could not see him and that he would wait another day just to be sure. The message was clear: André was coming ashore that night and Arnold would see him in the morning. But he awoke the next morning to find Samuel Cahoon in his courtyard bearing a message from Smith—he had not brought "John Anderson" ashore. The only hope was that the *Vulture* would stand by and Anderson be able to come ashore tonight.

 Arnold was furious. How was it that he had such damned nitwits working on his behalf as Squire Smith? He told Peggy what had happened, gathered up his coat and pistols and the West Point papers, carefully wrapped, and headed down to the wharf to take his boat to King's Ferry.

Out on the *Vulture*, Major André paced the quarterdeck restlessly with Captain Sutherland and Colonel Robinson. What had gone wrong? Was there any chance that the meeting would take place that night? As the adjutant general of the British Army, André was a very visible officer, his presence always noted. Could he spend another entire day aboard the *Vulture*? He had already missed two meetings with Arnold. He finally decided that it was such a long way from British headquarters that he might as well give it one more try. He wrote a letter to General Clinton explaining what had happened and saying that he would stay on the ship and feign some kind of illness, spending the entire day in his cabin. Then at midnight he would be on deck to see if the boat had come from the shore. If it did not, he would have to go back to headquarters to start the process all over again—and perhaps not be able to come for the fourth try.

 Meanwhile, Colonel Robinson drafted a note to Arnold saying that he would wait one more day and sent it ashore to the American post at Stony Point. Inserted in the envelope was a protest against an action the day before when one of the *Vulture*'s boats was fired upon as it approached shore with a flag of truce. The protest was from the captain, but the handwriting was André's—telling Arnold that he was aboard the ship.

Arnold arrived at Stony Point in the early afternoon and was handed the communication from Robinson. He read the two letters quickly and was satisfied to know that the meeting *would* take place that night. He learned that Squire Smith had obtained the rowboat from the Stony Point landing. Arnold told James Larvey, his coxswain, to stand by at Stony Point overnight and expect to see him sometime the next morning. Arnold requisitioned a horse and disappeared down the path toward Haverstraw.

 It was dusk by the time Arnold reached Belmont. He found Squire Smith having an argument with Samuel Cahoon, who had no interest in rowing a boat out on the Hudson River late in the night. When Arnold arrived, resplendent in his blue-and-buff uniform, Cahoon began to shift uneasily. Arnold told him he was needed for the river that night.

Cahoon began twisting his cap in his hands. "I don't want to go, sir. They's guard boats out there. They're dangerous."

"Nonsense," Arnold said. "This is important for our cause. You're a patriot, aren't you?"

"Yes, suh, I be a patriot. But I was up last night to go to your place. I'm too tired to go."

"My mission is very important. I've got to have my secret agent picked up this very night."

"He could wait 'til morning."

Arnold stifled his anger and resentment and said in a deep, measured tone that his business was so important that everything depended on fetching the agent that night. Cahoon shuffled his feet and then said he couldn't row that far alone.

"Go get your brother," Smith impatiently ordered.

He left, only to return in a few minutes. He hadn't fetched his brother because he spoke to his wife and she had forbid his going. Arnold leaped up, his anger bursting out, and smashed his hand on the table. "You'll go, damn it, or I'll have you both arrested!" Cahoon backed out of the room to get Joseph and Smith accompanied him.

In half an hour, Smith returned to say that all was settled. The Cahoon brothers would row. After supper, the time was nearing for departure. The Cahoon boys reappeared to say they couldn't go. Arnold and Smith went down to the courtyard to remonstrate with them.

"I'm the military commander of this district," Arnold explained. "I'm the law. What I say goes. Either you do this very important mission tonight or I'll put you in jail. And then, when you get out, it's into the army for you for three years. Either that or you go tonight."

The brothers displayed some fear at this threat, but were still reluctant to move. Arnold switched tactics, offering each of them a fifty-dollar sack of flour. Smith gave each of the Cahoon brothers a stiff drink. Arnold again asked them to think about being in the army for three years.

Arnold sent Smith's young black slave down to the creek to make sure the boat was ready. When he returned to say that it was, Arnold ordered the Cahoon brothers to go. They resisted. Then, sorrowfully, Arnold said he was going to get the guard to arrest them. Samuel shuffled off a bit. Joseph followed him. Smith joined them. They were going down to the boat anchorage.

Smith and the brothers clambered into the boat. The oars were muffled with sheepskin, per Arnold's orders. With Smith sitting at the tiller, the brothers poled the boat out into the creek and rowed forward to the river, where the tidal current moved along, heading for the *Vulture* some three miles away. With the slave boy, Arnold rode over to the river shore and watched until the boat disappeared in the dark. Then Arnold rode back to Belmont. It would be several hours before he could expect it to return.

As the boat glided up to the *Vulture,* a startled British watch officer uttered a volley of oaths and threatened to blow them out of the water. *Where were they from and what did they want?* Smith climbed a rope ladder to the deck and asked to see the captain. Just then Colonel Robinson, having heard the noise, appeared at the door to the captain's quarters and welcomed Smith on board. He took him below and introduced him to Captain Sutherland, who was in his berth, having come down ill that day.

The two officers examined Smith's letter and the pass for "John Anderson" to come ashore. Robinson went to fetch André from his cabin and found him buttoning his uniform tunic. It was clear to Robinson that André would insist on going. He put on his large cloak, which easily obscured his uniform, and followed Robinson to the captain's cabin where he was introduced to Smith as "John Anderson."

There was some discussion of the trip to the shore. Robinson opined that it would be difficult, rowing against the current with four men in a small boat. A larger British boat would go much faster. Smith said that would violate the flag of truce, although in fact there was no flag. The idea was dropped, and Robinson and Sutherland thus consigned their adjutant general to Benedict Arnold's care. They would wait for André's return, confident that Arnold would deliver him.

Out on deck, André bid farewell to Robinson. He clambered down the rope ladder into the small boat, nodding to the Cahoon brothers. Smith came down and took the tiller, and the boat shoved off, Smith talking most of the time, but hearing few return comments as André stared piercingly toward the shore. It was again a clear night with good starlight and no moon, and the boat plowed ahead slowly.

Too restless and nervous to be comfortable at Belmont, Arnold had come down to the shore to watch for the boat. When he finally discerned its shape, he could see that the boat was struggling and coming into shore some distance downstream from Haverstraw Creek. He rode to the landing. It was past two o'clock. Arnold positioned himself in a copse of fir trees as the boat edged into the sand shore.

Smith came ashore and found Arnold. "We have him," he hissed. "I'll bring him to you."

Soon Major André came up to Arnold. It was so dark that the two men could scarcely see each other's features. "General Arnold, I presume," André said.

"Yes, indeed, Mr. Anderson, it is I. Welcome ashore."

Chapter 53

Haverstraw Bay, New York
September 22-23, 1780

The two Cahoon brothers curled up in the boat and slept. Squire Smith was ready to play an exciting role in this unusual meeting when Arnold whispered to him that he had to meet with John Anderson alone. Smith was left to walk up and down the beach, bitterly frustrated, while Arnold and André disappeared up the bank into the growth of underbrush in the clump of fir trees.

"I must apologize to you for the quality of my help," Arnold said to André. "The two oarsmen I won't even comment on. The squire, Joshua Smith, is a local landowner who loves to meddle in the war. He's the brother of your chief justice."

"Yes, I've heard of him," André said.

"He's a good fellow, but rather gullible and not too bright. He knows you only as 'John Anderson,' and it's important to keep it that way. He thinks you're here as an American agent."

"So he comes out to a British warship to bring an American agent on shore. Rather odd thing to do, isn't it?"

"It may be, but he believes it. I've taken only one person into my confidence on our side regarding what I'm proposing to do, and you know who that is. Mrs. Arnold. The only one. Now, we have to decide. We can stay here or we can ride up to Squire Smith's house. I've got the plans of West Point there and some other important papers. It's not very far and I've brought you a horse."

"I would really rather stay here, if you don't mind. Sir Henry Clinton is very conservative about my visit. This is a neutral shore, is it not?"

The shore was loosely held, but those holding it were Americans. "Well, certainly, it's isolated. I think we have no fear here. It's cold and I have no light—that *would* alert someone, possibly. But we can accomplish much here."

"Very good," André said, settling down on the pine needles and leaning back against a tree. "I shall feel much better."

Arnold sank down, his back to the tree next to André. All he could tell was that his visitor was a youthful, trim figure. He tried to see André's facial features, but it was pitch-black. André seemed to have the same thought: "One of the purposes of this meeting is to make sure that we're really dealing with General Arnold. But it's so dark, I can't even see you. Even if it were bright daylight, I wouldn't know you."

"I could show you the wound your comrades gave me at Saratoga," Arnold smiled, stroking his left leg.

"It's too dark for that as well," André said. "I could ask you about Peggy—Mrs. Arnold. Did you know that I knew her quite well in Philadelphia?"

"Indeed I do. I've even suspected that you knew her too well."

"No, no, nothing like that. We were truly good friends, but that was all. I'm sure she's told you that."

"Yes, that is what she says. And I believe her. We are very close."

"General, the thought has occurred to me, and I wonder if I may ask you. Was your idea of coming to our side primarily Peggy's doing?"

Arnold's reply was quick. "No. She was immediately supportive. But I had thought of this well before our wedding. In the beginning I fought very hard, as was my duty to do so. But I was not appreciated. We have no government. Thirteen little countries. Continually starving the army. Nothing but anarchy and greed. Sooner or later, one wakes up. Especially given the generous conditions England has been offering for the past several years. It's idiotic for us to fight. The French are our real enemy. No, sir, I was ready."

"I'm very glad of it, sir, I must tell you. Your decision gives us a new chance, a priceless opportunity. I think we had best concentrate on that now. I have much to learn from you."

"Yes, I agree. Before we go too far, let me say that I think it proper if we first settle the money questions. If I were not married, if I had no children, I wouldn't talk of money at all. But I can't risk their futures."

André instantly regretted rhapsodizing about a "priceless" opportunity. "I assumed we were already in agreement on this question," he said.

"I believe Sir Henry has agreed to twenty thousand pounds for West Point. Correct?"

"Yes."

"But he has never responded with a figure for indemnification."

"He has authorized me to offer six thousand pounds."

"I asked for ten thousand pounds."

"We're so close. It seems absurd to argue about failure."

"Yes, we're very close. The chance of failure grows slimmer. But it's not absurd to have a full agreement on the table. I insist on the full amount for indemnification."

André thought for a long moment. Time was passing and there was so much to talk about. He made his decision. "All right. I will guarantee you ten thousand pounds in the event of failure of the mission. To your wife and children if you are a casualty. I will make certain that Sir Henry pays. On my word of honor."

"That is acceptable to me," Arnold said. "Now we should get on to the plan itself. But before we do, we should consider General Washington."

"Yes," André breathed, "what a triumph that would be! Sir Henry was beside himself with elation at the prospect."

"When you think of all of our efforts and our mistakes in trying to meet for a year and a half, to consider that when we do actually meet we have *two* such prospects—West Point *and* the commander-in-chief," Arnold said. "It's as if the fates were smiling upon us. But it's an illusion, I'm afraid. We're going to *miss* this opportunity by a matter of days or hours."

"I have to tell you that Sir Henry was very pessimistic about it before I left yesterday morning. Not enough time, he said. And then we lost a day today." André spoke glumly. "I take it there's been no change from your note—when you said he'd be staying at Robinson House tomorrow night."

"That was an approximation. He told me five or six days. He could be delayed, depending on his negotiations with Rochambeau. I gather they're meeting at Hartford. But even if he doesn't come until Sunday, or even Monday, I still don't think there's enough time."

"Especially if you have no way of communicating with us in time. The truth is, Washington's presence only complicates things."

"I agree," Arnold said.

André shook his head sadly. "I do hate to give it up. But it's such a long shot. We could jeopardize the taking of West Point. I think we had better plan that, to perfection, and set a time a week or ten days hence. Then if Washington is significantly delayed and you can get word to us—we can decide whether to try to take him."

"Good. We'll keep it alive, as a contingency. But let's get our plan for West Point set first. I have so much to tell you—much of it's on paper up at the house. The ordnance, the garrison, the approaches, how the defense will be arrayed, how best to time the attack and from where. We need to discuss these and agree on a precise set of steps."

For nearly two more hours, the two men went over every detail of West Point and painted several scenarios for a British attack, always including a naval armada and troop ships coming up the river, but also landings at various points to capture isolated units and attack from the rear of the fort complex. Arnold said that between his Life Guard and troops from Fishkill, Newburgh, and other towns, he could muster 3,086 men, and then disburse them in isolated units near West Point for easy capture.

The first rays of dawn were visible to Smith down on the shore, but not to Arnold and André in their secluded area. Smith decided it was time to intervene in the conference. He came up to alert the negotiators. Arnold checked his watch and realized that he could make out the dial. It was nearly five o'clock. "We haven't finished yet," he said to André.

"I've got to go while it's still dark," André said anxiously. The men clambered down to the shore where the Cahoon brothers were visible in the boat, looking grumpy and loutish.

"You should really have the papers I've prepared," Arnold said in an aside to André. "Plans of the fort. Schedules I've made up for most of the things we've talked about."

By now, it was evident that a beautiful clear day was dawning on the Hudson River Valley. André looked out at the *Vulture,* sitting at anchor some several miles away. "I can still make it," he said.

"It'll be bright sunlight before you get halfway," Arnold said. "Every soldier in these hills will be watching the river."

"I'm afraid I have some unhappy news," Smith interjected. "The Cahoon brothers are saying they don't want to go. They seem very firm."

"Dammit, I'll take a club to them," Arnold shouted, loud enough for the Cahoons to hear.

"No," André said. "Let's go get the papers. And then we'll decide whether a daylight trip is feasible."

While Smith joined the Cahoons to row the boat back to its mooring in Haverstraw Creek, André and Arnold mounted their horses and began riding up toward the road to the north. As they entered the sleepy village of Haverstraw, a sentry challenged them but smiled and stepped aside the moment he recognized Arnold. André was in high spirits, full of the exciting adventure he was engaged in, but the challenge of the sentry brought him back quickly to Sir Henry Clinton's words. He was concealing his role as a British officer, wearing his uniform but keeping it hidden, and entering into American-held territory. But it was so easy—Arnold was known everywhere in his territory and either being with him or having a pass from him worked equally well in defraying danger. André's high spirits returned—he had decided that he wanted the papers that were up at the house.

He glanced sideways at his companion, at Arnold's hawk-nosed profile and intent gaze, giving his rugged features a somewhat ferocious cast. André was surprised at how cultivated Arnold was, in both speech and manners.

Arnold also was managing to appraise André, curious about his personal habits as described by Peggy, whether or not he truly was a lover of men. The sight of André's handsome face and graceful frame was disconcerting, as well as the sparkling personality he was displaying as they turned their horses up the long driveway to Belmont. Arnold could easily see how a maiden's heart could be turned by such a man, and he felt a wrenching in his stomach at the thought. He was tempted to probe André, but the importance of the mission dominated everything. Personal matters could wait until they were colleagues in the same army in New York.

At that moment, a booming sound and echo came from a distance, in the direction of the river. The two men glanced at each other and then spurred their horses up to a turning point at the plateau, which afforded a spectacular view of the waterway below and the hills surrounding it. They saw a red flash of light and white smoke at Teller's Point, clearly another cannon round aimed at the *Vulture* offshore. Another blast followed, and then another, the last scoring a hit, as some of the ship's rigging gave way. Finally, a blast came from the *Vulture,* aimed at the source of the enemy firing, and then a salvo followed.

"Damnation!" Arnold roared. "I told him not to do it."

"What? What's happening?" André choked.

"Colonel Livingston. He's the commander in this sector. He was irritated by the *Vulture* anchoring so near. He told me he was trying to get some six-pounders to teach her a lesson. I told him to forget it."

"Obviously, he didn't."

"No. C'mon, let's get up to the house."

Dismounting in the courtyard, Arnold led the way up to a second-floor bedroom that had a porch. The two men climbed through the window to the porch and had a more elevated vantage point for seeing the battle going on some three miles away. British sailors were trying to unfurl sails in the light winds. The cannonading continued for a long while as Arnold and André watched, with the *Vulture* taking a number of hits.

André sputtered: "Damn, I wish I were aboard her right now!"

"I think we'd better forget any daylight passage," Arnold said.

Smith and the Cahoon brothers had witnessed the opening rounds a few miles away as they labored to bring the boat around into Haverstraw Creek. They watched in awe as the land station and the warship exchanged volleys.

"My God, we coulda bin out in the middle of that," Samuel muttered. Joseph's face was blanched. "I ain't rowin' nobody nowhere tonight—or any other night."

Clearly, the Cahoons were out of it. Squire Smith's own ardor for trips by water had cooled. He made up his mind that General Arnold's agent could return to British lines by land. When they had the boat tied up, Smith leaped on his waiting horse and took off for his home. On the way, he heard a much louder explosion than any of the preceding ones. When he reached a height in the road, he reined up to examine the scene across the river. Clouds of smoke arose from Teller's Point. Clearly the British had hit the gun emplacement's magazine. And the *Vulture,* its sails flying, was moving downstream away from the scene of action.

Once at the house, Smith rushed up to the bedroom where Arnold and André were. Anxious to join in their discussion, he burst into the room, and then stopped, astonished. Mr. Anderson was wearing a British officer's uniform! In the growing warmth of the day, André had removed his cloak. Arnold got up, put an arm around Smith's shoulders, and guided him out into the hallway. "My dear fellow, you could do wonders for us by fixing up a little breakfast." Then, in a lower tone, he said: "Don't be surprised at the uniform. It's just his peculiar pride. He borrowed it from an officer before he came."

"Oh. Well, it does seem strange. But you can never tell what people will do."

"No, you can't."

"I don't think he should wear it around here," Smith tossed over his shoulder as he went down the stairs.

Later, the three men ate a cold breakfast, their conversation desultory. André was still depressed by the gunfight and the disappearance of the *Vulture*. Arnold was anxious to get home, to proceed with preparations for Washington's visit and for West Point.

"Do you think she'll come back up river tonight?" André asked.

"She probably will," Arnold said. "You'll have to consider whether it'll be safe to row out to her. You can return by land after dark, too. Even better."

"How would one go?"

"Go up to cross the river at King's Ferry, go inland a ways, and then turn south, down toward the Croton River and from there to White Plains, or another British border post. Squire Smith would go with you as a guide, at least until no-man's-land, south of the Croton. Am I correct, Squire?"

Smith was on the point of saying that return by boat was just not possible, but he held himself. Better to let events play their way out. "Of course, I would be happy to accompany you, as far as I can."

"The first part is through fortified American territory," André said.

"Yes," Arnold said, "but you'd have my passport. I'll make out two passports, for you and Squire Smith, either way, by land or sea. Then when it starts getting dark, you can choose the alternative that seems safest."

That was the judgment that André finally accepted. Arnold made out the two passports. He then gave André the West Point papers and suggested that he put them between his stockings and his feet. "If there's any sign of trouble, be sure to get rid of them," Arnold said. "Most of them are in my handwriting." Then he bid André farewell.

André spent a fitful day indoors, alternating between cursing his luck and hoping that the *Vulture* would reappear. Once he heard Squire Smith outside, speaking to a man who had come to deliver two cows. The man wanted Smith to come down to the road to see the animals, but Smith whispered excitedly that he had General Arnold's spy upstairs and could not leave the house. André shook his head at the squire's foolishness.

As dusk arrived, Smith came to André and told him they had best get ready for the return by land, inasmuch as there had been no sign of the *Vulture* on the river. André protested vigorously but was met with nothing but smiles and smooth arguments from Smith. He believed the *Vulture* would not attempt to come up river while it could still be seen from Teller's Point. If it came at all, it would be only after dark, and Smith said that trying to reach it would be too dangerous. He couldn't get oarsmen to take the risk. André finally gave in and exchanged his officer's tunic for a civilian coat of claret-colored cloth with gold button holes, loaned to him by Smith. Because his nankeen breeches, waistcoat, and boots could pass as civilian attire, he continued to wear them, after wrapping the West Point papers carefully around his feet and lower legs. He accepted a round civilian hat from Smith as the final item in his costume. The two men mounted and, accompanied by the youthful slave, set out to the north for Stony Point, the portal to King's Ferry on the west bank of the Hudson.

Arnold arrived home highly satisfied over his meeting with André, only to find that his household was in the grip of tension. There was no mistaking the sullen expressions of Varick and Franks and their monosyllabic responses to Arnold's questions. He went upstairs to find Peggy, who was in control of herself, though her face was flushed. She greeted her husband warmly, and then said: "Now I'm the court of appeal for the two gentlemen of your military family."

"What does that mean?"

"When you didn't return last night, Varick instinctively knew you were with Squire Smith. He became nearly insane with rage. He shouted that you'd listened to nothing he'd said about Smith. He told Franks he was going to resign, too. Then they came to me and tried to enlist me to convince you that Smith is not a person for you to be so intimate with." She added wryly: "I told them I would try to remonstrate with you."

"Those two become more difficult by the day," Arnold growled. "We won't have to put up with them much longer." His expression changed to one of delight. "In a matter of only one week or a little more, we'll be rich. We'll be safe in New York and on the right side!" He told the rapt Peggy of his negotiations with John André. She was thrilled at the story of her husband's meeting with the man she once thought she had loved—on such earth-shaking business—and by the fact that everything now seemed in readiness.

"I found André to be as likeable as everyone seems to think he is," Arnold said. "But I bring you no enlightenment on his sexual proclivities." He smiled. "He made no advances on me."

Peggy's stern expression was intended as a rebuke. Then she said: "I have one piece of news for you. A note came from General Washington. He'll not be arriving tomorrow. He's been delayed. He'll come for breakfast with us on Monday. He now expects to come Sunday afternoon and will confirm that beforehand."

"Damn," Arnold said softly. "I wish I'd known that. André and I decided to leave Washington out of the plan. The attack is set for a week from today. There wasn't enough time to take Washington, too. But now, with two days' more time—I wish I'd known."

"I think it's better this way," Peggy said.

*   *   *

As André and Smith rode toward Stony Point in the gathering darkness, they overtook another horseman, an American major named John Burrowes. To André's consternation, Smith slowed down to allow Burrowes to ride between them, chatting away light-heartedly. Soon Burrowes took a fork in the road to the left.

André was nervous about passing through Stony Point to the ferry dock. The year before, he had negotiated the surrender of the American garrison to Sir Henry Clinton's army. His face might be familiar to any men who had served there, were paroled, and now served there again. As they rode down a steep incline toward the ferry, they came upon a group of American soldiers carousing before a tent, passing a bowl of spirits from hand to hand. André tried to look invisible and kept going, but Smith pulled up to banter with the men. André came to a stop at the steps to the ferry. He could hear Smith laughing that the bowl was already empty. Smith was having a hilarious time, as André sat there nervously, the small black boy standing next to him.

After a few more minutes of jollity with the American troops, Smith came over and the two men pulled their horses aboard the ferry, manned by six oarsman and a coxswain. Once again, Smith was the picture of a happy good neighbor to the crew, as André stared over the side of the boat. He sidled over to whisper to Smith that haste was important, and Smith made a big-hearted gesture to the crew, saying that he would give them something to revive their spirits if they sped up the pace.

Once they reached Verplanck's Point on the eastern side of the river, André could not dissuade Smith from stopping in the office to see the commander, Colonel James Livingston, the man who had engineered the shelling of the *Vulture*. André, left to sit anxiously on his horse outside, was glad that it was now dark. His anxiety increased sharply as he heard Smith boasting of his intimacy with General Arnold and confiding that he was escorting one of Arnold's agents on some mysterious business. Livingston's voice urged Smith to bring in his friend for a drink and some dinner. To his vast relief, André heard Smith decline, saying they were in too much of a hurry. Livingston argued, and André felt a charge of panic. But Smith persevered, saying that the issue was too important for the American cause to be delayed, and eventually he came out.

Now they were in the countryside, trotting down a desolate road. Smith chattered away and André said nothing. They had gone almost six miles when a voice cried out from the darkness: "Who goes there?"

"Friends!" Smith shouted.

A sentry stepped onto the road, his musket poised. Smith talked with him for a minute, and then Captain Ebenezer Boyd came out, his face mired in suspicion. Smith dismounted, as Boyd stepped back into the bushes and then returned with a light in his hands. He grilled Smith about who he was and where he and his companion were headed. Boyd looked to André like the thugs he had known in Carlisle, a stubborn, set expression to his square-jawed face. Smith kept insisting that they were on an important mission for General Arnold, the nature of which he couldn't reveal. Boyd was not satisfied with the answer, and Smith kept proffering the passport Arnold had given him. Finally Smith came back and mounted his horse again.

"He's concerned that we're out at night," Smith said. "Says a band of the pro-British raiders, the cowboys, are on the prowl in this neck of the woods. He says we'd better find some place to stay and I think he's right."

Arnold had spoken of the gangs of ruffians that roamed in the area, mainly in no-man's-land, the cowboys and the Rebel Skinners. André would have been happy to fall into the hands of the cowboys, but he couldn't say so. There was no course but to reluctantly follow Smith as he backtracked, looking for a house where they might stay the night.

After a brief search, Smith knocked on the door of Andreas Miller's farmhouse. There was no answer, so Smith kept pounding for five minutes. Finally the door cracked. The family had been cringing inside, fearful of raiders. Smith and André were regarded suspiciously. When they entered a bedroom, Miller shut the door behind them and André heard a key turn in the lock.

André stalked the room nervously for a while and then lay down on the single bed next to Smith to try for some tortured sleep.

Chapter 54

Westchester County
September 23–24, 1780

The first dull grey of dawn woke André instantly. He leaped out of the bed where he had tossed and turned all night and went to the window. He pulled it open and began shouting for Smith's young servant. The boy soon appeared and André told him to get the horses ready—they were leaving. By this time, Smith's snoring had degenerated to a series of snorts as he lifted himself up by one arm.

"What—what are you doing?"

"It's time to leave," André said. He pounded on the bedroom door.

Smith puffed his cheeks. "My God, you're an active man in bed. Bumps and bruises all night long. I hardly slept." He swung his legs over and reached for his breeches.

Andreas Miller opened the door, and in a matter of a few minutes Smith and André were mounted and on their way with no breakfast, the servant boy padding along behind them on foot.

The disconsolate Smith, still half asleep, muttered: "I'm hungry."

"Perhaps we can stop at a farmhouse," André said.

Smith was his usual chattering self, while André was grim and determined. After a few miles, they rounded a curve in a wooded area to come upon a party of horsemen moving toward them. An American officer was leading four troopers. André's heart sank—he *knew* the officer. He was Colonel Samuel Webb, a former prisoner of war who had been paroled in New York. Webb stared at André as they neared, and André thought he was undone. But Smith waved a cheery hello and the riders passed. As soon as they were gone, André felt an exhilarating flush of excitement. He knew he was going to make it now.

They saw a number of scattered farmhouses over the next half dozen miles, but no people—everyone was inside. The autumnal beauty of the Westchester countryside seemed to inspire André, for he suddenly began to talk, even more than Smith had. He discoursed on history and peace and artistic concerns, occasionally pointing out some feature of the landscape, the tints of the season that were already in evidence, the warmth of the sun in late September, the rich blue of the Hudson peeking between the hills every now and then.

Smith marveled at André's good spirits, but he finally could no longer tolerate his hunger. He spotted a one-story farmhouse by the side of the road and stopped. "Let's see if we can get something to eat," he proposed, dismounting. André was hungry, too. He hadn't eaten since late the afternoon of the day before, at Belmont.

A Dutch housewife emerged from the house and said she had almost nothing to offer. She had been raided by one of the outlaw gangs the day before. In response to André's question, she said she didn't know who the culprits were or what side they represented. She did have some Indian meal, which she boiled with water to make suppon. André had mocked the primitive dish in the *Cow Chace,* but he took a bowl now, sat on the stone step to the house, and wolfed it down.

"We're only a mile or two from the Croton River," Smith said. "I don't want to go any further. You're coming on to territory where the British have more influence than the patriots. And the cowboy gangs roam this area."

André said: "It's all right. I can go on alone. I'm almost there."

The big British outpost at White Plains was fifteen miles away, but there were smaller ones closer, and British patrols roamed the area. The Croton River was the traditional limit for rebel patrols.

"Just go on straight here," Smith said. "Cross Pine Bridge, and when the road forks, take the right one. That'll keep you off the Kings Road. Fewer people to deal with."

"I don't have any money," André said, "no weapon either."

"I can give you some coins, but no guns. You won't need one."

"I'll give you my gold watch in return for your money—until I see you again."

"Don't be foolish," Smith said. "I wouldn't take your watch. Here," he handed some paper money and a few coins to André. "Godspeed to you, John!"

André smiled and thanked Smith. "And Godspeed to you, squire!"

The two men mounted and rode off in different directions, Smith followed by his faithful servant.

André was in good spirits. What seemed like a nightmare was now behind him. He would be with British troops soon and on his way to Manhattan to see Sir Henry and make the final plans for the assault. His horse's hooves clattered on the wooden planks of Pine Bridge. There would be no rebel patrols on the south side of the bridge. He took the fork that Smith had suggested and rode on for several miles, seeing not a soul. He was thirsty as he came upon a farm where he saw the first human being he had encountered since the Dutch farmhouse. A young girl was playing in the front yard. He reined up under a tree and dismounted, stretching his limbs.

"Hello," André said, leaning on the fence. "Could my horse and I have some water?"

The girl was frightened, but André's good appearance and smile eased her fears. She carried a half-filled bucket and ladle over to him. He drank, using the ladle, and the horse bowed his head and drank from the bucket.

"Thank you very much," André said as he handed the ladle back. He was tempted to stay a while and rest and talk to the child. But he had to get along. "This is for you." André extracted a coin and gave it to the girl, who returned a wondrous smile. He mounted his horse and waved to the girl as he rode away.

He continued on in country that was desolate for its lack of people but beautiful in its natural abundance. He must be getting near a British sentry now. Several miles passed by, and André realized that he was nearing Tarrytown, a village well beyond the rebel lines. Not much longer to go. And then three scruffy-looking men stepped out onto the road from the underbrush to bar his way, brandishing muskets. One of them grabbed his horse's bit.

André stared at the three men. "Gentlemen, I hope you belong to our party."

"What party?" asked a huge man, who seemed to be the leader.

"The lower party." When the big man nodded absently, André rushed on: "I'm glad to see you. I'm an officer in the British service, and I've been on particular business in the country, and I hope you'll not detain me. And for a token to let you know that I'm a gentleman, please take this." He pulled out his gold watch.

The big man paid no attention and ordered André to dismount. The dirty and torn jaeger coat in red and green that the man wore had encouraged André. Suddenly fearing that these were not cowboys, but the skinners who were partial to the rebel cause, André nervously exclaimed, "My God, I must do anything to get along!" He searched his pocket for Arnold's pass and held it up. The big man took it and slowly scanned it, eyes concentrating on each word.

"Damn Arnold's pass," he shouted. "You said you was a British officer. Where's your money?"

André quickly dismounted, talking authoritatively: "Gentlemen, you had best let me go, or you'll get yourselves into trouble. By stopping me, you're detaining General Arnold's business."

Two of the men moved closer, poking their weapons. "Goddammit, where's your money?" a smaller weasely-faced man sputtered.

"I'm telling you, I don't have any money! Only a few Continental dollars."

"You're a British officer and no real money?" the little man snarled.

"Let's search him," the giant decided. He grabbed the collar of André's coat and half-pulled him off the road into a thicket. He ordered him to strip. André's mind swam. He realized he'd made a terrible mistake. If these men were cowboys, they'd take him to British lines. If not, his pass from Arnold would have sufficed, had he not already said he was a British officer. The three men looked evil, the giant having close-cropped hair and a permanent woeful expression, the other two with eager, avaricious faces. Once again, André's dreams of the ruffians of Carlisle flooded into his mind. Each article of clothing he shedded was snatched, quickly examined, and thrown to the ground. All that was yielded was the watch and his few Continental dollars from Smith.

From the muttered conversation of the men, André could now identify them. The big man was John; the other two, David and Isaac. André stood there naked except for his boots and socks. Disgusted at the small haul, John had taken out a knife and was ripping the lining of André's coat. Then he went to the saddle and examined it, ripping some of the stitching to search for hidden money.

"That's all there is," he said sadly.

For a moment, it seemed that they were going to let André go. Then Isaac said: "Damn him, he may have his money in his boots." He and David threw André on the ground and began tugging off a boot. Nothing—and then they peeled his stocking and found three papers wrapped around his ankle and calf. Both men were unable to read. They passed the papers to John, who could barely do so. He labored over them, and gradually their significance dawned.

"By Jesus, he's a spy!" John exclaimed. The other leg yielded even more papers of the same kind. "Get dressed," John ordered.

His three captors fell to arguing about what to do with him. David asked: "Will you give us your horse, saddle, watch, and a hunded gold guineas if we let you go?"

"Yes," André said. "I'll have the guineas brought back here or sent to wherever you want."

"Would you give us even more?"

John snorted. "Don't be a fool. There's no way he can do that."

"Yes, I can!" André exclaimed. "Just deliver me to Kingsbridge, and you shall have five hundred guineas!"

John had been released from a British prison only four days earlier. "Yes," he said, "and all three of us would be arrested and you'd be scot-free!"

"No, two of you stay here with me and the third go to Kingsbridge with a note from me. You'll come back with a thousand guineas!"

"If we did that, a British party would come back and we'd all be prisoners," John said. He was thinking that André would be worth something to the Americans as well—and a much safer prospect. "Let's take him to the colonel."

The three men argued for a while and then concluded that John was right. They would take André to the nearest American outpost, which was at North Castle, less than a half dozen miles to the northeast. André was prodded out into the road. David took the bridle of his horse, and the procession started out. In a short distance, four other men joined them from a watch point on a nearby road.

As the party of eight trudged along the road, André's mood alternated between hope and gloom. There was some chance that a commander at an American outpost might be confused and would have him taken back to Arnold, which, very likely, would save him. And then, at one point, he said aloud: "I would to God you'd blown my brains out when you stopped me!"

After leaving André near Pine Bridge, Joshua Smith rode back to Peekskill and then on up the river to the Robinson House, en route to joining his family in Fishkill. When he jogged into the compound, Arnold spotted him and greeted him joyously. The sight of Smith was convincing evidence to Arnold that "John Anderson" had made it safely back to Manhattan.

"All's well, I take it," Arnold said.

"Yes. I stayed with him 'til British territory. No problem."

Arnold gave a reassuring nod to Peggy as she emerged from the house. She came forward to greet Smith enthusiastically, forgetting for the moment her recent pledge to Varick and Franks to persuade her husband to stop seeing the squire. This was observed by David Franks from the large office on the ground floor. He expostulated bitterly and described the scene for Varick, who was lying on a couch, not feeling well.

Colonel John Lamb had been invited to dinner at Robinson House and arrived at two P.M. Arnold and Peggy, with the two military aides, sat down to dinner at three o'clock with Lamb and Smith. Varick and Franks were sullen and curt with Smith, who was entirely unaware of their hostility. He chatted away easily as dinner proceeded.

Colonel Lamb asked for the butter and then realized there was none. "Ah, but it's scarce," he said.

Peggy called to the serving girl to bring some, but the girl replied that the household was out of butter.

Arnold said: "Bless me, but I've forgotten the olive oil I bought in Philadelphia." He looked to the servant. "Bring us a pitcher of that, it'll go well with salt fish."

After a few moments, the girl returned with a pitcher and set it on the table. "That cask of olive oil cost me eighty dollars," Arnold said.

"More like eighty pence!" Smith laughed.

The implication that a Continental dollar was worth only one English penny, nearly true as it was, broke through Varick's cold mask. "You're mistaken," he cried in a loud voice.

"Oh, I say," Smith retorted. "What are you talking about? Of course, it's true!"

Now feeling more acutely the fever that was coming upon him, his face flushed, Varick snarled: "You damned Tory. You'd say anything to embarrass the patriots!"

Smith shouted a denial, and then Franks joined in, criticizing Smith in his high-pitched, nervous voice. "Quiet!" Arnold snapped, but he was drowned out as the argument escalated and the volume rose. Lamb looked on, astonished, and Peggy, seeing that her husband was about to lose control, cried out. "Stop it, stop it," she pleaded. "I beg you to stop!"

Instantly, where clamorous voices had reigned, there now was deathly silence, until the meal was finished. Squire Smith abruptly left for Fishkill to his family, and Colonel Lamb returned to West Point. As soon as both were gone, Arnold strode into the large office and grabbed Franks by the arm.

"Dammit!" he swore, "if I ask the devil to dine with me, I expect the gentlemen of my family to be civil to him. What the hell is the matter with you?"

Franks responded bitterly: "If he'd been at any house but yours, I'd have taken the bottle to his head—and treated him like the rascal he is."

The two men glared each other as Varick slowly rose from the couch where he had lain again. Franks tore himself away and shouted over his shoulder as he left the room: "I'm going to Newburgh. And I don't know if I'll be back. I'm resigning your service."

"Why are you picking on Franks when I'm the one who started the argument?" Varick demanded, his face flushed and his eyes feverish.

"You're sick."

"Damn right, I'm sick of Smith. He's a damned rascal, a scoundrel, and a spy! You'd better be careful if you want to stand well in this State." He ranted on with inflamed passion, while Arnold listened in icy composure.

"If you're finally through," Arnold said, "let me tell you that I'm always willing to be advised by members of my family, but, by God, I will not be dictated to by them!" He stalked out of the room.

Arnold's mind was churning. He'd have to put up with these two malcontents for only a few more days. He sat on a bench in the dying sun on the porch and gradually began to calm down. As dusk settled in, he finally rose and said aloud, "I'd best put some peace on it." He went searching for Varick and found him in his small bedroom lying on his bed, wrapped in a blanket. He sat on the chair by the side of the bed.

"You really are sick, aren't you?"

"Yes," came the sullen response. "I'm chilled and I ache all over."

"It could be that wicked influenza," Arnold said. "It's too late to get Dr. Eustis from West Point. I'll send for him in the morning. And I'll send Peggy down to see if she can find something to comfort you." Arnold paused for a while. Then he said: "Listen, Dirk, I'm sorry we had that argument. I've thought about it, and I can tell you that I'll never go to Smith's house again or be seen with him, unless it's in company."

Varick was astonished at the apology, but his expression did not change. Arnold patted him on the arm and then rose to go. "I'll send Peggy," he said as he left the room. On his way, the thought in his mind was of Varick and Franks in prison a few days from now.

Lieutenant-Colonel John Jameson watched out the window of his outpost as a band of men approached with a prisoner, about the same time of day that Squire Smith arrived at Robinson House. A Virginia gentleman, affable and easy to talk to, Jameson turned to Lieutenant Solomon Allen and said: "My goodness, here comes big John Paulding and his gang. Looks like they're bringing us somebody."

The two men walked outside and greeted Paulding, without much enthusiasm. He and his gang were becoming something of a pest to them.

"We got a spy, Colonel," Paulding said, bringing André forward.

"Is that right?"

"Indeed it is. His name is John Anderson. Has a pass from General Arnold, but he's also got some spy papers." He handed over the wad of papers to Jameson. "We caught him goin' south to British lines. He tried to bribe us."

"Well, it was good of you to resist that," Jameson said with mild irony. "We'll take Mr. Anderson and find out what's going on. Thank you, John."

"Beggin' your pardon, sir, but if he's a spy, there ought to be some kind of reward."

"Well, that could be. Why don't you come back tomorrow?" He turned to André. "Would you come in, sir?"

"We'll wait for a while," Paulding said, as he and his men started to move away.

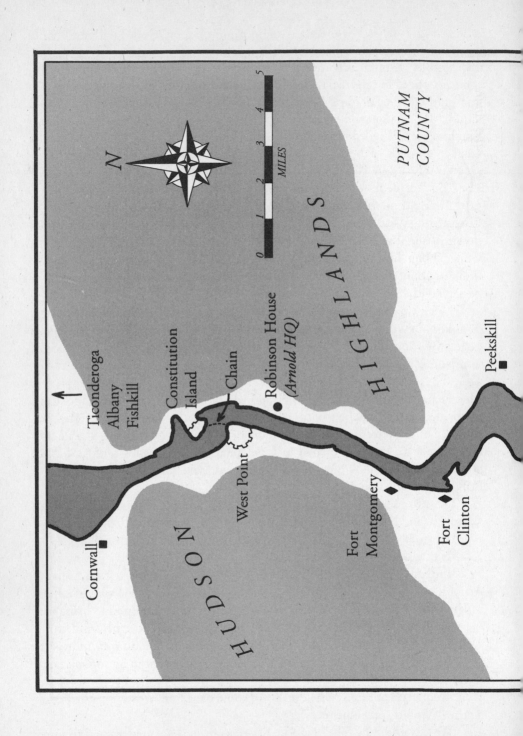

N

0 1 2 3 4 5
MILES

PUTNAM COUNTY

HIGHLANDS

Peekskill

Robinson House
(Arnold HQ)

Chain

Constitution
Island

Ticonderoga
Albany
Fishkill

West Point

Fort
Montgomery

Fort
Clinton

HUDSON

Cornwall

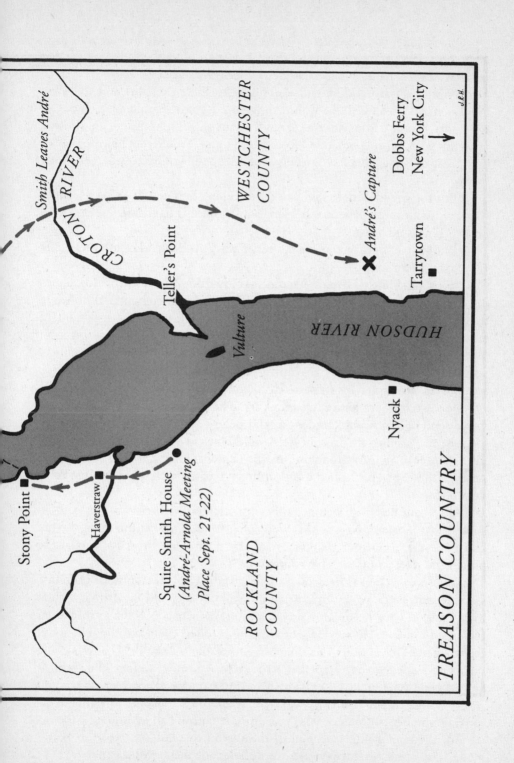

Smith Leaves André

CROTON RIVER

WESTCHESTER
COUNTY

Teller's Point

Vulture

× André's Capture

Tarrytown

Dobbs Ferry
New York City →

HUDSON RIVER

Nyack

Stony Point

Haverstraw

Squire Smith House
(André-Arnold Meeting
Place Sept. 21-22)

ROCKLAND
COUNTY

TREASON COUNTRY

J.R.H.

Once inside, Jameson said to André, "I believe we can take off your rope now." He beckoned to Allen who began working on the knot to the rope that secured André's hands behind his back. "Sit down, please."

Jameson sat at his desk and examined Arnold's passport and the West Point papers. He looked up. "John Anderson. I know that name. A few days ago I got a message from General Arnold, saying that if John Anderson showed up at my post, to bring him on to Robinson House. Would that be you, sir?"

"Yes, sir, it is. I'm on business for General Arnold, until these men stopped—"

"But the general's note said you'd be coming *to* him, not going the other way. And with these papers, too." Jameson shook his handsome, grey-haired head. "This is puzzling."

"But his passport directs me the other way," André said calmly. "On specific business for him."

"That's definitely General Arnold's handwriting," Jameson said, examining the passport again. He picked up the West Point documents. "But five of the six papers here are also Arnold's handwriting." He seemed lost in thought for a while. "Well, let me think this over, sir." He smiled. "You'll have to accept our hospitality for a while. You can rest a bit. And if you're hungry, we'll get you something a little later." He indicated to Allen to usher the visitor into a small room. He turned his wrist to tell Allen to lock the door from the outside.

He sat at his desk for a while, thinking. Then he told Allen: "Well, I'm going to send him to Arnold, under guard, I believe. But I'll also send a message to General Washington, just in case Arnold is up to something. Solomon, get me a courier to go to Washington." As the lieutenant left, Jameson began composing a message. He finished it and stuffed it into a pouch with the West Point documents.

Allen returned with another officer, a Lieutenant Prescott. Jameson assumed that Washington would be returning from Hartford the same way he had gone there—on the Danbury road. He instructed Prescott to take the pouch and intercept General Washington.

Jameson watched as Prescott took off, heading northeast toward Danbury, Connecticut. Paulding and his men were still outside, and they tried to elicit from Prescott what his mission was. Jameson was satisfied as Prescott ignored them and rode on. He sat down heavily on a stuffed chair and thought about the wisdom of his notion of sending Mr. Anderson to Arnold. What was going on? The evidence suggested that Arnold was turning traitor. The thought chilled Jameson. On the other hand, Mr. Anderson was being very calm about it all. "Damn, I wish Tallmadge was here," Jameson said aloud, referring to his ranking number two officer, who was off on a patrol. Failing to follow the orders of the commanding general of the region to send Anderson to him—made, it was true, several days ago—would be rank insubordination.

With a sigh, Jameson summoned Allen and told him to pick a guard of four enlisted men and take Anderson to Arnold's headquarters at Robinson House. While Allen was off getting ready, Jameson sat down to compose a note to Arnold:

I have sent Lieutenant Allen with a certain John Anderson taken going into New York. He has a passport signed in your name. He had a parcel of papers taken from under his stockings, which I think of a very dangerous tendency. The papers I have sent on to General Washington.

Allen arrived back and he and Jameson released their visitor from his room. Jameson noticed that Anderson did not seem at all perturbed to be led off, his hands tied once again. He was surrounded by four enlisted men, while Allen rode on a horse, as the procession began moving toward the northwest.

It was dark by the time Major Benjamin Tallmadge returned from his patrol, and Jameson told him all that had happened. Tallmadge was a star among the middle-ranked officers of Washington's army, bright and competent. He already was engaged at times in some of Washington's spying activities. Immediately concerned at what Jameson had done, he suggested that they bring Anderson back. He could not shake Jameson's conviction that Arnold must be informed, but Jameson agreed to a pretext for avoiding Arnold's order that Anderson be sent to him—the threat of enemy action in the area. They would bring Anderson back to protect him, but allow the message to go through.

Allen had been on the road for two hours before Jameson's messenger caught up to call the party back to North Castle. André's spirits fell when he heard the order. His hopes rose again when the soldiers began arguing with Allen and the messenger. They were anxious to get to West Point and away from the dreary outpost. In the end, Allen won out and the party returned.

When he arrived at North Castle, Allen was instructed by Jameson and Tallmadge to take Anderson to South Salem, a post fifteen miles inland from the river, where they had decided the prisoner could be kept more securely. Then Allen could set out for Robinson House. Jameson wrote another message to add to the one he had already given to Allen to deliver to Arnold, merely explaining that Anderson had been kept back under guard.

Sunday was a gloomy, rainy day in the region. At Robinson House, Dr. Eustis arrived from West Point to pronounce that Varick indeed seemed to have influenza. He was to stay in bed in a room that had been virtually quarantined. Eustis decided to stay at Robinson House to be present when Washington arrived later in the day.

Peggy was involved in preparing for the arrival of Washington and his party that afternoon when a message came from the chief saying that he had been delayed again. He would come for breakfast the following morning.

Franks returned that afternoon and went directly to his room, nodding to Peggy and ignoring Arnold. A kind of deceptive peace settled over Robinson House, as Arnold sat on the porch and dreamed about the glowing future that awaited him and Peggy, while she talked with the cook about the breakfast party for the next morning.

It was not peaceful aboard the *Vulture,* which had been at anchor since Friday morning near Sing Sing, south of Teller's Point, waiting for the return of the adjutant general of the British Army in North America. Robinson and Sutherland were exhausted from keeping a constant vigil for any sign of Major André. Robinson finally sat down to write a report to General Clinton: *"It is with the greatest concern that I must now acquaint Your Excellency that we have not heard the least account of him since he left the ship . . ."*

In South Salem, André had been confined to a small bedroom with guards at the door and window. Having arrived after midnight, André had slept the sleep of the exhausted. He awoke late Sunday morning and was taken for a stroll in a large yard by Lieutenant Joshua King. Sentries surrounded the yard. King already suspected that John Anderson was a well-placed gentleman, having been informed that there was powder in his hair when the ribbon was removed from his queue. André wore clothes loaned to him by King while his were being washed.

André was deep in thought as he and King strolled along. He realized that he would not escape and that Arnold's conspiracy was surely exposed. He finally told King that he needed to make a confidant out of someone. He said he was not John Anderson, American agent, but John André, adjutant general of the British Army. King was astonished, but not as much as he would have been had not some suspicions already occurred to him.

André asked for pen and paper. He wanted to write to General Washington to explain the circumstances under which he had been arrested. Late that afternoon, Lieutenant Prescott showed up at South Salem, on his way back from Danbury where he had been told that General Washington had taken a different route back, over to Fishkill and then down the riverside. South Salem lay on the road from Danbury to North Castle. Prescott added André's letter to the materials he already carried and set out on his way to sleep a few hours at North Castle before proceeding to find Washington somewhere along the river.

John André watched him leave and wondered what on earth would happen next.

Chapter 55

Robinson House
September 25, 1780

From three different locations, men began to move toward a fateful rendezvous at Robinson House on Monday. Inappropriately, it was a bright and cheerful day over the Hudson Valley region, after the rain and gloom of the day before.

In Fishkill, George Washington rose as usual just before dawn. Within an hour, his column of more than one hundred men set out for Robinson House, approximately twelve miles to the south, where Washington and his aides would breakfast with Arnold. He had started on this route the day before, but unexpectedly had met the French minister, Chevalier La Luzerne, on the road and had returned to Fishkill for a conference and to spend an extra night. Included at his large dinner table in Fishkill were Squire Joshua Smith and his family.

Lieutenant Solomon Allen had slept at South Salem after delivering his prisoner and had awakened late Sunday morning to find that his horse was lame. No other horses were available. He sent three of his enlisted men back to North Castle and took one man with him on a long walk, some twenty-five miles, to Robinson House. He and his companion had spent Sunday night in a farmhouse seven miles from his destination. It was past seven Monday morning when they set out for the final leg to Robinson House.

Lieutenant Charles Prescott, the courier sent in vain to Danbury to find Washington, had returned to South Salem and then to North Castle late on Sunday. He had slept for six hours Sunday night before setting out once again on horseback very early Monday to try to find Washington, this time somewhere on the River Road, heading south from Fishkill.

At Robinson House, Benedict Arnold woke early after a good night's sleep. He found that his wife was not feeling well.

"I have a headache and I feel flushed," Peggy said. "I think I have a fever, a small one at least."

"Damn that Varick!" Arnold said. "I never should've asked you to help him last night. I pray you and the baby don't catch his illness."

"No, darling, I'm all right. I feel a little faint, that's all."

"Don't try to come to breakfast."

"I couldn't eat anything. If I rest I'm sure I can come down and see General Washington before you leave for West Point."

"Or later in the day when we come back. Just don't tax yourself." Arnold patted her arm and kissed her cheek, then went downstairs to check on preparations for the visitors.

Arnold knew how early Washington rose and figured that his column was already on the move. But it would not be moving at a quick pace. Half of his escort were foot soldiers; the others, light horsemen. Arnold reckoned they could not arrive much before nine o'clock, if then. He figured on six guests in the dining room—three generals and three aides. Washington's troops would be billeted with Arnold's own Life Guard on the Robinson House property.

He walked through the kitchen and out into the courtyard and found bustling activity in both places. To the right, he could see that members of his Life Guard were busily preparing for the arrival of Washington's escort. He gazed up the River Road to the north, a dusty, rocky trail that seemed to end in a dark hole, so dense were the overarching trees that shaded it. Before long, Washington's column would be coming down that way.

He turned to his left, to the view of the Hudson River flowing peacefully by, now catching the early sun. West Point lay out of sight beyond the bluffs and the trees, two miles to the north. Across River Road, a rocky trail descended down the slope to the dock, where his barge was moored.

Arnold felt a nagging irriation that today was not the day of his coup. How close they had come! One or two days more of warning and they might have been able to accomplish both great purposes—capturing Washington *and* West Point. But it was probably better this way, even though he would have to bow to Washington one more time and take the great man on an annoying visit to West Point. Washington would spot many of the weaknesses Arnold had built in to the defense, express irritation, and leave behind a volume of orders. They would not be obeyed.

When Arnold turned to enter the house, he saw Franks coming out the front door. Franks had threatened to resign several times before and Arnold had ignored him. Arnold was sure he wouldn't be following through on his most recent threat to resign, either. But he decided he'd better make peace on this occasion. He went over to Franks and said: "David, I'm sorry we quarreled—and I'm sorry if I've been unpleasant to you. I've been under some stress. As I told Varick the other night, I won't be seeing Squire Smith anymore. Now I want you to relax and enjoy General Washington's visit."

It took a little while, but Franks finally produced a weak smile and said: "Yes, sir."

"Good," Arnold said. "I'm going to need you. Varick is quite ill with influenza and Mrs. Arnold may be coming down with something. If you'd please be alert to their needs."

Washington's column proceeded at a leisurely pace, stretched out a long distance on the trail. Enjoying the cool air and the dappled shade as the sun rose, Washington rode abreast with Generals Knox and Lafayette, each man followed by an aide, Colonel Hamilton, Major Shaw, and Major McHenry. Washington was disappointed by his meetings with Rochambeau. He thought the time had finally come to retake New York City, if the French army would cooperate. But Rochambeau pointed out that his army was blockaded by a British fleet at Narragansett Bay, while his own fleet was also blockaded, in Brest, France. The other French fleet, under Admiral Degrasse, was far away in the Caribbean. The opportunity was lost, for this campaigning season at least.

"There's another gun emplacement coming up, General," Knox said. "Do you want to see it?" he asked.

Washington nodded. "I don't know when I'll come this way again."

The Marquis de Lafayette was hungry, and he was anxious to enjoy the company of the beautiful Peggy Arnold again. The column had already lost half an hour by stopping at the first gun emplacement.

"We'll be very late for our engagement, General," Lafayette said.

Washington reined up. He was always the soul of punctuality. "You're right. I want you to go ahead. Let the breakfast start. Present my apologies to General and Mrs. Arnold, and tell them I'll be along as soon as I can."

"But, sir, I don't want—"

"Nonsense! Go ahead. Hamilton and McHenry should go, too. General Knox and Major Shaw will stay with me. These are their cannon we'll be looking at, after all." Washington smiled. "I know all of you young men are still half in love with Mrs. Arnold, so go on with you!"

Peggy had changed to her morning gown by the time Arnold returned to the large, sunny bedchamber to check on her. She smiled at her husband, looking healthier and more beautiful than ever. "Major Franks was here a few minutes ago. I'm so glad you talked to him. He seems so much happier. He's gone to the orchard to get some peaches for me," she exclaimed delightedly.

"Well, you're looking better," Arnold said. "That's good news."

"I do feel better. My headache's gone and I don't really think I have a fever. But I'm not going to try breakfast."

"No, it's all men in any case. You'll come down afterward? I know they'll all want to see you."

"Of course." Her expression turned serious and she spoke in a low voice. "I'm so glad we didn't plan with John André for today. I think I really would be ill if we had."

Arnold sat on the bed next to her and put his arm around her shoulders. "I don't want you to dwell on it. We'll get through this day and then three more days—and it will happen. Before you know it we'll be in New York with a new life."

"I can't help worrying—about André. Whether he really made it back successfully."

"I told you!"

"But you don't really *know*."

"Don't worry so much. Right now, André is planning the advance with General Clinton. Squire Smith told me he escorted Mr. John Anderson almost right up to the British lines. He passed through territory in *my* district, controlled by *me*—with a passport *signed* by me. No American officer would detain him."

"I'm sorry. I'll be all right. Until it's all over I don't think the fear will leave me that something might go wrong."

At that moment, footsteps could be heard in the hall outside and the voice of Major Franks. "Excuse me, sir. A message has come for you. From Colonel Jameson. His man won't give it to me. For you personally. And I have some peaches for Mrs. Arnold, if I may."

Arnold rubbed Peggy's moist cheeks, drew her to him, and kissed her fervently. "Courage, my dear," he whispered. "No one here knows anything. Not Squire Smith, not Franks, not Varick. Nothing can go wrong."

In the courtyard, Arnold saw a dust-stained officer and an enlisted man waiting for him. He recognized the man, Lieutenant Solomon Allen of North Castle.

"What are you doing here?" Arnold asked, genuinely puzzled.

"I have an important message, for you only, sir. From Colonel Jameson."

Arnold took no notice of the quizzical expression of Lieutenant Allen, who was staring at him. He took the despatch case, and then became aware that four light horsemen had ridden into the compound. Behind them came three other men on horseback. Arnold saw Hamilton and Lafayette, and another officer he did not know. He spoke to Allen: "You've come at a bad time. You and your man can wash up and get something to eat. I'll read your message in a moment."

Arnold greeted the newcomers. Introductions were made all around as Lafayette explained why Washington was delayed. He was dismayed that Peggy could not join them for breakfast, but cheered when Arnold told him she would be down later. The men took turns at the necessary house before coming into the dining room. Arnold sat down with them at the table and chatted for a few minutes. He asked whether they would like some food now or would rather wait for General Washington.

"He'll be here soon," Hamilton said. "Perhaps another fifteen or twenty minutes."

"Longer than that," Lafayette said, "and frankly, I'm starving. Is there something we can start with?"

Arnold rose. "I think the cook baked some nice rolls. I'll have them brought in, with some coffee."

In the kitchen he gave the message to the serving girl. Outside, he caught sight of Lieutenant Allen. He had left the despatch case in the dining room. He went there and told the others some food was on the way. "Forgive me for a moment, I have a message," he said. He opened the despatch case to find that there were two messages from Colonel Jameson. He tore one open and read:

Sir:

I have sent Lieutenant Allen with a certain John Anderson taken going into New York. He had a pass signed with your name. He had a parcel of papers taken from under his stockings, which I think of a dangerous tendency. The papers I have sent to General Washington.

Arnold froze. He read the message again, the awful implications sinking in. He opened the second message. Jameson had changed his mind and had decided to keep "John Anderson" back because of the threat of enemy action in the area, until Lieutenant Allen returned with Arnold's instructions for what to do with him.

Arnold's mind careened. Somehow John André had been taken captive. How could that possibly have happened? Arnold realized that, except for one fact, he might have been able to handle the situation somehow, send for André as his own prisoner until he could find a way to cover up the plot. That one fact destroyed any such possibility: *Jameson had sent a messenger to Washington, too.* That messenger was bearing the incriminating documents that would instantly reveal the plot to Washington—the plans and papers about West Point in Arnold's own handwriting. And Washington was due to arrive here at any moment. Had the other messenger reached him? Neither Hamilton nor Lafayette had given any sign that anything was amiss.

There was only one penalty for treason—death by hanging. And, under these circumstances, Washington would not hesitate. Arnold knew instantly that he had to flee for his life, that he might have only minutes to spare, but that he must warn Peggy, tell her what had happened, tell her that she would have to stay behind. He shuddered at the thought. Somehow she would have to steel herself to play the injured wife, to deny everything, to convince Washington that she had no part in the plot, that it was only her husband.

How could he flee without being run down like a common criminal? There was only one real hope for escaping. He excused himself, unconscious of the blank stares the three guests were giving him. He went outside and saw his manservant, Punch, appear at the kitchen doorway. He beckoned to him. He told Punch to saddle his horse and make sure both pistols were in their saddle holsters, then run down to the dock to tell Arnold's own barge crew to be ready to leave in a moment's notice.

As he rushed back into the house, he saw Franks coming down the stairway. Grabbing him by the arm, Arnold said: "I've got to go to West Point. Immediately. Go into the dining room and entertain the guests until General Washington arrives. Tell him I'll be back soon."

Leaving a puzzled Franks behind, Arnold ran up three stairs at a time. He burst into the bedroom, nearly scaring Peggy to death.

"My God, what's the matter?" she cried.

Gasping for breath, Arnold sank back against the door. "It's all over," he said in an anguished voice. "André's been captured. There's a messenger here. I've got to flee before Washington arrives."

"Oh no, no," Peggy cried, rushing to him. He embraced her.

"I've only got a minute," he said between grated teeth. "If I don't want to hang."

Peggy shuddered convulsively and showed signs of fainting.

"I'm going to try for New York. You have to stay. They'll question you. Remember, you know *nothing* about it. You know *nothing* of what I've been trying to do!" He grabbed her by her arms and shook her, staring into the half-crazed eyes. "Do you understand me?"

"Yes," Peggy gasped.

"Can you do it?"

"Yes. When will I see you again?"

"I don't know. With luck, you'll be able to come to New York eventually. If you can convince them you had nothing to do with it, Washington will let you go to New York, to join your husband."

They were startled by a voice at the door. It was Franks again. "Sir, one of Washington's servants just arrived, saying the general is nigh at hand."

Arnold managed to speak: "Thank you, Franks." To Peggy, he said: "Good-bye, my dear. God bless you and the baby." He kissed her and was gone.

Arnold rushed downstairs and outside. He saw his saddled horse. Punch was gone, down to the dock. Arnold leaped aboard the horse and galloped out of the yard and down the trail to the boat dock. He saw that Punch had alerted the crew. He dismounted and began unbuckling his saddle. He tossed it into the boat and leaped in after it. "Let's go!" he shouted.

Coxswain James Larvey began the count and the boat surged from the dock. "No, not to West Point!" Arnold shouted. "Down river, to Stony Point!"

As the boat turned, another vessel from West Point came in, heading for the dock. Arnold yelled at her crew. "Go up to the house for some food. Tell Washington I'll be back before dinner."

His oarsmen pulled well, but before they could go into Stony Point, Arnold said: "No. Keep going. I've got particular business for His Excellency aboard the *Vulture*." At the hesitancy among the men, Arnold urged them to go faster. "Two gallons of rum for you, my lads!"

He scanned both shores as the boat moved downstream. No special activity, no American gunboats setting out. He was going to make it. He thought of Peggy and the trauma it meant for her to be left alone. If she managed to keep her senses, she'd be all right. She would come to him in New York soon, he was sure of it. The capture of West Point had failed, but he was safe. He had his reputation as a soldier and a hero, and he would be invaluable to the British. He gave no thought to John André.

Aboard the *Vulture,* Robinson and Sutherland saw the boat coming, now under a white flag. "By God, it's André!" Robinson shouted.

"No, I don't see him," Sutherland said, as the boat neared.

Arnold was the first up the gangway after the boat was secured. He quickly told the waiting men what had happened. Robinson covered his face with his hands, genuinely fearful for André—and also of Sir Henry's reaction. Arnold's bargemen had come aboard and were gossiping with the tars. Arnold turned to them and made a dramatic announcement. "I'm no longer a rebel, boys. I'm a British general now! And if you'll join me I'll make sergeants and corporals of you all, and for you, James Larvey, something more!"

The men were stunned, looking at each other in disbelief. Finally Larvey spoke up: "Beggin' your pardon, sir, but I guess one uniform is enough for me." The others began nodding.

Arnold turned to Sutherland. "Put them below as prisoners, Captain."

Peggy lay on her bed sobbing after Arnold left. She heard noises from below that indicated Washington had arrived. She could hear the deep tones of his voice. She buried her face in the bedclothes to mask her sobbing. She and her baby were entirely alone now. No one to help them. Waves of panic engulfed her as she tried to think of what to do.

Washington was puzzled by Arnold's disappearance, but thought, on the whole, that it was a good thing he had gone to West Point to prepare for the visit. After breakfast, he and Knox and Lafayette and their aides left on Colonel Lamb's barge for West Point as Hamilton stayed behind, in charge at Robinson House in the absence of all higher-ranking officers.

Richard Varick felt slightly better this morning. He was lying in his bed thinking pleasant thoughts of Peggy Arnold, who had come to him the evening before. She had tea with him and paid him much attention. He was wondering if she would come again this morning when he heard a shriek from down the hall. Varick hurriedly dressed and ran to the Arnolds' room, as he heard more cries. It was Peggy, standing in the doorway, her hair disheveled and flowing about her neck. Varick was embarrassed by the fact that she wore only her morning gown, loosely tied. She seemed desperate, and, with a wild look, she asked: "Colonel Varick, have you ordered my child to be killed?" She slid to the floor, her arms around Varick's legs, begging for her child to be spared. He tried to lift her, but lacked the strength. Dr. Eustis and Franks came up the stairs, also attracted by the cries. Between the three of them, they got Mrs. Arnold back into bed.

She moaned that she had no friends there. Varick told her that she had him and Franks, and General Arnold soon would be back from West Point with General Washington. She cried, "No, no, General Arnold will never return. He is gone forever, *there, there, there,* the spirits have carried him up there. They have put hot irons on his head."

Varick and Franks managed to withdraw from the bedroom, as Dr. Eustis tried to calm Peggy. Franks clutched Varick's arm. "Listen, I was talking to that courier from North Castle. Allen's his name. He brought a message here. He says that Jameson thinks Arnold is a spy!"

"No, that's not possible."

"Well, that's what he says."

By midafternoon, Washington and his party were back from West Point. Washington was in a foul mood. Benedict Arnold had not been seen there, and the post was in terrible shape. What the hell was going on?

Hamilton handed Washington some papers that had arrived during his absence. Most prominent was the message from Colonel Jameson and its enclosures, which had arrived only half an hour earlier. Hamilton watched as Washington opened and read it. His face turned ashen. He looked up. "My God! Arnold has betrayed us. Gone over to the British." He shook his head and looked desperately at Hamilton. "Who can we trust now?"

Chapter 56

The Hudson River Valley
September 25–30, 1780

Washington was immobilized by what Arnold had done. For a long time, he sat still, hand to his forehead, as his aides milled about, trying to decide on a course of action. Finally, Hamilton came to him and said he had talked to a sentry who said he'd seen Arnold leave on his barge, heading south on the Hudson River. He proposed to give chase, if not to catch up with Arnold, to at least find out where he had gone. Washington nodded, and, with McHenry, Hamilton rode hard down the River Road toward Verplanck's Point.

Anything could happen, Washington thought, from a widespread conspiracy masterminded by Arnold to nothing at all, just a series of mistakes. Perhaps Arnold was away on some other urgent business and the rest was a case of mistaken judgments. As much as Washington hoped that was true, he knew in his heart that it wasn't. The Benedict Arnold he had known over the past year was not the same man as the brilliant fighter in the north. He had had hardships, had been treated poorly, had only grudgingly received the rewards that he had earned. But that was true of other officers in the Continental Army. And very few had deserted the cause.

Were others thinking of it now? That was the terrible thing about Arnold's heresy—it endangered one's faith in other people. If Arnold could do it, who could not?

Washington shook such thoughts from his head. He had to consider a possible British attack already in motion. Was he the target of Arnold's treason, or was it West Point—or both? There were actions he should take. He decided to wait a while, to take a risk to allow other elements of the conspiracy to play their hand. He instructed his aides not to spread the alarm for the time being, especially not to talk to Varick or Franks, who were suspect.

Dr. Eustis came to Washington to tell him of Mrs. Arnold's plight. "She's asked for you. Will you come, sir?"

Washington joined Eustis and Varick in going to see Mrs. Arnold, who was still in pitiable shape. Varick told her that General Washington had come, but she cried out: "No, that is not General Washington. That is the man who is going to help Colonel Varick in killing my child!" Peggy writhed on the bedsheets, clutching her baby, and muttering about "hot irons" on her head, and that General Arnold was gone forever.

There seemed no way to calm her. Washington soon left, moved at the sight of her, and convinced that she could not have been involved in the treason.

A despatch arrived from Hamilton enclosing three letters from the *Vulture* that had been sent ashore at Verplanck's Point. One was from Colonel Robinson, a defense of André, holding that he had acted under a flag of truce. Another, for Peggy from Arnold, Washington sent up to her without opening it, and the third was addressed to him from Arnold. He claimed that he "ever acted from a principle of love for my country," and that the same principle "actuates my present conduct." He asked for the protection of Mrs. Arnold: "She is as good and as innocent as an angel and is incapable of doing wrong. I beg that she may be permitted to return to her friends in Philadelphia, or to come to me, as she may choose." In a postscript, Arnold stated that Smith, Varick, and Franks were totally ignorant of his designs.

After Washington, Knox, and Lafayette had a very somber dinner, in which the chief was completely silent and reserved, Hamilton and McHenry returned and Washington called for a conference.

Hamilton told the story of the *Vulture* and said that on his own authority he had asked General Greene to bring the Continental Army northward and to send a battalion to West Point. Washington told the group that their prisoner in South Salem was Major John André, adjutant general of the British Army.

"The fact that Major André is our prisoner," Washington said, "means that he never reached British lines with his information. Presumably, that means the British attack has not started. But we must be on the alert. Major André has written me a very polite letter, delivered by Lieutenant Prescott this afternoon. Although he wants to be treated as a gentleman, his actions seem to be those of a spy. He mentions no one by name, not even Arnold, but it is clear, I think, that they met to plot the treason. I am not inclined to see this man or interrogate him, but instead to have him dealt with by a court-martial as soon as feasible. Do you agree?"

After nodding heads signaled assent, Washington turned to Hamilton and said: "Colonel, please make a list of actions to be taken and see that they are carried out. First, send a company of light horsemen under a very good officer to South Salem to take custody of Major André—and I need not say, to watch him very closely. They are to take him to Tappan to be imprisoned and to await his court-martial. We shall go there ourselves as soon as possible.

"Second, a message to Greene, confirming your instructions and asking him to take temporary command of West Point.

"Third, send an officer and several men to arrest Squire Joshua Smith and bring him here for interrogation."

"Fourth, a message relieving Colonel Livingston of command at King's Ferry until his name is cleared. It all happened in his area and we must consider him under suspicion for the present." Washington shook his head. "I am tempted to relieve Colonel Jameson as well. What stupidity. But for his bewildered conception of his job, we'd have Arnold in our grasp."

Hamilton left on his errands and Washington said to the rest: "Now, let us interview Mr. Varick and Mr. Franks. Arnold says both are innocent of any knowledge, but of course, we no longer trust anything Arnold says."

The two men were brought in separately, each facing a barrage of questions from the three generals. Both men told the truth and protested their innocence—and their outrage at what Arnold had done. Both asked for a court-martial to clear their names, and Washington acquiesced.

Afterward, Knox said: "They're either telling the truth or they rehearsed their stories endlessly. They jibe very well."

"Their court-martial will tell us the answer," Washington said. "Now we await Squire Smith."

When Hamilton finished his missions, he went upstairs to see Peggy. She was still in the throes of her form of dementia, although somewhat sedated by now. Her eyes were hollow, her skin pale, but she was still uncommonly lovely. He had come to her somewhat skeptical but left convinced that Washington was right. She was innocent.

That evening, Hamilton wrote of Peggy to his fiancée, Elizabeth, the daughter of General Philip Schuyler: "All the sweetness of beauty, all the loveliness of innocence, all the tenderness of a wife, and all the fondness of a mother showed themselves in her appearance and conduct."

Late that night, Squire Smith arrived at Robinson House under guard. He had been arrested in his night clothes at the home of his in-laws in Fishkill. Washington lost his temper and berated Smith angrily as either a rank traitor or a blithering idiot. Smith staunchly protested his innocence but wilted under the assault by Washington to end up blubbering. He was ordered imprisoned, to be court-martialed.

The next morning Hamilton came again to Peggy's bedside to assess her condition for travel. Though she was still miserable and distraught, he found her somewhat improved, able to answer questions in the real world. She asked Hamilton to intercede for her with General Washington to allow her to be taken to her family and friends in Philadelphia. Within minutes, Hamilton was back, saying that a carriage would be prepared for Mrs. Arnold's trip to Philadelphia, to depart the following morning, the 27th, unless her condition prevented it.

At midday, Washington took a walk with David Franks and told him that he would be detailed to take Peggy to Philadelphia, along with a servant and a nurse, if he pledged to return for his court-martial. Franks readily agreed.

The *Vulture* reached the dock at Spuyten Duyvil at dark on the 25th. Arnold was taken by carriage to the home of the royal governor of New York State, James Robertson, at Fort George at the foot of Manhattan. The next morning, still clad in the only clothes he had with him, the uniform of a major-general of the Continental Army, he was brought to the office of Sir Henry Clinton, commanding general of the British Army.

Arnold still possessed the self-confidence that greeted every problem as something to be challenged and overcome. What had happened was regrettable. The West Point opportunity was gone and the British had lost one officer to captivity. But they had gained the most heroic commander from the American side, who would draw thousands of his former soldiers to him as he spread the message that democracy was anarchic and venal, while the British were just and generous. It would be a difficult job, it would take longer, but it would still work—it would win the war.

He was therefore somewhat surprised to find Sir Henry to be older looking and sadder than he had imagined, and interested not in Arnold's future at the moment, but with the rescue of John André. To be sure, he offered Arnold a somewhat distant greeting and welcome, but shunted aside his desire to talk about his command and the role he would play.

"There'll be plenty of time for that, my dear sir," Clinton said, his eyes redrimmed and bleary. "Now we must bend every effort to bring Major André back to us. I would not be surprised to learn that Washington has in mind a gallows for him. We must immediately make it clear that André operated under a flag of truce until he came under your orders. I am writing my second letter to Washington now, and I would appreciate it, sir, if you would also write your account of the matter to be sent off with it. Address it to me, if you wish."

Thus it was that Arnold found himself with ink, pen, and paper and seated at a desk in an adjoining room. He wrote that André had been operating legally under a flag of truce and should be immediately released: "Thinking it much properer he should return by land, I directed him to make use of the feigned name of John Anderson under which he had by my direction come on shore. This officer cannot fail of being immediately sent to New York, as he was invited to a conversation with me, for which I sent him a flag of truce."

The first day of Peggy's trip to her parents' home was under a brooding sky that periodically released great sheets of rain. She had been mistress of Robinson House only twenty-four days. In the genteel atmosphere of Washington's headquarters, she had been coddled and beloved for the past two days, perceived as the most poignant victim of Arnold's crime.

Now, as she traveled in the outer world, she soon found that word of what her husband had done had spread quickly and made a profound impact. At every American post her carriage passed, she experienced hostile stares from officers and enlisted men alike. Several times, David Franks had to stand outside in the rain arguing with the soldiers until the party was finally let go, even though Mrs. Arnold had a passport signed by George Washington.

The first day's travel was the shortest stint, however, as the carriage stopped in Paramus, New Jersey, at the residence of the beautiful Theodosia Prevost, a friend of Peggy's and the widow of a British officer. Her lover, Major Aaron Burr, was not present. Once in a Loyalist household, the weary and disheartened Peggy let down every guard. She told Theodosia the true story of her husband's treason, including the fact that she was involved from the beginning.

Franks overheard her say to Theodosia, "I am heartily tired of the theatricals I've been forced to play."

On the following days the contrast to Peggy's happy, triumphal ride from Philadelphia to Robinson House, a little more than three weeks earlier, was heightened. At several places along the road, where she had stayed previously under the easy itinerary arranged by her husband, Peggy was refused service.

When she finally reached her family in Philadelphia, Peggy was greeted with love and warmth by every member of the family. To them, Arnold was the consummate villain, while Peggy was the wounded angel. In this atmosphere, she seemed to regress, to become a child again, under the protection of her father. It was indeed a trying time for Judge Shippen, since the prevailing sentiment in Philadelphia was that Peggy was guilty.

As soon as Arnold's treason was known, Joseph Reed's police had seized Arnold's papers from the care of Judge Shippen. They found evidence that Arnold had, in fact, profited from some of the escapades on which he had been tried and acquitted. More important was a copy of a letter from Peggy to John André in New York. Though entirely a letter about getting help in shopping, it was seen as the beginning of a treasonous correspondence. A movement began to banish Peggy from her hometown, just as she was leaning toward staying.

John André was innocent of any knowledge of the energies that had been released at Robinson House and British headquarters by his capture. He was isolated in confinement at South Salem until the company of light horsemen arrived on the 26th and took custody of him. Changing directions several times, the procession finally reached Tappan in the afternoon, and André was imprisoned in a stone house, within eyesight of Washington's headquarters.

André's bedroom was small, but he had a large and comfortable living room. The rest of the house was occupied by his detachment of guards. Through his windows, André could see much of the surrounding area, which had an unmistakably Dutch character, as if he were in a village in the Low Countries instead of the much more primitive United States. Down a short distance on a lane that could be seen from his living room was a small Dutch church. André would soon learn that that was where his court-martial would be held.

On the afternoon of the 27th, after Washington's party had reached his Tappan headquarters, Alexander Hamilton made an official visit to André in his prison. He told the prisoner that his trial would be held on Friday, September 29th, in the deWindt Church before a court of fourteen general officers, chaired by Major-General Nathanael Greene. The case would be handled by the judge advocate general of the Continental Army, John Laurence.

Hamilton found his visit to be oddly satisfying. André was not a dull, depressed wretch, but a lively, intelligent, and good-humored man. Details were handled quickly—a request would be sent to Sir Henry for a trunk of André's clothes and his manservant to come to the prison, breakfast would be brought to André every morning from General Washington's own nearby table, and writing and sketching materials would be provided to him. With that done, the two men, both young, handsome, and very competent in their roles as aides to high-ranking generals, found they had much in common.

After an hour of the pleasant meeting, Hamilton rose to leave. André sprang up, and said: "I do hope you will be able to visit me again, sir. It's been a long time since I so enjoyed conversation."

"Indeed, I shall. I'll come to see you tomorrow. Now, is there anything I can do for you?"

André thought for a moment. "I can think of nothing for the present, sir.

The two guard officers here, Captain Hughes and Lieutenant Burrows, have been most kind."

Another visitor was Major Benjamin Tallmadge, the man who had arranged to have André called back after Jameson had sent him off to be reunited with Arnold. He, too, found André to be an unusually likeable man: "He endeared himself to me exceedingly," he wrote to a friend. "I never saw a man whose fate I foresaw whom I pitied so sincerely."

André had charmed all of his captors by the time Hughes and Burrows led him down the old world path to the deWindt Church for his trial—and his composure stayed with him throughout the process. He gave prompt and forthright responses to all the questions asked him by Laurence and by members of the panel. He made no claim that he had come ashore under the protection of a flag of truce, being unaware that General Clinton, Beverly Robinson, and Benedict Arnold all had stated that he had in their letters to Washington.

The crucial moment of the trial came when Greene asked André directly if he had left the *Vulture* under a flag of truce. André seemed surprised. "It's impossible for me to believe that I came under that sanction," André said, "because if I had, I might certainly have returned under it."

André insisted that he had become a spy by accident. He had expected to meet Arnold on board the *Vulture*. Once he went ashore, things progressively got out of hand. Though he regarded himself as carrying out a high-level mission for his commanding general, he had become, in effect, Arnold's prisoner. The board did not accept André's story. The members felt that he had clearly confessed to espionage, and that all of the evidence pointed overwhelmingly in that direction. For this reason, no witnesses were called. André had spoken of no collaborators except Arnold, not mentioning either Mrs. Arnold or Squire Smith.

General Greene asked André whether he had any final statement to make before the officers retired to find a verdict. André said he had none, that he felt he had been treated fairly and he left the facts to operate with the board. The court recessed and André was led back to his prison. In the lively conversation of the board's deliberations, there was much praise of André's candor and demeanor. And the comment was heard many times that Arnold ought to be standing trial, not André. But, unfortunately, he was not a prisoner, and the board had a duty to perform.

That afternoon André was summoned again, and Greene read the findings: *"Major André, Adjutant General of the British Army, ought to be considered a spy from the enemy, and that, agreeable to the law and usage of nations, it is their opinion he ought to suffer death."*

André lived up to the board's estimation of his courage by making no emotional response to the verdict, but rather thanking the judges for their participation. He knew that the finding would be presented to General Washington, who would then set the date for his sentence. He was pleased when his first caller after the finding was Hamilton, who by this time had spent a number of hours with André and had become a friend.

"I'm very grateful for the generosity with which the board treated me," André told Hamilton. "They gave me every mark of indulgence, and they didn't press me to answer questions which could embarrass my feelings." He smiled at his friend. "If I ever felt any prejudice against the Americans, my present experience would obliterate them."

André soon grew somber. "When I was first captured, I never thought it would result in my death. Now I know I must die. There is only one thing that truly disturbs me. Sir Henry Clinton has been too good to me. I would not for the world leave a sting in his mind that would embitter his future days." Here André's voice trembled and he broke down, weeping. With great difficulty, he collected himself and asked if he could write to Sir Henry.

"Of course you can," Hamilton said. "I'll make sure your letter goes as soon as you've finished it."

On Saturday, Washington approved the sentence and set the execution for the next day, Sunday, October 1st, at five P.M. Hamilton carried this unhappy news to André's place of imprisonment.

After Hamilton informed him, André was silent, betraying no emotion, although he stared at the wall with unseeing eyes. Finally, he said: "Since it's my lot to die, there's still a choice in the mode. It would make a great deal of difference to me if I were shot like an officer and a gentleman—instead of being hanged like a peasant and a spy."

"I don't see how General Washington could refuse you. Write your request and I'll take it to him."

Later, André worked on his request, and Hamilton returned to retrieve it and deliver it to Washington. André wrote:

I trust that the request I make to Your Excellency at this serious period, and which is to soften my last moments, will not be rejected. Sympathy toward a soldier will surely induce Your Excellency and a military tribunal to adapt the mode of my death to the feelings of a man of honor.

Chapter 57

Tappan and New York City
September 30–October 2, 1780

On Saturday morning, Hamilton came to Washington's office with two thoughts in mind. One was André's request to change his mode of death. The other was an exchange of André for Arnold. He found Washington completing a short letter to General Clinton, notifying him of the verdict of the court-martial and André's impending execution. He was preparing a despatch box to be sent to the British commander. Inside were André's letter to Clinton and a letter that had arrived from Peggy Arnold for her husband. Washington explained the contents and asked if there were anything else to be sent.

"I have a suggestion to make," Hamilton said. "Perhaps you don't want to take official notice of it. It's a thought that, I have no doubt, has occurred to everyone. Arnold is the truly guilty party. Return André to British lines and take Arnold in exchange."

Washington allowed himself a small smile. "I wish we had captured Arnold and not André. I would give anything for that eventuality. But we must play the hand that is dealt to us. There is no question that Major André is guilty. Everyone knows that. For us to bargain with his life is to confess a weakness—perhaps that we're not certain he's guilty. In any case, Sir Henry cannot accept the bargain. As a matter of policy."

"Suppose he might? He and André are very close, I judge."

"If the suggestion came from him, we would be in a different position."

"So, as a matter of policy, we cannot officially propose such an exchange?"

"Yes."

Hamilton mused for a moment. Then he said: "Well, on to another subject. A much easier one, I should think. Please, sir, read this note from André."

Washington took the letter and read it. When he had finished, he put his hand to his brow and sighed. "Why does everything have to be so difficult?" He shook his head. "As much as I am tempted by the fate of such a decent fellow, we can't do this, either."

"But, sir! He's not questioning the sentence of death at all. He's quite reconciled! All he wants to do is die like an officer and gentleman. Not like a common thief."

"I understand. Unfortunately, he's been convicted of espionage. The only sentence for that is by the gibbet. Once again, it's a matter of policy. Consider the French. They're watching what we do. If we bend the rules out of compassion for the prisoner, we'll be seen as weak and indecisive. Everyone will question our judgment. We can't do it. I'm sorry."

Hamilton was overcome with anguish. "A matter of policy! This is a human being who—"

"Colonel, please contain yourself."

Hamilton stood there a moment, fighting back desperation. Through the window, he could see the house where André was a prisoner. André believed that Hamilton could convince the chief to change the sentence. And now Hamilton was up against this monstrous slave to policy. He abruptly turned and left the room.

Later, Hamilton caught Colonel Ogden when he emerged from Washington's office. He explained the idea of exchanging André for Arnold and found Ogden in complete agreement. He accepted a note that Hamilton had penned in a disguised hand and inserted it into the despatch case.

During the crisis of Major André's imprisonment, there no longer were half days for the British officers. The lights burned late at One Broadway as Sir Henry paced back and forth, an emotional wreck who was starved for information. At dusk on Saturday, an American courier, Colonel Aaron Ogden, entered New York City under flag of truce and was conducted to Sir Henry's office. He carried a despatch with four letters in it.

Sir Henry took the despatch case into his private office, asking his advisers to wait outside. One letter was from Peggy Arnold to her husband. Sir Henry put that aside to give to Arnold. Another was the folded note written by Alexander Hamilton, but in a disguised hand. It proposed the exchange of André for Arnold. The note said: "Major André's character and situation seem to demand this of your justice and friendship. Arnold appears to have been the guilty author of the mischief and ought more properly to be the victim."

The British commander was appalled at this proposal. Since the first day of the war, an unbreakable rule of the ministry had been that no deserter would ever be returned. No American would ever come over to the British side if deserters were returned to the enemy to receive their dire punishment. Sir Henry was sorely tempted by the notion—but he could not do it.

The third letter was from Washington, presumably in response to Sir Henry's letters, and the fourth a personal note from André. Sir Henry opened the Washington letter first and was shocked to read that André had already been tried and was sentenced to die. Washington's letter said that André had committed acts that flags "were never meant to authorize or countenance in the least degree." He had "with great candor" confessed to his court-martial that he had *not* been under the sanction of a flag. Therefore, the board of officers had no choice but to condemn him as a spy.

Devastated by this letter, Sir Henry ran the gamut of emotions, from fear to anger to despair. This must not happen! He would summon all of his general officers and Loyalist leaders to find a way to stop it.

With trembling fingers, he opened the last letter, the personal one written to him by John André. The letter spoke of "the rigorous determination that is impending," and sought to remove all thoughts of blame from Sir Henry for the circumstances that led to André's predicament. It said: "I am perfectly tranquil within my mind, and prepared for any fate to which an honest zeal for the King's service may have devoted me. . . . With all the warmth of my heart, I give you thanks for Your Excellency's profuse kindness to me, and I send you the most earnest wishes for your welfare which a faithful, affectionate, and respectful attendant can frame."

With brimming eyes, Sir Henry sat still for a long moment, and then broke into choking sobs.

Benedict Arnold had found that older officers were cordial to him at a distance, while younger officers ignored him. It was becoming clear to him that the fate of John André would mean a great deal as to how he was accepted by the British. He had found a patron, the Royal Governor of New York, General James Robertson. He pressed Arnold's case with Clinton and came back with an appointment as a brigadier-general in the provisional force and a permanent rank of regimental colonel in the British military establishment. He was certain that Lord Jeffrey Amherst, the famed arbiter of service promotions, would acquiesce.

Arnold thought the matter of rank had been affected by the André affair. But he said nothing for the present. Once André were saved, then it would be time to raise the issue. He had just tried on his new red regimentals at the royal governor's house when he received a message summoning him to a meeting with Sir Henry. It was nearly eleven o'clock Saturday night.

At headquarters, Arnold found that all of the British generals had arrived, as well as a number of Loyalist leaders. He noticed that some of them looked askance at his uniform. Stressing the gravity of the situation, Sir Henry opened the meeting, pointing out that André had been condemned to die on the gibbet, the precise time as yet unknown. When the initial shock at this news passed, several of the questions from the group seemed aligned with the view that André had, in fact, been a spy. The anguish to Sir Henry was noticeable, causing the questioners to desist. Eventually, the group voted unanimously that André was being illegally held.

At this point, Sir Henry said he wished to present his letter of appeal to Washington, reading aloud in a weary voice betrayed by his emotions. Arnold could tell that opinion of the letter within the group was not good. It was too personal and pleading a note, with a reference to Washington's "humanity." As the discussion proceeded, Sir Henry suddenly became bellicose, speaking of twenty individuals he had rounded up in Manhattan under suspicion of espionage. They could be hanged, as well as forty leading individuals being held in South Carolina under the charge of collaborating with the rebels. In the end, the group agreed a meeting should be held with the Americans to negotiate, instead of relying only on a letter. The civilian leadership of New York would take the lead—James Robertson; Andrew Elliott, lieutenant governor; and William Smith, chief justice. Robertson would write a short note requesting the meeting.

A courier was brought in to take Robertson's note to the American camp, and the three delegates were told where they would board their vessel Sunday morning for the trip up the river to Dobbs Ferry, across from Tappan. As the leaders filed out of Sir Henry's office, Arnold was asked to stay behind a moment. When the office was cleared, the British commander asked Arnold to write a letter to Washington specifying the dire result if he did not release André as requested. Though it was nearly two in the morning, Arnold sat down at a desk and wrote a threatening letter to his former chief. Before he did so, Arnold opened the letter from Peggy that Sir Henry had given him and was chagrined to learn that she had decided to go to Philadelphia rather than come directly to him. Although she said that she would wait to join him until he could give her more information, there was a lack of certainty about her coming. Arnold was deeply depressed, and it affected him as he worked on his letter to Washington. He wrote that if André were not released, he would be bound "by every tie of duty and honor to retaliate on such unhappy persons of your army as may fall within my power, that the respect due to flags and to the law of nations may be better understood and observed." He concluded: "I call heaven and earth to witness, that Your Excellency will be justly answerable for the torrent of blood that may be spilled in consequence."

On Sunday morning, October 1st, Hamilton came to pay his last visit to Major André. He intended to tell him that he had failed in trying to persuade General Washington to change the mode of death in his sentence, but once in the presence of André, his resolve failed him. He found André completely reconciled to his death, his morale much improved since the day before, as the time drew very near. He chatted gaily and showed Hamilton sketches he had made of his guards and a self-portrait of the young prisoner sitting at his writing table.

At that point, a guard brought in a message for André from Washington. André opened it and smiled at Hamilton. "Well, I shall have another day to live. Instead of this evening, General Washington has postponed my execution for a day."

Hamilton felt a surge of hope. Something was happening. "I'm so glad to hear it. If you'll forgive me, I'm going to try to find out what's going on."

*   *   *

A short time later, Hamilton found Washington in his office. "You've postponed his execution!" he said.

"Yes," Washington replied. "Just one day. To give the British a little time. They're sending a delegation. We can't receive them officially. I'm sending Greene to meet with them, informally."

Another matter of policy, Hamilton thought bitterly. "Is there no hope you'll change the method of execution? It is not much to ask."

Washington shook his head grimly. "Don't you think I would like to? I understand that he's a frank and courageous man, that he's an accomplished and gallant officer. It would be a popular thing to do, I have no doubt. But it would be wrong and I will not do it."

He watched as the cloud of anger and depression suffused Hamilton's face. "However," he said pointedly, "the British may have another suggestion."

There was a silence, as Hamilton's mind worked. Was Washington alluding to a trade of André for Arnold? "May I accompany General Greene, sir?" he asked.

"Yes, you may."

Several hours later, an American party led by General Greene set out across the Hudson to meet the British at Dobbs Ferry. As he shook hands with James Robertson, Greene explained that this was an informal meeting, since British interference with American justice could not be accepted, but he would be happy to speak to Robertson "as a friend." Robertson waved aside this technicality and launched into an argument that André was mistaken in his testimony that he was not under a flag, as Arnold maintained.

"Well, there's your answer," Greene said. "Arnold is a rascal. André is a man of honor whom we all believe. Whom would you really believe?"

Undeterred, Robertson tried several other approaches, such as appointing two foreign generals—Rochambeau and von Knyphausen—as mediators. He stressed that Clinton was so emotionally upset that he would repay sympathy to André many times over. On the other hand—Robertson showed Greene Arnold's letter.

Shaking his head, Greene did not comment on Arnold's threat. He said quietly that an exchange of Arnold for André was in the realm of possibility. Hamilton was slipping another note proposing the same idea into the pocket of Robertson's aide. Robertson also did not comment, merely giving Greene a look that said volumes. They could not do it. No American would ever cross to British lines again if Arnold were given up.

The two main guards, Hughes and Burrows, called on André Monday morning, October 2nd, to tell him that General Washington had set the execution for noon that very day. At that news, André's manservant, who had brought him a splendid British officer's uniform, broke into sobs.

"If you can't stop that unmanly display, please leave the room," André said.

In contrast to his guards, who were deeply saddened, André showed no emotion. He washed, shaved, ate breakfast, and slowly dressed in his uniform. As time passed, he could see that somehow word had spread, and apparently quite widely. Crowds of people could be seen through his windows, tramping through the fields on a fine autumn day. The buzz of a large mass of people could be heard, along with the sound of wagons, of troops being mustered, of a fife and drum corps.

Finally, André stood erect and laid down his hat. "I am ready at any moment, gentlemen, to wait upon you," he said to Hughes and Burrows. He took the arm of each man and pulled them out of the house and to his place in the funeral parade.

A company of well-dressed soldiers led the procession, followed by a brace of horses hauling a cart on which rested John André's coffin. He marched directly behind that, flanked by his senior guards. Behind him came the fife and drum corps, which now began the death march.

The procession moved forward slowly, André walking with a dignified air, Hughes and Burrows on either side. Occasionally a word passed among them, with André displaying a small smile. There were people as far as the eye could see, thousands of people who were drawn to this spectacle, both civilians and soldiers. When André caught sight of an officer he knew, he would nod slightly.

There was a face he recognized, a long, perpetually sad face on a large frame. It was John Paulding, leader of the group that had captured him. He saw Tallmadge, and his eye searched for Hamilton, but did not see him. Nearly every officer of the American army for a radius of more than twenty miles had come to witness the death of the British officer.

A short distance away, in his headquarters house, sat one officer who had not come. George Washington could see the crowd and the procession, and hear the sounds of the event. He called for an orderly and instructed him to close all the shutters of the house. This was the eighth time that Washington had ordered the hanging of a British spy. It was never easy. This instance was especially difficult. He knew that he was right, but that did not make it any easier. He sat there in the artificial gloom of his enclosed office and suffered quietly.

Alexander Hamilton was in the crowd, but not where he could be easily seen. He had not returned to forewarn André that he would be hanged, instead of shot. He told himself it was better that André did not know until the last few minutes. Yet he could not bring himself to be seen by André. And now, as he watched, he could tell the exact moment that André knew.

The procession went up a small hill and made a right turn, and suddenly the gibbet was in full sight. André abruptly stopped, his face ashen. Hughes asked him what was the matter. André shook his head. "It was just the sudden sight." He began walking again. "I'm ready to die, but I hate the means. I tell myself it will be just a momentary pang."

The gallows consisted of two very high poles, with a beam crossing their top, from which another pole protruded. André strode up with his head erect and came to a halt as the executioner worked to bring a team of horses and a wagon into position. It was to act as the drop. While he waited, André bowed his head and appeared to choke for a moment. With a toe, he dislodged a stone from the ground. When the wagon was in position, he nimbly climbed up on it by himself. Now he was in full sight of the multitude, which gave out a sort of sigh.

Colonel Scammell, of the New Hampshire regiment, was the officer in charge. He read the death sentence in a loud but wavering voice. "Major André," Scammell concluded, "if you have anything to say, you can speak, for you have but a short time to live."

André spoke in a firm, clear voice. "I have nothing more to say, gentlemen, but this: you all bear me witness that I meet my fate as a brave man."

The executioner, an unshaven man whose face was covered with soot, leaped up onto the wagon. As he attempted to put the noose over André's head, André pulled the rope from his hand. He took off his neckcloth and put it in a pocket, and then slipped the noose over his own head, drawing the knot close on the right side of his neck. Then he tied a white handkerchief over his eyes.

Scammell announced that his hands must be tied. André took off his blindfold, extracted a second handkerchief, and handed it to the executioner, and then replaced the blindfold. The executioner tied his arms behind his back above the elbows. Then he shinnied up a gallows post and tied the other end of the rope to the protruding beam. The murmur of the crowd grew in intensity. Then there was silence as the executioner came down to the wagon bed. André stood motionless.

The executioner leaped to the ground, grabbed a whip, and struck the flanks of the horses. They bolted forward and André was suspended in the air by the neck.

The buzz of conversation filled the ward room. It was past ten o'clock that night. More than sixty British officers had come at the request of Sir Henry Clinton to hear an announcement. In his new British uniform, Benedict Arnold was talking with Major-General Will Phillips, his old adversary of the northern theater. Like most of Burgoyne's army, Phillips had been a prisoner of war since Saratoga. Only recently had he been exchanged for Major-General Benjamin Lincoln.

Their rehashing of old stories was cut short by a booming voice: *"Ten-*

shun!" Sir Henry Clinton entered the room, accompanied by Generals Robertson and von Knyphausen, and by a man a few officers recognized as André's manservant. Clinton looked emotionally drained. His voice was hoarse and trembling. "Gentlemen, I have called you here so that you may all hear at once of the fate of our colleague, Major John André, adjutant general of His Majesty's Army. We have the eyewitness account of his manservant." Sir Henry glanced briefly at the small, somber man next to him.

"At noon today, Major André was executed by the enemy." A wailing sound grew in the room, and some officers shouted, "No! No!"

Sir Henry continued, quieting the din. "He was hanged by the neck until dead." He could not continue for a moment. The room was deathly silent. Finally, Sir Henry could speak again: "He was buried at the spot by American soldiers and his servant, Mr. Caulfield. His last words were"—Sir Henry paused for a moment to regain control—"were: 'I pray you will all bear witness that I meet my fate like a brave man.'"

It was a chilling moment. Not a sound was heard. Officers began turning to stare at Arnold. He felt their glares as well as saw them. It appeared that everyone in the room was staring at him. He began backing up to the wall. His hand found the door, and he opened it and withdrew from the room.

He stood in the hall a moment, trying to make sense of what had happened. Then he began limping slowly down the corridor to the street.

EPILOGUE

Letters to the Author from Eyewitnesses

From Richard Varick

Prospect House, Jersey City
January 17th, 1828

My dear Sir,

With the dramatic failure of Benedict Arnold's treasonous plot, I have come to the end of my narrative, save for my final comments in this letter. Yes, indeed, Arnold failed, but escaped to save his life, while the benighted John André was captured, tried, and hanged. André was martyred by his execution, much beloved in England and widely admired in America—while Arnold could not prevent himself from becoming the most reviled person in American history.

If you will pardon a personal reference, I must own that I have changed my views as a result of immersion in this project. You will recall that I saw Arnold as an archfiend in hell at the beginning. A careful review of the record and the longer path of history have combined to bring a more human quality to the story. I still despise what Arnold attempted—but I understand better <u>why</u> he acted.

Though he lived for another twenty-one years, still relentlessly driven by ambition and energy, he never again played an important role on the world stage. He lived as an exile, a despised traitor, who eventually came to regret his fateful action, and so he suffered in a purgatory he had created for himself on earth. It is a fate I would not wish upon any man.

So thoroughly was Arnold demonized as the lone villain that the conservatives who had befriended him—Schuyler, Deane, Wilson, et al.—emerged untarnished by the affair. David Franks and I were exonerated by our joint court-martial, although, as I narrated earlier, my reputation suffered for a time. Joshua Hett Smith escaped conviction in his civilian trial, although he was properly labeled as a gullible fool. Judge Shippen and his family survived, he rebuilding his legal career to become chief justice of Pennsylvania.

Arnold, meanwhile, was disliked by most of his new British colleagues. The execution of John André was an important reason, especially for Sir Henry Clinton, who never overcame his bitterness. He would not listen to Arnold's pleas to lead an offensive, and Arnold began writing to superiors in London. Finally, Clinton allowed Arnold to lead the Loyalist Legion in two raids, one to Virginia, where he sent Governor Thomas Jefferson fleeing for his life, and the second to Arnold's birth area, New London on the Connecticut coast, a base for privateers. Two atrocities happened on this action: a privateer loaded with ammunition exploded, setting fire to the town, and the defenders of Fort Griswold were massacred by a wing of Arnold's force, men who were infuriated by their losses in attacking the fort. Arnold intended neither action, but so low was his reputation that he was blamed for both, further blackening his name in the eyes of Americans.

After Cornwallis was defeated at Yorktown, he joined the Arnold family in sailing for England in January 1782. Arnold and Cornwallis were determined to take control of British forces in America from Sir Henry Clinton. I understand that Arnold did meet with King George and Lord Germain, but it was too late. Sentiment in England was overwhelmingly in favor of ending the war, and the peace faction soon took power. General Clinton was replaced by Sir Guy Carleton and in 1783 came the Treaty of Paris, formally bringing the war to a close.

From David Solebury Franks

Philadelphia
January 30th, 1828

My dear Sir,
Perhaps it is not amiss to follow my narrative with some description of Peggy Arnold after the failed treason attempt. As you know, I was closer to her than I was to Arnold, and I followed her later life with mixed feelings of dismay and admiration.

When I brought her to her parents' loving embrace in Philadelphia, it was plain to me that she had been crushed by events. She wanted to stay there, secluded, almost becoming childlike again, not wishing to hear anything of what had happened, even as the populace poured forth in the street parades that usually included burning Arnold in effigy. The radical leadership of Philadelphia was highly suspicious of her, despite the belief in her innocence by Washington and Hamilton. Lacking proof, the Supreme Executive Council finally took the step of banishing Peggy from Philadelphia for the duration of the Revolutionary War.

There had been no surge in desertions by other military officers to follow Arnold across the lines, making it clear that he had acted alone (aside from the uncertainty about Peggy). Joseph Reed was thereby denied the opportunity to seek retribution, and in due course his radical regime was removed by the voters of Pennsylvania in favor of a moderate form of government typical of the other States.

Poor old Judge Shippen had the unpleasant task of taking Peggy to American lines near New York and bidding her farewell as she crossed over to rejoin her husband. She apparently experienced a conversion, a coming of age, at this time. She was depressed at first, but as the Arnolds moved to London in 1782 Peggy became almost an ideal wife and mother, a much more favored individual than her husband to the British and Loyalist societies. To Arnold's credit, he never told anyone of her role, allowing her to be pitied as the innocent wife of the traitor.

When his efforts to prolong the war failed and the peace party took over in London, Arnold became just another retired colonel on half-pay pension. Peggy had a pension directly from George III, and she also succeeded in getting small ones for each of her children, which began growing in number. Over the ensuing years, she was to bear six more children, two dying in infancy.

With their various pensions, the Arnolds were living a moderate existence in fashionable Portman Square, but Arnold was as restive and energetic as ever. He unsuccessfully spent his time petitioning for claims to cover his losses in America and proposing new adventures to the ministry. His effort to go to India to join his friend Lord Cornwallis ended when he was blackballed by the East India Company.

With no war in sight, Arnold's patience ran out. He sailed away to Canada, setting up a trading establishment in Saint John, New Brunswick, a town almost totally inhabited by Loyalists, most of them hostile to him. Peggy and the children were to join Arnold in the following year, while Hannah and his sons by his first marriage came up from the United States. Arnold's commercial instincts were still good. Although a peace treaty had been signed, Britain did not revoke her ban on American trading with British Caribbean colonies. This meant that Canada had the opportunity of trading with both England and the Caribbean without American competition. Even though New Brunswick gradually sank into the throes of an economic depression, Arnold still managed to profit. He had a number of seagoing vessels in the trade.

The war being over, Peggy was able to travel from Canada to visit her home in Philadelphia for more than five months, over the winter of 1789 and 1790. I saw her in the city several times, though the animus against her prevented her from socializing very much. It also gradually affected her mother's health, so Peggy finally decided to return to New Brunswick. My last sight of her was on the day of her departure. The expression on her face was revealing. She knew that she would never be able to return to American soil and would never see her family again.

From Sir Thomas Stanley, KB

Knowsley, Lancashire
England
11 March 1828

My dear Sir,

Now that the narrative proper has ended, I believe all that remains is to acquaint the reader with the Arnolds' sad years in London. I can be of assistance inasmuch as I came to know them somewhat and kept up with their doings through the knowledge of others, including my uncle and Lord Cornwallis.

I saw Arnold only briefly during his first stay in London, since I arrived home in 1783 whilst he left for Canada only a year later. I heard on good authority at this time that the Arnolds were seen in Westminster Abbey, gazing at the new memorial for John André in the Poets' Corner that had been erected by order of the King. The inscription reads that André "fell a sacrifice to his zeal for King and Country" in an "important but hazardous enterprise." Anna Seward's poem "Monodony to John André" was immensely popular at the time, causing tears to fall in many English drawing rooms and boudoirs. The prevalence of such sentiments must have nearly maddened Arnold.

He was in Canada for seven years, and eventually fell upon hard times, due to the animosity of the local population. He became the victim of sabotage, his finest ship run aground intentionally and his warehouses burned. He saw salvation, however, when war with revolutionary France loomed. Arnold was happy to leave commerce behind and return to fight for England. However, he encountered the same lack of trust as he had before. Unable to gain any rank or position, Arnold volunteered, raising funds to buy his own ship and sailing her to the Caribbean as a privateer. I was among those he approached in his quest for financing.

Arnold profited for a time by taking prizes at sea, but then was captured by the French at Guadeloupe Island. While the French governor was making the decision to execute him, Arnold once again escaped. Bribing the guards on the prison ship, he slipped overboard at night to a small rowboat. A French cutter spotted him, but Arnold made it to a British warship outside the harbor.

For a year Arnold served as volunteer quartermaster to the British commander Sir Charles "No Flint" Grey, John André's former chief. Arnold played such a heroic role that the British planters and merchants of the area sent a resolution to the ministry to return him to the Caribbean at the head of a relief *mission. But again, his past intervened. The ministry could not bring itself to place Arnold over British officers—but it did reward him with a grant of 13,400 acres of land in Canada.*

While Arnold had been gone, Peggy was forced to move from Portman Square to a smaller house on Gloucester Street, and she bore her seventh and last child. She devoted herself to her children's welfare, striving to establish them in English society. Four of her sons served in the British military, one rising to very high rank. Two of Arnold's older sons, also veterans, had settled on a farm in Canada with his sister, Hannah. The eldest son, Arnold's namesake, was killed in 1796 as a captain in the British Army fighting the French in the Caribbean.

As the century died out, Arnold's health began to fail. His gout returned, to the point that he could no longer go to sea. He continued to speculate, sending trading ships and then another privateer abroad with other commanders. In all cases, these ventures failed. By 1801 Arnold was in a wretched state. On June 14th he died at the age of sixty-one of the combined effects of gout, dropsy, asthma, and a tropical cough. His wife believed that he "literally fell sacrifice" to a "perturbed mind." He was buried in the unfashionable St. Mary's Church in Battersea, across the Thames, where Peggy would also lie.

Peggy was shocked to find in Arnold's will that he had left land and an income to one John Sage, a boy of fourteen in New Brunswick, who apparently was the child of his mistress. But Arnold also made Peggy his executrix, and she fulfilled his wishes to the letter. The estate was debt-ridden, but Peggy heroically satisfied every one of her husband's creditors in the several years that followed. Her own health soon failed. On August 24th, 1804, at the age of only forty-four, she died painfully of cancer of the womb.

In a cameo she left behind was a blond lock of John André's hair.

FOR THE BEST IN PAPERBACKS, LOOK FOR THE

In every corner of the world, on every subject under the sun, Penguin represents quality and variety—the very best in publishing today.

For complete information about books available from Penguin—including Puffins, Penguin Classics, and Arkana—and how to order them, write to us at the appropriate address below. Please note that for copyright reasons the selection of books varies from country to country.

In the United Kingdom: Please write to *Dept. EP, Penguin Books Ltd, Bath Road, Harmondsworth, West Drayton, Middlesex UB7 0DA.*

In the United States: Please write to *Penguin Putnam Inc., P.O. Box 12289 Dept. B, Newark, New Jersey 07101-5289* or call 1-800-788-6262.

In Canada: Please write to *Penguin Books Canada Ltd, 10 Alcorn Avenue, Suite 300, Toronto, Ontario M4V 3B2.*

In Australia: Please write to *Penguin Books Australia Ltd, P.O. Box 257, Ringwood, Victoria 3134.*

In New Zealand: Please write to *Penguin Books (NZ) Ltd, Private Bag 102902, North Shore Mail Centre, Auckland 10.*

In India: Please write to *Penguin Books India Pvt Ltd, 11 Panchsheel Shopping Centre, Panchsheel Park, New Delhi 110 017.*

In the Netherlands: Please write to *Penguin Books Netherlands bv, Postbus 3507, NL-1001 AH Amsterdam.*

In Germany: Please write to *Penguin Books Deutschland GmbH, Metzlerstrasse 26, 60594 Frankfurt am Main.*

In Spain: Please write to *Penguin Books S. A., Bravo Murillo 19, 1° B, 28015 Madrid.*

In Italy: Please write to *Penguin Italia s.r.l., Via Benedetto Croce 2, 20094 Corsico, Milano.*

In France: Please write to *Penguin France, Le Carré Wilson, 62 rue Benjamin Baillaud, 31500 Toulouse.*

In Japan: Please write to *Penguin Books Japan Ltd, Kaneko Building, 2-3-25 Koraku, Bunkyo-Ku, Tokyo 112.*

In South Africa: Please write to *Penguin Books South Africa (Pty) Ltd, Private Bag X14, Parkview, 2122 Johannesburg.*